Acquisition
The Complete Series

Celia Aaron

i

Acquisition: The Complete Series

Celia Aaron

Cover art by PopKitty
Editing by J. Brooks
ISBN: 1535478608
ISBN-13: 978-1535478601

OTHER BOOKS BY CELIA AARON

Kicked

An American Football Romance

***

Tempting Eden

***

The Cleat Chaser Duet

A Baseball Romantic Comedy
Co-written with Sloane Howell

***

Cash Remington and the Missing Heiress

Sexy Dreadfuls, Book 1

Cash Remington and the Rum Run

Sexy Dreadfuls, Book 2

***

The Forced Series

***

The Hard and Dirty Holidays

Sign up for my newsletter at AaronErotica.com and be the first to learn about new releases (no spam, just free stuff and book news.)

Twitter: @aaronerotica

CONTENTS

SINCLAIR

COUNSELLOR

MAGNATE

SOVEREIGN

SINCLAIR

CHAPTER ONE

Past

BLOOD STREAKED MY MOTHER'S face and dripped down the front of her yellow sun dress. Screams ricocheted through the night, and flames leapt into the sky from the neighboring property.

The house was eerily quiet. Mom and I were the only ones inside. I blinked hard, trying to erase the horrors I'd seen from my vision. But when I opened my eyes, Mom was still there, still staring down at me.

"Why are you crying?" She grabbed my wrist and yanked me toward the wide front doors.

I wiped my tears with my free hand as she lifted the bar from the doors and tossed it onto the floor, marring the wooden planks. She wrenched the door inward. The screams were no longer muffled. Agonized cries rose from the fields of sugar cane that stretched as far as I could see in the pale moonlight. The neighboring fields were on fire, the acrid smoke making my eyes water even more.

She ripped me down the front steps. I yelled as my ankle turned on the last stair, but she only pulled me harder

1

toward the fields.

"Mom, please!" I tried to dig my heels into the hardened dirt.

She whirled and stabbed her index finger into my chest. "Don't you *ever* beg *anyone*! You hear me? You're a Vinemont. You don't cry. You don't beg. You do what you have to do to keep this family on top. Do you understand me?"

My chest ached where she'd poked me, and her harsh words only made me cry harder. "I-I'm sorry, Mom. Let's go back."

The blood around her mouth had crusted a deep brown, but the streaks along her cheeks glimmered like fresh paint. She bent down and wiped a tear from my face with her thumb.

"There is no going back." She stared into my eyes, a cruel smirk on her face. My mother, but I didn't recognize her. Something had happened to her during the last year. Something bad. "No going back. Never. Never again."

"Mom." I took her hand. "Let's just go. Let's go. Please!"

Her stinging slap rocked me back on my heels. "Not yet."

I clutched my cheek. She'd never hit me before. I couldn't hold back the sob that shot from my lungs. I wanted to wake up. It had to be a nightmare.

She dashed to the edge of the sugar cane field and yanked down a stalk. She pulled off a set of green leaves and turned back to me as her foreman sauntered around the side of the house. Two men behind him dragged a third.

"Señora Vinemont!"

She grinned and took my hand, pulling me back toward the house. The man lifted his head, a bloody gash running along his bald pate.

"Rebecca?" He blinked, his eyes teary from the heavy smoke, or perhaps from something else.

"That's Sovereign, to you." Her voice was hard, like

stone grinding against stone, but she curtsied like a little girl. "Edward Rose. So nice to see you again." To the foreman, she said, "Take him inside."

The men dragged Mr. Rose up the front steps as we followed behind, my hand clamped firmly in my mother's strong grip. A cold tingle ran down my spine. Instead of going inside, I wanted to escape. But the screams in the fields at my back kept me hemmed in. There was nowhere to run. And my mother was gone, though she looked the same, had the same voice.

Once we were all inside, the foreman barred the heavy front doors again. The men set Mr. Rose on his feet. Mother circled around him, her skirt swaying as she perused him with eyes that were foreign to me. Gone was the mother who used to read to me, hold me in her lap, and chase me around the house when I rode my bike indoors. This woman—the one with the cold blue eyes and the blood-streaked face—was a stranger.

She circled Mr. Rose one more time as he finally stood on his own. His eyes remained downcast.

"Sovereign, I-I—"

"Shh." She stood in front of him as the other men smirked and backed away. Mr. Rose swayed, but stayed on his feet. Then she held out her right hand, her fair skin still delicate even though it was tinged with crimson.

The foreman put a pistol in her hand, and she handed the sugar cane leaves to me.

Mr. Rose began to quake and shake his head, the gash oozing blood down to his ear. "I-I'm sorry about the supply issues. I promise, it won't happen again. Now that you're Sovereign, I w-won't … please"—his voice broke—"please, Sovereign, I beg you, please."

Mother pulled me forward so I stood next to her. She handled the gun with delicate, deadly fingers.

"I think you know it's too late for that." She pulled the hammer back, the click somehow loud even with the noise outside.

"It doesn't have to be." Mr. Rose finally looked up, his mouth turned down at the corners, his chin quivering. "I'll give you whatever you want."

"I'm already *taking* what I want." She pressed the gun against his forehead.

He pulled away, but the two men were on him, holding him in place by his elbows.

I grabbed her hand. "Mom?"

"This is what you need to learn, Sinclair. This is what you have to be." She never took her eyes from Mr. Rose.

"No." Mr. Rose cried and sniffed, a line of snot rolling to his lips. "Please. My family."

Mother laughed. "Dead. All dead. All gone. Did you have fun at the Christmas trial?"

He shook his head. "Wh-what?"

"Answer my question. Did you have fun at the Christmas trial?"

"I only did what everyone else—"

She cracked the butt of the gun along his cheek. "I asked you if *you* had fun. Not everyone else."

"I-I- don't remember... Please, Rebecca."

She cracked him again in the same spot and he screamed, but the men held him steady as more blood mixed with his tears.

"Yes, Sovereign. I did. Yes."

"Remember my Acquisition? Remember what you did to her? I can still hear her screams as you violated her, hurt her. I know every word you said, every time you told her to take it and called her a slut, every time you said she was a cunt who loved getting fucked in her ass. Do you remember all that?"

My stomach lurched, and I turned to the side. What little contents I had in my stomach emptied onto the floor in one powerful heave. The foreman laughed and stepped back.

"Sinclair!" Mom grabbed my chin and wrenched my face around to hers. "Watch every moment of this. Don't turn away. You have to learn."

I shuddered at her touch, her nails digging into my face. "Okay."

"Better. Now, where was I?" She tapped the gun barrel on her cheek. "Oh, right. You raping my Acquisition over, and over, and over again."

Mr. Rose didn't respond, but his eyes pleaded with Mom. I clutched the sugar cane leaves until my fingers broke through them.

Mom backed up a few feet and pulled me with her. "Don't look away, Sinclair," she said as she raised the gun. "Never look away."

"Please—" Mr. Rose's plea was cut off by the deafening roar of the pistol. His right cheek exploded, the white of his teeth showing through, and he slumped to the ground. The men who'd been holding him backed away and wiped his blood from their faces.

I screamed. The sound ripped from me as Mom gave the gun back to the foreman with a steady hand.

The foreman nodded and smiled. "*Muy bien*, Señora Vinemont."

The cry died in my throat as my lungs burned for want of air. I gasped and stared at Mr. Rose, unmoving on the floor. One of the men kicked him over onto his back. Only one eye remained intact, and it stared at me. If his mouth could move, it would tell me this was all my fault somehow.

"Get him out of here and clean this up." She waved a dismissive hand at the men and grabbed my upper arm.

"Mom?" I let her pull me to the dining room. She shoved me into a chair, took the one across from me, then snatched the sugar cane leaves from my numb fingers. My ears rang in a high note, nothing like the deep sound of the gun. And I couldn't stop the tears.

"Mommy?" I needed her more than I'd ever needed anything. Where was she?

The woman across from me smiled. "Hold your hand out."

I shook so hard my teeth chattered. "N-no."

5

"Sinclair, put your hand on the table." Her voice darkened. "Now."

I swallowed hard and placed my hand on the edge of the table. She reached across and yanked it so I was leaning over, my arm outstretched. My tears plopped onto the dark wood beneath me.

She plucked a sugar cane leaf and felt along the stiff side. As she slid her finger down the sharp edge, red welled up from a smooth cut on her fingertip.

She smiled and placed her other hand, palm down, next to mine. "Now, let's begin."

CHAPTER TWO

Present

"HAVE YOU HEARD WHO'S gotten picked for this year?" Judge Montagnet sipped his bourbon, his black robe open as he lounged in his chambers.

I pulled on my sleeves, ensuring that my cuff links were perfectly turned.

"No, Judge, I sure haven't. Should be an interesting year with Cal in charge." I smiled. It was mechanical. Sometimes I would have to actively think about how a normal person would react to a statement or an action, and then attempt to mold my response in the same fashion.

"I really can't wait. Christmas trial is always my favorite. Did you attend during the year Cal won?" He shifted his hips higher, the law clerk between his legs making sloppy noises as he bobbed his head on the judge's cock.

"No, I'm afraid to say the sugar business called me away to foreign lands quite a bit that year." I finished my bourbon and set the glass on the polished wood table to my right.

Judge Montagnet closed his eyes and gripped the young man's head, pulling him close. After a series of choking noises and some low grunts from the judge, it was over. The law clerk sat back, sputtering and gasping for air. He wiped his sleeve across his eyes, and it came away wet with tears.

No pity for him welled in my deadened heart. I had no concept of what that word even meant. Was it a feeling? A thought? I was better off without it, not that I had a choice in the matter. I couldn't miss something I'd never experienced in the first place.

Boredom swirled around me, and I wanted to get the hearing over with as soon as possible. As the district attorney for the parish, I had to prosecute all criminal offenses while Judge Montagnet made a show of presiding over the trials. The job only became fun when I found a really nasty rat and made him squeal.

Luckily, I'd found just such a rat in Leon Rousseau. His arraignment was set on the docket, and I had big plans to investigate every scrap of paper and every dime flowing to and from his accounts. Making his life a living hell would amuse me for a time, at least until I found something better.

Judge Montagnet zipped up and patted the law clerk on the head. "Good work. Run along now and let them know I'll be on the bench in a moment."

The clerk stood, crimson painting his cheeks, and left.

"I guess that's my cue." I rose as the judge straightened his robes and smoothed his white hair.

"I'll see you out there. Anyone you want me to roast today?"

I smirked. "I think I can handle the roasting at the moment. You've had all the fun so far. Now it's my turn."

He smiled, his wrinkles turning his thin skin into accordions around his mouth. "I sure have."

I fastened my top coat button and strode out into the courtroom. The bailiff nodded at me as I skirted the bench and headed toward the counsel tables. The public defender had already set up his files on his side. My side was bare. I knew my cases; no files necessary.

I scanned the gallery behind the short wooden wall separating the front and back of the courtroom. Leon Rousseau sat and stared at me with his beady eyes. But he wasn't what caught my attention. I didn't break my step, but

I couldn't take my eyes off the redhead sitting beside him.

Her head was bowed, and she wore a black suit, the skirt too long for my tastes and the cut too modest. So prim and proper. I wanted to toy with her, bat her around like a cat playing with a mortally wounded mouse.

I'd never been drawn to another human being. The sensation was odd, irritating. Even so, her red hair would look perfect clenched in my fist, and I had to take a sharp breath at the thought of her skin bearing marks from my belt.

I walked the remaining steps to my table, but she didn't look up. The flame of desire began to burn lower when I realized she was too tame. I would break her in an instant, and I didn't want to play with broken toys. Pity.

She looked up at me. Her green eyes pinned me to the spot, and my heart kicked against my ribs. She was more. So much more. Her hateful gaze scorched me like a firebrand, and I wanted the burn. I wanted to give it back to her, make her scream and call my name—in agony or pleasure, or that perfect mix of both. She held me there, as if the hate in her eyes had snared me in a trap.

"Counsellor Vinemont?" Judge Montagnet's voice echoed around the wood-paneled walls. "Which case would you like to handle first?"

I cut my eyes from her to Leon Rousseau and back again. He gripped her hand with his. A name flitted around my mind. A daughter, he had a daughter. *Stella.* I smirked as her name came to me, and she kicked her chin up a notch in response.

Still meeting her gaze, I called, "Judge, I'd like to take Leon Rousseau's case first, if that's all right with you."

When her eyes fell, the beast who lived in my hollow heart roared. She was fire, but she could be contained. Dominated. By me. And I already felt the need to do it again.

CHAPTER THREE

THE VICTORIAN HOUSE NEEDED work—the paint on the window casing was peeling, and some areas of the roof bowed. The grass was neatly mowed, and a porch swing with fluffy pillows moved with the breeze. Something about the swing made me think that she often dallied there. Perhaps she liked to read.

"Ready?" Sheriff Wood's voice crackled over the handheld radio in my car.

I clicked the button on the side. "Hit it."

Several lawmen rushed from the unmarked vehicles along the narrow street. Most converged on the front porch, while a few others rushed around the back. After Mr. Rousseau pleaded not guilty at his arraignment two weeks prior, I set the wheels in motion to crush him. His life was mine to destroy, and I looked forward to watching it crumble.

I climbed out of my car and leaned against it, the sunlight warming my skin and trying to penetrate my dark glasses.

After a swift knock, Sheriff Wood leaned back and kicked the door in. The deputies swarmed inside as if they were looking for the number one man on the most wanted list. In reality, Mr. Rousseau was just a low level schemer and a high level liar.

But I liked the flair of going big, and more than that, I wanted to rattle his daughter's cage. Just the one glimpse of Stella had haunted me. Her soulful eyes, the emotions that roiled beneath her surface, were ingrained in my mind. She was something different. Something wild. While I was a placid lake, nothing daring to touch the treacherous surface, she was a cascading river. Alive where I was dead, making noise while I lay silent.

She was a mystery. One I needed to unravel and devour.

I'd pulled everything on her that I could find—her high school yearbook photo, and a news clipping about her mother's suicide were the highlights. Stella's own suicide attempt intrigued me, and I'd only discovered it after getting her medical records from Dr. Ward, a Vinemont family friend. Her father had found her after she'd slit her wrists. What drove her to it? Him?

Shouting brought me back to the task at hand. Voices rose inside the house, and then quieted. Once satisfied everything was on lockdown, I strolled through the broken front door. A small library was to my left, a sitting room to my right. I continued down the narrow hallway, my shoes silent on the threadbare rug.

"—bust up in here and do whatever you want!"

I turned the corner into a den area where Mr. Rousseau, Stella, and a young man with blond hair stood under the guard of two deputies. The other deputies ransacked Mr. Rousseau's desk. Noise from upstairs told me the deputies were destroying things for fun during their 'search'.

Just as I'd instructed.

"Son, don't make me take you in. Spending the night in a jail cell—"

"You wouldn't dare. My mother is—"

"I don't give a good goddamn who your mother is. This is an official parish investigation. If you keep interfering, I'll arrest you. Got me?"

"That won't be necessary." I strolled to the deputy as

another crash sounded from upstairs.

"You." Mr. Rousseau narrowed his eyes and wrapped his arm around Stella's waist. She wore a white T-shirt and jeans. A simple ensemble that hugged her curves. It would look even better stained with blood or tears, maybe both.

The young man bristled. "Don't look at her."

I met his gaze for a moment. He was muscled with a thick neck. Based on his clothes, he played lacrosse. Based on his muscles, he had a penchant for steroids. I gave him a withering glare and turned to Mr. Rousseau. "I have a warrant. Everything is in order, I assure you."

"Signed by that snake, Judge Montagnet, no doubt." Stella scowled.

A smear of blue paint colored her cheek, and her fingers carried a mix of the same blue and streaks of yellow. I'd visited the small gallery in town and studied the few paintings of hers that hung there. They were dark and brooding. I rather liked them. But her current palette was lighter. I'd work on the colors, pushing her back into darker and darker shades. After all, this was only the first search of many. I intended to turn the screws until Leon Rousseau jumped at every sound and feared I was the monster under his bed.

"Snake, Ms. Rousseau? It isn't wise to impugn a judge's honor, especially one presiding over your father's case."

"We aren't blind, Mr. Vinemont. I saw you in his chambers before the arraignment." Her shoulders moved back, her challenge obvious. My gaze flicked to her hardening nipples. She wasn't wearing a bra. She must have been spending a comfortable day in her house of straw until the big bad wolf came to her door. Now the wolf was inside, and all I wanted to do was eat her up.

"You're impugning my honor as well?" I smirked.

"What do you know about honor?" She threw it back in my face with a quickness that had my blood racing. If I slapped her, would she quiet down or hit me back? I hoped the latter.

"More than the Rousseaus, apparently." I surveyed the room. Sketches and paintings lined the back wall near the tall, narrow windows looking out onto the rear yard. A deputy went to one and ripped it down.

"No." I kept my voice low, but the deputy glanced at me, seemed to shudder, and placed the drawing on a nearby table. He didn't touch any more of the art.

"You can't do this." Mr. Rousseau shook his head and leaned on Stella. He was like a parasite, sucking her life away.

"It's done." I gave Stella one more long, appraising look. Her red hair fell in waves down her shoulders. I wanted to mark her alabaster skin with my teeth.

"I said, stop looking at her." The young man stepped forward.

"Dylan, don't." A warning note laced through her voice. She was smart. One more step and I would drop Dylan on his ass.

"And you are?" I walked past Dylan and studied the closest sketch. I already knew who he was, but I might as well ask to be polite. Mother always wanted me to be polite, though not particularly to trash like the Rousseaus. None of them mattered to me, not even Stella. We were a different species.

"Dylan Devereaux, Leon's stepson."

The sketch appeared to be of a knife, the smooth edge almost glinting on the paper. The handle was a deep mahogany brown, and I smiled at the pool of blood drawn beneath it, some of the drops still on the blade.

"I think we're about done here." Sheriff Wood called as deputies carried boxes of material out to their cars. They'd emptied the entire contents of Mr. Rousseau's desk and taken various other papers they'd found in the house.

"How much for this drawing?" I turned and peered into Stella's eyes—still fascinating, still full of hatred.

This was only the beginning. Her hatred would build until her other emotions were weak whispers next to how much she wanted to destroy me. I needed to taste her rage, to savor it on my tongue.

"It's not for sale." Her words were even, but I could see the rapid flutter in the vein at her neck. Her heart was racing.

I shot a glance to her father. "Don't be silly. Everything's for sale, right Mr. Rousseau?"

"Get out of here." He scowled.

"While your false disdain is amusing, I'm afraid a jury won't find you quite as believable as your daughter does. So, what's the price?" I kept my gaze on Stella. I wanted her to give in, though I knew she wouldn't.

"I'd rather burn it than sell it to you." Her voice lowered to a hiss as the last of the deputies cleared out.

Her hatred was like a blast of heat on a frigid day. I wanted to strip her flames away, bit by bit, until I reached her core. Once there, would I snuff her fire out, or stoke it until it raged beyond control?

I didn't know the answer. But I knew I wanted her beneath me, my hands on her body, and her blood in my mouth.

"Counsellor?" Sheriff Wood leaned against the doorframe and flipped the strap on his holster off, popped it back on, off, on, off, on.

Stella held my gaze as I strode past.

"Maybe we can continue negotiations the next time I visit."

"You already took everything you wanted." Her father's voice was like a claw in my eardrum.

I turned on my heel and eyed Stella up and down. The line of her legs, the flare of her hips, trim waist, and high, round tits. She shifted uncomfortably under my scrutiny.

I held her defiant gaze. "I'll decide when I've taken everything I want."

CHAPTER FOUR

I LAY IN MY bed and studied Stella's photo. It was already etched into my mind, no need to look at it any longer. But I did.

Someone from my office had snapped it as she left the courthouse after the arraignment. Her hair appeared even more vibrantly red in the sun. Her eyes, though, were sad. I wanted to see them glimmering with tears.

My cock surged at the thought of hurting her. Would she beg? The fire in her eyes told me she wouldn't. Perhaps she would beg me to make it burn, to push her to the edge. The way she'd looked at me during the last search, and the one before that, and the initial one when she'd openly challenged me. *Fuck.*

She wanted to tear me apart. I wanted her to rail against me until she gave in, beaten and defeated. I'd savor every last tear, every cry of pain, and finally, every scream of pleasure.

The violence I'd seen in her eyes made me groan, and my hips surged upward. I slid my hand down to my cock, stroking it slowly as I stared at her photo. Her delicate neck would fit perfectly in my hands. I dropped the picture and clenched my eyes shut, imagining her pale body, the scars on her wrists, the feel of her soft skin. I wanted to bend her to my will, to force her onto her knees and use her—vengeance in her eyes and my cock in her mouth.

I kicked the sheet off. Her mouth was wrapped around me, her smooth tongue weaving along my shaft. I'd tied her hands behind her back, and her ass already bore red welts from my hand and belt.

Licking my lips, I imagined her taste on them as she sucked me, her eyes never wavering from mine. I fisted her hair and pulled her forward until my cock was lodged deep in her throat. Her eyes watered, and I knew she couldn't breathe. I didn't want her to. I held her life in my hands, and I could kill her without a second thought.

Still, her eyes burned with hate, and she tried to fight me off. I didn't let her go, not until her eyes began to glaze and flutter closed. I pulled out and she gasped. I needed to be inside her hot cunt, so I threw her onto the bed. She cried out from the pain of her hands being crushed behind her back, and I savored the sweet sound. I spread her legs and plunged inside her, no warning. I took what I wanted. Her eyes widened with surprise and that delicious spark of agony.

My hand sped, squeezing me just like her pussy would. She fought, trying to buck me off. I only thrust more deeply into her. My balls drew up tight to my body as I clapped my hand over her mouth to muffle her screams.

I sank myself inside her and matched every bit of rage I saw in her eyes with my punishing strokes. She wouldn't break. I had to work harder. I could. I sped my pace, each impact bruising her thighs, her pussy. I reached down and palmed her tit, squeezing mercilessly. Her eyes narrowed, the challenge alive and well. I moved my hand up so it covered both her mouth and nose.

She tried to turn her head, but couldn't escape my strong grip. No air moved inside her body. She fought some more, but I kept taking from her, shoving inside her because I owned her. I didn't let up, suffocating her as I glared down into her rebellious eyes. Her body jerked, still trying to get air.

When she realized I wasn't going to stop, something else lit her gaze, the one thing I'd wanted from her all along. Fear. I came, my cock jolting in my hand as my release spurted onto my stomach. I gasped at how intense the orgasm was, rolling over me and constricting every blood vessel in my body. My cock kicked once more as I relaxed into the bed, my hand still and my heart pounding.

"Fuck." I stared at the ceiling, trying to put all my pieces back into place. *She's no one. No one.* She was nothing to me, other than a body I wanted to use. Nothing.

This time she sat on the swing reading when the cruisers rolled up to the house. She glanced up, shook her head, then went back to her book. The deputies got out and strolled up the front porch. They flashed a warrant. She ignored it.

She said something I couldn't hear and waved at the door. Ten men entered the house. I'd asked them to get even rowdier than the last couple of times. More than a few items would be destroyed during this 'search' I smirked and continued to stare at her. A hot summer breeze rustled the first of the fallen leaves on the lawns nearby. Fall was almost here, and her father's trial was set for the following week.

Two days of testimony and he'd be convicted. There was no other option for a parish jury, especially given the dirt I had on the old man. Then sentencing. I'd have him sent to the nastiest pen in the state. His suffering would only weaken her, make her ripe for the taking.

She continued perusing her book, only turning her head to the side a couple of times—likely when she heard something break inside. I was a little disappointed she didn't get up to investigate or make a scene, but I'd rather keep my eyes on her anyway. I knew it bothered her, so it was the best of both worlds.

I slid my gaze down her v-neck shirt—the bare swell of her breasts just visible. Her athletic shorts showed plenty of leg, and I admired the way her calves tapered to narrow ankles. I wanted to knot rope around them and spread them wide. A flogger to the pussy would shake any woman's resolve, even Stella's.

The breeze picked up again and splayed tendrils of her hair across her face. She brushed them out of the way and stretched. Her back arched. My cock swelled to a painful degree. She brought her arms back down and glanced out to the road. She froze, her eyes locked with mine.

She cocked her head to the side again, listening to the sounds inside the house, and scowled. The deputies must have been following my instructions with verve. Tossing her book to the side, she rose, her eyes never leaving me as she strode down the front walk, her bare feet silent on the cracked concrete.

I couldn't stop the smirk that turned my lip at the corner. She wanted a confrontation. I would give it to her. Rolling my passenger window down, I waited. She arrived and bent over. I saw her simple white bra. I could rip it off in two seconds, and I wanted to. When I caught her lilac scent, my cock went from hard to painfully hard. My jacket hid it. She held my gaze, that fire inside her burning brighter by the second.

"Pleased with yourself?" Even when she was harsh, her voice still had a melodic quality.

"I'm sorry, Ms. Rousseau. I don't quite take your meaning." My mask was in place—I was the parish prosecutor, a public servant to the core. Everything I did was in the name of the law.

"There is nothing here. There hasn't been anything here since the first time you came. Why are you doing this?" She peered at me, but she didn't see me. Just my mask.

"I have to make sure every piece of evidence is collected.

After all, you wouldn't want me to miss the one document or item that could exonerate your father, would you? I have to be thorough."

She dug her nails into the trim along the window sill. "You don't fool me for a second. You just like to torment him. That's all you're doing."

"I'm only doing the job I was elected to do. Keeping the parish safe from fraudulent operators like your father."

"You're lying."

Always. "I'm sorry to hear you think so. I truly am."

"We'll see at the trial. No one will believe your lies then."

I tsked at her and shook my head. "You think he'll win, don't you?" I laughed. "Foolish. Then again, I never took you as particularly clever. Not like he is."

"Insult me all you like, but the truth will come out. My father will be found innocent, because that's what he is."

She actually believed her father's lies. Why was it so hard for her to believe mine?

"We'll see. Now, I have much more important affairs to tend to than your diatribes. If you'll excuse me." I cranked the car.

She didn't move, her green gaze still taking in my mask. There were no cracks in it, nowhere she could see inside. I'd crafted it so well that people had no idea it was actually a mask to begin with.

"I see you." She spoke through gritted teeth.

"That makes sense as I'm sitting right in front of you in broad daylight." The hackles on the back of my neck rose as she stared harder, her eyes glinting.

"No. I see the real you. Don't think for a second that you're fooling me. It may work on everyone else. But I see what you really are." She pulled her hands away. "And you disgust me."

"If that was some sort of threat, it fell flat, Ms. Rousseau. Maybe work on your inflection and try again next time. I'll attempt to act sufficiently frightened." I turned the wheel.

She backed away as I hit the gas and cruised down the

street. I stared at her in my rearview mirror, her arms crossed over her chest and her mouth drawn down in a scowl.

I didn't want to leave. What I'd wanted to do was grip her shirt and yank her into the car. Kidnapping her in broad daylight wasn't an option, unfortunately. But if I had, how long would it take before she screamed? Before true fear overcame the steel lining her spine?

I didn't know, but I wanted to find out.

CHAPTER FIVE

"I HAVE NO FURTHER questions." Mr. Rousseau's attorney sat down. The fool had put Mr. Rousseau on the witness stand when he should have remained silent.

I cracked my knuckles, and Judge Montagnet turned away from the jury to hide his grin. This would be fun.

The gallery was filled with Mr. Rousseau's victims, each one of them having already testified in the State's case in chief. The jury had listened to every word, every syllable about what a dirty schemer Mr. Rousseau was.

Stella sat behind her father, the circles under her eyes growing darker with each passing day. We'd just come back from lunch, and I was more than ready to take my time with her father, squeeze out every last lie and hold it up for the jury—and Stella—to see.

I couldn't help myself. I shot a glance at her over my shoulder as I rose and buttoned my suit coat. She kept her gaze on her father. Good.

"I have a few questions, if you don't mind, Your Honor."

"You may examine the witness." Montagnet had composed himself and leaned back in his chair, ready for the show.

I strode forward and positioned myself directly in front of the jury. Leon Rousseau was on trial, but I was the star of the show.

I clutched my hands in front of me, humbleness in every calculated movement. "Mr. Rousseau, I'm Sinclair Vinemont, the parish prosecutor. We've met before—"

"I know who you are." His snarl, though understandable, did not play well to the jury. Two of the ladies on the back row shifted uncomfortably in their seats.

"You remember meeting Mrs. Caldwell?" I motioned to the elderly woman with the tennis balls attached to her walker. She sat in the front row, her aged face in a permanent frown.

Mr. Rousseau, sweat beading along his upper lip, nodded. "Yes."

"You told her to invest in Mirabella, a tenants-in-common product?"

"Yes."

I turned to the jury, affecting a teaching tone. "Tenants-in-common means that several investors go in together to buy a property, one that is usually fully leased and provides steady income via rent payments and increase in value in the property market. Is that correct, Mr. Rousseau?"

"Yes."

"Mirabella was a good investment for Mrs. Caldwell?"

"Yes." His tone turned warier with each affirmative response.

"It would provide steady income to pay her living expenses?"

"Yes."

"Especially when the housing market is on an upswing, like now?"

"Yes."

"So." I turned to the jury. "It was a highly suitable and wise investment?"

"Yes."

"But you didn't invest her money into Mirabella, did you,

Mr. Rousseau?"

He swallowed hard and looked away.

"Mr. Rousseau, did you invest her money into Mirabella?"

"I-I..."

"It's a simple yes or no answer. Which is it?"

His watery eyes fell. "No."

"You told her you did?"

"Yes."

"But you actually put that money into another account?"

"Yes."

"An interest-bearing account with your name on it?"

"Yes, but I was going to transfer her investment—"

"You never put her money in any other investment, did you?"

"No, but I was going to." He talked quickly. "I was waiting until the market bounce—"

"Mrs. Caldwell never received a dime of interest?"

"No. But if you'd just let me explain. She'd been in a series of annuities that actually depleted her principal at a far faster rate. I would have transferred her money over into the Mirabella accounts once I received all of her principal from the annuity companies, but you froze my accounts before I had the chance."

"I see." I nodded as if I agreed with his assessment. "So, you were trying to help Mrs. Caldwell?"

"Yes." He surveyed the jurors, trying to make eye contact with each one.

"Are you aware of a rule for financial advisors, like yourself, that states any commingling of funds results in a total disbarment?"

"Yes, but—"

"And isn't it true that you were barred from working as a financial advisor by the financial regulatory agency three months ago?"

He turned his gaze toward me. "Because of you. Because you testified to all these lies about me. I did nothing wrong."

"Nothing wrong? Didn't you just admit to putting Mrs. Caldwell's money into your personal account?"

"Yes, but—"

"Do you remember the first time you met Mr. Calgary?" I pointed to an elderly man in a wheelchair who glared at Mr. Rousseau.

Mrs. Caldwell, Mr. Calgary, Mrs. Green, Mr. Bradley, Mr. Hess, Mr. Graves, Mrs. Oppen, Mr. Travis—I went through each elderly victim, each transaction, each instance of misappropriation. Mr. Rousseau had an excuse each time I pointed out that their funds always wound up in his personal accounts. By the end of my cross examination, several of the jurors leaned back with their arms crossed. They didn't believe him, were repulsed by him, just like I was.

When I finished, and Mr. Rousseau's excuses finally died out, I turned to the judge. "The State rests, Your Honor, but we would move for a judgment of guilt as a matter of law, given Mr. Rousseau's own testimony here today."

"Mr. Rousseau, you may step down." Judge Montagnet looked to Mr. Rousseau's counsel table. "You have anything to say about that?"

The mediocre attorney stood and bumbled with his file. "I, uh, I object and move for a judgment of acquittal."

"Both motions denied. I'll let the jury have it." He peered at his wrist watch.

"It's quarter to four, Judge."

"Thank you, Counsellor Vinemont." He shook his head. "These old eyes can't quite see how they used to. I'll go ahead and charge the jury and let them begin deliberations."

I strode to my table, giving Stella a long look as I walked. She tried to school her features, but it didn't work. Venom, rage, and pain were writ large across her pale face. I savored every bit of emotion that skittered off her like sparks.

The judge instructed the jury concerning the elements of each charge and how they should go about making their decision. Then he sent them to deliberate. As soon as the last juror left the room, Stella rushed through the swinging wooden door and hugged her father. Dylan followed and put his meaty hand on Stella's back.

I sized him up again. He was big, but I'd killed bigger with nothing more than my bare hands. The way he touched her set something off inside me. I didn't know what. It was as if a slimy eel swirled in my stomach. It mixed with the one feeling I could recognize with ease—hatred.

"Come on, Dad. Let's get some air."

I smiled. "Yes, take him outside while you still can. He won't be a free man for much longer." The elderly people seated behind me mumbled and grunted in agreement.

Stella whirled and took a step toward me. Her fine hands were fisted, and I could sense how badly she wanted to hurt me. My cold blood heated a degree or two, and a flash of me yanking up her skirt and bending her over the counsel table went straight to my cock.

Taking a deep breath, she un-balled her fists and stretched her paint-stained fingers out straight. She must have thought better of going toe-to-toe with me. Too bad. She turned and took her father's elbow. Dylan sneered as he walked past, but I didn't give him the satisfaction of even looking in his direction.

I kept the image of Stella in my mind, relishing the way her hate kept me warm.

The jury returned in less than an hour.

They filed in one by one, and the foreman handed the judge their verdict. The jurors wouldn't meet Mr. Rousseau's eyes. Their verdict couldn't have been more obvious.

"All rise." The bailiff's voice brought the courtroom to its feet as Judge Montagnet skimmed down the verdict form, his mouth moving with silent words.

"I think everything is in order here." The judge handed the verdict form back to the foreman, who returned to the jury box. "Has the jury reached a verdict?"

"We have, Your Honor," the foreman responded.

"Please read it aloud."

The foreman cleared his throat and shot a quick look to Mr. Rousseau. "We, the jury, find Leon Rousseau guilty on all counts."

Sighs and murmurs of approval erupted from the gallery. Mr. Rousseau sank into his chair, and Stella rushed up and put her hand on his shoulder.

"Daddy, it'll be okay. It'll be okay." Her fervent whisper was a lie. I would make sure of that.

"Would you like me to poll the jury?" Judge Montagnet asked.

"Not for the State, Your Honor." I buttoned my suit jacket and stepped around the counsel table.

"Defense?"

"No, Your Honor."

He turned to the jury. "In that case, you all are free to go. Thank you for your service." Judge Montagnet banged his gavel, and the crowd at my back grew loud with chatter.

The jurors filed out of the box. I shook each one's hand as they passed and assured them they'd done the right thing. They smiled and nodded, because I was telling them exactly what they wanted to hear.

Once I'd shaken all their hands, I walked into the gallery and received pats on the back and 'bless you's' from the teary victims. I figured I'd have to burn this suit after all the touching. These people disgusted me only slightly less than Mr. Rousseau, but I slapped on what I knew was a pleasant smile and accepted their congratulations and grimy thanks.

The victims eventually cleared out of the gallery and headed toward the courthouse elevator. The room emptied until only the defendant, Stella, Dylan, and I remained.

Stella hadn't shed a tear even as her father turned into a blubbering mess. Dylan tried to comfort him with nonsense like 'appeal' and 'they can't do this'. Mr. Rousseau would be long dead before his appeal was ever heard.

I should have left. Then again, I'd never been one to pass up a final twist of the knife. I walked around the table to face all three of them.

"I'll have Judge Montagnet bump your sentencing up to next week. That way you can start serving your time as soon as possible. It'll give you a better chance of getting out before you die. Though, sorry to say, that is still quite unlikely."

Mr. Rousseau's blubbering increased.

"Do you lack even a shred of decency?" Stella's accusation missed the mark, given I had quite a bit more decency than anyone on her side of the table.

"I was only trying to be helpful." I smirked.

She straightened her back, the dark gray of her skirt suit giving her eyes a steely quality. "You're a bully. A menace parading as a saint. I see right through you."

"As you keep telling me. But, I don't think the jury had the same vision."

"Sin?" Judge Montagnet called through the door to his chambers.

Stella's mouth compressed into a thin line, and Dylan edged closer to her.

"Coming, Judge," I called. "I'll see you all next week. Don't be late, Mr. Rousseau. You're still out on bond for now. Just keep in mind that I'll have Sheriff Wood drag you up here if I have to." I gave Stella a congenial smile and turned on my heel, walking straight back to the judge's chambers.

"I see you." Her voice wafted to my ears as the door swung closed behind me.

CHAPTER SIX

"CAN I COME?" TEDDY plopped down on my bed.

I smoothed my button-down shirt, though it had already been ironed to crisp perfection. "No."

"Why not?" He tossed a baseball in the air and caught it. Tossed it again, missed it, and it hit himself in the nose.

I laughed as he cursed and rolled back and forth on my bed. "Good one, Ted."

If there was one bright spot in my dark existence, it was my youngest brother. Somehow, my fucked up family hadn't managed to erase whatever spark he kept inside. Did I ever have a spark?

"Shut up." He pinched his nose and winced, his voice coming out as a nasal whine. "Why can't I go?"

"Because you weren't invited. Besides, it's at Cal's house."

He grimaced. "Never mind. I'm glad I wasn't invited."

"Was I invited?" Lucius strode in and took the ball from Teddy.

"That's mine."

"Not anymore." Lucius threw it up and caught it right above Teddy's crotch.

"Not cool, man." Teddy scowled.

31

"No, what wouldn't have been cool is if I hadn't caught it."

"You two are dicks. I'm going to my room." Teddy stood and gingerly touched his nose.

"You're still pretty. Get over it." Lucius took Teddy's spot on my bed.

"I'll see you when I get back, Ted. Okay?" I smiled at him in the mirror. I couldn't tell if I was faking it or not.

He returned it, so perhaps it had been genuine after all. "Yeah. See you later."

"Don't worry, little bro." Lucius grinned. "I'll be here to take care of you, wipe your ass, rub on the baby lotion, hold your dick when you piss—all that." Teddy flipped him off and walked down the hall.

"You shouldn't taunt him so much." I threaded my tie around my neck and began to knot it.

"He needs to toughen up if he wants to hang with us."

"I hope that he won't have to hang with us. Medical school will get him out of here. Away from all this, from us."

"What's so bad about us?" He tossed the ball up and caught it again.

"He isn't…" My fingers hesitated on my tie. "He doesn't deserve this life."

Lucius shrugged. "I think you're underestimating him."

"I'm not saying it's a bad thing." I finished my tie and checked it. The knot was perfect, the deep blue of the tie setting off the lighter hue of my shirt. "I want him to stay the way he is. I don't want him to turn into…"

"You?" Lucius finished for me.

I cocked my head at him in the mirror. "There are worse things he could be. *You*, for instance."

"He should be so lucky."

I'd showered and shaved. My dark hair was smoothed down. Nothing was out of place. Perfection was my favorite form of control.

"You think he'll ever man up and get inked?" he asked.

"It doesn't matter either way. He's a Vinemont with or without the crest on his skin."

"I think he will. All the girls in Baton Rouge will be on his dick if he shows up with the vines on his arms."

I plucked my cuff links from the small box on top of my dresser. "Maybe."

"Fuck, no 'maybe' about it. Chicks love tats. I wouldn't mind trolling sorority row myself. Get some fresh pussy."

"They might be interested in him, but I've noticed him giving the new cook more than a few looks."

"You going to let him hit that?"

"No." I raised an eyebrow at him in the mirror as he continued tossing the baseball. "You know that sort of fraternization isn't allowed. She's a peasant. He's a Vinemont."

"But, come on, you've fucked chicks who aren't top stock."

Once my sleeves were perfected, I slid my arms into the jacket. "Not ones who are servants in my house. No."

"I don't think it would be so terrible if he got his dick wet with her. That's all I'm saying."

"You'd be wrong, as usual." I chose a pair of black oxfords and laced them while pondering what was in store for me at Cal's house.

An invitation to the Oakman Estate wasn't something to be taken lightly. Cal Oakman, as Sovereign, controlled too much, had too many allies, and had grown more dangerous each year of his reign. I didn't know what the party was for, but I was certain it couldn't be a good thing. Over the past ten years, he'd left the Vinemonts alone most of the time, only sending word when he decided to increase his cut of our family's sugar business.

We were living quietly under his thumb until a week ago when his invitation arrived, the wax seal imprinted with the all-too-familiar oak. Dread had spread across my mind as I'd opened the letter. A dinner at Cal Oakman's house on the eve of the Acquisition trials—nothing good could come of it. I straightened and turned to leave my room.

"You sure I can't come?"

"I'm sure."

Lucius followed me into the hall and down the front stairs. "You have any idea what he wants?"

"The same thing he always wants. Too much."

"Do you think…" Lucius hesitated on the bottom step as Farns, our butler, opened the front door for me.

I stopped and let Lucius ask. The same question had been haunting me from the moment the invitation arrived.

"Do you think it'll be us this year?" The anticipation in his voice told me he was thinking about it like a business arrangement. Being chosen could lead to wealth and, obviously, position. But there was another side—a much darker side—to it all. One he didn't know about.

"I'm about to find out." I squared my shoulders and walked out into the night.

CHAPTER SEVEN

ABOUT TWENTY CARS LINED the drive to the overdone Oakman estate. Modelled on Versailles, but even gaudier, it dominated the acres of perfectly-mowed lawn surrounding it. The windows sparkled into the gloom, and a handful of guests climbed the stairs to the front entrance.

Luke, my driver, pulled to the front. The valet opened my door, and I stepped out into the muggy southern heat. I made quick work of the stairs and entered the sprawling chateau. Crystal chandeliers hung in a line down the main hallway as party guests broke into cliques.

"Sinclair, my man!" Cal strode up and shook my hand. "Welcome, welcome. So glad you could make it."

As if I had any choice in the matter. Turning down an invitation from the Sovereign would result in a myriad of consequences that I didn't even want to contemplate.

"Thanks for having me." I smiled at him as a tall, willowy redhead in a light blue dress walked up and linked her arm in his.

"Gretchen, my love, where have you been?" Cal slid his hand down to her ass.

She winced.

"Still sore from our earlier fun, sweetheart?" He slapped

her ass and she bit her lip, wetness brimming in her glassy eyes. "That's what I like to see." He watched as a tear rolled down her overpainted cheek. "Sin, head on down to the dining room. We're about to start."

"Sounds good." I turned and heard another slap coupled with a pained squeal. Cal had always been a sadist. The redhead didn't realize it, but she was getting off easy. He was capable of much, much worse.

Another slap and another cry followed me down the long hallway. I smiled whenever it seemed appropriate and shook hands with other party guests.

"They invited the Vinemonts? And here I was thinking this was going to be a classy affair." Red Witherington scowled at me from his group of chuckling friends.

"Sad to see that the beating I gave you last spring didn't temper your bad manners any." I smirked as his face fell. "But I'm always up to try again."

"You're lucky we're at Cal's place." He stepped toward me. "Anywhere else, I'd take you the fuck out."

I laughed. "You've always been such an entertainer. I'll tell your sister about this little show tonight once she's done calling me daddy. She's a real screamer. Did you know—"

"Fucking prick!" He lunged at me, but one of his friends held him back. Lucky for Red.

I remained still, even as he tried to surge forward and attack. "See you at dinner, Red. I hope you'll be on your best behavior in front of the Sovereign."

"Motherfucker!"

"Maybe after your sister, sure." I strode past him as his friends tried to talk him down.

I was more than happy to step outside and beat Red unconscious, but I had more pressing matters. Returning greetings, I continued down the hall.

Only select families of the Louisiana elite were in attendance, though I couldn't tell what the significance of the guest list was. There were other sugar producers, yes, but also bankers, politicians, jewelers, textile manufacturers, and a host of others.

Even without any hints from the assemblage, the timing couldn't be missed. We were only a week away from the start of the Acquisition. The rumor was that Cal had already chosen and met with the competitors. Perhaps this was simply a party to congratulate them. The unease in the pit of my stomach said otherwise.

My discomfort grew with each step toward the dining room. A few guests were already inside, chatting among themselves.

"Sin." Sophia glided over, her silvery dress shimmering in the light. "Haven't seen you in a while. Where's Lucius?"

I smiled down into her dark eyes. "He wasn't invited. Besides, am I not enough?"

She let her eyes travel down my body and then back up. "You're more than enough. I haven't seen you for a while, though. How's the public servant routine going?"

"Fine. I have to deal with the rabble far too much for my tastes, but I'll live. How about in-house counsel work? Still enjoying it?"

She wrinkled her perfect nose. "I would hate to have to deal with the lower classes on a daily basis. I don't know how you manage it." She flipped her smooth dark hair over her bare shoulder, the skin smooth and tan. "In-house work is much more enjoyable, though time consuming. I still manage to travel quite a—"

Cal's voice boomed down the hall. "Let's get started, everyone."

"I'll see you around." She gave me a silky smile before retreating toward the other end of the table.

I chose a seat near the far end, the better to observe Cal and the other guests. He walked in, his chest puffed out and his arms spread wide. "Welcome, welcome. Take your seats." Striding to the head of the table, he motioned for everyone to sit.

Cordelia Shaw sat on my right, Bob Eagleton on my left. We exchanged pleasantries as the servers brought bread and salad to the table.

"What do you think we're here for?" Cordelia whispered through her crimson lips. She was the eldest Shaw, her blond hair and bright blue eyes marking her as one of the most attractive women at the table.

"No idea." I speared a piece of lettuce. "But the ball is next week."

She shuddered at my elbow, her pert breast rubbing against me through her thin dress. "I hope it's not me."

I shared her sentiment on most levels, but there was one part of me that wanted to take the crown and all the perks that came with it. Ruling over the nobility would bring me wealth and power beyond anything I could imagine. I considered the row of people, their jewels sparkling, their very demeanors soaked in luxury and privilege. To rule them would be an engaging game, one that would keep me satisfied for the next decade. But the specter of my mother warned me away from any such ambition—her broken mind was a powerful blow against competing in the Acquisition trials.

"Think it'll be you?" she whispered and took a sip of her wine.

I maintained my nonchalant air as I carefully buttered my bread. "I heard he'd already chosen."

She shook her head, her large diamond earring wobbling. "That's just a rumor. I think—I think this is it."

"We'll see."

Talk continued around us as the first course was cleared away, and the servers brought out the entrées. Bob spilled his wine halfway through the main course and proceeded to blame the staff for his ruined shirt and suit. His round belly took the brunt of the damage, a wine stain spreading across the taut fabric like blood. Despite his setback, he made quick work of his fillet, likely never even tasting the savory notes of rosemary and garlic infused into the meat.

Once we reached the end of the entrées, Cal stood. The table chatter ceased immediately.

"Bring the dessert."

A wave of servers entered, carrying petite chocolate cakes atop thin bars of gold. My stomach lurched. I recognized the golden 'plates'. They were invitations to the Acquisition Ball. I'd seen a similar one ten years prior, but I didn't attend the ball or any of the trials. This year, with Cal in charge, would be different. He apparently wanted to kick off the trials with a bang.

A server set one of the cakes in front of me, the chocolate concoction in the form of a small mound with a dimple in the center.

Cal clapped his hands, the sound like a shot. "As you all know, the Acquisition Ball will be held here next Friday. The rest of the invitations are, even as we sit here, going out across the South—and the country, for that matter—to attendees. It's going to be an amazing year." He grinned and stroked his hand down his tie. "You will all remember this Acquisition as the most momentous one of your lifetimes. I guarantee it."

A smattering of polite applause rippled around the room.

"Stop, stop. You flatter me." His grin grew even wider, his too-white teeth splitting his face into halves. "But there's one more thing I need to do before we get started. I have to pick the competitors."

The room was so silent that it seemed most of its occupants were holding their breaths.

"Before you, sits a decadent dessert." Cal waved down the table.

I eyed the innocuous cake. Was something rotten inside?

"It's tasty. I may have sampled one before dinner." He rubbed his stomach for emphasis. "As you all know, I love surprises. So, my three chosen Acquirers will have a little something different inside their cakes. You'll know it when you see it, ladies and gents."

He raised his glass. "Pick up your spoons and dig in."

The guests hesitated, some of them clenching their eyes

shut to avoid finding out. I took my spoon and perched it over the smooth cake, trying to discern if it would blow up in my face or simply ooze into a chocolaty mess.

"Thank God." Cordelia had cut into her cake. Dark chocolate cascaded from it, and she split it all the way open just to be sure. It was just a dessert, nothing more. She dropped her spoon as if it had burned her. Quiet sighs of relief rose from the table.

"Oh." Bob spit into his napkin. "This tastes horrible."

His golden plate was covered with crimson and the distinct scent of copper rose from the cake's warm interior.

"It's blood."

He shrugged and wiped the red from his lips. Disgusting.

A whoop sounded from the end of the table near Cal. It was Red Witherington. "Fuck yeah!" He laughed.

Cal grinned at him and then glanced around the table. When his eyes landed on me and stayed, the hairs at the back of my neck stood on end.

"One more." He didn't look away. Others caught on and began to stare, waiting for the reveal.

There was no way out, no way to stop the inevitable. I eased the spoon into the cake. It slid easily. No filling escaped as the edge of the spoon tapped against the gold beneath. I twisted the spoon slightly. A stream of blood flowed around the silver and pooled on the gold.

It sank into the grooves of the invitation and put the letters in sharp relief. There was no mistaking the words that had been cut into the golden surface, now darkened with crimson. Sinclair Vinemont, Acquirer.

CHAPTER EIGHT

I STARED AT THE ceiling. I'd been doing it for the past few nights—ever since Cal's dinner. The rules played over and over in my mind as I traced the corners of the room with my gaze. Three Acquirers, one victor. Winning would cement the Vinemonts at the top of society. Wealth, privilege, and the freedom to live our lives in any way we chose.

Losing. I closed my eyes. I wouldn't think about losing. Tossing the sheet off, I stood and strode to the shower. Mr. Rousseau's sentencing was set to start in two hours.

I left the bathroom light off, soaking up the darkness as the warm liquid cascaded down my body. In the inky black of the bathroom, I couldn't tell if it was water or something worse.

Red hair, green eyes, fair skin—Stella floated along the river of blood that ran through my mind. I'd wanted her for myself. I'd wanted to claim her on my own terms, to master her and break her my way. The fire that burned inside her lured me closer because I wanted so badly to feel the burn. But the game was no longer my own. I'd wanted her before. Now, I needed her.

Would the fire that burned inside her be enough to see her through the trials?

I soaped up and rinsed off, ready to put my plans into

41

motion. After I shaved and dressed, I headed into town. Specifically, to Judge Montagnet's chambers. He waited inside, his law clerk nude and on all fours on the floor. A thin trickle of blood ran down the young man's thigh, and I ignored his tears as I sank down onto the judge's sofa. He puffed on a cigar and blew the smoke into the sniffling clerk's face.

"Got my morning started off right." Montagnet smiled. "Get dressed and get out." He kicked the clerk, who hurriedly dressed and escaped into the adjoining office.

"I heard about Cal's selections." He took a hard drag on the cigar, the tip flaming orange.

I nodded and smoothed my hands along my thighs. "Yes."

"You picked who you're going to acquire?"

"Yes." I pulled a sheaf of paper from my pocket and handed it to him.

He glanced it over and smiled. "Smart boy." He rose and shuffled to his desk. Drawing out a fountain pen, he signed the document with a flourish, then folded it up. He used his lighter to heat a small nub of wax, pressed it to the paper, and then affixed his seal to it. "All done here." He handed it back.

I blew on the seal. He watched me and licked his lips.

Once satisfied it was cooled, I placed it in my pocket next to its counterparts.

He sank back down and rubbed his knees. "Damn, these floors grow harder the older I get."

I nodded in empty agreement despite my revulsion.

He zipped his robe all the way up, his appearance of fairness complete. "I guess we'd better hop to it. Time for the sentencing to start." After lurching to his feet, he lumbered to the door leading to the courtroom. He peeked over his shoulder, his eyebrows high. "So, *Counsellor*, you think you'll get her?"

I stood and followed him through the door, my mask firmly in place. "I know I will."

COUNSELLOR

CHAPTER ONE
SINCLAIR

IN THE HEART of every man is a darkness. Primal. Instinctive.

At its most basic, it's a desirous nature—one that covets, demands, takes. Most men brick it up behind a wall of self-control. They invest time and effort in maintaining the separation. These men, good men, control the darkness until it withers away and becomes nothing more than a shadow haunting their innermost thoughts. Something easily forgotten, dismissed, erased.

I've never been a good man.

My darkness is neither restrained nor buried. It lives right at the surface. The only thing that hides it is my mask.

My mask is the law, the light, the pursuit of justice. It is forthright and airy. It is the appearance of righteousness in a fallen world.

The mask I wear is purely the act of a predator. Theater. Pageantry. Deceptive and lethal. It allows me to get close and closer still until it is time to strike.

I stalk so near that my prey can feel the tickle of my breath, the coldness of my heart, the depth of my depravity. Only a whisper separates me from what I desire.

Then the mask falls away, and all my victim sees is darkness.

CHAPTER TWO
STELLA

THE DISTRICT ATTORNEY sat completely still at the dark, polished table across the courtroom. My father sat in front of me at an identical table, but he was full of nervous energy. He shifted, ran a hand through his silver hair, and leaned over to whisper to his attorney.

I clasped my hands in my lap until the ring on my index finger dug into my flesh. This was the last chance my father had for freedom, the last day he would be able to throw himself on the mercy of the court. My gaze wandered back to the district attorney, the one who had my father arrested. Investigators scrutinized every last cent the old man ever invested or borrowed. And, just like that, my world became a smoldering heap of ashes. All because of one man.

Sinclair Vinemont was unmoving, like a spider poised on a web, waiting for the slightest sensation of movement from a hapless moth. My father was the moth, and Vinemont was about to destroy him. The investigation and prosecution had been the careful work of a master. Vinemont had woven the cocoon tighter and tighter until my father was caught from all sides. He had nowhere to run, nowhere to try and hide from Vinemont's poison. Dad was being systematically dismantled by the silent monster in a perfect suit.

I wanted to crumble. I couldn't. Dad needed me. No

45

matter the long list of allegations and the even longer list of evidence against him, he was my father. He had always been there for me. Always protected me, stood by me, and encouraged me. Even after what my mother had done. Even after what I had done.

I would not leave his side. He was staring down a hefty prison sentence. Even if the worst happened, I would visit him, call him, write him, and keep him company until the day he got out. I owed him that and much more.

I stared at Vinemont so hard I hoped he would burst into flames from the sheer heat of my hatred. I'd wished for his demise for so long it had become like second nature to me. I hated him, hated every slick word from his mouth, every breath he took. Vinemont's downfall was stuck on replay in my mind. As I glared at his back, he remained tranquil, completely at ease despite my father coming apart with worry at the table next to him.

I forced myself to drop my gaze, lest anyone see me glaring at him with embittered rage. I couldn't bear for my father to suffer any further torment, especially not if it was based on any of my actions. My hands were pale in my lap, a white contrast to my dark pinstriped skirt. I took a deep breath and settled myself. It would do no good for me to fall apart now. Not in the face of my father's sentencing. I let out my breath slowly and looked up.

Something was different. I darted my gaze to the side. Sinclair Vinemont sat just as still, but now his eyes were trained on me. His gaze pierced me, as if he were seeing more than my exterior. I refused to turn away and, instead, gave him a matching stare full of righteous anger. We were locked in a battle, though not a word was said and no one threw a punch. I wouldn't look away. I wouldn't let him win even more than he already had. I perused his appearance more fully than I had ever dared. He would have been handsome—dark hair, blue eyes, and a strong jaw. He was tall, broad, fit. The perfect man except for the ice I knew coated his heart.

The internet had told me everything I needed to know about him. Single, old money, career in public service, and at twenty-nine years old, he was the youngest district attorney in parish history. The only thing I didn't know about him was why he would dare look at me, why he thought he had any right to pin me with his gaze after he'd ruined my life. I wanted to spit in his face, claw his eyes, and make him hurt the same way he'd hurt my father and me.

The door at the front of the courtroom opened and the judge entered, a stark, elderly man in black robes. Vinemont finally turned away, vanquished for the time being. Everyone in the courtroom stood. The judge shuffled to his seat behind a high wall of wood and state insignias, far above the spectators and lawyers.

"Be seated." Despite his apparent age, his voice boomed, echoing off the dusty shutters and up into the gallery above. "Counsellor Vinemont..." He trailed off, sorting through the papers on his desk.

My father sank into his chair and turned to grant me a thin smile. I tried to smile back to give him some sort of comfort, but it was too late. He'd already faced forward, watching the judge. I willed the judge to let my father go, to suspend his sentence, to do anything except take him away from me. I had no one else. No mother. No one except Dylan, and I refused to rely on him for anything.

Vinemont stood and fastened the top button of his suit coat before stepping from behind the table. He was tall, and like so many dangerous things, effortlessly beautiful.

The bespectacled, bearded judge was still rifling through sheets upon sheets of documents when Vinemont spoke.

"Judge Montagnet, I have several victims lined up to speak against Mr. Rousseau." His deep Southern drawl was an affront to my ears. Even so, words spilled off his tongue with ease. He could charm the devil himself. As far as I was concerned, Sinclair Vinemont *was* the devil.

I wished we'd never left New York, never travelled to this backwoods bayou full of snakes. Vinemont condemned my father with airy ease every chance he got. No one spoke against him. No one countered his venomous lies other than the ham-handed defense attorney my father hired. So many of the people we'd met in this town were good, forthright souls—or so I'd thought. They weren't here. They didn't sit on my father's side to give him support against Vinemont's false charges. They hadn't come to testify that my father's sentence should be reduced or that he should be granted mercy. It was only me and rows upon rows of empty, cold pews. We were alone.

On Vinemont's side of the courtroom, two rows full of people, maybe twenty in all, sat and glared at Dad and me. Most of them were elderly men and women who had invested with my father. They blamed him for losing their money when all he did was invest as they requested. He had no control over the market, or the crashes, or the resulting instability. My father wasn't the monster Vinemont had made him out to be.

One of the women, gray and wrinkly, met my gaze and made the sign of the evil eye. I only knew what it was because she'd done it before, the last time I'd seen her in court during my father's trial. I'd looked it up and realized she was cursing me. With each movement of her hand, she was willing destruction down on my head. I looked away, back to the true reason for my father's disgrace and my desperation. Sinclair Vinemont.

The judge nodded. "Bring up your first witness, Counsellor."

I steeled myself as one by one, the alleged victims walked, limped, or wheeled past me to testify against my father. Their tears should have moved me, their tales of trust broken and fortunes lost should have forced some shred of empathy from my heart. All I felt was anger. Anger at them for getting my father into this mess. More than that, anger at Vinemont as he stood and patted the "victims" on the shoulder or the arm and gave out hugs like he was running for office. Every so often I could have sworn he leered back at me, some sort of smug satisfaction on his hard face.

The day droned on with story after story. With each witness, Dad slumped down farther in his chair, as if trying to melt away into the floor. I wanted to put my hand on his shoulder, tell him things could be fixed. Instead, I sat like a statue and listened.

The accusations stung me like a swarm of hornets. After the sixth or seventh witness, I went numb from their venom. Despite the breadth of the charges, I did not doubt my father. Not for a moment. Vinemont had done all this to ensure his reelection or for some other, similarly vile purpose.

When the last witness finally turned her walker around and shuffled back to her seat, the silence became a separate presence. Heavy, ominous, and draining, like a specter haunting the empty spaces of the room. My father remained hunched forward, his head bowed.

"Well, judge, I think you've heard enough." Vinemont held his hands out beside him, the show at an end.

"I have. I'm going to need the evening to think on the sentence." He glanced around the courtroom, his impassive gaze stopping on me for a moment longer than anyone else. "I'll have my verdict in the morning."

Vinemont turned to the judge and gave him a slight nod. Judge Montagnet returned the nod and then banged his gavel. "Court is adjourned."

"Just let me make you feel better." Dylan leaned over me, pushing me sideways onto the ancient leather sofa in my father's library.

"I can't do this right now." I tried to push him off but he pressed harder, overcoming my balance so I fell on my back beneath him.

He put his mouth to my neck, sucking my skin between his teeth. He was large and well-muscled thanks to endless lacrosse and rowing. He crushed me and constricted my chest.

"Please, Dylan." I gasped. I should have been afraid. I wasn't. I was still dazed from the courthouse. Dylan was just adding to the long line of disappointments I'd suffered over the past six months.

He pushed his knee between my legs.

"I can make it all go away for you," he murmured against me. "Just let me make you feel good for a minute. You need a break."

He forced his hand up my skirt.

"Stella? Where are you?" My father's voice calling my name had my stepbrother off me in a heartbeat.

Dylan gripped my hand and yanked me into a sitting position as he straightened his button-down and smoothed his blonde hair. He winked at me. The bastard.

When Dad didn't show up in the doorway, I knew it was the "come here" sort of call.

"I have to go."

"Later," Dylan whispered.

Not if I can help it. Dylan had taken one youthful mistake committed years ago and turned it into some sort of lifelong flame. No matter how many times I told him, he just didn't believe that twenty-five year-old me wasn't the same as the foolish, needy nineteen-year-old I once was.

When my father and I had moved to Louisiana, we were despondent. Mom had left this world without saying goodbye or giving an explanation. Dad and I were adrift, trying to come up with some way to carry on even though our heart was gone, buried in the cold ground of a New York cemetery.

Dad eventually took a liking to Dylan's mother and tried to make a new start with her and, admittedly, her family fortune. Neither venture worked out and they divorced after only six months. Dylan and I were mismatched step-siblings if ever there were any. I painted and read. He loved sports and abhorred learning of any sort if it didn't have to do with Xs and Os on a whiteboard.

Still, I was sad and desperately looking to feel something, anything, in the wake of my mother's death. Dylan was there and more than willing. So, I did something foolish. It was my first time—my only time—and I didn't exactly regret it afterward, I just didn't think about it. It was a non-event for me. That wasn't the case for Dylan, unfortunately.

I shook thoughts of him from my mind as I followed my father's voice to the back of the house and into his study.

Dad had sunk our last few dimes into this turn-of-the-century Victorian home. The whimsical façade was charming. The leaking ceilings and drafty windows? Not so much. Even so, it had been a safe place until Vinemont's tendrils had begun to invade, first with visits from investigators, then the arrest, then the searches. Vinemont had shown up each step of the way, reveling in the torment he inflicted.

For the millionth time that day, I hoped Vinemont would spontaneously combust. Then I strode into my dad's study.

The fire was crackling, and the room smelled of my father's pipe. The atmosphere in that room always had a way of putting me at ease, making me feel safe. Even now, after all we'd been through, I still felt a familiar comfort when I walked in.

Along the back wall near the high windows, he'd arranged the draft paintings and sketches I hadn't sent to the local gallery. I'd caught him so many times just standing in front of whichever piece he'd decided to peruse for the moment, staring into it as if it held some sort of answer. My mother had taught me to paint. Maybe he was seeing her in the strokes and lines?

My feet hit the soft Persian rug that I used to play on as a child, bringing me back to the here and now. My father sat in his favorite wingback chair near the fire. The room felt fuller, somehow more occupied than usual, as if there was less air or not enough space.

Despite the crackling flames, the room was colder, darker. My familiar comfort drained away. Someone else was sitting in the matching chair facing my father, though I couldn't see who it was.

My pace slowed as I saw my father's stricken look. His wrinkled, yet still handsome face was pale, even in the flickering firelight. The first coils of dread snaked around my heart, constricting it slowly.

"Dad?"

Then I caught the scent of *him*. Whenever I passed him in the courthouse or when he came too close to where my father and I sat, I'd gotten a taste of this same scent. Woodsy and masculine with a hint of some sort of sophisticated tinge. My knees threatened to buckle but I kept going until I stood behind my father's chair and faced my enemy.

Vinemont's cold gaze appraised every inch of my body. "Stella."

I'd never heard him say my name. He spoke it with his signature arrogance, as if just uttering the word was somehow beneath him.

I scowled. "What is this? What are you doing here?"

"I was just discussing a business arrangement with your father. He doesn't seem inclined to accept my terms, so I thought I would run them past you. See if I got a different result."

"Get out," I hissed.

He smirked, though there was no joy in his eyes, just an inscrutable coldness that radiated out and made my skin tingle.

"I think you should leave." Dad's voice broke on the last word.

"Do you, now?" Vinemont never took his eyes from me. "Before I've had the chance to give Stella the particulars?"

I put my shaking hands on the back of my father's chair. "What are you talking about?"

"Nothing. Mr. Vinemont should be leaving." My father's voice grew a bit stronger.

"Y-you can't be here talking to my father without his attorney." I forced the tremor to leave my voice. "I know the law, Vinemont."

Vinemont shrugged, his impeccable dark gray suit rising and falling with the movement. "If you aren't interested in keeping your father out of prison, then I'll go."

He didn't move, simply watched me with the same dark intensity. Goosebumps rose along the back of my neck and shoulders.

What is this?

"What do you mean?" I asked. "How?"

"As I was just explaining to your father, I have a certain deal to offer. If you accept it, then he'll stay out of prison. If not, then he'll be going away for the maximum sentence—fifteen years."

"A plea deal? But you've refused this whole time to make any deal at all." My voice rose, anger influencing every word. "You were in the papers, telling anyone and everyone that you would do nothing short of seeing my father rotting in prison."

"Plea deal? I never said anything about a plea deal. I didn't realize you were this foolish." He steepled his fingers and canted his head to the side. He looked like Satan, the firelight dancing along his strong features. "No, Stella. I already have a conviction, nothing left but sentencing for him. And I have no doubt he'll get the max. I've made sure of it."

He spoke as if I was a small, slow child in need of extra after-school help.

"Then what? What are you offering?" My hands fisted, my fingernails digging into my palms. "And what do you want in return?"

"Ding ding ding, she finally catches on." His smirk grew into a wicked grin that chilled every chamber of my heart. His teeth were even and white. If there had been actual warmth in the smile, he would have been beautiful. Instead, he was the monster from my nightmares.

"The deal is simple. Even simple enough for you to understand, Stella." He reached into his inner suit coat pocket and drew out a folded sheaf of papers with some sort of wax seal. "All you have to do is sign this and your father will never see the inside of a prison cell."

"No. I've heard enough. Get out of my house." My father stood and came around the chair to stand by my side.

Vinemont finally tore his gaze from me and glowered at my father. "Are you certain, Mr. Rousseau? You do realize that a Louisiana prison is hell on earth as it is, but I have ways to make it even more unbearable. Cell mates and such? It would be a shame for you to get paired with a violent— or amorous—sort, especially at your age. You wouldn't last long. Maybe a month or two until you broke. And after you're broken, well, let's just say the prison system isn't exactly known for spending medical dollars on old, decrepit thieves."

"Get out!" My father's voice rang out stronger than I'd ever heard it, even as he trembled next to me.

Vinemont's smile never faltered. "Fine. See you in court."

He tucked the papers back into his coat, rose, and strode from the room. Confidence permeated his movements as he stalked out like some big, dangerous animal. The sureness of his words, the conviction of his gait left me feeling at once chilled yet burning to know why he'd come.

What the hell is going on?

When he was gone, I was finally able to take a full breath. I clutched the back of the chair. "What was that?"

My father pulled me into his chest, his familiar smell of tobacco and books cutting through Vinemont's more seductive scent. He was quaking violently. "No. Nothing. Forget about it. About him."

"What did he want? What was in those papers?"

"I don't know. I don't care. If it has anything to do with

you, I don't want it. I don't want him near you."

I leaned away and looked into my father's eyes. He didn't meet my gaze, only watched the fire behind me the same way he would stare into my paintings. He studied something far away, past the flames and the bricks and the mortar.

Fatigue was written in every line on his face. Not even the flickering orange glow could hide how drained, how frightened he truly was. He hadn't looked this haunted since the night he found me lying on the floor, almost two years ago. I rubbed my eyes, trying to erase his fear and the memories from my mind.

He let out a labored groan and fell back against the chair.

"Dylan!" I called.

My stepbrother appeared in the doorway within moments. "What's going on? Was that the dick prosecutor I passed in the hall?"

"It doesn't matter, just please help Dad to his room. He needs to rest."

"No, no. I'm fine." Dad clutched me to him again, his grasp weaker, fading. "I love you, Stella. Don't forget that. No matter what happens tomorrow."

I forced my heart to stay together. If it shattered, I would be of no use. I couldn't become a quivering heap of regret, not yet. Not until I found out what Sinclair Vinemont wanted from me.

CHAPTER THREE
SINCLAIR

I TAPPED MY fingers along the top of my thigh as I waited. I hated waiting. Something about it made me itch to do something, anything, to keep my life moving. Good or bad, it didn't matter. Given my history, most likely bad.

I wouldn't have to wait long. I knew she would come. The dutiful daughter, rushing after any salvation for her father she could find. Poor little idiot. Salvation had a price—the highest one imaginable—and I knew she would pay it the moment I first laid eyes on her.

She'd been sitting at her father's side at his arraignment. Her red hair had been pulled back in a tight bun and she wore a black suit, as if she were in mourning. She wasn't. Not yet. She would be soon enough. I'd caught sight of her as I walked through the door from Judge Montagnet's chambers.

It had been immediate—I wanted her. More than that, I wanted to break her, to make her mine and take everything from her until I was the only thing she thought, or dreamed, or breathed.

She seemed easily breakable. Her pale skin and delicate wrists with the tell-tale scars were like a lure to me, and her understated curves would look perfect when reddened by my hand or belt. But my momentary infatuation faded with each step closer I came to her downcast eyes. She'd be too easy, too quickly cowed and brought to heel. She wasn't a challenge, and I wouldn't waste my time.

But then she'd looked at me. Her eyes were fire, heat, hate. I wanted to stoke the flames, to make her despise me with even more ferocity. I knew how to get her there, to drag her down into the darkness and twist her beyond recognition. I would do it, too. There was no longer an 'if', only a 'when'. Things had been set in motion that were beyond even my control. She was my Acquisition.

I shifted in my seat and willed her to come to me. The sooner the ink dried on our deal, the sooner I could begin her education. The front door of the Rousseau estate opened, casting yellow rays of light onto the wide, curved stoop. Her small figure took the few steps down the stairs, and she strode toward my car with purpose. I couldn't see her face in the dark, but her movements were enough. She had steeled herself for this, strengthened every fiber of her being. I would tear it down piece by piece until she was naked, shivering, and begging for more.

My driver, Luke, got out and opened the back passenger door for her. She slid in next to me, though she took care to come no nearer than absolutely necessary. She still wore the light blue blouse and black skirt from earlier. The coat was gone, and she'd put on some unbecoming flats. I frowned.

"I should've known you'd be waiting out here like a spider."

I smiled at her. She would come to regret that statement. "What can I do for you, Stella?"

"What's this deal?"

I reached into my coat pocket and she jumped. She pressed herself back into the car door. Her fear made my cock spring to attention, annoying me. This wasn't about fucking her. This was about defiling her. Destroying her.

Adding her to a gruesome menagerie.

"As I said before, Stella, it's simple." I drew the document from my pocket and handed it to her.

She looked at it as if it were a particularly venomous snake before darting her hand out and taking it.

"Luke." At my command, my driver flipped on the interior lights.

Stella turned the documents over in her hand and stared at the large 'V' wax seal, covered in the classic vines that adorned the Vinemont crest and estate. "What is it?"

"A contract."

Her gaze shot up. She had dark half-moons under her eyes, and her skin seemed almost sallow in this light. She was worn down, or at least she thought she was. This was nothing compared to the coming months.

She studied my mask. Finding nothing there to enlighten her, she broke the seal and unfolded the contract. I'd written it myself in perfect calligraphy. She read through the recitals on the first page, which stated the parties to the contract, dates, duration, and other boring particulars.

"One year?" She said it to herself more than to me as she flipped to the second page.

Her eyes grew wider with each line she read, until a look of utter horror painted her face. It was beautiful. The paper shook as a tremor settled into her hands. She finished the page and flipped once more. The last page was simply for her signature.

It seemed impossible, but she shrank even further back, melding herself against the leather and metal of the car door. "You can't do this." Her eyes were glassy, fearful.

"I'm not doing anything. I've simply presented you with terms. You can agree to them or not. It's up to you."

"What will happen if I don't agree?"

"That's the question of a child, Stella. Worse, you already know the answer to it."

Her chin shook and her green eyes welled. "You'll send my father to prison."

"No, I'll make sure your father *dies* in prison."

Her breath left her so quickly it was as if I'd punched her in the gut. And I had, in a way.

She recovered, though her voice was no more than a whisper. "But if I do agree—"

"Then you are mine for one year. To do with as I please when I please. You will live with me at the Vinemont estate. You will do as you're told. You will serve me and whoever else I want. I will own you, body and soul."

Though she trembled, she lifted her chin the slightest bit. "No one can own my soul."

I already do. "What's it going to be, Stella? This offer is quite time sensitive. Your father's sentencing is at eight a.m. sharp. And it's," I made a show of checking my watch, "ten fifteen p.m. right now. Tick tock."

"How do I even know you have the power to do this? How do I know you'll do what you say? I'm supposed to take the word of a man like you?"

A flame of anger licked around my heart. "Are you questioning my honor, Stella? I wouldn't do that if I were you."

She laughed, the sound shaded with exhaustion. "What is the word of a man like you worth? What sort of man presents someone with a slave contract and says 'sign it or your father dies in prison'? This isn't even enforceable. I may not be a *counsellor*, but even I know that."

She threw the pages back at me, adding more to her punishment. She was already poised to endure more pain in the next twelve months than she had for her entire sheltered life.

I neatly arranged the papers and pulled the final document from my coat pocket. This was sealed with a wax 'M'. I held it out to her. She ripped it from my hand and tore through the seal.

When her face fell, I was disappointed. No more fight? No disbelief? No amazement at how completely I'd caught her in my trap? Instead, she just looked defeated. She *was* defeated, of course, but would it hurt her to lament her situation a bit more loudly?

"Judge Montagnet?" Her voice was barely audible now.

"Old family friend. You see, in this parish, old money has its own ways. This happens to be one of them. The North may have won the war, but slavery has always been in vogue around these parts. I don't choose based on color. That's barbaric. I choose based on certain other factors."

"Like what? Finding someone who will do anything to save the father she loves? Desperation? Is that it, you sick fuck?" The fire in her eyes was indulgent, alive.

Her punishments were adding up each time she opened her lips. Too bad I wouldn't taste them for a while yet. Not until she was broken beyond all repair and begged me to take her.

"Not quite. But that's all you need to know for now. What I need to know is whether you agree to my terms. As you see, Judge Montagnet has agreed to suspend your father's sentence for the year's time you agree to be mine. If at any time you breach this contract, Montagnet will immediately sentence your father and have him taken to the prison of my choosing. I rather like Dunwoody—no air conditioning and a widespread rodent infestation." I waited a beat, just to let the idea of rats crawling over her father while he slept sink into her mind. Then I continued, "So, as I've said from the start, it's up to you. The choice is yours."

I handed her back the contract. She took it, though I still wasn't sure if she'd rip it to pieces before my eyes. Her anger was unpredictable, wild. I wanted to taste it, take it in and relish it.

"Choice? You call this a choice?" She pushed her hair behind her ear in a violent movement.

"That's exactly what it is. Don't sign. Let your father meet his fate. Or do sign, and give him a total reprieve." I relaxed back into my seat, though I kept my gaze on her.

She chewed her lower lip hard enough to draw blood. She didn't seem to notice. I wanted to run my thumb across her mouth and sample the flavor.

She stared past me, back into the warm light cascading through the front door of her house. "I can't decide on this right now. I need to get out of here. Away from you."

"I'm afraid that's not possible, Stella. I'm an early riser and, what with how late it already is, I'll need to be getting back home. So, you either stay here and I'll see you at the sentencing, or you come with me now and put the whole unpleasantness of the court system behind you and your father."

I smiled.

She cringed. Perfection.

I couldn't let her out of the car, not now that she was so close to signing. I could tell she was standing at the edge of the precipice, looking over the side and pondering the jump. Would the fall kill her? *Perhaps.*

She dropped her gaze to her lap. "How can you do this? You're supposed to uphold the law."

My hand itched to slap her for such a foolish question. For the pure naïve idiocy of it. But she wasn't mine yet.

"Public offices like mine are just a remnant of the *noblesse oblige.* It means nothing to me or my family. We couldn't care less if people like you rape and murder each other, or get hooked on drugs, or hurt their own kind. Enough questions. What's it going to be, Stella?"

"People like me?" Her eyes, shimmering with tears, found mine again.

My anger had reached its zenith. Her futile display of emotion wasn't going to change my plans. Nothing would. "For fuck's sake, Stella, sign it!"

She recoiled at my words and turned to open the car door.

Shit. I forced myself to remain still. I wanted to grab her by the hair and drag her to me. I didn't. I let her finally find and pull the handle before she ran away and back into the house. The door slammed behind her, smothering the yellow light and leaving everything dark.

CHAPTER FOUR
STELLA

I DASHED PAST the library, narrowly avoiding Dylan as he came out into the hall.

"What—"

I ignored him and took the stairs two at time until I came to my room. I heard his heavy steps behind me but I slammed my door and clicked the lock over. I leaned back against the solid wood, my heart beating so loud that I thought my ears would burst from the pressure.

A hard knock at the door.

"Dylan, go away." It was more of a plea than a command.

"What's wrong?"

"I don't want to talk."

"Let me in." He twisted the handle, the metal parts clicking and scraping but not giving way.

"No. Just go. Please, Dylan."

"Who was that guy? Do I need to do something?"

Yes, you need to kill Sinclair Vinemont. "No. Just go."

The floorboards creaked, as if Dylan was walking in a

circle outside my door.

"Dylan, please, just go back to your mom's house. I need to rest. The sentencing tomorrow…"

The creaks stopped and a thump sounded, his hand hitting the door. "I'm sorry, Stella. About earlier. I just thought it would help is all. I didn't mean to cock things up even worse."

"You didn't. Really. I just, I just need to rest is all."

Another, lighter thump. "Okay. You're right. I'll go. See you in the morning. I'll be there for you."

I breathed a silent sigh of relief. "Thank you, Dylan."

His footsteps retreated and I sank down, my legs no longer willing to hold up the weight that grew heavier by the moment. I still clutched the contract to my chest. The infernal sheets of paper threatened to burn me down to nothing more than cold cinders.

I flipped the pages open and stared at the swirls and curves of ink. They had no meaning in the semi-darkness of my room. They were only drawings on a cave wall that told a story of violence and degradation. The elegant curlicues hid nothing from me. The words were stark, cruel—just like the man who'd written them.

I dropped the pages as if they scorched my fingers. The agreement fluttered to the floor and lay there as if it were just harmless paper. I knew better. I pulled my knees up and rested my head on them. How could I sign over my life to a man who I knew would hurt me? I had no doubt of it. The way he'd watched me in the car, as if I was a plaything, still haunted me. I'd been fearful of him before, of something I couldn't quite put my finger on. I still couldn't explain it, but now I was terrified.

Tears welled and leaked down my nose before landing on my knee and rolling down my leg. I sat like that for a long time. Minutes, hours. However long it took for me to go through my memories of my father. How strong he'd been when my mother had checked out of this life. How much stronger he had to be when I'd tried to do the same thing. Could I let him go to his death, all the while knowing I could have saved him?

One year. It wasn't so long. I'd wasted a year recovering from my suicide attempt. Would it be such a loss for me to disappear for one year? I'd never graduated college. My mother took her life the summer before I was to attend NYU. My life was put on hold indefinitely. Then Dad had decided to move us here so we could get on with our lives. Dylan's mother helped ease my father's pain for a time, though I withered away, locked in my room, painting dark scenes of even darker thoughts until it all became too much.

I shuddered at the memory of what I'd done. I'd vowed to never be weak again, to never let myself get to the point of wanting the oblivion badly enough to run headlong into it. I couldn't go to that place again. And just as I refused to rush to a dark fate, I refused to send my father to one equally grim.

I stood, my back stiff from resting against the unforgiving door. My decision made, I dragged a carry-on bag from my closet and began packing clothes, not caring whether they were fashionable. The basics would do— shirts, shorts, jeans, bras, socks, panties. I scooped up some toiletries from my bathroom and snagged the photo of my mother and me from my nightstand. I changed into a pair of jeans, a dark t-shirt, and a navy cardigan to protect against the chill in the fall air. After making quick work of my belongings, I pondered whether I should leave a note.

It tore at my heart not to say any goodbyes. I pulled out my stationery with the swirling 'S' along the top. I stood for a while with the pen poised over the page. My hand shook. There was so much to say. Or maybe there was nothing. The pen clattered from my fingertips.

I didn't trust myself. If I put what I felt down on paper, my resolve could waver. My father would know where I went, anyway. He wasn't a fool on any count. I only hoped he wouldn't do anything stupid to try and save me. He had no chance. The look on Vinemont's face when he'd proffered his bargain was one of certainty. If what I'd read about him was true—his family owning the largest sugar factories in America and some of the most expansive sugar cane plantations in a number of other countries—he had ways to keep my father at a distance. He and that snake Judge Montagnet would no doubt see to it.

I opened my bottom drawer and reached up for the knife I'd stashed there. I'd taped it to the bottom of the second drawer so that I was the only one who'd ever know where it was. It was the same blade I'd used on myself. My blood no longer stained the metal, but I knew parts of me were still there, ingrained in the steel. I shoved it into a side pocket of my bag, hiding it among some toiletries and underwear.

I gave one last glance around my room, saying a quiet goodbye, before creeping down the stairs and out to the garage.

I threw my few belongings into my trunk and started the car. It didn't take long to find Vinemont's address on my phone. It was an hour from town, out in the more rural area of the parish. Once satisfied I knew my way, I lay my phone on the small table next to the garage door. I couldn't risk anyone calling me and changing my mind. A plea from my father could break my resolve, and I was determined to see this through. For his sake.

I reversed down the driveway and settled in for the trip, watching the retreating façade of the house instead of the lane behind me. One year, and I would be back. One year, and my father would be safe.

What was one year to someone who should already be dead?

The drive was somber and dark. Though the moon was high, it was only a sliver in the vast expanse of inky black and scattered stars. The farther I drove from town, the more opaque my surroundings became. Night covered the fields of cotton, the groves of trees, and the brambles cloistering the dark waterways.

Soon the road withered down to two narrow lanes with woods encroaching on either side. I continued onward, though no cars passed anymore. It was just me, alone, being drawn ever forward into Vinemont's trap. I chewed at my lip, the taste of copper the only thing that stopped me from worrying away my flesh.

The road curved around to the left and the GPS told me the turn was up ahead on the right. All I saw were trees and thick underbrush, no sign of a house. I drove a little farther until I saw an opening. There was a drive of no more than a hundred feet that ended at a massive gate. I turned and idled up to it. It was wider than four cars sitting side by side and high. It was black wrought iron with metal vines twining and ensnaring the bars. In the center was a 'V', the vines slithering around the letter and creating an impenetrable barrier.

My breath caught in my chest. I looked around each side and saw the same high wrought iron fence flowing away from the gate and disappearing into the shadowy woods. I stopped and tried to calm my heart, to slow the hammering sensation of blood pounding through my veins.

Fear. There was no other word for it. The cold sweat along my temples, the sinking sensation pulling me down into despair. The deepest sort of dread overtook me, and I reached down to the gear shift, ready to put it in reverse and leave. Maybe there was some other way? Something I could do to save my father that didn't involve Vinemont, didn't involve whatever lurked beyond the sinister gate?

The metal shifted, swinging silently inward. There was no guard tower, no obvious camera anywhere along the unyielding metal fence. Still, he must have been watching me. I knew it just as sure as I knew I would be here, with him, for the next year.

I pulled my hand away from the shifter and rubbed a damp palm along my jeans. With a deep breath, I hit the gas and passed through the gate, lurching unsteadily forward into an unknown and uncertain future.

The driveway was initially hemmed in by the same forest and thick brush as the roadway. It was claustrophobic, even with the moon still high and clear in the sky. Slowly, the woods began to recede, leaving well-trimmed grass at the sides of the smooth drive. I'd gone what felt like a mile along the road, seeing nothing other than Louisiana landscape. Here and there would be a bridge crossing over dark waters as I flew past.

Ahead, the grass became expansive, a wide river of rippling emerald in the night breeze. Far in the distance, I finally saw lights glowing through the night. It must have been a house. *His* house.

I let off the accelerator, no longer fearing what dwelled in the dense woods and bayou inlets. Vinemont was a real, tangible danger, not one from my imagination.

Even as the grass expanded, more trees loomed ahead, forming an arch over the drive. These were the classic Southern oaks, moss hanging low from their limbs. Beyond the graceful trees was the home, a structure so tall that I couldn't see its roof for the blocking boughs. Three, possibly four stories of antebellum splendor—large columns anchored the palatial home, and it gleamed a ghostly white in the moonlight.

The windows were wide and tall, warm light spilling onto the porches. I could imagine rocking chairs and children playing tag, running through the grass, or having a picnic. But not here, not while Vinemont ruled over this estate. Despite the home's charm, its occupant lacked even basic human warmth. The magnificent façade was just that—charming camouflage for the depraved soul within.

I slowed and pulled up near the front door. The drive continued off to the right, further into the estate grounds. I took my keys from the ignition and was about to drop them into my purse. I stopped. Why? Would this car be sitting out here waiting for me for the year?

The thought made me laugh. My beat up American-made sedan sitting out in front of this mansion for a year, its battery going dead, parts rusting. It was absurd, just like everything that had happened over the past few months. I let the laughter pour from me. Some turn of the century medical pamphlet would say I had a case of 'hysteria' and advise that I be shipped off to the sanitarium. The giggles tapered off, as if I were sobering up. I didn't know if I'd have the chance to smile or laugh at anything again. Not for a year, at least, and something told me this year would leave scars to last a lifetime.

I dropped the keys in the cup holder and looped my purse over my shoulder before stepping out. I grabbed my bag from the trunk and rolled it to the steps. Mums, perfectly full of fall blooms, lined the flower beds next to the porch. I lifted my bag and rolled over the wide plank floor to the double front doors.

I didn't have to knock. A door swung inward to reveal an elderly butler. He looked stuffy and proper, though he had a smile for me. He was tall and wiry with white hair and light blue eyes. He seemed friendly, if reserved. The only odd thing was that he was getting the door for me at well past midnight.

"Miss." He gave me a small nod.

"Um, hi." I didn't expect this. I expected Vinemont to drag me in and beat me, hurt me, and throw me into a dungeon.

"Would you like to come in?" He smiled the slightest bit, as if amused by my hesitancy on the doorstep.

"I-I thought—"

"You thought what?" Vinemont stalked into the foyer. He wore a pair of dark jeans and a gray t-shirt. I'd never seen him in anything other than a perfectly-tailored suit. He seemed almost human. His chest was somehow broader than I remembered, tapering down to narrow hips and long legs. A five o'clock shadow covered the hard lines of his jaw and fluttered down his neck. His eyes were still cold, though, and as calculating as ever.

And there was something else about him I never thought

possible—dark vines of ink snaked from under his sleeves and down to his forearms. He was like the wrought iron gate—cold, hard, and choked with equally unyielding greenery. His unexpected tattoos shocked me more than the surreal nature of my situation.

I closed my mouth, determined not to answer any of his questions.

"Do come in, Stella. We won't bite." He smiled.

I wanted to slap the look right off his face.

"Farns, this is our newest Acquisition."

The butler blanched and swayed. Vinemont put a hand on the old man's elbow to steady him. That one tiny act of kindness made me feel like I'd fallen into some alternate dimension. I didn't think 'kind' was something ever attributable to the spider standing before me.

Farns turned his head from Vinemont then back to me, his friendly smile faltering. "I see." He sighed. "This year? I see. May I?"

He held a shaking hand to take my luggage. I passed it to him.

"Thank you, Miss—?"

"It's Stella Rousseau," Vinemont said. "Go ahead and get the quilt room ready for her. I would have told you earlier, but I wasn't sure if she'd accept." The cold smile crept back into place as Vinemont continued assessing me.

I bristled. "I think you *were* sure. You knew all along, you bastard."

Farns coughed delicately. "Oh, well, I'll just go get everything straightened out for you, Miss Rousseau." Farns gave Vinemont a strange look, almost pitying, before taking my bag and heading toward the sweeping stairs.

I peered around, ignoring Vinemont. The house was just as beautiful inside as out. Antique wood and plaster work graced every surface I could see. The floors were a warm honey color, reflecting the light of chandeliers and sconces that bathed the rooms in warmth. The furniture was dark, providing a contrast and making everything look even more luxurious.

The room to the right had couches and an elegant writing desk. The one to the left appeared to be a music room. A piano, guitars, and a few other instruments were displayed. I realized the wall paper was actual sheet music, pieces pasted over other pieces until the room was a paper mache made of melody and harmony.

The Rousseau home back in town was large. This house would have swallowed it whole and come back for seconds.

"When you're finished gawking, we can get down to business." Vinemont was still sizing me up, maybe deciding how badly he intended to treat me. I didn't know. Everything was so foreign, so overwhelming. Even so, I forced my spine to straighten. I wouldn't let him intimidate me.

"Fine." I glared back at him.

He turned and walked past the staircase, leading me deeper into the house. The grandeur didn't end. Paintings and rich tapestries lined the halls. Some of the artists I recognized, others were a mystery, but I wanted to stop and inspect each one. Instead, I followed my captor. He drew me into a dining room with two bright crystal chandeliers overhead. The table sat at least two dozen people.

He went to a sideboard with a decanter and glasses atop it. "Have a seat. Want a drink?"

I was confused before. Now I was utterly lost. "A drink?"

He looked at me over his shoulder as he poured perfectly. "Yes, Stella. In everyday parlance it means a liquid refreshment. In this context, I'm suggesting an alcoholic beverage."

Asshole. "Yes."

"What's your poison?"

"Whatever you have."

"We'll have to work on your tastes."

I winced at the thought of Vinemont working on anything of mine.

I sank down into the nearest chair and lay my head on the back of my hands.

"What is this?" I mumbled. I wasn't sure if I was asking him or me.

"This is you and I having a drink as we discuss the contract. I assume you brought it?" He put a glass next to me, setting it down with a slight clunk.

He took the seat across from me.

I dug in my purse and pulled the pages out. "Yes."

"Good. Have you signed?" He took a drink from his glass, appearing nonchalant. He didn't fool me. There was eagerness in his eyes, the spider hungry for its next meal.

"No."

"But you're here, so I assume you intend to sign it?"

I leaned back and returned his direct stare. "Why won't you just let my father go?"

"Because he's a criminal."

"So are you."

He drained his drink. "No, I'm not."

"So slavery is legal all of a sudden? No one told me we'd revoked the Emancipation Proclamation."

The corner of his mouth twitched the slightest bit, as if his cruel smile wanted to surface. It didn't. "The real question, the one you keep avoiding, is whether you believe your father is a criminal." He stood and poured himself another drink before returning to the table.

I took my glass and turned it between my palms, the condensation wetting my fingers. Back and forth. "He's not."

"Then you really are as dumb as I think you are."

"That's fair, given I already know you're as evil as I think you are."

He smirked. "Evil? You haven't seen anything yet, Stella."

"Funny, I feel like I've already seen more than enough." I gave him a pointed look.

He pushed back from the table and walked around to

my side before picking up the contract. His scent enveloped me. I could feel him, his eyes on me, as he stood at my back. He bent over and smoothed the paper with his large hand. I noticed a series of scars along the back of his wrist. They were faint, barely noticeable, but there all the same. A crisscross of damage marking his otherwise perfect hand. I had the wild instinct to run my fingertip along the scratches, to see if he really was made of flesh and blood. I didn't. I wouldn't.

"Just so happens I have a pen right here, Stella." He slapped down a fountain pen next to the signature page.

He leaned in closer, his mouth at my ear though he never touched me. "Sign it."

I closed my eyes, hoping I would open them and the nightmare would be over. It didn't work. The paper with my signature line was still in front of me, held in place by his strong hand.

I picked up the pen and poised it over the page. "Are you going to hurt me?" I hated the weakness in my voice, the weakness of the question, but I had to ask.

His warm breath tickled my ear. "Definitely."

My hand began to shake, my resolve faltering.

"But that doesn't mean you won't like it." He reached around me, his hard chest pressing into my back, as he steadied my hand with his own. "Sign it, Stella."

His voice was somehow hypnotic, seductive. Instead of loathing, something else bloomed inside me. It was sick, wrong. Even so, I leaned back into him the slightest bit, searching for some sort of comfort. He didn't withdraw.

His hand was warm, unlike his heart. He pressed down until pen met paper, the ink spreading like blood from a wound.

I should have tried to fight him, to burn the house down and run. But the wall of muscle at my back told me just how futile such thinking truly was. I would have to use other tools at my disposal if I wanted to make it through this ordeal.

I took a deep breath. *For Dad.* I moved my hand under his, making the swirling signature that bound me to Vinemont, that made me his, his to rule and ruin, for a year. When my signature was finished, the last letter inked, he leaned in even closer, the tips of his lips pressing against my earlobe, raising goosebumps down my neck and lower.

"Now you're mine, Stella."

With that, he seized the papers and stalked from the room.

CHAPTER FIVE
SINCLAIR

FUCK. THAT WAS not the way it was supposed to go. I paced around my study as Farns escorted Stella up to her room. What was I doing? It didn't help that my erection was siphoning blood away from my brain. No wonder I couldn't think straight.

I went to the closest half bath and locked myself in. I unzipped my pants, angry at the complication my dick was causing. It wasn't supposed to be like this. This transaction was solely business for me. Something that needed to be done. The same as it had been for other generations of Vinemonts. The same as it had been for centuries. I wasn't a special fucking snowflake. I was a Vinemont.

Of course, the last Acquisition had been done by my mother when I was still a small child, but I don't remember it going so badly straight out of the gate. She had followed the rules, respected the tradition. She was a true Vinemont, whereas I was standing in a water closet with my cock bossing me around. *Motherfucker.*

I pulled the traitorous length from my boxer briefs and began stroking. If I could just squeeze out a release, I would be able to calm down and do this the right way. I closed my eyes and saw her red hair, the way it fell around her shoulders as I'd stood behind her, the way it was begging to be fisted as I fucked her mouth. *No.* I forced my eyes open and looked at my own reflection.

I wouldn't think about her, not like that, not anymore. The time would come when I would fuck her, but not out of any real desire on my part, except for the desire to fully break her.

I fisted myself harder, pumping up and down as my hips bucked. An unwanted image of her guileless green eyes flitted across my mind. It was then my balls drew up tight and my cock jerked, shooting my seed into the delicate, hand-painted sink. Once I was done, I placed my hands on either side of the vanity and took a deep breath.

I had to maintain control. It was the only way to win. This year's Acquisition prize was mine for the taking. All I had to do was stay strong. I stared at myself in the mirror, willing the mask back into place. Once satisfied I was what I needed to be, I straightened.

I cleaned up, rinsed my seed down the drain, and tucked my cock back in. With this little momentary insanity behind me, I knew I would be able to maintain, to win, to ultimately defile Stella Rousseau.

CHAPTER SIX
STELLA

FARNS LED ME to an upstairs bedroom. He flicked on the light and showed me inside. The room was large and somehow light. I thought I'd be led to a cell with shackles and a metal bed. But no, this was a sweet country bedroom, even homier than my drafty room in town. It was along the side of the house, and two expansive windows filled one wall. Quilts hung along the other walls from floor to ceiling.

They were displayed with pride, some folded on racks and some spread out and exhibited. I scrutinized the nearest one with tired eyes. It bore a repeating pattern of a little boy in overalls and a wide straw hat. The fabrics were mixed, though all seemed well used.

"That one dates to 1897, I believe." Farns stood behind me.

"Does he collect these or something?"

"No, miss, he doesn't. His mother did, as did her father, and so on up the Vinemont tree."

"Who made them?"

"This one was done by a great-great grandmother of the late Mr. Vinemont. The rest were done by other Vinemont women and sometimes men, if they had the knack of it."

There were so many others, some done in a similar style, others with art deco influences, some oddly modern. The room was a mix of old and new.

"This one," he pointed to a smaller square of material that was far darker than the others in the room, "was done by Mr. Sinclair's mother."

I ran my finger down a particularly straight seam. There was no pattern to the material, just jagged edges on blue and green fabric. The stitching was a deep crimson, discordant and striking.

"I didn't think people who have been rich forever bothered themselves with being useful."

"Forever is a long time, Miss Rousseau. Most things aren't quite so constant." He gave a slight bow and left, clicking the door shut behind him.

I needed more than veiled information, but I was too tired to follow Farns and ask questions. He wouldn't give me any real answers, anyway. Still, I went to the door and opened it. It hadn't been padlocked from the outside or anything. They had a strange way of keeping prisoners.

I pressed the door shut and eyed the bed. It was a four poster affair with a fluffy white comforter and welcoming pillows. I went to the closet and found it mostly empty. Farns had deposited my bag inside. Quilting fabric and thread were perched on the upper shelves, far from my reach.

I pulled out some toiletries from my bag and took them to the en suite bathroom. It was large for such an old house. Soaking tub, small walk-in shower, vanity, and toilet. I arranged my items in the cabinet and along the sink before getting ready for bed. It was odd, doing these things in a strange house, but I did them anyway. Brushing my teeth and changing into a t-shirt somehow put a veil of normalcy on the whole sinister affair.

I returned to my bag and dug out the knife. Tape still lingered on the blade. I pulled out the third drawer of the bedside table and affixed the knife to the bottom of the second drawer, just like at home. No one would find it there. It was like an insurance policy of sorts. I didn't intend for it to ever spill my blood again. But Vinemont's? That was a definite possibility.

Once satisfied it was hidden, I sat down on the bed. It was plush, luxurious. I was through the looking glass—nothing made sense and everything seemed somehow backwards. Was it a trick? Would Vinemont drag me from my bed after I'd fallen asleep and throw me into a musty dungeon?

I rubbed my eyes, too confused and exhausted to ponder what would happen in the next few minutes, much less in the hours to follow.

I got up and hit the lights. The darkness was almost a comfort to me, like it was cloaking me from prying eyes. I crawled into the unfamiliar bed, sliding between the smooth sheets. They smelled like linen and faintly of detergent. Clean and cool against my skin. These things, this room, they were all meant to seduce me, just like Vinemont's voice in my ear. I wasn't in a fairy tale. Vinemont wasn't my prince.

I snuggled in deeper, hugging an extra pillow against me. It was down-filled, soft and fluffy. I breathed in deeply and let it out. I would enjoy what I could while I could, because I didn't know what tomorrow would bring. Sleep fell like a curtain in front of the stage, slowly obscuring me from view.

A knock at the door jarred me awake. Light streamed in through the windows, giving my cell the appearance of a traditional Southern room.

"Who-who is it?"

"Farns, miss."

"Oh, come in." I sat up and pulled my blanket to my

neck.

He opened the door and took only a single step inside. "Breakfast is ready downstairs. I wanted to let you sleep for a while longer, but Mr. Sinclair has requested your presence."

"I haven't even showered." I pushed my hair back from my eyes, knowing it was a tangled mess.

"Even so." He didn't look at me. In fact, he looked everywhere but in my direction. Modest much?

"Fine. I'll be down in a few minutes." I paused, realizing I had no idea which way to go to get down to breakfast.

"I'll wait while you ready yourself and then I'll escort you, if you'd like," Farns said.

"Yes, please." I dropped the blanket and swung my legs over the side of the bed.

Farns backed out of the room and eased the door shut with a soft click.

I rose and stretched before going to the bathroom, washing my face, and running a brush through my hair. Presentable. But why should I be? Maybe when Farns said "breakfast" he really meant "guillotine" or "the rack." I had no way of knowing at this point. Were his kindly words and face just another put-on like Vinemont's?

I donned another pair of jeans, a tank top, and a cardigan. I wasn't sure about shoes, so I put on some sneakers. I sat for a moment to collect myself, to try and sort through what was true and what was the lie. It was impossible. I only knew one thing for certain—Vinemont was my enemy. Anyone connected with him was suspect, if not an outright danger to me. With that cold thought, I took a deep breath, straightened my back, and went to the door.

Farns was, as he promised, waiting outside. "Right this way, miss."

I followed him down the long hallway. I peered into rooms as I passed. They were all bedrooms in this part of the house, each with a different theme. Some were flowery, others done in rich, dark fabrics.

"So, do you treat all your prisoners like this?" It came off even more snide that I'd meant it to. I was testy, angry, a seething bubble of emotions that seemed to have simmered overnight while I slept and only now erupted at my surface.

Farns stopped and then took another step, as if unsure whether to continue. "I'm not entirely sure how to answer that."

"Why? I'm sure I'm not the first slave Vinemont has owned."

"I, ah. Well, miss, you are the first Acquisition we've had for the past twenty years, if that's what you mean."

"Acquisition? I keep hearing that word. What does it even mean? Is it some code so you don't have to say 'slave'?"

He turned toward me, his eyes kind. He made it hard for me to be cross with him. "I take it Mr. Sinclair hasn't explained the Acquisition trials to you yet?"

"There are *trials?*"

"Yes, there are." Vinemont strode down the hall toward us. "And if you would come downstairs to breakfast, I would explain them to you."

I crossed my arms over my chest. "What's the rush?"

"Farns." Vinemont's gaze darkened and he waved the butler away.

Farns hesitated and then obeyed, retreating back the way we'd come until it was just Vinemont and me. He wore another pair of dark jeans with a black t-shirt, his inked vines snaking down his arms from beneath the fabric. In the morning light, I saw they were a deep green, small leaves done in an emerald, and vicious thorns done in almost black.

He gripped my upper arm and yanked me to walk alongside him.

"Hey—"

"You are testing my patience, Stella." He stopped and pushed me up against the wall. His eyes bored into me. "Don't ask Farns questions like that. He can't help you."

"I can ask whatever the hell I want." The cocktail of emotions roiling inside me had made me bold, even in the face of Vinemont's wrath.

His gaze travelled over my face, down to my lips and then back to my eyes. "That's where you're wrong."

He gripped my hair and pulled my head to the side. His mouth was at my ear again, his Southern drawl whispering darkly to me. "I thought I made it clear that I own you now. You do as I say. If you don't, I'll make sure your father feels the brunt of your punishment."

He stepped into me, pressing my back into the wall and crushing me painfully. I yelped at the sudden aggression. He clapped his free hand over my mouth. I hit ineffectually at his sides, his back. I even tried to knee him, but he took advantage of my efforts and pushed one of his large thighs between my legs and lifted so I was straddling him.

"Fuck." It was a gravelly whisper.

My heart beat faster and faster, panic welling up inside and drowning out any other emotion. He was going to hurt me. Right here, right now in this sunny hallway.

He pulled my hair harder and harder until I thought he would rip it out. I stopped struggling.

"Better. Here's how this is going to go, Stella. You are going to stop trying to make trouble. You are going to do as you're told. This year will pass by much easier for you if you just follow my orders. You can fight me." His lips moved down to my neck, a hairsbreadth from making contact. "And I'm not going to lie, I like it when you fight. It makes this easier for me. But you won't like the results."

He released me and backed away. He ran a hand through his hair as he continued to stare me down. My heart hammered, demanding that I run as far and as fast as I could.

He licked his lips, reminding me of a hungry killer that had scented blood. *My* blood. I shivered under his gaze, hating that my nipples had hardened from the sensation of him rubbing against me.

Vinemont stabbed a finger in the air in the direction he'd come. "Go."

I bolted from the wall and tore down the hallway. I found the stairs to my right and maneuvered down them so quickly I almost fell on the second landing. His steps sounded behind me, heavy and deliberate.

I whirled when I reached the bottom, my stomach growling from the smell of food on the air. I turned right, spotting the front door. I didn't make a choice. My body made it for me.

I ran to the door and wrenched it open. I took off across the porch and down the stairs. The morning sun made the wide expanse of grass seem manageable. The air was crisp, fall had finally settled even this far south.

My sneakers barely touched the pavement of the driveway before I was treading on the soft earth. I ran as hard as I could. I was small. I would make it to the trees and hide. Just curl up somewhere in the roots of a cypress or maybe even climb and hide in the branches. Maybe Vinemont was lying about having the judge in his pocket. Maybe I could go to the police or someone else. I was desperate to believe it as I hurtled through the sunlit lawn.

None of my hopes were true, I knew that, but I didn't care as long as my legs kept pumping, carrying me closer to the salvation of the tree line. I had to get away from him, from the terror, from the flare of unwanted heat he sparked in me.

My lungs began burning, making me painfully aware of my need to stop and take deep gulps of air. I didn't. I pushed myself harder, ignoring the pain in my side, ignoring everything except the approaching sanctuary. I'd made it more than halfway across the emerald field.

I fell. Hard. Arms had encircled my waist and dragged me down so I was lying on my stomach. The grass had softened the fall, but not much. The air whooshed from my already tortured lungs, and my ribs felt on the verge of cracking apart and spearing the organs inside. The smell of fertile earth and verdant green invaded my nose, but his scent mixed in as well.

He was on my back. He gripped my arm and pulled me over roughly. He straddled me, his thighs against my hips. I couldn't see his face. The sun was high behind his head, blinding me. I screamed and tried to slap him, scratch him, draw any sort of blood I could. He captured my wrists easily and pinned them over my head. He leaned over me, blocking the sun yet showing me the scorching anger in his eyes. He was fierce, far worse than he had been upstairs.

"I warned you, Stella. I told you." His breaths were shuddering even as I gasped for air.

He transferred both my wrists to one of his hands and drew back his palm to strike me. I held his gaze. I wanted him to feel it, to know how much I loathed him, to know what I thought of his twisted soul.

His eyes opened a little wider at my stark stare.

"Fuck!" He stayed his hand and, instead, slammed his fist into the ground next to my head. He let out a roar, guttural and full of pent up rage.

He let my hands go and sat back, crushing my thighs. His head was thrown back, as if he were pondering the shape of the lazy white clouds above instead of thinking about how to hurt me. I lay still, once again blinded by the sun.

"You're killing your father." He brought his head back down slowly. His face was calm again, as if some switch had flipped.

"N-no." My breaths were finally evening out, though my head pounded from the adrenaline and lack of food.

"Yes, you are." He leaned down over me, bringing his face only an inch from mine. His erection was hard against my thigh. "If you had escaped, what do you think I would have done? Nothing?"

"I-I didn't think—"

"Exactly. That's your problem." He drew a hand up and fastened his palm around my throat.

I tried to pry his fingers off, scratching him and pulling. He didn't move, only squeezed harder the more I fought. It was as if he were pinching my windpipe, stopping even the slightest flow of air. When the edges of my vision started to dim, I relaxed.

"I thought I made it clear upstairs. I guess I didn't. What do I have to do to get through to you? Hurt you more? Take more?" He ran his free hand down my side, my stomach, and finally to the vee of my thighs.

I whimpered as he rubbed against the seam of my jeans, right over my clit.

"I will, if that's what you want, if that's what it takes for you to understand how completely I own you." He rubbed harder, building a heat inside me. My stomach clenched. I didn't want his pleasure, not like this, but my body wasn't discriminating.

"Is that it, Stella?" He eased his mouth closer to mine as his fingers continued to work. He was so close I could feel his warm, minty breath on my lips. "I've wanted you from the moment I saw you. Before I even planned on making you my Acquisition. What do you taste like? I wonder. I've wondered it for quite some time. Would you like me to find out?"

His fingers continued their maddening pace, forcing desire to swell where there should have been none, where there should be terror and anger instead. I couldn't stop the breathy sound that erupted from my lips.

He laughed, low and husky. "You would like for me to taste you, wouldn't you?"

My hips rose toward his hand of their own accord, wanting more from him. He froze and blinked, as if realizing what he was doing.

"Shit!" He rose up and fell back as if I'd burned him. He sat in the grass at my feet, looking at me like I was a live grenade.

I sat up, blood rushing to my cheeks at how I'd reacted to his unwelcome touch. I saw movement behind him. I shielded my eyes from the glare of the sun and saw a young man, late teens or early twenties, walking up. He had sandy blonde hair, much lighter than Vinemont's, and his features, though similar, were softer, friendlier. He waved.

I dazedly returned it, not knowing what to do. Vinemont turned and saw the newcomer.

"Teddy, go back inside." It was a command, but lacking Vinemont's usual viciousness.

"What's going on, Sin?" The young man kept on his path until he stood at Vinemont's back. "Who's she?"

"She's none of your concern." Vinemont stood and faced him. "Go on in. We'll be in for breakfast in two minutes."

Teddy looked from me and back to Vinemont. "You sure?"

"Yes, I'm sure. It's nothing. Trust me."

Teddy's gaze landed on me, no doubt taking in my disheveled appearance. "Okay, Sin, if you say so. It's nice to meet you, um…"

"Stella. Her name is Stella Rousseau."

"I guess I'll see you at breakfast, Stella." Teddy wrinkled his brow, but eventually took Vinemont at his word. I was glad to see I wasn't the only one who made the same mistake.

Vinemont ruffled the boy's hair as he turned to trudge back to the house.

Are you shitting me? A hair ruffle from Vinemont?

"Up, Stella. Now." A growl for me.

I could either keep fighting and running or acquiesce. Vinemont had already threatened my father again. I believed him. He was serious, lethal. The thought of my father in prison grounded me, reminded me of what I had to do.

I had no choice. I'd signed it away. Running had been instinctive. Now, I needed to calculate, to somehow figure a way out of this mess and keep my father and myself alive.

Vinemont offered his hand with an irritated sigh.

CHAPTER SEVEN
STELLA

FARNS GREETED US at the door. He didn't say a word as we walked by, but he gave me a kindly smile. I followed Vinemont past the now familiar stairs and into the main hallway that led deeper into the house. We passed the dining room from the night before and kept going, the smell of bacon and biscuits increasing the farther we went.

"Try and behave yourself for once," he grated, and turned left into a sunny breakfast room. The table here was smaller than the dining room's, able to seat only twelve. Teddy, the young man from the yard, sat toward the far end and chatted with a pretty maid. When we walked in she stiffened and scurried away.

"You know that's not allowed, Ted."

"What? Talking to the staff is a bad thing?" He grinned.

"Talking, no. Anything else, yes. You're a Vinemont. You can't lower yourself."

Teddy rolled his eyes. "C'mon Sin, I was just getting to know her a little. No big deal." He forked a piece of pancake and stuffed it in his mouth unceremoniously. He pointed the tines at me and mumbled something around his food that could have been "who's this?"

"I told you. Stella Rousseau." Vinemont motioned for me to sit across from Teddy while he took the seat at the head of the table.

The young maid from earlier brought in two plates already piled high with grits, pancakes, bacon, and scrambled eggs.

"If you'd like more of anything, or something different, please let me know." She curtsied and smiled, showing a youthful beauty. "Would you like coffee, tea, juice, or water?"

"I'd love some coffee." My system needed a jolt of caffeine to recover from the run.

"Yes, ma'am." She left and promptly returned with a coffee decanter and cups for both Vinemont and me. She asked my preferences on cream and sugar, but didn't ask Vinemont. She already seemed to know his desires. Once done, she gave Teddy a small smile and returned through the door behind him, to what I supposed was the kitchen. Teddy winked at me. He was a flirt, for certain.

"Okay, now we're alone. Tell me what's going on. You've never brought a woman to breakfast. Honestly, I don't think you've ever brought a woman to the house." Teddy stuffed another piece of pancake in his mouth and smiled.

"If you must know, she's my Acquisition." Vinemont took a long swig of the coffee, even though it was still far too hot.

Teddy sputtered around his pancake before swallowing hard and almost choking. His face reddened, his eyes watering. "That's us? It's us this year?"

I listened intently as I sampled the array the maid had provided. The food was delicious and much needed. I felt like I hadn't eaten in days. The information flying back and forth was even more satisfying.

"It is." Vinemont ripped off a piece of bacon and chewed slowly.

"What is it, really? I know sort of what it is, but not the

whole thing." Teddy looked at me, all his prior flirtation gone.

"I'm not going to discuss this right now. I'm the eldest brother so it falls to me to take care of it. You don't have to worry about it. Needless to say, I want you to treat her with respect, and also to respect my decisions as they pertain to her. Understand, Teddy?"

He put his fork down. "What does that mean?"

"That means you may disagree or even hate some of the things you see or hear, but she is my responsibility and these things must be done."

"Why?"

Vinemont pinched the bridge of his nose. "Because they must."

"Okay, but *why*?"

"Goddammit, Teddy!" Vinemont slammed his fist down on the table.

Teddy jumped and seemed genuinely uneasy. Had he never seen his brother act like this? I could give him a lesson or two about the real Vinemont.

Vinemont placed both palms flat on the table and took a deep breath. He seemed as if he were trying to hold himself together somehow. "Let me give you an idea of what I mean." He turned to face me. "Stella, take off your clothes and stand on the table."

I stopped mid-chew. "What?"

"You heard me."

I looked at Teddy. His eyes were wide, the blood fading from his face as it did the same from mine.

"Don't look at him, Stella. You're not his. You're mine. You will do as you're told or you will be punished. Strip. Unless you'd like me to call Judge Montagnet?"

His threat spurred me into action. I stood.

Teddy did, too. "No, Sin."

"Teddy, sit down. You need to learn how things are done. I've coddled you for far too long."

Teddy backed away from the table as I lifted the hem of

my shirt, pulling it over my head with shaking hands. Tears burned behind my eyes, at the back of my throat, but I did what he said. I couldn't risk not obeying.

"No, Sin, make her stop!" Panic filled Teddy's plea.

"Sit. Down." Vinemont's jaw was tight.

Teddy obeyed. Just like I did. Just like everyone under this roof must.

I unbuttoned my pants and drew down the zipper before shimmying out of them. I took a deep breath, hatred burning in my breast for Vinemont, even though he wasn't looking at me. He was focused on Teddy, where the real battle for control was being waged.

Now only wearing my bra and panties, I put a foot on the nearest chair to climb onto the table.

"I said all of it, Stella, or did you not hear me?" Vinemont's cold voice was quiet.

Bastard. A sob tried to escape, but I wouldn't let it. I reached behind my back and unclasped my bra, a single tear sliding down my face. My mind was screaming, roaring, crying. On the outside, I was placid. Only the uneven fall of tears gave me away.

I pulled my bra off and dropped it in the chair where I'd been sitting moments before. Teddy darted his gaze away. With shaking fingers, I pulled my panties down and kicked them aside.

"Look at her, Teddy." Vinemont fixated on Teddy. "Look!"

Teddy turned his face to mine, his kind eyes now fearful.

"Up on the table. Stand there."

I pulled a chair back and stepped into it before climbing up onto the table. The polished wood was slick and cold beneath my bare feet.

"Face me, Stella." He still stared down Teddy, forcing the boy to watch my every move.

More tears escaped, landing on my breasts and rolling down to my stomach. I dropped my head, fixating on the table beneath me. Humiliation flowed through me like blood, or maybe more like gasoline, fueling my hatred yet explosive at the same time.

"Do you understand now, Teddy? Is it clear?"

"Y-yes."

"Good. Now finish your breakfast." Vinemont took another long swig from his coffee and attacked his food.

Teddy picked at what remained on his plate. "Are you just going to make her stand there?"

"I can make her do more, if you'd like."

Teddy slammed down his fork. "That's not what I meant and you know it."

"This is necessary. It's what has to be done. Get used to it." That was the Vinemont I knew, cold and unforgiving. Maybe he was right. Maybe the sooner Teddy realized his brother was a monster, the better.

Vinemont still hadn't looked at me. Coward.

A whistle sounded at my back. Vinemont's head whipped up, but he didn't look past me. Instead, he focused on me, taking me in, taking everything from me. His expression turned from anger to something else. He stood and froze, tension rolling off him in waves.

"Lucius, glad you could join us." Vinemont's gaze travelled my body. His stare was possessive, desirous.

I wanted to cross my legs, cover myself somehow. I knew he wouldn't allow it. So I stood, letting the degradation wash over me.

"So this is the Acquisition?" A man, his voice similar in tone to Vinemont's, yet silkier.

"Yes." Vinemont's gaze was still on me, as if he didn't want to give me up.

I maintained eye contact, damning him for doing this to me. I hoped he felt every flame of my rage. I hoped it charred his already black heart to ash.

A hand running up the back of my leg startled me and I jumped away. My foot tripped over the edge of the table. I hurtled down.

Someone caught me and set me on my feet. Vinemont

pressed me into him, my face lying against his hard chest. For once, I was happy to be near him, happy to be at least somewhat covered. His hands were warm on my skin, his palms damp. Had he been sweating my forced exhibition?

"She's skittish, huh?"

I whipped my head around. Lucius was tall, lanky, and had similar tattoos as Vinemont. He wore a blue plaid shirt, the buttons at the top casually undone and the sleeves rolled up. His hair was a tousled brown, slightly lighter than Vinemont's and darker than Teddy's. Another brother?

"She's mine, Lucius. I was just teaching our little brother that lesson." Vinemont's voice rumbled against my ear.

Lucius arched an eyebrow before snagging a piece of bacon from my plate and devouring it. "I think all you taught Teddy was that a wanking is absolutely necessary ASAP."

Teddy stood. "I can't take any more of this mindfuck. I'm going into town for the day."

He fled the room in a huff. I envied him.

Lucius kept his gaze on my ass, the one piece of me that wasn't pressed against Vinemont. "She's definitely a prize. Think you'll get to be Sovereign? I'm still not clear on all the rules, by the way."

"Only the firstborn knows the rules. You're just guessing," Vinemont growled.

The tension in the room took on another dimension, thickening the air like invisible smoke.

"Then tell me already." Lucius pointedly licked the bacon grease from his index finger as he continued staring at my exposed rear.

Vinemont released his hold and pushed me behind him. I was beginning to agree with Teddy about the mindfuck. First he wanted to exhibit me and now he wanted to hide me?

"That would be breaking the rules. You aren't a firstborn."

I peeked around Vinemont.

"Fine." Lucius shrugged. "I'll just enjoy the show. I know enough from what Mother told us. This should get entertaining pretty fast. When's the ball?"

"Friday."

"You mean tomorrow? Damn. You waited pretty late to collar your Acquisition." He sprawled in the chair next to mine. "Laura!"

The pretty maid hurried in but stopped as soon as she saw me. Vinemont put a hand on my hip, possessive. She recovered far more quickly than I would have in this situation and poured Lucius a cup of coffee before fetching a plate of food for him.

"Thanks, babe." Lucius grinned at her.

She retreated, but not before casting another worried glance in my direction.

"I trust you'll stay out of my way as far as the Acquisition is concerned?" Vinemont's fingertips dug into me.

"Yeah, what do I care? It would be nice if you'd share, though you've never been particularly good at that."

The pressure increased, his whole hand palming my hip. "Just stay out of my way."

Lucius waved his fork in the air. "Fine. Carry on with your sadism. Ignore the man behind the breakfast plate."

"Get your clothes." Vinemont removed his hand, the warmth gone and leaving goosebumps in its wake.

I crept from behind Vinemont. Lucius watched every move intently as he chewed. I darted around behind him and snagged my jeans, shirt, bra, socks, and shoes, but I couldn't find my underwear.

I pulled the shirt on over my head and hastily yanked on my jeans. Once covered, I peered around the base of the chairs looking for any sign of my wayward panties. They weren't where I'd left them, and I couldn't find them on the floor.

"Lucius, give them up," Vinemont said.

"Give what up?" He shrugged and turned to me. His eyes were lighter than his brother's, sky blue instead of the dark depths of Vinemont's. Lucius gave me lascivious wink.

I didn't think it was possible to like someone less than I liked Vinemont. I may have been wrong.

Vinemont stabbed his fingers through his hair and let out a particularly vile curse before turning toward the door. "Come on, Stella."

I followed Vinemont, but before I left the room, I turned. "I haven't had a shower yet today. Just so you know."

Lucius smiled. "Mmm, I like it best when they've soaked a bit."

Motherfucker.

"You're only encouraging him." Vinemont pulled me down the hall.

"Get your hands off me." I yanked my arm away from him.

"Fine," he snarled. "Just go the fuck upstairs. I can't deal with this right now."

"*You* can't deal with this? Are you kidding me?"

"Stella, I'm warning you." He advanced, crowding me back into the wall.

"I'm not afraid of you." I tried to put the force of my conviction into my words. It was a lie. I was scared, confused, and more alone than I'd ever been.

His hand was at my throat in an instant. "You and I both know that's not true. Get the fuck upstairs. Stay there until I come for you." He squeezed for emphasis before letting me go.

I slipped away from him, stumbling over the edge of the hall runner before righting myself and hurrying away. I looked over my shoulder. He stood perfectly still and watched me. I got the strange feeling that I was one wrong move away from him pouncing on me.

He was a predator by nature.

Right then I knew. If he acted on instinct, he would rip me to shreds.

CHAPTER EIGHT
SINCLAIR

THE MEMORY OF her naked body was forever seared into my mind. I was weak, so fucking weak. I'd thought forcing her to stand on the table was a show of strength, some way to teach Teddy the realities of our lives. Instead, I'd made myself almost blind with lust and gave Lucius a reason to torment Stella. She was *mine* to torment, no one else's.

I wanted to destroy every fucking thing in the house, then rage through the grounds like a tornado before lighting the woods on fire. Instead, I stepped out the front door and into the cool air. I needed a ride. Something to clear my mind and get me focused on the Acquisition trials.

I walked the few hundred yards to the shop out back. It was two stories of distraction. Fast cars, even faster bikes, and all the tools needed to repair each one of them. I ran my fingers down the McLaren, thinking it might be the one to take me far away from here—and as quickly as I needed. But the air was too nice to miss.

I snagged my leather jacket from the wall and chose Emelia instead. She was a revved up American stunner, a motorcycle my father and I had brought back to life years ago. I threw a leg over and cranked her up. She rumbled and purred beneath me. I tore from the shop, taking the road deeper into the Vinemont property.

The helicopter waited on the pad to my left as I cruised by. It wasn't an option. I had to keep my feet on the ground. It would be a simple feat to climb into the cockpit and simply fly away from this house, my responsibilities, and my Acquisition. I wouldn't. I needed to stay, to shepherd Stella through the trials.

Despite the setbacks, breaking her would be a singular treat. What I'd shown Teddy had only been a taste, just the tip of the proverbial iceberg. She had no idea what was in store. I wasn't even sure how far I'd go, but I knew I had to win. Losing wasn't an option.

I gunned the engine harder, rushing past the lake, the scattered cattails bleeding into a brown and green blur as I drove to the levee.

But the way she'd looked, the way she'd reacted to me in the grass, her smell, the way she fought. *Fuck.* I was screwed. I had to stop thinking about her as a *her.* She was an Acquisition—my Acquisition—and nothing more. If I didn't get my head on straight, and get her outbursts under control, tomorrow night would be a disaster. The Sovereign needed to leave the party knowing that my Acquisition was the one to beat, literally and figuratively.

I'd never actually attended an Acquisition Ball, but Mother had told me plenty in her attempts to strengthen me. The depravity in her tales had shocked me, intimidated me. She didn't go easy, telling me exactly what I'd have to do to win. In the process, she'd told me what she'd had to do to win during her Acquisition year. How a piece of her had died. She'd wanted me to endure, to make it through unscathed. To be even stronger than she had been.

I slowed to a stop in the middle of the levee, water sparkling on either side. My thoughts strayed back to the scars on Stella's wrists and the knife she'd hidden in her nightstand. I'd almost taken it from her as she slept. My fingers had traced the handle, the blade. Somehow I knew it was the same one she'd used on herself. Ultimately I'd left it there. I shouldn't have. Another mistake.

The engine roared to life beneath me and the bike ate up the smooth road through the woods and over the waterways. Wild turkeys scattered as I raced through their territory. I made the entire loop around the property before cruising down the winding lane and out to the front gate.

Approaching the bottleneck of woods and metal, I saw the glint of something metallic through the bars. A car sat on the outside, foolishly seeking entrance to my territory. I grimaced at the idiocy of the attempt, the sheer lack of understanding this visit revealed. Still, I knew he'd come.

I pulled to the right so I could stand broadside against the wrought iron. When I killed the engine, a heavy silence fell.

"Mr. Rousseau. Nice to see you."

He peered through the bars and vines, his eyes red and watery. There was nothing to see. Only me.

"Let her go." His wavering voice made me sick.

"No."

"You, motherfucker!" A younger man leapt from the car and rushed over. "Bring her out or we're coming in."

I laughed. "That's adorable. If there's nothing else, I'd best be going. Pressing matters and all."

He gripped the bars and tried to shake them. Nothing. This fence could withstand a lot more than some prep school prick in lacrosse gear.

"Dylan, stop. We can't win that way."

"Listen to the old man, Dylan." I let the venom that had welled up inside me over the past twenty-four hours infect my words.

"Please." It was a teary plea from Mr. Rousseau. "Just let her go. I-I'll go to prison willingly if you'll just let her go."

Pathetic. "Too late. The deal's done. If that's all the business you have to transact, I'm sorry to say you wasted your trip. Goodbye, Mr. Rousseau."

Dylan erupted in yells and a respectable amount of profanity.

I cut off his cries with the fire of my engine, and left them standing at the gate as I screamed along the smooth road toward the house.

They were fools.

She was mine. No one could take her from me. Not even her own blood.

CHAPTER NINE
STELLA

I STAYED IN my room for the rest of the day. There was nowhere I could run, nothing to do. I took a long, hot shower. While I'd been out for breakfast—and the run across the lawn, and the nude exhibition—someone had come in and put luxurious shampoos, soaps, and other thoughtful amenities in my bathroom. The mental image of Farns daintily stacking tampon boxes actually pulled a laugh from me. So, that was something.

After my shower I lay on my bed, cooling off, wearing just a towel around my hair. I clicked on the overhead fan with the remote from the bedside table, letting the cool air waft down over me. The quilts along the walls ruffled with the breeze.

I was warm, relatively well fed, and had a modicum of safety in this room. It didn't erase my unease as much as I would have liked. I was still caught in a web, even if the silken threads that bound me were soft and beautiful.

My eyelids drooped, the heat from the shower and the run from the morning pulling me downward into sleep. But I wouldn't go. Whenever my eyes finally closed, I saw Vinemont's face. His anger. And something else, too. The heat when he'd been on top of me in the grass, his hand between my thighs.

I knew it was a transgression. I shouldn't have wanted it. His voice was a subtle poison, creeping into my system, luring me deeper into his hell. My nipples pearled as I remembered the feel of his hard shaft against my thigh. *What would it feel like inside me?*

I tried to swat the thought out of my mind, but my fingers crept down to my still damp pussy. I teased my hard clit with the tip of my finger, sending a jolt of need pulsing through my body. I tried to pull my fingers away, hating the image of Vinemont in my mind, looming over me, his mouth cruel and sensual.

How much of him was covered in the vine tattoos? How low did the ink go?

My finger disobeyed, dipping lower, swirling around my aching clit. My hips rocked up to meet each stroke, the tension rising like someone slowly pulling a string taut. My breaths came in quick pants as I continued working myself, visions of Vinemont's face between my legs driving me wild with the need for release. When I imagined his eyes lit with desire for me and only me, I couldn't hold back the wave of pleasure. I bit my cheek to keep from crying out, though I still made some high-pitched noises that couldn't be mistaken for anything else.

Something slammed somewhere nearby in the house, like a heavy book falling from a high shelf. Embarrassment and worry cooled my brief, blissful high. I whipped the blanket over my body. After a few moments, my breathing returned to normal. I wasn't sated exactly, but I had cleared my head enough to remember that Vinemont was my enemy, nothing more.

I began to drift into sleep when there was a knock at my door. I sat up and glanced to the closet where my few clothes were hanging.

"It's just me, miss." A woman's voice.

"Oh, come in?" I didn't know who 'me' was, but she

sounded harmless enough.

She entered, a middle aged woman in an understated maid's uniform, black except for the white Peter Pan collar. Her hair was strikingly dark, cascading down her back in a shiny mane. If there were any grays, I couldn't see them. She could have been no older than 45.

She smiled, warm and friendly, despite a distinct look of sadness written in the wrinkles around her dark eyes. "Welcome. I'll be your personal maid during your stay with us. If you need anything, just ask for me. I'm Renee."

"So you're the one who put all the good soaps and things in the bathroom?"

"Yes, ma'am. I also took the liberty of ordering some more clothing items in your sizes. Of course, Mr. Sinclair assisted me in choosing for you."

I frowned. The thought of Vinemont choosing my clothes was beyond irritating. I wasn't his pet or a doll he could dress. I was a prisoner.

She folded her hands in front of her. "I know how you feel. It's all more than a little off-putting, but things will fall together in time."

I pulled the towel from my head and rubbed my temple with one hand, the other still holding up the blanket. "You know how I feel? Are you a slave, Renee?"

Her deep brown eyes lit for just a hint of a moment. "I am not, ma'am."

"Then I don't think you could possibly know how I feel. No offense."

"None taken, ma'am." Her gracious smile returned despite my barb.

I sighed. I'd been an Acquisition for less than a day and parts of me—the kind ones, the gentle ones—were already splintering. "I'm sorry," I said as she retreated to my bathroom. "This isn't your fault."

I was the one who signed the contract. Renee didn't force me into it.

She came back with a brush and sat down on the bed

next to me. "Here." She put her hands out, offering to brush my hair.

I scooted around to her, still keeping the blanket pressed to my chest.

"It's fine. I'd be more surprised if you weren't angry." She started at the ends of my hair just like my mother used to do. "*The path of least resistance*" Mom used to call it, working out the kinks from the bottom up until my hair was smooth.

"How many of me have there been?"

She kept brushing with careful strokes. "How many Acquisitions?"

"Yes."

"I'm not sure if I'm supposed to say."

I sighed and let my chin fall to my chest.

She dropped her voice to a whisper. "Two that I know of in the Vinemont family in the past twenty years. There were more before that, but I don't know all the details."

"So few? It isn't an annual sort of thing?"

"No, ma'am."

"You said 'in the Vinemont family'? Are there Acquisitions in other families or something?"

"Yes."

"But why? What's the purpose?" Why would they do this? What could possibly be the reason for enslaving people just for the sake of enslaving them? Maybe that would be the best outcome—a kept slave for a year. No labor, no punishments, no ill treatment. I shook my head. It was all too good to be true. Fear crept up my spine as my question lingered in the air. Something told me there was more, far more to all of it than I could even guess.

"Just tell me why." My tone had gone from curious to desperate.

She hesitated, the brush in the middle of my locks. "You'll see tomorrow."

"What's tomorrow?" Dread settled like an anchor in my gut.

The brush continued, smoothing the waves as it went.

"The Acquisition Ball."

Lucius and Vinemont had spoken about a ball over breakfast, but I hadn't realized I would be going.

"A ball? I'm a slave and I'm going to a ball?"

"I really can't say any more."

My mind was whirling. What was this ball? Was it the actual reason, however twisted, for Vinemont to have forced me into the contract?

She reached the crown of my head, still easing the bristles down through the strands. "There, I think we're done."

She rose and then stopped, noticing the photo of my mother and me on my nightstand. "She's beautiful."

I nodded. "She was."

"Your mother?"

"Yes." I studied the picture right along with Renee. I'd been trying for years to divine what she was thinking, why she would leave my father and me the way she did. I supposed I shouldn't have looked too hard, especially given that I'd done the same thing. I just didn't see it all the way through the way she had.

"I'm sorry." Renee put a comforting hand on my shoulder.

She gave me a light squeeze and returned the brush to the bathroom. "I'll have Laura bring your lunch in fifteen minutes if that's all right. Or you can take it downstairs with Mr. Sinclair and Mr. Luciu—"

"Here is fine." The thought of having to see either of them in the same dining room turned my stomach.

She gave a slight bow and left. I dressed in a t-shirt and some pajama bottoms and sank down on the window seat, letting the sun bathe me in afternoon light. The trees were starting to give away their leaves, a brown and orange carpet amassing at the edges of the grass expanse. I pushed the window open and let the cool breeze rush into the room. It carried the smells of grass and woods and water.

I breathed it in, reminding myself I was alive. Even if my

life belonged to another for some ridiculous expanse of time, I was alive and I would fight to stay that way. I ran my hand along the scars on one of my wrists. I wouldn't break. I wouldn't go willingly into darkness. Never again.

I spent the rest of the day in my room. Thankfully, I was able to talk Laura into bringing me a sampling of books from the library downstairs. The books were older, but well worth reading, especially the few bodice rippers she'd found.

I'd wanted to wander around the house and investigate, but I kept getting the mental image of two knights in armor crossing their swords in front of me and blocking my way. More than that, the thought of running into Lucius without anyone else around was a chance I wasn't willing to take.

Vinemont didn't summon or visit me at all, which was a relief. He'd gone into town, apparently, to handle some official district attorney business. *Sure.* I supposed the work of railroading innocent citizens was a constant, thankless job.

When Laura brought my dinner, I asked if she could get me some painting supplies. She promised to make my request to Renee. If I were going to spend all my time hiding in my room, which was my game plan so far, then I would need plenty to keep me occupied.

The night passed without incident or even a hint of Vinemont.

The next morning, I was already up and dressed in a light sweater and jeans when the knock came at my door.

"Come in."

Instead of Farns, it was Renee. She was still dressed in all black with the white collar, and her dark hair was arranged in flowing waves.

"Good morning, ma'am."

"Morning, Renee. And please call me Stella. What happened to Farns?"

"He's with Mr. Sinclair all day. I'm with you. I hope that's all right." Her gaze dropped to the floor.

"Oh, no, no. I didn't mean it that way at all. I was just curious. I'm happy to see you again."

After the words fell out, I realized they were true. I was happy to have someone to talk to. Maybe I could even call her a friend, such as they were in this new world.

She raised her face, her smile making her luminous in the morning light. "I'm happy to see you, too. I must admit, I asked to be assigned to you as soon as I heard about your arrival."

"Why?"

She put her hands in her skirt pockets. "I just feel like we may have some things in common is all."

"Oh, so you hate Sinclair Vinemont, too?"

She laughed. It was an open, inviting sound that held nothing back. "I certainly don't, and I don't believe you do either."

I leaned back against my bedpost. "Pretty sure I do."

"Well, in any case, you have a big day and an even bigger night. I'm here to help you through all of it."

"You told me about the ball tonight. So, what are we doing today?"

"Getting ready, of course. Mr. Sinclair gave me explicit instructions on how he wants you prepared. He ordered your gown the night you arrived, and he picked out your jewels and accessories with me this morning." She walked to me and took my arm. "You are going to be the most beautiful Acquisition they've ever seen."

I pulled my arm from her grasp, anger rushing through me like a wildfire. "You're excited? About putting Vinemont's property on display before some other loathsome people just like him?"

She returned her hands to her pockets. "I was only trying

to…" She shrugged and met my eyes again. "I can't undo the contract. I can't stop the ball or anything else that goes on, but I can help you if you'll let me. I can see you through until the end when your year is up and you can leave. That's all I want to do."

The earnestness of her words struck me like a bolt to my heart. She was right. I had signed the contract and now I was bound to it. If she wanted to help, then I would be wise to let her. I only wished I knew more about the Acquisition. Still, I would take whatever allies I could get.

"I'm sorry, Renee. I'm just…"

Emboldened by my apology, she took my arm again. "I know. Like I said yesterday, I understand. Now, let's get you to the spa."

I almost fell back against the bed. "The spa?"

"Here on the property, of course. Mr. Vinemont called in professionals from all over the country for this. You're going to get the royal treatment."

She pulled me out into the hallway and down the front steps.

"What does this entail, exactly?"

"First, breakfast."

I dug in my heels and stopped despite the angry rumble of my stomach. "I don't want to see them."

"The boys are already out and about today. Don't worry."

"*Boys?* You mean the two sadistic men who live here with their third clueless brother?"

She walked me into the thankfully empty breakfast room. "I've known them since they were wee ones, so I still think of them as boys."

She called for Laura, effectively cutting off my incredulous commentary with the sight of a breakfast tray piled high with deliciousness.

Renee sipped her coffee as I demolished my breakfast. If she was right about having a big day planned, I certainly had a big enough breakfast to power through it.

I wiped my mouth daintily, though it did nothing to undo my earlier lack of manners.

Renee finished her coffee. "Ready to get started?"

I stood and stretched like a lazy cat. "Lead the way."

"One more thing." She showed me down the hallway, leading me deeper into the house than I'd been as of yet. "You are about to meet some new people. They're outsiders. They wouldn't understand what's going on. It would be best if you told them as little as possible in order to avoid any unpleasant complications. They know you're going to a ball. Just keep it at that."

"So I shouldn't tell them that I'm an Acquisition and utterly at the mercy of Vinemont?"

Her quick step faltered for a second but then she regained her pace. "Exactly."

The spa was in a wing toward the back of the house. It was in what seemed to be a converted sunroom. The walls and ceiling were made of paned glass, letting in natural light and warmth. It was an open area with river stone floors, a sunken hot tub in the center of the room, a large wood sauna set to one side, and massage tables to the other. It smelled wonderful, like expensive bath oils and some sort of woodsy incense.

Two men and two women stood waiting for us. Renee went in first and introduced me down the row of staff.

"This is Alex. He's from New Orleans. He'll be in charge of your hair and makeup for the night."

He was a young man with a bright orange faux hawk, multiple piercings in his eyebrows, peacock-colored eyeshadow, and colorful tattoos on each arm.

"Nice to meet you, Ms. Rousseau. When I'm done, you are going to be the belle of the ball."

I looked at Renee, my eyebrows high. "Does everyone know about the ball but me?"

Alex placed a well-manicured hand on my arm. "Oh no, honey. I had to sign a non-disclosure agreement longer than my di—um, longer than my arm, just to get this job, and I still have no idea what you're up to." He winked. "I just know that whatever it is, you are going to look fabulous."

Renee moved me along to the next person. "This is Juliet. She'll be buffing your skin and doing your nails."

"Buffing my skin?"

"Gets rid of all the dead skin cells, makes your skin look like an 18-year-old's." She ran her fingers down my neck and peered at me almost scientifically. "Doesn't look like you've gotten much sun. Perfect. I'll have you shined up like a new penny." She took my hands in hers and examined my nails. They were permanently stained various colors from my paints.

She frowned, her blonde bob falling against her plump cheek as she surveyed the damage. "These will take some work. We may need to use gel to cover the staining."

"Okay I guess?" I'd never really paid much attention to things like my fingernails.

She flipped my hands over and pushed up my sleeves, inspecting further. When she saw the scars along my wrists, she dropped my hands.

Her light blue eyes found mine. "Oh, I'm sorry."

"It's fine. That was a long time ago." I didn't know these people. Still, they were people, and like Renee, they seemed to want to help me. I smiled at her. "It doesn't bother me. You can look at them."

She reclaimed my wrists and ran her fingers over the raised skin. "I think I may have a few tricks to make these less noticeable." She returned my smile, seemingly at ease again.

The next woman had dark hair, a unibrow, and was by far the shortest person in the room.

"Yong will do your waxing."

I whipped my head around to Renee. "Wait, waxing?"

Yong nodded and put a hand on my shoulder, pulling me down so she could inspect my face. "Brows need work...lip looks okay...I'll do full face anyway. Everything else looks fine. When's the last time you had a Brazilian?"

My thighs clenched together involuntarily. "The wax? Never. I don't generally wax anything."

Yong frowned, her unibrow like a dark caterpillar encroaching on her eyes. "I can tell. This will take some work. When I'm done, you'll be smooth as a baby everywhere."

"Um, thanks, I guess?"

She grinned. "I'll go start getting everything ready. It's going to sting some, but you'll love the results."

She passed through an adjoining door, walking quickly and with purpose.

"And this is Dmitri." Renee introduced me to the last person in the row. He stood almost seven feet tall and seemed built of pure muscle. His head was shaved, though dark hair obviously grew there in abundance. He took my hand, his beefy palm swallowing mine whole.

"Very nice to meet you." His Russian accent was so thick it made his words almost unintelligible. But like the others, he had a smile and warmth for me. I appreciated any compassion they had to offer.

"And what do you do, Dmitri?"

He released my hand and held his palms in front of me. "Massage."

"Oh." I swallowed hard.

"I no hurt you." He squeezed my hand encouragingly. "Well, maybe a little. You like. Promise."

"First, into the hot tub," Juliet said. "I need your skin nice and pruny." She stepped toward the massage tables. "Come on, get on in. We have a lot to do."

"You want me to just strip in front of everyone?" I looked from Renee to Juliet and then up at Dmitri.

I crossed my arms over my chest. They could clean me

up and dress me like a doll, but I wasn't going to run around naked for their amusement.

Dmitri laughed, the sound filling the large room and making it seem somehow small. "Nothing new to me, Miss Stella. But I wait over there if make you more comfortable." He shrugged and went through the same door as Yong.

"Needless to say, this"—Alex waved his hand up and down at my body—"does nothing for me. But I'll still be a gentleman and wait in my booth. I'm going to need to send out for a bit more color, anyway. I'm thinking we're going to make your red a bit more strawberry and maybe a touch of…" His words trailed off as he left the room.

Renee backed up and took a seat near the door before pulling a small book from her pocket. "I'll stay with you in case you need anything. Just try to relax. Enjoy it. Mr. Sinclair has spared no expense."

"First class ticket from L.A. and a sweet paycheck," Juliet agreed.

I smirked. "Well, we definitely want Vinemont to get his money's worth." I stripped without ceremony and stepped into the bubbling water in the center of the room.

"I met him for all of five seconds. That man is absolutely dreamy." Juliet knelt in a corner of the room and began removing various equipment from a large rolling case.

Was she going to use all that on me?

"Yeah, if you like tall, dark, and psychotic," I said.

Renee snorted.

I slid further down into the enveloping warmth, and lay my head back.

"So are you really going to a ball?" Juliet asked.

"That's what I keep hearing."

Juliet squealed a little. "That's just so, so exciting! And like, romantic. We don't do stuff like balls in L.A.—I should have been born Southern. I wish I could go with you."

"No, you don't." I closed my eyes and let my whispered words fade into the bubbling heat around me.

Four hours later, I was putty in Dmitri's strong hands. I lay completely naked—my sense of modesty waxed away right along with all my body hair—and let his magical fingers work me over.

"You so tense, *Krasivaya*." Dmitri had taken to referring to me as krasivaya. I didn't know what it meant and I honestly didn't care as long as he kept smoothing his hands over my body and making my muscles sing.

I'd been buffed, oiled, manicured, pedicured, handfed by Renee as my nails dried, and now I was being turned into a limp noodle by Dmitri.

"It's almost my turn. I can't wait." Alex clapped his hands as he stood next to me. "You know, I've never really cared for the female form, but I might make an exception for yours. It's actually pretty. If you had a dick, I'd definitely fuck you."

I snickered as Dmitri's large palm pressed into my lower back.

"Why so many girl-men in this country? In Russia, we have no such men. Only real men." Dmitri moved to my ass and rubbed from there down to my thighs in strong strokes, as if squeegeeing my stress away.

"Is that so? I have an ex-boyfriend who came straight from Russia with man love. That St. Petersburg boy could power bottom like a son of a bitch."

"Truly?" Dmitri squeezed and rolled my thighs.

"I had the orgasms to prove it."

I moaned as Dmitri's hands worked the tension from me. Had I been afraid of him? He was a massage god.

"Ah, hear that? That is what real men desire to hear. To make woman tremble with desire for him. You need to learn this. Then you be real man."

"Yeah, I'll get right to work on that." Alex patted my

behind. "You're mine next. And I promise, unlike some *real men*"—he mimicked a Russian accent—"I won't have a raging boner when I'm touching you."

I giggled. I didn't care if Dmitri was jacking off all over me, just so long as he kept pushing my tension all the way down my body and out my toes. I'd gotten massages before, but nothing compared to this. Not even close.

"How's the Acquisition doing?"

Lucius' voice undid Dmitri's work and made my muscles seize.

Dmitri must have felt the change because he let out a litany in angry Russian. His hands rested possessively on my lower back as Lucius leisurely made his way to me. Whereas Vinemont was a methodical serial killer, Lucius was more of a smooth assassin. His fluid movements and swimmer's body hinted at quickness and wiry strength.

Renee stood and pocketed her book, but didn't move.

I couldn't get up, because Lucius would see me fully naked. His seeing only my ass, once again, seemed like the lesser of two evils.

"Krasivaya doesn't like you, comrade. You interfere with her pleasure." Dmitri's voice was a cautionary rumble.

Lucius stopped next to me, his black boots filling my vision. "I'm certain that's not so. I could give her plenty more pleasure if we had this room all to ourselves."

"Well, you don't." Dmitri stepped around the table and stood chest to chest with Lucius.

"What, because you're here? A hired set of hands?" Lucius placed his hand on my ass and squeezed.

I tried to jerk away from him, but I had nowhere to go. Dmitri yanked Lucius' hand away from me. I scrambled off the table and backed away from them, nudity be damned.

Dmitri and Lucius faced off against each other, neither man backing down.

Lucius smiled up at Dmitri, as if declaring a truce with the bigger man. Instead of walking away, Lucius struck quickly with a vicious haymaker across Dmitri's jaw. A classic sucker punch. Dmitri staggered back. Rage lit the Russian's face and he swung, catching Lucius on the chin and sending him reeling away. Instead of falling, Lucius seemed emboldened and charged the larger man.

Juliet and Alex each came to either side of me.

"Now this is entertainment," Alex said. "I wish they hadn't confiscated my cell. I'd post a vid of this hunk on hunk action and make a fortune."

"Lucius!" Vinemont rushed into the room. He saw me and stopped, his mouth opening slightly.

I slung an arm across my breasts and crossed my legs, though it didn't do much good. I was completely bare down there now, with nothing left to the imagination.

Lucius turned and looked at me too, his signature lascivious smile returning to his otherwise handsome face. Dmitri took the opportunity to get him in a headlock. They struggled against each other, Lucius trying to buck Dmitri's vice-like hold around his neck. Lucius shoved an elbow back hard into Dmitri's ribs, breaking the Russian's hold and slipping away.

Vinemont appeared to come back to himself and darted between the two men. "Lucius, get the hell out of here!"

"This is my house, too, Sin," Lucius said. "I can go wherever the fuck I want. We're brothers, remember?" He glanced over his shoulder at me. "We share."

"Not this we don't," Vinemont growled.

"We'll see." Lucius dragged his thumb across his chin, wiping the blood from his split lip. He squared off against Dmitri again. "You hit pretty good for a red."

"You hit pretty good for a *devushka*."

"*Ya yebat' etu devochku pryamo pered vami*," Lucius replied with a matching accent. He glanced over at me again.

Dmitri took a threatening step forward, menace oozing from his pores.

I wanted Dmitri to smash Lucius to a bloody pulp, to wipe the self-satisfied grin from his face.

Vinemont pushed each man backward. "Stop!"

"Is it hot in here? It definitely feels hot in here." Alex used his hand as a fan.

"Agreed." Juliet's hand was at her throat as she watched the men, her tongue darting at the corners of her mouth.

Vinemont jabbed a finger into his brother's chest. "Lucius, I'm warning you. Get out."

"You aren't the Sovereign. Stop acting like you are."

Vinemont advanced on Lucius until both men were almost nose to nose.

"Stand down, Lucius."

The staring competition lasted for a few tense moments before Lucius blinked and backed away. "I didn't know you'd get your panties so bunched over an Acquisition. I should have. You've always been a royal cockblock."

Lucius sauntered toward the exit before glancing over his shoulder. "See you around, Stella."

Alex let out a bated breath. "I want to see him around. More accurately, I want to see my mouth around his—"

"Stella, for Christ's sake, cover yourself." Vinemont didn't move and kept his gaze trained on me.

Yong bustled in from the waxing room—or as I called it, the room of intense pain and humiliation—and tossed me a towel. I grabbed it and wrapped it around myself so fast I almost dropped it.

Vinemont watched every single movement, as if he were attuned to me on some primitive level. He blinked slowly and scrubbed a hand down his face. "How much longer before she's ready?"

"Three hours," Alex said.

"Have her ready in two. The seamstress should be here any minute to fit her. I don't want any delays."

"Stop talking about me like I'm not here."

Vinemont turned his wrathful gaze back to me. "Fine. Be ready in two hours. If you disappointment me, there will be a high price to pay and *you* will pay it."

He turned on his heel and left, fury in his steps.

"That. Was. Intense." Alex leaned on the massage table.

"I kind of want to make you late just so you get some sort of naughty punishment. Sweet Jesus, do I want some BDSM lovin' right about now."

Juliet sagged with relief. "Both of those hotties want to get with you. You know that, right?"

"That first one does not deserve to even look at you, much less enjoy your kiska." Dmitri's face darkened anew with anger.

"Don't worry," I said, "my kiska is mine alone, if I take your meaning. By the way, what did Lucius say to you in Russian?"

I didn't think it was possible, but Dmitri's glower deepened. "He is, how you say, confident your kiska will be his."

"Well." Alex took my hand. "I may not have a taste for kiska, but if we only have two hours, you're mine, sugar."

Dmitri grumbled about not finishing the massage, and promised he would be back to take care of me.

Alex plopped me into his chair and got to work. He was a madman with scissors and chemicals that smelled like a mix of turpentine and overripe fruit. He foiled, heated, rinsed, and cut, turning my scalp into a beauty battleground. My hair was still the same red, but with highlights and lowlights to set off the color. He put it up in big hot rollers and sprayed it down with an obscene amount of hairspray.

He then set about to do my makeup. I was a bit worried, given the peacock colors above his eyes and his bright lips. He made it worse by not letting me look into the mirror until he was done. After what felt like over an hour of brushing, shadowing, highlighting, contouring, and coloring, I finally got a chance to see the finished product.

"Voila!" He whirled me around and held the swivel chair steady before the mirror.

I'd never thought of myself as a ten. I was self-aware enough to know I was pretty by most standards, but nothing about me said movie star or model. When I looked at what Alex had done, there was more than just a tinge of amazement in my stare. He'd highlighted my high cheekbones and plump lips. He'd given me dramatic eyebrows with a killer arch. Most of all, he'd brought out the deep green color of my eyes. They'd never looked so bright.

"Wow," was all I could muster.

"Wow is right, honey. That right there is the money shot. That face, that hair. One in a million, trust me." He smiled back at me from the mirror.

Renee walked in and clasped her hands in front of her. "This is… You are… I've never…" It ended in no words but a high pitched gleeful sound.

The reserved maid looked positively girlish. "You are absolute perfection."

"Why, thank you." Alex gave a small bow.

I laughed. I was beginning to enjoy my ragtag band of beauty assistants. I tried not to think about how I may never see them again after today. It was hard to think of a reason why Vinemont would send for them again. I couldn't imagine going to too many balls. In fact, I had a suspicion that this "ball" was quite a bit more than it seemed.

It didn't matter what it was. I would go. I would do what I had to so that my father would remain free and alive. There was no going back, only forward. And forward meant I had to get through the ball and the 363 days thereafter.

"The seamstress is outside." Renee calmed herself and motioned for me to rejoin the others in the main room.

The seamstress was an economical woman in a pantsuit and flats, chalk in her fingers and a pencil behind her ears. What she'd brought me to wear wasn't practical in the least. It was perched on a model form. I had never seen anything like it short of the pages in fashion magazines. It was a deep green gown with a plunging neckline, lace straps, and a ball gown skirt made entirely of black peacock feathers.

Alex gasped and ran to the gown. "Oh my god, oh my god. I have never seen anything as fabulous in all my years and, trust me, I've seen more than my fair share of fabulous things. Who's the designer and when can I have one?"

"I designed it and, I assure you, it's a one of a kind." The seamstress eyed me. I got the distinct feeling she was somehow taking my measurements through my towel. She quirked up a corner of her lip, as if pleased. "I think it should be an almost perfect fit with a few tucks here and there."

Alex was gushing as I gaped at the dress. It was extravagant, over-the-top. I wanted to sketch it, not wear it.

Renee walked around the garment, examining it with a hyper-critical eye. I couldn't imagine what a woman who dressed in plain black, wore no makeup, and seemed to do nothing to pretty herself in the least could find lacking in the dream creation before her.

"I think you are very close, Enid." Renee tapped her finger on her chin. "Where's the vine detail?"

"Her cloak." Enid snapped her fingers and what seemed like a harried assistant rushed in, glasses askew, pushing a wheeled mannequin ahead of her. It was covered in a black cloak with embroidered deep green vines twining all around the material.

"And her jewels." Enid motioned the assistant closer. She held a red velvet box under her arm.

Enid took it and undid the delicate clasp, opening the box and blinding me with sparkle. Inside lay a silver necklace with emeralds arranged in the same vine motif. A pair of large emerald earrings completed the set.

Renee's eyes brightened when she saw the fantastic jewels. "I haven't seen these for twenty years." She reached a hand out, as if to touch them, but simply held it above the priceless array.

Enid clapped her hands. "Well, we're burning daylight. Drop the towel, let's get you dressed."

I shifted from one foot to the next. "Did you bring underwear? I'll need to go to my room to get some before I can put all this on."

Enid put her hands on her hips. "Do you think I'm going to let you ruin my splendid gown with some bunchy cotton

117

panties?"

I put a matching hand on my hip. "I can't go to a ball commando, now can I?"

"You can and you will."

"What?"

"Strip." Enid's mouth was set in a firm line.

"Do it, do it, do it!" Alex tried to yank the towel off me. "I have to see it in motion. It may kill me from fashion overload, but I'll die happy."

I glanced over at Dmitri. He sighed, as if hoping I'd forgotten he was there. "Fine, fine. I won't watch. Even though you let girl-man see." He frowned at Alex and turned his back.

I finally let Alex tug the towel free and stepped toward the feathery cloud.

CHAPTER TEN
SINCLAIR

WHERE IS SHE? I waited out in front of the house in a black sports car. I was too on edge to even bother with my usual driver. I needed control any way I could get it.

Going to the Acquisition Ball was something I had never done before. All the preparation in the world likely wouldn't ready me for what was about to happen. I would get through it. Making sure Stella performed—that she stood out—was my main goal. I gripped the steering wheel, trying to decide if I needed to go inside and drag her out, when the front door opened.

Renee stepped out first, and then I saw her. The late afternoon sun blinked off the jewels at her throat, barely visible above the dark cloak tied at her neck. Her dress was the signature Vinemont green, and Enid had outdone herself on the skirt. The black peacock feathers would turn more than a few heads. I only hoped one of them belonged to the Sovereign.

If that weren't enough, Stella's face was radiant. Even as she crossed the threshold, uncertainty painting her features, she made something inside me click into a higher gear. Her bright green gaze tried to ensnare me, tried to make me feel

119

something. I didn't. I wouldn't.

Still, I wanted to see her—all of her. Damn that cloak. I imagined ripping it all off her except the jewels, and my cock thickened in my tuxedo pants. *Fuck.* Now was neither the time nor the place.

It was going to take everything I had to get through this night. It was going to take even more out of Stella. Once it was all over, she wouldn't want to have anything to do with me. She probably already felt that way after what had happened in the yard yesterday. Tonight would seal the deal. Not that she'd have any choice. She would do as I told her. She cared about her father too damned much not to.

She wore a pair of breakneck high heels. I imagined how long her legs would look, bare and smooth, wearing nothing but her stilettos. I shifted in my seat. The large Russian walked out the door behind her and helped her down the front steps. He smiled easily as she spoke to him. I wanted to destroy him for even thinking of talking to what was mine, to take him down and show her I could do it. I could hurt, kill. I could do even worse.

She took the last few steps to my car, and the Russian bastard had the nerve to open the door for her. She maneuvered into the tight space, tucking her dress in and almost falling into the seat.

"Easy *krasivaya*," he said.

A muscle ticked in my jaw as he called her beautiful. She was my pet. If anyone were to give her a special name in Russian or any other fucking language, it would be me.

"I see you when you return." He closed the door and moved away from the car.

No, you won't. I put the car in reverse and backed away from the house. Lucius stood in one of the downstairs windows and watched us leave. Actually, he didn't watch *us*, his gaze was fixed on Stella.

"He creeps me out." Her eyes were trained on the same window.

"Don't talk about my brother like that." He was blood.

She was an Acquisition. Even if I wanted to beat the desirous look out of his eyes until all I saw was gore, some bonds were unbreakable.

"Fine." She sank back in the seat as far as she could and stared out the window. I glanced at her, taking in her stunning profile. Creamy, smooth skin, delicate nose, sumptuous pout… Her lips were painted a blood red, the perfect complement to the emeralds at her throat.

I wore classic black tie. I didn't need to stand out. I was nothing more than background noise. Stella was the attraction, the star.

We fell into an uncomfortable silence as I cycled the gears, sped through the estate, and maneuvered out onto the road. The ball was held at the Oakman estate, and had been for as long as anyone cared to remember. This year's affair promised to be even more extravagant than previous years, given that Cal Oakman was the current Sovereign.

The bastard was revered throughout our community. His winning Acquisition ten years ago had cemented him at the top of Louisiana society. I hadn't attended that ball, despite the engraved platinum invitation. Now I wished I had. At least I would know more of what to expect. Hopefully my mother's recollections of her Acquisition Ball twenty years ago would still hold true. They should. Tradition and ritual were the bedrock principles beneath the entire system.

"What's going to happen?"

I ignored her question. If I described what I expected to go on at the ball, she might put up enough fight to be a problem. I needed her just as she was, a perfectly tantalizing morsel, wide-eyed and beautiful. I needed her eventual downfall to be spectacular. I needed to win.

Twilight fell as we sped along country roads, past vast estates hidden behind walls of trees and dark bayous.

"I won't run." Her voice was quiet, but resolute.

"What?" I downshifted as we came closer to the Oakman gate.

"If you tell me what's going to happen, I won't run. I know there's nowhere to go and you'll hurt my father if I do. So, just tell me."

I pulled the car over so quickly she yelped. The freshly fallen leaves crunched under the tires as we skidded to a halt.

"You want to know what the most powerful people in the South, maybe the entire fucking country, are going to do to you tonight?"

She winced and then turned her wide, angry eyes to me. "Yes."

"Remember how I said I would hurt you?"

"Yes."

"Tonight, I won't be the only one inflicting the pain. That's all you need to know."

I wanted to be the only one to hurt her, the only one to make her cry or bleed or scream. Instead, Cal fucking Oakman would be sharing the duties, and for an audience. She was mine—not because I cared about her, but because I owned her.

I hit the steering wheel and turned to her, pinching her chin between my thumb and forefinger. "You just have to get through it. No matter what happens."

Her breaths came faster and she leaned toward me, her cloak falling to the side and revealing the swells of her breasts. "But you'll be there? With me?"

She was drawing me toward her somehow until my lips were only a whisper away from hers. She smelled like rosewater and honey, a scent I'd chosen for her for the evening. It was meant to be intoxicating, to draw people in, but it wasn't supposed to work against me like this. Her eyes closed, her lips in full bloom and ready for a kiss.

Once again, I was letting my family down. She was property. I needed to stop acting like she was anything more than that. But she didn't make it easy. The day before when she'd lain on her bed and stroked herself, making quiet cries and grinding her hips against her hand, it took every ounce of willpower I possessed not to burst into her room and fuck her until she screamed my name. The memory went straight to my dick, making a bad situation even worse.

Her question came back to me. Would I be there with her? Yes. Would she be happy about it? No. Definitely not. Her lips begged for solace I could not and would not give. I pulled away and made a show of wiping my fingers on my handkerchief.

"You must be desperate if you think I offer you any more safety than the strangers you're about to meet. I don't."

She recoiled, stung by my words, by my actions. Good. She needed to hate me. It would make it all easier.

I put the car back into gear and pulled from the shoulder. I was desperate to get out of this enclosed space, away from her eyes, her scent, her lips, her breath.

As I wished for an escape, the wide gates of the Oakman estate loomed ahead of us. Several cars passed through after their occupants showed the guards the distinctive engraved invitation—this year's was solid gold. I hefted the plate from my inner coat pocket and flashed it before I was waved through to the tree-lined lane. The Oakman home rose from the landscape, a French chateau built in the style of Versailles. Stella took a deep, steadying breath beside me. Nervousness? Excitement? Dread? Any one of those, or all at once, maybe.

I mimicked her quietly, trying to calm my nerves right along with hers. So much was riding on this. On her. She would either save the Vinemonts or break us. Tonight was her first step toward either destiny.

CHAPTER ELEVEN
STELLA

THE HOUSE IN the oak grove was ominous despite the fact that the outside was lit up as bright as day. Ballgoers climbed the wide stone stairs to the open and bright front entrance. I shivered.

I'd almost had him only moments before, but the iota of control I wielded over Vinemont wasn't enough. My lips, my words, none of it was enough to make him change his course. I entertained the ridiculous fantasy that if I could get him to care about me, then he wouldn't hurt me. I knew he wouldn't let me go, not until the year was up. But maybe I could convince him to leave me alone, to let me paint, to let me do anything besides standing naked for his amusement or enduring any of his cruel intentions.

But then he'd pulled away, becoming his usual cold self. At the last moment, I'd lost him.

Even though I hadn't been able to shake him, whatever lay within the chateau put Vinemont on edge. I didn't think anything could make him nervous. He tried to hide it beneath his usual snobby veneer, but I saw it clearly. He could hide plenty from me, but not that. Even he didn't look forward to the dark deeds that awaited in this place.

125

He pulled up to a valet. For the first time, I noticed all of the people walking past the car were wearing masks. I turned back to Vinemont to find he'd already donned a simple black mask covered with the vine motif, his blue eyes showing through the material like patches of dark sky. His jaw was tight, the clean shaven lines perfection beneath his disguise. He pulled a far more extravagant mask from behind my seat, made with the same black peacock feathers on my dress.

"Put it on."

I slipped the ribbons around my head and tied them in the back. Alex would have had a fit if he had seen me so much as touch my hair. I felt a pang in my breast at the thought of never seeing my short-lived friends again. After Mom had died, I didn't do much besides keep my father company, paint, and read. I had no friends to speak of, no one to notice I was gone.

Now that I didn't belong to myself anymore, I realized what a sheltered, useless existence I'd truly had. I was utterly unprepared for the world, for Vinemont, for the shadows that threatened to smother the very life from my body. I could feel it, the darkness, swirling near me, taking the air from my lungs like a greedy parasite.

The valet had been holding his hand out for an awkward moment before I took it and allowed him to help me from the car. He wore a silver mask with what looked like an oak branch pattern in stark black lines.

"Thank you."

"My pleasure," the valet said. "Welcome to the Oakman chateau."

"Not a scratch." Vinemont threw the keys. The valet caught them easily.

Vinemont came around and offered his arm to me. I would have refused had it not been for the too-high heels strapped to my feet. As it was, I would need help climbing the wide stairs unless I wanted to break my neck.

I pushed my cloak out of the way and took his arm.

Warmth radiated from him, seeping through his tuxedo and into my bare arm. With the shoes, I was tall enough to get a good look at his face, despite the mask hiding him from me. His jaw was tight, stress written in the tension.

We began our climb as others crowded around us. I tried to listen to the snippets of conversation.

"—picked this year?"

"I heard the same thing! Cal is apparently very interested in the new Acquisitions to the point he—"

"I hope the Witheringtons win. Have you seen their eldest? He's still a bachel—"

The blood drained from my face. The tips of my ears went cold. I stopped even as Vinemont tried to tug me along with him. "This is some sort of sick competition?"

A couple of masked people near us turned to look.

"Her first ball," Vinemont said cheerily.

"Oh, my dear, you're in for a real treat!" A female ballgoer in a sparkling mask with a grotesquely long nose took my other arm.

She and Vinemont walked me up the stairs.

"This year is going to be especially interesting," the beast at my other elbow trilled. "The three families are really the crème de la crème. Top notch. And Cal is going to be the greatest master of ceremonies we've ever seen if his Acquisition was any indication. He really set the bar high that year. Have you heard what he has planned for tonight?"

"Don't spoil it for her," Vinemont said with a smile in his voice. "I want her to get the full experience."

I cursed him silently for cutting off my only flow of information.

We reached the top step and fell in line behind some other couples.

"In that case, I'll say no more. See you inside. I'll tell you one thing, though, this year's Acquisitions are going to be much the worse for wear when it's over." With that, she giggled and rejoined her party.

I faltered, my heel catching as the corners of my vision

darkened. Blood roared in my ears. Vinemont held me up and wrapped his arm around my waist, pulling me into his side.

"Keep it together, Stella." His voice was low.

"Just tell me what's going to happen." Desperation colored my words, only hinting at the panic escalating in my breast.

He continued moving me inexorably forward. Panic rose up from within me, threatening to overtake the thin veneer of control I had. I wanted to scream, to run, to do anything but go inside this house with the monster at my elbow.

"Please, Sinclair, please."

He stiffened as I used his first name. He pulled me to the side and let others pass ahead of us.

"Goddammit, Stella." His voice was a low growl as his eyes flashed behind the black mask. "Stop asking questions. In fact, don't speak again until you're spoken to. Understand?"

"I'll stop and I won't speak if you just answer my question. Just tell me."

He brought me closer to him, pretending we were embracing each other, solely for the benefit of the other ballgoers around us, no doubt.

His mouth was at my ear. "I haven't told you for a reason, Stella."

He put a hand to my throat before smoothing it around to the back of my neck in a move of utter possession.

"They will mark you." He ran his fingers across the skin at the nape of my neck, making a vivid heat tear through my body from the points of contact. "Here."

His other hand snaked under my cloak and around to the open back of my dress. His fingers played at my exposed skin. "And here."

I shook so hard that he spread his large palm against my bare back and pressed me to him. "I warned you, Stella. I didn't want you to know ahead of time. Fear is your enemy. Fear will make it hurt more than it has to. Now, look at you." He slid his hand up my spine. "Trembling against me, the one who stole you away from your life, the one who's going to take everything from you. You are cozying up to the spider you detest."

His lips brushed my earlobe and the strange heat pulsed through me again, scorching a path straight to my core. His evil words weren't igniting fear in me. They were making me need him, need his wicked tongue to do things other than taunt me with pain.

I knew I should be afraid. I was. But not of him.

He moved his hand around to the front of my dress and teased my hardened nipple with his thumb. He groaned low in his throat. The cloak hid his movements, but I felt every single touch. When he cupped my breast and squeezed, I hitched in my breath.

"You'd let me fuck you right now, wouldn't you? In front of all these people. Right here." He released my nape, grabbed my hand, and guided it to the hard length in his pants. "You'd take this."

My heart fluttered even faster. I slid my hand along him and his hips jerked toward me. I couldn't think, couldn't waste my thoughts on fear when he created an inferno that scorched me in my most secret places.

"Yes," I breathed. "I would."

"And I'd take you, too. In fact, I will, but not here. Business first. Get through this, and I'll grant you a reward." With that, he let me go and backed away. His step was steady but his eyes were wild.

My skin was needy, demanding his touch and more. What was wrong with me? I *hated* Vinemont. Maybe it was because of what I'd done to myself. Maybe I felt like I deserved some sort of punishment for being so weak throughout my life? I didn't know. All I knew was that I wanted him to rekindle the same fire in me, to make me burn for him, no matter the cost.

He held out his arm for me again. I took it and allowed him to escort me into the glowing hell of the Oakman chateau.

Masked greeters welcomed us and offered to take my cloak. Vinemont declined and swept me further inside the mansion. It was alight with conversation and alcohol. Servers in harlequin masks wove through the revelers, offering drinks and taking already empty glasses.

One whisked towards us, his tray laden with champagne.

"No, thank you," I said.

Vinemont grabbed two glasses and handed me one. "Drink. It'll help."

I took a sip and then another. We walked further inside. Everything was gilded, golden, and sparkling. Dozens of chandeliers lined the high ceilings, and the walls were covered with intricate murals of romanticized scenes from the old South. It reflected a whitewashed history, the lighter paint hiding a bloody and violent past.

I waved my glass at the images of cotton fields and smiling slaves. "This is disgusting."

"Thank you for your fascinating art critique. Now, drink," Vinemont urged.

I swallowed another mouthful of the champagne, my stomach warming. And then the delicious liquid was gone. Vinemont handed the second glass to me.

"Finish it."

I did as he instructed, suddenly thirsty and starving. My lunch at Renee's hands seemed to have happened days ago.

"Good." He passed the empty glasses to a particularly horrific server dressed in complete maudlin. His mask was skeletal even as the bells jingled merrily along his crown.

What sounded like a full orchestra began playing somewhere deeper in the house. Vinemont and I fell into the stream of masked strangers, some of them in gorgeous gowns that seemed to have come right off a runway. The men were all in staid black tie, the only things marking them as different were the varied masks that hid their faces. Some were pure peacocks, others in simple black. All seemed eager, almost excited. A buzz was in the crowd, elation at what came next, whatever that might be, creating an expectant energy.

A man plucked the edge of my cape and stared down at me.

I cringed back into Vinemont.

The stranger didn't seem to notice, or care. "A Vinemont, I take it?"

The hum of the music grew, the whine of violins echoing down the wide marble hallway before the sound coalesced into beauty along with the other instruments.

"Yes." Vinemont pulled me into his side, forcing the stranger to release my cloak.

The stranger smiled, his eyes lighting behind his midnight blue mask. "There are no female Vinemont heirs. So you must be an Acquisition."

"I'm just—"

"She's mine. Back the fuck off, Charles." Vinemont tightened his grip at my waist, pressing the already tight dress into me even more.

The stranger laughed. "Nice to see you, too, Sinclair." He stared down into my eyes again. "And I'm very much looking forward to seeing you, all of you, very shortly."

The floor lurched beneath my feet. The only thing that kept me upright was Vinemont's arm around my waist. He was a prison made of flesh and blood. My very own cage.

The stranger, Charles, stepped away and whispered something to the woman at his side. She frowned at me, giving me an up and down sweep with a critical gaze, her crimson mask turning her into a particularly vicious foe.

The orchestra was playing some elegant tune, one made for the opera or a symphony, not for this. It was so out of place that I wanted to laugh. I stifled my giggle as I glanced away from the crimson bitch.

I ignored the priceless canvases that graced the walls, and the ornate doors and moldings. Instead of letting the beauty of the house lull me, I stared into the masked faces, many of them now staring back at me as word spread that I was an Acquisition, whatever that really meant. Was I so rare? How many Acquisitions were there?

Though light glanced from every surface and sprang from the bright walls and polished floor, I was in a nightmare. The home was only gilded, gold covering the rotten core. I was surrounded by ghouls, all of them hungering for a piece of my flesh. The glitz and glamour did nothing to hide their true natures. No mask ever could.

The quick beat of my heart resounded in my ears, deafening even the smooth sound of the instruments. Vinemont didn't stop, didn't say a word, just kept moving forward. Toward what, I didn't know. We passed through a wide set of high doors and into a ballroom. The floor was a light oak and shone like everything else in the vile mansion.

In the center was a high platform that towered over the ballgoers. It was circular and done in brilliant gold. A fabricated oak tree shot up through the middle, the leaves sprouting artificially green and full almost up to the ceiling, which must have been forty feet overhead, if not more.

Vinemont swept me through the crowd, moving closer to the tree. I wanted to dig in my heels, to stop his resolute forward momentum. It was no use. The nearer we drew to the platform, the louder my instinct screamed for me to run. Something metallic along the trunk caught my eye and my knees almost gave way. Three sets of silver shackles hung from the tree, each attached to chains that ascended into the branches above.

"No." I pushed back against Vinemont.

"Calm down." He changed course and led me around the tree and further toward the orchestra.

Another platform was set up toward the back of the room near the floor-to-ceiling windows. Three men sat atop it, each with a table in front of them at knee level. Each was shirtless. Every bare piece of their muscular skin was covered in ink—naked women, skulls, tribal, even flowers. One in a goblin mask seemed to pick Vinemont and me from the crowd.

"He's staring at us," I said. "The goblin, up there."

"Everyone's staring at us."

Vinemont led me toward the goblin. I didn't want to go, but I didn't want to retreat and get any closer to the tree, either. We stopped midway between the two, far too close to the tree for my liking.

The orchestra suddenly quieted and then the hall fell utterly silent. All masks turned toward the platform where a man stood, his arms outstretched, a microphone in one hand. Someone worked up in the rafters of the hall, training a spotlight down on the apparent star of the show. His mask seemed to be an array of oak leaves, the same that decorated the tree behind him.

"Welcome to the twenty-fifth Acquisition Ball!" he shouted into his microphone.

A cheer went up from the crowd and then they all clapped as if they were at the opening of the Kentucky Derby.

After a ridiculous span of applause, the man held his hands out to quiet crowd.

"This year, we have an amazing slate of competitors." He gazed around at the people beneath him, clearly a showman. "Though, of course, not as amazing as my Acquisition year. Cal Oakman for the win!"

Laughter sounded through the cavernous hall. Vinemont neither clapped nor laughed, just stood with me at his side. Tension was etched in his bearing just as fear must have been etched into mine.

"It has been an honor to be your Sovereign for the past decade, and I am pleased to say that any of the three firstborns chosen for this year's Acquisition will make an excellent addition to the Sovereign legacy I leave behind.

And now, without further ado, let's introduce the Acquiring families!"

Another roar from the crowd.

The Acquiring firstborns were *chosen*? Vinemont hadn't volunteered to ruin me, humiliate me? Of course he had. He was a cruel man who enjoyed hurting me. Wasn't he? I couldn't tell what was real anymore. And why were there three? I glanced around. Out of all these masked faces, only two could be my allies.

"First up. Robert Eagleton. Come on up, Bob, and show us what you brought with you!"

Someone moved through the crowd to our right. A middle-aged balding man in an eagle mask led a much larger man wearing a nearly identical mask. They took the stairs to the top of the platform and shared the spotlight with Oakman. The balding man puffed a bit, but the taller, younger man just stood and surveyed the crowd below.

"All right Bob, tell us who we have here." Oakman should have hosted a game show. He held the microphone out for Bob.

"This is, well, this is Gavin. He's my, um, Acquisition. And we will win this year." Bob let out a sigh of relief, as if he'd gotten past the hardest part.

"Ready for the first reveal, everyone?"

Another bloodthirsty cheer. Or maybe the champagne bubbles playing in my mind just thought it was bloodthirsty.

Oakman removed the man's mask. He looked to be in his early twenties, dark eyes, pale skin, short brown hair, handsome even from this distance. The crowd twittered and some wolf whistles rang out.

"Looks like we have a competition." Oakman clapped Bob and Gavin off the stage along with the crowd.

"Up next, the Witheringtons. Red, you out there?"

More cheers.

Another man weaved through the crowd on the opposite side of the platform. He pulled a woman in a feather mask behind him, practically dragging her to the top of the platform.

The man, Red, took the microphone from Oakman. "This is Brianne, this year's winning Acquisition."

Red stripped her mask away, revealing a small, scared blonde. Her eyes were huge, and she visibly quaked under the spotlight.

"Oh, my," Oakman stepped back and gave an over-the-top up and down look. "We've got some stiff competition, if you folks know what I mean!"

Hoots and whistles, mixed with laughter, echoed around the hall.

"We're next." Vinemont's voice was in my ear, each syllable laced with rigid determination. Any hint of the heat he'd shown me outside was gone. He released my waist and took my hand. His palms were damp, the only indication that he was at all nervous.

Brianne and Red retreated from the platform.

"Now, last but never least, the Vinemonts. Counsellor Sinclair, show us your wares!"

He strode forward, confidence in every movement, and pulled me behind him. The tree loomed ahead, the shackles glinting in the spotlight. Foreboding rose inside me and blotted out my voice, my heart, and my soul. I followed. There was nowhere else to go.

We took the stairs one at a time, each step adding a weight to my shoulders, a rock to my stomach. Finally, we stood next to Oakman. Everything beyond the glittering stage was a dark blur. The spotlight was a blinding sun, focused on me as if by a cruel child with a magnifying glass.

"Her name is Stella, not that it matters." Vinemont was cold, his words like frost in my mind.

He untied my mask and yanked it from my face. Then he ripped the cloak from me, my skin tingling from the sudden onslaught of open air. A collective gasp rose up from the crowd, followed by thunderous applause.

"Oh my, my. Now, Sinclair, you know I've always had a thing for redheads. And this is one is too choice to pass up."

135

"I'll tell you what, Cal, when I'm Sovereign, I'll send you a new redhead each week," Vinemont said to raucous laughter from the crowd below.

"I like the confidence. I've got my eye on this one, ladies and gents. Now, let's get this party started right. Branding time!"

The orchestra started back up and Vinemont pulled me down from the platform. No longer hidden by the ornate mask or my cloak, I felt naked. The ghouls stared and leered as I walked past, Vinemont dragging me along through the pressing bodies.

Wait, *branding time?*

He was leading me toward the tattooed goblin again. The male Acquisition, Gavin, was already shirtless and lying on his stomach, one of the other artists inking him in front of the masked onlookers.

"Bigger," Bob directed.

The artist nodded and continued free-handing the outline of an eagle on Gavin's shoulder blade.

The orchestra changed to a waltz, and many ballgoers paired off to dance, skirts swirling, their laughter melding with the music.

Red led his Acquisition, Brianne, over to one of the tables and shoved her down onto her back. He pulled the strap of her dark purple dress down so her left breast was exposed. "Over her heart. My name."

Her eyes were squeezed shut, tension written along her vibrating body. I took an unsteady step toward Red, prepared to do my best to knee him in the balls. Before I got the chance, Vinemont's iron grip encircled my upper arm and pushed me up onto the platform in the same rough fashion. He dropped me onto the table in front of the goblin and pushed me down until I lay prone.

The buzzing noise of the two other tattoo guns, mixed with poor Brianne's whimpers, reached my ears over the waves of music.

"What's it gonna be, Sin?"

The goblin knew Vinemont?

"The traditional V," Vinemont replied.

"Where?"

"Here." Vinemont's hand swiped the hair off my nape and let it hang down beside me in a curling cascade. He moved the emerald necklace up and out of the way. Then his cold finger traced a V on the back of my neck.

"Can do."

I had never gotten a tattoo. I'd thought about it plenty of times, but never had the conviction to get anything in particular. I used my body to make art. I didn't intend to be the art. And now, I was getting a tattoo forced on me. Nothing was my choice anymore. I'd signed it away.

For the millionth time since this ordeal started, I pictured my father. He was sitting by the fire in his favorite chair—safe, warm, no doubt sad, but alive. I would do what I had to do. I would cover my entire body in ink if it would save him.

Despite knowing this sacrifice was worth it, I wanted to go numb, to stop experiencing the horror of what was happening. I couldn't. I felt the cold table beneath me, felt the eyes of the masked people watching me as I was "branded," and I felt Vinemont standing next to me, no doubt enjoying my degradation moment by moment.

The goblin leaned down and whispered in my ear. "It's going to hurt, but I'll be as nice as I can."

"Thanks." *Did I just thank my torturer?*

The buzzing started close to my ear. I fisted my hands as the first stinging pain erupted at the back of my neck.

"Good girl," the goblin said. "Just relax. I'm quick." Some more buzzing pain followed, punctuated by Red telling Brianne to shut her fucking mouth. "Well, at least all the girls say I'm quick."

Cruelty interspersed with sex jokes. This is what my life had become. I closed my eyes and let my arms fall, my knuckles brushing the floor as more pain ricocheted down my spine. I was an Acquisition, a possession to Vinemont.

Nothing more. He would let the goblin mark my skin. He didn't care. He was still the cold spider I'd known him to be since the first time I saw him. I was in his web now, caught and dangling as he fed off me slowly. How would he win this competition? What would victory entail? My death?

I let the pain flow into me, trapping it inside a box in my heart. I'd store it up, feed it, make it grow stronger until it turned into rage. Then I would let it out and bring Vinemont and the rest of these accursed people to their knees.

CHAPTER TWELVE
SINCLAIR

SHE'D GONE LIMP. Given up. Tony continued his work, making a better V than even the one gracing my chest. He was my personal tattoo artist. His shop in Mobile was the toast of the South. People came from all over the country, all over the world, just to bear his ink.

He finished up the last of the thorns, done in the same deep green as mine, when I leaned down and added a little something extra.

"I want a small spider." I pointed to one of the inner curves of vines. "Here."

I whispered it low enough that Stella wouldn't hear it over the music and the buzzing. She always referred to me as a spider. Now, I would be on her body permanently.

"I like it, man." Tony switched to a deep crimson ink and drew in the small accent. "Nice."

One of the buzzing sounds stopped. Red's Acquisition sat up and yanked her dress back in place over her bare breast. I almost pitied her. That little show of skin was nothing compared to what came next.

I pitied her more for the garish tattoo Red had forced on her—his name in bright red ink with blue flames licking the letters. What a fucking prick to ruin a beautiful woman that way.

I shook my head. No, Red has his head in the game. Ruination was the goal. I was over here dicking around and ensuring Stella's brand was art, not something to mar her perfect skin. I'd told myself too many times to stop thinking of her as a person. But here I was, doing it again and letting my dick lead me around.

I'd already given in to her, promised her a reward for making it through this night. It was foolish. Still, if it worked even a little to keep her in line, it was worth it. This was spectacle, all of it. I needed the families, and especially Cal, to come away from this seeing me as the frontrunner for Sovereign.

Bob's Acquisition didn't fare much better than Red's. At least the eagle on his man's back had some artistry in it. It was nothing compared to Tony's work, but it turned out far better than the travesty on Brianne's chest.

"All right. She's all done." Tony sat back and admired his handiwork before rubbing some salve along Stella's skin.

It was a wasted effort. Her tattoo was the least of her worries.

Stella sat up and gave me the most vicious glare I'd ever seen on her face. Not even after the day in the yard had she flashed at me with such hate.

"Here, angel, check it in the mirror. It's not so bad."

Tony handed Stella a mirror and held one up behind her so she could see the design. Her crimson lips fell open. "That goddamn V? And what's the red thing. It looks like…" Her gaze shot up to my eyes. "A spider."

"Yes, indeed." Tony took her mirror and began packing up his tattoo gear.

"Head on out, Tony," I said. "Money's already in your account."

Tony popped his head up and surveyed the room. "Sure I can't stay and see if I can convince one of these masked freaky chicks to go home with me?"

Tony had no idea what was going on. I'd told him this was a fancy party with paid staff and entertainment, Stella and the other Acquisitions being the entertainment. He thought all this was voluntary and just a night of fun. If he stayed any longer, he would know just how non-consensual the whole thing was. I didn't want to alienate one of the true friends I actually had, and nothing alienates like slavery and whippings.

"No, man. No offense, but you don't have a chance with these women. Well, unless your bank account is bigger than I think."

"Definitely not. Okay, then. I'm out. Thanks again, Sin. And it was lovely working on you." He took Stella's hand and kissed it. "I'd love to see you in my shop sometime. Color you in some other areas."

She smiled at him. Actually smiled. "I'd like that."

Something roared to life inside me. It ripped at my ribs and tried to claw through my chest. Jealousy. Petty, overbearing, jealousy. I took her hand from his.

Tony laughed and jumped down from the platform. He gave a salute and then cut through the crowd and out one of the side doors.

"Why did you smile at him?" The ridiculousness of the question hit me only after I asked it.

"Because he was nice to me and he clearly had no idea what sort of fucked up shit you all are doing out here," She held my gaze, challenge in her bearing. "It's not his fault you dragged him into it."

"I didn't drag him into anything. I paid him well to create art on your body, and that's exactly what he did."

She raised her eyebrows and straightened her back. "You think the taint of this place doesn't rub off on people? You think he's unscathed?"

I grabbed her by the elbow. "He's a lot more unscathed than you're going to be."

"Fuck you."

Shit. Her anger shot straight to my cock, even in the

141

middle of this crowd of devils. Her eyes flashed at me in unbridled fury.

"In time." I gave her the smile I knew she hated, the one that got under her skin.

She lifted a hand to strike me. I caught it and pulled it down, squeezing her wrist hard. "Do that again, and I'll hit back much, much harder. Understand?"

I wanted her to do it again, to knock my mask off so she could see the real me, the one who wanted to make it hurt, to fuck her, to make her scream. Her fear was easier for me to deal with than her anger. Her anger made me want to push her further, to take her to the edge, to make her beg me for something, anything. Her anger spurred me on to break her. Her fear let me know I was getting close.

The music piped down, the circling vultures slowing to a stop as Cal climbed atop the central platform again. "All right folks, brandings are done. Looks like we're ready for the big show."

Masked servants rushed in through the side doors with various pieces of equipment and furniture. Whips, chains, clamps, dildoes, spanking benches, couches, and too many beds to count. Once everything was in place, a cavalcade of prostitutes entered through the doors. Masked and nude, there was something for everyone—thin, ample, old, and young; they stood like low-hanging fruit, ready for the taking. The ballgoers flitted out and picked this one or that one, dragging the choice morsels back to their chosen spot of depravity.

I glanced down to Stella. She stood mesmerized. She'd unconsciously stepped closer to me as the hall geared up for the main event. Now, she was frozen in her horror, perhaps unable to comprehend the well of the evil in this room. It was deep, far too deep for anyone to plumb its depths. Especially not her. Naiveté swirled around her like a priceless perfume. The vein at her neck fluttered in a distressed rhythm. It was beautiful, like the pale wings of a butterfly—and just as fragile.

The orchestra kept playing softly as the dance floor became a sea of debauchery. Only a center strip was left open. The parade route.

"Come on, Acquisitions, don't be shy. Step on up. Time to really show us what you have to offer." Cal was gleeful.

I took Stella's hand and pulled her through the crowd, many of them already disrobing and setting on each other like wild animals. Fucking, biting, scratching. They left their masks on, as if it made any difference. The guest list was expertly curated. Any number of governors, wealthy socialites, business magnates, and others were congregated here tonight. The entire power structure south of the Mason Dixon was in this room, rutting like pigs and enjoying the show.

I dragged my sacrificial lamb behind me as she gasped at the spectacle all around her. Men and women clawed at her as she rushed past, their hunger bleeding over onto anyone and anything. Stella's purity was like a beacon. I sensed it, too. I wanted to drag her down and feast on her just like they did. But that wasn't what she was here for. Not yet.

We made it to the end of the cleared section of floor that bisected the entire hall and took our place behind Bob, Gavin, Red, and Brianne. The servants had quickly placed risers along the ground in a straight line so the walkway was elevated above the thriving mass of wickedness all around. Cries rose up and were drowned out by others. The orchestra continued playing as if nothing out of place were happening.

"Time to walk the walk, Acquisitions." Cal was crowing atop the podium as one of the prostitutes sucked his cock.

I hated the idea of him seeing Stella, of any of them seeing her. She was mine. But I kept having to share her.

Bob pushed Gavin up the stairs. "Walk."

Gavin obeyed, tentatively placing one foot in front of the other. Once he'd made it a little way across, he was emboldened, holding his head a bit higher, his shoulders back. It made sense. After all, walking was easy.

He picked up his pace. When he got to the end of the walk, he turned to come back. Two men grabbed him, stripped off his coat, and then ripped his shirt away. He started to fight them but stopped when one held up a cattle prod. The other one pointed back down the runway.

Stella trembled next to me as Brianne broke down into gut-wrenching sobs. Red grabbed her by the hair and shook her. She screamed, high and piercing.

Stella reached out, fast as a cat, and gripped Red's arm, trying to wrest his grip from Brianne. Her small hands did nothing to stop him.

"Get your bitch under control, Vinemont, before I do it for you."

I wrapped my arm around Stella's waist and pulled her back. "Stop, Stella. You're making it worse."

She lunged at Red again as Brianne still suffered in his grasp. I held her back and away from him.

"What, you don't like this?" Red asked and shook Brianne again. He used his other hand and ripped down the back of her dress, leaving her top fully exposed. "What about this? Stella, is it? Do you like this?" Red ripped her dress again until the fabric fell to the floor.

"You, son of a bitch!" Stella cried.

"Oh, look over here. We have a wild one." Cal's voice grated on my ears as it boomed around the room.

I put my hand around Stella's throat and squeezed until she fell back against me gasping for air.

"Stop fighting," I hissed in her ear.

"Motherfucker. You, motherfuckers," was all she managed to get out.

Red sneered and stepped toward us.

"Back the fuck up, Red."

"Or what?"

"Or I'll stomp another mud hole in your ass, same as I did at your sister's wedding last year. Remember that?"

"Fuck you, Sin."

"Right back at you, Red."

He returned to his toy, palming her ass so hard it had to hurt as she waited her turn. He leered at Stella as he did it, but she didn't make another move.

"You're all best friends, aren't you?" Stella's voice was quiet. "You're all the same. Let me go. I'll be *good*." She put an acid inflection on the last word.

Her comment should have stung me, but it was true. Red and I were the same breed. He was just playing the game better than I was at the moment. That would be remedied before the night ended.

I released Stella, but stayed ready to hold her again. I didn't know what Red would do if she actually managed to hurt him. It wouldn't be pretty. Not that I'd let him hurt her. That wasn't his right.

She stood in front of me, careful not to touch me. The back of her dress was open so I could see her smooth skin. She was so pale against the deep green of the dress. Flawless, radiant skin. I stared, knowing that it would never look this way again, not after tonight.

Gavin was on his final run, fully nude and halfway across the walkway back to us. Men and women rose from below to touch him. I froze at the thought of one of them touching Stella. But they would. There was nothing I could do to stop them.

"Go on, whore." Red pushed the shivering Brianne up onto the walkway. She wore only heels as she made her way between the revelers.

Many rushed to her, their fingers reaching to touch her pussy, her ass, her tits. Towards the middle, one man actually pulled her down and threw her on the nearest bed before trying to force her legs apart. Her scream blended with the others. Two servants approached and pulled the man off before setting her back on the platform. Now her shoes were missing and she was sobbing as she walked.

She made it to the other end and tried to stay there. It took a near miss with the cattle prod to get her moving again. By the time she made it back to us, her makeup was streaked from tears and her body shook with sobs.

"Again," Red demanded.

She shook her head. Red advanced on her with a menacing step.

"Go, just go. Get it over with." Stella urged the girl to pass through hell one more time. "You can do it. You have to."

Brianne focused on Stella who was nodding at her, encouraging her.

"I'll be here when you get back, okay? The faster you go, the faster it'll be done. And then it'll be my turn."

Red turned and put two fingers to his mouth in a 'V' before sticking out his tongue at Stella. "I can't wait."

I wanted to take out his knees, pound him into the ground, and then piss on his fucking corpse. Stella ignored him.

Brianne took the steps back up and made her final pass, far more quickly this time without heels. When she got back, Stella moved to embrace her but Red cut her off.

"Excellent work, whore. Maybe I'll only beat you once tonight." He turned to Stella. "Strip, bitch."

I hit him. I dropped him. I didn't even think. I just acted. Mistakes always seem to happen that way.

He rolled on the ground, hands to his face. He pushed his mask off and felt around his eye. "The fuck, Sin?"

Shit. This was not the plan. Getting angry and decking one of our number was definitely not part of a winning Acquisition.

Cal's laughing voice boomed over the sound system. "Now *that's* a show, ladies and gents!"

CHAPTER THIRTEEN
STELLA

RED PICKED HIMSELF up. He was shorter and smaller than Vinemont, but clearly angry. "You want to go outside?"

"No. But I may go over to your mother's place and release some aggression later." Vinemont smirked, clearly baiting Red.

Red swung. Vinemont backed out of the way easily and rushed forward, tackling Red to the ground. They devolved into a rolling, punching mass on the floor. I looked around. The nearest guests were focused on the fight. I took a few steps backwards, then a few steps more, then I was in the thick of the masked crowd. Some of them glanced at me and went back to their work. Others couldn't tear their attention away from the fight.

I turned and ran. I had no thought except escape. It was as if a host of klaxons were ringing in my head, my heart, alerting me to the mortal danger. I cut through the reaching hands and past the servants around the edges. I ran through the first open set of doors, my heels almost going out from under me as I turned the corner. I sped faster until a man stepped in front of me. I slammed into his chest and he

147

wrapped his arms around me.

"Going somewhere, Stella?"

I knew that voice. "Lucius?"

He dragged me sideways into an antechamber off the main hall and kicked the door closed behind us.

"The one and only." He held me close to him, his hands pressing into the bare skin at my back. A deep emerald mask hid his face, but I could see his eyes, light yet piercing. "Where were you going?"

"I-just away from there."

"Wouldn't that kill your father?" He slid a hand lower down my back.

Guilt crashed down on me. I had run from pure instinct, just as if I'd pulled my hand away from the fire. I couldn't do things like that. I had to leave my hand in the flames until it crisped and charred. My father's life depended on it.

"Yes."

"I could save you, you know?" His hand went lower, and slid beneath the fabric of my dress.

"What?"

"I mean, you'll still be an Acquisition for a year, nothing to be done about that. But you could choose me. You could tell Sin you'd rather be mine."

"You're even worse than he is." I tried to back away, but he held me fast and pinned me against his chest.

"Am I? Am I the one who threatened your father? Who prosecuted him? Who forced you into the contract?"

No. Vinemont had done all those things and more.

"See, Stella. I haven't hurt you or trapped you." His hand smoothed along my ass as he put his other hand at my chin and pulled my face up to his. "I could make this whole thing more bearable for you."

"I don't trust you." My voice was so breathy, like he'd taken the air from the room with his seductive words.

"You shouldn't." He leaned down, his lips so close to mine.

The door burst open as Vinemont crashed in. "Stella?"

"Another time, then?" Lucius whispered to me.

"What the fuck are you doing here?" Vinemont rushed to me, a trickle of blood flowing from his busted lip. "Get away from her."

Lucius released me. "I was just talking to her."

"Like hell you were." Anger rippled off Vinemont. "She's mine, Lucius. Leave her alone."

Vinemont stood behind me and wrapped a possessive hand around my neck. "Mine." It was more of a growl than a word.

Two servants rushed in behind Vinemont.

"I think you'll find this man doesn't have an invitation. You'll need to escort him out. Roughly."

"Come on, Sin." Lucius smiled.

Lucius's snake-like charm didn't work on Vinemont. "Out."

Each servant grabbed one of Lucius' elbows and hustled him from the room.

"Later, Stella," he called. His voice echoed along the now-empty marble hallway.

Vinemont turned me around so I was forced to stare up into his unmasked face. "Did he hurt you?"

"Did *he* hurt me? Do you even hear yourself?"

Oakman strolled into the room. "Come on. Can't wait forever. The natives are getting restless for her walk and the rest of the festivities."

"Just another minute, Cal, if you don't mind." Vinemont didn't even turn to look at the host.

"That's all you'll get." The gameshow host tone drained from Cal's voice like water through a sieve. "Tradition can't be broken."

He shut the door behind him as he left.

"You can't run, Stella. I'll catch you. *They'll* catch you."

"The only one who caught me was Lucius."

"And you were lucky this time. You won't be so lucky again. Trust me."

This was such a mindfuck. He acted like he cared one

way or another what happened, but I knew all he cared about was winning this twisted competition. He wasn't fooling me. No one was. Fuck him. Fuck all of them. I stepped away from him and walked to the door.

"Where are you going?"

"To do my walk of shame. Are you going to help me out of this dress or what?"

I'd never seen shock on his face. If he weren't a monster, it would have been almost cute. He followed me back into the ballroom, new debauches going on all around as the ballgoers got their second wind. I didn't see the other Acquisitions.

Once lined up at the walkway, I reached behind me to unhook my dress. Then I realized I had no idea how Enid had put the thing on me.

Vinemont was at my back then, his fingers pulling the fabric together and unhooking the closures that must have held it together along the center seam. He moved his hands up to my shoulders and inhaled deeply before slipping his fingers beneath the lace straps and letting the dress fall to the floor in a feathery heap.

Cold air rushed over my body, and the nearest revelers stopped what they were doing to watch me.

Vinemont moved his hands down my sides, feeling my curves before his hands settled at my hips. His breath was warm against my shoulder. His familiar scent was oddly comforting.

I took one step, and then another. I kept my head high as I walked. I fixed my gaze far across the room on one of the particularly beautiful chandeliers. Crystal drops hung from it, multi-faceted and shimmering despite the mass of human ugliness beneath it. It was untouched by the hideous inhabitants of the room. Maybe I could be, too.

I slapped away hands and fingers, refusing to let them degrade me any more than they already had. I ignored catcalls and whistles. When I reached the end, I turned and repeated my travel, glaring at Oakman as defiantly as I could. He stared back intently before unzipping his fly and motioning for one of the women below to "assist" him.

I dropped my attention and caught Vinemont staring at me, fire in his eyes like never before. He didn't look down my body, just held my gaze as I walked, as if he were pulling me toward him with some strange gravity. I reached him and turned, making the circuit one more time under the watchful eyes and the grasping hands.

I reached the far end where a wrinkled man with a protruding erection waited for me.

"Ms. Rousseau, so pleased to see you again." He grinned, a red mask obscuring his eyes, while his date for the night— a handsome man of no more than twenty—stood close behind him.

I knew his voice. My stomach flipped and soured. "Judge Montagnet?"

The judge's date reached around and began stroking Montagnet's cock, though the set of the young man's mouth was less excited and more apathetic.

"Well, I must get back," Montagnet said. "I just wanted to congratulate you. Keep up the good work, lovely girl, and I certainly hope the Vinemonts prevail this year. Don't worry. I'll keep an eye on your father for you." He disentangled himself from the younger man's grip and knelt down on all fours on a nearby divan. I turned my head away before I saw anything more.

The judge's threat was a strangling vine around my heart, choking out any love or warmth, leaving only cold fear. I was foolish, so foolish for running. Never again. I was captured, bound by the invisible vise of these people, their power. There was nowhere to run, nowhere to turn. I scanned the crowd, wishing I could burn the chateau down on their heads.

One of the servants motioned toward me with the prod. I took a deep breath and finished my walk. I kept my eyes up, trying to distance myself from the horror of the scene. I refused to give in to the helpless feeling of being nude and on display for the faceless horde. They thrashed around me like damned souls in hell, their breaths hot and their hands clawing at me. I fought them off and hurried my pace.

No one managed more than a brushing swipe against my bare skin. I counted it as a win. Vinemont's gaze was still rapt, though every so often he would stare daggers at the ones who reached out to touch me.

When I made it back to him, he offered his hand to me as I stepped down. I didn't take it.

"Well, now that we've got the easy parts over with, let's get on to the main attraction!" Oakman, as ever, kept the entertainment fresh.

I glared up at Vinemont. "Wait, *that* wasn't the main attraction?"

He showed no emotion, just held my gaze. He was somehow steady even as I felt the storm rising around me.

"Bring them on up," the voice boomed.

Vinemont squeezed my arm and pushed me in front of him, toward the stairs and to the tree. Gavin and Brianne were ahead of me. As they made it to the top, I heard metallic clanging sounds above. Brianne shrieked.

"We haven't even hurt you yet." Oakman's laughter infected the room until it was a cacophony of soulless mirth.

I took the final step. Brianne was sobbing again. Gavin just looked catatonic, as if none of this was registering any more. They were both chained, their fronts facing the tree. Vinemont guided me to the one empty spot against the trunk. He raised my wrists and clamped the shackles down around each one. He pulled the chain down from above and hooked it to the chain in the center of the restraints. Then he fastened my ankles with the restraints at the base of the tree.

I shook. I couldn't stop it. I couldn't stay strong in the face of what I knew was coming. Oakman stood and trailed the end of a whip through his hand lovingly. Moving slowly, I bet the leather was smooth and supple. Moving as he swung, it would tear my flesh. My tremor grew until the shackles were shaking, clanging against each other.

"Oh, I can fix that." Oakman yanked on a chain hanging from a pulley next to him. It pulled our arms upward until all three of us were pressed against the tree, the metal digging into our wrists and ankles and our backs on display.

"Everyone, the years just keep getting better don't they?"

A smattering of approval rose from below. Even with the spotlight in my face, I could sense they were all still, watching. A tremor roared through me at the realization. What could be so fascinating to stop the roiling beasts from clamoring and rutting?

I tried to turn, to look at Vinemont. To try and will him to free me, save me, let me go. I couldn't see him. The blinding light and tight bonds mastered me. I was held fast, blood already running down my forearms from the shackles. The pain in my wrists and ankles was growing by the second, the metal cutting deeper with each of my breaths.

"Two-hundred and fifty years of pride. And this year is the best of all. Twenty-five Acquisition Balls, twenty-five strokes of the whip for each of our guests."

The crowd roared with approval.

I couldn't stop the sob that rattled up from my lungs. Brianne began screaming, her voice a high, blood-curdling shriek. It died away, muffled by Red's handkerchief or some similar gag.

My thoughts scattered, unable to focus on anything. I clamped my eyes shut and forced myself to focus on why I was here. Dad. He was there on the back of my eyelids. Standing over me as I awoke in the hospital. He smoothed my hair from my face even as I was bandaged and strapped to the bed. Was this so different? I bled, I was bound, I was wavering between the world I'd known and one I could only imagine. But now, instead of breaking him, my suffering would save him. Tears slid down my cheeks and disappeared. I would endure it. All of it.

"Now, who wants to go first?" Cal broke through my

memories.

"That'd be me." Vinemont spoke, his voice harsh and strong.

"That's my good man. Here you go. Make them count." Oakman laughed.

Vinemont stood behind me and ran a lingering hand down my skin, the whip hanging from his other hand. His touch was warm, somehow gentle. I let myself feel it, if only for a second. Let myself imagine he cared for me, that his was a lover's touch. That he wouldn't hurt me.

The warmth disappeared. He backed away.

I held my breath. I felt like the entire room held its breath. And then I was awash in pain. I didn't know I'd screamed until the sound died in my lungs from the force of the next hit.

"He's really going all out. This may be your next Sovereign ladies and—"

I couldn't hear his words, couldn't hear anything except the sound of my pain. It was my scream, eating up the space inside me, bleeding out my ears. Agony like I had never felt before erupted along my back. Lines of destruction. I could feel my skin separating with each of his vicious strokes. Blood leaked and trailed down my legs. It felt the same as I remembered it from those years ago, the same way as my blood felt dripping from my arms. But this time the damage was bigger and offered no promise of release from this life.

I screamed until my voice left me, the air no longer cooperating with my lungs. I burned everywhere. My blood sprayed against Brianne whose stifled scream replaced my own.

I couldn't breathe. I couldn't see. I was gone.

CHAPTER FOURTEEN
STELLA

MY MOM STROKED her warm hand down my face. Even in the dark I knew it was her. She whispered comforting words to me, telling me the pain was temporary and would fade. The sharp stings were far away now. Everything beneath me was soft, warm. I was loved. I was content.

My back was cool, numb. What happened?

I tried to tell her how much I missed her, how glad I was she was back. She'd been gone so long. Where had she gone?

"Shh, sleep now." Mom pulled a blanket up to my waist, making my legs toasty.

"Go ahead and push more before she feels anything." She was speaking to someone else now.

Deep dreamless sleep.

The sound of birds pulled me up from the pleasant

darkness. Light streamed in through the windows of the room. I faintly recognized the walls, the windows, the quilts, all jogging my memories. I was lying on my stomach.

I blinked the sleep away and lifted my head. An aching pain shot through my back. I dropped my head back down with a groan.

"Stella." It was my mother's voice. No. No, it was Renee's. Mom was dead.

"Renee?" I could barely speak, my voice hoarse.

Is there a tube in my arm?

"I'm here. Don't worry. You're healing up nicely. Do you want to go back under again?"

"Under?"

"Asleep. The Vinemont family doctor has been staying for the past three days and keeping you asleep so you could recover. I can have him put you out for longer if it bothers you too much."

My mind was having trouble clicking into the 'on' position. An IV was suspended above me, some clear liquid dripping through it at a leisurely pace.

I shifted my head so I could see Renee. Her concerned face brought the flood of horror back. The ball, the tortures, Vinemont flaying the skin from my back.

A sob rose up and stuck in my dry throat.

Renee wrung her hands. "I'll fetch Dr. Yarbrough."

"No," I croaked.

I fought the tears back, though a few escaped and dropped onto my white pillow. We were silent for a long time. The ball replayed through my mind like a particularly vivid nightmare—the masks, the cruelty, the violence, and the pain. More than anything, I remembered Vinemont, how he'd volunteered to whip me first, how he'd swung harder and harder until I blacked out from the pain.

Had I actually almost felt something for him? Each lash killed whatever twisted emotion had grown in my heart. I was glad. My feeling of betrayal was replaced with rage, raw anger. I added these to the box in my chest, the one where

I had hidden away my sadness. It was full to bursting with every negative emotion I possessed. Still, I stuffed more inside, poisoning myself by saving the bitterness and hate.

I tried to calm my breathing. Anytime my lungs expanded too fully, my back felt as if it would rip apart. Renee looked almost as white as my pillowcase and kept wringing her hands.

"Vinemont?"

"I haven't seen him. Not since he brought you back. He was, well, he was in a bad way. Lucius and Teddy had to come get him."

"Tired out from whipping me, was he?"

"No, not that. It did something to him. I don't know."

"Did something to *him*, huh?" I tried to yell, but it only came out in a hoarse burst of sound. The effort made my back scream.

"I meant. I-I meant—" She rose abruptly and came to take my hand.

I wanted to rip it away, but I didn't dare move.

"I mean, I've never seen him like that. He kept begging me to fix it, to heal you. He tried to clean your wounds himself before Dr. Yarbrough arrived. He wouldn't let anyone else touch you. He sat here with you and told you he was sorry over and over. He wouldn't leave. Not until Lucius and Teddy came. Only Teddy could get through to him. I haven't seen Mr. Sinclair since."

I couldn't imagine any of what she was saying. Remorse seemed a completely foreign emotion to Vinemont. The way he'd whipped me was an assault on more than just my body. He'd struck at my soul, instilling dread so deeply that I didn't know if I'd ever recover.

When I'd hurt myself, it gave me a release, a chance at oblivion. When he'd done it, he trapped me even more inside myself. Every lash was a fresh set of bars, hemming me in and holding me captive. If he could do that to me, what else would he be willing to do to win the Acquisition? And what was even required to win?

"I know it's hard. I know." Renee's voice broke through my shadowy thoughts.

"You know? No, you don't." I slid my fingers away from her, out of her warm grip.

She knelt by my bed, getting at eye level with me.

"I do, Stella."

No you don't.

"How? Have you been branded and whipped? Have you had a year of your life stolen? Have you had to endure a man like Vinemont?" My tears were flowing, making slight plops onto the pillow beneath me.

Renee's dark eyes were troubled, a storm seeming to rage in her breast. She took a deep breath, as if she had come to a decision. She began unbuttoning her black shirt, her fingers nimble. Then she turned and swept her hair away from her nape. There in the stark green and black was the same 'V' that had been seared into me in ink.

She pulled her top down further so I could see the beginnings of lash marks crisscrossing her fair skin.

"What—"

"I was Mrs. Sinclair's Acquisition twenty years ago." She faced me again, her frank gaze disarming me.

If she had hit me, I couldn't have been more stunned. A million questions tumbled through my mind, one building on the next before stumbling in front of an even bigger curiosity. Why would she stay? What had her year been like? Could she help me?

She stood and refastened her top. When she moved to step away from me, I reached for her. The pain shot like lightning down my back. It went so deep I wondered if my heart hadn't somehow been lashed right along with my skin. I screamed and dropped my head.

"I'll get the doctor. Don't move, sweet Stella. Please don't." She rushed from the room.

My mind spun with revelations and harsh sensations. Renee had known all along. She knew what would happen to me at the ball. Why didn't she warn me? Vinemont's words came back to me—the more I knew, the more afraid I would be, and the more it all would hurt.

A dark figure rushed through the door, Renee sweeping in behind. Before I could protest—did I want to protest?—he fiddled with my IV and I was out.

This time I dreamed. Vinemont was in there in all of them—tormenting me or loving me. Were they one and the same? Then my father was sitting in his favorite chair telling me a story, though I couldn't hear the words. Finally, my mother arrived, her hair up in the messy bun I remembered. She was sad. Always sad. Water flowed from her mouth and then it changed to blood, more blood than a person could lose and still live. She was drowning in the very thing that gave her life. I couldn't save her. I couldn't even save myself. I sat in a pool of my own blood, the droplets slowing right along with my heartbeat. Steps in the hallway—my father. I dreaded him finding me before it was over. I didn't want him to see me die. The footsteps grew louder and then stopped.

"Stella?"

I knew that voice. It wasn't my father's. It was the voice of a demon, one that made me burn with desire and hate until both emotions mixed in a funeral pyre of black smoke.

I opened my eyes. He was here. Vinemont.

"Going to hit me again?" It came out as a whisper, but he winced as if I'd yelled at him.

"I don't know."

I was still lying on my stomach. My eyes finally adjusted to the dark. He sat near the door, his face unshaven, his clothes wrinkled and disheveled. He looked like I felt.

"What sort of an answer is that?"

"An honest one." He leaned over, resting his elbows on his thighs.

"You sick fuck." I refused to cry. *I would not cry.*

"Yes." He scrubbed a hand over his face. The sound of his palm rubbing against his stubble was loud in my ears.

"What now? Are you going to hurt me some more?

Maybe cut some fingers off and send them to my dad? Fuck you. Whatever it is, just get it over with." Tiredness had settled into every muscle and bone of my body. It must have been the drugs. My back no longer felt so raw; only a low ache emanated from it. My skin felt as if it had stitched back together, but I could already sense the scars forming, solidifying, forever marking me.

"No, I would never…"

I laughed but it was a rough, ugly sound. "You would *never*? Never what? Never enslave me? Never strip me naked and make me bleed for an audience?" My eyes welled with unshed tears. The hurt inside me seemed too much for my body to bear.

He dropped his head, his defeat just as out of character as his unshaven face and mussed hair. "I can't change what I did, Stella. I would do it again."

I wanted to scream, to rage at him, to demand to know why he sat here appearing contrite, while at the same time telling me he would do it all over again if given the chance. Was this the mental torture to go along with the physical?

"Do me a favor. When you become Sovereign, how about you make your first decree for you to go royally fuck yourself?"

He sighed and shook his head. "I don't expect you to understand. I didn't want—"

"Get out." I turned my head away from him, my neck stiff and unused to the movement.

He stayed. I could sense him there, unmoving, his gaze still on me.

There was nothing more to say. He'd whipped me like an animal. Worse, really. The memory of Cal Oakman's voice rattled around in my mind. The way he crowed over Vinemont's fevered strokes that drew my blood so easily. My tears went from sadness to rage.

I was a furious tempest of hatred and loathing but I was trapped in my battered body. All I could do was wish my tears away and accept that Vinemont had damned me to this existence. This life of pain and hurt and darkness. So many shadows that I never even knew existed had eclipsed any faint light I may have once had. I had been snuffed out, destroyed by the man who now looked so lost.

After a long moment, the floor creaked, and I heard his retreating footsteps.

"Wait," I said.

He returned with a quicker step, standing behind me now.

"You said I could have a reward if I got through the ball."

"Yes." His voice crackled, almost hopeful.

"I want to see my father and stepbrother."

He shifted and another long silence fell like deep winter snow, muffling and burying us. He touched the edge of my bed, the hesitant movement making me angry, making me want to hurt him.

"Okay." He sighed, resignation in the rush of air.

"You're going to keep your word?"

He ghosted his fingers through my hair. I closed my eyes, wondering if he had any chance of calming the firestorm that raged in my breast.

"I always do." His voice was as soft as his caress.

I wanted to believe this was truly who he was—the man who seemed just as wrecked by what he'd done as my tattered flesh. But which one of him was real? The destroyer or the destroyed? Either way, my tears still fell, my pain still stung, my heart still ached. He had done this and would do it again. I pushed any tender thoughts away.

"I want to see them soon. But not until I'm healed all the way. Or at least as much as I can heal from what you did. I don't want them to see me like this."

"You just tell me when and I'll arrange it." He gave my hair one last gentle stroke. He hesitated. Words were on his lips. I could sense them lingering there in the dark. Instead of voicing them, he turned and strode out, his pace clipped.

I was left alone with my pain, all the varying shades of it.

161

I turned my head back to look at the chair where he'd sat. My gaze roamed further up and seized on the discordant quilt created by Vinemont's mother. What sort of person made it through the Acquisition and won?

I heard more steps, and recognized them as Renee's. She slowed to a quiet tiptoe by the time she reached my door. Her black skirt rustled softly as she sat and folded her hands in front of her.

"I want to get up."

She rose and smoothed my hair over my shoulder. "Sunrise is in an hour. Rest until then."

Comfort was in her movements, her touch. I didn't want comfort. I wanted to stop crumbling, to shore up what pieces of me I had left.

"No, I'm done resting. Help me sit up or I'll do it by myself."

I couldn't lie in bed for another minute. I couldn't stand being helpless and weak. I wouldn't be. Not anymore.

With Renee's help, I recovered over the next few weeks. I didn't see Vinemont or Lucius at all during that time. I would pass Teddy in the hallway sometimes. He would smile and exchange pleasantries. Underneath, I could sense he was troubled. I had too many problems of my own to even begin to care about his. He seemed like a nice guy, but he was born into a pit of vipers. It would be foolish to think he wouldn't bite just as surely as Vinemont and Lucius did.

I began to realize he was the only one who knew less than I did about what was going on. Renee wouldn't tell me anything new, only that Vinemont didn't volunteer for the Acquisition. It was done on some sort of lottery basis.

I'd figured as much at the ball when the names of the families were called. Oakman made it seem as if it were some "luck of the draw" situation, though it seemed like a stroke of bad fortune to be chosen. Even so, I couldn't forgive Vinemont. He didn't have to choose *me*. He didn't have to threaten my father and force me into the contract. I didn't wish this on another soul, but I couldn't excuse his turning a bad stroke of luck on his part into a year-long suffering on mine.

"I honestly still don't know how they're picked," she said one day over a steaming mug of tea after I'd pestered her for the better part of an hour.

The weather had finally turned cooler, leaves swirling in the yard and the grass fading into a dormant brown. I preferred hot chocolate, and stirred the marshmallows around in the foam before taking a scorching sip.

"Well, tell me something, anything. What's next? Is there something next?" I hoped there wasn't. I hoped it would be just a year of captivity spent here with her. I wasn't a total idiot, though. I knew that little fairy tale was too good to be true.

She set the mug down and stared into the rolling steam. "I'll tell you this and no more. There are more trials. The next one is at Christmas."

I raised an eyebrow at the all-around fucked up quality of holiday-based tortures.

"And then there's another in the spring, and the final one in the summer. I won't give details."

After that revelation, she was close-lipped, and always answered my questions with a deflection or a suggestion that I get it directly from the source—Vinemont. No matter how many times she reiterated the fact that Vinemont didn't choose to participate in the Acquisition, I couldn't forget the verve with which he pursued the Sovereign title, the way he'd played to the audience of masked ghouls. I still didn't know what it would take for him to win, but if the exhibition of my body and the whipping were any indication, it wouldn't be a pleasant outcome for me. So, no, I wouldn't speak to him.

Despite her stonewalling on the Acquisition process, Renee and I fell into a happy pretend friendship, as if we didn't share a dark secret of slavery and sadism. She was more than happy to discuss just about any subject I could think of other than the one I was desperate to learn about. We'd spend time in the house's library, reading quietly as the days faded. No one ever stopped us from exploring, and Renee showed me the ins and outs of the kitchen wing, the guest wing, and several other areas that had rooms upon rooms full of remarkable possessions and ornate furniture. Farns was always happy to see us, and gave us the history of various antiques and treasures scattered around the common rooms.

We even stopped in Vinemont's room once. It had his scent, masculine and clean. It drew me. I wanted to know more about him, to pick him apart in an effort to find out how he ticked so maybe I could somehow gum up the mechanism.

His room was modest, more modern and Spartan than the rest of the house. A king size bed with white duvet, navy walls, and minimal furniture filled the large space. No photos of him or his family graced the walls. I wandered to his nightstand when Renee wasn't looking and pulled the top drawer open.

Instead of skin mags or back issues of "Psychotic Monthly," there was nothing except for a single black feather. I recognized it immediately. It had come from the dress I'd worn to the ball. It mocked me, reminiscent of the forsaken glass slipper. Except Vinemont was no prince. He was the devil.

I slammed the drawer shut.

Lucius' room was more colorful, white walls covered with tons of art—much of it good, to my surprise. He was messier than Vinemont. Books and magazines were scattered across his desk. There was an iPod and earbuds that somehow managed to make their way into my pocket.

"Where are they anyway?"

"Mr. Sinclair is in town for work, I believe. Mr. Lucius is in South America visiting two of the sugar cane plantations. He's in charge of the business while Mr. Sinclair handles the legal issues and keeps up appearances as parish district attorney. He never wanted the position, but the Sovereign decreed that Mr. Sinclair would take the post, and that was that."

"I thought the parish district attorney was elected?"

Renee raised a cynical black eyebrow. "And I thought slavery was illegal."

"Touché. What about Teddy?"

"He's in school still, in Baton Rouge. I'm not sure what he intends to do. It's not as if he has too many options."

"How does a rich, handsome young man like Teddy not have many options?"

"Depends on what the Sovereign says. If Oakman decides Teddy should be a lawyer, then off to law school he goes. If he decides being a doctor would be better, then med school."

"The Sovereign wields that much power?"

"More than you can even imagine. Who do you think decides the winning Acquisition? And it's worse for the Vinemonts, really. Even though they've been part of the ruling faction for well over a hundred and fifty years, some families still remember that it wasn't always so. The others try and lord it over them. The Vinemonts used to be poor sharecroppers and seamstresses. Worked for the Oakmans for years and years until..." Renee put her hand to her mouth as if that would somehow stop her words from spilling out.

"What? Until what?" I didn't want her to stop. All this was news to me and I was starved for information.

"Oh, nothing. I shouldn't have said. It's all ancient history. It's just, those things aren't really talked about. Not in the house, especially."

"If it's ancient history, then why can't you talk about it? What harm could there be?"

"Mr. Lucius should be home in a couple of days." I'd learned that Renee's subject change signaled the end of the conversation, despite my many unsuccessful attempts to make it otherwise.

There was only one part of the house we never visited—the top floor.

"It's mostly shut off and dusty. No one goes up there, really. Not anymore." Renee always led me away from the stairs to the third floor, even when I had placed a foot hesitantly on the bottom step. The steps weren't dusty, and I got the feeling Renee's hurried explanation was hiding something more. Then again, this house was full of secrets—Renee's not the least among them.

A few days later Renee and I were whiling away the afternoon in the library. I still hadn't set eyes on Lucius or Vinemont since my recovery. I sometimes caught myself wondering what Vinemont was doing, where he was. Then I reminded myself of the scars on my back and turned my thoughts elsewhere.

Renee sat under a throw blanket and read as I tried to paint. She had ordered every supply I could think of to get my art started again. But for the third day in a row, I just stared at the blank canvas.

Before, I would let whatever I was feeling meld itself to the canvas. Now, it was as if my emotions were in too much of a vicious muddle to do anything other than a Picasso imitation, my pieces scattered in ways that reflected how fragmented I was inside.

My back had healed. It no longer stung or ached, but I knew it was different, scarred. Renee smeared some sort of specialty cream she'd ordered from Juliet over my back every night. She said my scars had already faded much more than her own. Even then, she wouldn't tell me about her Acquisition, about why she lingered here in this house.

While I was lost in my thoughts, my hands worked on the canvas of their own accord. Before I knew it, I'd drawn out a harsh line, then another, then another. I worked feverishly, sketching a body drawn impossibly tight and covered with the crisscrossing lines. I drew and shaded until the image came forth from the white background just as it had done in my mind.

The canvas was macabre even without color. The woman's head lolled to the side. A hand with a whip reared back as if the aggressor stood where I did, on this side of the easel, ready to inflict more violence. When I finally changed to paint, mixing the colors with a rough hand, I realized it had grown late. Renee slept on the couch, a book resting against her softly rising and falling chest.

I woke her gently and sent her on to bed before returning to my work, intent on finishing what I'd begun. I smoothed on the crimson, letting the painting run in streaky rivers before sweeping through them with the edge of my brush. I let that part dry and worked on the edges and background. I swiped my hand on my long skirt, leaving a streak that I knew would never come out.

Vines in blacks and greens—matted, twisting, and snakelike—grew from my brush strokes. They looked as venomous as I'd intended, threatening from the canvas, seeking to taste the crimson of the foreground. They wrapped around the nude woman's ankles and wrists.

When I finished, I stepped away, giving a critical eye to the piece. It was dark and needed a good deal of touching up, but it was my soul in pencil and paint. The darkness infecting me had leached onto the bristles and then the threads. Would getting it out keep the rot from going any deeper?

"You captured it."

I whirled. Vinemont stood behind me, so close that I didn't know how I hadn't heard him. He was clean shaven again, well put together. He wore a suit, the tie loosened and his top button undone. His eyes, though, were haunted. They were still his deep, turbulent blue. Beneath them were gray circles, unease or worry having left its mark.

"You look well," he said.

167

"Do I?" I crossed my arms over my chest, not caring that I got paint all over my shirt. It wasn't the first time. "Maybe you should see my back. It might change your mind."

He finished the job on his tie, pulling it loose so it hung open around his neck. "I did what I had to do, Stella."

A burning rage erupted in my chest, my mind. My anger had simmered for so long that seeing his face forced it to boil over. But what made it worse, what really sent me over the edge, was that some part of me recognized a change in him. The things he'd said to me that night in my room, the way he looked now—none of it fit with what he'd said about willingly hurting me again.

"Why?" I met his gaze.

"Because you're my Acquisition. Because I have to win."

"So you'd do anything it takes to win, to be Sovereign?"

"To win? Yes." His face hardened, becoming the cruel mask I knew so well. "I will do everything in my power to win."

"Then why are you here? Why even come speak to me until it's time for my yuletide whipping?"

"Renee told you?" He shook his head and anger flashed in his tired eyes.

"Yes. She told me I have a very busy holiday schedule over the next few months."

"What else did she tell you?"

"Nothing. You've got her well trained."

He ran a hand through his dark hair. "Not me."

"Then who?"

He took a step toward me. I matched it, stepping backward.

A shadow crossed his face—pain? Then it was gone and he fisted his hands at his sides, hell in his eyes.

"Look, Stella, this is something that neither of us can avoid. I'm doing what I have to do. That's all you need to know about it. Once your year is up, you can leave and never look back. Until that time, I need you to do as I ask and just accept it. No more questions. No more trying to run."

"I'm not running."

"Keep it that way." He took another step toward me, menacing.

I held my ground. He could hurt me, but I wouldn't give him the benefit of my fear. I stared into him, past the blue and deeper, watching as they turned from anger to heat. The air in the room shifted, like an electrical current hummed between us.

All the concern that he'd walked in with was gone. He looked...hungry, as if the moon had emerged from behind a cloud and revealed him to be some sort of ravenous wolf.

His gaze travelled my face, my body. When heat erupted along my skin as if he'd touched me, I knew I was damned. To want the touch of the devil was nothing short of a mortal sin.

I struck him, my open palm whipping across his face with a satisfying slap. He didn't retaliate, just tilted his head to the side until his neck popped in the most unnerving fashion. What had been fire in his eyes was now a raging inferno.

He advanced, only inches from me now. I pulled my hand back to strike him again, but he caught it, squeezing my wrist painfully. I tilted my chin up, meeting his vicious encroachment with defiance. He wouldn't frighten me out of this space. It was mine. I didn't care if the entire place was covered in fucking vines, I would slash and burn them until I'd cleared an area for me, my paint, my books, and my own bit of freedom.

Quick as an adder, he put his free hand to my face. I didn't flinch, though I expected him to strike me. The heat in his gaze spoke of something explosive—violence or desire, maybe a heady mix of both. When his palm touched my skin, my eyes closed involuntarily.

"So soft." His voice was tinged with wonder.

I was down the rabbit hole, everything topsy-turvy and wrong, because his touch—god, his touch. It was like I'd

CELIA AARON

been starving for it this entire time but didn't know it. When I opened my eyes, he leaned down, his lips teasing mine with the bare millimeters of distance. He was a gorgeous villain, a predator dressed up as a man.

I raised my unrestrained hand to hit him again, but he caught it, too, and wrenched both of them behind my back. He pressed me into his chest, caging me with his body. I could feel the blaze emanating from him, the desire like a heat wave. Could he feel mine? His gaze held me fast, furious and possessive. He looked at me like I was *his*. Not because of a contract, not because of the Acquisition, but because the intensity of his desire made it so. He would have what he wanted. His gaze flicked down to my mouth and he dipped his head lower, his breath grazing my lips.

I burned to destroy him, to leave him in flames as I walked away from the ashes. But first … just a kiss. I pushed up on my tip toes.

Our lips met.

I was lost.

He wasn't gentle. I knew he wouldn't be. I still wanted him. His lips were soft and firm, taking everything and demanding more. His tongue probed against my lips. When he pulled my hair back, I arched into him and opened my mouth. His tongue was a wicked explorer, caressing mine and tasting me in a way no one ever had.

He groaned and wrapped an arm around me, crushing me against him. His scent was in my nose, floating in my lungs like a whirlwind, putting me even further under his spell. My nipples rubbed against him, the tips hard and wanting. They ached for his touch, his mouth. I had never known the sheer need that welled up inside me, the wetness between my thighs, the desperate feeling of wanting more and still more.

He lifted me and carried me to the sofa, laying me down and looking over his prize. He yanked off his blazer and pulled his shirt away, buttons flying as his hard abs were revealed. The same V as mine was inked over his heart, the

170

intricate vines spreading and roping along his chest and down his arms.

I licked my lips, and his gaze went straight to the movement. He was the spider I'd always imagined him to be, lethal and beautiful.

He stalked on top of me, wedging himself between my thighs. His hands were at the hem of my shirt, pushing it up and peeling it off my body. He hitched in a breath when he saw I wasn't wearing a bra.

"Fuck, Stella," he rasped.

He pressed a hard kiss on each nipple. My stomach tightened and clenched.

I dug my fingers through his hair, scratching him as he took a nipple in his mouth. I arched my back off the sofa. His mouth was hot as he teased the hard tip. He circled his tongue around the pearled peak before pulling it in his mouth against his teeth. The sensation went straight to my pussy, making it pulse with want. When he sucked my nipple hard enough to bruise, I couldn't stifle my cry. He was going to devour me, just like his eyes had always promised.

He relinquished my breast to move up and reclaim my mouth. His hard length rested against my pussy. It promised more pleasure than I'd ever felt. I dug my nails into his shoulders, wanting to hurt him, to mark him just as he'd done to me. I bit his lip, drawing blood. He groaned and kissed me roughly, making me taste his copper on my tongue. I was on fire, rage and hatred mixing with the most primal need. I wanted him bleeding, but I also wanted him buried deep inside me. I wanted him screaming in pain but also in the most resplendent pleasure.

As our mouths warred, blood welled around my nails where I broke his skin. He rocked his hips against me, making my clit buzz with the power of his stroke. He gripped my hair, pulling until I cried out. When I opened my mouth, he sank his tongue inside me, claiming me. I gave in. I opened for him, letting him taste me, letting him own me. He kissed me so ferociously that my breath was gone and I was breathing only him.

He slid a hand down to my neglected breast and palmed it as he rubbed a thumb over my nipple. I moaned into his mouth, his tongue swirling the sound around before he swallowed it. He was possessing me, branding me far more than any ink on my neck or any scars on my back. His touch, his insistent kiss marked me deeper, surer than any lash ever could. I was betraying myself. I knew it. I didn't care. I didn't want anything other than him, his hands, his body, his kiss. I had never felt more alive.

He pushed a hand between us, yanking my skirt up before roughly pulling my panties to the side. When he touched my wet core, he groaned. I wanted him inside me. I wanted him wild, desperate. I wanted him to come for me, only me.

"You are so wet," he grated. He released my breast and gripped my hair, yanking my head to the side and sucking on the tender skin of my neck.

His fingers strummed me, playing me until I writhed beneath him. Wanton and desperate for his touch. He was the most delicious thing I had ever felt.

"You like that, Stella?" he murmured against me.

"Yes," I breathed.

"How about this?" He sank a finger inside.

I gasped, the breath hitching in my throat at the unbridled pleasure. He withdrew it and pushed it in again. My hips ground up into him.

"Fucking my finger, Stella? Just wait until it's my cock, filling every last bit of your tight cunt."

I thought I might come just from his words. No one had ever spoken to me that way. I needed more.

He sat back on his haunches. "Don't move." A growl to match the animal look on his face.

He pushed my skirt up past my hips. With one hand, he ripped my panties away. Then he fixed his gaze on my pussy. I was bare to him, completely open and at his mercy in a way I'd never been, not even when I was chained and whipped. This was the most intimate moment I'd ever had.

"I can't stop." He slowly brought his gaze to mine. "I won't."

I swallowed hard, his taste still on my lips. "Don't."

CHAPTER FIFTEEN
SINCLAIR

IT TOOK EVERY remaining shred of self-control I had not to rip my fly open and shove into her. Her glistening pink flesh was something I'd fantasized about and now…to have it laid out before me like an offering was almost too much.

I drew down my zipper and pulled my cock from my boxers. It throbbed in my palm. I didn't want my skin. I wanted hers. Every inch of it.

Her eyes grew wide as she saw my cock, hard and ready for her. I slid my tip against her slick folds and almost lost my seed all over her. I gripped up on the base, keeping myself in check.

She scooted back from me. Not happening. I dragged her back down beneath me and caged her throat with my hand.

"It's too big, Sinclair. I-I don't think I can."

She said my name. I always wanted her to call me Sinclair, though she insisted on Vinemont. The former was a surrender, the latter a curse. All I needed from her right now was total surrender, submission. I would have it.

"I haven't done this since Dylan and I—"

I silenced her by forcing two fingers inside. She moaned and closed her eyes. I didn't want to hear about anyone else touching what was mine. After tonight, they would be erased. I would fuck her so completely that I was her first, her last, her everything. My cum on her—in her—would mark her as mine.

Still holding her fast with one hand, I stroked her clit with my fingertips. The fear drained from her as I worked her into a frenzy. Her clit was a delicious little nub that demanded to be sated. I would give Stella what she wanted, what she needed.

I swirled the tip of my index finger around her clit and rubbed it in increasingly strong strokes. She was going wild, her hips meeting my movements with more and more urgency. She ground against me, begging for a release she wouldn't get until every inch of me was buried in her tight heat.

I brought my wet fingers to my mouth and licked her sweetness from them.

She watched, her eyes glazed with lust, just like I wanted her.

I slid my cock to her opening. Her flesh was no longer hot, but molten. The muscles along my back shook with the need to plunge into her, to take what I wanted just as roughly as I wanted it. I couldn't. I wouldn't hurt her. Not this time. Not yet.

"Sinclair." It was a reverent prayer from her bruised lips.

I pushed inside, my head squeezing into her exquisite velvet. She moaned and clutched at my chest. I couldn't tell if she wanted to push me away or pull me closer. Either way, I couldn't stop. I needed her more than I'd ever needed anything in my life. I watched as I fed myself slowly into her, inch by inch. Further in, then out, then even further. When I was seated as deeply as I could go, her muscles clenched around me, pulling me farther inside. Still, I wanted more. I wanted it all.

I wrenched her hands above her head and pinned them

as I drew back and filled her completely.

"Fuck."

"Sinclair, please."

I had never heard a sexier sound in my life.

"Please what?"

She rubbed up against me, her clit begging for release just as her mouth did.

"Please just, just…I want to come."

Fuck. My cock pulsed inside her, perilously close to the edge. I steadied my breathing.

"Do you want me to make you come, Stella?"

"Yes."

I pulled out and slid all the way back in before starting a slow rhythm. Her face was a mix of pleasure and pain as I slowly made her mine.

"Look at me, Stella."

Her eyes were half mast, but locked on mine all the same. I wanted her to watch me as I brought her pleasure. The fucking barbarian who lived in my breast demanded it, demanded that she acknowledge I was the only one who could give her the release she was begging for.

I licked into her open lips before taking her mouth again. I claimed her fully, my cock and my tongue embedded in her and giving her gratification. I knew my seed was close to bursting, my balls drawn up tight against me. I wouldn't come, not until she did. Once I felt her muscles milking me, I would coat her pussy lips. The picture in my mind almost sent me over the edge.

I pulled out to my tip and kissed down to her hard nipple. When I released her hands, she put them in my hair, pulling until it hurt and I growled against her tender flesh. I bit down on her nipple and fucked her harder, ramming my cock deep into her. Her hips rose up to meet me, marking my rhythm.

I knew she was close, the tension building in her as I'd intended. Each shuddering thrust went right to her clit. She arched off the couch, her gorgeous breasts shaking from my impacts as she rubbed her clit into me stroke for stroke.

"Don't stop! Please, Sinclair. Don't stop." Her voice was sex, raw and low.

As if I had a choice. There was no stopping, not now, not when I was so deep in her slick pink.

"Come for me, Stella. I own this body. Now I want it to come."

"Sinclair." She thrashed her head from side to side.

I couldn't tell if she was refusing me or lost in her own passion. Either way, she needed to focus on me. I gripped her hair and forced her to meet my eyes.

I plunged into her, my skin slapping into her with each vicious strike. The sound reverberated around the room. I fucked her like an animal, vicious and base. Her moans spurred me on harder and faster.

I gripped her hair tightly, the fine strands catching on my fingers. I wanted her to feel nothing but me, think nothing but me. "You're mine. Come for me Stella. Now."

At my words, her pussy convulsed and she cried out my name in a river of release. The sound was unbearable. I pulled from her and lashed her clenching flesh with ropes of cum. My release was ripped from me, my body seizing from head to toe as I fisted my length and coated her with my seed. Her gaze was fastened on me as I came. There in her eyes was something I never even imagined to see. It was possessive, proud even.

When my last ounce of cum rested on her perfect skin, I sat up and let my head fall back. I gulped in deep breaths as she panted beneath me.

"That was, that was…" She sputtered beneath me, her eyes glassy.

"I know," I said.

As I stared at the ceiling, invisible guilt and responsibility crashed down on me. What had I done? Weren't things already complicated enough?

"Don't do that." Her voice was soft now, the release liquefying her tension.

"Do what?"

"Regret it. Regret me."

How could I not?

A sound like a gunshot echoed around the room, then another. I snapped my head back down. Lucius stood in the doorway, slow clapping. I fell back, grabbed my coat from the floor, and covered Stella.

"Very nice, big bro. I'm going to have to go rub one out after that."

Stella covered her face with both hands.

"Don't be shy, Stella. I really enjoyed the whole show. Your tits are, in a word, epic. And I can only imagine how sweet that pussy is for Sin here to bust a nut so quickly."

"Get out." I stood and yanked my pants up.

"I was just up for a midnight snack, is all. You can't blame me for making sure there wasn't a burglar. You know, the kind that fucks really loudly before robbing the place blind." He smirked. I hated it, mostly because it was almost the perfect mirror of mine.

I advanced on him. He backed away laughing. "I'm going. Because, seriously, going to have to stroke it before I can even think of sleeping again. I'll, of course, have to replace you with me in the reenactment, but I'm sure you understand."

I stalked toward him, ready to murder my own blood. How fitting.

He turned on his heel and disappeared down the hallway, his smug laugh shredding my already non-existent composure.

I returned to Stella and used my coat to clean her off. She draped an arm over her tits and then pushed her skirt down to cover herself. When she sat up and turned to get her shirt, I saw the scars on her back.

My guts wrenched, the memory of that night making my stomach churn and bile rise into my throat. So much pain. Her blood had soaked into my clothes. As soon as the spotlight was gone and the ballgoers' attention was turned elsewhere, I'd carried her out, clutched closely to my breast. I couldn't bear for anyone else to touch her, look at her. Her blood soaked through the vining cloak, painting everything a gruesome crimson and scenting the air with copper.

Her blood still covered my hands, though only I could see it. And now I'd taken even more from her. Remorse wasn't an option for me, not anymore. I'd set out to be this, to do this, to become the monster I had to be.

I reached out and ran my hand across one of the marks. She froze and glared at me over her shoulder. The accusation in her eyes was warranted, more than fair. It still struck me hard, embedding in my chest and spreading its barbs into my heart.

She yanked her top down, hiding what I'd done to her. Her cheeks were red, shame or some other emotion tingeing them with rose.

"It's time for you to make good on your promise. I want to see my father and stepbrother."

"What? Now?" I hadn't seen that coming. I should have.

"Yes. You said you'd arrange it when I asked. So, I'm asking."

I didn't want them here, poisoning her against me. Though that was a ridiculous thought. I was doing it plenty well on my own.

She bristled at my hesitation. "Well, are you going to be true to your word or not?"

My mother would have struck her for such an impertinent question. I didn't move. "I'm always true to my word. What day would you like to see them?"

"Tomorrow, in the afternoon."

"Fine, but only for an hour. No more."

"An hour? That's not enough time t-to—"

"I never promised you how long they could visit, I just agreed that they could." I hated the thought of her stepbrother here, speaking to her, thinking he had any sway over her. He didn't. He never would again.

She stood and smoothed her skirt down with quick,

angry movements. "You know what? I was wrong before. You should regret it. You should regret all of it."

She left, never looking back and taking more of me with her than I should have allowed.

CHAPTER SIXTEEN
STELLA

I FIDGETED WITH my hair, pulling it to the back and ensuring it covered the tattoo. I didn't want Dad or Dylan seeing the permanent brand. I wore a simple black sweater and a gray skirt. To their eyes, I would no doubt look the same as I had a month ago. Only I knew that the woman they remembered was long gone.

The front door opened and footsteps approached. I stood, nerves making my movements jerky. I was desperate to see my father, but I worried he would get too worked up. He didn't need to suffer any more than necessary.

Dad rushed in and embraced me. I didn't realize my tears were falling until they rolled down to my lips, salty on my tongue.

"Daddy," was all I could choke out.

Dylan stood a few steps back, bowed up with rage. Vinemont stood behind them, leaning against the wide doorway into the sitting room.

My father held me for the longest time. He stroked my hair and kept saying he was sorry.

I pulled away and looked into his watery blue eyes. "Don't be sorry. I chose to do this. I would do anything to keep you safe."

He shook his head, now covered in even more gray than I remembered. "That's what I'm supposed to do. Not you."

"We're going to get you out of here, Stella." Dylan crushed me in his thick arms, squeezing me to him.

"I will get you back," he whispered in my ear.

I rested my chin on his shoulder and caught Vinemont staring daggers at Dylan.

Jealous, Vinemont?

I placed a chaste kiss on Dylan's cheek and glanced at Vinemont. He fisted his hands at his sides, the impeccable suit and tie he wore doing a poor job of hiding the animal underneath.

Dylan set me back and looked me up and down. "Has he hurt you?"

"I-I—"

Dylan whirled and advanced on Vinemont who just stood and smirked. He was taunting Dylan, drawing him in so he could hurt him. I knew the power in Vinemont's body, the way he could break even a man like Dylan.

"No one has hurt me," I lied. "Please, just, let's just sit down. We only have an hour. Please."

He stopped only a few feet from Vinemont, and the men engaged in a testosterone-laden stare down. I went to Dylan and tried to pull him away.

"Come on, Dylan. Sit with me."

He laid a hand over mine and an arm around my waist. Vinemont crossed his arms over his chest, muscles popping even through his dress shirt.

I led Dylan away before my hour was stolen with pointless violence. I'd already had enough of that for a lifetime.

Dad sank down in a fluffy side chair as Dylan and I sat on the floral sofa. Sun poured into the room, belying the chilly air outside. My father was thinner, though he seemed well put together, his clothes new and pressed. Dylan wore his usual rugby shirt and jeans.

Vinemont didn't move from the door. I glared up at him, willing him away. He smiled back, daring me to ask him to leave. I knew it was useless. Instead, I put my hand in Dylan's and laced our fingers together.

Enjoy the show, asshole.

From the corner of my eye, I saw him shift from one foot to the other, tension in his taut muscles. I'd seen them, intimately, closely. I brushed those thoughts away and focused on my father.

"How have you been?"

He looked at the floor before bringing his gaze back to mine. "I know I keep saying it, but I'm sorry. I should have just let him lock me up. I should have... You never should have come here."

"I don't want to talk about should haves or could haves. We only have a short time and I want to hear about you. How's the house? Have you had any more trouble from your old clients? Did any of my paintings sell?"

I forced a smile to my face, encouraging my father to engage with me like we were normal human beings, not as a grieving father and an enslaved daughter.

"Oh, your paintings." He almost managed a smile. "Yes, yes. The gallery called. Just a few days ago, some highbrow collector came in and bought every last one of your works."

"Someone bought out the gallery?"

"No, not the whole gallery, just your pieces. It was the damnedest thing. Paid full for each one and had them shipped. I don't know who it was, and the gallery kept their information confidential. But the check was real enough." His gaze dropped again. "I put it in your account. It'll be there when you get back."

My heart soared at the thought of my art gracing some collector's walls. I'd never sold more than a few paintings every so often. Certainly, no one had ever bought two at once. This news was like Christmas... Then I remembered what my real Christmas would entail.

My smile faltered a bit before I plastered it back across

185

my face. "Dylan, how's school?"

"Same old, same old. My lacrosse team is leading the SEC like it does every year…" He gave the broad strokes of his life outside, the start of a new school year. Instead of making me feel better, it only reinforced my isolation here at the Vinemont estate.

I resolved to get outdoors more, especially now that my back had healed. Renee had spoken of stables on the property. I'd always been a decent rider.

When Dylan wound down, my father leaned forward and took my hands. "Please tell me what you've been doing for the past month. I think about you every moment."

I glanced to Vinemont. His gaze bored into me.

"I mostly stay in the house. I read and paint. There are others here. I have a good friend, Renee. And Vinemont's brothers are pleasant, especially the youngest, Teddy." Okay, I may have fibbed a bit—well, a lot—but I couldn't exactly explain that I was whipped bloody and paraded around naked.

"Has he hurt you? Has anyone? I couldn't bear to think of them hurting you." The tears welled in Dad's eyes again.

I shook my head in vehement denial. "No, no. They're all very nice here. I'm fine, really. It's like an upscale prison, really. Food's good, too. Far better than anything you ever made, Dad."

That would have made him laugh a month ago. Now, though, he only smiled sadly.

"If they just keep you around as a pet, what's the point?" Dylan asked.

"I, um, I don't really know." Lies were rolling off my tongue more easily by the minute. "I think it's just some sort of traditional thing they do here."

"Why don't you enlighten us, asshole?" Dylan turned to Vinemont.

"Oh, suffice it to say, I like owning beautiful things. As you know, your stepsister is particularly lovely, especially when unencumbered with trifles like clothing." Vinemont didn't miss a beat.

I gripped Dylan's hand hard, keeping him next to me on the couch instead of challenging the devil in the doorway.

"I have an idea, Stella. Why don't you show Dylan who you belong to?"

Ice water flowed through my heart. "What?"

"If he wants to know why I keep you and what I do to you, just give him a peek at your neck. I realize he's slow, but maybe a little demonstration will help him figure it out."

Dylan was already searching my throat with his gaze. "What's he talking about, Stella?"

"Nothing." I smoothed my hair down.

"Did he do something to you?" Dad asked. The sadness in his voice broke off a piece of my heart, leaving a bloody, jagged edge.

"No, he's just talking."

"Show them, Stella." It was a command now, no longer a suggestion.

"No." I pleaded with him, humiliation rising to color my cheeks.

"Is this a road you want to go down?" Vinemont looked from my father to me, the threat lingering in the air. "Do it."

"Don't talk to her like that." Dylan's anger mixed with the already-dangerous current of emotions in the room.

"No, I'll show you. Just don't antagonize him."

"I'm not scared of him." Dylan rose and faced Vinemont. "Of *you*. Let's take this outside, motherfucker."

"Wait, no, Dylan. He's right. He owns me. I let him, okay? I'm his. Look." I bent my head and pulled my hair to the side. "See? I'm his. I chose to be here, chose to be his."

My father gasped. "No, Stella."

"See, *Dylan*?" Vinemont's self-satisfied tone made me want to claw his eyes out.

"All I see is a pussy who gets his rocks off hurting women," Dylan snarled.

Score one for Dylan.

187

"Let's not be so reductive. I enjoy hurting men, too, especially dumb brutes like you. Want me to show you?" Vinemont pushed off the doorframe and stood at the ready.

I smoothed my hair back over the mark. "Stop, both of you! Dylan, please, for me, just talk to me a while longer. Ignore him. Don't you see? He wants you to go outside and fight him."

"Time's wasting, Dylan," Vinemont added not-so-helpfully.

Dad dropped his head in his hands. I'd never seen him so defeated. I sank to my knees at his feet. "Please don't, Dad. It's going to be okay. All of it. Eleven months left? That's nothing. I'll be back before you know it."

"I'll never forgive myself." He shuddered as a sob ripped through him.

"There's nothing to forgive," I said. "Please don't torture yourself. I want you to be healthy and happy when I come home. I want you to be waiting for me with open arms. I'll be there, Daddy. You'll see. It's not that long at all." I pressed my forehead to his.

He offered no more words as his tears overcame him. I wrapped my arms around his shaking frame. I pulled from some deep well of strength inside myself—one I didn't even know was there—as I held him.

"Time's up." Vinemont scowled at us.

"Look at him! Do you truly have no heart?" I hissed.

"In this case? No. No, I don't. Now, gents, I suggest you get the fuck out of my house."

"And if we don't?" Dylan asked.

"Lucius," Vinemont called.

His brother appeared, the two of them presenting a solid wall of muscle. They were almost a matching set. Both were glowering, their threat palpable. They could beat Dylan and my father senseless, and they would if given the opportunity.

"I'll walk you out. Come on." I refused to allow them to hurt Dad or Dylan.

My father rose with difficulty, and I helped him to the front door. Dylan took his other elbow as we maneuvered down the front steps. A black BMW waited out front.

"Did your mom get you a new car?" I asked.

"No, it's his." Dylan gestured to Dad.

"Oh." I supposed his old, beat up Camry finally died.

I gave Dad another long hug. "I'll see you again soon. I promise."

He put a shaking hand to my cheek. "I'll count the moments."

Vinemont snorted as if Dad had told a joke. I shot him a corrosive glare.

Dylan and I helped Dad into the driver's seat. Once he was in, I gave Dylan a long hug. Both Vinemont and Lucius smirked, no doubt feeling like they'd won some sort of victory. I'd show them.

When Dylan pulled away, I stood on my tiptoes and kissed him on the mouth. At first he was surprised, but then he deepened it, bending me back and clutching me to him. His tongue sank in my mouth, trying to get the fullest taste possible. It wasn't exactly enjoyable, but when he pulled me back upright and I broke the embrace, the fire in the Vinemont brothers' eyes was more than worth it.

"That was..." Dylan ran a hand through his hay-colored locks. "That was nice."

"I'll see you again soon." I put my hand on his chest, playing it up like an Oscar was hanging in the balance.

He sobered. "I'll get you out of here. I swear I will."

I smiled at him, though I knew his oath would be broken. There was no getting out of here. Not for me. Not until my time was up.

Dylan walked to the passenger side and dropped in. I waved them away down the driveway. When the car disappeared in the glare of the sun, I turned and floated back up the stairs.

Vinemont grabbed my arm. "What was that?"

"What?" I fluttered my lashes innocently.

"You know what."

I shrugged, enjoying the muscle ticking in his jaw. "I'm just an affectionate stepsister. What can I say?" I pulled my arm from his grasp and strode past an equally pissed Lucius.

"Good afternoon, boys," I called, and closed the front door behind me, my heart full to bursting with my petty victory.

CHAPTER SEVENTEEN
STELLA

THE NEXT MORNING, I breakfasted with Teddy. He was back from school for the weekend. We actually had a long discussion about his art appreciation class. Like Lucius, he seemed to have an eye for good art.

He started out throwing major shade at Jackson Pollack, but by the end of his second coffee, he was coming around to the idea that all art didn't have to be still lifes and flowers in vases. I was growing fonder of him despite myself. He seemed so normal, like a young man trying to figure himself out and make his way in the world.

I wondered how such a well-adjusted person could have come from the likes of the Vinemont family. Then again, I'd only ever met Lucius and Sinclair. I didn't know what their parents had been like.

"So, now that we've gotten your art classes straightened out," I said, "I have a few questions of my own. I'm tired of being cooped up in here, and I think you can help me out. Are there horses I could ride?"

"Like here, on the estate?" He tore through a piece of bacon and winked at the pretty maid as she refilled my cup.

"Yeah."

"Sure. I'll take you. I can't ride with you, though. I have to finish some homework, and then I have a date." His gaze slid back to the maid, Laura.

"Oh? Something romantic?" I asked.

"We'll see." He stood. "Come on."

I followed him out to the hallway.

"Hang on, Stella. You can't wear tennis shoes to ride. Got any boots?"

I looked down at my outfit. "You're right. I'll meet you back here in five minutes."

I rushed upstairs and threw on some jeans, a t-shirt, a light jacket, and boots before returning to Teddy. Laura scurried away when I hit the bottom step. Teddy smiled, his lips a little redder than they were when I left him.

"Don't say anything to Sin, okay?" He led me through the kitchen and then out through a back hallway.

"I don't intend to say anything to him, period. So that should be easy."

"Yeah, you two have some kind of crazy thing going on. I don't really understand it. I've learned just to not ask any questions anymore. They don't tell me anything, anyway." He shrugged. His hair was lighter than Vinemont's but he was just as tall and almost as built. It was no wonder Laura had taken a liking to him.

He led me to some sort of ATV that was parked behind the house and motioned for me to get on the back. He swung a leg over and cranked it up.

"Where are the, um, helmets?" I asked over the sound of the engine.

"Scared?" He smiled, and I realized he was a lady killer hidden in the body of a young, sweet man.

I snugged up behind him and wrapped my arms around his middle. "Go fast."

He laughed, a deep rumble I could feel through his back. "Yes, ma'am."

The day was uncharacteristically warm, but the breeze created by the speeding ATV was delicious. The smell of fall was in the air, crisp and familiar. Many trees still bore some seasonal color, while others had already given up, their branches bare and dormant.

He gunned it down the curving drive. I squealed with the pleasure of movement and freedom. The barn loomed up ahead, large and classically red. Bales of hay were lined up out front, and chickens pecked around from a nearby coop. It was a lovely picture, really—the sky mostly blue with a few fluffy clouds, the red of the barn, and the color in the trees, all working together to create something idyllic.

We flew past the barn and came to the stables, painted the same iconic red. He parked out front and helped me off the ATV.

"That was fun."

He smiled again, beautiful. "Anytime. I'll get you set up. Come on."

We went into the stables and he disappeared into what I assumed was the tack room. There were several horses in the expansive enclosure. Two struck my fancy. One, large and dark. He nickered at me in greeting. I held out my hand and rubbed his nose lightly. He was proud but still friendly.

The next was a white mare, so light she looked almost silver. She watched me approach and nuzzled my hand.

"Oh, you've gone for Gloria. She's my favorite. I would have picked her for you, myself."

"Do you take care of the horses all the time?"

"No. I'd love to, though. Just don't have the time with school. We have a stable master and a few grooms. They keep the horses and take them to shows and things like that. They're out at a show right now. Should be back tomorrow."

Teddy carried a saddle to Gloria's stall.

"Come on Gloria, how does a nice ride sound?" She nickered and nodded her head.

I laughed. "She certainly knows how to get her point across."

"You'll never meet a smarter horse." He threw a glance

over his shoulder at the black gelding. "No offense, Shadow."

Shadow didn't respond.

"That's Sin's horse," he explained.

"I should have guessed."

Teddy led Gloria from the stall and got her all set up for me. Once the bridle was set, he helped me up and adjusted the stirrups.

"Feel good?" He ran a hand down Gloria's mane.

"Yep. I think this is just right. Thanks, Teddy." I loved being astride a horse. It made me feel so tall, powerful.

"My pleasure." He led Gloria and me from the shady stables out into the dappled light.

"Now, like I said, I don't know the deal, but I'm pretty sure I'd be in big trouble if you rode off into the sunset and never came back." He squinted up at me.

"Not on your watch, Teddy. I promise."

"All right then. Head that way if you want to ride past the lake and over the levee. There are some pulp woods over there if you want trees above you, or you could ride back toward the house. It's up to you."

"I think I'll see the lake."

"Good choice." He looked up. "Don't stay out here too long. When it's warm like this, storms aren't far behind."

"I won't. It's been a long time since I've ridden. My ass will be sore in no time." I blushed. *What did I just say?*

He chuckled. "Fair enough."

I set off at a slow trot, following the road. Teddy roared off on his ATV back to the house. I hoped his date went well.

He was right about the day being unseasonably warm. I shed my jacket and tied it around my waist. I spurred Gloria on a little faster and she was happy to oblige. Maybe she'd been cooped up for too long, just like me. She was a smooth ride, her pace perfect. Someone had clearly loved on her and trained her well.

Before long, we were racing through the grass. The wind

whipped against my face and my hair flew out behind me. I loved every second of it. Fear mixed with exhilaration as I leaned down and gripped her mane. The sun bathed my face in light and delicious heat.

We'd sped for miles, the stables long gone and only the encroaching woods and the thinner strip of grass next to the road in our view. Out here, away from the house, the grounds were far less manicured, the grass high and wild.

We startled some deer in an open field as we hurtled past, sending them scattering for the trees, their white tails up in alarm. Gloria didn't seem to mind. She powered ahead, free and fast, the wind a song of liberation in our ears.

After a few more minutes of a full-on gallop, I pulled back on the reins, slowing her down and sitting back upright. I guided her back onto the road and we clip-clopped over a bridge spanning a wide bayou branch. Fish swam in the waters beneath us and frogs sang in the trees. A few hundred yards ahead I caught the sparkle of a large span of water. The levee. We trotted up to the edge. It was a sizeable reservoir, the lake disappearing into wooded inlets far off in the distance.

On the far edge, I could just make out the straight lines of a cottage in the woods.

"Think there are alligators in there, Gloria?"

She nickered and nipped at the high grass.

Cattails grew along the sides of the water and lilypads floated here and there. A ramshackle dock and small wooden boat were abandoned nearby. The water darkened toward the center. How deep was it?

I guided Gloria further up the bank where a small retaining pond split off from the larger lake. A grassy berm separated the bodies of water. At the top, I dismounted and dropped to the ground. The last few cicadas of the summer played their song in the pines that hemmed in the water on all sides. I always associated the sound with hot days.

I let Gloria eat the high grass as I lay out on the ground,

staring up at the passing clouds. I popped in the stolen earbuds and set Lucius' iPod to random, listening to his eclectic mix of music as the sun smiled down, warming me with comforting beams.

I laced my fingers behind my head and closed my eyes.

Gloria's loud whinny woke me. I must have dozed off in the warm sun. It was gone now, dark clouds hovering above, promising a downpour. A rumble of thunder had Gloria nuzzling at my head with her nose.

I got to my knees and then stood. "I'm up. I'm up. We'd better get back."

I stowed the purloined iPod. As I clambered onto Gloria's back, the clouds erupted, huge raindrops pelting us. Then the hail came, larger than anything that should ever fall from the sky. The size of golf balls, the ice hurt with each stinging impact. It would take half an hour, likely more, to get back to the stables. The only other shelter was the cottage in the woods I'd spotted earlier. I couldn't see it anymore for the curtains of rain and the pelting hail, but it wasn't far.

A piece struck my forehead and I felt warm blood running down my face.

Shit.

I couldn't stay out in the open. I made my decision and urged Gloria toward the woods. We would have to ride the storm out in the cottage. The thunder grew louder, the booming reverberating in my chest as lightning streaked across the sky.

We made it to the tree line, the branches above blocking out or at least slowing down the balls of hail. Gloria whinnied as a streak of lightning led to a deafening crack of thunder. I stroked her mane.

"It's okay, girl. We just have to make it to the cottage."

I led her through the trees, heading to where I remembered the cottage sat. Or at least I thought I was. We were in the heart of the storm, gloom and sheets of rain cutting visibility down to nearly nothing.

I urged her on. The cottage had to be nearby. I hoped I hadn't missed it in the murky woods. We went a little farther, but there was still no sign of the cottage. We must have just passed it. I turned Gloria around to double back.

The rain seemed to let up a little bit, a brief respite. Maybe the storm was passing and we could head back to the stables instead of trying to ride it out? Then, a strange sensation shot through my body, like a tingling. *Oh, no.*

"Gloria, go!" I cried.

Too late. Lightning struck so near us that Gloria reared back and threw me. I hit a tree trunk. The deafening boom of thunder was the last thing I heard.

CHAPTER EIGHTEEN
SINCLAIR

I MADE IT to the front porch before a heavy rain began to fall. Then came the hail. Good thing I'd parked in the garage. Once inside, I pulled my coat off and handed it to Farns before loosening my tie.

"She in the library?" I asked.

"No, Mr. Sinclair. I believe she and Teddy went out for a ride."

"Not smart." Teddy would take care of her, at least. An image of Stella in a wet t-shirt floated through my mind. The thought of her with Teddy was no longer so palatable. "I guess I'll go see if they made it out of the rain."

"Very good, sir." Farns smiled.

I climbed the stairs two at a time to my room. I stripped out of my suit and dressed in a t-shirt and jeans. I was ripping a raincoat from its hanger when a rhythmic banging wafted to my ears.

Lucius was still at the plant. I'd spoken to him on the phone, so no one else should have been in our wing of the house. I yanked on some boots and headed down the hall, creeping along the runner so my steps were silent.

The closer I got to Teddy's room, the louder the sound

grew, and it was interspersed with grunts and feminine moans. My hands clenched. Fire laced around my heart, squeezing like a lasso of flames, drawing me inexorably closer to his door. The image of Stella was back, but this time she was beneath Teddy, writhing in pleasure as he fucked her. I had to lean a hand on the wall as my sight grew hazy, rage coloring everything a shade darker.

No. Well, Farns did say they'd gone for a ride. I would have laughed if anything were funny. Nothing was. Murder might be entertaining, but definitely not amusing. I gripped the door handle, steeling myself for what I was about to see. The cries grew louder and beneath them was the sound of skin slapping on skin.

I flung the door open. Teddy was on top of the maid from the kitchen, Laura. He rolled off her when he saw me.

"Sin!" Teddy threw his blanket across her naked body.

I let out a pent up breath. Relief washed through me, replacing the bitter taste of hate and rage.

"Don't you fucking knock anymore?"

"Fuck, Teddy. I thought you were…" I shook my head.

"With Stella?" Teddy asked.

"I should go." Laura's voice quavered.

"No, stay." Teddy smoothed a hand over her knee.

Her face looked pinched as she stared up at me.

I sighed. "I'm not going to fire you, Laura." *Though I should.*

I should have ordered her to pack up and leave then and there. Instead, my mind was whirring away with where Stella was, what she was doing. Teddy's discipline could wait.

She let out a pent up breath, the blood returning to her face with a vengeance.

"Of course he's not going to fire you." Teddy glared at me.

"Teddy. We've talked about this. You can't fuck the help."

"Just like you can't fuck the Acquisition?"

I returned his glare. "Stella is none of your business. I

told you to stay out of it."

"It's kind of hard for me to stay out of it when you force her to stand naked on the table or whip her so badly—"

"Teddy!" I barked. I glanced to Laura. She looked away, pretending to be deaf.

He shrugged and dropped his gaze. "You know what I mean."

"Teddy, please believe me when I tell you that you don't know shit about any of it. Not the Acquisition, and definitely not Stella." I regretted the words as soon as they were out. Teddy looked stung. Lucius was fair game, but Teddy—he wasn't like us. He had a good heart.

I balled my anger up and pushed it down before resuming in an even tone. "I'm sorry, Teddy. I didn't mean it that way."

"I'd know more about it if you'd tell me. Maybe I could help." He stood and ran a hand through his hair. He didn't seem to notice his half-mast dick was waving around.

"You don't need to know. It's only for the firstborn." I'd had this conversation about six times with him ever since Stella arrived.

"Then why does Lucius know?"

"Lucius just thinks he knows. He doesn't. Trust me. When you're older and if you have to deal with this shit, you'll know. And you'll regret it, okay?"

He grumbled and sat back down. He shot a glance to Laura and his demeanor brightened the slightest bit.

The silence became more than awkward. Laura coughed.

"So, where's Stella?" The question that had been on my lips from the moment I walked in the door finally broke free.

"She went for a ride." Teddy turned to look out the window. "Shit. I didn't realize that was thunder I was hearing. I thought it was—"

"Your bed busting through the wall, stallion?" I needed to break the tension. Teddy was worth protecting and I didn't want him to feel like I did—caught in an unfair trap.

He smiled, blushing. "Something like that."

I followed his gaze out into the downpour.

Fuck. If Stella was out in this, she'd be soaked through and lucky if she avoided the hail. The temperature was dropping now that the cold front was moving through. I needed to find her. Fast.

"She was heading to the levee, if that helps," Teddy said.

"It does. Thanks, Ted. Sorry for the interruption."

I swung the door closed. As I hit the stairs, the rhythm began wafting from his room again.

I dashed to the garage and started my car. The rain was a milky barrier and the hail pinged off the luxury vehicle. It was painful hearing the damage, but I was too worried to care. I broke through the sheets of opaque water and raced down the slick drive into the back part of the estate. I contemplated driving down toward the levee, but realized if I did and she'd gone off in the woods, I wouldn't be able to find her. I pulled up into the stables and killed the engine.

I hoped she was inside, warm and dry, waiting for the rain to stop. I ran down the stalls, looking for her. She wasn't there, and the mare Gloria was gone. Something unsettling and queasy swirled in my stomach. It was a feeling I wasn't very familiar with, not anymore. Fear.

Shadow whinnied at a particularly loud blast of thunder and stomped his disapproval. The tack room door was open and a saddle was missing. I wasted no time getting my horse saddled and ready. He stood calmly as the thunder rumbled, as if desperate to get out for a ride, storm be damned.

"It's going to be a wet trip." I climbed into the saddle and spurred him out of the stables and into the rain. At least the hail had stopped.

The droplets stung as I urged Shadow into the deluge. We set a hellish pace. It wasn't simply raining, the sky was jettisoning the water, throwing it forcefully earthward. Lightning split the sky above us, the flash and resulting sound making Shadow rear.

"Steady. Steady, boy." I held onto the reins for dear life

and eased him back down. "Keep it together." I ran my hand along his nape, smoothing his mane as the rain soaked through me, the jacket doing nothing against the onslaught.

He resumed a moderate gallop, and I guided him onto the road as the grass along the sides became muck. It was harder on his hooves, but made it easier for him to maneuver, so he picked up his pace. I felt as if I were racing the clock—a burning need to get to Stella had settled deep in my gut.

What was she thinking going for a ride alone? If she wanted to ride she should have asked me. I would have taken her. Now, she'd gotten herself into a mess. Even as I silently berated her, that same queasy fear overcame my ire.

I saw movement in the gloomy sheets of rain ahead. A horse. My heart rose. I pulled back on the reins. I could lead Stella back to the stables and get her warmed up in no time. I ignored the intense relief that settled over me and squinted against the wall of water. A gust of wind pushed the watery curtain aside for a split second. My heart sank.

Fuck.

Gloria emerged from the downpour and flew past us, back toward the stables. She was riderless and beyond spooked. My momentary reprieve sent me into an even deeper state of panic once I realized it was nothing more than a mirage. Stella was somewhere out in the storm.

My thoughts came in a torrent to match the deluge all around me. Teddy said she went toward the levee. Where would she have wandered?

"Faster, Shadow." I dug my heels in and he shot forward.

I ignored the bite of the water droplets lashing my face. The cold was seeping into my pores, leeching away my body heat as I urged Shadow forward. The streaking lightning and rolling thunder became just another part of the blur of scenery. We were full gallop, a breakneck pace, racing into the heart of the raging storm.

We crossed the narrow bridge leading to the levee. I

pulled him to the left, up to the top of the knoll where I felt Stella may have tarried. We slowed and turned in a circle around the area. She must have been here. I could barely see, but the grass had been chewed, and some of the blades were smoothed down, as if someone had lain there recently. She'd been here. Where did she go?

Though I couldn't see it, I knew the old hunting camp was nearby. She may have tried to make it to the log cabin. I spurred Shadow up and around the edge of the lake and into the pine woods. I kept a tight hold on the reins. Shadow was spooked, ready to bolt. I kept his gait slow. If Stella were trying to shelter under the branches, I couldn't afford to miss her. Shadow's feet were sinking in the muddy ground beneath the trees and he kept trying to move faster.

"Easy boy. Slow. Keep it slow." The roar of the rain hitting every surface stifled my voice, but Shadow obeyed.

I angled him toward where I knew the log cabin sat in the woods. We'd gone about a hundred yards before the smell of ozone overcame the fresh scent of water in the air. A blackened tree, scarred and hewn in two lay to our right. It must have been struck recently.

Shit. Where is she?

We cantered a little further before I saw her. She lay in a crumpled mass on the ground. My heart, already racing, felt like it could have stopped altogether, never to beat again. I jumped from Shadow, keeping a hard grip on the reins as I dragged him to her.

"Stella!" I yelled against the rain, my voice barely carrying above the howling wind.

She didn't move. Blood streamed from a wound along her brow and she was pale, far too white. I scooped her into my arms, the fear in my soul real, almost palpable.

She was breathing. When her chest moved against me, I carefully draped her limp body across Shadow's back. With one hand holding her secure and the other still squeezing the reins, I led Shadow through the trees, the rumbles of thunder no match for the booming beat of my heart. I pushed forward, ripping my boots from the soaked and muddy ground again and again. After a while, my legs burned from the effort. I ignored the pain. Nothing would stop me from getting her to safety. I kept pushing until the cabin came into view.

I pulled Shadow up onto the wide porch and fastened his reins to the railing. "You'll be safe here." I hoisted Stella from his back and carried her inside.

The cabin was old, but we kept it up. Recently remodeled with modern amenities, it was much more than a usual hunting camp. I tracked mud onto the Carrera marble floors and laid Stella, dirty and bloody, onto the leather sofa. The storm still raged outside, but the cabin was like a cocoon, muffling the raw fury of the elements.

We were soaked. I brushed matted hair from her face and examined the cut along her temple. It was shallow, but bleeding like a son of a bitch. I felt around through her hair and discovered a golf ball sized knot on the side of her head. *Fuck.*

"Stella, wake up for me. Stella?"

She shivered. I set to work stripping her, yanking her boots off first before getting her down to her bra and panties. I checked her over, looking for blood or any broken bones. The dread left me incrementally, each piece of her that was intact wicked it away.

She seemed fine except for her head. Which was the exact opposite of fine, really. More than anything, I needed to get her warm. I picked her up and lay her down on the fluffy rug in front of the fireplace. I grabbed the remote from the mantle and clicked on the flames, forcing them higher and higher until warmth rushed forward and onto us.

I hurriedly stripped my clothes and pulled her close, her back to my front as we lay in front of the roaring fire. I pulled her hair away from her face and smoothed it down.

"Stella, I need you to wake up for me." I ran my hand down her side. Her skin was clammy and cold despite the blast of heat.

I grabbed the edge of the rug and flung it over us. We were wrapped in sheepskin and directly in front of the fire. We would either warm up or burn to death.

"Come on, Stella." I needed her to be all right. I told myself it was because I needed her for the Acquisition. It was a lie. I wanted her. I cared for her. And wasn't that just a fucking problem of epic proportions.

I kept rubbing my hand down her side, willing my heat into her. Slowly, her skin warmed under my touch. She shifted, her eyelids fluttering, and I breathed a sigh that carried more angst than I knew I was capable of holding.

"Sinclair?"

"Yes. I'm here."

"What happened?"

"You'll have to tell me. I found you in the woods. How's your head?"

"It hurts." Her voice was small.

I put my hands on her shoulders and turned her around so she faced me. The cut had stopped bleeding, but red still remained along the edges of her hair and in her eyebrow. I ran my hand over the bump on her head. It seemed to have shrunk a bit. I tilted her chin up so I could look into her eyes. The pupils appeared to match. No concussion. Maybe.

I shook my head and pulled her closer to me so her head fell into the crook of my neck. "You are a mess."

"You should see the other guy."

I laughed. I hadn't actually laughed from pure amusement at anyone except for my brothers in so long it felt odd, but also right.

"Mmm, I don't think I've ever heard you laugh. Well, maybe you do whenever you're drowning puppies or something. I've just never heard it."

I nuzzled into her wet hair. "Puppy drowning is every Thursday. You'll just have to catch me at the right time."

She giggled and draped an arm over me. The air between us expanded, somehow becoming bigger, fuller; maybe even a little expectant. We were lying on a rug in front of a fire while the storm raged outside. We should be drinking wine and laughing and fucking. But this wasn't a romance or a fairy tale. She was my Acquisition.

"Stop thinking." She lifted her lips to mine and brushed against them softly. A delicious tease.

"I don't know if I can."

"If I can then you can. After all, I'm the captive, the slave, the Acquisition, the one you whip and humili—"

I claimed her mouth because, fuck, I wanted to and to shut her up. Hearing her recite my long list of sins was too much truth. At that moment in front of the fire, I wanted the fairy tale. I wanted to be her knight instead of her demon. I kissed her like I meant it, like I felt something more for her than ownership. I let myself go. Just this one time.

She answered with more verve than I had any right to deserve or expect. She had surprised me so many times over the past weeks that I should have been accustomed to it. I wasn't. When she brought her hand to my cheek and caressed it lovingly, I was caught up in her more than I could stand. I threw the rug from us and pulled her on top of me, never breaking our desperate kiss.

She straddled me, the fabric of her panties a maddening barrier between her delectable skin and mine. I unhooked her bra. She sat up and took it off, her nipples puckered and hard in the dancing firelight. I palmed her breasts, the weight of each perfect in my hands. She closed her eyes and dropped her head back as I touched and stroked and teased. I leaned up and caught one of the pearled tips in my mouth. She tasted like rain and sweat and sweetness. Perfection. I licked and sucked her in, rubbing the nub against my tongue. Her hips moved against my cock, giving me a glimpse of what awaited me beneath the fabric—hot, wet, and wanting.

I hooked my fingers in the side of her panties and ripped them. I did the same on the other side and yanked them from her. My cock jumped at the promise of euphoria her pussy offered. I knew it was tight, slick, perfect. She rubbed her needy clit over my shaft, giving herself a cheating pleasure just as she gave me the same. I wanted it all.

I gripped her hips and raised her. She wrapped her small hand around my cock. She'd gone from cold to scorching hot in moments, and her touch made me hiss.

"Fucking hell, Stella." I could barely get the words out through my gritted teeth.

She teased me, rubbing my head against her clit as her hips rocked against me. I wasn't waiting any more. I pulled her forward, positioning my head at her opening. When she slid down on my shaft, I groaned from the demanding need to thrust up into her. My fingertips dug into her soft hips. She gave me a sultry gaze, eyes green and partly hidden beneath her lashes. When she raised up and settled down again, pushing me as deeply as I could go, it took every ounce of willpower I had not to flip her over and fuck her hard and fast.

She leaned down over me, brushing her perfect tits against my chest. She set a slow rhythm, as if trying to get used to my length inside her. It wasn't enough. I thrust up into her, meeting her strokes with pure animal lust to take everything she had. She was panting, each breath hot between her parted lips. I spread one palm over her ass and fisted her hair with the other.

I crushed our mouths together as our bodies melded into one. She moaned and sped her pace, gliding back and forth on my shaft and rubbing her clit against me. I wanted it in my mouth, but my cock wouldn't relinquish her tight heat for anything. I was rough, claiming her mouth and pulling her hair. She dug her nails into my chest as she rode me, all reservations gone, surrendered to our mutual pleasure.

I couldn't wait any longer. I flipped her onto her back and spread her legs wide beneath me. I sat back and fed each inch into her flushed pussy. It was the hottest thing I'd ever seen, making my balls pull up even tighter against me.

"Fucking beautiful, Stella."

"Sin," she breathed.

She'd never called me that. I would put that one rasping word on replay in my mind every time I stroked off to thoughts of her tight body.

I rammed myself home, all gentleness gone. I needed her, all of her. She gasped as I lay on top of her and pistoned into her. She grabbed tight onto my shoulders as I fastened my mouth to her neck, the slight salt of her sweat delicious on my tongue. She dug her heels into my back as I ground my cock into her softest skin.

Her hips were pinned, but she still managed to push against me, adding even more roughness to our frantic fucking.

"You like that, Stella? My cock deep inside you?"

"God, yes," she cried.

"Not god, Stella." I gave her some longer, harder strokes, and my cock demanded I explode inside her.

"Sin." She arched her back, rubbing her tits against me.

"Better." I bent my head down and pulled a stiff nipple into my mouth, sucking it as I pounded into her.

She scored her hands through my hair. "I'm so close."

I grazed her nipple with my teeth before I raised my head up to meet her lusty gaze. "Yeah?"

I smoothed my hand down her stomach and leaned back, watching her tits bounce beautifully with each impact. I pulled her hips further up to me so I could stay just as deep. Because I was a selfish asshole.

I put one hand on her hip to keep her pinned beneath me then licked my other thumb and pressed the pad against her clit.

She bucked when I touched her sensitive nub.

"Look at me, Stella. I want you to tell me when you come, and I want you to tell me who made you come."

She nodded and gasped when I increased the pressure on her clit, still fucking her hard. My cock demanded release. I wouldn't give in, not until she was clamping around me.

Her gaze locked on mine as I swirled my thumb around

her clit in small circles. Her pussy pulsed, and I knew she was near the edge. I pushed her over, rubbing her clit faster until her wet walls tensed and squeezed.

"Sin!" She came with crushing pressure on my cock.

Her pussy convulsed as she gripped the rug and repeated that one word. My cock couldn't take any more, not when I had this beautiful sight before me and her cunt milking me. I gave a final hard thrust and groaned as I shot into her, deep and hard. I filled her, each hot kick of my cock a blissful release until I was spent.

I let myself fall on top of her, feeling her last shudders as I remained buried deep inside.

CHAPTER NINETEEN
STELLA

MY BODY WAS sated. My soul, bereft. What had I done? This man who had just given me the most erotic moment of my life was hell-bent on my destruction.

I turned my head toward the fire as he dropped light kisses along my neck. A traitor was here in this room, and she lived inside my breast. I thought I was playing the game, making Vinemont care about me enough to keep me safe. But an ache in my heart, one that told me I'd taken these stolen moments in too deeply, was an accusatory slap in my face.

I tried to lure him to me, to make him care. I'd done the opposite, and my heart was the one caught in the trap. Even now, I wanted to taste his lips again, to make him hard and wanting under my touch. I let out a deep breath.

"Stop." He dropped kisses along my jaw.

"Stop what?"

"Thinking." He took my mouth again, gentle now, reverent.

I wanted him so much it twisted my heart. I wanted him to want me, to treasure me. But he'd always been upfront. Hell, he'd even told me he would gladly torture me

211

all over again. He swept his tongue into my mouth, trying to erase all thought from my mind and nearly accomplishing it. His scent was all over me, marking me as his. I loved it and hated it at once.

I broke the kiss before I fell back under his spell. "I can't."

"My dick is still inside you, Stella, and now you can't?" He moved his hips for emphasis, sending a thrill back to my clit.

I pushed on his chest and he withdrew, pulling from me. I wanted him back immediately. He took in my body, the bruises coloring my nipples where he'd bitten me, the marks on my neck, his fingertips imprinted on my hips. He still looked hungry. I wanted to feed him.

I couldn't.

I pulled the fluffy rug up to my chest. He met my eyes.

"This was a mistake," I said.

"I know." He searched around, found his boxers, and pulled them on.

His words stung me more than they should have. The heat from the fire was oppressive now. He grabbed a remote and turned it down to a low flame. He ran a hand through his hair in what I now recognized as the classic "Vinemont man in distress" move.

"This can't happen again," he said. "None of it. We just have to make it through the year. That's all." He put a resolve into his words that I knew he didn't feel. "This was just…circumstances." He waved a hand at the windows where sunlight now poured through.

More pain bloomed in my chest. I ignored it because he was right. I was still his Acquisition, his plaything. He was still my captor. I dropped the rug and searched around for my clothes. He stared hard at my bare skin before looking away, his jaw tight.

The fire had mostly dried my clothes except for my jeans. I pulled them on anyway. He dressed, too, his movements quick and angry.

He led me through the front door.

Shadow stood on the front porch, his head almost brushing the rafters. He nickered as we emerged and nuzzled Vinemont's hand. He was so gentle with the animal, obvious affection in his touches. Shadow responded, resting his head on Vinemont's shoulder. They were a gorgeous set, dark and handsome.

Vinemont led him down the steps and into the wet grass. I followed, and Vinemont helped me up before seating himself behind me.

"Come on, Shadow, let's go home."

We rode in silence. A cold breeze had kicked up in the wake of the storm. Winter wouldn't be far behind. I lay back into Vinemont for warmth, or so I told myself. He wrapped his arms around me, keeping at least some of the chill wind at bay. Shadow maintained an easy pace, none of us seeming to be in a hurry to return.

My thoughts couldn't seem to focus on anything other than the man at my back, his actions and words. I still wanted to believe something was different between us. That our stolen moments in the library and at the cottage meant something more than just sex.

I wondered what was going through his mind. Was he worrying just like I was? He was unreadable at best. I relaxed back into him more, snuggling against his hard chest. He pulled me in closer, barely holding the reins as Shadow leisurely walked home.

As we approached the stables, I remembered my own horse that had bolted.

"Gloria?"

"I'm sure she's munching on some hay inside. She galloped past us in the thick of the downpour."

The storm, my accident – Vinemont had seen me through all of it. "Thanks, by the way."

"For what?"

"For...well, for saving me."

He leaned away. "I didn't. I haven't."

He pulled his arms from around me, letting the outside chill seep into my bones for the short distance before we trotted into the stables.

We skirted a sleek black car, still wet and slightly dinged. Gloria waited there, just as he'd said, grazing on a hay bale.

Vinemont dropped to the ground and then helped me down. He dug in his pocket and handed me his car key. "Take it back to the house. I need to get Gloria and Shadow settled. You need to warm up."

"I can stay and—"

"No. Just go." It was a dismissal. He turned his back and started unburdening Shadow.

Asshole. I opened the fancy car's door and slid into the driver's seat. I glanced down at the transmission. It was a stick. I hadn't driven a stick in years and wasn't much good at it to begin with. I smirked at Vinemont's broad back. This would hurt him more than it hurt me. I pushed the button on the ignition and the engine purred to life.

I depressed the clutch and easily put the car into reverse. I hit the gas and let off the clutch. It lurched forward and sputtered.

Not reverse.

Vinemont glanced over his shoulder and shook his head. I moved the gear shift into what was, most likely, reverse and tried it again. This time I slid backward out of the stables so quickly I had to slam on the brakes once I reached the smooth drive.

Vinemont had completely turned now, watching me with his arms crossed over his chest. I couldn't tell if he wore a look of chagrin or regret. Either way, I was going to make the next gear shift hurt. I ground it into first gear, the transmission screaming an angry noise, and hit the gas. I was off like a shot, leaving Vinemont and the stables behind me.

I moved it into second gear, imagining the look on Vinemont's face as I ground that one even harder, the transmission making a vicious metal on metal sound. I smiled and whipped the rest of the way to the house. I parked out front, satisfied with myself.

Renee was sitting in the library and followed me up the stairs when I dashed in. I stripped in my room as she entered.

"Where have you been? What's happened?" Her curious gaze settled on my neck. "Are those love bites?"

"I, uh, I'm freezing. I need a bath and then I'll tell you about it."

She kicked into maid mode and ran me a hot bath while I tossed off my remaining clothes. As I soaked, letting the warmth soothe my aching body—some of the soreness from the riding accident, some of it from Vinemont's attentions—I told her about my day. I left out most of the sexy details, but she got the picture well enough.

The hand wringing began almost instantly. I closed my eyes and leaned my head back against the tub.

"Is it really as bad as all that, Renee?"

"Yes, and worse."

"Why?"

"If his mother finds out—"

My eyes shot open and I whipped my head around to her. She clapped her hand over her mouth.

"Vinemont's mother is *alive*? You told me she was dead!"

Epic hand wringing ensued. "I never said she was dead. You just drew your own conclusions."

Realization dawned. "The third floor?"

She nodded, a troubled look overcoming her features.

"Why does it matter? Where is she? Can she do anything about this, about the Acquisition?" My mind raced from thought to thought. Why was Vinemont's mother such a secret?

"It matters, and no, she can't help you. She wouldn't even if she could. She was Sovereign for ten years, you see."

I turned in the water so quickly it sloshed against the sides of the tub and splashed to the floor. "No, I don't see.

215

You keep all these secrets from me. How could I possibly have any idea?"

"It's just that Rebecca doesn't want to have anything to do with it, with the Acquisition. She can't."

"Why not?" This was the most Renee had told me about the Acquisition since she revealed the multiple trials. I needed her to keep talking.

She sank to the floor next to the tub, resting on the bath mat. "I don't see why I should keep it from you anymore, not now that you and Mr. Sinclair have..."

"Tell me."

"It's going to make everything so much worse for you." Tears welled in her eyes.

I was glad I hadn't told her about what we did that night in the library. She may have had a total come-apart.

"Rebecca found me at a time in my life when I had no purpose. I-I..." She examined her hands. "I was young and was selling my body in New Orleans." Red rose from her collar and flowed into her face.

"I'm not judging you, Renee." I had no right to pass judgment on anything anyone did to get by.

"Well, she found me there. Just happened across me, really. It was almost time for the Acquisition Ball, and the Vinemonts had been chosen that year. She was the eldest, so it fell to her to go through the process. I didn't realize it then, but she was desperate to find her Acquisition. I was it. I was desperate to get out of New Orleans. So, it was fate." The sorrow in her voice, the sense of betrayal, tore at me.

"I'm sorry, Renee."

"Oh, it was a long time ago." She swiped a tear away. "It was just that Rebecca was so kind and caring. And she truly was, even though the Acquisition was hanging over her head. Her maid at the time became my ally and told me how Rebecca had always been a lovely, sweet person. She was also a doting mother. I saw that myself. The way she loved on those boys of hers was beautiful."

She paused and took a deep breath. "And she was good

to me, too. She really was, until she couldn't be anymore."

"The ball?"

Renee nodded and absentmindedly picked at her collar. "Yes, there and then Christmas." She blanched. "And then spring and summer."

"What happened, Renee? What happens at those trials?"

"It depends on the Sovereign. My year—" Her voice caught in her throat. "They say my year was one of the most brutal in Acquisition history. They say it with pride, like it was a feather in their cap to enjoy so much suffering."

Though the water was still warm, chills ran up and down my spine.

"Each trial has the same bent—in accordance with tradition—but the Sovereign can choose to add little twists to 'enhance' the experience. Christmas was the worst for me." Her dark eyes sought mine. They were haunted, immensely sad. "The worst for both of us, Rebecca and me. And now I'm afraid it'll be the worst for you, too."

"What happened at Christmas, Renee?" I needed to know but dreaded her answer.

"My year? My year, they chained us out in the cold. It was freezing. The three of us shivered and cried. Have you ever been truly cold, to the point where your skin goes numb, but underneath there are a million needle pricks?" Her voice took on a faraway tone, and I realized she was no longer looking at me. She was still chained, cold, and afraid.

"They sat in heated tents and watched, drinking, laughing, and giving in to their most basic desires while we suffered." She ran her hands up and down her arms. "Then, when they were ready for us, they brought us inside. We were on the verge of hypothermia. One of us even lost a toe from frostbite, though I heard that losing body parts was a rule violation. Everything in moderation." She laughed, high and desperate.

"They laid us out on the tables in their tents. I was glad to be in the warmth…and then I wasn't. They took turns.

There were so many." A tremor shot through her.

Horror welled in me. Is that what Vinemont intended to do to me? Let me be raped by the masked ghouls from the ball?

"They hurt me. I can't lie. They did. But at some point during it, I sort of...disconnected. I was gone, burned away for the rest of the trial and for quite some time after. Rebecca wasn't so lucky. We had been, we were..."

I reached out and smoothed her hair away from her face with my damp hand. "It's okay, Renee. It's okay. I'm sorry."

I regretted reopening her wounds, but I needed to know. It was now or never.

She rubbed her tears away on her sleeve. "I loved her. I was certain she loved me. But that trial, what they did to me. It changed her, made her cold, hard. That's how they win. Do you understand? The only way to win is to become one of them, to *really* be the sort of monster that can rule the entire depraved aristocracy with an iron fist. Do you see? That's what they'll do to Mr. Sinclair. He'll fall. He'll break. But he'll win. And when he does..."

Her sad eyes captured mine, foretelling my own dark future by retelling her past. "Rebecca won, but she lost herself."

CHAPTER TWENTY
SINCLAIR

"I CAN'T DO anything about it, Lucius." I sank down into a chair in the study while Lucius paced around the room.

"I'm tired of the Sovereign taking such a huge cut," Lucius said. "We work our asses off—well at least I do while you're out playing public servant—and then fucking Cal comes in here and demands a goddamn ransom."

"You know we have to pay." I pinched the bridge of my nose. "We've been over this a million times."

Being Sovereign came with an untold number perks, the main one being a cut of all the income from the other ruling families. There was a yearly price and it was due within the month. Pay or suffer the consequences.

I was already dealing with far too many consequences to add non-payment to the list.

Lucius kicked the waste basket next to my desk. "We're working the fucking Brazilians to death and putting even more pressure on our already troubled relations with our Mexican producers. Sugar cane isn't as lucrative as it used to be. Even a fuckwit like Cal should be able to do the simple math."

"I'm aware. It doesn't matter. We have to pay Cal." I couldn't say it any other way. The facts were what they were.

He stopped pacing and stared out the window into the deepening night. "What else are we going to have to give him?"

"What do you mean?"

"You know what I mean, *who* I mean—Stella." He turned to me, giving me the same pissed off look he'd worn ever since he realized I was the oldest and, therefore, in charge of him.

"Stella is none of your concern. She's mine."

His eyes narrowed. "She doesn't have to be."

I stood, suddenly seething. Did he know? "What are you talking about?"

He crossed his arms over his chest, a self-satisfied grin on his face. "Mom told me some of the rules. She said if Stella chose me, I could take your place in the Acquisition."

Fuck.

I was bone tired after the long day with Stella. I had a short fuse and Lucius was doing his damnedest to light it. "Oh did she? Did she tell you the rest of the rules? Did she tell you what happens if you lose?"

"You don't get to be Sovereign." He shrugged. "So what? That's not a loss. We'd be in the same situation we're already in."

I hesitated on the verge of telling him the true penalty, the blood that would be required for us to keep our position. It was an exhausting secret, one that weighed more heavily on me every day. Maybe if I shared the burden, it wouldn't be so crushing. I opened my mouth to speak the lethal truth when Farns knocked and entered.

"What?" I snapped.

"We've had a call from the hospital in town. It seems Ms. Rousseau's father has taken ill. He is in intensive care. Her stepbrother has requested she come. I wasn't sure what you would like me to do with this news."

"I know what *I'd* like you to do." Stella entered behind

Farns, her quiet steps masked by Lucius' and my argument. How long had she been listening?

"It's probably some sort of trick cooked up by your stepbrother," I said. "I forbid you to go." Surely, she realized it was nothing more than a desperate ruse? Transparent and dumb, just like her stepbrother.

She strode to me and stared into my eyes, my soul. "You can't forbid me from seeing my father in intensive care."

I gave Farns a look. He took the hint and backed into the hallway and closed the door.

"I can and I just did. Go back to your room." I wasn't letting her out of this house again, not after what had happened in the cabin earlier. She'd gotten to me, lanced through my rotten core and into the one piece of true heart I had left. I didn't even know it was there until she'd clawed her way in there, too. Goddamn her.

"I'm not going anywhere until I speak to my father." She kicked her chin up and put her hands on her hips.

Lucius walked up behind her. "Sin, it's her dad, maybe you should—"

"Maybe you should shut the fuck up, Lucius." Seeing them together, standing like a united front against me, finally lit the powder keg. I grabbed Stella's arm and ripped her away from him, pressing her back into my chest and putting my hand at her throat. She tried to scratch me, but I squeezed harder, cutting off her airway until she complied. I held Lucius' gaze the entire time.

"She's mine. All of this." I slid my hand down her side, around her thigh, and cupped her pussy like the piece of shit caveman I was. "It's all mine. So, back the fuck off."

Lucius glowered and tensed. "I've had it with your shit."

I held her fast, taunting him. "What, you want to fight me? Won't you be embarrassed when I kick the shit out of you in front of your little crush here? Maybe then I'll fuck her while you're bleeding on the ground?"

Lucius raised his fists. "Let her go, and I'm going to knock your fucking teeth out."

A sharp pain in my ribs shocked me out of our stare down. Stella had managed to sneak in an elbow while Lucius had me distracted. She pulled away from me and darted to stand behind Lucius, her hand on his arm. I thought I was a powder keg before. Now I was a fucking black powder factory going up in a blaze of heat and sound. He reached back, put a possessive hand on her hip, and smirked at me.

"I just want to see my father. That's all. Please, Vinemont." Her plea, delivered behind my leering brother, pushed me far past my limit.

"You do? Are you sure?" I turned my back and went to my desk, digging for a certain sheaf of papers.

"Yes, I'm sure. Please, I'll come back. I promise. I just need to see him."

"I'll tell you what, Stella." Venom laced every word. "I want you to do a little light reading. Then tell me if you still want to see him. If you do, you can go and visit him. How about it?"

"Fine." She sounded relieved.

I laughed, the sound cruel and harsh even on my ears. I found the papers I was looking for and held them in my hand. She'd have to come to me.

"Hand them over," Lucius said.

"Go fuck yourself. Stella, come here."

She stepped out from behind him and tentatively approached me. She wasn't fearful, but she wasn't trusting, either. I gripped the papers tighter.

Lucius trailed his hand down her arm. I wanted to pummel his face until he was no longer capable of begging me to stop.

Her fear was back. I needed it. I ate it up. It reminded me of what I needed to do, what I *had* to do. Even so, it tore at my heart, leaving a part of me shredded and raw. I wanted to say I'd never hurt her. Never give her reason to fear me. But it would be a lie.

I passed her the papers and then held my hands up to show her I meant no harm. But I did. The papers were the dagger, her reading them would twist the blade deep into her back. She took them over to one of the sofas next to a bright lamp. Darkness had fallen outside, painting the grounds in somber gray tones.

She read the first page, then flipped to the second. I knew when she understood. I knew the exact moment when she read the words, when she flipped to the third page to see her father's signature.

"He sold you to me, Stella."

Her gaze rose to mine, horror shining in her eyes along with myriad other emotions—all black, all painful.

"Before you even came in that night, into the room where he and I sat, he'd already signed that contract in your hands. One million dollars. I was so pleased with my good fortune. That was a pittance for a woman like you. He eagerly agreed, signing the paper and sending you to me. He even told me how to phrase my offer to you before you came in. Very helpful, really. And it worked. Oh, how it worked. You came out to the car as planned. Then you came here, as planned. He knew you'd sacrifice yourself for him. The one man you thought loved you was actually the one man who sold you to me. And, just so you know, he was guilty of every single charge against him. I give you my word."

Her hand rose to her face, covering her mouth as she gasped for air. I hadn't hit her, hadn't touched her, but I knew as surely as she sat there that I'd destroyed some deep piece of her heart. It was blasted away, spoiled so that nothing could ever grow there again. Loathing rose in me— for myself, for her father, for everything.

She dropped the papers and stood, turning her back on me and staggering to the dark windows. Lucius rushed to her, steadying her by the shoulder. I could do nothing but wish him harm and wish her comfort. After all I'd done and all I would have to do, I still just wanted her to look at me again the way she had in the cabin. It was only hours ago, but now seemed like a lifetime.

I thought I'd seen love in her eyes, or something like it, as if I knew. I didn't know anything about that particular emotion, not really. But, I didn't remember anyone ever looking at me that way, with so much genuine feeling. It was guarded, but it was there. I wanted it back. I'd strangled any fledgling feelings she may have had with the documents that now lay on the floor, but I still wanted her. I wanted her to come to me for comfort, for support.

Lucius pulled her into his side as her sobs rose and fell. I willed her to leave him and come to me, to return to me and throw her arms around my shoulders. I would hold her while she cried. I would whisper sweet words into her ear. I would soothe her and bring her out of her despair.

My heart swelled, as if drunk on her tears. I could make it right. Somehow. I would try.

Her sobs stopped and her breathing slowed. She lifted her head, staring out into the inky gray of night.

I would tell her. I didn't care if Lucius heard. I was sorry, so fucking sorry.

"Stella—"

"I choose Lucius."

"What?" Her words were a jolt to my system—unbelievable, false. She couldn't mean it, not after what we'd been through, what we'd shared in the cabin.

She turned to me, her tear-streaked face bearing an expression that was a mix of heartbreak and hatred.

"I said I choose Lucius as my owner instead of you," she spat.

"You can't—"

"You heard her, Sin." Lucius wrapped his arm around her waist. "She chose me. She's mine now."

She stepped back from him, pushing his arm away in disgust. "Don't touch me. Leave me alone, both of you."

She rushed through the room, running as if demons were at her heels. We both watched her go—one brother destroyed, and the other exhilarated.

She wouldn't look at me, though she was all I could see.

She retreated down the hallway, disappearing from my view. My soul seemed to have left with her; my legs were no longer strong enough to hold up the empty shell of my body. I sank into the chair.

What have I done?

After a few moments of silence, a door slammed somewhere far away in the house. Her door.

The sound jarred Lucius into motion. He followed Stella's trail like a seasoned hunter, smooth and focused.

I wanted to stop him, to work the same violence on him that I had on Stella's heart.

"Leave her alone, Lucius." Though my soul was gone, my rage still burned.

He glanced over his shoulder, triumphant and vicious. "She's mine now. I know the rules. I call the shots, and I have no intentions of ever leaving her alone."

"I will fucking end you." I forced myself to move and followed him into the hall.

He flipped me off and took the stairs two at a time.

"Game on, big brother."

.

MAGNATE

CHAPTER ONE
STELLA

THE SUN'S RAYS floated through the clear water, shining on me in dappled waves. My lungs burned. They'd been burning for a while, ever since I'd dived down to the bottom and forced myself to stay. I could almost see the edge of oblivion hovering in the distance, the darkness submerged here with me. The tile beneath my feet was a pattern of tangled vines, all emanating from the dark green 'V' in the center. The same one that graced the back of my neck.

I winced when I remembered how I got the mark. Not because of the pain it took to get it, but because of the man who had given it to me. The man with a matching one over his heart. Sinclair Vinemont. Another bubble of air escaped. My last. It wobbled this way and that before it floated to freedom.

The burning grew until my vision blurred. I propelled myself upward and broke the surface in a burst of speed. I sputtered and took in huge gulps of life. Grasping the side of pool, I coughed until my breathing calmed, my heart settled, and the water quieted. It was only moments before

227

the surface became a smooth mirror again, reflecting the blue sky above. Nothing had changed. Would anything have changed if I'd stayed beneath the water?

I shook the thought from my head and swam to the stairs. Once out of the pool, I dropped onto my chaise and lay back. The sun was high, beating down, yet somehow failing to dissolve the humidity that hung in the air. Winter in Cuba was a lot like Louisiana in summertime, hot and bright. But there were differences.

An acre or so of verdant grass surrounded the pool patio. Palm trees dotted the lawn here and there, offering a small bit of shade from the unforgiving sun. Beyond the grass was nothing but an impenetrable wall of green—sugar cane.

I scanned the horizon. The fields stretched out around the Vinemont plantation for as far as the eye could see, a wave of emerald disappearing into the horizon. The tall, slim leaves danced on the breeze. Whenever the wind hit just right, the smell from the nearby sugar plant would sweep over the estate, encompassing me with a lingering sweetness that I didn't feel. Just like the sun bathed my skin, drenching it in warmth that never penetrated any deeper.

I turned my head to the side, away from the open sky and toward the classic Spanish style mansion. The stucco was a muted pink and the roof consisted of neat rows of brown clay shingles. It was three stories of rooms upon rooms that were a mix of modern and antique. I leaned back on the chaise, water sliding from my skin and dripping to the fabric. Even with my shades, the sun was unbearable. I closed my eyes and willed the warm light to infuse something into my heart—some flicker, some sign of life.

But when I closed my eyes, I glimpsed Vinemont's blue ones. He was always there, hidden inside, waiting for me to close my eyes or fall asleep. In my dreams or waking, I saw him. I clamped my eyes shut tighter, trying to erase him. It never worked. I hadn't had a good night's sleep in the two weeks since I'd left Louisiana.

Lucius had followed me that night—the one when my world shattered and Vinemont was the cause—back to my room. He'd promised me escape, a chance to leave the world of Acquisitions and pain. But he didn't promise me for how long. I sighed and shifted, the raised scars along my back sliding against the damp fabric.

I kept my eyes closed, even though Vinemont was there, his dark blue eyes always piercing through to my heart, the one he'd destroyed. The warm sun and light breeze lulled me to sleep under Vinemont's watchful gaze. He followed me down into the abyss. A whip in his hand, but a loving touch along my cheek. His whispers were in my ear, promising me pain, pleasure, and so much more. He ran a hand down my back, his fingertips caressing the lines of suffering he'd embedded there. I let out a soft moan when he brushed his lips against my neck.

I wanted to put my palm to his face, to look into his eyes and feel that surge of heat, but my hands were bound. I struggled against the manacles. He smiled without warmth. Cruelty lived in his eyes, his mouth. I shivered. But not from pure fear. And that was the worst part—I always wanted him. Even when he visited me with a whip, with vicious words, with pain, I wanted it all. I wanted *him*.

Vinemont's gaze darkened, what little light was in his eyes snuffed out.

"Stella?"

He reared back with the whip. My breath caught in my throat.

"Stella?"

I strained to free my wrists. It was no use. He started his swing, the whip lashing through the air. A strangled scream erupted from me.

"Stella!" Not Vinemont's voice. Someone else.

I opened my eyes, my heart racing and the scream only then dying on my lips. Lucius leaned over me, kneeling at my side and blocking the sun. He brushed a hand across my cheek.

229

"Are you all right?" His other hand rested on my bare waist, above the line of my bathing suit bottoms. For a moment, I caught a flash of Vinemont, but it was replaced with his brother Lucius, his chocolate hair and lighter eyes. Handsome, made even more so by the concern written in his features. I wasn't falling for it. He was just another viper.

"Fine. Just fell asleep." I tried to shrink away from him, but his hand on my waist kept me where I was.

He leaned in closer, his clean, sandalwood scent filling my nose. "It doesn't have to be like this. You don't have to be afraid, not of me."

He slid my sunglasses up my head and peered into my eyes before wiping a tear that had escaped during the dream.

"I'm not afraid of you, Lucius." I returned his stare.

"Then why are you trembling?" His voice was silky, seductive as he leaned closer.

I had to escape his gaze, his touch. "Because you remind me of your brother."

He shook his head slightly. "I'm not Sin, Stella. I thought you knew that when you chose me."

My barb about his brother hadn't worked. Lucius was still too close, his hands too warm, his words too easy. If anything, he was emboldened by my sharp tone, his gaze darting to my lips.

This is the closest he'd come since our flight to the island and subsequent Jeep ride to the estate. We had been in Cuba for two weeks. Most of the time I had remained in my room, trying to figure out what I was going to do. I couldn't go back home. I didn't have one. Not anymore. My father sold me like a piece of cattle. The memory of his signature beneath Vinemont's elegant script made my stomach churn. Bought and paid for by one Vinemont, and now another was trying to take even more of me.

"No, Lucius." The steel in my words strengthened my resolve. I gripped his wrist and pulled his hand away from my face. "I've been played enough. By my father. By Vinemont. Now you're trying to play me. Not anymore. I'm not the same naive girl from two months ago."

He allowed me to move away from his touch, but he gripped my hand. "Stella, I won't deny I've wanted you since the first time I saw you." He smirked. "It didn't hurt that you were naked at the time."

I sat up but he didn't release me. Instead, his hold tightened. He was kneeling so it was as if we were sitting face to face. Too close.

"But you need to know you're mine now. You chose me. You are my Acquisition and you'll stay that way. Your contract is just as binding as it ever was. Your father? He still has the same sword over his head as he's always had. I can have him in prison with a phone call."

"You think I care what happens to him?" I tried to yank my wrist from his grip. It was like trying to pry it from steel.

"I know you do. I know deep down you don't want him to suffer and die in prison. Even though he sold you like a worthless trinket. I know you, Stella. I could be your ally instead of your captor. If you'd only let me." His gaze flicked to my lips again.

The worst part was that he was right. I still cared for my father. I hated myself for it, hated the stupid little girl who lived in my breast and held out hope that this was all a trick or a mistake. It wasn't. Anger rose inside me like the waves of heat from the cobblestone patio around the pool. "You don't know anything about me, Lucius. All you know is I'm an Acquisition, sold to your godforsaken family and enslaved first by your brother and now you. You own me for a year. I have nowhere to go. So stop with the mindfuck."

"That's not what this is Stella."

"Then why don't you just let me go?"

"I can't do that." His face hardened.

"Why not? If you don't want to be my *captor*, then that's the quickest way to alleviate your concern."

"The Acquisition. It's too late for that now, Stella. You're mine." The velvet faded. He was made of stone.

231

"Am I? I remember Vinemont telling me the same thing. Wasn't true then, either."

His eyes bored into me. "I would never let you go, not like that. Sin didn't know what he had. I do. I'm good at three things, Stella. Three. One is running the family business. The second is valuing assets. Whereas Sin undervalued you, I see your true worth."

Lucius let the words hang in the humid air. The ghost of the man who'd taken my heart and left a black, twisted hulk in its place haunted us even in the bright daylight.

Don't fall for it. Lucius was just manipulating me, the same as his brother. I let out a hitched breath as he drew even closer, his minty breath mingling with mine.

Three things? "What's the third thing?"

He smiled, wickedness in every crease. "You'll find out about that one soon enough."

A shiver shot through me at his words.

He released my hand and I got to my feet, feeling exposed in my bathing suit while he was fully clothed in jeans and a white button down. Even so, he held my gaze, never darting his eyes down my body like I would have expected from him.

"*Jefe?*" A voice carried down to us from the upper terrace.

Javier, the man who'd driven us from the airfield, and who I'd learned was the head of the operation in Cuba when Lucius was gone, appeared over the railing. I suspected he had connections with the dictator, the only explanation for how the Vinemonts maintained their foothold in Cuba. He and Lucius spent most of their days away from the plantation, leaving early and coming back well after sundown. I was glad Lucius was preoccupied with the sugar business. I didn't want to deal with anything—not the Acquisition, not Lucius, not Vinemont, not my father. For the first time in my life, I was steeped in uncertainty, but I didn't care. I just wanted to be left alone.

"I'm coming." Lucius ran a hand through his hair,

ruffling it in the same way his brother did when he was frustrated.

My stomach fluttered at the familiar movement. I clamped my shades down over my eyes like some sort of shield from the onslaught of memories. I didn't want to feel anything.

"Look, Stella, just give me a chance here, okay? I'm trying to get you through this, all of it. I don't want to have to threaten you or keep you under lock and key. I will." He smirked. "Don't doubt that for a second. But it doesn't have to be so black and white. I just want…"

"What?" I flicked my damp hair over one shoulder and put my hands on my hips. My heart was hammering, a mix of anger and indignation pumping through my veins. "What do you want from me?"

"Jefe!" Javier called again.

Lucius let out a string of invective in Spanish at the foreman before turning back to me and lowering his voice. "Everything." His familiar, wolfish grin surfaced, eating me up bit by bit.

I knew it. "You'll get nothing."

"We'll see, Stella." He turned on his heel and ascended the curving staircase to the terrace, his broad back straining against his shirt. With one final look at me, he disappeared into the house with Javier.

I sank back down onto the chaise, my heart thundering in my chest, the beat in my ears, my temples. The first Acquisition trial was over, but we were still playing the game. I was still a pawn, a piece to be sacrificed so a Vinemont could rule the depraved cabal of moneyed southern families.

I eyed the pool again, the water still reflecting the perfect blue sky. Playing the fingertips of my left hand along the scar at my right wrist, the ridges reminded me of why I could never sink to the bottom of the water and stay there. I would survive. I would make it out of this nightmare, and I would never be the same weak fool again.

Gathering up my towel, I wrapped it around my body and climbed the stairs to the upper terrace. I peered in the back windows and, once assured Lucius was out of sight, I hurried across the palazzo floor and to the right.

My room was at the end of the hall. With its own private balcony and massive en suite, the luxury it entailed was far beyond the wildest dreams of the people who lived in the surrounding countryside. The Vinemonts turned the sugar cane into gold and kept the resulting wealth to themselves. It was as if they had a particular talent for injustice, no matter where they went or what they did.

I trudged to my bathroom, turned on the shower, and took off my top before shimmying my bottoms off.

A calloused hand clapped hard over my mouth and a wide, rusty blade grazed my neck. I was yanked back and an arm wrapped around my ribs, crushing the air out of me. My scream made it no further than the palm against my lips.

CHAPTER TWO
STELLA

"NOT A WORD." The voice in my ear was low and heavily accented. "Where is jefe? What room is his? This one?"

I shook my head. I hung lifeless in his arms lest I give him any reason to cut me.

"Where?" He loosened his grip on my mouth, but kept the blade poised at my throat.

"D-down the hall. I can show you."

"I bet you can show me a lot of things, eh *mi puta?*" He slid a hand up to my breast and squeezed.

I forced my scream to stay put in my throat.

Another man spoke from behind us, near the balcony. He was clearly irritated and giving instructions in Spanish to the one who held me.

"Later, mi puta." He crushed my breast in his palm, pain roaring through me until he let up.

He shoved me forward and the other man grabbed my upper arm hard.

These were rough men. Their calloused hands and rugged faces telling a story of years of toil. And they hadn't come to talk, judging by their machetes.

"Now show us where he is. If you make a sound, I'll give you to Franco." He jerked his chin at the man who'd first grabbed me. "*Comprende?*"

"Yes." I'd heard bits of gossip here and there about how the local workers weren't happy with their cut of the sugar cane profits. It was as if the Vinemonts had started squeezing more over the past few months, increasing their own income while ignoring the burden it put on the already-strained farmers.

The tension seemed to have reached the point of no return. Would they kill Lucius? The thought thrilled me, but what would happen to me if there was no more jefe? I glanced over my shoulder at Franco, his low brow and toothy leer. I didn't think it possible until that moment, but I would fare worse if Lucius were gone.

"Go." The man shoved me forward and I began to walk, hyperaware of the attackers, their weapons, and my own nudity.

I turned toward the left, the direction of the main house, hoping someone would see us and sound the alarm. It was broad daylight, after all, and the house had a few servants. We passed some bedrooms, and I saw a glimmer of hope as Raul, one of the butlers, turned the corner ahead of us. He froze, his mouth falling open as he saw me. Then he stared at the man who held my elbow. I willed him to run, to yell, to do something.

Instead, he dropped his gaze and retreated into the nearest bedroom, closing the door behind him. *Fuck.*

Franco laughed low at my back. "*Coño.*"

I kept walking, leading them toward Lucius' study. We didn't pass any more servants, and the house seemed eerily quiet. The adrenaline in my system amped up another notch, my heart beating loudly in my ears as my steps began to falter.

"Keep up." The man lifted me by my arm, forcing my gait to stay steady.

I took a few more steps toward the closed French doors leading to Lucius' study.

"Here?"

I nodded.

Franco seized my shoulder. "Run, *puta*. I will find you soon enough."

The men shoved me to the side and took the last step to the doors. Franco brought his knee up and kicked through them. The other man followed close behind as they rushed forward, blades drawn.

I darted away. My ruse had worked. Lucius and Javier worked the evening hours away in the library, not the study. I ran down the corridor, my feet slapping against the tile floor. Footsteps echoed behind me, Franco and the other man hot on my heels.

"Lucius!" I screamed and flew into the library. He and Javier rose as I threw the doors shut and turned the lock.

"What the fuck, Stella?" Lucius eyed my body.

"Men," I gasped, "here to kill you." I pointed to the door and scrambled back.

Javier yanked his pistol from his belt holster, and Lucius pulled out a handgun from his desk. The door handles began to rattle.

"Stella, hide!" Lucius barked and pointed to the space beneath his desk.

I was naked and weaponless. There was no other choice but to do what he said. I ran to him as the door began to give way. He shoved me under the desk.

"Don't come out until I say." His sky blue eyes were full of turmoil before he rose and disappeared.

There was an even harder thud and then the whine of wood against wood as the door splintered. Gunshots rang out so loud that I covered my ears. Shouts and curses, English and Spanish – all of it mixed as the booming noises died out and nothing was left but silence.

Lucius and Javier exchanged some words in Spanish that I couldn't follow.

"Stella, how many?" Lucius called.

"Two."

"You sure?"

"I don't know. I only saw two." Raul's frightened face flashed through my mind. "And Raul saw them with me, but he just… He did nothing."

"I'll check the grounds." Javier's voice.

"Be careful. I don't trust anyone. The staff, no one. Not now."

"Understood, Jefe."

Footsteps, then Lucius knelt down and held his hand out to me. "Come on. They won't be bothering us anymore."

There wasn't a scratch on him, but he'd just killed two men. He was calm, as if he'd only swatted a fly.

I reached out to him, only then noticing how badly my body shook. He pulled me out from beneath the desk and tilted my chin up with his thumb and index finger. Inspecting my neck, he said, "You're bleeding."

"I am?" A haze had settled over me, and my ears were ringing. The smell of burnt gunpowder hung in the air. I glanced past him and fixated on the two bodies, blood pooling around them in a crimson sea that blocked the door. How would we get out without getting their blood on us? I'd lured them in here, straight to their deaths. I was already covered in their blood, I just couldn't see it.

"Stella?" Lucius pulled my gaze back to his, a crease forming in his brow. "Come on. Let's get you out of here." He scooped me up in his arms, his pistol still in the hand at my knees.

I stiffened. "I can walk."

He shook his head at me, his light brown hair falling into his eyes. "You're in shock."

"I've been through worse."

He grazed his fingers along my back, feeling the ridges of my scars. "I know. Close your eyes. I'm going to step over them and take you back to your room."

"No." My voice shook and I looked down again, the bodies drawing my gaze like a magnet. "That's where they found me."

"Close your eyes. Do it now." Lucius' tone was harsh.

I turned back to him and buried my face in his shoulder, but I could still feel their lifeless stares. He moved through the library, taking a final, big step across the pool of blood, and then we were out in the hallway. I opened my eyes as he turned to the right, away from my room and toward his. He moved quietly and swiveled this way and that each time he came to a door, searching for any more unwanted guests.

Easing his bedroom door open, he peered around before walking in and setting me down on the bed. I drew his blanket to my chin and watched as he checked the bathroom, the closet, and then closed and locked his balcony doors.

"You'll be safe here. I'm going to go find Javier and make sure there were only two." He clicked something on the gun and the magazine slid out. He checked the bullets and nodded to himself before looking back to me. "Don't move from this room."

I stared at the crimson stain along the side of his boot. Blood. So much of it had flowed around me. My mother's, mine, the men on the floor. How much of it was my fault? All of it?

He stalked to me, his light eyes flashing even in the now-darkened room. "Stella. Tell me you'll stay here. I need you safe."

That got through to me, his one half-truth. He needed me. He needed his Acquisition untouched until he said otherwise. Until three weeks from now at Christmas when the second trial was set to begin. Would he keep me safe then? Renee's story of torture and violation replayed through my mind, forming a lattice work of pain over the pool of blood that had already seared into my vision.

I looked up and met his focused stare. "I'll stay here."

"Good. I'll be back in a short while. Don't open this door for anyone else. Not even Javier. Got it?" He pulled back the gun's action and checked the round in the chamber. His hands were steady, as if killing was what they were made for.

He released the metal, a smooth *shick* sound that spoke of death. Reaching out toward my face, he pushed a lock of hair behind my ear. I leaned away from his touch.

His eyes narrowed. "Stay here. No one but me gets through that door. Tell me you understand, Stella."

"Yes." I wanted him gone. I wanted all of it gone.

He raised his gun and went to the door. "Lock it behind me."

He opened it silently, peeking out, and then slid through before pulling it shut behind him. I rose, pulling the blanket with me, and clicked the bolt over. It was just a deterrent. If others wanted to get in, they would.

I scanned the room for a weapon. There wasn't much to choose from, unless I could somehow fashion a dagger from some local art or decorative tobacco baskets. I went to Lucius' bedside table. Nothing there of use. I whirled and caught his fireplace in my peripheral vision. I grabbed an iron poker, gripping it hard and getting a feel for its weight. It wouldn't do much if the intruder had a gun, but it was better than nothing.

Tossing the blanket back onto the bed, I hurried into his walk-in closet. I closed the door behind me and yanked down a white button up. I slipped it on and rolled up the sleeves, ignoring the fact that I wasn't wearing panties. The wooden racks and drawers gave me nowhere to hide.

I scratched the idea of sheltering in the closet and returned to the bed to sit and wait. It didn't matter anyway. If someone came here to kill me, hiding wouldn't stop them. They would find me.

Tension roiled along my body, every commonplace sound in the house like a bomb going off, shocking my system. The ticking of a clock, the sound of a bird on the roof nearby, the slow drip of Lucius' faucet in his bathroom. I edged back until I was sitting against the headboard, the fireplace poker next to me, the unyielding metal a strange comfort.

Would I die here instead of in the Acquisition? Maybe

this end was better. Maybe this farmer uprising—if that's what it truly was—was a blessing in disguise. I absentmindedly trailed my fingertips along the scars on my left wrist. I'd wished for death back then. I still toyed with it, flirting with it from across the room with glances and coy smiles. Death watched me as if I were its next dance partner, its next sumptuous feast of flesh. How long would our flirtation last before he dragged me into the swirling mass of dancers, swallowed up by flowing skirts and dark smiles?

The air remained still, the whole house turned into a sepulcher by the two bodies, maybe more, that filled its walls. I focused intently on every noise, every creak of the house. After an hour or so, a sharp crack shattered the stillness. A single gunshot that was soon joined by others. Booming shots mixed with the sporadic cracks of pistols as I huddled under the blanket, my gaze fixed unwaveringly on the door.

The sun slowly faded through the window as I waited. The room became steeped in gloom, hours passing without word from anyone and no more shots. I didn't dare turn on a light. The adrenaline was long-since drained from my body. I scooted down in the bed, propping my head on pillows so I could keep an eye on the door. Lucius' scent surrounded me, sandalwood and sophistication sinking into my pores.

My eyes grew heavy. I should have sat up, should have moved around. Instead, I let the darkness lull me. It wasn't the first time.

The door burst open, and I scrambled from the bed. Sleep was gone and a surge of murder took its place. The poker was in my hand as I rushed forward toward the dark figure advancing into the room. Drawing my arm back, I waited for the gunshots to sound, for my blood to spill. Nothing.

I swung with all my strength but the figure caught my wrist and squeezed hard. The pressure increased until my bones ached and I dropped the metal with a cry. He clapped his hand over my mouth and snaked an arm around my waist, pulling me to him. Fear engulfed me like quicksand, dragging me down until I knew I would suffocate.

I peered up to get a better look at the person who would snuff me out. I breathed in through my nose and got a taste of his scent—woodsy, masculine. My heart drummed in my chest. I recognized him, the hard body against my breasts, the feel of his arms caging me against him.

"Stella." The deep rumble of his voice made my knees weak but also poured kerosene on the ember of hate that burned in my heart. The flame leapt, catching the rest of me on fire, setting every nerve ablaze.

I renewed my fight, kicking and opening my mouth wide so I could dig my teeth into his palm. The bastard dared touch me after everything he'd put me through—my contract, the Acquisition ball, and my father selling me. He needed to bleed, to suffer. I bit harder. He grunted but didn't release me. Even as I tasted copper and he constricted me so tightly to him that my vision dimmed, he wouldn't let go.

"Stop," Vinemont ordered, impatience dripping from his tone.

Getting nowhere, I relaxed my jaw and he withdrew his hand, but he kept the arm around me, walking me backward so he could close the door behind him.

"Where's Lucius?"

He was already drawn tighter than a piano wire, but my question made him vibrate with intensity.

"He's here tending to his foreman."

"Is Javier hurt?"

"Took a slug in the shoulder. Through and through, but still hurt like a son of a bitch based on his whining." He pushed me back until my knees hit the bed and I sat.

He took a step back and peered around, slivers of moon peeking through the windows the only light in the room. He strode back to the door and flipped the light switch. I was momentarily blinded but it didn't matter. He blotted out everything else. Vinemont, standing before me, his dark hair wild and blood running from cuts along his cheek, his neck, his arms. His right pant leg was stained a vivid crimson and still wet.

But more striking than any of that were his eyes. Deep blue, turbulent, and filled with a mix of possession and pain that rent my already tattered soul into even smaller pieces before scattering them away into the four winds.

"What—"

"We're safe." His gaze took me in, every inch from head to toe. "For now."

"What's happened?"

He ignored my question and strode to the bathroom. Though he hid it well, I saw a slight wince each time he put weight on his right leg.

He ripped open the linen closet and dug around until he found a first aid kit. I followed, lingering in the doorway as he sank onto the edge of the tub and yanked the case apart. Supplies spilled into the floor, and he grabbed the small bottle of alcohol before tearing the lid off and dousing the cuts on his arms and neck. Some were deep, the alcohol making the blood flow more freely. He'd lain a gun to his right, within easy reach.

He needed help. His arms and neck would heal, but the crimson stain spreading along his leg looked much, much worse. Should I help my enemy? The man who'd whipped me, tortured me, and told me he'd do it all again without hesitation? I chewed my lip as he dabbed at the wounds with gauze and glanced up at me every few moments, as if making sure I hadn't bolted.

When I noticed the slight tremor in his hand, I acted.

"Here." I grabbed some towels and wash cloths from

the closet and sank down in front of him.

He raised his eyebrows and froze, surprise in the clear windows of his eyes. Then he looked away, closing my one glimpse into his depths. I took his hand and inspected the arm that was the worst for wear. The slashes were straight, clearly caused by a knife, and one was particularly deep. It cut through one of the thick, snaking vines of ink at the upper end of his forearm. The wound needed stitches to stanch the blood that dripped down to the white tile floor. I searched the first aid contents and found a small staple gun. It would have to do.

"I want to see your leg before I do anything else."

"It's fine. I'll heal." He reached for the half full alcohol bottle, but his tremor had increased and he knocked it into the tub. I bent over his legs and grabbed it before the entire contents rushed down the drain.

"Just let me see." I sat back on my knees. "Take your pants off."

He smirked. "Missed me?"

I was a moth trying to aid the spider. *What was I thinking?* I started to get up. "Go fuck yourself."

"Stop." His voice shook the slightest bit. "Please." He reached to his dark leather belt and unbuckled it before unfastening his pants.

I swallowed hard, giving him an angry stare before I gripped his jeans at the sides of his hips and pulled as he lifted up a bit. He settled back down heavily, the hand I'd bloodied with my teeth slipping as he sank and painting a bright red smear along the white porcelain. His boxer briefs were the only article of clothing not soaked with crimson. I drew the pants the rest of the way down and gasped when I found the stab wound through his calf. It was longer and deeper than the gash on his arm. The edges were ragged, oozing blood.

"How?" I looked up into his sapphire eyes.

"He came at me." He lifted his arms and I could tell the wounds were defensive. "I fought back." He rotated his wrist so I could see his bloodied knuckles. "And when he fell, he got one last good stab in before I..." He turned his hands over and stared at his palms, his brow wrinkling. He looked back at me, his eyes haunted.

What little compassion I had left was his, though he had no right to it. "You did what you had to. It's going to be okay."

He snorted a tiny laugh, but there was no smile, no spark to him. "I seem to keep doing that."

"What?"

"What I have to do, no matter what. No matter who gets hurt. No matter who I destroy." His voice thickened, mournfulness in every note, before he straightened his back and looked away.

Remorse? I would have laughed. I wanted to, the crazy impulse bubbling up and almost spilling from my lips. Instead, I pulled the belt from his jeans and looped it around his thigh, yanking it tight to momentarily slow the blood flow. When he winced, I felt somehow vindicated. Then I removed his boots and stripped his socks and pants the rest of the way off.

I soaked a washcloth with the alcohol and dabbed at his wound. He hissed but kept still. It had to hurt like hell. *Good.* I cleaned the wound more as his breathing grew ragged. The white washcloth soaked up his blood, his life with each swipe. Once I was satisfied the gash was as clean as I could get it, I gripped the stapler with one hand and used my other to squeeze his damaged skin together.

"Ready?"

He turned to me, his face back to its angular stonewall, and nodded. I squeezed the trigger and the machine made a loud *tick* as the staple clamped. He fisted his hands but gave no other sign that it hurt. I did another, then another, continuing until the wound was sealed. Blood still flowed around the edges, but most of the damage was contained so I could release the makeshift tourniquet. After stripping off his shirt, the now-familiar Vinemont emblem blazing from his chest, I moved to his arm and did the same. Once the largest gash was sealed, I used gauze and medical tape on the rest.

When I was done, the shirt I was wearing was a mottled crimson and white. I wiped the sweat from my brow with the back of my arm and sat next to him on the edge of the tub.

"Thank you." He stared straight ahead, his neck tight, his jaw tighter.

I'd healed the spider, gotten him into tip-top shape so that he could destroy me even more thoroughly the next chance he got. I had no doubt he would. My flesh would be ripped, my blood spilled, and he would be the one to do it, just like before. I was a fool.

My gaze dropped to the gun only inches away, and I itched to take it. Could I kill him? End him and run? As much as my head wanted to say yes, my heart remained treacherous and refused.

As if reading my thoughts, he palmed the gun and stood, but swayed on his feet. He'd lost too much blood—the towels were soaked right along with his clothes. I pushed up and put my arm around his waist, helping him to Lucius' bed. He eased down, set the gun on the pillow beside him, and looked around, a haze over his eyes.

"Just rest for a minute. You need to recover. I'll go to the kitchen and get you some juice and whatever else I can find." Distance. I needed it to clear my head, to cope with the shock of him bursting into my life again. I got one step away before he grabbed my wrist.

"Stay."

"No. You need liquids. To replenish your blood." I pulled my wrist, but it was useless.

His palm rested over my scars, the very reason I knew how to help him build his blood back up. I'd been hooked to an IV for days even after a transfusion.

I sighed. "I'll come right back."

"No." He yanked and I fell into the bed next to him.

"It's not safe." He wrapped his bandaged arms around me and pulled me to him, his hard chest pressing into my back.

"Vinemont!" I tried to push away from him, but I was caught.

"You aren't going anywhere. Too dangerous." His fingers played along the edge of my shirt, no doubt feeling the dampness of blood. "Take this off."

I stiffened. There was no way I was going to lie in bed with him naked. "No."

"Off." He growled and gripped one side, yanking the shirt apart, buttons bouncing off the hardwood floors as he pulled the shirt roughly down my arms and tossed it.

"What the fuck do you think you're doing?" His body was hot, alive, and hard at my back. I couldn't stay here. Not with him. Not in this bed like we were lovers, like we were two people who could seek solace from each other. We weren't. We never could be those people. "Stop!"

He caged me, my struggles nothing to him even in his weakened state. "You aren't leaving this bed. Get used to it. Don't fucking try anything."

I stopped fighting. There was no point. I would just have to wait until he fell asleep.

"You're mine, Stella." He tightened his grip with each word. "I don't care where you run, who you choose, what you say, or what you fucking do. You, all of you, belongs to me."

"I'm not a thing you can own," I hissed.

He laughed, the sound low and full of heat. "You can hop countries like a skipping stone for all I care. I'll find you, and you'll wind up right where you are now."

I tried another tack, one designed to knock him back to reality. "Besides, if I belong to anyone, it's Lucius."

He stopped laughing and drew his free hand up to my hair, stroking through the strands before gripping so tight it hurt. I yelped.

"Has he touched you?" His voice was in my ear, danger and seduction cutting through me like the knife had his skin.

"Fuck off."

He yanked. "Has he?"

I barked out a harsh laugh. "Yes. Every night. Every night he fucks me until I scream his name. He gives it to me so good he's all I can think about. I want it from him. I dream about him. When he puts his cock in my mouth I've never been happier. I beg him to fuck me in the ass. When he does, I come so hard I black out."

He relaxed his grip and nuzzled into my hair. "You done?" His laugh was low, seductive. "Or do you have some more lies for me?"

My body warmed under his touch, his breath, his voice. I willed the memory of him whipping me into my mind, the memory of him showing me the contract where he'd bought me from my father. I wouldn't fall for his tricks. Not again. I was done being his plaything.

He released me for a moment and gripped the white duvet, throwing it over us and marring it with blood. I edged away from him, separating our bodies, but it didn't matter, he reached across me and turned off the light with the remote before crushing me against him. This time I felt his half mast dick pressing into my ass.

"Stop." My voice quavered, the turmoil inside me spilling out in uncertain notes.

He spread his fingers along my bare stomach, his index finger brushing against the bottom curve of my breast. "Tell me to stop again. Please, Stella. Tell me again and see what happens."

His words were a dark promise that sent a thread of electricity straight between my thighs. I was in his web again, caught and cocooned as he slowly sank his fangs into every bit of me.

I remained silent. I had no other choice.

"No?" He teased his lips down my neck. "You don't want to find out? You don't want me to put you on your stomach, slap your ass, fist your hair, and fuck your tight pussy until I make you come on a scream? Tie you up, make you come again and again while I'm deep in your ass until you beg me to stop? You don't want all the things you just lied to me about? I can make them true, Stella. Every last one." His fingertip moved back and forth against the sensitive skin of my breast, every nerve in my body focusing on that one small movement. "I could break you and you'd love every minute of it."

"You will never break me. Never." The venom in my voice surprised me. I realized then how much I meant it. How much I intended to fight. There would be no more sinking to the bottom of the pool. No more toying with death over drinks and dancing. I intended to walk across the room, wrap my arms around death's neck and pull him down to me. Kiss him like there was no tomorrow and dare him to do a thing about it. Fuck him. Fuck Vinemont, too.

"We'll see." Though his voice spoke of exhaustion, his grip on me didn't falter.

He fell asleep soon after, his breaths becoming deep and even, tickling my neck.

I tried to slip away twice after he lost consciousness, but I only managed to put a few inches between us before he wrapped his arm around me like a vise and yanked me back, a growl in his throat.

Eventually, I drifted off to sleep, awash in Vinemont, regret, and the faint scent of Lucius.

CHAPTER THREE
SINCLAIR

STELLA SLUMBERED PEACEFULLY on my chest, her red locks fanned out along my upper arm as if entwining with the vines that covered me. The sun had risen without any more bloodshed, though there had been plenty the night before. I'd killed men. My fair share, maybe more, to keep the Vinemont stronghold alive and well.

I didn't blame the farmers, or the instigators, or even the paid mercenaries our competitors hired to keep the unrest churning. No, I blamed the Sovereign. If Cal wasn't squeezing us for an even bigger cut of profits, then none of this would have happened. The farmers were just collateral damage, pawns in a much larger war that was going on hundreds of miles north of here in the bayous of Louisiana.

I smoothed my hand down Stella's back. The tiny ridges marred her skin like braille beneath my fingertips. I'd written our story on her fair flesh in blood and violence. Regret tolled in me, but what I'd done was necessary. Just like all the trials.

Her eyelashes fluttered against my chest and she let out an angelic sigh. Her breasts were pressed into me and her smooth thigh was slung over mine. She was soft and warm, a wet dream come to life in my arms. I breathed her in, her hair smelling of lavender and vanilla.

251

I moved my hand back up and dug my fingers into her hair. I didn't want her sighing. I wanted her screaming, my name on her lips, my ecstasy pulsing through her veins. But it wasn't so simple. It never had been. I needed so much more from her than simple surrender. And the past two weeks without her under my control had been nothing short of torture.

She had run away. My fist tightened.

Away from *me*. Her eyes opened.

She chose Lucius. I gripped her hard right at her scalp.

"Vinem—"

Before she could even say my curse of a name, I settled on top her, pushing my knee between her legs as she struggled. Her attempts to buck me only made my cock harder. She was my Acquisition. Mine. She needed to know it. I was foolish to indulge her for as long as I did. Foolish to let her hope, to let her think that she could hold any sway over my heart. Maybe if I could do this, if I could commit this transgression, I'd finally stop seeing her as something more than a possession.

"Don't." Her eyes went wide, all traces of sleep gone and fear in its place.

This was what I needed. Her fear. Her loathing. I slapped my hand over her mouth and stared into her eyes. She dug her nails into my back with her free hand while I pinned the other above her head. My cock was against her hot core, only the fabric of my boxer briefs separating us. I could take her. Take everything.

"I should have done this the first day you showed up at my house, Stella." I crushed my palm into her lips, surely bruising them. "I was weak. You made me weak. From the first moment I saw you, you were a fucking poison."

But then something sparked in her emerald depths. Not fear. Defiance.

Her eyebrows lowered the tiniest bit, as if daring me onward. She let out a roaring sound against my palm, deep and guttural. The heat between her thighs had me pushing my hips against her. She was wet and wanting even as her eyes were full of vengeance. I wanted her, wanted every last morsel of her rage, her hate.

Even so, I knew if I did this, she would never forgive me. And then I would have truly lost her. Could I bear it? It didn't matter. I had to do it. Breaking her was the only way to win. And I would win no matter what.

A searing pain exploded through my calf at the same time she bucked hard. She'd dug her heal into the wound. I rolled to my side and reached for my injured leg as she slid out from under me and off the bed. She scrambled away, the skin of her knees squealing against the polished hardwoods. I recovered and lunged after her, jumping on my good leg before sinking to my knees and gripping her by the hair. I landed on her back as she cried out, pinned beneath me.

"Do it. Just fucking do it, you psycho!" Despite her words, she still fought me, pulling against the hold I had on her hair.

She was helpless. I pushed my hips against her, the friction of my hard cock on her soft ass almost unbearable. I pulled her head to the side and licked her ear before capturing it between my teeth and biting down.

She whimpered, her nails scratching at the floor as I kissed down her neck, tasting her skin the same way I'd thought about every second she'd been away. I'd waited for her to come back, to realize she'd made a mistake. She didn't. She hadn't. I bit the flesh over her jugular, wanting to punish her for running, for taking what was left of my heart with her when she did.

She surged beneath me, one last effort to escape. Not a chance. I rose and flipped her onto her back, pinning her wrists to the floor and studying her face. Her chest heaved and her pussy was on fire, making my cock leak. The morning light made her eyes sparkle even through the hate I found in them.

"You are pathetic. All of you. Just get it over with." She

fisted her hands, but couldn't do a thing with them. Her gaze was nothing short of scorching.

As she goaded me on, I knew I couldn't. And that knowledge sealed my fate. If I couldn't break her, I would have to pay the price. The Acquisition demanded it.

A sudden flash of light at my temple turned into a gloomy dark and then a pair of hands were on me, lifting me up and throwing me down onto my back. My vision cleared. Stella shrieked and turned over to her side, rolling into a ball. Lucius stood over me, his brow wrinkled in fury.

"Don't you fucking touch her, Sin!" He went to her and scooped her up in his arms. She clung to him and buried her face in his neck.

I tried to get up, but my injured leg gave way and I landed back on my ass. Lucius backed out of the room, Stella clutching him.

She gave me one last look, her eyes awash in tears and pain. Then she was gone, all hope right along with her.

CHAPTER FOUR
STELLA

LUCIUS SAT ME on the edge of my bed and pulled my duvet up around me. He eased down next to me and rested his palm on my cheek. I flinched away, but he wrapped his other arm around my waist, holding me still.

"Did he hurt you?" His sky blue gaze searched my face.

"No." I shook my head, ignoring the tremor in my voice.

"He'll never hurt you again." His jaw tightened, but his touch remained soft.

"I'm fine." I shuddered at what Vinemont had done. His threat had grown in the two weeks since we'd been apart, not lessened.

"You're not fine. Don't lie to me."

I pushed him away. I refused to be manhandled or bullied by any of them. Not anymore.

He sighed and released me. "I'm not him."

I let my gaze travel the ink peeking from the edges of his sleeves. Even if the brothers didn't see eye to eye, they would always be bound together, on the same side.

His face softened a bit. "Stella, listen—"

"What happened yesterday? Is it safe?" I didn't want any more mind games. I only wanted to know if I'd survive the day.

He glowered, fine wrinkles turning the corners of his mouth. "Local unrest spurred on by outside interests. It's taken care of for now. I had to fix up Javier and then meet with useless government officials until late."

Blood stained his shirt in several places, most of it already brown in the morning light. He seemed none the worse for wear, save a few scratches, making me wonder whose blood he carried in the threads.

He continued, "That was the only reason I didn't come back to you. I sent Sin to protect you because I couldn't. I run the business here, so I'm the one who had to calm things down. I didn't realize he would…"

"Looks like you don't know your brother as well as you thought." I pulled the blanket up higher, covering every inch of skin below my neck. "Don't worry. Your little investment is protected and plenty *useable* for the next Acquisition trial. No harm done."

He slumped the slightest bit. Whether it was fatigue from the long night or my sharp words, I didn't know. "There are traditions. Things have to be done a certain way. You wouldn't understand."

I arched an eyebrow. "Do *you* understand? Vinemont says you don't even know the rules yet you jumped right in and started playing."

"I don't need to know any rules to win, Stella." He met my eyes.

I didn't lean away. I wouldn't cower for him or anyone. I could play the game, too. "You're full of shit. Playing second fiddle to your brother has made you rash."

He pulled at the duvet slowly until my shoulders were uncovered, though his eyes never left mine. A heat kindled in them, intense and immediate. "I've always been rash. This is nothing new."

He stroked his fingertips along my collarbone, the gentle sensation so at odds with the ravenous look in his eyes. "I've given you two weeks. Two weeks to adjust to being mine. I would never try to force you. I'm not my brother, Stella. Two weeks—has it been enough time?" He slid his fingers lower, pushing the duvet down my bare skin and to the swell of my breast.

My breath hitched in my throat as I glared at him. "I'm not yours. It doesn't matter what some contract says or what some bullshit Acquisition rules say. I will never be yours."

He smirked and shoved the duvet the rest of the way down before pulling me into him. His mouth was hot on mine, his tongue desirous and seeking. I shoved against his chest, but his grip on me was unshakeable. His lips were firm, insistent.

He sank his tongue inside, exploring and groaning as he tasted me. Heat pulsed through me but it was all wrong— his scent, his voice, his lips. Even as my body warmed to his advance, my thoughts strayed to his brother. The way he'd handled me before, the feel of him between my legs, the pain and determination in his eyes as he told me I was his poison.

Vinemont was right. I intended to poison them both. So I opened my mouth further, letting Lucius hold sway over me. Letting him think I chose him. He pushed me back on the bed and moved one hand to my breast, kneading it as his hard length rested against my thigh.

I faked a moan. His touch was pleasurable, but didn't send the shock of adrenaline through me like Vinemont. It didn't matter. I would use Lucius. I would do what I had to do to truly turn him against his brother. I tangled my hands in his hair and he moved his knee between my thighs. I lifted my hips to him, my pussy tingling at the friction.

"Jefe?" Javier's tentative voice came through the door.

Lucius broke the kiss and sat up, pulling me with him. I yanked the cover back in place.

"What?" he barked.

"The jet is ready. I found Mr. Sinclair in your room. One of the hands is helping him."

"We're coming." Lucius smoothed a hand through my

257

hair and rested it on my cheek. "This isn't over," he whispered.

No, it isn't.

He stood and squared his shoulders, all business again. "We're leaving?" I asked.

"Now that we've tamped down the uprising, Javier will run the plantation until after the Christmas trial." He glanced away at the last words, unable to look me in the eye. *Coward.*

Reaching out, I brushed my fingers along his. "Tell me what the trial is."

He lifted his fingers, seeking more contact. I let my hand stay there, our skin heating wherever we touched.

"I'm not sure. I haven't spoken to Sin since we left, not until yesterday when I got word of trouble. And then we didn't have time to discuss the trial. I know generally what it is." He glanced away again. "But that rat bastard Cal will be sure to make it more interesting since it's his year."

I dropped my hand, a deadness spreading in my chest. "Renee told me about her year. I know what's going to happen to me."

"It can't be helped." He knelt in front of me, his eyes pleading. "All I can tell you is that once I'm Sovereign, I'll make it all up to you."

"Just let me go." I ran my fingertips down his chiseled jaw, the stubble sharp and thick. "You could let me leave. Or we could leave together."

"No, Stella. You don't know what you're asking me. When I'm Sovereign, I can give you anything you want. Anything you've ever dreamed about. These trials will just be some hazy memory when we're flying on our private jet or vacationing in the Maldives or having tea with the fucking royal family. Don't you see? If I lose, then all of that's gone. The Vinemonts will spend another ten years under someone else's thumb. Someone who may be even worse than Cal. Stella, look at me. We can do this." His face appeared almost boyish in its earnestness.

I laughed, the sound cold even to my ears. "Now it's a team sport? 'We'? Are you going to watch as your friends rape me? Hold me down? Cheer them on? Keep count? Gag me to cover my screams? Will all of that be a hazy dream to you once you're Sovereign?"

He rose, towering over me. "I will do what I have to do to become Sovereign. It's the right play, Stella. You'll see."

Turning his back, he strode away with renewed purpose, as if our chat about my defilement put his head back in the game. "Be ready to leave in half an hour."

My chin dropped to my chest as he closed the door. Lucius had made up his mind, just like Vinemont, to win at all costs. To them, the value of being Sovereign outweighed my well-being, my freedom, my everything. I stood and dropped the duvet before going to the shutters and throwing them open.

The fields of sugar cane waved in the light breeze as the sun blazed down. The rays were painful, sharp, and unrelenting, but the sugar cane soaked up the punishment and grew stronger, sweeter—more valuable. Every moment under the oppressive heat was a gift, a dose of life when there would otherwise be none. Surviving and thriving.

Was strength always born of fire, of torment? I nodded at the silent question. I would have to suffer to survive. But I would come out the other side. And when I did, I would burn the entire Acquisition to the ground.

CHAPTER FIVE
STELLA

THE JET RIDE lasted a few hours, the sun already fading from the sky as we neared land. The dark waters of the Gulf retreated and a twinkle of lights sprouted along the horizon. New Orleans was ablaze, the city vibrant even from the air.

Neither Vinemont nor Lucius spoke to me or each other as they piloted the plane from the open cockpit. Despite the lack of words, the animosity between the brothers had grown into something almost palpable. It swirled around the cabin, making every moment strained. I smiled and relaxed back into my seat, enjoying the tension in both of their backs as they sat at the controls in front of me. Maybe tearing them apart wouldn't be as difficult as I'd first imagined.

We landed at a private airfield outside the city and taxied over to a hangar. A driver waited out front next to a black limo. Once we came to a stop, Lucius stood and opened the hatch, letting the stairs down so we could exit. He held his hand out for me.

"Don't touch her," Vinemont growled.

"Fuck off." Lucius didn't waver.

I took his hand and stepped down, glad to be out of the tight cabin. The weather was chilly for Louisiana; winter was in full swing despite the high, bright sun.

The driver greeted me with a smile and opened the back door. I slid in as he went to help gather the bags and other items from the plane's storage hatch. The car was running, and Christmas music was playing low on the radio. I almost laughed. *Merry Christmas to me.* Gallows humor had taken on a particular relevance for me in the past few months.

Even though I was here for the Acquisition trial, I was still glad to be back in the States. I allowed my thoughts to flit to my father for a split second before forcing them down. The last I'd heard he was in ICU. I hadn't inquired any further. I couldn't. Not after seeing his name on Vinemont's contract. Had the hospital stay truly been a ruse as Vinemont suggested, or was my father ill? I shouldn't have cared, but I did.

My eyes stung, the wound still fresh. He'd committed an unforgivable sin against me. Even so, I couldn't wish for his destruction, no matter how much I wanted to. Too much of me was caught up in him, too many memories, too many years of relying on each other and surviving despite the weight of Mom's death slowly crushing us. I blinked the unshed tears away and tilted my head up until they receded. I may not have wanted my father dead, but I'd be damned if I cried for him.

The car shook as the driver loaded up some belongings in the trunk. Vinemont slid in next to me and locked both of the back doors. Lucius stood outside and glared at his brother before climbing into the front passenger seat.

"Back to the house?" the driver asked.

"Yes, Luke." Lucius kept me in his peripheral vision.

I edged away from Vinemont. He was still banged up, fresh bandages down his arms and angry red wounds along his neck. He was healing, but it would take time. He studied me, his eyes fixing on mine as he tapped his fingers on his knee. What could he be thinking after what he'd tried to do earlier that morning?

The memory of his hard body on top of mine sent a rush of heat spiraling through me. I'd been afraid at first, but then

I'd become something more. Livid. I dared him to do it. I wanted him to take that last step, to seal his doom even further.

My body may have been fooled by him, desperate for his touch. My mind was anything but. I knew he couldn't follow through. I knew he wanted me as more than just his Acquisition. His twisted heart had a glimmer of love left and I'd touched it, felt it. Now I would use it to break him.

Luke sped down the interstate, farther into the Louisiana countryside toward the Vinemont estate. Lucius kept glancing back like a chaperone insistent there would be no funny business on his watch. Vinemont said nothing, just continued studying me, as if he were dissecting me piece by piece to discover what particular magic made me tick.

The Christmas music persisted for the entire drive, telling us all to be joyful as we pulled up to the vine-covered gates and I entered enemy territory once again. It felt like a homecoming of sorts—the winding road, the secret bayous, and the familiar oaks. My eyes strayed above the tops of the trees to the dormer windows on the third floor. A light glowed into the night from one of them. Was Vinemont's mother watching our approach?

We arrived at the house, the stately white façade and wide porch greeting us like always. The front door opened, and Farns and Renee appeared, both smiling as I got out and clambered up the steps.

Renee folded me in her arms and squeezed hard. "I missed you."

"I missed you, too." I buried my face in her familiar jet black hair.

"Ms. Rousseau, so nice to see you again." Farns gave a slight bow.

I smiled up into his weathered face. "Ever the gentleman."

"Why, thank you. The house wasn't the same without you." His smile faltered, as if remembering I wasn't exactly a willing guest. He covered by telling Luke he'd help with the bags, though he eased down the stairs with ginger steps.

Renee pulled her shawl tighter around her narrow shoulders. "Come in, come in. Too cold out here to be standing around."

A biting wind blew past, as if to illustrate her point, and I followed her into the foyer. Everything was the same—honey oak floors, glittering chandeliers, and impeccable southern architecture. Still, a shift had occurred in my bones, maybe even at my most basic level. The last time I'd arrive here and entered those doors, I hadn't known what to expect. This time I did. This time I could face my future and, hopefully, have a chance of weathering the storm.

"When I got word you were on your way, I went ahead and drew you a nice hot bath. How's that sound?" Renee led me up the stairs and into my room. Lavender and vanilla permeated the air and drew me into the bathroom.

She didn't need to tell me twice. I stripped out of my jeans and t-shirt and slipped into the fragrant water. I moaned in sheer pleasure as Renee bustled around making sure I had towels and anything else I needed.

I finally waved her toward the small hamper. "Sit down and tell me what happened while I was gone."

She laughed and took her seat. "I think you need to tell me why you're back so soon first. I heard there was trouble brewing, but from the looks of Mr. Sinclair, it seems to have boiled over and scorched."

I nodded and lay back, letting the heat relax my muscles. I recounted my two weeks of wandering around the Cuban estate, swimming in the pool, and doing everything in my power to avoid thinking about Vinemont. When I told her about the uprising she clucked her tongue.

"That sort of trouble has happened before, but it was a long time ago."

"When was that?"

Her dark eyes scrutinized me and she furrowed her brow as if she were trying to make a choice.

I willed her to tell me something, anything. Information

was like to gold to me. It always had been in this house.

She sighed. "Well, I guess it doesn't matter. I'll tell. Maybe it'll help."

I leaned forward and propped my chin on my knees. Renee must have missed me to be so ready to spill information.

Her fingers were already in a twisting war with each other. "When Rebecca was Sovereign, she had a problem with a neighboring sugar cane plantation in Brazil. It was owned by another family, the Roses. The Roses had been steadily eating up the open farmland around the Vinemont fields and gained a stranglehold on the crop in that particular area with the help of paramilitaries. It was a lawless place that far inland. Still is. Anyway, once Rebecca won Sovereign, the Roses had already been doing everything they could to get the Vinemonts out of Brazil." More hand wringing.

"Go on."

"Well, the Sovereign has a certain set of powers." She halted, clearly wondering how much information she should give.

"What powers?" I had to keep her talking.

"Well, the Sovereign can bring families in."

"Like the Vinemonts?"

"Yes." She avoided my gaze. "Like them."

She scratched at her neck before forcing her hand back to her lap. "And the Sovereign can cast families out."

"What happens when a family gets cast out?" I asked.

"It means that, should the Sovereign will it, the family's assets and lives are forfeit."

I cocked my head sideways at the idea of such a one-sided remedy. "Why doesn't the Sovereign just do that to everyone and take everything and call it a goddamn day. To hell with the Acquisition?"

"Because the Sovereign may only do it to one family during their entire reign. He can bring one in and he can kick one out. It helps keep everyone in line, you see?"

It made sense. Casting a family out fortified the Sovereign's wealth and position. And just the threat of it was likely enough to keep the families under the Sovereign's thumb. Being able to add an ally? Priceless. It was like stacking up pieces around the king on a chess board. "What happens to the family that gets the boot?"

"It depends. Some are allowed to go, move away, try and rebuild. Some aren't so lucky. The Sovereign controls fortunes, controls life or death…" She dropped her gaze to the floor, a pall falling over her.

"What happened with Rebecca and the Roses?" The water couldn't have cooled in such a short time, but I felt a chill rush down my spine all the same.

"The Vinemonts weren't always one of the main families. Some of the older families looked down on them, tried to take advantage—"

"Families like the Roses?"

She nodded but still didn't meet my gaze. "By the time Rebecca became Sovereign, she was a different person. Before, she would work with the local farmers and try and sort out the issues the Roses were creating at the plantation. But after the trials, she decided to make an example of them. She waited until they instigated another supply problem— Rose trucks blocking the roads and keeping the workers from getting the sugar cane to the processing plant. She went down to the farm, flew herself as she used to do, and took Mr. Sinclair with her. I told her he was too young. She didn't listen. That poor boy…" She finally returned my stare, her dark eyes swimming with unshed tears.

"What happened?"

Renee took a deep shuddering breath. "I really shouldn't be telling you this."

"Tell me." I needed to know the rest of the story like I needed my next breath.

Her eyes flickered to the ceiling and then back to me, and she dropped her voice to barely above a whisper. "She rounded up every farmer on the Vinemont property, armed them, and set them on the Rose plantation. It was burned to the ground within hours. The fields charred. The workers killed. Mr. Rose was down there at the time. He never returned. A month after that, the Rose plantations were Vinemont plantations, and the Rose clan was no more. The little boy that left with his mother never came back, either."

"Why would you tell me this now?" I couldn't keep the anger from my voice. She had so much more information that she wasn't sharing. She doled it out in tiny spoonfuls and I was hungry within seconds after each bite.

"Because I've seen the way Mr. Sinclair looks at you. I saw how he was for the two weeks you were gone. He needs you, Stella. More than he's ever needed anyone. I think…I hope." She chose her words haltingly. "I hope that you may be the one thing between him and a lifetime of regret. I wasn't strong enough to save Rebecca. But you're different." A tear rolled down her cheek, hesitating in the small crease next to her mouth before falling to the floor.

"You want *me* to save *him*?" I couldn't begin to wrap my head around the mix of Stockholm Syndrome and pure fucked up insanity she'd just said. "I'm his prisoner, his plaything, the ant he likes to use a magnifying glass on. I have no power to save myself, much less him. Whatever feelings he may have for me are nothing compared to the darkness inside him. You've seen it."

"I've seen it." She held my gaze. "But he's not the only one with darkness inside him, Stella. We all have it."

I closed my eyes and sank beneath the water, for once sated with information. I didn't want to think or hear any more about the child Sinclair, how scared he must have been, how horrified at the violence he no doubt witnessed. I had to think of myself. It didn't matter what sort of rules he adhered to now. The fact was he could still let me go if he chose. He could leave my father alone. He could still turn his back on the whole Acquisition. He only stayed in it to reap the rewards and benefits of a system that was built on darkness, on the vilest impulses of human nature. He was a part of it, participating willingly.

No, I wouldn't save him. I refused. But I would save myself.

When I emerged from beneath the surface, Renee had disappeared.

After I'd soaked as long as I could in the hot water, I rose and dressed in some new pajamas I found in my dresser. Renee had been busy during my absence, the closet full of new clothes and the dresser bursting with even more. I ate in my room that night, not willing to sit through a meal with the Vinemont clan. I picked through the roast chicken and vegetables Renee had brought until there was a knock at my door.

Adjusting my tank top, I pulled the blanket up over my shorts. "Come in."

A blond head of hair peeked through. "Hi."

"Hi, yourself." I smiled, happy to see Teddy. Of all the Vinemont brothers, he was the most genuine. Teddy telegraphed his motives clear as a bell and his boyish manners endeared him to me, though he was only a handful of years younger than I was.

He came in and shut the door behind him before easing onto the foot of my bed.

"I heard some things about Cuba. You okay?"

I set my plate on the nightstand and drew my knees up. "Things were hairy there for a minute, but I'm safe."

"Yeah, Sin doesn't look so good. Dr. Yarbrough is patching him up right now. But Sin said you took care of him, doing staples and all that?"

I nodded, remembering the way Vinemont had watched me as I knelt before him, cleaning his wounds. "I did."

"Why?" He angled his head so I could look down the line of his strong jaw.

It wasn't an easy question, and I had no easy answer. "He needed help."

"But why would you help him after he..." He glanced up to my shoulder, as if he could see the lash marks there.

I shrugged. "I don't know."

He traced the stitching on the quilt at the foot of my bed with his fingertip. "I think I know why."

"Enlighten me."

He met my gaze, his hazel eyes shy but also seeking. "I think it's the same thing I feel with Laura. Like, you would do anything for that person, even if you're mad at them or even if they've done something terrible."

I tilted my head to the side. "Are you talking about love?"

He shrugged, his lanky arms rising and falling with the movement. "I guess, yeah. I don't know. I've never been in love. I just know that if someone hurt her, I'd make that someone pay, and then I'd do everything I could to help her. Does that make sense?"

"It does. For you and Laura it does."

"But not for you and Sin?"

I sighed and leaned back against the pillows. "I think whatever is between me and your brother is much more complicated than what you've described. And I think you know why."

"Because of the Acquisition?" He kept tracing the same pattern of seams over and over, his index finger moving to its own silent beat.

"Yes." In some other life, there may have been love. Maybe if Vinemont hadn't been born into his role and I hadn't been born into mine, then maybe. But as it was, we had no future and our past was murky at best.

"I just wish..."

"What?"

He shook his head and rose. "I'll let you get back to your dinner. I just heard you were back and wanted to come say hi and that I missed you. And thank you for taking care of Sin when he needed it."

I held my arms out and he came and gave me a hug, squeezing me almost as tightly as Renee did, but not quite.

"You're welcome," I whispered.

"Okay." He stood and retreated to the door. "I'll see you in the morning at breakfast then?"

I couldn't refuse his honest smile. "Yes, I guess so."

"Good."

Once he left, I snuggled down into my bed. Why did the other two have to be so vile when Teddy had turned out so normal?

I tried to fall asleep but couldn't. Not until I dropped to my knees and reached up into my nightstand. Once I felt the familiar blade still securely taped to the underside of the drawer, I crawled back into bed. I'd brought the knife here as a weapon, but the simple act of touching it strengthened my resolve. It was more of a talisman than anything else at this point.

I didn't need it to keep me safe. I could do that on my own. And I would.

CHAPTER SIX
STELLA

BREAKFAST THE NEXT morning was oddly calm. Vinemont was already at the table, sipping his coffee and watching my every move as I walked in and took a seat next to Teddy.

"Happy to be back?" Vinemont set his cup down and leaned forward, his perfectly pressed business shirt doing nothing to hide the muscles underneath.

"I wouldn't say that." My sharp tone made the corners of his mouth turn up, a smile trying to break free. The half-smile died as Lucius entered the room.

He was on a call, fluent Spanish rolling off his tongue as he gave orders to someone, most likely Javier. He wore a navy polo and jeans that fit his narrow waist and lean hips perfectly. When he was done, he tossed his phone down on the table.

"Well?" Vinemont asked.

"Javier says it's all over. But now we have to pay the local militia for their *assistance*."

Vinemont glanced to Teddy and shook his head at Lucius. "We'll finish this discussion later."

"I'm not a kid anymore, Sin. You two can tell me what's

going on." Teddy swept his hair off his forehead, perhaps aiming for a more serious look.

"It's nothing." Vinemont waved his hand as if a militia fighting a farmer uprising was nothing more than a simple labor disagreement.

"Sure." Teddy wasn't convinced.

"All under control, lil bro. Don't worry, we're keeping your trust fund stocked." Lucius grinned.

"Douche." Teddy crossed his arms over his chest as Lucius' grin broadened.

I elbowed him. "Ignore him. Tell me what life is like out there. What's going on at school?"

He smiled. "I aced my classes this semester—"

"And every semester, dork." Lucius cut in.

Teddy raised an eyebrow at his brother. "So I'm almost done with my pre-med coursework."

"So you're well on your way to being Dr. Teddy, then?" I asked.

"Yep. I've already been accepted. I should graduate undergrad in the spring and roll right on into med school."

A surge of misplaced pride welled inside me. After all, Teddy wasn't my blood. Still, I smiled at him and patted him on the back. "Well done."

"Thanks."

Laura came in and set out plates full of biscuits, gravy, country ham, and eggs. She and Teddy avoided each other's eyes. It was glaringly obvious they were in love and trying desperately to hide it.

Vinemont scowled and speared a chunk of ham. Lucius smirked and gave me a wink.

I decided to help Teddy out and erase some of the awkward. "What sort of doctor do you want to be?"

"Gynecologist, right?" Lucius didn't miss a beat.

Teddy choked on his orange juice. I clapped him on the back a few times and glared at Lucius.

Teddy tried twice to speak before he could do it without sounding strangled. "No, I was thinking cardiology."

"What do you know about hearts?" Lucius grinned at Laura as she came around and refilled our coffees.

"Nothing yet. That's what the medical degree is for."

"Touché." Lucius laughed.

Vinemont remained silent. I thought he'd at least encourage Teddy to do something other than hang around this house and its godforsaken occupants. But he didn't say a word.

"And how many years will you have to be in school?" I tried again.

"Four years of school, three years of residency, and maybe another three years of fellowship after that."

I elbowed him. "You'll be an old man by the time you finish all that. I'm glad you started young."

Vinemont's fork and knife clattered to his plate. He fixed Teddy with an inscrutable stare before turning his burning gaze on me.

"Sin, what gives?" Lucius said. "Shouldn't you applaud the little bro's fine, upstanding life plans? Better than running a sugar business and playing lawyer like we do. Let's toast." He raised his mimosa.

Teddy and I reached across the table and clinked glasses with Lucius. Vinemont rose, threw his napkin down, and stormed out.

Teddy's cheeks bloomed red and his shoulders fell.

"Sin!" Lucius stood and strode after his brother.

What the hell just happened? I put my hand on Teddy's arm and squeezed. I was just as in the dark as he was.

A door slammed down the hall—Vinemont's study.

Knocking and banging echoed through the corridor. "Open this fucking door, douchebag, and apologize to Teddy!"

Nothing.

Before long, Lucius returned and sat down. "He's just being a dick as usual, Ted. Don't worry about him. He's told me before that he's all for you getting a medical degree."

"He's told me that, too. So, I'm just..." Teddy shrugged

273

and placed his napkin next to his plate. "I'm going to go upstairs for a while." He pushed his chair back and walked out, head down.

"What the hell?" I asked.

Lucius shook his head. "Not a fucking clue."

Laura came in to check on us, but her pleasant smile faded when she noticed Teddy was gone.

"He's upstairs." I said. "Some company might be welcome right now."

She blushed and retreated back to the kitchen.

"You shouldn't encourage that." Lucius leaned back and linked his hands behind his head, the broad expanse of his chest appearing even wider.

"I don't live by your snobby rules." I wiped my mouth and set my napkin on the table.

He raised an eyebrow. "No?"

"No."

"I'm pretty sure you're bound by quite a few more rules than I am." He smiled, wolfishness taking the place of his anger at Vinemont.

"I'm not in the mood, Lucius."

He let his gaze run down the scoop neck of my sweater and lower. I stood and moved toward the door. He darted faster down his side of the table and blocked me in.

"I think you are." He shoved me into the corner, caging me in with his hands at either side of my head. "Want to know what I've been thinking about? What I thought about last night while I stroked my cock?"

I met his light eyes and fisted my hands at my sides. "No, but I'm sure you'll tell me."

He moved closer. I tilted my head back so I could hold his gaze. He was dangerous. Taking my eyes off him wasn't an option.

"I thought of you." Pressing his fingertip into my jugular, he traced down my bare skin to the edge of my sweater. "The way you looked in Cuba, naked underneath me. The way these were hard." He pinched my nipple and I pressed back into the corner. "Just like they are now. How much I wanted them in my mouth. How deep I wanted to be in your pussy. You know what got me off, what pushed me over the edge?"

I forced myself to stay put, to see this part of the game through. "What?"

"This." When he pressed his lips to mine, I closed my eyes. He tasted like champagne and oranges, heady and sweet.

I clung to the front of his shirt. He sank his hand down in my pants, gripping my ass hard and pulling my hips forward.

I tried to shove him away, but he growled into my mouth and ground his thigh against my pussy. I dug my nails into his chest, but he only kissed me harder, his tongue plundering my mouth. Heat raced through my body, pooling between my thighs. He grabbed my hair and pulled my head back before kissing down my neck, biting my throat and then fastening his lips to my collarbone.

"Lucius." I was panting, caught up in a man who was no better than the devil I'd given my heart to. "Please."

"Beg me. That's right, Stella. It's time to finish what we started." He kissed lower, his mouth hot and luscious on my skin. "Beg me to give you what you want, what you need."

He rubbed against my clit, the friction making my head spin. I gasped.

"Beg me to sink myself so deep in you that you can't tell where I end and you begin."

"Don't." I breathed as he released my hair and pulled my sweater and the cup of my bra down.

I moaned—not a fake—when cool air hit my nipple, his mouth following close behind.

This was wrong. All wrong. I dug my fingers into his hair and pulled, but he sucked me in harder, his teeth grazing along the hard peak of my breast. He groaned into my skin and palmed my ass viciously, rubbing me against him in a slow, teasing rhythm.

"We can't." I sounded unsure even to myself.

He swirled his tongue once more around my nipple before coming back up and resting his forehead against mine, his hand on my cheek. "You're already mine. I'm going to taste every bit of you. Every inch of skin. You're going to take all of me, Stella, and beg for more. And I'll give it. I'll give it every time you ask and even when you don't."

His words buzzed around my mind like a swarm of bees, stinging me but with the promise of something sweet.

He leaned in to kiss me again but I pushed harder. I couldn't do this. Not here. Not now. I wanted to snare him, but not with Vinemont a few doors down.

He gripped my wrists and pinned them above my head. "I know you want it, Stella. I know you want everything I have. If you say you don't, you're lying to yourself." He brushed his lips against mine again, making me believe his lies. *Were they lies?*

"I could take you right now. I could yank your jeans down and feast on your sweet cunt." He shoved his hips into me, his hard cock substantial in his pants. "I want to, Stella. Oh, how I want to."

"Please, don't. I-I can't." I was stumbling, falling, begging the wolf in front of me to catch me.

He stole another kiss, this one lingering. My heartbeat was like a drum in my ears as his tongue swirled against mine, teasing and tasting. He pulled my wrists down from the wall and wrapped them around my back at my waist, making my breasts jut out against him.

He kissed to my ear. "I'm going to take it all, Stella."

"Never." I tried to shake myself out of the haze he'd put me in.

His deep laugh was in my head as he nipped at my neck. "We'll see."

He pulled away and stared down at me, his eyes calculating. "I'll give you a pass this one time, Stella. Just once. But the next time I get you alone and you try to tease me—" He grabbed my palm and ran it down his hard length "—you're going to get all of this. And then you're going to thank me when I'm done."

He dropped my wrists and backed up another step. "Go," he commanded, "before I change my mind."

Stunned, I brushed past him and into the hallway. All the oxygen had been out here, not in the dining room where Lucius had made it impossible to think. I stumbled over the runner before gaining my feet and taking the next few steps. I pulled my top back into place as I fled. The doorbell stopped me. I turned and glimpsed a figure through the transom windows.

Lucius was already in the hallway, adjusting himself in his pants before striding to the door and swinging it open.

The visitor wore an old-fashioned servant's livery—even stuffier than Farns'—who ambled up and shook his head at Lucius. The man handed Lucius a card, gave a perfunctory bow, and whirled on his heel.

"You shouldn't get the door. That's my job, Mr. Lucius," Farns chided gently.

"I've gotten my hands dirty plenty over the last few days, Farns. Trust me. This is nothing."

Vinemont appeared, his dark hair a tousled mess as if he'd been running his hands through it. He glanced up at me and quickly looked away. I felt a surge of guilt that I batted away. We weren't together. We never would be. Seducing Lucius was part of the plan. Or was Lucius seducing me?

"What is it?" Vinemont's voice was gruff.

"Invitation." Lucius swiped his finger under the wax seal and broke it open before unfolding the parchment.

The brothers read it together as I walked to them, curiosity overcoming my shaken cocktail of emotions.

"Fuck!" Vinemont whirled and punched a hole in the foyer wall, plaster falling in a heap at his feet. I flinched and went to stand at Lucius' elbow to get a better look.

Farns shook his head and scurried down the hallway,

most likely for a dustpan and broom.

"What is it?" I asked.

"Cal wants us to come to his New Orleans house tomorrow night. Welcome party for some new family or something." Lucius flipped the page over, as if searching for more writing on the empty back.

"All of us have to go?" I thought I was done with the bastards until Christmas.

"Invite says Sin, you, and me."

"He knows." Vinemont shook his head, his brows pinched.

"Knows what?" I scanned the invitation, the stark lines of a New Orleans address and a time with an oak tree watermark.

"He knows my Acquisition has changed hands. He knows or he never would have invited Lucius." Vinemont's violence had reopened the wounds in his knuckles. Blood dripped to the floor, but he didn't notice. A vein thrummed in his neck as he stared murder at Lucius.

"Hey, I didn't tell him. But what does it matter?" Lucius put his hand around my waist. "It's true."

Bad move. Vinemont was already on a hair trigger. He lunged for Lucius, grabbing him by the neck as they fell in a heap on the floor. I stumbled backward and sat down hard.

With a guttural roar, Vinemont flexed his bloodied knuckles as he choked his brother.

Lucius gripped Vinemont's hands and ripped one free before leaning up and head-butting him. Vinemont groaned at the impact and slammed Lucius back down, pressing harder with the one hand still at his brother's throat. Lucius reared back with his right hand and aimed a fist at Vinemont's jaw, the blow sending him crashing to the floor. Lucius jumped on top of his brother, both men slugging away.

I should have been happy. My plan was working. This was what I'd wanted—them tearing each other apart so that

I could stand over their shredded remains. But as they fought, I wanted nothing more than for it to stop. The sickening thuds of fists on flesh, the blood, the grunts and anger.

I covered my ears. "Stop!" I didn't realize I was capable of the scream that tore from my lungs.

Lucius held his fist ready to strike before pushing himself off Vinemont, landing with a heavy clunk that made the chandelier overhead rattle. Both men stayed put, breathing heavily and eyeing each other as if waiting for it to start again.

I heard footsteps on the staircase behind me, and then Teddy's voice. "What the fuck is going on?"

"Don't worry about it." Lucius grinned and put his hand in the air, giving Teddy a thumbs up, though he didn't take his eyes from Vinemont. "Everything's fine, Teddy."

"Fine." Vinemont agreed and sat up.

"Sure. Right." Teddy offered me his hand. "Nothing in this house is fine. Come on, Stella."

I took it and he pulled me to my feet. I could feel two sets of eyes on my back the whole way up the staircase until I turned the corner toward my room.

"Are you okay? What was that about?" Teddy asked.

We hurried down the hallway and into my bedroom. I dropped down on my bed before digging the heels of my palms into my eyes. Teddy sat next to me and put his hand on my back, rubbing it gently.

"I'm okay. Thanks, Teddy. And that was about me. Well, actually, I think it was about me and Cal Oakman."

Teddy blanched. "I hate that guy. Always have."

"You and me both."

He wrapped his arm around me and pulled me over so my head rested on his shoulder.

"Are we going to make it through all this, Stella?" He sounded tired, far beyond his years.

"Honestly? I don't know. But I think your chances are a smidge better than mine." I smiled weakly. "So there's that."

He rested his chin on top of my head. "I would have taken that whipping for you. If I'd known about it. Which I didn't."

His unexpected kindness was like a balm, though tears stung my eyes and I swallowed hard. "I wish you didn't know about that. And I don't think that's how it works, anyway. But I appreciate the sentiment."

He took a deep breath. "I wish a lot of things. I wish there was no Acquisition. I wish we weren't here. I wish Laura and I could be together. I wish…"

"I know. I have my fair share of wishes, too." A flash of images sparked through my mind—Mom, Dad, and the spider who haunted my waking moments along with my dreams. Wishes for each of them. Some good. Some bad.

We sat silently for long enough to hear Vinemont and Lucius go to their respective corners, and to hear Farns start cleaning up downstairs.

When Teddy left, I realized all three Vinemont men had made inroads into my heart.

And I cursed them for it.

CHAPTER SEVEN
STELLA

RENEE FLITTED ABOUT, bobby pins hanging from her mouth and test smudges of eye shadow along the back of her hand. She had been working on me for over an hour, but it was obvious that getting ready for a fancy party was a bit out of her skill set. Still, she gave it her best—rolling my hair, curling my lashes, doing my makeup. I'd argued at first, told her I could do it myself. With a raised eyebrow and a shake of her head, she'd whisked me off to my room.

Now, I was as close to ready as I was going to get. She'd pinned the sides of my hair up, and the rest flowed down my back in red waves. My skin appeared luminous under the vanity lights.

She'd gone heavy on the dark brown eye shadow, but otherwise I was fine with everything. It didn't matter to me. Not really. I didn't want to impress anyone. Maybe I should have gone the dowdy route, made myself less appealing for the upcoming Christmas trial. Though I knew what they had planned for me wasn't about sex. Not really. It was about violence. About taking something from me.

I took a deep breath and did my best to smile at Renee in the mirror. She tossed the last bobby pins on the counter and returned my smile. "I think I've done it. You look amazing. Maybe not as fabulous as you did for the ball, but you had professionals helping you…"

She let her words trail off when I dropped my gaze to my hands.

She placed a hand on my shoulder. "I'm sorry. I shouldn't have brought that up."

I placed my hand over hers and met her dark eyes in the mirror once again. "It's fine. It's my life now, after all. And we're sort of in this together, right? Just twenty years apart."

"That's exactly how I feel." She sighed. "I know it's you. I know you're the one going through it, but I still feel it, you know? It's like a wound that never fully healed. When you went to the ball, I knew I couldn't save you, but I felt it as if I were there again, reliving it. Instead of a fresh pain, it was a dull ache. The emotions—they were the same. I-I felt it. I understand."

If she still felt this pain, would I twenty years from now? Would I still be here, helping the next sacrificial lamb prepare to have its throat slit? I shuddered at the thought. *Never.*

"And there's one more thing." She pulled open the small drawer on the far left of the vanity and plucked out a syringe.

A ribbon of worry streaked through me. "What's that for?"

"For you. It's your usual prescription." She wrinkled her brow. "To be effective, you need it now. Just in case… at the trial, you see…"

I studied the syringe and my eyes widened with recognition. Birth control. My last shot had been three months prior, so Renee was right on time. Vinemont had left no stone unturned, getting my medical information and keeping me in tip top shape for the Christmas trial. My eyes burned with angry tears.

"This is so twisted, Renee." I balled my hands into fists, my fingernails digging into my palms. "So fucking twisted."

"I'm sorry. I just—"

"No. It's fine." I fought the tears, not letting a single one drop. "Just do it."

I offered my arm and she ripped open an alcohol wipe, cleaned a spot, and injected me. A slight sting and then nothing. *Now I'm protected.* I didn't know if I wanted to laugh or cry at the ridiculousness of the thought. I would never be protected, never be safe until I was free of the Acquisition.

She tossed the syringe into the waste basket. "I'm sorry."

"It's not your fault." I shuddered at the thought of carrying a child as a result of the Christmas trial. "And thank you … For doing it for me, I mean."

Renee kissed the crown of my head before laying her cheek against my hair for a few moments. I was surprised such a small gesture could impart so much solace. But by the time she straightened, I felt her warmth flowing through me like a mild transfusion.

She smiled big enough to almost convince me it was genuine. "Wait 'til you see the gown I picked for you."

"If it's got feathers—" I grimaced. "—I'll pass."

She laughed and shook her head, her dark hair shining. "No feathers. Not this time. Come on."

I followed her into my bedroom and stopped when I spied the dress she'd laid out on my bed. It was black with a plunging neckline. The hem would fall to my ankle, but the high slit would leave little to the imagination.

I frowned and crossed my arms over my chest. "I don't think I can pull that off, Renee."

Renee threw her hands on her hips. "Modesty is confidence's ugly sister."

I laughed. For a woman who'd I never seen in anything other than prim black and white, Renee surprised me.

She pushed me forward. "Put it on. I know it'll be perfect."

"Fine. For you. I'll try it for you." I shrugged out of my robe and trudged to my dresser for some underwear.

Renee cleared her throat. I turned to look at her over my

shoulder. "What?"

She pointed to a thin piece of black material that I hadn't noticed next to the dress.

"Is that a g-string?"

She smoothed her skirt. "Well, that dress clings, and you can't have panty lines. Or you can go no panties if you like that better."

I definitely did not like that better. I gave up my quest for comfortable cotton panties and pulled on the barely-there thong. My ass was totally exposed, but at least my pussy had some semblance of fabric over it.

"I'm guessing no bra, either?"

She shook her head and eyed her feet. "The back is open, so no."

"Fine." I lifted the dress and dropped it over my head. Renee was right, it clung as it slid down my body and settled. The front dipped low between my breasts in a draping cowl that thinned into spaghetti straps and tied at the top of my shoulders. The straps multiplied into three thin strips that flowed down my back and joined the sides at elbow level, leaving the rest of the back open almost down to my ass. The slit was so high that I was glad I chose to wear the panties.

"You are perfect."

"I take it this isn't a jeans and t-shirt event?" I snorted and walked to the full length mirror to get a better look. Renee had created a fashion plate in record time.

"Never. You need to impress the Sovereign. Play to your strengths."

"To help Vinemont?" I narrowed my eyes at her in the mirror. "I have to dress like a street walker to help my captor?"

"Yes." Renee pushed my hair over my shoulder and perused my tattoo. "Though I never had a dress this nice when I was a working girl."

That raised my eyebrows.

Renee shrugged and blushed. "I told you about my past,

and I'm not proud of it. But I'm just saying that yes, you are being taken somewhere to be shown off as an Acquisition, but enjoy the little pleasures. That's all. One day you won't even have those. So—"

"Did you just tell me to *carpe diem*?" I turned and smiled at her, willing away her embarrassment.

"I did." She smiled back, the clouds of memory giving way to the present. "Now let's see about your shoes and, the best part, your jewels."

She went into the closet and brought out a pair of velvet stilettos with red soles.

"I don't know if I can manage those. Got anything with a shorter heel?"

"Nope. These are the ones." She set them down in front of me and I stepped into them. They were almost impossible, but not quite. As long as I was on an even surface and not doing any running, I might survive.

"And these." She practically pranced to a box on my dresser and flipped the lid before pulling out a dazzling necklace. An array of emeralds in an art deco layout. The jewels dangled from silver chains, with the center emerald hanging lower than the rest.

"Do the Vinemonts own all the choicest emeralds in the world or what?" I walked over to her and lifted my hair so she could fasten the priceless strand around my neck.

The earrings were similar threads of silver with an emerald dangling at the end. I put them in and smoothed my hair back down.

Renee clasped her hands in front of her. "This is going to help us. It has to."

"Us?" I turned to her, searching her dark eyes for some clue as to what she meant. Obviously, I wasn't in this to help the Vinemonts. I couldn't care less who became Sovereign.

"Winning will help everyone, Stella. You included."

I peered down at her. "Did winning help you? You're still here, aren't you? Are you living out your wildest dreams? Did things perk up after your lover was ruined by becoming Sovereign?"

She waved my comment away with an impatient flick of her wrist. "Rebecca was strong, but Mr. Sinclair is stronger. Even Lucius is stronger. When either one of them is Sovereign, there will be so much they can do for you, for their mother, for the family, for all of us." She closed the jewel case, her fingers shaking slightly. "Now that we're in the running, winning would be the best outcome. There's no way around the trials. But if you win," she turned, an iron glint in her eye that I'd never seen before, "and you've played your cards right, you have a great deal of power at your fingertips. Power to destroy the ones who hurt you."

"Like the Roses?"

She nodded. "Like them and others."

I'd meant it as a barb, but she wore the Roses' destruction like a badge of honor.

"Have you destroyed people, Renee? The ones who tortured you most during the trials?"

She took my elbow. "We should get you downstairs. Mr. Sinclair will be antsy to leave."

"Renee, you can't just cut me off. I need to know." I hadn't actually considered the proposal Lucius made in Cuba—the power he would have after winning Sovereign. But Renee was echoing his sentiments: win, and then everything else will fall into place. Was Renee right? Was helping the Vinemonts win the surest route to destroy the entire game? Take it all down from the inside? Maybe, but it hadn't worked for Renee.

"You need to go. You can't be late for Cal's party. That would be a bad start to your night." Renee swept past me and opened the door before ushering me through it.

I'd been around her long enough to know that the discussion was tabled. She was practiced at evading my questions. I just wished I could break down her walls, see everything inside and leave with the spoils of information. It would never happen. Not with Renee. Whether she'd always been evasive or was forced to be so because of the

Acquisition trials, I'd never know.

I maneuvered slowly down the stairs in my heels with Renee at my side. Once downstairs, I heard voices on the front porch. Lucius and Sinclair.

"Tell me all about it when you get back." She pulled a long, dark fur from the foyer closet.

"Is that for me?" I didn't do fur, but the coat glowed with an amazing luster and begged to be touched.

"I had it brought from the climate controlled storage this morning. It's the sable." She held it out.

"I'm not sure." I ran my fingers down the front, each strand of fur silkier than the last.

"I am. Come on. It's cold out there."

I turned and slipped one arm and then the next into the coat. It was heavy and warm, the softest thing I'd ever felt. I studied my appearance in the foyer mirror. Even in the few months I'd been involved in this cruel game, my eyes seem to have hardened. Or maybe it was what was inside that had changed, grown stronger. I tilted my chin up the slightest bit, as if steeling myself for what was to come.

Renee swept my hair from the coat and draped it over my shoulder. "Everything will be fine. They won't harm you between trials."

"Do you know that for certain?" I opened the front door.

"Nothing is ever certain." Renee gave me a wry smile.

With that cryptic bit of wisdom, I walked into the cold night. Vinemont and Lucius quieted as I approached, but a heavy tension roiled in the air.

"Stella—" Lucius began.

Vinemont turned and stepped in front of his brother before offering me his arm.

Both men wore clean black tuxes, expertly fitted. Lucius's hair was tamed down in smooth waves while Vinemont's was his usual dark and tousled perfection. Clean shaven lady killers. They were beautiful, each in their own way. Lucius sleek and refined. Vinemont rough, almost gritty, even though everything about him was polished.

Luke waited in the drive, the limousine competing with the inky black of night. I ignored Vinemont and gripped the stair rail, holding on for dear life while I clicked down each step in my stilettos. I let out a silent sigh of relief once I was on level ground again.

"Ms. Rousseau." Luke tipped his hat and opened the back passenger door for me. I slid in, the fur moving across the leather like butter in a warm pan.

"Don't fucking try it." Vinemont's voice wafted past the engine noise and he sank down next to me.

Lucius took the front passenger seat once again, turning and giving me a winning smile. "You are fucking gorgeous."

Even though I knew it was a trick, just words, I couldn't stop the heat in my cheeks. "Thank you."

"Drive," Vinemont barked at Luke.

The limo eased down the driveway, and soon we were whistling along the interstate, heading into the heart of New Orleans.

Vinemont's eyes bored into me until I turned and matched his glare. His gaze slid to my mouth, then lower to the open top of my coat. Warmth raced through me, and I was thankful the fur covered my hardened nipples. His tongue wetted his bottom lip and I found I couldn't look away.

His mouth, the sharp line of his jaw, the elegant silhouette of his neck in the darkness of the car—all of it was somehow a lure. And like every other lure, there was a sharp hook in it, ready to catch and draw blood. I dropped my gaze, though I could still feel his burning into me, making me hotter than I should be to the point where I wanted to shrug out of the rich coat.

"Take a fucking picture, Sin. Jesus. You're making her uncomfortable." Lucius caught my eye and winked at me, his white teeth momentarily glinting in a passing street lamp.

"You don't know a thing about her comfort."

"Oh, I think I may have a few ideas. Don't I, Stella?"

I shifted in my seat, away from both of them.

"What is he talking about?" Vinemont smoothed a hand down my sleeve before gripping me lightly through the coat. "Stella?"

I ripped my arm away and sank even further back. "You two play your twisted game. I'm going to sit this one out."

Lucius laughed and faced forward again before cranking up the music to an almost painful level. Some angry rock song with a thumping beat. At least it cut off the conversation. I stared out the window at the passing cars, wishing I was in one of them. Any would do, just so long as it was going away from these people, from the Acquisition.

The rest of the drive was filled with Lucius' brash musical stylings. The city loomed ahead of us, the lights beaming out into the night like a million lighthouses luring us toward safe harbor. Luke took us into the city's beating heart, live music on the street corners and the smells of fried food seeping through the vents. The houses grew statelier the farther we drove, until we were in the midst of the Garden District. Mansions rose on every side, elegant and stylish, with high wrought iron fences separating their inhabitants from the rest of the tumultuous city.

We eventually pulled up in front of a three-story Victorian that seemed to take up half a block. It was almost garish in its ornate grandeur; turrets and a widow's walk ran along the roof. Two hulking magnolia trees stood guard over the walkway, and a sweeping porch wrapped around the entire house. Every light in the windows burned, and people congregated on the porch and spilled out the front doors.

Luke stopped out front and opened my door. I rose and made it to the sidewalk without tripping. It was a win. But my next step landed on a rock or something else I couldn't see in the dark. My ankle turned and I made a strangled noise as I started to fall.

A strong hand grabbed my elbow and righted me easily. I looked up, but somehow I already knew it was Vinemont.

Suspicion confirmed as Lucius came to my other elbow. Vinemont offered his arm again, this time a slight smirk on his face.

I accepted it for no other reason than to avoid breaking an ankle. We climbed the three steps to the yard, strode down the wide walk, and then ascended a few more steps to the front porch. The impulse to run grew stronger with each moment. Vinemont must have sensed it because he pulled my arm into him, steadying me more as we walked past some guests and into the brightly lit entryway.

A servant came for my coat. Vinemont helped me take it off and froze when he saw my dress. His gaze tore down my figure, as if memorizing every line, every curve before he met my eyes again.

Lucius strolled up next to me and pulled on his cuffed shirt sleeves. "This should be fun."

The house was beautiful with exquisite woodwork on every corner, above the wide doorways, and along the sweeping stair. Partygoers milled around, all dressed in black tie or dresses that screamed Hollywood glamor. Music played upstairs, a deep beat drifting down and completely at odds with the antique, elegant nature of the home.

"The Vinemonts made it!" Cal was halfway down the stairs, his gaze fastened on me and a huge grin plastered on his face. He pulled a petite blonde along with him. I recognized her—Brianne, Red's Acquisition. She stumbled trying to keep up, but Cal just pulled her into him and dragged her the rest of the way down before setting her back on her feet. He was just as much a showman as he had been at the ball—his tux flashy, his salt and pepper hair perfectly coifed, and every word spoken two tones too loud.

Brianne clung to him, her red dress revealing the tattoo along her chest and a fair amount of skin. I could only assume Red had chosen her attire for the evening. Her eyes were glassy and she looked through me, no recognition sparking to life in her face.

"Glad you could come to my little soiree." Cal shook

Vinemont's hand, then Lucius'. I didn't offer my hand, so he grabbed both of them and pulled my arms out, staring down my body as he licked his lips. "You look good enough to eat, Stella."

Vinemont twitched at my side, but did nothing. Cal released me and cocked his head up the stairs. "Come on. The real fun is on the second floor. And Stella, if you're lucky, I'll invite you up to the third and give you a surprise."

A cold tremor ran down my spine. I wanted to stay as far away from the third floor as possible. Even so, Vinemont took my elbow and led me forward as we followed Cal and Brianne upward toward the pounding music. *Is the second floor a rave?*

Brianne swayed, but Cal gripped her ass firmly, sinking his index finger deeply between her cheeks as he lifted her up stair after stair. He glanced at me over his shoulder and winked. Anger gurgled in my throat, threatening to come out of my mouth in a scream. I wouldn't let it. Renee and Lucius had made me think more about seeing the entire game board before making any decisions on moving pieces. If playing along got me in a better position to destroy these people, then I would do it.

We reached the landing and the beat was even deeper, vibrating in my chest and shaking the chandelier that hung above the foyer. Cal continued forward toward an open set of double doors, exchanging pleasantries with the partygoers that crowded around. People gawked and stared, but I kept my eyes straight ahead. They could look and leer, but I held on to what Renee had told me. They couldn't hurt me. Not tonight.

A man pushed through some guests and came up to us. Auburn hair and beady eyes—Red.

"Oh, there you are." He glowered at Brianne.

"She's just helping me greet my guests, Red."

"You're welcome to her, Cal. Anytime." Red flicked his eyes to me before letting his gaze fall to my breasts. "Nice to see you again, Stella."

"I can't say likewise." I still wanted to scratch his eyes out for how he'd treated Brianne. Then again, I was standing here holding onto a man who'd whipped my back until I bled. The scars were on display even now in this backless dress. Is that why Renee had chosen it?

Red flipped his too-long hair out of his eyes. "Still a cunt, I see."

"Shut the fuck up, Red." Vinemont tensed next to me, a warning.

"Don't like it when I insult your whore?" He laughed, his teeth slightly purpled from wine.

Vinemont took a step forward and Red drew up his fists.

"Boys, boys. Save it for Christmas!" Cal laughed and patted them both on the back. "I've come up with a pretty clever way for you to release your aggressions, trust me."

Fight or flight kicked alive inside me again. My stomach churned and bile rose in my throat. Renee's tale of her Christmas trial was bad enough, but I knew Cal would make mine as horrible as possible. I had a momentary flash of trying to kill him. Maybe slipping down to the kitchen and grabbing a knife and slitting his throat right in front of all these ghouls. Would that end it? Would that stop the entire corrupted machinery from turning? Or would I just put a new Sovereign in charge sooner than expected?

"You and I are going to have a very Merry Christmas, Stella. Count on it." Red backed away and grabbed the nearest woman before sinking his tongue into her mouth. She moaned and went limp, letting him reach up her short skirt and finger her.

Vinemont took my elbow, roughly this time.

Cal clapped his hands and gripped Brianne. "That's more like it. Now, come on. I want to show you the fun."

We followed him toward the large double doors where the sound emanated from. The room beyond was dark, but we plunged ahead. The music grew louder, a techno beat. It was a ballroom on a much smaller scale than the one at the Oakman estate. Still, it was large and took up almost the whole second floor.

Nude men and women writhed to the music on four platforms that dotted the room. Stuffy paintings and ornate sconces lined the walls, totally discordant with the scene. Couches sat against the periphery, some occupied by people doing drugs or having sex, sometimes a mix of both. I couldn't tell if they were more frightening now that they were unmasked.

I should have realized at the ball that these people had no limits. But now I knew the ball wasn't an anomaly. It was them. *This*—the woman snorting coke off a man's hard cock, the two men fucking while a semi-circle formed to watch, the needles and the glassy eyed women—this was what these people were.

"Isn't it something?" Cal yelled over the din.

"Impressive." Lucius nodded, his gaze glued to the nearest platform where one woman knelt and licked between another's legs.

"I like to throw these parties every so often. Keep things fun as Sovereign. This one is a welcome party, of course. But I certainly hope the next Sovereign keeps the tradition of impromptu get-togethers alive." He yanked Brianne into his side and looked from Vinemont to Lucius. "But which one of you is in the running?"

"I am." Vinemont and Lucius spoke in unison, though their voices barely carried over the music.

Cal shook his head and glanced to Brianne. He grabbed her chin roughly and pulled her face to his. "Only *one*, isn't that right little Acquisition?"

"Y-yes. One." She nodded, seemingly even more out of it than she had been downstairs.

Cal turned back to us, his face stone cold sober, all hint of a smile gone. "Sinclair, you know the rules. Did she choose him or not?"

Vinemont snaked his arm around my middle. "She did, but—"

"But nothing, Sin." Cal's face broke in a wide smile, the

façade back in place. "Lucius, my favorite sugar magnate, looks like you're in the running."

"I am. She's mine." Lucius stepped closer to me.

"Excellent, excellent. Now, has Sinclair given you all the rules or do I need to give a little lesson?"

Vinemont's fingers pressed into my waist hard enough to leave bruises. I didn't protest, hoping Cal would enlighten me on the rules.

"I'll handle it," Vinemont said.

Lucius cut his gaze toward his brother and then back to Cal. "I'm sure Sin will give me all the details."

Cal nodded and grabbed a cocktail from a passing waiter with a tray. "He better." He toasted to nothing and no one before downing his drink. "Now let's have some fun."

CHAPTER EIGHT
SINCLAIR

IT WAS DONE. Even though I pulled her close to me, even though I wanted nothing but her, she was no longer mine. Her scent, her skin, everything about her had sunk even more deeply into my bones since she'd returned. And now, I'd lost her.

Cal leered and pulled Brianne away to a nearby sofa. No doubt he would drug her again. I toyed with drugging Stella to make this night seem more transitory, less sharp edges, but I couldn't. She deserved to see it, to feel it all. I couldn't save her from it any more than I could save myself. We would all have to play our parts, damned as they were.

"Vinemont." Stella's sharp tone cut through my thoughts. "You're hurting me." Her green eyes were luminous with each flare of light from an adjacent strobe. I eased my hold on her waist, though I didn't want to. I wanted to pick her up and run with her. I couldn't. I was just as shackled to the Acquisition as she was, and now Lucius had unwittingly wandered into the same trap.

"Let's get a drink." Lucius took her hand and led her away, farther into the room.

I followed. I didn't intend to let her out of my sights no

matter what my fool brother had done. Her leg showed through the slit with each of her steps, giving me a chance glimpse of the dark fabric covering her tender flesh at the juncture of her thighs. I didn't care if Lucius claimed her, I still owned her, especially there where I'd already tasted. My cock grew hard at the memory of her spread before me, her soft moans and the frantic movement of her hips. I wanted it again. I hadn't been able to think about anything but her for quite some time.

We wound through the crowd, halted by several people who wanted to shake hands. At least the music was too loud for chit chat. A wide bar was set up along the back wall, and servants poured, rolled, or razored into a line any substance imaginable. Lucius shouted out a drink order and leaned down to take a line. Stella's eyes widened as he snorted it and then pinched his nose. He smiled and handed her the straw.

"Try it."

She eyed the lines of coke.

I knocked the straw from her hand. "Lucius, I'm warning you."

She glared up at me. "I'm a grown woman, Vinemont. I don't need your permission."

"You already have mine, Stella. Go ahead." Lucius handed her another straw.

"I don't need your permission either. Jesus!" She turned and peered over my shoulder before the ghost of a smile graced her face. "You two do me a favor and go have a pissing contest with Cal. I see someone I know."

She brushed past me, her flower and citrus scent wafting over the smell of lust and liquor. *Who could she possibly recognize?*

She maneuvered through the dancers and shook her head at a couple of eager gentlemen. Her destination reached, she stopped in front of one man in particular. He turned. Gavin from the ball.

Lucius handed me a drink as we watched her. "Who the

fuck is that?"

"Eagleton's Acquisition."

"Want to fuck him up?" Lucius downed his drink and motioned for another, the coke already speeding up his movements.

"That's against the rules."

Lucius laughed. "Guess you'll have to tell me all of them now."

I took a drink, the bitter flavor hitting my tongue just right. "I will."

He studied me before following my gaze to Stella. "You know the difference between you and me, Sin?"

"I know of several."

Lucius smirked and leaned against the bar. "I can do what needs to be done to her. I can win this. I can make her cry, make her hurt, leave her in a bloody heap, and never look back. I can win this for us. The Vinemonts can rule it all again. But you..." He drained another glass. "You can't. That hot pussy of hers has got you on your knees. That's why it needs to be this way. That's why it's a good thing she chose me. I'll break her and become Sovereign. You'll see."

As if it were that simple. As if all he had to do was make her cry, make her bleed. I shook my head. I let Lucius talk despite the acid that roiled in my gut. That's all it was—talk. I'd seen the way he looked at her when he thought no one was watching. I'd hated him for it, for his desirousness that edged on something more.

He may have fooled everyone else, but not me. His boldness would falter, and he would fail. And the consequences would destroy us all. I had to get her back, to somehow remedy the situation, but I was out of plays. I had to wait for other pieces to go into motion before I could make a move. I chafed at the waiting, just as I always had.

"Look at that motherfucker." Lucius shot his hand out toward Gavin.

Gavin smiled down at Stella, genuine pleasure at seeing her written all over his handsome face. I wanted to break his nose. It was ridiculous, that aggression, that need to keep her to myself. But it was there and I couldn't ignore it. I'd done far worse than beat a man over a slight, but I'd never fought over a woman. Not until Stella. I swallowed more of the bitterness, letting it run down to my center and mix with my own.

"I still want to fuck that guy up." Lucius slammed his glass down. "Is it against the rules if no one sees us do it?"

I wanted to say we could take Gavin out back and bloody him for even speaking to Stella. That we could end him and dust off our hands like we'd just taken out the trash. But we couldn't. Too much was at stake to break the rules now.

The rules. I shook my head and finished my drink.

"You don't know what you've done." I said it too softly for my brother to hear me over the din. But the words were true.

Lucius had taken my spot in hell. He just didn't realize it yet.

CHAPTER NINE
STELLA

"I GET THREE squares a day and a bed. That's more than I got when I was on the streets." Gavin shrugged, his eyes a deep amber. "I don't even see Bob. I saw him for the ball. Otherwise, I sort of have the run of the guest house on his property. Nobody bothers me. I guess I could try to run, but he's assured me he'd find me and drag me back. Nowhere to go even if I did. I'm just going to see it through. I don't really have any other option at this point." He sighed. "How about you? How'd you get talked into this?"

I sipped the drink he'd handed me. "Betrayal, deceit, lies, and a contract. Same song, different verse."

"I get it. Trust me, I do." He glanced around, the glaring strobe flashing in his face, making him ghostly one second and solid the next. "Hey, do you want to get out of this room? Go somewhere we can talk without so much noise and so many ears?"

"Yes, please." The cacophony of music and the blur of bodies was overwhelming, and I couldn't help but notice some of the guests pointing at Gavin and me. They knew who we were.

He took my hand and pulled me through the dance

floor, past the frenetic dancers and the sex performers. The hall still thumped from the beat within the ballroom, but it was calmer. Delving further into the house, we turned a corner and found a small alcove backed with a stained glass window in a floral pattern. We sat on the window seat thigh to thigh, both silent as our senses became accustomed to the light and freedom from prying eyes. He was warm next to me, his body heat seeping into my bare leg that was revealed by the high slit.

"You look beautiful tonight, by the way." He leaned back and let his head rest against the panes.

"Thanks. You do, too. Handsome, I mean." I followed his lead, leaning out of sight from anyone further down the hall.

"Thanks."

I glanced up at him, his eyes even warmer now that light reflected from them. "Are we going to survive?"

"Yes." He answered so quickly that I wondered if he misheard my question.

"How do you know?"

"I've always been a survivor, and something tells me you have, too."

I wobbled my head back and forth on the glass. "No, I've given up before."

"Maybe, but I knew the moment I saw you at the ball that you had steel in your spine. The way you stared out into the crowd as if you were above all of them, the way you tried to help Brianne, the way you took the…"

"The whipping?"

He nodded and his hand found mine. "I don't remember much of that night. Maybe I blocked it out, but I do remember how strong you were, how I wished I could be strong like that, too."

"I think you have me confused with some other helpless woman caught in an antiquated trial for supremacy among rich sadists."

He snorted and squeezed my hand. "No, it's you. And

nothing about you is helpless."

"Don't let the jewels fool you. I'm just as caged as you are."

"I know you are, but your strength gives me hope. Don't make me doubt it. I need it to keep going." His voice was somber, pleading.

"Okay. I'll try."

"That's all any of us can do."

We fell into a comfortable silence, listening to the music and watching as guests staggered past, high and lit. I kept my hand in his, forming some sort of bond that I hoped strengthened the both of us.

After a brief respite where we were simply able to exist, someone laughed raucously and stumbled down the hall in our direction. I recognized the voice—Red. I tensed and tried to shrink into the alcove.

"What is it?" Gavin dropped my hand and put a steadying palm on my thigh.

"Red," I whispered.

The steps came closer. I shivered.

"Oh, fuck. That guy?"

"That guy." If he noticed me, I wasn't sure if we could avoid an even worse confrontation.

Gavin looked down the hall and then back at me. "Trust me?"

I nodded. Then his lips were on mine, his body crushing into me and shielding me from the hallway. His eyes slowly closed as he slanted his mouth more, covering my face so that all Red would be able to see was Gavin's dark hair.

I'd frozen at Red's voice, but Gavin's body heat tried to thaw me. He rested one hand at my waist and planted his mouth on mine. He didn't seek entry with his tongue, just kept himself poised over my lips. Red's voice grew closer, and I closed my eyes, praying he wouldn't see me.

Red bellowed a string of profanities. He was so close it startled me and I opened my mouth. Gavin took the small chance I gave him and lightly darted his tongue inside, teasing along the tip of mine. He tasted like vodka and some sweet mixer. I gripped the lapel of his jacket as his hand slid up my bare thigh.

"Well look at this shit." Red's voice. "We got Acquisitions fucking each other now?"

Damn. Gavin broke the kiss, his brow creased, before pulling away from me.

"You horning in on Sin's little cunt here?" Red swayed and leaned against the wall opposite us, his head almost bumping into an ornate sconce.

"Fuck you." I stood and stared him down.

He leered at me. "Wait 'til Christmas, little cunt, then I'm going to be balls deep in your ass while you scream for me to stop."

Rage lit me from the inside out and before I knew what I was doing, I'd slapped him, leaving an angry red handprint along his cheek.

"You fucking—" He lunged for me, his eyes wide with wrath. His hands were at my throat, pressing the metal of the necklace into my skin as he constricted my airway. I clawed at his wrists, drawing blood and wanting to do much, much worse.

Gavin yanked him off me, but I wasn't finished. While Gavin was pulling Red backward, I walked up and kneed him right in the crotch with every ounce of anger I had. Red yowled and bent over. Gavin released him and held his hands up as if he'd just touched something filthy.

"You fucking bitch, you fucking bitch." Red kept saying the same thing over and over with wheezing breaths as he cupped his balls and stared up at me from his hunched position.

Gavin came back to my side. "Stella, we need to go—"

I couldn't look anywhere but at Red. The desire to inflict more pain blotted out any thought about Acquisitions or trials or who was watching or consequences. "You are never going to touch me, you sick fuck! You got that?" I seethed with hate, and pulled my hand back to strike him again, but

Gavin gripped my forearm.

"Don't."

"That's right, bitch. Don't." Red was trying to stand up straight, but kept clutching his crotch. "I'll get you back. Don't worry. In a few weeks, I'm going to fuck every hole you got. And there's not a fucking thing you can do about it, you stupid cunt. Merry Christmas to me." He laughed in a high-pitched cough.

I struggled against Gavin's hold, desperate to hurt Red, to make him feel even an ounce of the pain I'd already endured.

"Gavin?" A voice floated down the hall. "Gavin, where are you?"

"Shit. It's Bob." Gavin pulled me next to him and forced me to turn my back on Red and walk away.

Red was still laughing. "Oh, I'm going to have a good time with you Stella. Such a good time. Can't wait to see you at the Christmas trial. Come hungry."

Gavin kept leading me away even though I wished I could go toe to toe with Red and win. I wouldn't. He would beat me. And worse, I feared his words were true. There was nothing I could do about the Christmas trial, no way to pull myself back from the brink. Red would capitalize on it, make me hurt in ways I never had before. He would always have the last laugh, just like everyone here. Even so, I still held onto the slim hope that I could somehow stop it.

"Gavin?" Bob's voice, closer now.

"Right here." We turned the corner to find Bob, Lucius, and Vinemont.

My expression must have tipped Vinemont off that something happened because he was towering over me in an instant. "What?"

"What do you mean?" I dropped my gaze to the floor. I didn't need his help and I certainly didn't want it.

He leaned back to get a view down the hall we'd come from. Red barreled around the corner, mirth still lighting his eyes.

Vinemont advanced on him until they were standing chest to chest. "Red, stay the fuck away from her. I'm not going to tell you again."

"You don't have to. I'm done. Don't worry, I'm a patient man. I'll get my turn at Christmas." He winked at me, though he still kept a protective hand over his crotch.

I hoped his dick was bruised and swollen. I only regretted that I hadn't tried to rip it off.

Lucius stepped up next to his brother. "Stella belongs to me now, Red. If you touch her, speak to her, do anything to her without asking me first, I will skull fuck your little sister." Lucius smirked. "She eighteen yet? Not that it matters."

"Don't you fucking talk about my sister!" Red screamed. His anger was raw, unexpected, the sound catching in his throat.

Somehow, this anger was far more real than any other emotion I'd seen from him. It was strange to think he cared for someone other than himself. But there was no mistaking it. Lucius' jab had hit home. Why?

Vinemont put a hand on Lucius' arm. "Come on. Let's get the meet and greet done and then we can bow out." Vinemont pulled Lucius back, reining in his younger brother.

Red shook his head as if to clear it, the auburn strands sticking to his sweaty forehead.

"Gavin, come." Bob tottered away, his round body swaying like humpty dumpty as he headed toward the staircase to the third floor.

Gavin gave me a small smile and turned to follow.

"We're going, too." Vinemont placed his hand on my lower back, his fingertips hot against my bare skin, and led me forward.

Lucius was close behind and Red followed. We climbed the stairs. The music faded as we rose, until it was only a slight rhythmic bump.

We turned right at the landing and entered a solarium.

The glass ceiling above opened to the night sky. Exotic plants that were painstakingly curated to give the appearance of wildness filled the room.

Branching ropes of wisteria climbed central pillars and fanned out across the panes, creating a patchwork of bark and greenery. I imagined how it must look in the spring, heavy lavender blooms hanging beneath the blue heavens. I closed my eyes, etching the image into my mind so I could paint it later. It would have been beautiful, but tonight the sky was nothing but a dark blur through the glass, no stars, no moon. The air stagnated with conversation and stale cigar smoke. Whatever beauty this room might hold was covered with a fine layer of grime from its occupants.

About two dozen more guests settled here, lounging, talking, drinking. Several older ladies in one group turned toward us, whispering and eyeing me with haughty disdain. Though they were long past their prime, their faces were frozen in an impression of youth—lips too plump, brows too unlined, smiles too improbably white. Like some of the plants in the room, they were sickly sweet and entirely predatory. I shivered and edged closer to Vinemont.

He wrapped his arm around my waist and something inside me calmed. The tempest of emotions Red, and now this room, had whipped up mellowed under Vinemont's touch, and even though I knew I wasn't, I felt safe.

I glanced up and caught his eye, the dark sapphire blue stopping my breath for a second. The memory of him in the cabin that day during the storm, the way he'd worshipped my flesh with his, flitted through my mind. A distant echo of those same feelings scattered through my heart and multiplied until the only thing inside me was his name, a whispered prayer. *Sin.*

He leaned toward me until his lips were at my ear. "I should have told you before. But I have never seen anything more beautiful."

My heart stopped, and then a warmth spread from it to the rest of me. His words were unexpected, and my steps faltered as I tried to keep his pace.

He straightened and looked ahead so that all I could see was his strong profile against the backdrop of the shadowy sky. His grip never failed, I gained my feet again, and we glided through the room.

Unlike the dance floor below, the atmosphere was almost cloyingly serene, and a string quartet played in a corner. The older guests here were sedate, perhaps having swum long enough in an ocean of privilege and depravity that they were now content to sit on the shore and watch the rest of the swimmers struggle and drown.

Cal rose from his perch on a love seat, Brianne sitting next to him, and greeted us. "Welcome, welcome. Make yourselves comfortable. Relax. It's a party after all."

He stepped forward and took my hand. My skin crawled, and Vinemont's fingertips pressed more firmly into my waist.

"Come, let me chat you up. These boys can do without you for a few minutes, right Sin?"

Vinemont froze and focused on me. *Would he refuse?*

Cal faked a laugh. "But, wait, what was I thinking? Lucius is the proud owner now. I was confused, what with the girl on your arm, Sin, instead of your brother's." He gave Vinemont an acid smile and turned to Lucius. "So, may I speak with Stella for a moment?"

Lucius grinned and pulled Brianne up from her seat. Her eyes still bore a glassy sheen, and I wondered if she would even remember tonight. "You talk to that one. I want to *talk* to this one."

"That's my man." Cal laughed as Lucius dragged Brianne a couple of sofas over and hauled her into his lap. "Now, Sin, if you don't mind? I do believe Lucius gave permission." There was an edge in Cal's voice, and his fingers started to crush mine.

"Sin?" Red jerked his head toward the door. "Can I speak to you?"

"You're speaking to me right now." Vinemont didn't

look at Red.

"I mean in private, asshole." Red's anger flared like the head of a match in the dark.

I held my breath. Maybe Vinemont would refuse Cal. Maybe something had changed. I was desperate for it to be true.

It wasn't. Vinemont dropped his hand. Cal sat and yanked me down next to him, the seat still warm from Brianne's presence.

Vinemont held my gaze, unwavering even as Cal put an arm around me and pulled me closer. Renee's words about playing along echoed in my mind, but I still had the urge to fight Cal off, to do anything other than submit. I wanted Vinemont to pull me up and take me out of here. Instead, after a second prompting from a jittery Red, Vinemont broke our connection and walked away to speak with him.

Lucius had long since gotten lost in Brianne, his hand in her dress and his mouth on her neck. I was left with Cal.

"So," he leaned in and inhaled at my ear, "tell me about you, Stella."

"What, you aren't going to drug me first like Brianne?" I tried to shift away from him but his grip tightened on my upper arm.

"You think I drugged her?" He tsked and pierced me with a withering look. "She drugged herself when she got here. She's weak. Can't handle it. You, on the other hand, handle all of it with surprising grace. The way you took that whipping..." He made a humming sound, as if the memory was particularly tasty for him. "I'll never forget the blood on your pale skin."

He released my arm and ran his fingers down my back. I struggled to stay calm.

"You're something special." He moved closer, his mouth at my ear. "Did Sin know you were special when he chose you? Or did he only figure it out once he had a taste?"

"Get off me." I leaned away from him but he clutched my waist and kept me tucked to his side.

"Do you ever behave?" He laughed and let his gaze drop to the deep neckline of my dress and then to the slit at my thigh.

"I'll scream." My heart was racing, fear oozing along my body wherever Cal touched me.

"Do you think anyone here will care? Come now. I just want a little taste is all. I have a thing for redheads." When his lips hit my neck, I had to tamp down my cry. I scanned the room for Vinemont, but he and Red must have stepped into the hall. I couldn't see Lucius, though I had no hope of help from him anyway.

Cal licked up my neck and I couldn't bottle the sound of revulsion that leapt from my lips.

"It's not so bad, is it?" He gripped my chin and wrenched my face to his while he eyed my mouth. I pushed on his chest, ready to scratch and bite if I had to. I couldn't play along, not with this.

"Cal?" A woman's warbling voice sounded from behind us.

Cal released me and I was finally able to breathe again. I scooted away from him until my back hit the arm of the love seat.

He adjusted his bow tie and stood, the fake smile already back on his face. "Ms. Devereaux, back so soon?"

Wait, *Devereaux*? She spoke again. I knew her voice. Something like déjà vu but darker swirled in my stomach. I turned. There, standing at my back were my former stepmother, Marguerite Devereaux and my stepbrother, Dylan.

CHAPTER TEN
STELLA

"DYLAN?"

My stepbrother rushed around the love seat and sat next to me before folding me in his arms.

"How?" My vision swam, hope trying to fire in my breast but unsure if this was some trick by Cal.

"Are you okay?" His embrace crushed me to the point I had to push away just to breathe.

"I am now. But how are you here?" I searched his eyes, willing it all to be real.

"Because, Stella," Cal interrupted, "the Devereauxs have long been a family in the upper echelons of society." He gave Dylan's mother a respectful nod. "But in just this past month, the lovely Marguerite expressed an interest in finally joining our particular party—the very pinnacle of all society. And we are more than happy to have her and her son, of course." Cal smiled like a toothy shark.

I wondered how much Marguerite had to pay to be accepted into this den of monsters. We had never been close when she was briefly married to my father. She saw me as more of an inconvenience than anything else. This must have been Dylan's doing.

Dylan smoothed a hand across my cheek. "Are you okay?"

"I'm fine. I just don't understand—"

"And you never will, Stella. Because we're different breeds." Cal looked down at me, as if I were an unruly child who needed to learn her manners. "Dylan here has an affection for you, clearly, but how much affection can a lion truly have for a lamb? He doesn't realize it, but you're beneath him, just like you're beneath everyone else in this room. It doesn't matter if we dress you up, put jewels on you, or whatever else."

"You don't have to talk to her like that." Dylan's voice was gruff, though he still palmed my cheek tenderly.

"I'm just stating the facts, Dylan. That's all. No need for unpleasantness. Marguerite, may I show you my particular favorite orchid here in the solarium? Give these two a chance to catch up?"

Marguerite stared at me and then her son before shaking her head and taking Cal's arm. She'd studied me the same way the entire time I'd known her, like I was a curious animal or insect. Interesting enough to examine, but too low to approach or engage. Without a word, she walked away as Cal began waxing poetic about plants.

Dylan hugged me again just as fiercely before holding me away from him. "It worked. I can't believe we're in and I'm here with you." He smiled, youth beaming from his tanned skin and light brown eyes.

"Can you get me out?"

His face soured, the corners of his mouth turning downward. "I don't know. Cal hasn't been very forthcoming about the whole process you're caught up in."

"The Acquisition?"

He nodded. "Right. He says there's going to be a big Christmas party next weekend where we'll get the idea of what it's all about."

"Next weekend?" I thought I had more time. I thought I had at least two more weeks. But no, Christmas was coming early. A wave of nausea washed over me, but I had to focus. I needed information.

"Yeah, he says it's a big to-do out at someone's house in a forest up north of here. Two-day party. I have no idea. I'm not much of an outdoorsman, but Cal assured me I'd enjoy the hunting." He shrugged, completely oblivious.

My heart sank and tears burned in my eyes. "So you're coming to the Christmas trial?"

"Yeah, we kind of have to. It's part of the whole joining the club thing. And maybe once I get more in with them, I can get you out. You'll be there, right?"

"Yes." I stared at the floor.

"Stella, what?" He gripped my hands. "And what do you mean by trial?"

"Christmas. It's a trial."

"Like with your dad?"

I shook my head and looked at him again, my tears barely held at bay. "I've already been through one trial."

"I'm not following." He held my hands tighter, as if the pressure would somehow make him understand. But there was only one way he would comprehend what I was talking about. I had to show him.

I twisted my body so I faced away from him. The gasp when he saw my back and the touch of his fingers along my skin made two tears fall—perfect, transitory drops that were lost in the black fabric of my dress.

"Who did this to you?" Dylan's voice was a strangled whisper.

"They all did."

"Cal?" His fingertips stroked across each mark.

"No, but it doesn't matter who did it. It's them. All of them. They all do it." Why didn't I want to tell him Vinemont had inflicted the wounds? I could have said, could have named him, but I didn't.

I looked up and caught Lucius staring at me, his eyes burning even as Brianne was pliant under his touch. She was straddling him now, her skirt hiked up and her hands in his hair. He palmed one of her tits, his other hand on her ass, as she kissed his neck. Even so, his direct gaze was on me, pinning me to the spot. My mind spun out of the conversation with Dylan even as his fingers still traced the memory of the tortures written on my skin.

Lucius gripped Brianne's breast harder, her head lolling back as he twisted her nipple. I swallowed hard, a tingling erupting along my same breast. He pulled down Brianne's dress and latched his mouth on her nipple, his eyes never leaving mine. Her moan cut through the string ensemble and my heart sped up. When he gripped her hair and yanked her head back so that she arched into him, I let out a pent up breath.

"—Stella?"

I forced myself to look away from him, to engage with the one man in this cursed place who I knew cared about me.

"Are they going to do that to your back again at Christmas?" Dylan's face was pale, the color drained like water from a sink.

"No."

He let out a sigh of relief. "Thank God. I don't think I could handle something like that."

"Have you seen my dad?" I blurted it out. I shouldn't have cared what happened to him, but seeing Dylan brought my mangled feelings for my father back to the forefront. Had Dylan's message that my father was ill been true?

"He's fine. Not sick or anything. Don't worry. Just concerned about you. He's the one that thought of this. There was no way to get you out, he said. But maybe if the Devereauxs could get in, we could help you. You're all he talks about. Trust me, he wants you away from here. He wants you safe and back with him."

Dylan's words were meant to comfort me, but they were a rusty blade in my stomach. My father had not only betrayed me, but now he'd betrayed Marguerite and Dylan. Entering this realm was not something done lightly, and though I didn't know for certain, I was sure there was no easy way out. My father had doomed Dylan to become one of the monsters that was seated around us now, the villains in beautiful clothes with perfect manners and a taste for blood.

"Don't change the subject, Stella. What happens at Christmas?" He furrowed his brow.

How can I tell him?

"What happened before…to my back." I shook my head. "Christmas will be worse."

"What could be worse?" He pulled me into his arms and ran his palms down my shoulders. "What could be worse than this?"

A shadow fell across us. "Get your hands off her." Vinemont glowered at Dylan, his hands fisted at his sides, the still-bruised knuckles turning white.

"You bastard. You did this to her, didn't you?" Dylan stood, rage already turning his cheeks a bright shade of crimson.

Vinemont sneered and affected a bored air. "You don't know what you're talking—"

Dylan shoved him, and Vinemont took a few steps back before smirking. "I've been wanting a good fight since I got back from Cuba." He appraised Dylan. "Too bad I still won't get one."

Vinemont was fast, his fist crushing into Dylan's jaw in a scant moment. But Dylan didn't fall. He was strong, well-muscled from rowing and lacrosse. He took the impact and rushed forward, seizing Vinemont around the chest and slamming him into the marble floor. The other guests, smelling blood, stopped their small chatter and watched the show.

"Dylan, stop." I stood and stepped toward them, but they both ignored me.

Vinemont laughed as Dylan caged him with his knees and started raining blows on his face. Vinemont wasn't blocking them, just taking the vicious hits until he saw his moment. Then he aimed a powerful fist to Dylan's ribs. Dylan wailed and fell sideways, clutching his side. Vinemont pushed Dylan onto his back and put a knee on his chest before raising his fist.

"No. Please, don't." I grabbed Vinemont's arm. I knew what he could do, what he was capable of. "Don't."

He turned to me, his eyes wild and wrathful. I let go of his arm and ran my hand down his face, brushing my thumb over his split lip. His flesh burned beneath my touch, but his eyes cooled and he leaned into my palm the slightest bit. I felt it then, the one thing I wished had completely died that night when he'd shown me how truly alone I was. The string that bound us together, the inexorable link that ran from his heart to mine, came back to life. The connection tightened, and he rose as Dylan sputtered. Vinemont took my hand in his and leaned over me. He was so close. Everything stopped. My eyes closed of their own accord and I wanted his kiss, his blood, him. I just wanted him.

"Fuck, Sin. If you aren't going to finish it, I will."

I opened my eyes to see Lucius aiming a kick at Dylan's side. "Stop!"

Too late. Dylan howled with pain as Lucius' foot connected. I dropped to my knees and draped my arm across Dylan as he curled into a ball. I held my free hand up, trying to ward off Lucius.

Lucius straightened his coat and smiled. "Lesson of the day, *Dylan*. Don't fuck with us or our property."

"She's not property." Dylan coughed and rolled to his back.

The chatter started again, the momentary blood sport at an end.

"She's mine, you little shit. That's all you need to know."

"Ignore him. Come on." I helped Dylan into a sitting position. "Are you okay?" I felt along his ribs and he winced. They could have been broken for all I knew. "Can you walk?"

"I-I think so."

Lucius stepped over Dylan's legs to stand at my side and peered down at me. "Come on, Stella."

I glared at him, acid in my gaze. "No! Back off, Lucius."

I hitched my hand under Dylan's arm to try and help him to his feet, but a searing pain along my scalp had me crying out. Lucius wrenched me from the floor by my hair and brought my face to his.

"You will do as I say, Stella. Every—fucking—time." His eyes flashed and his voice was thick with malice.

I spat in his face, anger flowing up through me like lava. "Fuck you."

"Enough," Vinemont growled, and wrapped his arm around my waist, pulling me away from Lucius. I dug my fingers into him and tried to pry his hand loose. His mouth was at my ear. "Stop making a scene. Stop making us have to hurt you."

I stilled against his chest, but scowled at Lucius. He drew out his kerchief and popped it before wiping his face. He smiled as he did it, as if enjoying some private joke.

Everything had turned into a fight. More blood, more pain—I was awash in the cruelest of emotions, and in a few days, things would only get worse.

Dylan struggled to his feet, his breath coming in quick pants. I wanted to go to him, but I didn't. Vinemont's strong arms had me rooted to the spot.

Cal and Marguerite emerged from amongst the fronds and fountains, laughing politely. Dylan smoothed his jacket and shot Lucius a dark look before turning to his mother.

"How was it?" he asked.

"The orchid? Glorious," Marguerite simpered. "Makes me think of having the greenhouse at the Acres rebuilt."

Cal gave a slight bow and handed Marguerite off to Dylan, who smiled despite what must have been an aching pain in his ribs on both sides.

"What did I miss?" Cal asked.

Given his narrowed gaze and even haughtier demeanor, I surmised Cal never missed much of anything.

"Just some rough and tumble antics. You know how it is when boys get together." Vinemont's smooth words covered the jagged scrapes and bruises of only moments before.

"I do. But we want to treat our new guests with utmost respect at all times. We are so pleased to have them here in our midst." Cal's chiding tone was buried in an over-friendly smile as he patted Dylan on the back.

"Of course. Glad to be here." Dylan fell into his easy manners, learned through a life of the best schools, fancy dinners, debutante balls, and the like. He wasn't rocking the boat in front of Cal. Maybe he was smarter than I'd given him credit for in the past.

When he shook Cal's hand, I realized that some of what Cal had said was true. Dylan was one of them. He was born and bred to fall right in step with these people. Doubt crept into my mind. Marguerite must have made a sizeable investment to get into this party. Dylan would be risking his family fortune and his future if he tried to take my side in anything having to do with the Acquisition.

"Well, it's been fun, but Stella here will turn into a peasant—I mean pumpkin—if we don't get her back home soon." Lucius patted Dylan on the back far too hard, and Dylan gritted his teeth at the second assault.

Vinemont stayed at my back the entire time, his clean scent enveloping me, and his heart beating against me. His arm was still at my waist, a sturdy band of bone and muscle that kept me locked tight to his body. I got the feeling that if Cal asked for me to sit with him now, Vinemont would tell him to go to hell.

Once Lucius was done with Dylan, he stalked over to me. I kicked my chin up and met his stare. I was trapped between the two Vinemont men, the one at my back an enigma, the one in front an open book of deceit.

"Take my arm and walk out of here, Stella." Lucius' voice was a low, dangerous purr.

"Do it." Vinemont's voice in my ear. He shifted and

pulled his arm away, his fingers trailing along my stomach and making my skin tingle as he went. I wanted to stay with him. I wanted to believe that maybe something was different, that maybe he felt the same connection I couldn't escape. But he'd turned me over to Lucius.

Dylan gave me the slightest smile, a hidden "chin up" that tried to warm my heart, but fell short. He didn't know what Christmas would bring. I did.

The string quartet began playing "Silent Night" as I took Lucius' arm and turned my back on the one small bit of sanctuary I'd found since all this began.

The car ride back was silent. I chose the front passenger seat before another idiotic fight could break out. Luke smiled as he got the door for me, perhaps aware of what I was doing.

As soon as we stopped at the house, I darted out of the car and up the front steps, my shoes left behind in the car. Farns opened the front door and I blew past him, seeking the shelter of my room. I had to think about what happened, to sort out what Dylan's presence might mean for me. And, most of all, I needed to talk to the one person who might be able to shed more light—Renee.

Though I didn't hear following steps, I closed my door and leaned against it. It felt as if the filth of the party coated me, Cal's fingerprints meshing with my skin and tainting me just like everything else he touched. I stripped the dress off, not caring that I left it in a heap in the floor along with the panties and jewels.

I ran a hot shower and stood beneath the steaming rain, my makeup running down my face and my hair wilting. I just wanted to be clean, to have not a single trace of Cal or Red or anyone else left on my skin. I picked the bobby pins from my hair and shampooed all of it. Then I lathered myself up, scrubbing until my skin was raw. I rinsed off and stepped out.

I reached for my towel, but it wasn't on the bar. Movement behind me had me whirling. It was Vinemont, the towel in his hands. He wrapped it around my shoulders and clutched it closed in front of me. He still wore his tuxedo pants, but his jacket was gone and his shirt halfway unbuttoned, as if he'd been in the middle of disrobing when he'd changed course and come to see me. His eyes were half hooded, lust and heat wafting from him like a fire.

My body tingled, anticipation and fear playing along my skin. "Were you watching me?"

"Yes." His voice was a low rasp. He was so still, but his jaw was tight and the sinews in his neck even tighter.

I moved the towel down under my arms and tucked one end into the other over my chest. "If you're done with your peep show, I'd like to get dressed and get some sleep."

I edged past him even though he took up so much space. The room, my head, and my heart were all filled with him.

"Dylan can't save you." His words were cold, far colder than the heat of his eyes.

"I don't expect anyone to save me. I expect to save myself." I forced myself to walk slowly to my dresser, not even looking as Vinemont approached. I grabbed a pair of panties and shimmied them up my legs beneath the towel. Then I chose a tank top and pulled it over my head, dropping the towel once it was in place. I turned back to him, my hands on my hips. He was so close, having crept up behind me while I dressed.

"What do you want?"

"Do you think this will stop me?" He plucked the hem of my tank top and ran his fingers over the edge.

"One minute I'm beautiful, the next you're in here threatening me?"

"This isn't a threat. I'm simply telling you." His eyes bored into me as he fisted the material of my top and pulled me to him. "Dylan can't save you. You can't get out of this. I will never let you out of it. Understand?"

"Understand what? That you want me, that you have feelings for me, but you'll also gladly let me be raped by all your friends so you can win some game? I got it. Now get the fuck out." His fist had tightened as I spoke, drawing me closer.

Without heels, I had to crane my head up to see him, to look into the dark pools of his eyes. "I will do anything to win, to make sure Lucius wins, to beat the others. Anything, Stella. Even if that means that every fucking man in Louisiana rapes you a hundred times over. No matter how much that sickens me. Yes."

I should have seen it coming, should have known that nothing I thought about him was real. No one who had feelings for me could say such a thing. My eyes watered. I should have been used to pain. I'd endured so much of it over the past weeks, but his words struck at my very center, like a shard of ice skewering my soul.

"Get out." I stared at the floor, not wanting him to see my tears when they fell.

"If Dylan contacts you, I'll know." He gripped my hair and wrenched my eyes back to his. Tears ran down my temples as he spoke in a harsh whisper. "Don't try anything. If I find out you've been speaking or even trying to speak to him, you can say goodbye to this room, these nice things." He yanked my shirt hard, the seams splitting under my arms. "These clothes. Everything. I'll have you kept naked and bound in the stables with a horse blanket for warmth. See, Stella? That was a threat. And I intend to make good on it if you even so much as think about trying to fuck us in this Acquisition. Do I make myself clear?"

I swallowed hard, tears thickening in my throat as terror pounded in my heart. Vinemont shook me, my arms flailing before I latched onto his shirt. My already scattered mind exploded in waves of desperation. I had to get away from him.

319

"I asked if you understood, Stella." His intense gaze crushed me more than his hands ever could. "Do you?"

"Yes."

He shoved me back into the dresser.

"I'm glad we had this little chat." He turned and walked out, slamming my door behind him.

I sank to my knees, the sobs uncontrollable. I thought I had something figured out. I thought I was getting Vinemont to turn, to put me ahead of being Sovereign. I was wrong. So wrong. I sobbed until I couldn't breathe, until I thought I would vomit. I cried for what felt like hours. So much of me poured out and into the rug beneath me.

Where was Renee? She should have come. She had to know I was here. I lay on my side and clutched my arms to me until the last tear fell and I was silent. Everything inside me was fractured and broken. Vinemont had taken what I was and smashed it into the ground.

But I was the one who'd given him the ability, who'd let him in. I'd allowed him to hurt me by foolishly hoping I could change him. I was the one who'd changed, who'd let myself be taken in by a man whose sole desire was to use me in every way possible before tossing me aside. When would I learn?

I picked myself up and crawled into my bed, the soft whir of the ceiling fan the only thing competing with the sluggish beat of my heart. My thoughts flickered to the hidden knife before I shoved the thought back in its box and turned the lock.

This was a setback, and, I forced myself to believe, a good thing. Now I could seduce Lucius and turn him on Vinemont without any second thoughts. I burrowed into my crisp linen sheets and forced my breathing to even out, forced my eyes to close, and forced myself to give up any hope of warming Vinemont's cold heart.

CHAPTER ELEVEN
SINCLAIR

I PACED MY study, tossing back a bourbon before pouring another. It was close to daybreak. I'd been in here for a couple of hours, steeling myself for what had to be done next. A dull ache emanated from my chest and I wondered if it would ever go away. But it was necessary. All of it.

I should have gone even further with Stella, but I couldn't. The pain in her eyes was enough. The fear—even better. I wanted her afraid. It was the only thing I could use to keep her in line now that she knew about her father. So much was riding on her, how she behaved, how I, and now Lucius, treated her. It was all a skillful dance put on for the entertainment of the Sovereign. Tonight, I could feel his favor slipping. And after my conversation with Red, I realized things were even more precarious than I'd thought.

I had to tell Lucius. It was time. After his performance at Cal's party, he needed to know the real stakes, the real penalty. And our grasp on Stella was weakening by the moment now that Dylan was a possible player. Could I trust Lucius to stay strong with the weight of the truth bearing down on him?

I poured another glass and left my study as the first rays of the sun shot out across the dead grass and peeked through the leafless trees. My legs were heavy on the stairs, each step painful in more ways than one. Stella had done well fixing up my leg, but our doctor had cleaned the wound and re-stitched it just the day before. It still burned like a son of a bitch. Fatigue clouded my vision. I only hoped it hadn't clouded my judgment.

I passed my bedroom on the way to Lucius'. I wanted nothing more than to sink into my bed and into a dreamless sleep. No, that wasn't true. The one thing I wanted more was to walk to the other wing of the house and get in Stella's bed, pull her close, and fall asleep with her head above my heart. But that would require her trust and something more—her love. I almost laughed, my chest shaking from the strained chuckle caught beneath my ribs.

I'd heard her sobs, stood outside her door and listened to the aftermath of what I'd done. She would never let me in again; not in her bed, and definitely not in her heart. It was better for her this way. I had to destroy her or watch my brother do it. Wanting her, feeling her entwined in my very soul, had nothing to do with the Acquisition. And it couldn't. I wouldn't let it interfere.

I tucked a glass under my arm and swung Lucius' door open. His room was dark, his curtains drawn so that only a slice of the growing daylight showed through.

"What?" An orange circle flamed in the dark and then faded.

"Mom would kill you if she knew you were smoking in the house." Wisps of smoke circled in the air across the room, folding back in on themselves before spreading into nothing.

"Good thing she doesn't know, then. What do you want?"

"We need to talk." I closed the door behind me before settling at the foot of his bed and holding out the second drink.

"Your good bourbon?" He took the glass and stubbed out his cigarette. "Did shit just get real, or what?"

"It got real a while ago. As soon as I was chosen for the Acquisition this year."

"You finally going to tell me the rules?" He sat up higher against his pillow and sipped his drink.

"Yes." I sighed and drained my glass, wishing the alcohol would kill the stings that ricocheted inside and out of me.

"About fucking time. Shit. Hit me. I'm ready, drama queen."

"There are only seven." *Seven rules to see you through. Seven rules to live by. Seven rules to make it hurt. Seven rules to kill by.* Mom's voice when I'd told her we were chosen this year echoed in my mind. I'd known for quite some time that the mother from my earliest memories was gone. But I didn't know how far gone until I'd heard her scratchy song, sung with glee.

"Seven rules? I'm all ears." He leaned forward, the strip of daylight cutting across his face.

"Let's start with the first, and most important rule." I wondered if a weight would lift after I'd told him, if I'd suddenly be lighter or freer. I doubted it.

"What's that?" He polished off his drink.

I met his eyes, knowing I was about to knock the wind out of him worse than I ever could with my fists. It would kill him just as sure as it was killing me, but it couldn't be helped. Not anymore.

CHAPTER TWELVE
STELLA

THE MORNING CAME, and with it, still no Renee. Then another dawn, and another. I hadn't seen Vinemont or Lucius in the days since the party. Farns apologized profusely, but gave me no information about what had become of Renee. Laura took over Renee's duties in my room. She was tight-lipped, far more than she had ever been before.

It was as if the house had just shut down around me, shunning me and making me the outsider I was. No information, no interaction. Just me, sitting here, and waiting until the Christmas trial. Four days away and still no sign of my friend. The only person I spoke to other than Farns and Laura was Teddy.

"Want to go for a ride today?"

I glanced out the window behind him as we ate breakfast. "Is it going to rain? Or storm? Or hail? Or *lightning*?"

He grinned and checked his phone. "Nope, only sunny and cold. It'll be fun. I'll save you from any danger, promise."

"Aren't you the valiant one?" I smiled and took a bite of French toast. Cinnamon and sugar played on my tongue to the point I wanted to moan.

"At your service, my lady," Teddy said. "I've been meaning to go out for a ride. Get some air and just cruise, especially since Sin and Lucius aren't around to tell me no."

"Where are they? Do you know?" I'd already tried to get some Renee information out of him to no avail. Might as well take my chances and see if he'd spill about his brothers.

"There was more trouble in Cuba. Lucius flew down a couple days ago." He finished his orange juice. "I don't know where Sin got off to. He was here yesterday on a conference call with Lucius and some investors, but then he was gone again. Maybe back in town? I'm not sure. He keeps tabs on *me*, not the other way around." He shrugged, his broad shoulders pulling at the buttons on his plaid flannel shirt.

"Will Lucius be back by Friday?" That was when the trial was supposed to start. If Lucius wasn't back, did that mean I wouldn't have to go? I didn't dare to hope, not for a second.

"I don't know. What happens Friday?" He leaned back and set his napkin on the table before patting his stomach like it was full. Even under the shirt I could tell he was all lean muscle, just like his brothers.

"Nothing. I'm not really sure." The Stella who lived in this house, who wore my clothes, and answered to my name was a liar. I wondered if that would be something that remained, something I would never be able to shake, just like so many other dark souvenirs from my time here.

"Stella?" He put his warm hand on mine. "What is it?"

I forced a smile. "Let's ride. I think it'll do me good and clear my head."

"All right. Don't tell me. Just like everyone else here never tells me anything." He rolled his eyes. "Come on. I need to change. You do, too. Got any leather?" He stood.

"Leather?"

He grinned. "Yeah, for riding."

"I need leather to ride a horse?"

He looked over my head and out toward the garage.

"Depends on what sort of horse we're talking about."

I took his meaning and crossed my arms over my chest. "I don't ride motorcycles."

"You do today." He gripped under my arm and pulled me up. "Live a little. Come on."

Maybe he was right. It wasn't like I had a lot to lose. Not anymore. I grabbed my coffee and downed it before slapping the cup back onto the table. "All right, hell on wheels, let's do it."

We went upstairs, and I inspected my closet. Renee had, in fact, gotten me a brown leather jacket. I pulled it from the hanger and inhaled deeply, the smell delicious and strong. I yanked on some jeans, socks, and boots. Then a tank, sweater, and the jacket, along with some gloves. After pulling my hair into a low, messy ponytail, and snagging some sunglasses from the back of my closet, I felt almost badass enough to ride a motorcycle.

Teddy swung my door open and strolled in, his shitkickers making steady clumps as he walked around my room.

"Don't knock or anything." I stepped out of the closet.

"I gave you plenty of time not to be naked. And like you said before, I'm valiant. I wouldn't have looked or anything." He waggled his eyebrows. "Well, let me rephrase. I wouldn't have taken pictures, but I definitely would have looked."

"Perv." I gave him the finger and walked past him. "I'm ready to meet my maker. Let's go."

We pounded down the stairs and took the short walk to the garage. I'd glanced in here a few times, but I'd never actually been inside. Cars and bikes filled every bit of free space. I had no clue what I was actually looking at, especially given that most of the cars bore emblems I didn't even recognize.

Teddy stepped toward the back to a row of polished bikes. He chose one on the end, its black metal glinting under the shop lights.

"This one's mine. I named her Black Widow."

"That's not a very reassuring name for a motorcycle." I ran my fingers down the smooth leather seat. The chrome was rubbed to a high shine, and the bike was low and sleek. If it was half as fast as it looked, I might be screaming my head off before we even made it off the property.

"You'll love it. Here." He tinkered with a black helmet and handed it to me. I removed my sunglasses, slid the helmet on, and then snugged my sunglasses back over my eyes.

He slipped his helmet on, and his voice crackled to life in my ear. "It has Bluetooth, so we can talk as we ride. Also, music." He tapped the screen of his phone and a deep bass starting pumping, backed by someone shredding a guitar. "I've already got some tunes picked out."

"Born to be wild." I couldn't help but smile.

He walked the bike out to the front of the garage and threw his leg over. I followed and climbed on behind him.

"Hang on to me. I don't mind." The music dimmed as his voice sounded clearly.

"Yeah, I'm sure you don't." I wrapped my arms lightly around him as he fired it up. The rumble shook me in all the right places and made my thighs tense against the seat.

"Sounds like heaven, doesn't it? You ready?"

I propped my chin on his shoulder, our helmets touching. "I'm ready."

He gunned the engine and we were gone, shooting up the drive, past the house, under the trees, and out into the daylight that filtered down through feathery clouds.

The wind whipped around us as he sped up, the tires devouring the distance to the gate. It was already opening by the time we reached it. He must have had a remote key somewhere on the bike. He turned right, toward town and away from the interstate.

I clung even more tightly to him through the curves and twists in the road, pressing my chest into his back as we tore through the barren countryside. The fields were gray, crops long since harvested. His music changed from hard rock to some sort of electronic dance music. We kept going until the road widened into more lanes, the traffic increasing slightly as the area became more populated. I didn't know how long we would ride, but I didn't care. I wanted to fly with him, to just be alive for a little while and not worry about the trial.

"Ready to go a little faster?"

"Faster than this?" I asked as the countryside whizzed by.

"Way faster. Straightaway up ahead. Hold on to your tits, Stella."

I laughed, but the roar of the engine drowned out the sound as he pushed the bike harder and we hurtled forward, passing a couple of cars until we made it to the straightaway. The road rose up to meet us as he leaned forward, me glued to his back. We sped so fast that we were nothing but a whoosh of speed and sound, oncoming cars only a transitory blip. My heart pounded, pure adrenaline pumping through my veins.

"Wooo!" Teddy's voice in my ear. No, it was both of ours. Both of us let out the exhilaration and soaked up the danger, the life, and the realness of the moment.

His heart pounded against my palm, matching the chaotic beat of my own. This was the freedom I longed for, a beautiful escape, if only fleeting.

We glided for a little while longer before he let off the accelerator, the bike calming down though our hearts still raced.

He reached back and squeezed my knee. "Fuckin' A, right?"

"Couldn't have said it better myself."

We rumbled into town, the familiar streets no longer holding the same charm for me they once did. He drove through the town square. We passed the courthouse where my father's trial had been held and the jail where he'd been taken after his arrest. Dark memories tempered the excitement of only moments before.

"Can we go left here?" I asked.

"Sure. Whatever you want." He turned as I'd directed, and I gave him a few more instructions before we cruised down my old street.

"Down toward the end." Toward my father's house. There was no reason for me to do it, to torture myself like this. But I had to see.

We rolled up and I gasped. The house's roof was gone, the top of the windows blackened, and the front porch fallen in.

"What is it?" Teddy cut the music. "What's wrong?"

"That's my father's house." Worry twisted my insides.

Teddy pulled into the drive and stopped, shutting the engine off and kicking out the stand. He helped me off and I walked up to my home, or what was left of it. I pulled off my helmet and tucked it under my arm.

"What happened?" Teddy stood beside me and craned his head back to see the charred tips of what remained of the sloping eaves.

"I don't know. I had no idea…" All I could do was stare, shell-shocked that this piece of my past had been erased. All my paintings, the mementos I had to remember my mother—gone.

Teddy pulled a glove off and went to the nearest window before pressing his fingers along the wood. "Not wet and the inside looks dry, too. It must have happened a while ago."

"Why would no one tell me?"

"Because you didn't need to know." Vinemont's hand clapped down on my shoulder and I jumped.

Teddy turned. "Sin—"

Vinemont cut him off. "Imagine my surprise when I was driving home after spending all night at the office and I saw a bike speeding past me at an insane clip. Who could it be?" He squeezed my shoulder so I couldn't turn around and face him. "I wondered who was foolhardy enough to drive at such a breakneck pace, who was dumb enough to ride at his back, and further, who did I know that had such a fast bike?"

I gripped his fingers and pried two of them loose before darting forward and whirling. "Keep your fucking hands off me, Vinemont."

He wore a dark blue dress shirt, the throat open, and a pair of black slacks. The sun lit his hair, coloring the deep brown a milk chocolate. He had a shadow of light stubble across his cheeks, rough and masculine. In his eyes I saw a seething anger.

"Look, Sin. I'm sorry. It was my idea, though. Not hers." Teddy walked up beside me. "You don't need to like, punish her or anything."

"I don't need to be having this discussion while at least two neighbors are watching through their curtains, no." He kept his voice low, but each word was tinged with wrath. "But here we are anyway. One big happy fucking family."

"Sin, we'll go the speed limit on the way back, okay?" Teddy grabbed my helmet and lifted it above my head.

Before he could put it on, Vinemont said, "Leave it. She's riding with me. You are riding ahead of me the whole way and *we* are going the speed limit. Got it?"

"I'm not a kid, Sin. I don't have to do what you say." Teddy handed my helmet back to me and squared his shoulders.

"I have ways of keeping you in line. Don't make me use them."

"What, are you going to cut me off?" Teddy threw his hands out to his sides and his voice rose. "Make me pay for college? What are you going to do?"

"No. None of that. But do you remember the first day you met Stella?"

Teddy shifted from one foot to the other. "Yes."

"I can make her do a lot more than just stand naked. And I can make you watch all of it. Is that what you want? Would you like that? And another thing, in case that's not enough to get your attention. Laura. I can make sure you never see her again."

Teddy slammed his helmet on the ground. "Goddammit, Sin! Why are you like this? What happened to the you that existed before the Acquisition? The one who helped me with homework because Mom was too drugged up or spaced out to notice I was even there? The one who encouraged me to go to med school? The one who taught me how to ride a fucking bike?" He pointed to Black Widow. "Where did you go?"

Vinemont remained completely unmoved. His placid demeanor in the face of such a heartfelt plea sent a chill down my spine. How had I thought for one moment that he was anything other than a monster?

"The same place you're going. Right back to the house, in front of me, and at a reasonable speed. Now shut the fuck up, get your helmet on, and get on the bike. Stella, get in the goddamn car." He turned on his heel and stalked through the unkempt grass, back to the car.

"Just go." Teddy was defeated, crushed under Vinemont's elegant shoe. Just like me. "There's no talking to him like this. I'll see you back at the house."

"I'm sorry, Teddy."

"It's not your fault." He glared at his brother but then his expression softened. "If I told you he wasn't like this, not really, would you believe me?"

I didn't want to give him the bad news—I already knew this was the real Vinemont.

"Ride safe." I gave him a weak smile before walking to the black sedan. I tossed the helmet into the back and sank into the passenger side before slamming the door shut.

"Did you do this?" I asked as he pulled from the curb.

"Do what?" Vinemont sighed and waited for Teddy to ride out ahead of him.

"Burn down my house."

He laughed, the sound filling the car's interior and making me flinch. "Are you still laying your father's crimes at my feet?"

"What?" I glanced back at the ruined house that held so many memories for me, good and bad. "Are you saying my father did it?"

"Oh, look who finally figured something out. Well done, Stella, really. I'd clap, but as you can see, I'm driving." His sneer had me looking away, looking at anything but him. "You don't believe me?"

"I didn't say that." After what my father had done to me, I wouldn't put anything past him.

"Money, Stella. Insurance money, to be exact. He torched it all. He cashed in on that house, just like he cashed in on you."

He drove around the square and turned onto the highway that led back to my prison. My breathing turned shallow as I thought of everything that had happened to me in the burned-out husk behind me, how the last time I'd left it, I thought I was doing it for all the right reasons. The betrayals layered on betrayals began to suffocate me like dirt on my grave, and I couldn't get enough air. The metal and glass closed in on me, and I clamped my eyes shut, trying to ward off my rising panic.

"Stella?" Vinemont's voice came through like we were at opposite ends of a tin can telephone.

I gulped in more air, trying to stay alive, to breathe. I just had to make it to the next moment, to keep going to the next and the next until they all fell over like a long line of dominoes, and at the end was freedom, *my* freedom. But my thoughts began to dim and I still couldn't get enough air.

"Stella!"

The car stopped and hands were on my shoulders, pulling me out and into the cold winter wind.

"Breathe, Stella. Slowly. Slowly."

I opened my eyes and stared up into Vinemont's face. I staggered back, shrinking away from him even as something in me reacted to the worry in his eyes. I shook my head. He was only worried I wouldn't be able to win for him. He would violate me. They all would. I couldn't breathe. I couldn't see. I stumbled and fell back against the passenger door as he advanced.

"No," I croaked.

"Stella, please." His voice, so different from just a few moments ago, was soaked in the same pain that burned in my lungs, in my mind.

He took another step. I finally got my breath and used it to scream. I screamed and screamed, the sound ripped from my throat and piercing the air. Each peel of despair carried every horror, every unwanted touch, every painful lash, and every desolate thought. I couldn't breathe, I couldn't be free, but I could scream. I screamed until I crumpled. He caught me in his arms and crushed me to his chest as my lungs gave out, the last shriek dying on the wind as he held me close.

No one heard. Only the desolate fields, the withered scarecrows, and Vinemont.

CHAPTER THIRTEEN
STELLA

I COULDN'T SLEEP. The last full night of rest I'd gotten was when Vinemont had brought me home after my meltdown on the roadside. That restful night had more to do with a dose of narcotics from the family doctor than anything else. I hadn't cared about being drugged. I was emptied out. Every last bit of me had been screamed into the cold air as my tormentor held me.

But the trial was here. Lucius had returned from Cuba the previous night. I knew he would. There was no escape for me. I would be abused, likely many times over, and it would start today. The sun had risen an hour ago, the rays illuminating the quilts, each one telling a story I didn't care to hear.

Renee was still missing. Her absence added to the long list of disappointments already lodged in my heart. I'd stopped by her room several times, but she was never there. Her bed was always neatly made. I'd peered at the stairs to the third floor, and even taken a few steps once before Laura hurried down the hall and shook her head, warning in her eyes. After that, I'd stopped asking about Renee.

A knock at my door made me turn my head. "Yes?" My

335

voice was scratchy.

"It's time." Lucius didn't barge in and order me around. He stayed out of sight.

"I'm coming."

"Downstairs in an hour. Dress warm, and wear comfortable shoes."

Before I could get in a snide reply, his footsteps were already retreating down the hallway. *Dress warm.*

I rose and showered, taking my time to feel every bit of the hot water. I ignored the paleness of my face in the mirror, the shake in my hands as I brushed my hair. Dressing as instructed, I donned a dark green sweater, black puffer jacket, jeans, and boots. I couldn't shake the feeling I was dressing myself for my own funeral. I didn't bother with makeup. I knelt next to my nightstand and took out the knife. The unyielding metal gave me an odd sense of comfort and served an even more basic purpose—defense. I turned the blade over and over in my hands before I wrapped the tape around it and shoved it down into my boot.

I met Lucius and Vinemont downstairs in the breakfast room. Lucius had dressed warmly in a black sweater and jeans, and Vinemont wore his usual work attire. Neither man looked at me.

I took my seat and picked at my food. If I ate a bite, I was sure it would come right back up. Lucius didn't seem particularly hungry either, and Vinemont only drank coffee.

I stopped even attempting to look interested, laying my fork down and sitting back in my chair. "I hate the waiting. Let's go."

Lucius nodded in agreement and stood. Vinemont ignored him, staring straight ahead as if he watched a ghost known only to him. I rose and followed Lucius out of the dining room and down the hall. In the foyer, he turned, his face more solemn than I'd ever seen it. There wasn't so much as a hint of amusement or his acerbic wit. Only focus.

His seriousness scared me more than anything. I

couldn't control the shudder that went through me.

He grabbed my hands and brought them to his chest. "You can do this. We can do this, okay? Remember what I said to you in Cuba? All of it still stands. You just have to get through this."

I lifted my eyes to his. "And then I have to get through the next, and the next? What are the last two, Lucius? Are you going to flay my skin from my body? Scar me beyond recognition? What?"

"One thing at a time. And, no. None of those things. This one is…"

"The worst?" I finished for him.

"I think so. But I don't know what Cal is planning for the other two." He gripped my neck and pulled me toward him before dropping a kiss on the top of my head. "Trust me. We'll get through it. We'll get through all of them."

I wanted to be heartened, to take his words as some sort of comfort. But they were hollow. Getting through this trial was my cross to bear, not his. I would be crucified right along with the other two Acquisitions while Lucius threw dice at my feet.

I closed my eyes and remembered my father. The way he was before his arrest, before his trial, before any infernal contracts. The one that had held me as I cried for my mother on nights too numerous to count. The one who'd saved me from my own attempt at self annihilation. The one who, even as I felt the sting of his deceit, still lived in my heart. I needed my loving father there, giving me courage to do what I had to do, even if he was nothing more than a specter haunting my memories.

Farns rolled a couple of suitcases through the foyer, jarring me from my thoughts. I followed him onto the porch.

"I hope your trip isn't long." He smiled down at me, clueless about what was going to happen. If he'd known, he never would have smiled like that.

I hugged him. Just an instinct. He made a surprised noise

and hugged me back.

"Thanks, Farns. I just needed..." I stepped away from him. "Just thanks."

"Anytime, miss." Pink crept into his paper thin cheeks.

"Stella?" Vinemont appeared as Lucius took the bags down to Luke, the driver. "A word?" I couldn't read him—asking or intimidating all seemed to have merged into one.

Farns shuffled past him and into the house.

"What?" I didn't move toward him. I wouldn't.

He walked out to me, the sun highlighting his tired eyes and sunken cheeks. He looked like he hadn't slept or eaten in days. When he stuffed his hands in his pockets, the muscles in his forearms flexed, making the vines writhe. "I just wanted to say, not that it matters, not that it will help..." He sighed, as if having trouble grabbing ahold of his thoughts as they flittered away before him. "I would gladly take your place if I could. But I can't. And I need you to get through this. And I need..."

"What?" I asked again. He'd already taken so much, and now he was asking for even more. That connection between us, the one I'd felt so strongly, was withered now, dead on the vine. He couldn't ask any more of me. But I had to know, all the same.

"Stella?" Lucius called, but had the good sense to stay by the car.

I held Vinemont's gaze, demanding he finish his thought. "What else do you need from me?"

"I need you to come back to me." His words were so soft and low I almost missed them.

I stared at him and tried to misinterpret his words, tried to make it seem like he wanted me to come back so the Acquisition could continue and the Vinemonts could win. But seeing his eyes, and the sadness and pain welling in them, I knew it wasn't that. He wanted me to come back to him. No, he *needed* it. He'd only given me glimpses of this man—the one who hurt, who felt, who needed. And now he'd laid himself bare.

"Stella. We have to go. Come on."

Lucius' irritated command knocked me out of my reverie. I did have to go. I had an appointment to keep, one that would leave me scarred and broken for the rest of my life. And the reason I had to go was this man, the one whose regretful eyes and words were nothing compared to the pain I was about to feel. It took everything in me, but I wasn't going to help the spider anymore. I wasn't going to hasten my own downfall by jumping into his web. Not again.

I turned without a word and hurried down the stairs. Luke helped me into the back seat and closed the door. I didn't look at Vinemont, even though I knew he hadn't moved, his gaze still seeking me out even behind the privacy glass. Lucius slid in and settled next to me as Luke drove away. I kept my eyes down, never turning back.

Lucius and I didn't speak as we drove steadily northward. He took some calls, half of them conducted in Spanish as we cruised along the smooth pavement. My hands couldn't stay still, worrying away at each other or twisting the hem of my sweater. Eventually, Lucius reached out mid-conversation and snagged my right hand in his, pulling it over onto his thigh as he kept talking about sugar cane crops and the costs of production.

I let him keep it. I could worry away on the inside just as well with or without that hand. I kept trying to clear my mind. Thinking about Vinemont's words or, alternatively, replaying Renee's story of hypothermia and unforgivable violations only made the fear roar louder than my hatred. I wanted the hatred to win out, to suffocate my fear until I was nothing but a raging flame of anger. Even as I tried to master it, the dread seeped in, coloring every thought with a dirty film.

The landscape changed during the drive, the trees getting thicker as more pines mixed in with the dormant oaks and hardwoods. We were in the middle of national forest land when Luke pulled off the interstate onto a two-lane highway. Our route took us farther into the woods, the bleak trees creeping up close to the road on either side.

Lucius tapped his phone off, finally ending a particularly heated call with Javier. He gave my hand a light squeeze but didn't look at me.

After another half hour, Luke turned into a paved lane blocked by a gate similar to that on the Vinemont property. At the top of each door was a stag, its horns magnificent and overdone. Luke rolled down his window and spoke to the attendant standing out front. Then we passed through the gate and into the encroaching woods. The drive meandered through rolling hills, the sun shining with ease through the barren trees.

Before long, we spied the glint of a car ahead of us, and we joined what seemed to be a long procession winding along the narrow drive. Eventually, the woods opened into a wide clearing, and a massive log structure rose from the side of a hill. It was enormous, the size of a small hotel, out in the middle of nowhere. The roof had several apexes, each one an A-frame with a large sheet of glass enclosing the front of the house. The oak logs were rustic, but the glass was modern, glinting in the early afternoon sun.

The cars moved in an orderly row, each pausing at a valet station before parking in a field off to the right. Luke pulled to the front of the line, and the valet greeted us and opened our doors. I stepped out into the bitter air and stuffed my hands in my pockets. I didn't want anyone to touch me.

Lucius walked around to me after telling Luke to bring up the bags.

We climbed the stairs behind an elderly couple who had a hard time managing it. Neither Lucius nor I offered to assist. If they fell down and broke their necks, it was all the better for me as far as I was concerned.

We made it to the upper deck where all the windows opened out onto the landscape. I looked back and realized the house was situated on the highest ridge of the area, giving an expansive vista of the forest beyond.

"Come in, come in." Cal's voice had me slowing my

pace. I could stand the frigid air more than I could stand his presence.

"Sheriff Wood! Welcome. Glad you could make it." Cal rattled off names with his usual exuberance as the greeting line moved along.

The elderly couple finally made it into the house through a pair of rustic wood and metal front doors. Lucius put a hand on my lower back and guided me forward. Cal, wearing a ridiculous Christmas sweater, gripped my upper arms and air kissed me on each cheek.

"So nice to see you again, Stella. Lucius, welcome."

Thankfully, Cal went on greeting the people behind us so we slipped in without any more fanfare. The house was a work of art—beams in a lattice work across the high ceiling, and glass giving a full 180-degree view of the ridges and valleys in the distance.

People were everywhere, talking, drinking, and mingling. The sound system played jaunty Christmas tunes as I caught pieces of conversations about the "fun of the last Acquisition Christmas trial" and "what does Cal have up his sleeve for this year?" My stomach churned as they crowed about what a good time they intended to have over the weekend.

I spotted Gavin ahead, his tall frame giving him a boost above most of the surrounding guests. Surging forward, I pushed through to him.

"Stella." He hugged me.

"Hi."

"I can't exactly say I'm glad you made it." He pulled me away and shook his head, the dark circles under his eyes telling me he hadn't slept, either. "But, if we have to be here, at least we're together."

"You aren't together." Lucius caught up to me. "Bob, get your Acquisition on a fucking leash, would you?"

Bob began stuttering, his face turning red almost instantly. "Gavin. Stop talking to her. She's the enemy."

Gavin bent down by my ear and quickly whispered. "I

got your back."

He straightened and moved away toward Bob before I could reciprocate. I didn't know if it would be true, me saying I had his back, but I would do my best.

"What did he say?" Lucius maneuvered us toward another set of stairs with an attendant at the top.

"Nothing."

"Lucius?" A blonde woman in skin-tight jeans and a thin white sweater rested her hand on Lucius' arm.

"Oh, hey…"

It was obvious he couldn't remember her name, but that didn't stop her. "I'd heard you'd somehow jumped into the running. It's been a while. What, last year sometime?" Her voice dropped to as much of a husky whisper as possible to still be heard over the multitude of other people chatting.

Lucius nodded. "Yeah, I think that's right. I had a great time."

I stared at him as the lies rolled off his tongue. He clearly had no clue who she was or when he'd fucked her.

She moved her hands to his shoulders and tiptoed to whisper in his ear, rubbing her breasts all over his chest while she did it. He only smiled when she dropped back down and stared up into his eyes.

"Sounds good. Soon then."

"Soon." She winked and turned back to her conversation as Lucius pushed me even faster through the throng. We finally made it to the stairs and climbed until we came to another attendant. He was dressed all in black which did nothing to hide his portly girth. He had an air of self-importance that rankled.

"We need our room," Lucius said. "Lucius Vinemont and Stella Rousseau."

The attendant flipped through screen after screen on his tablet. "Oh, you're one of the competitors. Your room will be up one more flight of stairs, last door on the left. It's one of the larger suites."

"Key?" Lucius held his palm out.

The attendant shook his head. "No keys, sir. Trust is implicit."

"Come on, Stella," Lucius said.

The attendant cleared his throat. "Oh, no. I'm sorry. I didn't make it clear. The suite is solely for you, Mr. Vinemont. She will be staying with the other Acquisitions."

"What?" Lucius turned back to the attendant. "No, she stays with me."

"Those are my instructions from Mr. Oakman. I'm sorry if they aren't palatable, sir." He didn't seem the least bit sorry.

"But one of the other Acquisitions has a dick." Lucius was fuming.

"No need to worry about that. She won't be sullied until it's time."

Sullied? I tried to stay calm, to keep up what little barrier I had to these people and their minions. But this was already too much. I snatched the tablet from his hands and tossed it over the rail. Someone below yelped but the sound was quickly drowned out by the clamor of voices.

The attendant's nostrils flared and he scowled at me. "You can't do that."

"I just did." I may not have been able to stand up to anyone else here, but this guy? I was more than happy to grind him under my heel and piss on the dust that was left.

The attendant's eyes narrowed. "Michael," he called over his shoulder, "please escort the Acquisition to her quarters and hand me your tablet."

One of the other attendants, a younger man, stepped forward and handed his computer over before looking at me.

Lucius pulled me aside and spoke in my ear. "You have to go with them, but if you need me, you heard what he said. My room's up the stairs, last door on the left. Come find me if anything happens, okay?"

"This way, Acquisition." Michael grabbed my elbow.

"Back the fuck off, asshole," Lucius said. "And address

her as Ms. Rousseau or I'll rip your goddamn tongue out, you fucking prick."

Michael stepped away in a hurry.

Lucius reached up as if to touch my cheek but glanced around and thought better of it. "Just tell me you'll come to me, okay?"

"I will." I wouldn't. He couldn't help me.

"All right. Go with him, but don't take any shit." Lucius took my hand and squeezed my fingers. "I'll see you soon."

His words were like a judge pronouncing a sentence. He was right that he would see me soon. I pulled my hand away from his and followed Michael down the hall.

"Where are we going?" I asked Michael's retreating back.

"As was already clearly stated to you, to the Acquisition quarters, *Ms. Rousseau.*"

This kid was getting under my skin almost as badly as Mr. Tablet Overboard. "I have another question."

"What?" He let out an exasperated sigh.

"Why are you such a douche?"

He stiffened, but kept walking. *Score one for Stella.*

He led me around a few more corners before coming to a set of oaken double doors. He pushed through and we entered a room with three twin beds and an en suite bathroom. It was small, but not cramped. A tiny window in the upper rafter let in natural light, and high track lighting shined down from the wooden beams.

"These will be your quarters for the duration of your stay with us. Don't leave until someone comes for you." He backed out of the room, smirking at me and closing the doors as he went.

Brianne stepped out of the bathroom. She was in a cutoff t-shirt and shorty shorts.

I panicked. "Why are you dressed for spring break? You need to be warm."

"Why, we're going to be inside, right?" She plopped onto the nearest bed.

"No. Well, I mean, I don't know, but—"

"Red said not to worry about it. That it wasn't a big deal." She stared at the small window. "It's just supposed to be a little fun for them."

Red was an even bigger piece of shit than I'd ever imagined. I sank down next to Brianne and took one of her hands. "We have to get you dressed warmer. Did you bring any clothes?"

She finally looked at me and her eyes had the same glassy quality as they did at the party in New Orleans.

"Did you take something?" I asked.

"No. What do you mean?" She pulled her hand away from mine.

"I mean, are you high?" I had no idea what having drugs in your system would do when faced with hypothermia or worse.

She narrowed her eyes. "Don't think I don't know what you're doing. Red told me this was a competition between you and me and that powder puff Gavin. You aren't going to beat me."

My eyes rounded in disbelief. "You think we're competing against each other?"

"We are. Now get the fuck off my bed and mind your own goddamn business," she hissed.

"Brianne, please, you have to listen—"

"I said go!" Her scream was crazed.

I stood and backed away. Red had already destroyed the girl I'd seen at the ball. Brianne had broken. Would I?

My legs hit one of the other beds and I sat as Brianne went back to staring out the window at the patch of blue sky. I dropped my head into my hands, resting my elbows on my knees. Despair leeched from the air around Brianne and into my skin.

The doors opened and Gavin strode in, the rude attendant giving the same spiel about staying in the room until someone came for us.

Once he was gone, Gavin hitched a thumb over his shoulder. "Can you believe that guy?"

I rose and ran a hand through my hair. "Yeah, I called him a douche."

"He is definitely that and then some." Gavin surveyed the room before walking over and sitting next to me. "Hey Brianne, how's it going?"

"I'm not talking to either of you, so stop trying to get up in my head." She lay down with her back to us.

Gavin raised an eyebrow at me.

I shook my head, the insane urge to laugh mixing with my desire to cry. "She thinks we're competing against each other. That somehow we're the ones who need to win the competition. I'm not sure what she thinks we'll win, but there it is." I dropped my voice even lower. "She's on something. Same thing as at Cal's party."

Gavin pressed his lips into a thin line and shook his head. "Hate to say I'm not surprised. By the time this trial is over, I may be wishing I'd brought some pharmaceuticals."

"So you know?" It was a relief that I wouldn't have to tell him.

"I do." He scrubbed a hand down his clean shaven face.

"What do you think they'll do to us? I mean other than the…" I shivered.

"I don't know. I just know we have to get through it. And we can." His amber eyes were kind, and I leaned into him.

"I wish it was over already."

"Me too."

We sat like that for a long while, Brianne silent on her bed and Gavin and I huddling for some sort of comfort. No one bothered us until night fell. Then some plates arrived with a smattering of various foods. Brianne didn't eat a thing. Gavin and I tried, if only to keep our strength up, but the food made me queasy before I'd even had a mouthful.

The room was silent except for raucous cheers every so often from some other part of the house. They must have been stoking themselves up for the next day, for our humiliation.

Footsteps sounded in the hallway and the three of us stared at the door. It opened, and Lucius, Red, and Bob walked in. Gavin put a protective arm around me, and I shrank back against him. Not that it mattered. Not that any of us could stop what was going to happen.

Lucius narrowed his eyes and came straight to me. He took my hand and pulled me up, my cheek brushing against the softness of his black cashmere sweater, and his sandalwood scent in my nose. Maybe this was how it started—a gentle touch before the betrayal, before I was feasted on until there was nothing left but bones and sorrow.

He pulled me from the room, and the others followed.

"Where are we going?" I asked.

He gripped my elbow. "To the party. Don't speak unless you're spoken to. Got it?"

I bristled but remained silent. I had nothing to say to these people. The wooden floorboards were sturdy under my feet, my boots barely making a sound as we meandered through the halls toward the sound of voices. We entered a sea of people drinking and talking. The smell of roasted meat and wood smoke floated through the air.

Cal was speaking over a microphone; his favorite. "—so let's get another look at our little morsels. Ah, and here they are. Come on up!"

Lucius led me toward the raised stage in front of one of the high windows where Cal held court.

"Yes, yes." Cal narrated. "First up, looks like the Vinemont Acquisition, Stella. And, folks, I'll tell you a secret. I may have sampled a little taste—"

The people crowed and whistled as Lucius pushed me to stand next to Cal.

"Now, now. Just a taste is all I said. Not the whole meal. Don't get jealous. But I can tell you that little Miss Stella here is sweet as sugar, and I can only imagine the rest of her will melt right in your mouth."

Laughter, wolf whistles, and a few raised glasses. More movement to the bottom right of the stage caught my eye. My heart soared when I noticed Dylan standing below, waving at me to get my attention. His familiar face gave me strength and I straightened, shouldering my burden a bit more confidently just from his presence.

"Oh, and then Gavin. Now, he isn't to my tastes." Cal put his arm around Gavin's wide shoulders. "Nothing personal, of course. But I know quite a few of you ladies and gents who are salivating for a piece of this hunk, am I right?"

Cal held the crowd in the palm of his hand, their yells and laughter feeding into his frenzy of showmanship.

He moved down the row and pulled Brianne into his side. "And, I'll admit folks, I've had more than just a sample of little Brianne here. And she was good to the very last bite, I can promise you."

Brianne was still checked out, and waved to the throng like she was a homecoming queen instead of slave whose rape was the topic of discussion.

"Now that they're all here, I have a question for all of you good people out in the audience. Which one of you is going to fuck little Brianne here?"

A roar went up, and some of the men on the front row moved in closer.

"And how about Gavin?"

Another roar with quite a few high-pitched cat calls from the women.

"And finally, Stella?"

The room shook with stomping feet and yells, one of the men below climbing the first two stairs before some others pulled him back down, all laughing.

"That's what I like to hear! Now, I'm going to let them mingle a bit, and I expect everyone to be on their best behavior." He glowered at the younger men hovering near the front of the stage. "We do this the right way. The real fun won't start until tomorrow. So, behave with the

Acquisitions, but of course, you are welcome to misbehave with each other to your hearts' content."

Cal bowed, and applause coursed through the room. Lucius gripped my hand and pulled me down the stairs. He elbowed through the men hanging around the stage, and I kept my eyes down to avoid their leers. I still heard their voices, their words, their promises of violence and violation.

"Back the fuck up." Lucius shoved one of them and barreled the rest of the way through the crowd and to the bar. He pushed me ahead of him and caged my body from behind. It was protective, but also too close for me. I needed air. I'd rather be in my quarters than here.

I craned my neck around to search for Dylan, but the mass of people blocked my line of sight.

"Give me an old-fashioned. Two of them." Lucius' chest was warm against me, his hands on my hips. "You're doing fine," he whispered in my ear. "That was the big show for the evening."

The bartender poured the drinks and set them down in front of us. I took mine; the taste was bitter on my tongue, but the rush of warmth from the alcohol was welcome. I drank quickly, the liquid burning as I downed it.

"Easy, Stella." Lucius took my almost empty glass.

I leaned my head back on his shoulder and spoke into his ear. "Please, Lucius. I don't want to feel it."

His fingertips pressed into my hip. "Getting drunk tonight will only make tomorrow worse. You have to stay strong."

"Why?"

"You know why."

"I don't." I did. I just needed to hear it, to know how much worse things could get.

"Because if you can't stay strong, I'll make sure your father suffers. I'll make sure you suffer."

I snorted and snatched the drink back from him, downing it. "Yeah. I think my suffering is a given with or without my good behavior." I avoided the topic of my

349

father. His kind eyes flashed through my mind, though I supposed they weren't truly kind, not anymore. "Got anything else? Anything to stop me from marching right back up to that stage over there and telling all your pals to go shove their Acquisition right up their asses?" I ordered another drink.

"Plenty. Are you going to suffer tomorrow? Yes. But I can make you suffer every day after." His voice darkened and he gripped my hip painfully. When the bartender set the drink down, Lucius knocked it away. "You're mine for months and months. I can think of all sorts of nasty things, Stella. Far worse than anything you could ever dream up. Pain, torture, violations that will make tomorrow seem like a pleasant memory." He moved his hand around the front of my thigh and cupped my pussy as he pushed me into the bar, my ribs crushing painfully against the wood. "If that's what you want, then by all means, go on up to the stage."

I tried to squirm away from him, but he only pressed me harder and his fingers sank farther between my legs, massaging my core through my jeans.

"Get off me," I growled.

He ignored me, his fingers making my body come alive when I wanted to stay numb.

"But," he let off and moved his hand back to my hip, "if you do what I want you to do, then I will do everything I can to protect you. And once this is over—"

"Lunch with the queen. I got it. Now get the fuck off me." I pushed away from the bar.

"Stella!" Dylan shoved past a couple of guests and embraced me, picking me up off the floor and squeezing me to the point where I wished I hadn't had that drink.

"You're here." I was starved for an honest touch, for someone who I knew cared about me and not because of some stupid game.

He set me down. "Yes." His cheeks were red and his breath smelled of something strong.

"Are you drunk?"

"No. I mean, Cal shared some choice whiskey, but I'm not drunk." He shook his head, the movement slow.

"You're drunk." A shock of pain hit my chest. "You came here and got drunk with these people?"

"I was just trying to play along. Calm down." He put his heavy arms on my shoulders and pressed his forehead to mine. "I'm going to be the one, Stella. Tomorrow. It'll be me."

"You'll be the one to what?"

He grinned, his perfect smile unnerving more than comforting. "You'll see. But it'll be me. I'll take care of you."

"I think that's enough." Lucius menaced from behind me.

"I can talk to my sister if I want to."

"Your former stepsister, you mean?"

"Yeah, so what?"

"She's not your blood. She's no concern of yours."

"She's not your blood either, asshole." Dylan had a point.

"She doesn't have to be. I own her. Now step the fuck back before I drop you and kick you while you're down again."

"We're just talking," I said. "Can't I talk to someone? Please?" I'd never tried asking him nicely. Maybe it would work.

"Yeah, you can talk to me." Lucius put his arm across my neck, pulling me back into him. "Fuck off, Dylan."

"Stop." I elbowed him, but he didn't let go.

Dylan glowered and dropped his gaze back to me. "Remember what I said." Then he turned and moved away in the crowd.

"Get off." I rolled my shoulders and Lucius lowered his arm, but not before grazing my breast.

I turned and glared at him. "Asshole."

He smirked and took another swig. "So?"

"I'm going back to my room."

"No."

"Why not?"

"Because I need you to be seen." He set his glass on the bar and took me by the arm. "Just smile and fucking nod. That's all you have to do."

He waded through the horde of people and dragged me with him. He knew so many of them, striking up easy conversations about childhood events, fun times in college, or how the sugar business was going. But no matter who he spoke to, the conversation always worked its way back around to me.

"Stella's an artist," Lucius said for the tenth time that night.

A woman, perhaps no more than fifty, and impeccably dressed in winter white, smiled and sipped her wine. "So am I. Several pieces on display in New York and Los Angeles. What sort of galleries have you been in?"

"A gallery in my hometown has, well, had a few of my pieces," I said.

"Hometown gallery?" She raised a perfectly-drawn eyebrow and took a sip of her wine. "How quaint."

Lucius smiled. "I heard one of Stella's pieces was recently on display in New York at one of the hottest up and coming galleries. It sold for fifty thousand dollars just last week."

I cocked my head at Lucius. He certainly knew how to spin a lie.

"Oh, is that so?" She simpered at me over her glass.

Lucius didn't miss a beat. "It is. I don't know if you know the piece, but it was called *The North Star.*"

Something was off. I did have a piece called *The North Star*, but it sold at the town gallery a month ago, not in New York last week. And definitely not for $50,000.

Her eyes widened. "That was you?"

"It was her." Lucius squeezed my hip and crushed me into his side, pride written into his smile.

"Congratulations. I actually saw that piece in person at La Vie Gallery and was impressed. I had no idea someone of your—" she waved her hand at me like I was some interesting animal behind glass at a zoo "— situation could create something like that."

"I would take that as a compliment, but since it wasn't, I won't." I smiled at her, wishing for her death.

Lucius forced a laugh as the woman's expression soured.

"Good luck tomorrow, dear." She gave me a tight smile, and Lucius pulled me away toward another group of people.

"Bad form, Stella," he whispered in my ear. "Try again."

We visited several more clusters of people who chatted about mundane first world problems before turning to my enslavement like it was just another topic.

The next cluster we visited included Dylan's mother, Marguerite. She didn't speak, only listened to Lucius while the other ladies laughed. Her lips were pressed into a narrow line, and her gaze never left me. I wanted to speak to her, to ask if she knew anything that could help me. And, I admitted, I wanted to ask about my father. But her face was impassable, hard.

The next group was younger; Lucius fit in easily, though I kept glancing back to Marguerite as she whispered to the ladies around her. They would glance to me from time to time. I was obviously the topic of their hushed conversation, and none of the information looked good, given their expressions of distaste.

The hour grew late and, though I knew I couldn't sleep, I was ready to be alone. At least, as alone as I could be. I didn't want to be looked at or talked about anymore. If I couldn't be numb, then I'd rather fight my fears alone instead of in front of an audience.

"Are we done?" I asked after we walked away from a particularly nasty pair of older men who leered at me and spoke of nothing other than the trial.

"We can be. Come on, I'll walk you back."

"I can find it. It's just down that hall."

"I know you can find it." His light eyes were shrewd, the liquor doing nothing to dim them. "I just want to make sure you get there."

"Fine."

He led me away, his hand at my lower back as we wove between furniture and people. The hallway was cooler, the air less full of talk and noise.

"You did well. Except for Ms. Thibodeaux. I'll never hear the end of that little art slight."

"How did you come up with that lie about my art selling in New York??"

We turned the corner toward the Acquisition quarters.

"It wasn't a lie. Your *North Star* piece did sell last week for $50,000."

"No, it didn't."

"Yes, it did."

I stopped and faced him. "How?"

"You'll have to ask Sin. I'm not sure about all the details."

I resumed my pace. "Vinemont sold my art? What for?"

"Like I said, ask him. I don't invest in art. I just know good art when I see it."

"Did you tell him my art was good?"

He shrugged. "Maybe. Is this your room?"

We arrived at the double doors. "Yes."

Lucius pushed inside. "Which bed is yours?"

"We haven't really picked, though I think Brianne took that one over to the left."

"So yours is next to Gavin's?" He stepped between the beds and pushed one all the way to the far wall. "That's better."

"That's juvenile." I crossed my arms over my chest.

"Maybe. But I don't want him touching you."

"Well, when you're living it up in your suite tonight and we're down here afraid, I doubt there's much you could do to stop us from touching."

He strode to me. "If he touches you, we're going to have a problem, Stella. A big one. We clear?"

"Sure. He won't touch me. Don't you worry." I put the

least amount of conviction into my words as possible. I didn't know why I was trying to get a rise out of Lucius, but I was. Perhaps to repay him for his Dylan tirade.

He yanked me into his chest, the movement so sudden I gasped. "Do you ever shut up?" He kissed me.

I shoved him away. "Are you trying to cheat and get first dibs? Won't that piss off the sadistic buddies you're trying to impress?" I sneered. He'd shown me off for hours, parroting his talking points like he was running for office.

"Come here." He fisted his hands at his sides.

"No."

"Come. Here. I won't tell you again, Stella."

"Fuck you." I stepped up onto the bed and then down the other side and turned back to face him.

"You want to do this right now?" He grinned and pulled his sweater and t-shirt over his head. His skin was smooth, light brown hair at the center of his chest and disappearing into his slacks. The V tattoo swirled out of his heart, the thick brambles snaring him. He was leaner than Vinemont, but just as fast. And he was determined, given the look in his eye.

"I want you to leave right now." I was playing with fire. Something was so wrong about all of this. But I needed to feel something other than fear, other than horror.

"I don't think that's true." He let his gaze run down my body, lingering at my neck, breasts, and thighs before returning to my face. "Your pulse is racing, your nipples hard, and I can just bet your pussy is wet, Stella."

"Guess you'll never know." I backed away.

In one smooth movement, he leapt over the bed and tackled me onto the other bed against the wall. The air was squeezed out of my lungs as he wrestled my hands over my head. He stared down at me, his eyes alight with passion and need.

He claimed my mouth, his tongue sure as it swirled around mine, tasting and touching as he spread my knees apart with his. He was hard, his cock rubbing against me as his hips moved slowly. His kiss was hypnotic, the way he took me over, took my breath, and lit up every nerve ending. I wanted this, something to take my mind off the rest of it. Some small bit of fleeting pleasure before the devastating weight of reality crashed back down.

He moved to my neck, his lips worshipping my jugular as he switched my wrists to one hand. When he slid his hand under my top and squeezed my breast, I moaned. He ripped the cup of my bra down and twisted my nipple between his thumb and forefinger. My hips rose against him, his cock giving more delicious friction. I ignored the flash of deep sapphire eyes that crossed my vision.

Lucius hissed when I raised my hips again, working him through his pants.

"Lucius," I breathed, though another name was on my mind, hovering right along my lips. He sank lower, his mouth on my breast as his free hand yanked at the button and the zipper on my jeans.

He bit me hard, and I arched up to him as he slid his fingers into my panties. I was wet, and my skin was on fire wherever he grazed me with his mouth or his hands.

"Fuck." He reached farther, pulling wetness from my entrance and smoothing it around my clit.

I squirmed and moaned as he circled my hard, sensitive nub. He relinquished my nipple and kissed back up to my mouth, his bare chest pressing into my skin.

He sank a finger inside me and groaned. "I need you, Stella."

The words grated on me. Someone else had needed me, too. Vinemont—his eyes were there again in my vision. He was the ghost that lingered in every corner of my mind.

Lucius brought his fingers up to his mouth and licked them clean. He kissed me again, but his taste was wrong. Everything was wrong. I was a furnace that had burned out, the flame gone, the room cold.

I turned my head. "I don't want this."

"Yes you do." He bit my neck.

"No. I mean it."

The tone in my voice froze him, and he brought his face back to mine. "Are you fucking serious?"

"Yes. Please, just go."

He let go of my hands and sat back, his eyebrows knit together in confusion. "Why?"

I shook my head and yanked down my top. "Please, Lucius."

He stood and stared down at me. "It's Sin, isn't it?"

I looked away.

He didn't need any more confirmation. He turned and retreated, his movements jerky and full of anger, before swiping his sweater off the floor.

I jumped when he slammed the door behind him.

What am I doing? I bounced my head on the mattress, trying to sort through what the hell I was thinking. Seducing Lucius was a necessary part of the plan and a welcome distraction. And I'd just blown it all up because Vinemont said he *needed* me. Because of a single sentence from a man who ran hot and cold faster than a tap.

I stood up and straightened my clothes before going to the bathroom. I splashed warm water in my face and stared at the mirror me. She was just as inscrutable as before, the reflection doing nothing more than reiterating how lost I was.

The bedroom door opened. I dried my face and walked out to find Gavin and Brianne. Gavin looked at the rumpled bed, then up at me, but I scooted past him with my head down.

Brianne went into the bathroom and took an inordinately long time getting ready for bed.

"So, um, the bed? Anything I need to know about?" he asked.

"No. I'm sad to say." I rubbed my eyes. "Nothing happened. Well, nothing substantial."

"Second base?"

I looked up and he was grinning at me. How he managed

to smile so big on the eve of an Acquisition trial was beyond me. But his smile was contagious, because the corners of my mouth turned up despite my mood.

"Something like that. I'm not even sure what the bases are. But let's stick to second."

"I can do that." He kicked his shoes off as Brianne walked out of the bathroom.

She crashed on her bed, not even bothering to get under the covers.

While Gavin was in the bathroom, I took off my boots, feeling inside for the knife. The warm metal was comforting. Then I stripped my jeans and sweater off, but kept my undershirt on. Gavin came out, removed his shirt and pants, and slipped into his sheets. I did the same, pulling my covers up to my chin. We lay silently for a while, listening to Brianne's steady breathing.

"I'm too afraid to turn the light off," Gavin whispered.

"Same here." I flipped over to my side and looked at his profile as he stared at the ceiling.

"Do you think they'll do it in the morning or the afternoon?"

"I don't know, but I intend to be ready to go at sun up."

He turned his head toward me. "How can you be ready for something like this?"

"You can't, I guess. We just have to survive." My voice was small and I felt even smaller. One person in the huge crush of malevolent strangers scattered throughout this mountain retreat.

"Stella?"

"Hm?"

"Can I sleep with you?"

What? "You want to …"

"I mean, in your bed." He smiled. "I mean actually sleep. Not the other thing. I just thought maybe it would make it easier is all."

"Oh," my face reddened. "Sure."

He got out of bed and padded over behind me. The bed

shifted and then his warmth was at my back. He pulled the blanket up and slung an arm over me. "Is this okay?"

"Yes." I barely knew him, but his arms were the safest place to be for miles and miles. I settled back into him.

"If it makes you feel any better, that kiss we shared last week was the first time I'd ever kissed a woman."

"Oh." So that's what Brianne had meant by "powder puff Gavin." *What a bitch.* "Well, I'm glad to be your first?"

He must have heard the smile in my voice because he laughed lightly. "Yeah, I was just trying to help. But it wasn't bad. Not really. Just different, I guess."

"Your hand sure went up my skirt fast." I reached behind me and pulled his arm under my neck so he could get more comfortable.

"Thanks. And I was just playing the role. Apparently, I need to work on it since Red still jumped on us."

"A for effort. Nicely done."

"I appreciate it."

We fell silent. His presence was a comfort in and of itself. I was afraid if I kept talking, I would focus on what would happen tomorrow. I didn't want to think about that pain until I had to, until I couldn't escape it.

Our breathing evened out, but neither of us slept. I worried away one hour, then another.

"It's okay, Stella. Sleep. I've got you." Gavin's voice was colored with exhaustion as he pulled me so I turned over to face him.

I let my head fall into the crook of his neck. He rubbed his hand up and down my back in a soothing motion until he drifted off.

"I've got your back," I whispered as sleep took me, too.

CHAPTER FOURTEEN
STELLA

SOUND. SO MUCH of it that I instinctively covered my ears. My eyes flew open, my vision sharpening on a multitude of bodies crushing through the suite door. People swarmed into the room, black batons in their hands. They wore white masks, holes cut for their eyes and mouths, with the rest of their features obscured.

I jolted up right along with Gavin.

The men chanted some rhythmic song, unintelligible but somehow vicious. I clutched at Gavin's arm as he gripped my thigh through the blanket. We were both frozen, fear eating up any response we could have mustered.

The throng quieted suddenly, the loss of sound almost as terrifying as the noise. A woman, her long dark hair flowing from the back of her mask walked through the center of the crowd and threw down two white dresses and a white shirt and pants. She retreated back into the mass and Cal, maskless, stepped forward. His gaze flitted about between the three of us before landing on mine.

"Acquisitions, we have something very special in store for you." He pointed to the clothes on the floor. "But first, strip."

Neither Gavin, Brianne, nor I moved. Cal held his hand out behind him and someone put a black baton in it. He walked up and slammed it down on the footboard of my bed, the sound like an explosion through the now cramped space.

"I said strip." He spoke to all of us, but his malevolent gaze was fixed on me.

Gavin pushed me out of the bed and stood next to me.

"Just do it." His whisper was loud in the silent room.

The dozens of masked devils watched as Gavin and I took our clothes off. Brianne did the same, her eyes wide and no longer quite so glassy. The drugs must have worn off, because she came and stood at my other side, shivering and trying to cover herself.

I draped an arm across my bare breasts and used my other hand to cover between my legs. I didn't look at Gavin, who stood on my other side. I wouldn't add to the unwanted eyes already on him. All those masked faces—was Lucius there, watching?

Cal walked forward and put his index finger under my chin, pulling my face up until our eyes met. His pupils were huge, taking in every last bit of me.

A tremor ran through me at his touch, his look.

He let me go and backed up before pointing at the clothes the woman had dropped on the floor. "Dress."

I grabbed a dress and threw it on over my head, wincing at how bare I was before the material covered me. It was short and thin, and would offer no reprieve from the elements. My fear had been stunned right along with me at the sudden intrusion, but it roared back to life. I tried to fasten the top button of the dress at my throat, but my fingers were numb and clumsy.

Cal surveyed us and grinned, apparently pleased with our outfits. "Now, we're going to play a little game. Sound like fun, Acquisitions?"

Some of the masked figures smiled, their teeth showing through the holes in their masks.

"This game is simple. It's about three a.m. right now. Perfect time for a little stroll in the woods. So, this is what we're going to do. We're going to take you outside and let you go. Let you enjoy the fresh, *cold* air. Stretch your legs."

Oh, god. I reached for Gavin's hand. His skin was like ice.

"Then at daybreak, we're coming for you."

A barrage of shouts went up, gleeful and bloodthirsty.

"Whoever catches you first, wins. That person will fuck you. That person will do whatever they want with your body, because your body was made for our enjoyment. When the winner is done, they may choose to pass you around or bring you back here for more of their own enjoyment. Anything goes. But the winner gets the first fuck and the final say. Simple, right?" Cal nodded and raised his eyebrows at us, as if wanting us to agree with him.

Brianne did. I just gripped Gavin's fingers tighter.

"Your time starts…" Cal glanced at his watch-less arm. "Now."

Another cheer, and the masked figures began filing out. Cal remained and approached, clearly reveling in the power he wielded over the three of us.

"Run, rabbit, run," he whispered. Then he turned and whistled as he followed the pack the rest of the way out of the room.

Only two stayed behind—one of the masked men and the woman with the long, dark hair.

"Come on. Outside." Her voice was harsh, but her nerves made the sound wobble.

I took a chance and darted to my bed and sat, pulling on my socks and boots before grabbing my jacket. The knife rubbed against my ankle, reminding me I still had some measure of defense.

"Gavin, clothes," I urged. "More clothes."

He yanked on his socks and shoes before throwing his coat on over the white pajamas he was wearing.

The woman came toward us, her baton held above her head. "I said let's go."

"Brianne, shoes!"

She jolted at my words and finally moved, the white dress hanging loosely from her as she pulled on her sneakers.

"Hit her." The male hadn't moved from the door, but his hand ran up and down his baton.

The woman swung at me. I ducked back, but she nailed me on the forearm when I held my arm up to ward her off. Pain exploded down to my wrist and up to my shoulder. I screamed, and gripped the injury.

Gavin finished donning his coat and advanced on her, but the male guard moved forward.

"Enough bullshit," the guard barked. "Let's go."

Brianne had no coat, nothing to keep her safe from the chill wind in the darkness. My arm stung and ached, but I stood and snagged my sweater off the floor and tossed it to Brianne. She yanked it down over her head as we filed out the door under the watchful eyes of our guards.

They led us through the house and then down to the road. A curve of silver moon hung in the sky, and my breath shuddered out in white puffs. Icy patches dotted the road, and the air was keen and cold, faintly burning my lungs on each inhale. The sting took my attention away from the throb in my arm.

Laughter rang out above. A host of masked ghouls crowded the deck and peeked through the windows of the home. Cal stood at the top of the stairs and raised a pistol into the air.

"As an added incentive to our little rabbits, I am offering them a prize beyond value." I couldn't see his eyes from this distance, but my skin crawled enough for me to know he was watching me. "If no one has caught you by noon, you will remain unscathed. No one will touch you."

The crowd booed and hissed. Cal laughed, the sound loud, fake, and booming. "Now, now calm down. We must have a carrot, after all. It can't always be the stick." He grabbed his crotch for emphasis, and the mob erupted in laughter.

May the best man, or woman, excuse me ladies—" a smattering of feminine laughter coursed through the crowd, "—win!" Cal pulled the trigger, and a hollow pop echoed across the ridges and back to my ears.

"Come on." Gavin tugged at my arm, and we both took off at a sprint away from the house.

I looked over my shoulder. Brianne remained still, staring at Cal and the masked assemblage above her.

"Brianne, come on!" I cried.

She turned and followed us at a jog.

"Which way should we go?" I asked.

"I don't know. Just away from here." Gavin took the lead, moving across the parking area, then through an open field, and finally to the tree line.

Brianne was several yards back, but still followed. I couldn't slow down. We had to make it, had to get far enough away somewhere and hide, or just run and run until the sun was high enough overhead that we knew we were safe.

The woods were shadowy, the crescent moon doing little to illuminate our path. We crashed through the underbrush, not caring what sort of trail we left as we jumped over logs and climbed the first hill. The house gleamed in the night, the windows brightly lit, and the sounds of laughter and music floating along the chilled air. They partied as we ran, enjoying themselves before sinking their claws into the three of us and ripping us apart.

We crested the hill and started down the other side, the house finally out of view. Knowing that they couldn't see me anymore gave me the slightest bit of comfort, but we had to keep moving and put as much distance between them and us as possible.

Gavin stopped and leaned against a tree as we waited for Brianne to catch up.

"Do you think we can hide?" I asked and peered up into the trees.

Gavin shook his head. "Not in the trees. No cover without leaves. We'd be sitting ducks."

Brianne was breathing hard already, and her cheeks burned a bright pink from the frigid air. My cable-knit sweater wouldn't keep her warm for long, especially not when the wind soughed through the trees as it did. My legs were cold above my boots, and hers must have been freezing. She wore only tennis shoes. I dug in my jacket pockets, ignoring the pain in my forearm, and found my gloves and the knit hat I'd stuffed inside.

"Here." I handed Brianne the hat and the gloves.

Her eyes opened wide. "Th-thank you."

"We aren't competing, Brianne. I promise. Red lied to you."

She took the hat and pulled it down over her blonde locks, which shined almost white in the moonlight. "I know. I don't know why I said all that. All he does is lie to me and, and…other things." She looked away as she pulled on the gloves.

"It's okay. This isn't easy." I slipped my chilled fingers inside my boot and drew out my blade before stuffing it into my pocket. "But we've got to stick together and keep moving. Can you do that?"

"Yes. I think I can."

"Good."

"Take mine." Gavin drew some leather gloves from his coat pockets and handed them to me.

"No, I'm good. I can just stick my hands in my pockets when they get cold. You wear them."

He shook his head and peered down at me. "I can do the same. Go ahead and take them. At least I'm wearing pants. This will make us even."

He wasn't fooling me. The white linen pajama bottoms offered him no more protection from the piercing wind than my bare legs had, but I took the gloves to cut off any more argument. We needed to get moving.

"I'm ready. Let's go." I pulled the too-large gloves on

and began picking my way down the slope. It was slow-going because the leaves were covered with a slick of frost, were wet underneath, and the terrain was uneven. It quickly became clear my boots were made more for looks than use, with each step turning into a balancing act.

Once we'd reached the bottom where a small stream ran, we paused.

"Up and over the next ridge, or should we break off to the right and follow the water?" I didn't want to keep moving in a straight line, but I also wanted to get as far from the party as possible.

"Let's follow the stream and then cut up the next hollow we come to." Gavin said.

Brianne nodded, her teeth chattering.

We stayed along the water's path, moving as quickly as we could with Brianne lagging behind. Large stone boulders dotted the landscape, and I wondered if we could hide against one of them. But it was still too out in the open. They would find us in no time. And they would expect us to hunker down, to try and wait them out. That's why we had to keep moving. We slogged through the dead leaves and cracking branches, grunting with the effort of climbing over trunks or boulders. The woods were silent except for our exertions and the inconsistent wind which whistled and pushed easily through the naked branches, chilling the sweat on our skin.

Gavin and I surged ahead, urging Brianne to step where we did to avoid any mishaps. We followed the stream for maybe a half mile before a long hollow opened up to our left. I was sweaty and cold, perspiration rolling down my back, though I didn't dare take my jacket off.

"Brianne, keep up," I called as we started to climb up the hollow.

A screech cut through the still woods, and I glanced over my shoulder. Brianne floundered, one leg in the icy stream as she tried to climb back to her feet.

"Shit." I raced back down to her and gripped her

forearm, dragging her from the shallow stream.

She shivered, her teeth chattering. "I-I slipped."

"Come on." I eyed her wet feet and legs.

"She okay?" Gavin made it back to us.

"I think so, but she got wet."

He shook his head, frustration creasing his brow.

"So cold." Her eyes squeezed shut, misery pouring out of them in delicate tears.

"I know." I had nothing else to say, no promises of help or warmth. We were hunted and freezing; hope was out of reach. "Let's go."

I took her arm and we resumed our trek, her one wet shoe squishing with each step. Our pace slowed even more as her breathing grew labored. The cold was seeping away her strength, her will. I felt it, too.

She paused to rest against a tree as Gavin and I kept going.

"Move, Brianne. Come on," Gavin barked.

Wiping her face with the back of her glove, she started trudging upward again. When we were halfway to the top of the ridge, I slipped on a wet pile of leaves and slid before Gavin caught my arm and hefted me up.

"Thanks."

"No problem."

We were both winded, but wouldn't stop. After more long minutes of climbing, we reached the top.

I bent over, gulping in air.

"Stand up straight and put your arms over your head," Gavin said through wheezes. "It helps."

I did as he'd instructed, though it was agony at first. I leaned my head back, gripping my wrists at the back of my neck. I inspected the sky. No longer an inky black, it was dotted with stars. The Milky Way split the center, its mass of blooming light like a road we could follow. A beautiful path, but cold and distant.

The burning in my lungs subsided as I scanned the bright dots marking the heavens. I dropped my gaze earthward as

Brianne sank to the ground at our feet, soiling her dress as she gasped for air.

The moon was lower now, and I could still make out the gleam of lights from the cabin over the last ridge. We were too close. We needed to travel faster.

"Brianne, get up. We have to move."

"I can't." She wiped her runny nose with my glove. "I can't go any further."

"You have to."

"I don't. It doesn't matter. They're going to catch me. They'll catch all of us." She looked up, her eyes brimming with tears. "There's no way out."

I knelt. "Brianne, if you just sit here and don't move, you could die of hypothermia before they even find you."

She dropped her gaze to her knees. "Would that be so bad?"

"Yes." I pulled up my sleeve and showed her my scars. "Yes. It would. Trust me. Now get the fuck up and let's go."

Gavin offered his hand, and Brianne took it. We were on our way again, moving down into the next valley, skidding on leaves and climbing over fallen trees. Once at the bottom, we decided to cut even farther sideways instead of continuing straight up the next ridge.

The moon lowered, its disappearance heralding the coming dawn.

"What's that?" Gavin stopped ahead of me.

I came to stand beside him. "What?"

"You see that light?" He pointed ahead.

Something glimmered between the trees, maybe fifty yards ahead. "Yeah. What is it?"

"I don't know. Let's go. Maybe it's help." He took off faster, his steps becoming less careful at the promise of salvation.

"No, Gavin, wait." Foreboding took hold inside me, and I struggled to catch up with him. "Don't."

"Stella!" Brianne fell to her hands and knees behind me. "I can't feel my feet. I-I can't walk."

"Shit." I dashed back to her, my feet sliding over the leaves and stones. I gripped under her arms and pulled her upright.

"Gavin, don't!" The frigid air swallowed up my voice. I could barely see him through the trees now, but I spied the light. It infused me with dread.

I slung Brianne's arm over my shoulder and half-dragged her.

Gavin's scream sliced through the air, through my mind.

Brianne stiffened at my side. "What happened? What was that?"

He screamed again, agonized and frantic.

"I don't know. But you have to keep walking." I dropped her arm and scrambled over a boulder before taking off toward the light and Gavin's screams.

"Stella." Brianne's voice cracked behind me, but I couldn't stop. Gavin's cries compelled me forward. I tripped as my muscles burned and my lungs struggled to pull in enough air, but I kept moving.

The light grew brighter as I lurched from tree to tree, trying to get a look at what it was.

Gavin's screams subsided into a gasping "Stella" that he repeated until my heart was shredded.

I slowed and crept closer. The light appeared to be a gas lantern hung in a tree. Beneath it dangled a bulbous net bag of clothing—knit hats, jackets, gloves—all warm and welcoming. Gavin lay beneath the bag in a shallow, concealed pit, a narrow bamboo shoot piercing his calf.

"Oh, shit." I dropped to my knees at the edge of the hole and reached down for him.

He grimaced and raised up on his elbow. "I am so stupid. So fucking stupid."

"No, no." I bent over toward him. "Can you get up? Give me your hand."

"It hurts." He stared at his calf, his eyes wide with shock.

"I know. But we have to keep moving. They'll come here first. Please, Gavin." Desperation colored my voice.

He nodded and turned on his side, more bamboo shoots rolling beneath his large frame.

"Is it just your leg?" I asked as he took my hand.

"I think so. Isn't that enough?" He pulled hard enough on my arm that I thought it might come out of the socket, but he managed to perch himself on the edge of the pit next to me. "So fucking dumb. I saw it and thought... I don't know what I thought." He examined the injury. "I guess I wasn't thinking."

The bloodied shoot had been sharpened into a curving tip, penetrating Gavin's flesh cleanly.

"We have to pull it out and keep moving." I took his booted foot in my hands and placed it on his other knee so I could get a better look at the spear. Blood soaked into the white fabric around the wound.

Gavin shook his head, a dazed expression in his eyes. "I don't know—"

"Oh, god." Brianne caught up and retched into the leaves behind me.

"I'm going to pull it from this direction, okay?" I gripped the longer end of the spike. "Just hold still."

"Fuck! I don't think I can do this." Gavin clutched my hand.

I put my gloved palms on his cheeks and stared into his amber eyes, now awash with pain. "We can do this. I've got your back."

He nodded, sweat running down his face.

I bent over him and gripped the underside of the shoot again. "On three."

He took a deep breath.

"One, two—" I ripped it free in one smooth jerk.

Gavin's scream pierced my ears, leaving them ringing long after the air was gone from his lungs.

He lay back and pulled his knee to his chest, his hands clutching at the punctured leg. I fought back my tears and glanced to the lightening sky.

"Here." I ripped the thin edge of my dress, tearing off a

long strip. Wrapping it around Gavin's wound, I pulled it tight to try and stem the flow of blood. He grunted as I tied it off.

"Brianne, help me get him up."

She sat on the stony ground, her chest heaving and her hands clapped over her ears.

"Brianne!" I took her forearms and shook her. "Snap the fuck out of it."

"I can't." She shook her head and her tone was reminiscent of a tired child.

The moon was gone, time running away from us just as we ran from our hunters. Bitterness welled in my stomach, then a seething hatred. I wasn't angry at Brianne, but I needed her to function. I grabbed her hair where it flowed from beneath her cap and ripped her to her feet. She screamed. I didn't care.

"Stella—" She protested.

I shook her again, this time by her hair, putting every ounce of nastiness into it that I could. "Shut the fuck up and help Gavin."

Her lip trembled, but when I released her, she didn't fall. Instead, she knelt next to Gavin. I took his other side and we lifted him.

"Can you walk?" I asked.

"It hurts, but I think everything still works." He grunted. After a few steps, he was able to walk on his own with a pronounced limp. Our pace slowed to a crawl, but we keep plodding through the never-ending trees.

My legs burned, the pain in my arm now a dull throbbing ache. My cheeks were wind-chapped and stinging. And, above all, I was cold. The sort of cold that nothing short of a soak in a hot bath or a long shower could alleviate. It was in my bones.

We trekked and trekked before coming to another shallow ravine crossing up the hill in the direction we were going.

Gavin and I turned and started heading up the slope

when Brianne collapsed behind us.

We rushed back to her. Her chest heaved, big white plumes of her breath floating in the air.

"You okay?" I asked. I yanked a glove off and smoothed her hair from her face. Her skin was cold and clammy. Had I pushed her too hard?

"No. I can't. I can't go on."

"You can." I wrapped my arms around her chest and lifted. "Get up."

She remained limp, every last bit of fight expended. "No, I can't. I'm tired. I'm too tired. Leave me." Her voice was weak.

I glanced up to Gavin. "What are we going to do?" I didn't want to face the truth. "We have to take her with us."

He leaned against a tree. "I would carry her, but I can't. I just can't." He gestured to the crimson stain on his pant leg.

"Just go. Please. It's all right. I knew what would happen. I knew." She closed her eyes as I kept my palm on her cheek. Her words came in shuddering breaths. "You did all you could. It's okay. I was never going to make it."

The knowledge that I couldn't save her ate at me like acid. She put her hand over mine and leaned into my touch, her eyes closed.

"I'm sorry." I choked down my sob.

"You did all you could." Her voice stuck in her throat, but she shed no more tears. She peered at me, her light eyes unfocused. "Run."

I scanned the hollow for any sort of camouflage, something to at least give her a chance. A fallen branch caught my eye. Several limbs sprouted from it, and the crisp leaves were still attached in places.

"Gavin, if we can get her to that limb, maybe we can hide her under it and cover her with leaves to keep her warm."

He stared up the hill. "That'll take time. Sunrise is soon."

"I know. But we have to. We can't just leave her."

He wiped a hand down his sweaty face. "You're right. I'm sorry. You're right."

I pulled my glove back on and dragged her to her feet. We made it to the fallen limb, and she climbed under the branches. I gathered up armfuls of leaves from a little farther up the slope and piled them around where she lay curled up. Gavin helped as best he could, and after a while, she was completely hidden. I got on my hands and knees and spread the leaves out around where we'd taken them to hide the disturbance.

The sky was brightening, the sun threatening. The hunt would begin soon.

I clambered back up from my aching knees. "Okay, Brianne. Just stay there until the sun is high. It'll be okay."

"Thank you." Brianne whispered her absolution, though I would never forgive myself for leaving her behind.

"Let's go." Gavin started ahead of me, using saplings to help pull himself up the steep incline. He groaned with each heavy step on his injured leg, but he kept moving.

I turned and followed, using the same sapling technique.

When we got to the top of the ridge, my legs shook, fatigue settling into my deepest parts.

"What's that?" Gavin pointed down into the next valley. Smoke rose through the darkness, floating along the tops of the skeletal trees. It must have been a cabin of some sort.

"I don't know, but it's probably another trap."

"A warm trap." His gaze lingered on the plume of smoke.

The smell of wood burning floated in the air, and I had never smelled anything more wonderful. I forced myself to scan farther down the ridge, away from the toasty lure of a roof and a fire.

"Come on." I trudged away from the beckoning cabin, toward the west and the dark azure sky.

Gavin fell in behind me, his injured leg crashing heavily with each step. We stuck to the crest of the ridge until it started sloping down into a ravine with hollows running up either side.

The sun peaked over the farthest ridge I could see, and a gunshot cracked in the distance.

Gavin gripped my gloved hand and squeezed. "This is it."

"I know." I leaned into him and we just stood together for a moment.

"We'll be alive, Stella. On the other side of this, we'll still be alive." His voice shook.

"My heart will still beat. I'll still draw breath, but I don't know if I'll still feel alive." My words flattened in the air and sank to our feet as we began to pick our way down the embankment.

Once we reached the relatively flat bottom of the ravine, we were able to pick up more speed. Maybe it was our second wind, or maybe fear fired our nerves and muscles to push harder. We continued a slow trot. Gavin favored his bad leg, but powered through all the same. Several hollows fell away as we continued deeper into the gorge. My heartbeat thundered in my ears until a buzzing noise cut through the rapid thump.

Gavin hauled me sideways until we hid against one of the large rock outcrops that dotted the forest. A square drone flew by, its four helicopter blades whirring as it eased down the ravine. The machine passed us by, then hovered for a moment. I held my breath and closed my eyes. I was in Cuba beneath the pool's surface again, the vines snaking around my ankles and holding me under.

The noise of blades cutting through the air increased, and Gavin pressed my fingers until I lost sensation. Then the sound retreated and the drone kept going, the morning light reflecting off its metal surface as it purred away in the lessening gloom.

"Did it see us?" I whispered.

"I don't know. I don't think so."

We stayed put until we were sure the drone was gone, and then took off again, running faster even though we were drained. Gavin's limp grew worse. The terrain turned rocky again, the sides closing in as the slopes became more treacherous and the hollows petered out. Over stones and up steep hills, we climbed and descended, hopped streams and ducked under fallen trees.

Every muscle in my body was on fire, but I forced myself forward. I wouldn't sit and wait for them. They would have to come get me.

The ravine ended in a wide open grassy plot. A hunting blind stood at one end of it, and some deer were munching in the field. As soon as we burst from the trees, they scattered, silently disappearing back into the woods. The sun had risen higher than I'd thought. We'd spent at least an hour in the ravine. What time was it? Nine, ten?

For the first time since we started running, I entertained the hope that we could make it. That we could get far enough away to where they'd never catch us. The stale, dead grass grew waist high as we picked up speed on the open terrain. We jetted across, the faded trees at the edge of the grass becoming an oasis in the desert. If we could just make it through the field and into the woods on the other side, we could outwit Cal, outwit them all. It was like turning a page. Gavin must have felt it too, his feet thundering unevenly on the dirt as we pushed ourselves as fast as we could.

Then we heard the buzz, the familiar whir of flight. The drone had come back.

"Down," Gavin hissed.

We both dropped, lying in the grass and hoping the drone hadn't seen us. I held my breath as the sound grew closer, the hiss of the helicopter blades like a hand at my throat, cutting off my air.

The drone passed overhead and I could breathe again. The whir lessened, and I was about to get up when the noise grew louder and louder until horror atrophied my senses. I turned my head to the side and it was hovering over us, sitting in place. They'd seen.

"Fuck. Run, Stella!" Gavin lunged from the ground and

took off.

I pushed my aching muscles, the stiffness already setting in even though I'd only been still for a few moments. I dashed after him as the machine lazily followed.

We finally made the tree line.

Gavin crashed ahead. Limbs scratched my face like clawing fingers as I tried to keep up.

The machine whirred above us now, floating above the trees and keeping track. Gavin stopped so quickly in front of me that I slammed into his back.

"What?"

"We have to split up." He ran a hand through his sweat-drenched hair.

"No." I peered up through the branches. I could feel the drone staring back.

"We have to. It can't follow us both. It's our only chance."

"No. I can't. I've got your back, remember?"

His eyes softened, and he ran a cool hand across my cheek. "I know you do. We'll still be alive. Remember that, okay? I'll see you again."

"Here." I shucked his gloves off and handed them back to him. "My hands are warm. You need them."

He tried to refuse but I shoved them into his palms. "Please."

"Fine." He pulled them on and hugged me tightly before glancing sideways at the woods around us. "Left or right?"

It didn't matter. "I'll go left."

"Okay." He kissed my forehead, his lips like ice. "Go."

He limped to the right, and I hopped the fallen tree trunk to my left, skittering across the leaves and rushing between the trees. I stood at the base of a gentle slope. Turning back, I caught a flash of Gavin's white pants before he was lost in the browns and grays of the woods. The rumble of engines cut over the sound of the drone, some sort of off-road vehicles moving far faster than I could ever hope to. I balled my hands into fists and forced myself to move, fear and rage mixing to give me one final jolt of energy.

I kept going, slower now, the pain in my body, the lack of food, and the constant exertion killing what little physical ability I had left. The sun still rose, the minutes ticking off the clock. The whir of the drone never stopped. It had chosen to follow me instead of Gavin. I couldn't do anything about it, just keep moving, keep striving.

When I reached the top of the slope, I stopped to catch my breath. I felt heavy, heavier than I'd ever felt in my life. My dress was drenched with sweat, and my legs were an ugly shade of red. The wind and cold had burned them. My face was tight, the skin stinging as my silent tears flowed down over them. The sun continued its climb, but I still had at least an hour before noon.

"Stella!" A man yelled out in a perfect mimic of Marlon Brando from "Streetcar," followed by howls of laughter from others. It was distant, but not distant enough. The yawning pit in my stomach opened even wider, dragging me down.

I pushed my legs into motion, ignoring the wave of nausea and aching hurt. My feet were blistered, and my socks dug into the swollen skin. Even so, I hobbled away from my pursuers. The drone flew toward my right, toward Gavin. It had abandoned me. Why? Was I as good as caught?

I tripped halfway down the slope and tumbled into the wet leaves and over a rock before skidding to a stop against a tree. My leg was bleeding. Still, I picked myself back up and kept going.

More yells, this time "Gavin" and "Brianne" added in. They must not have found her yet. I smiled, my chapped lip splitting as I did so. Maybe she would make it.

The sound of an engine grew louder and then died. Voices. They were close.

I stumbled and wrapped my arms around the nearest tree, catching myself before falling again. I retrieved the knife from my pocket, ripping the tape off as I lurched forward. No matter what happened, I would fight. The consequences be damned.

A desperate yell met my ears and then was quickly cut off. Gavin. They had him. I wiped the back of my hand across my face, erasing the tears as I put one foot in front of the other.

I was almost to the bottom of the hill when I glimpsed movement in the trees ahead of me. I stopped, but the multiple voices at the ridge to my back had me moving again. I prayed a deer was in front of me, running from the hunters just like me. I would have laughed at the absurdity of hope, but I didn't have the energy.

My steps lingered, my feet leaden and my limbs spent. I tripped over a root and caught myself, my hands on my knees as I raised my head and peered through the shadowy trees. More movement. A man strode right toward me. The hair on the back of my neck stood up and I rose, scurrying back the way I'd come. The man's steps didn't falter. He was large and not the least bit winded. He wore the same white mask as the others, the rest of him covered in camouflage.

Blood roared in my ears as I scrambled back up the slope, back toward the grasp of the others. In the open woods, the sun filtering down in orange rays, I was caged. The crackle of leaves and heavy footsteps behind me spurred me faster. I didn't turn around, only pushed my legs harder. The steps picked up their pace, the thuds growing louder. A scream built in my throat. I turned to face him.

He was only yards away, his large arms swinging as he advanced, my destruction balled into the palms of his hands. I froze. There was nowhere to go, no one to save me. Caught. I held my knife at my side. I wouldn't go down without a fight.

He slowed when he was but steps away, then stopped and stared. His white mask obscured everything but his mouth and eyes. He took another step.

I held the blade out in front of me.

He smiled and shook his head calmly. "Stella."

I peered into his eyes. I knew them. "Dylan?"

"I told you I'd take care of you."

"Oh my god." My knees buckled, and he rushed to me, taking me in his arms before I sank to the ground. The knife tumbled from my hand and landed in the leaves at my feet. "It's you."

"It's me." He pulled me to his warm chest.

Hope exploded in my heart. "Oh my god." I wrapped my arms around his neck and buried my face in his shoulder. I had never felt so grateful in my life. I was blinded by it. "Thank you. Oh my god! It's you."

"It's me. Calm down. Shh." He moved his hands up and down my back as I clung to him.

"But how?"

"I may have gotten a head start." He smirked and cocked his ear toward the sound of male voices along the ridge at my back.

I glanced behind me, but they were still out of sight. "We have to go."

"Don't worry. I won't share you. It'll be nice to have an audience, though."

I pulled my hands away from his neck as his words slithered around in my mind. "Audience?"

"For the big show." His hands ventured lower and gripped my ass.

"Dylan." I tried to back out of his grasp, but he squeezed me to him. "What—"

He crushed his mouth to mine, his tongue stabbing at my lips. Ice trickled down my spine.

I pushed as hard as I could. "Dylan, no!"

"Shut the fuck up." He pushed his fingers between my ass cheeks, only the thin dress separating us.

Panic rose in me, twisting like a tornado, until I was biting and scratching wherever I could find purchase.

He threw me back and ran his fingers along a deep scratch in his neck. "You fucking bitch."

I darted past him and took a few long strides down the

slope. His thudding steps were at my back in moments.

"Gotcha!" Dylan tackled me to the ground. We slid through the rotting leaves and careened to the base of the hill.

We rolled a few more times until I landed on top of him and tried to scramble off, but he gripped my throat and slammed me onto the ground before climbing on top of me.

"No!" I fought, scratching at his wrists, his neck.

He batted my hands away and unzipped my jacket. Then his warm hands were on my thighs, hiking up my dress.

"Dylan, please stop. What are you doing?" I let go of his neck and pushed at his shoulders, as if that simple movement would snap him out of whatever dark daydream had taken hold in his breast.

"What I have to do." His light brown eyes, the same ones I'd trusted, shown through the mask.

"No. You don't." My mind tumbled, the thoughts not connecting. I squirmed and tried to get out from beneath him. "Stop."

"I do. This is what you need. What I need. Mom was right. I need to stop having a fucking schoolboy crush." He squeezed my throat and reached between us with his other hand.

"Dylan, no. You aren't one of them." I could barely push the words past his palm at my neck.

"No, Stella. You aren't one of *us*." I felt his hard tip pushing against my thigh.

He gripped my breast so roughly it hurt, and a strangled scream burst from my lungs. I thrashed, fighting with all I had left, but he was too big, too strong. I didn't have a chance even at full strength. He reared back and slapped me, dimming my vision. My body stilled for a moment at the force of the hit.

"That's better." He squeezed my throat as my eyes watered. "One fuck when we were kids?" He shook his head. "God, I was such a fucking pussy. I should have taken all of this a long time ago. Every time I stood over you as you slept. Every time your dad left the house and I jerked off as I watched you shower. I should have fucked you like you deserved. Like the little cunt you are. But I didn't, because I was trying to be something I'm not."

"Please don't, Dylan. Please." I cried, my tears flowing in a never-ending river as I hit and kicked at him to no avail.

He leaned closer, his eyes boring into mine. "But I'm going to make up for it now. I'm going to show you what a filthy whore you are. And I can't wait until I get you back to the house so everyone can see how I treat cunts like you, especially Lucius. I want him to watch while I fuck you until you pass out from the pain."

The rough stones dug into my back and the smell of peat and earth sank into my pores as he crushed me. "Please."

"I like you this way." He smirked down at me as his cock pressed closer to my entrance. My skin screamed as his palm tightened at my throat, his fingertips digging into the back of my neck. His hot mouth was at my collarbone, and I thought I might vomit.

"Stop!" I screamed.

And then his weight was gone.

Another masked man stood over him, a pistol in his hand, butt out. Dylan had gone completely limp next to me. I skittered back, kicking at the leaves as the man advanced, his steps sure and steady.

"Please, don't." My progress stopped as I backed into a tree trunk and I put out a shaking hand. "Please, I'm begging you. Please, I won't survive. I can't survive it."

"Stella. It's me." He gripped my hand and pulled me up.

"Sin?" I couldn't trust my senses anymore. I glanced at Dylan's prone form and then quickly back to the man. I couldn't trust anyone.

He lifted the mask. It was him.

I wanted his warmth, his strength. I couldn't move.

He yanked the mask back down over his face.

"Are you going to do it?" I stared into his eyes, the tempestuous blue so familiar, the man behind them so strange.

His eyes narrowed, as if I'd hurt him. He stepped toward me, but I had nowhere to go. My stomach twisted in a knot as he glared down at me. Then he bent over and threw me over his shoulder.

"Play along or we're both dead. Got it?"

I didn't say anything. I didn't even know what he meant. The blood rushed to my head and my vision swam.

He slapped my ass, the sting worse because of the cold. "Got it?"

"Yes."

I heard shouts at the top of the ridge. More men coming for me.

He kicked a break of leaves down on top of Dylan and lumbered up the slope, me swinging limply at his back. "I raped you. You hate me. I'm going to take you back to the house and rape you some more. Oh, and I'm Lucius. All that clear?"

"Yes."

"Good." He hefted me higher on his shoulder, my ribs pressed against his back. "The hate part should be easy enough."

"Wait, my knife!" I scanned around the area where Dylan had first found me. There was a slight glint in the leaves. "There it is!"

"What knife?"

"Please, I need it. It's right behind you."

"Dammit, Stella." He whirled and knelt before standing back up, lifting my weight easily. "I got it. Hang on. This is actually a stroke of luck." He made a fast movement and then his left hand was all over my ass.

"What—"

"It's done." He growled. "Now, shut up. Or cry. Either would work."

The voices got louder. "Fuck, someone already got her."

"Shit!" A younger man's voice. "Hey man, you sharing?"

"No, I already bottomed her out anyway. Now I'm going

Celia Aaron

to take her back and rip the fuck out of her ass."

"Which one is that?"

"Stella."

"Goddammit. That one was my favorite."

As if I were a toy and he could collect them all. Rage rose in my worn-out body, but I stayed silent. I would do whatever it took to get out of here.

"Son, there's still one more. Come on. Let's keep hunting." An older man's voice, his antique drawl right out of the antebellum South. "But I am curious. Who is the lucky hunter?"

"Lucius," Vinemont called, his steps slow and steady up the hill.

The old man cawed out a laugh. "Well I'll be damned. The Vinemont boy caught his own goddamn Acquisition and took the cherry. Good work, my boy. Cal will definitely be impressed with that. Did she cry?"

"Of course she did. She's weak. Begged, pleaded, and screamed when I shoved it in. Fucking bitch didn't know when to shut up. I had to cover her mouth, and you know I hate that. I prefer it when they scream."

"As do I. As do I. Come on, Brent, let's get back to business. This little chat has my blood up. I'm going to tell Cal about your performance, Lucius."

Vinemont shifted, and I felt him shaking hands with the stranger. "You do that. Sovereign would look pretty damn good in front of my name."

Another laugh from the older man.

"You sure you're not sharing?" The other one—Brent—spoke, and a hand ran up my leg and gripped my ass.

"I'm sure. This cunt is just sweet enough for me. Go find your own, boys. Better luck next time. But if you catch Brianne, I might just trade up."

The man squeezed harder, and I cried out.

"Sounds good to me. We'll take you up on that when we find her." The hand released me.

"Good hunting."

384

"Congratulations again, Lucius. Keep up the good work." The older man said, his voice farther away now, and mixed with the sound of crunching leaves.

"Yes sir."

CHAPTER FIFTEEN
SINCLAIR

I WALKED PAST the dozens of congratulations and offers to fuck Stella. The house was abuzz with a Vinemont victory. I nodded and waved, smiled at them all as I still carried her slung over my shoulder like the spoils of war.

"Take the mask off. Let's see you." One of the older ladies crowed as I stomped up the stairs to Lucius' suite.

"No can do, ma'am. The mask makes her scream almost as much as the rest of me."

She laughed and smacked Stella on the ass. "Get her."

Once past the crone, I had one more set of stairs to ascend before she'd be safe.

"Caught your own girl?" Red leaned against the railing. From where he stood, he'd seen me from the moment I walked in with her over my shoulder.

I gave a curt nod. I wasn't sure if he'd recognize my voice. His gaze shifted to Stella, to the blood from my palm I'd smeared on her.

"Looks like you put it to her the way she deserves." He slid his hand up her leg and she tried to kick him. He dodged but backed up a step, still eyeing her. "I sure would like a little taste."

I shook my head. "Not sharing," I said as quickly as possible.

His eyes widened for a split second. Did he know who I was? I wasn't going to wait to find out. I walked past and felt Stella's hand pressing on my lower back. I glanced over my shoulder to see her pushing up from me so she could give Red the finger.

He gripped his crotch in response. "Next time, bitch."

I continued toward the suite, passing an open door on my right. I glanced in. Gavin was there, his hands tied behind his back and a gag in his mouth as Judge Montagnet rutted on him like a boar. *Fucking animals.* I glanced away from Gavin's mournful eyes. I had enough pain without sharing his. Stella swung hard against my back as I turned so she wouldn't glimpse her friend.

The rest of the way was smooth sailing to Lucius' room. I kicked the door, and he swung it open before shutting it tight behind us and propping a chair under the handle.

"Did you get to her first?"

"Mostly." I hurried through the main room and into the bedroom, setting her down on the bed and kneeling in front of her.

Her lip was split, her cheeks and forehead wind burned. There was a cut on her leg. She was dirty, with black dirt under her fingernails and smudges on her face. The urge to kill everyone who'd hurt her, chased her, tried to violate her rose up inside me and threatened to block out any rational thought.

She reached out with a trembling hand and stripped off my mask, tears welling in her eyes and spilling down her cheeks. "You came for me."

"I told you I always would."

"Jesus." Lucius kicked an accent table, breaking the leg off.

Usually, I would have scolded him for the outburst, but for this the noise was necessary, desired even. Everyone needed to believe Lucius was rough fucking her while she cried. The more brutal, the better.

"Get the first aid stuff I brought."

Lucius unzipped a case and yanked out some of my clothes and other items, including a bag full of medical supplies. He handed it over to me. "If that's all you need, I'm going into the other room."

"Go ahead. Make plenty of noise."

"Not a fucking problem." He slammed the bedroom door, cranked up the sound system with some angry metal, and then there were a series of crashes.

"Stella, I'll need you to scream for me. Can you do that?"

She nodded as I moved the pads of my thumbs over her cheeks, wiping away the tears. A shallow cut ran along my palm. I'd used her knife on myself and smeared the blood on the bottom of her dress, made it even more believable as I'd carried her around like a trophy.

"Go ahead. Scream."

She let out a peel of shrieks, her body quaking from the effort.

"Okay, that's good for now."

She stopped and shivered, shaking uncontrollably, her teeth chattering. She needed heat.

A scream sounded from somewhere else in the building. They must have found Brianne.

"No." Stella's faced crumpled and she covered it with her hands. "No. I hid her. I hid her."

"It's not your fault." It was mine. I'd seen Brianne's hiding spot when I'd first set out for Stella. I'd radioed back to another party that something appeared odd at that break in the forest and intentionally used an open channel so everyone heard. The ensuing search for Brianne bought more time for me to find Stella first. But I'd still failed. I could only hope that Dylan would keep his mouth shut about what happened. He'd turned out to be more intelligent than I'd originally thought, and definitely more devious. I might have even liked him if he weren't trying to take what was mine.

I gently pulled her wrists away, the coldness of her skin shocking me into action. I rose and went to the bathroom, finding a whirlpool tub with a forest mosaic of tiles surrounding it. I turned on the water and adjusted it until it was just north of lukewarm. Once the bath was running at the right temperature, I went back to her. She sat unmoved, fear and sadness painting her face, turning her eyes into sad emerald pools.

"Come on." I helped her up, but she groaned as she stood and fell back. "What is it?"

"Everything, but mostly my feet." She bent over and tried to unzip her boots, but her fingers couldn't grasp the tabs. I eased her hands away and slid the zipper down on each one.

Her legs were burned like her face, and I was as careful as I could be. I pulled the first boot off. Her sock was bloody, and she cried out as I stripped it from her foot. Blisters had risen and burst all along her feet and ankles.

"Shit." The bath would sting like hell, but I need to clean all her wounds. "Just hang on to my shoulders, okay? You can hurt me all you want. I don't care. Just hold on to me."

She grabbed me as I pulled the second boot away, her nails digging into my thermal shirt and the skin underneath. When I peeled the sock off, she let out a strangled scream, and I heard something break on the other side of the suite door.

"I got it. I got you." I looked up at her. The pain in her eyes tore me apart. I wanted nothing more than to stop her hurt.

I eased my hands to her shoulders, keeping it slow as I pushed her jacket off. Underneath was nothing more than a paltry white shift, the bottom hem ripped away. I clenched my jaw at the thought of her out in the woods, frightened, and wearing nothing more than a thin nightgown. Cal was a sadistic piece of shit.

I gripped the muddied hem. "I have to take this off."

She shivered more and placed her hands over mine.

"Don't."

"It's dirty, Stella. The bath is going to be nice and warm." I moved my hands up the slightest bit, lifting the skirt up her thighs. "It's okay. Here, just guide my hands."

I kept my grip on the nightie at her upper thigh until she pulled. I lifted it higher, almost to the apex of her thighs when she pushed against me and I stopped.

"I'm not going to prey on you, Stella. I just want to help." I knew my words sounded hollow to her after everything I'd done, but I held her gaze and tried to make her believe them.

She hesitated, then pulled more. I raised the shift higher and stood, drawing it from her arms and tossing it in the floor. An ugly bruise—purple edged with yellow and green—covered a large part of her forearm.

"What happened there?"

"A woman. She hit me." Stella blinked down at the injury. "Before we ran."

I made a mental note to find out who it was and punish the bitch accordingly. "I'm going to lift you and take you to the bath."

I bent over slowly, treating her like I would a skittish horse that was too afraid to be treated. I slid my hands under her knees and across her upper back.

She made a noise and bit her lip. "It hurts."

"I know." I carried her to the bath and lowered her into the tub.

Her face twisted in a mix of relief and pain as the water rushed up to meet her. Once she was in, I turned off the water and stripped off my wet shirt, tossing it out the door in the same heap with her dress.

She glanced up, taking in my chest and stomach before she closed her eyes and leaned her head back.

I sat on the edge of the tub, my gaze tracing the curves of her body beneath the water. I'd tried not to look when she was on the bed, but my cock was hard all the same. Because I was a bastard.

The water trembled as she shivered, the heat not seeping into her fast enough. Her hair floated around her shoulders, the red strands delicate against her pale skin and the white of the tub.

She shifted and groaned, but her teeth no longer chattered, and some color was returning to the parts of her skin that weren't chapped.

"You can't stay in here long. Hot water isn't the best for the blisters."

"Just let me sit for a little while longer." Her eyes didn't open, and her voice had a distant quality, relaxed and sleepy.

I went to the vanity and dug around in the cabinets, finding towels, shampoo, wash cloths, and soaps. I grabbed a bar, smelled it, tossed it, and then picked another. This one was more on point, sweet without being overpowering.

I sat on the edge of the tub again and dipped the cloth in the water before using the soap to lather it up. Stella's head lolled to the side as her breathing smoothed into a steady rhythm. Something warmed inside me at the thought that she felt safe enough to fall asleep in my presence. That, or she'd simply been pushed beyond exhausted.

I put my arm down in the tub and gingerly lifted her leg. The blisters were clean from the water, but still an angry red, with deflated skin around the wounds. They would hurt for a while. Good news was I had something in the first aid kit for it. Bad news was I didn't think Stella would willingly let me drug her. Not that it mattered. I would do it either way to help her through this mess.

I soaped up her foot and she woke, sucking in a pained breath.

"I'm done. I'm done." I moved up her calf and massaged as I cleaned.

She moaned.

"This okay?"

"Yes. Don't stop." Her throaty whisper had my cock straining against my pants, but I ignored it.

I continued working my fingers into her muscles, and

her mouth opened. She was panting as I got to her thigh and massaged out the knots there. When I neared her pussy, I forced myself to stop and place her leg back on the bottom of the tub. Then I lifted the other one and did the same.

By the time I was done, she watched me with half lidded eyes. I had the impulse to jump in the tub with her and sink between her thighs. Instead, I dutifully soaped the washcloth again and worked up another good lather. I gently scrubbed her face, her delicate neck, graceful shoulders, and arms. The bruise seemed even uglier now that the rest of her was clean.

I soaped her chest and ran the washcloth along her pert breasts, the nipples hard and begging for attention. I swiped lower, cleaning her before putting a hand behind her back and leaning her forward. I rested her upper chest on my palm as I washed her back. She was like dough in my hands, soft and pliable. Vulnerable.

I leaned her back and poured water in her hair. I shampooed her scalp, the first time in my life I'd ever done such a thing. Her neck bore ugly bruises from Dylan's hands. Anger coiled in my stomach like a snake waiting to strike, but I shut it down and concentrated on Stella. Once I rinsed the suds from her hair and she was clean, I hit the drain.

"No." Her protest was weak.

I gripped under her arms and lifted her until she stood, the water sluicing down her body. She was more than I could take, so beautiful that it hurt. I wrapped a towel around her and scooped her up again before carrying her back to the bedroom. The king size bed with the black comforter swallowed her whole.

I inspected her feet. They were still in a bad way and needed antibacterial ointment and bandages. Her eyes were closed, her wet hair fanning out against the pillow. I would kill two birds with one stone. I got the first aid items and laid out alcohol, ointment, gauze, tape, and one final thing—a syringe.

393

CELIA AARON

"Stella? This is going to hurt."

She murmured something unintelligible. With the syringe in one hand, I dabbed alcohol onto a blister with the other. She awoke on a scream, the sound raising the hair on the back of my neck. It was perfect.

I gripped her arm hard and kept it still as I slid the needle into her vein and depressed the plunger. She looked at me, lightly shaking her head as one tear fell. Then she was out. Hitting a vein on a struggling woman was one of my specialties, thanks to my mother.

Another crash from the living quarters. This time it sounded like Lucius had ripped the flat screen off the wall.

I took my time with her, cleaning every blister, every scratch. An hour later, she was bandaged and sleeping comfortably. I undressed and took a quick shower, though I hated letting her out of my sight. Lucius would guard us, not that I expected any guests. I'd made clear that Stella was mine and that I wasn't sharing. Or, that Lucius wasn't sharing, as they thought.

I was still amazed that he'd called me last night. That he'd given up and wanted to transfer her back to me. It didn't work that way, of course. He never gave me a reason why, though I suspected the rules had something to do with it. And when he'd explained this particular trial to me, I knew I had to get to Stella first. To be the one who took her or saved her, as the case may be.

I hated myself for knowing that I would have done it if I'd had to. If someone had been watching, I would have committed the act. I had no choice. It was the only way to keep her safe from the others, and the only way to win the Acquisition. Would she have ever forgiven me? I shook my head, not wanting to consider that alternate outcome.

She rested peacefully, her chest rising and falling, and every so often a sweet sigh escaped her lips as if she were in a pleasant dream. The drugs wouldn't wear off for a few hours. I dug through my bag, pulled on some boxers, and picked out some panties and pajamas for her. I slipped the

394

towel away from her body and my cock was rock hard in an instant. I slid a pair of panties up her legs, careful to avoid the bandages, followed by a pair of shorts. Once I pulled her top over her head and threaded her arms through it, I pulled the sheet down and lay down beside her.

I couldn't look away. She was the only thing I'd seen for months. Even when she wasn't in my presence, I saw her. More than that, I felt her. She'd taken up residence inside me. I shifted closer, her body so near mine that I could feel her heat. It was a comfort. I watched over her. I was here, with her, and she was safe.

CHAPTER SIXTEEN
STELLA

I WOKE WITH one thought. *He saved me*. I was warm, with my head on his chest and his arm around my shoulders. He was everywhere—his scent, his body, him. I stretched against him and my muscles ached. My feet stung, and my arm felt as if it were broken. The morning came back in a rush, and I sat straight up despite the pain.

Vinemont sat up with me and scanned the room before turning his gaze back to me.

Dusk had fallen outside. How long had I been here?

"You drugged me." I felt along my arm where the needle had gone in.

"You needed it."

"Maybe, but you can't just drug me!"

"It won't happen again." He smirked, the signature twist of his lips familiar enough to be comforting. "It won't happen again unless you are in extreme pain and by drugging you, I am easing that pain."

"Is this the shit they taught you in law school? Because it doesn't work."

"It does work." The smirk grew. "Just not on you."

"The others?" Gavin's yell played in my mind, joined by

397

Brianne's scream. My heart sank.

"I haven't heard a peep for an hour or so. I think they've finally been given a reprieve."

His nonchalance was like a slap in the face. I tried to scoot toward the end of the bed and stand, but the movement made my body scream. My left thigh cramped, and I rolled onto my side, gripping it. The tightness ramped up, like my muscle was being twisted around a corkscrew, and I gritted my teeth through the ache. Vinemont got on his knees, his strong hands rubbing the muscle hard until the pain subsided.

"I'm okay. It's gone now." I flipped to my back, and he fell next to me on his elbow. I met his eyes. "Just don't talk about them like that. They're people. It could have been me." I remembered Dylan, what he'd tried to do, and I put a hand to my throat. "It almost was me."

"Don't think about it." He slid his arm under my neck and pulled me into him. "I'm sorry. Just don't think about it."

"Did you just say sorry?"

He let out a low laugh, his Adam's apple bobbing. "Maybe."

"You did. I'm not falling for this again." I moved my head back so I could see into his eyes, and perhaps even deeper. "I know you're going to turn back into Mr. Hyde tomorrow."

"Likely." He clutched me to him, his fingers splayed across my back.

"Why can't you be like this all the time?"

"Because I can't."

"But why?" I wouldn't let him get away, not this time. I pushed back from him again so I could see his eyes, and I rested my palm on his cheek. "What changes?"

His eyes softened the slightest bit as he considered me, and he was here. The man I knew he could be. Not the vile monster he so often was. My heart burned to know why. But just as soon as the softness came, it was gone again.

"I remember my obligations." He rolled away and sat up before running both hands through his hair. "I won't discuss it further."

I lay back, shut out again like I had been so many times before. What wouldn't he tell me? What was the game within the game? Something more was happening. Something just beyond the periphery that I couldn't see.

"I need you to do something for me." He looked back over his shoulder.

"What?"

"I need you to tell Cal that you want to transfer your ownership back to me."

"Why?"

"I'll explain later. But you need to do it today. Will you?"

"Shouldn't we talk to Lucius?"

"No. It's already been decided between the two of us. Now it's up to you." He turned to face me, the late afternoon sun shining over his shoulder. "Will you be mine again?"

It was a twisted proposal, one that should have come with a ring and love. Instead, it came with a lock and key.

"It doesn't really matter who owns me, does it? It just matters that I'm owned." I sighed. "Fine. I'll tell him."

"Good. Now that that's settled, let's get the fuck out of here as soon as possible." He rose, the chiseled planes of his body on full display. Desire rushed through me like a wildfire. I intentionally pressed my foot into the bed for the sting of pain to cut off my need for him. It didn't work. The sting only heightened my arousal, the pressure between my thighs growing.

He contemplated me, his eyes locked on mine. I didn't have to look down to know he was hard, to know he wanted me.

I wanted him, too. But could I deal with the consequences? When he threatened me and hurt me again the next day, would I hate myself? I knew the answer and turned away, breaking the moment, severing the tie.

Vinemont helped me down the stairs with Lucius following a few steps behind. It seemed more believable since Lucius was my supposed rapist.

Cal was glad-handing guests as they left.

"That was one hell of a party." Judge Montagnet was ahead of us, grinning and patting Cal on the shoulder. "That boy Gavin, whew!"

"Glad you enjoyed him. I enjoyed watching, I can tell you that."

"Can't wait to see what spring holds."

Spring. My stomach churned at the thought of what happened to Gavin and the trials that remained.

"You're going to love it." Cal smiled as the judge made his way out into the falling night.

Cal's smile fell away as I hobbled up on Vinemont's arm. "I heard we had an unannounced guest."

"My apologies, Sovereign." Vinemont hefted me closer into his side, and I kept my eyes downcast.

"Lucius, my man." Cal beamed and patted the younger Vinemont on the back. "I heard quite a story from Senator Calgary about how you bagged Stella here."

"All true." Lucius shook Cal's hand, but I still didn't raise my eyes.

"Maybe you finally broke this little filly. Stella, look at me, darling. Let me see those gorgeous green eyes."

I shook my head.

"Do it." Cal's voice was instantly cold.

I raised my head slowly. He peered at me, his watchful eyes studying every inch of me.

"Oh, I don't know. I think I see some spirit left." He grinned. "All the more fun for the next trial."

Vinemont cleared his throat. "About that, Cal. Stella has

something she wants to say."

"And what's that, little Stella?"

I looked to Vinemont who gave me a small nod. "I want to go back to Sinclair."

Cal chuckled and glanced to the juncture of my thighs. "Was Lucius too rough on you?"

I dropped my gaze again.

"Do you even want her back, now that she's all used up, Sinclair?" Cal crossed his arms over his chest.

"Not particularly, but if Lucius has to spend all his time in Cuba fighting off threats from other families, sacrifices must be made."

"The Eagletons trying to cozy up to the regime again?" Cal asked, his tone conspiratorial.

"Not sure just yet," Lucius said.

"Well, the Acquisition does get to choose between first and second born." Cal tapped his chin. "I don't think we've ever had one change hands twice, though. This will set an interesting precedent. But I'll allow it. Of course, Lucius' performance at this trial won't carry much weight in my final determination, but if this is what you want, Sinclair, then it's fine with me. Just keep it this way, is all I ask. More paperwork for me, you see?" Cal clapped his hands, signaling an end to the conversation.

Vinemont helped me hobble away.

Cal's voice called out behind us. "You better perform the best at the next two, Sinclair, or you may be in for some trouble."

Vinemont stiffened but kept moving. "Got it, Cal."

The open air enveloped us, and I was finally able to breathe. Vinemont gave up trying to help me along and swung me up in his arms as he took the stairs down.

Luke held the back passenger door open and Vinemont placed me inside before joining me.

Lucius leaned over in the window. "I've got a ride with, um, Amanda over there. I'll catch you two later."

The woman we'd met on the way in the day before stood

next to a sports car, watching Lucius like a lion eyeing a gazelle. And I sincerely doubted her name was Amanda.

Lucius didn't look at me, just gave a sarcastic salute to Vinemont before straightening.

"Don't stay gone too long," Vinemont said. "We've got business."

'Fuck off." Lucius strode away toward 'his ride'.

"Dick." Vinemont shook his head with a slight smile. "Luke, take us home."

"Yes sir." Luke pulled around the circular drive and followed the line of cars down the lane.

I yawned, fatigue still so deep in my bones that I wondered if I would ever feel at full energy again. I rested my head against the window, the coolness giving my chapped skin the slightest relief before the glass warmed. The trees hurried by, along with the now too familiar hollows and boulders. I hoped I'd never see these woods again.

I sat up and leaned my head back, not wanting to see anymore. The dark material of the car's roof was a much more palatable view. I closed my eyes, but opened them again immediately. Brianne's frightened face, streaked with dirt and scratched by branches, had appeared. I couldn't think about her, about Gavin. Not yet.

Vinemont shifted. I let my head loll sideways toward him. He'd stripped off his long wool overcoat. "Come here." Before I could move, he'd put one hand at my back, the other at my knees, and pulled me into him, laying me down so my head rested in his lap.

"What are you doing?"

He gazed down at me, his dark hair shading his forehead. It was longer than I'd ever seen it. And I knew it was soft, perhaps even softer than mine. He seemed older now. Or maybe I was the one who'd aged in the months since we'd met. He draped his coat over me, and I slid my feet toward the door. I wasn't going to fight it. I didn't have the strength.

One of his hands rested lightly on my waist, and the

other trailed through my hair. "Sleep. I've got you. I know you're drained."

"I'm scared." I hated myself the moment I said it. Admitting things like that to him was like laying my neck bare and handing him a blade.

"I know." His fingers started at my scalp and smoothed another long lock of hair. He glanced up as we finally left the drive and entered the main road, his soft v-neck sweater falling right below his collarbones. His strong chin and jaw, along with the darker shadow on his cheeks, threw him in sharp relief. He was so beautiful. I moved my arm from under his coat and reached up, tracing my fingertips down his jaw and neck, feeling every little bit of stubble, every piece of sinew, every strong pulse of his blood.

He looked back down as I dropped my hand.

"Close your eyes."

I shook my head against him. Gavin and Brianne would be there, their bodies ruined, their hearts ripped apart.

"You're safe. I promise. And I always keep my word." He moved his hand from my waist and put his warm palm on my cheek. "Close them."

He ran his thumb over my lips lightly, the feeling more soothing than sexual.

Safe in his arms, I closed my eyes.

I didn't remember how I got to my bed, but I woke the next day to torrential rain. I glanced at the clock. It was already past noon. I lay still for a long time, letting my body slowly wake up, each sting of pain a reminder that I was alive, just like Gavin said I would be.

Gavin. I rolled to my side, the effort making the muscles in my legs try to seize. The hurt subdued me, and I focused on breathing through it. A tray was at my bedside with a sandwich, an apple, some chips, and a glass of tea. It looked like it hadn't been there long.

"Renee?" My voice was hoarse, but plenty loud enough.

I heard the creak of a floorboard and then heavy footfalls. Not Renee's. My door opened and Vinemont came into view. He flipped on the light. I closed my eyes against the sudden glare. The light flicked off again, and he strode to my window where he pulled back the curtains and let in the soft glow of sun through rain.

"Better?" His deep baritone washed over me.

"Yes, thank you."

He stood over me, inspecting my face before moving to the foot of the bed checking the bandages on my feet. Seemingly appeased, he returned to my side.

"You need to eat." He put his hands under my arms and pulled me into a sitting position before placing a pillow behind my back and resting me against it.

I ached all over, groaning even though he was gentle with me. Once I was settled, he drew the blanket back up and set the tray in my lap.

"Where's Renee?"

"Just eat. I'll have the doctor come in when you're done and fix you up proper." He opened the little bag of chips and placed it back in front of me.

"Will you just tell me if she's all right?" I placed my hand on his arm and wondered if the rest of him was as warm.

"Take a bite and I'll tell you if she's buried out back, okay?"

My eyes grew large, the loss too much for me to bear, but then I saw his mischievous look, the corners of his mouth turned up.

"Are you *teasing* me about killing Renee?"

"Maybe. Now take a big bite since you didn't do it when I asked the first time."

I did as he said. The sandwich was actually delicious, made just the way I liked with fresh tomatoes and turkey.

"She's fine." He slid his arm down, and I thought he was

going to pull away, but instead our fingers met and he entwined them. "She's here. She's just occupied elsewhere."

I swallowed, relief flooding me, before taking another bite. I was suddenly ravenous. Vinemont smiled and handed me a napkin. I took the hint and wiped my mouth, Dijon mustard coming away on the cloth.

"Elsewhere?" I asked between bites. "Do you mean upstairs?"

His fingers tightened on mine. "You know, then?"

"I know your mother's alive. Not much else. Feel free to fill me in." The chips were salty and perfect, and I downed the sweet tea to finish it all off.

"There's nothing to tell. She's been up there for years." He stared out the window at the sheets of rain, milky white in the gloom. He slipped his fingers from mine and took the tray before standing. "I'm going to send in Dr. Yarbrough and Laura. Keep resting."

When he got to the door, my emotions got the better of me. "When are you coming back?" I knew I was a fool for wanting him, for my weakness. I couldn't stop it any more than I could stop what happened to Gavin and Brianne.

"Soon." He walked away, and not long after I heard more footsteps—the doctor and Laura as promised.

Laura stripped my gauze and helped me bathe, then she ushered me back to the bed so Dr. Yarbrough could clean my injuries and re-bandage them. He laid out some pills on the bedside table and made sure I took one.

"For the pain." He didn't have much of a bedside manner. Perhaps he'd seen too much. With his age, I suspected he may have doctored Renee during her Acquisition year. He must have seen it all, become numb to it. Competent and distant—maybe it was the smartest way to be around these people.

"I'll be back around tomorrow." He picked up his black leather bag and left while Laura puttered around my room, a certain nervousness in her quick movements.

"What is it?" I asked as the faint rumble of thunder

rolled over the house.

"Nothing." She straightened my blanket, even though I would just kick it off once I was asleep.

"Something." I tilted my head at her and patted the bed. "Sit. What is it?"

She paused and then slowly walked over to me and sat, her small frame barely making an indention in the bed. The thunder grew louder, the rain pouring over the higher eaves, making a small waterfall outside my window.

"It's Renee."

I sat up. "What about her?"

"It's just," she glanced to the closed door and back to me, "I'm not supposed to talk about..." She looked up.

I took her meaning. "About Vinemont's mother?"

She nodded and dropped her voice to a whisper. "But I've heard things when I've been in Teddy's room." Her cheeks pinked. "Cleaning in Teddy's room," she corrected herself.

"Like what?"

"Bangs and yells and crying. All sorts of things that never happened before. I've never been allowed up there, and I know neither of us are supposed to go and see. But I know that's where Renee is. I prepare meals for two now instead of one, and send them up with Mr. Farns."

I gripped her arm. "Do you think Mrs. Vinemont is hurting Renee?"

"I think so." She shrugged, her narrow shoulders carrying more weight than seemed possible. "It's worse up there now. And it's worse down here, too. Teddy hears it and he sort of, I don't know. He just gets so sad, and it doesn't matter what I do or say; I can't help him." She wiped at her eyes with the hem of her white apron.

Something upstairs had changed. The silent partner in this Acquisition mess was making plenty of noise all the sudden. I moved my feet under the blanket. I winced as a stinging pain erupted along my injured skin. I didn't have a chance of getting upstairs anytime soon, especially not stealthily. Maybe a week or so. Then I could investigate.

"Why tell me?"

She sniffed and brought her gaze to mine. "You're the only one I've ever seen get to them. I mean, Teddy talks about you like a sister." She laughed. "I was even jealous at first when you came." Her giggle died on her tongue. "But then that morning in the dining room, when Mr. Sinclair made you stand and m-made Teddy watch. I didn't envy you. I still don't fully know what the Acquisition is—"

"Join the club."

"But I know it's ripping them all apart. I don't want Teddy hurt. I lo—" She stopped herself.

"It's okay to love him, Laura. He's a good boy. Man, I guess. He's a good man."

The two of them wouldn't have an easy road, but the love they shared was obvious. I hoped that one day they could leave the Vinemont legacy behind entirely and strike out on their own.

Tears rolled down her round cheeks. "I know. I'm worried about him. I'm worried about Renee." She picked at the hem of her apron. "I just don't know what to do. I would march right up to the third floor, but then I'd lose my job and my chance to see Teddy."

I patted her arm. "I'm already in hell. Going down another circle won't hurt me too much. I'll check it out as soon as I'm able." I waved at my legs and feet.

She turned her body toward me, staring at me head on. "How are you so brave? How do you do it?"

Brave? That's not a word I'd ever associated with myself. "I'm just surviving."

"You *are* brave." Tears still shone in her bright eyes. "I know what they did to your back. I heard a rumor about where you went the last couple of days, what they were going to do to you." She dropped her gaze. "I would have given up if I were you."

"No, you wouldn't." I leaned my head back, the pill starting to do its work. "You would do what you had to do.

You would go through hell. But you would be alive on the other side. You'd be different. I'm different. But I'm alive."

"Brave," she said again, and rose. The thunder boomed right overhead, the sound vibrating in my lungs, my mind.

I turned my head and stared out the window, the streaking rain becoming nothing but a gray blur as she left and clicked the door shut.

The next few days were spent in bed, Laura visiting more and more frequently. I sketched and sketched. Most of my drawings were of the wisteria in bloom from the house in New Orleans, or skeletal trees spiking in a desolate landscape.

I didn't see Vinemont or Lucius, though Laura told me they were out of the country on business. I wondered if that meant Cuba. Teddy came by to visit, though he avoided any questions about how I came to be laid up like I was.

By the third day, the weather had turned frigid, and Laura said we had a chance at some snow that night or the next day. It was Christmas Eve. I'd been up and around a few times, the pain in my feet subsiding and my bruises maturing into light yellow hues.

I sketched some more, this time a man's face. I roughed in the first few harsh lines and kept going. More strokes, and lines, and shading, until a familiar, square jaw emerged, and then full lips, and the sharp line of a nose. His eyes were difficult. They could be so emotive at times, so impassive at others. In the end, his look was something warm. The way he'd looked at me after the lightning strike, or when he cradled me in his lap on the way back from the woods. He'd worn the look enough for me to picture it, to capture it in charcoal.

The day grew late, the sun setting through a bevy of high,

billowing clouds. Music began drifting through the halls. I halted my drawing and listened. At first it was just the rumble of drums, the whine of a guitar, and the tinkling of piano keys—all of it a discordant mosh. Then, a song took shape, the drums setting the rhythm and the guitar playing the melody while the piano filled out the sound. Was there a party?

I set the drawing aside and swung my legs out of bed. The muscle soreness had thankfully diminished, but my feet were still tender. I snugged them into the fluffy slippers Laura had brought me and stood. I could stand the twinges of pain, so I slowly maneuvered around the room, slinging on a bath robe to cover my pajamas before creeping into the hallway.

The sound came from downstairs. The music room off the foyer. It took me a while, and the song seemed to be almost finished by the time I reached the bottom step, but I relished the feel of finally moving. By the time I turned the corner, the song was over and a new drum beat began. Lucius sat at the drums and counted off before Teddy began riffing on the guitar. Vinemont sat at the piano, his back straight, and his fingers at the ready.

I smiled. It was a genuine grin that I couldn't contain. It grew even bigger as the piano joined in, Vinemont picking up and playing to Teddy's notes. I eased into a high-backed chair and Vinemont looked up, his fingers still working the keys. He didn't miss a note, and his answering smile made my chest warm. Shots were lined up across the top of the piano, three sets of five glasses, though one of each had already been drained.

Teddy's nimble fingers ran back and forth on the frets and strings like he was in an eighties hairband. They played well together, following the squeals and improvisation of the guitar, but staying within the parameters of Lucius' beat. We all laughed when Teddy went even more over the top, started a run toward me, hit his knees and slid up to my chair, still wailing on the guitar.

"Big finish!" He hopped to his feet from his knees and bopped his head along to the beat before letting his fingers fly so fast over so many notes that Vinemont threw his hands up and leaned back, grinning at his brother.

With the piano out, Lucius kept the beat going until Teddy ended on a screechingly high pitch that made me want to cover my ears. Then he tossed his pick at me. I was more surprised than anyone when I actually caught it.

I applauded and heard more clapping; Laura and Farns stood in the doorway at my back.

"Another," I demanded.

"What would the lady like to hear?" Teddy swiped his hair off his forehead.

I glanced over my shoulder at Laura. "Requests?"

"Well, seeing how it's Christmas Eve, can we do a carol or something Christmasy?"

"Sin? You feeling it this year?" Teddy asked.

Vinemont looked at me, then quickly back down at the piano. "No, not that one."

Teddy grinned even bigger. "'Last Christmas' it is."

"Shots!" Lucius leaned over to pluck one from the piano.

Vinemont and Teddy grabbed their respective glasses, clinked with each other, and then drained them.

Teddy's face twisted up and he rubbed the back of his sleeve across his mouth. "Damn." He walked back over to me. "Um, I'm going to need that pick back."

I laughed and handed it to him. He shed the electric guitar and picked up an acoustic, slinging the strap over his shoulder.

He winked at Laura. "You'll love it. It's my fave." He backed up. "All right, Lucius. Hit it."

Lucius tapped the cymbal and then started a beat on the snare punctuated with the bass on the downbeats.

Vinemont smirked as he began playing lightly in the background. I knew the song. It was an eighties staple from some long-defunct boy band that played on the radio every year at the holidays.

Teddy's voice rang out, smooth and clear. I was shocked at how exquisitely and freely he sang. He made the notes sound easy as he played along, rocking slightly as he kept Lucius' beat. All three of them worked together beautifully.

This was how they were supposed to be. A team, a unit that functioned best when they were all in accord. Even Lucius was smiling, his happiness making him seem younger and far more carefree than I knew he was.

Teddy held Laura's eye for quite some time as he belted out the lyrics—heartfelt and cheesy at the same time. But he pulled it off, and the smile never faltered from my face, though I watched Vinemont watching me more than anything else. He swayed to the music, not at all like a concert pianist; more like someone who felt the beat but wasn't ruled by it.

My stomach fluttered as if I had joined in on the last round of shots. He wore a simple black t-shirt, the ever-present vines wrapping around his biceps and to his forearms. I studied each movement, each sway, each time he moved to the lower notes or the higher.

Teddy reached the end of the song, singing soulfully about giving his heart to someone special.

I leaned back and whispered to Laura. "Are you going to throw him your panties?"

She giggled and slapped at my shoulder.

The song wound down, and Teddy held the last note for longer than I could hold my breath. Everyone laughed, Farns gripping his stomach and looking positively gleeful. The only one missing was Renee, and I intended to make my inquiries as soon as possible. This little trip downstairs was proof I was ready to roam a little farther.

"What next?" Teddy asked.

"'It's Cold Outside'?" Laura suggested.

"Can we handle that, boys?" Teddy asked.

Lucius did a drum roll in response, and Vinemont matched it with a flourish.

Teddy grinned. "That's a duet, Laura. Come on up."

"Oh no. No." She backed away. "I couldn't carry a note in a bucket."

"We have to have the woman's part." Teddy strummed, searching for the right key.

"Stella?" Vinemont asked, raising an eyebrow at me.

I could sing. But I wasn't sure if I could sing in front of him. I shook my head, color heating my cheeks.

"Aww, she can sing. Look at that face." Teddy laughed and put his guitar on the floor. He hurried forward and scooped me up.

"Hey!" I cried. "Why does everyone manhandle me around here?"

He set me on the piano. "You okay?"

My legs hung over the edge and blood rushed to my feet, though the slight tingle of sensation didn't hurt. Despite my irritation, I couldn't help but smile at Teddy. "Yes."

"Good." He grabbed two glasses from his line of shots and handed me one.

Lucius and Vinemont seized theirs, and we toasted before throwing them back. The liquid stung my tongue, my nostrils, and burned all the way down. I sputtered and slapped the glass back on the gleaming dark wood of the piano.

"You're harmony." I pointed to Teddy and tried to clear the pure alcohol from my lungs with a cough.

"Not a problem." Teddy leaned against the piano next to me. "These pipes are lined with gold."

I peeked over my shoulder at Vinemont as he began the accompaniment. He nodded to me, urging me to start the song. I waited a few more bars and closed my eyes before singing, "I really can't stay." My voice wobbled, but hit the right notes. Teddy jumped right in, telling me it was cold outside and adding, "It really is."

Laura linked her arm in Farns' and they swayed back and forth as Teddy and I sang the tune about responsibility and desire, the two dancing around each other.

Teddy's perfect harmony made my voice sound even better, though alone it was middling at best. My nerves seeped away as Teddy got into it, putting his arm around me though I knew he was singing right to Laura's heart. It was working, her gaze glued to him.

We reached the end, our voices melding and joining in unison as Lucius tapped the cymbal and the piano softened and quieted.

Applause from Farns and Laura rang out. I peeked over my shoulder at Vinemont and the look was there—the one from my drawing. Kindness, and something else that was undefinable. Something even warmer, even deeper. The same feeling had a stranglehold on my heart, my soul. Even in the barren ground of the Acquisition, love still grew.

"Beautiful voice. Like a bell." Farns beamed. "I think—"

His words were cut off when a tall woman with flowing white hair barreled past him, ripped the front door open, and ran out into the freezing night.

CHAPTER SEVENTEEN
SINCLAIR

I'D BARELY SEEN her ghostly form flit past when the front door slammed. *Fuck*.

"Teddy, take Stella to your room and lock the door." I didn't think my mother would be violent, but I couldn't tell anymore.

Stella opened her mouth, no doubt in protest, as Teddy scooped her up and headed for the stairs.

"Laura, you and Farns stay in the kitchen," I said. "Run out the door to the garage if anything happens."

Laura helped Farns from the floor as Lucius and I rushed past, no time to don shoes or coats, and took off after her. A blast of arctic air rushed into the foyer and stung my exposed skin as we darted into the night.

She fled across the moonlit lawn, her hair glowing silver in the luminous rays, and her white nightgown floating around her ankles. Ethereal and determined, she was making decent time. All the same, Lucius and I gained on her. My feet burned from the frost on the freezing ground, but we pounded after her, ignoring the pain.

She was slowing, fatigue already making her lag. We caught up, both darting around to corral her. She stopped and shrieked, her eyes wild and glancing from Lucius and back to me. I barely recognized her. The woman who'd

415

raised me, tormented me, was now a screaming banshee on the same front lawn she used to rule.

"Mom!" Lucius tried to shout her down, holding his hands out in front of him as he crept nearer.

"Don't you touch her! Don't you touch her, you bastards!" She snarled, spit flying from her pale lips.

"Mom, it's me." I stepped closer and stared into her eyes, the ones I knew were the same shade as mine.

"Stop hurting her." She put a hand to her mouth, gasping as if someone had knocked the wind from her lungs. "Please stop."

"Mom! It's me, Sin." But she wasn't seeing me. She was seeing Renee's trials. They played over and over again in her mind as if she were sitting alone in a movie theater, strapped to a chair with her eyes pinned open.

"Stop!" she screamed and raked her nails down her face. "Take me instead. Please, take me."

I moved slowly, the individual blades of icy grass crunching under the soles of my feet with each step. She grimaced and tore at her hair, ripping at the silver strands as her wild gaze turned skyward. Lucius and I both darted in, grabbing her around the waist. Then the screams began in earnest as she clawed and fought.

"Mom, calm down." Her nails were on my neck, gouging deep lines as she bit at Lucius. She was feral, the mother I'd known long since gone.

A brutal wind whipped past, carrying her screams out into the night. She was barefoot. If my feet were any indication, we were all in danger of frostbite the longer we stayed out here.

"Get her legs," I yelled.

I gripped her upper body, pinning her arms to her sides, as Lucius grabbed her around the knees. Together, we lifted her and hurried back toward the house. Once we reached the steps, she stopped struggling and her screams ceased. Defeated and limp, she fell silent. I took her full weight, cradling her in my arms.

"Lucius, go on up and see about Renee."

"Oh, shit. I didn't even think about her. Mom, what did you do?"

She was unresponsive as Lucius took the steps two at a time.

"Can I help?" Farns came down the hall, wringing his hands as Laura gripped his arm.

"Everything's fine." A lie. "Just one of her episodes." I hurried up the stairs to the third floor.

The door to her room was open, and I carried her in before laying her on the bed. Renee sat on the floor by the fireplace, hand pressed to the side of her head. Blood trickled down her face.

Lucius knelt down beside her, pulling her hand away to check the wound.

"You okay?" I asked over my shoulder.

"I-I think so," Renee said.

Mom lay on the bed and stared at the light green ceiling. Her mouth moved, half-formed words passing through her lips that held meaning only to her.

She'd made this large suite her sanctuary, the place she'd retreated to when Lucius and I were old enough to take care of the estate and the sugar business. I'd thought it was a blessing to be rid of her at the time, but I didn't know how much darker her thoughts would grow while she stayed alone up here.

"What happened?" Lucius pulled Renee's hand away to inspect the damage. The wound seemed to be somewhere in her dark hair, and was bleeding profusely.

"I don't know," Renee said. "She was lucid. We were talking about you boys when you were little. She was telling me a story about how Teddy used to ride his tricycle into the house and how it drove her batty. We were laughing, actually laughing. Then she swung something at me. I don't know what. I don't remember anything until you two came in."

I knelt beside her and pulled her hair away. It was a small

417

gash that wouldn't need stitches, but the lump around it was troubling. I looked back at Mom, but she was still in her daze. Would she regret this when she came back to life? I doubted it.

"Give me the key to the medicine cabinet." I held my hand out. Renee dug in her black skirt and produced a key ring, but couldn't seem to focus on which key it was.

"It's fine. I got it." I went to the armoire, unlocked it, and swung it open. Two syringes were loaded and ready to go, but Mom was calm now, so I didn't bother. I grabbed up some alcohol and bandages. I handed some to Lucius and then took the rest over to Mom.

I worked on her feet, dabbing the alcohol on each small cut. It had to sting, but she didn't react at all, remaining perfectly still. I'd done this only days before on a different woman, one I hoped wouldn't end up as damaged as the woman who lay before me. Once I'd bandaged her, I checked Lucius' work on Renee. He'd done well, the wound clean and Renee comfortable. I sat next to him and we wiped the blood from our feet.

"This is fucked up." Lucius glanced to Mom. "Keeping her up here like this."

"If there was a better way, I'd do it."

"I just wish we could get her some sort of care."

"There's no care for what's wrong with her." Renee had looked like hell even before Mom clocked her. But she wouldn't leave Mom's side, no matter how many times I asked her to get some rest, to go downstairs, to visit Stella. Tired eyes, gaunt cheeks, and sallow skin were her reward.

When Mom was like this, the only person she could tolerate was Renee. And now she'd attacked her.

"She's fine now," Renee said. "I'll stay with her. She wore herself out with that little episode." She tried to gain her feet, but wobbled before Lucius caught her and helped her stand.

"No. You need to go and get some rest."

"But Mr. Sincl—"

"Go!" I pointed to the door. "I'll stay with her for a while. Lucius, take Renee to her room and have Laura sit with her tonight."

He paused like he was going to challenge me, but seemed to think better of it. Taking Renee's arm, he said, "Come on. Sin's right. You're beat. In every way." He gave her a smile that she didn't return before walking her out.

At the door she turned. "Rebecca, I'll be back to see you tomorrow. I'm okay. Don't worry about what happened. You didn't hurt me." Her pleading voice broke on the last few words, as if she were injured more by having to lie to her lover than by the bloody wound along her scalp.

Mom made no move, just kept staring at the ceiling, her mouth slightly open. Lucius closed the door and I scrubbed my hand down my jaw. This was her worst episode yet. It was as if her memories grew stronger every day, the fear gripping her more tightly and turning each of her thoughts dark.

I moved her slender body up the bed so her head rested on a pillow. After pulling the sheet and blanket over her, I sat on the edge of her bed. I took her cold hand, the back pale, each vein a blue ridge leading to her bony wrist. The small crisscross of raised scars was still there, a matching set on my right hand.

I sandwiched her hand between both of mine, trying to instill some warmth in her. I knew I couldn't. She'd never given me enough to start with, so I had none to give back.

"Mom. Come back." How many times had I made the same request? Countless. More so when I'd been a child. But the words were empty. The Mom I'd known before her Acquisition had long been gone. Only Renee still encountered her from time to time. Never me, or Lucius, or Teddy. To us, she remained the strict matriarch, ensuring we maintained our dominance over the other families by coercion, deceit, or force.

Her breathing was even, but her eyes remained open and unseeing. A knock sounded at the door, and Farns shuffled in.

"How is she?" He'd known my mother longer than anyone. His eyes swam with sadness as he contemplated her expressionless face.

"She's coming down. I'm going to give her something to help her sleep." I stood and returned to the armoire, pulling out a syringe before locking it up and pocketing the key.

Farns walked over and took my spot on the bed, patting her hand. "Everything's going to be all right. The boys are fine. Everyone's fine. We just have to get you well again."

She would never be well again. There was no cure for the regret that had blackened her heart and eaten away at her mind. There was only management. Farns held her wrist as I pushed the needle into a vein on the back of her hand and depressed the plunger. After a few moments, her eyes finally closed.

She was peaceful. I should have felt relief. Instead, I felt what I always did. Despair.

CHAPTER EIGHTEEN
STELLA

I SAT ON Teddy's bed as he paced the room. When we heard the commotion on the stairs that eventually settled on the third floor, we knew it was over.

"Does that happen a lot?" I hugged my knees and watched as he came apart with each fitful step.

"No. She's done…things before. But she's never done this." He sank next to me and cradled his head in his hands.

I leaned over against his back and listened to the rapid beat of his heart. "I'm sorry." It wasn't enough, but it was all I could say.

"She'll be okay, I think. They caught her quick, right?"

"Speaking from experience, I've made that same dash across the lawn and didn't make it far at all."

"I remember. That was a fucking weird day."

"You're preaching to the choir." The memory of Vinemont, the sun high and blinding as he glowered over me, was something I would never forget.

"I know." He sighed. "It's because of Christmas, you know? Why she's like this."

I put my hand on his shoulder. I'd guessed that the time of year had something to do with it, especially after Renee told me how hard her Christmas trial had been on both women.

"I understand." I didn't know if I meant that I understood Teddy or his mother. Maybe a little of both. My mother was dead by her own hand, and Teddy's seemed to have killed herself in much the same manner. Winning the Acquisition was a self-inflicted, fatal wound.

"She wouldn't hurt us." His eyes met mine, as if begging for agreement.

"I'm sure she wouldn't." I had no idea, but I would say anything to wipe the pain from his kind heart. "I think Vinemont just wanted us out of the way so he could tend to her."

"Yeah."

Footsteps sounded in the hallway. Two sets. Teddy unlocked the door and peeked out. Lucius walked by, Renee's arm slung over his shoulder as he helped her to her room.

"Is she okay?" Teddy asked.

"They both are. Sin is staying with Mom. I'm putting Renee to bed. She's exhausted. You can take Stella back to her room."

I wanted to run to Renee, but by the time I'd made it to the door on my sore feet, they'd turned the corner, and the house was quiet again.

Teddy offered his arm. "Come on. I'll take you over to your place."

I peeked down the hall. "I really want to see Renee, if that's all right? I promise I'll go straight to my room after."

He raised an eyebrow. "I don't think Sin would—"

"Teddy!" Laura rushed down the hallway and into his arms. "Is she okay?"

"Yeah, I think so."

I took my chance and began hobbling away as some wet noises erupted at my back.

Teddy broke their kiss for long enough to call over his shoulder. "If you don't get back to your room, Sin is going to kill me."

"Okay, okay. I'll go just as soon as I see Renee."

"You better." The kissing noises resumed as I turned the corner.

This was the same hall where Lucius' and Vinemont's rooms were. They stayed along the side of the house, and Renee's small suite was at the very back. I passed Lucius' door, a lamp burning on his desk and some rock music playing low. I kept going and came to Vinemont's door, but it was closed.

I leaned against his doorframe to give my feet a momentary reprieve. I stared at the closed door, and curiosity got the better of me. I turned the glass knob and swung it open just a bit.

A beam of moonlight lit the curves and lines of a piece of my soul—the painting I'd made after the first Acquisition trial. He'd hung it in his room, the stark image made even harsher in the low light. I pushed the door the rest of the way open and flipped the light switch. My breath left me.

Every painting I'd ever exhibited, save one—*The North Star*—covered his walls. I was everywhere, my heart, my thoughts, my emotions covering every bare inch of space in his room. I walked in and spun in a circle, disbelieving my own eyes. But it was real. All of me was here, in this room, with Vinemont.

"I bought them a little while back." Vinemont leaned on the doorframe and crossed his arms over his chest. His face and neck were scratched, but the marks appeared to have been cleaned. He no longer bore even a shred of the merriment from the music room. His mother had stripped it all away, leaving him cold and raw.

"Why?"

His eyes pierced me but he gave no answer.

My heart began to thump in my ears as we held eye contact. I wanted to turn away. I tried. I couldn't. His gaze dropped to my lips. Instead of cold, his eyes were suddenly alive with heat. He filled the door, his wide shoulders the

423

perfect barrier.

I felt the urge to run. It was instinctive. My breath caught in my throat.

"Stella, if you keep looking at me like that…" His strained words trailed off as he walked in and shut the door, clicking the lock in a smooth movement behind him.

I took a step back, but there was nowhere to go. One more step and I'd be against his bed.

He covered the short distance between us, his aggression hitting me like the wave of a turbulent sea. I placed my hands to his chest and found his heart beating just as fast as mine, if not faster. He put one hand in my hair and another at my throat.

I tilted my head back, wanting to see every bit of his emotion, his need. My own surged inside me and created a blaze in my core.

"You're still hurt." He squeezed my throat and used his thumb to turn my head to the side. His lips ran along my jaw as he ghosted his mouth to my ear. "And I won't be gentle."

The blast of heat that shot through me at his darkly whispered words was beyond reason, beyond anything I could comprehend. I didn't want gentle. I wanted everything he had. And I wanted it just as real, just as raw as he was.

"Then don't be."

"You don't know what you're saying." He moved his hand down my body and gripped my wrist, rubbing the palm of my hand against his hard cock. "I can't control myself with you, Stella. Especially not now. I want to make it hurt, make you scream."

Something in his words clicked inside my mind. He *wanted* to hurt me. My thoughts flickered back to the first trial—each time he'd hurt me, it was as if he was hurting, too. And he'd never wanted to bring me pain. The second trial proved that beyond doubt. But, here and now, we were two people who didn't have to be master and slave. Here and now, when I could choose, I wanted him to hurt me.

"I want you to." I rubbed my hand up and down his cock as it strained against his jeans. My pussy was already wet, and my heartbeat pulsed in my clit.

"You're making a mistake." He groaned and yanked my wrist away, twisting it up behind my back. The slight pain sent a buzz straight between my legs.

He grabbed a fistful of my hair right at my scalp and pulled so I was completely at his mercy, my body arching into him. His lips were at mine, his gaze bearing down on me. "If we do this, there is no safe word, Stella. There is no tapping out. I will hurt you. Do you understand? You're mine."

"Sin, please." I wanted every dark thought he'd ever had. I wanted to cede him control freely, not have it taken from me.

He closed his eyes when I used his name. "Say it. Say you're mine, and I'll show you how much I can make it hurt."

My knees grew weak and fear kicked in my breast like a snared rabbit. But fear didn't rule me. Not here in his arms.

"I'm yours," I breathed.

He released his hold on me and gripped my robe before yanking it down. His hands were all over me, his eyes locked on mine as he fisted my tank top and pulled it, the seams coming apart with a popping sound. My body jerked forward but he put a hand at my chest. Then, he gripped my shorts and panties with his left hand and yanked twice before ripping them off.

He stepped back, breathing hard, and raked his gaze down my naked body. Goose bumps rose along my flesh, and when he stopped at my pussy, the tightness inside me increased. I felt like I might come just from the pressure of his stare.

"Lay on the bed on your back, head toward me."

I backed away as he watched, his body completely still. When my knees hit the bed, I sat and then spun so I was on my back and looking at him upside down. His hands went to his belt, his strong fingers nimbly unbuckling it and pulling it slowly loose. He tossed it on the bed next to me. The faint smell of leather filled my nose. He unzipped and pushed his jeans and boxers down while drawing out his rigid cock. I swallowed hard.

His jeans at his hips, he walked to me and gripped my shoulders, pulling me so my head hung off the bed. Blood rushed to my brain, pooling there as the lust pooled between my thighs.

Oh my god. When he rubbed his wet tip across my lips, my nipples stiffened and I scissored my legs, my clit desperate for attention. I darted my tongue across his head and savored the salty taste.

He groaned. "Open."

I opened my mouth as wide as I could and he shoved into me, his head hitting my tongue and then moving to the back of my throat. I gagged, but he only pulled back and pushed in again. I closed my eyes and fastened my lips tightly around him, sucking and playing my tongue along the top of his shaft.

He leaned over and squeezed my breasts to the point of pain as he fucked my mouth in hard strokes.

"Spread your legs. I want to see what's mine." His voice was an animal growl.

I obeyed, parting my legs as I squeezed his thighs. He continued shoving in and out of my mouth.

"Wider!"

I pushed my heels as far apart as they could go, cool air against my hot, wet pussy.

"Fuck." He pushed in farther and my eyes watered, but I didn't stop sucking him, his cock filling my mouth and making my jaw ache. I wanted every last bit of him, though I couldn't possibly have taken him all in my mouth.

He pinched my nipples, making me squirm and moan around him. He backed away, and I gasped for breath. His cock stood at attention, out of reach and tantalizing.

"That's going to make me come, and we aren't anywhere near done yet."

He stripped his shirt over his head and pushed his jeans and boxers the rest of the way off. "Get on your stomach. Head on my pillow."

I rolled over and did as he said, burying my face in his clean, masculine scent as he prowled up to the bed. The jingle of his belt got my attention and I turned to stare at him. His eyes were wild, every muscle on his body tense.

"On your hands and knees."

I slid my legs under me and pushed up as he ran a hand down the line of my spine from my neck to my ass. I shivered under his touch.

"Spread your legs more." I shifted my knees apart and he teased a finger down my pussy and to my clit.

I moaned and pushed back into his hand. He withdrew his fingers. "Not yet."

He gripped the belt in his right hand and for a moment I was back at the first trial, chained to a tree. I hung my head, taking in a gulp of air, and tried to stay in the moment.

"Stella." He gripped the back of my neck. "Look at me."

I turned my head and caught his gaze. His body was drawn tight, tension infusing every muscle, but his eyes were steady, reassuring. "I've got you. I'm right here. Just you and me. I've got you."

I was doing this because I wanted to. Not because I was chained against my will. I nodded, and he placed his hand on my cheek, gentle for a moment before he reached behind my head and gripped my hair tight.

"When you scream, make sure it's my name."

"Yes."

"Yes what?"

"Yes, Sin." Hearing the words spill from my mouth made my pussy tighten even more, my arousal reaching new heights each time I gave in to his demands.

"Good." He let go and stood with his knees against the bed, his cock pointing at me straight and stiff.

427

He reared back, and a sting erupted along my ass, a sharp crack echoing around the room. I grunted and fisted the blanket.

"My name, Stella." He hit me again, harder this time.

"Sin!" I cried in unison with the sound of the leather on my skin.

He fisted his cock and hit me again, this time the leather grazing against my pussy lips and making me shudder.

The impact went straight to my clit. I gave him his name again and again and again. My ass stung, but I leaned back into every strike, begging for more. I wanted the pain. It was mine. I owned it. I'd chosen it.

One more stroke and I buried my face in his pillow, screaming his name and breathing hard. The belt jingled to the floor and the bed shifted. His hands were on my ass, spreading me apart and pushing me forward, and then his tongue was on the hot flesh between my legs. I jerked as he licked from my clit to my entrance.

He groaned and stabbed his tongue inside me, fucking me in and out with it. I rocked my hips back to him, and he moved to my clit, sucking it between his teeth as I pushed back into his face. He sucked until my moans grew louder, my pussy tensing. I was at the edge, so close, his tongue swirling and flicking me into a frenzy.

When he stopped, I yelled my frustration into the pillow and tried to flip over. He gripped my hips hard and kept me right where I was.

"Don't you fucking move." His voice was gravelly, filled with unrestrained lust. "Not until you have my permission, Stella."

He slapped my ass hard and I screamed at the sudden pain.

He hit me again on the other side even harder, and his name flew from my lips. I remained still, his cock pressing against my pussy as his hot palms marked my ass again and again. I jerked with each hit, his head teasing my clit until I was desperate for him to fill me.

"Sin, please," I said as he rubbed my ass, soothing the sting.

"Begging me, Stella?"

"Yes!" I pushed against him again, my hot clit seeking his cock for the slick friction.

"What do you want?" He slipped a finger between my cheeks and rubbed the wrinkled skin around my asshole. I made a keening sound and twisted so I could look at him.

"I want you to fuck me."

He gripped my hip so hard it hurt and shoved forward, my clit singing at the increased contact of his cock. Then he flipped me over with one rough movement and crashed down on top of me, crushing the air from my lungs. He pinned my wrists over my head with one hand, covered my mouth with the other, and thrust inside. I screamed into his palm as he sank to the hilt.

Pain and pleasure exploded within me as he started a hard, rough pace. I was still yelling into his hand as he dropped his mouth to my ear.

"Is this what you wanted, Stella?" He released my mouth and rose up on an elbow.

Yes.

He jarred my body with each impact and looked down to my bouncing breasts. He captured a nipple in his mouth and bit down. I moaned and writhed, his thrusts getting stronger as he reached down and gripped one thigh under the knee and yanked it up, spreading me wide for him. He groaned as he surged and surged, his cock so thick inside me and every crash hitting my clit. The slapping sounds of our skin reverberated off the paintings and mixed with my moans.

"Sin, I'm getting close."

"No, you aren't." He switched to my other nipple, sucking and taking me higher.

My pussy was screaming for release.

"Please, I'm going to come," I cried.

He released my nipple and wrapped his hand around my

throat. "Not until I say."

He maintained the same pace, a hard fuck that kept me perched at the edge, ready to tumble over at any second.

I was there. "Please!"

He withdrew and I wanted to cry. I growled with rage, but he just smirked and flipped me to my stomach again and pushed my legs together. He straddled me and raised my ass and spread my cheeks before shoving his cock into me again.

"Fuck, you're tight." He groaned and leaned over me.

I moaned at the sensation of being filled again as he fucked me in steady pumps. He grasped my hair and wrenched my head to the side before fastening his lips to the back of my neck, his tongue tracing the tangle of vines that lived there. My pussy clenched him tighter as he possessed every bit of me. I jerked against him, but he kept his other hand at my hip, yanking me into his cock with each thrust.

He kissed my shoulder, running his tongue along my skin, and I gripped the pillows. I was desperate to touch my clit. As if reading my mind, he snaked his hand beneath me and rubbed the swollen nub with two fingers. I arched my back, pushing my ass farther up into him so he could get even deeper.

"Sin." It was all I had. The only word on my tongue.

He grunted with the effort, the rough fuck taking everything out of him as I gave him all I was. He strummed my clit harder as his cock grew inside me. I teetered on the edge again, my pussy gripping him tightly, desperate for release.

"Please, Sin, please." It was a strangled cry.

He kissed to my ear and kept working me. I shook with the pleasure and fought against coming. I would wait for his permission. I had to.

"Sin!"

"Come on my cock." His voice was in my ear and I couldn't stop.

I cried out his name as he bit down on my shoulder. I shuddered as wave after wave of bliss blew through me, my pussy spasming as he kept pounding.

He grunted and bit harder. I felt his cock kick inside me, but I was too lost in my own high to do anything other than sink beneath him and take everything he gave me. He pulsed a few more times and kissed my shoulder where his bite had stung. Then he rolled off to my side and let out a whoosh of breath.

I was still floating, my mind and body in two separate locales. He reached over and moved my hair off my sweaty neck. I turned toward him and it was there again. The look that I'd drawn. It was mine. I'd never seen it any other time than when he looked at me.

My heart swelled, and so many emotions I thought I'd given up on rose to the surface, not the least of which was hope. Hope that this would change things. Hope that he would value me more than just a means of winning the Acquisition.

The warmth that bloomed in my heart was almost too much to bear, and I wanted to hide it, nurture it—let it grow under the harsh sun of the Acquisition. I slid over to him and rested my head on his chest, listening to his heartbeat slow and even out. He ran his hand up and down my back and my side.

I was awash in him, soaking up his heat, his sweat, his emotions. He sighed deeply and his hand stopped, resting at my waist. I held my breath, never wanting the spell to break.

"Sin?" Teddy's voice from the other side of the door made me jump.

Sin covered me with the blanket before tugging on his boxers and going to the door.

He clicked the lock and opened it a crack.

"What?" Sin's voice was rough.

"I know she's in there," Teddy said. "I just wanted to ask about Mom. Is she going to be okay?" The worry in his

431

voice was enough to make me turn toward the door, more concerned than embarrassed.

"I gave her something so she can sleep. You know how she gets this time of year."

"Yeah, but it's never been like that."

Sin ran a hand through his hair, his back muscles flexing with the movement. "I know."

"Can I go up and see her?"

"Yeah, she's out. Farns is sitting with her."

"Okay. I'll check on her. Bye, Stella."

"Bye, Teddy," I called.

Sin turned and lowered his eyebrows at me before closing the door and locking it again.

"You two think you're clever, don't you?" He smiled, warmth and hunger mixing in his eyes.

Yes. I shrugged. He stalked to the bed, ripped the blanket off and settled on top of me, pushing between my legs and wrapping his arms around me, pinning my elbows to my sides.

He kissed my collarbone, light caresses that made the butterflies in my stomach swirl and dip. His lips were warm and soft as he moved to my neck, sucking my skin between his teeth. I squirmed as my body awoke from its momentary reprieve, but I was trapped in his arms with nowhere to go.

He nibbled at my jaw and surged against me, his cock hard again and seeking entrance. The only thing to stop him was the material of his boxers. I moaned as he bit my ear, and I was hyper aware of every sensation—his mouth, my hard nipples pressing into his chest, the exquisite ache between my thighs.

When he took my mouth, I moaned. He swallowed the sound and sank his tongue into me, demanding and hot. I gasped when he slanted over me, his body hard against me as the softness of our mouths melded. I was on fire again, needing even more of him. He slid a hand down to my ass and I was free to run my fingers through his silky soft hair. When I gripped it hard, he thrusted against me, his head pushing at my veiled entrance.

He rose onto his knees and shucked his shorts before falling on top of me again. I moaned as he sank inside without warning, my pussy clenching at the sudden intrusion. I dug my heels into his ass, ignoring the sting of pain. He thrusted smoothly and bent his head to my breast, teasing around the nipple. I buried both hands in his hair.

He sucked me into his mouth as he surged deep and stayed, grinding against my clit with small movements of his hips. I was already panting, my body on a hair trigger from his touch.

"I want to see you." His deep voice was an aphrodisiac of its own.

Gripping my back, he flipped us over so I was on top. I sank down completely on him, his cock stretching into my deepest core as I threw my head back. His hands were at my hips as I rose and fell on him, working him in and out. I spread my knees even wider, and he thrust up into me, pulling a deep moan from my lungs.

I leaned forward, planting one hand on his chest and the other at the pillow next to his head.

"Fuck, yes, Stella. Look at me. Make yourself come on my cock." He palmed a breast with one hand while his other stayed at my hip, pulling me down tight as I ground my pussy against him.

I held his gaze as I worked him. His grunts and thrusts made my pleasure spiral higher and higher. And when he pinched my nipple hard I cried his name.

"I'm so close," I whispered, and put my forehead to his.

His cock hardened at my words, and my clit pulsed as I was filled so completely.

"It's mine. Every orgasm is mine, Stella. Tell me."

"Yes. Yours. All of me, Sin. I'm yours."

His jaw tightened even more. "Then give me what's mine."

My hips bore down even harder, the sweet friction on my core too much as I came.

"Sin—"

He kissed me, taking his name from my lips as I froze and shuddered. He thrust hard once more and tensed as he shot inside me. My orgasm was still rolling, burning me with skittering sparks of pleasure as I convulsed and moaned my bliss into his mouth. I was gone, my mind shattered as I broke our kiss and took in a gulp of air before dropping my head onto the pillow next to him.

He encircled his strong arms around my back and crushed me to him. I was limp, utterly spent. I didn't move, just lay on top of him and allowed myself to remain in pieces.

"Stella, look at me."

I lifted my head and stared into his eyes, the shutters to his soul open and giving me a view of something more beautiful than I could have ever imagined. The real him, the one he kept hidden, the one I knew existed deep beneath the cold exterior.

He kissed my lips softly and ran his hand over my cheek. The wonder in his gaze made so much inside me open and warm. Then a shadow flitted across his eyes, some dark thought or memory that clouded our connection. He gave me one more lingering kiss before pressing me to his chest and covering us with the blanket.

I began to drift to sleep as his fingertips stroked my back, my hair. Love was in every touch. I'd never felt so safe, so content. A comfortable darkness began to fall over me, but my last thought was about the shadow.

CHAPTER NINETEEN
STELLA

I STARED AT his face in the early morning light for far too long. Sleep wiped the cares away from his brow, making him seem young, almost reminiscent of Teddy. I wanted nothing more than to stay in his arms, in his bed, in the sanctuary that he'd covered with my art, but I needed to check on Renee.

The house was quiet, my steps the only sound as I crept down the hall. Her door was open when I got there, and she was gone, her bed made like usual. I stared at the ceiling, wondering if she was upstairs again.

I felt a deep ache in my body as I snuck downstairs to my room. Sin was still with me, his scent on me, his body still making mine feel everything we'd done the night before. My ginger steps told the tale of a night spent with him.

I showered and slid naked into my sheets, staring out the window as the cloudy, cold Christmas day began. I couldn't go back to sleep, the memories of Sin's mouth, his hands, and his eyes making me tingle.

I was toying with sneaking back to his room when there was a forceful knock at my door. *Renee?*

"Who is it?"

"Merry Christmas, *Krasivaya*."

My mouth dropped open. Dmitri, my manly masseuse

I'd met before the Acquisition ball.

The door swung open and Alex, his hair a bright shade of indigo, rushed in and jumped on my bed. "It's a Christmas miracle, beautiful!"

Dmitri scowled at Alex as he lumbered inside.

I put my hand to my mouth, joy rushing through me. "You're here!"

"Juliet's downstairs getting set up. Sadly, Yong couldn't make it. She's busy waxing an entire clan of reality stars in Hollywood. Serbians. Super hairy."

"But why?" I reached out and touched Alex to make sure he was real.

"Few days ago, the honorable counsellor Sinclair Vinemont requested our presence as a Christmas treat for you and offered some choice coin." Alex winked and lay back, threading his fingers beneath his faux hawk. "This ain't so bad." He surveyed the quilts. "Nice room. I didn't know you sewed."

"I don't." I finally accepted they were really here and wrapped my arms around Alex's neck.

"Eww, naked woman." He patted my back awkwardly.

I pulled back and yanked the sheet up, having totally forgotten I hadn't dressed yet.

Dmitri smiled, his large frame ridiculous against the backdrop of a particularly dainty white and pink quilt, and started cracking his knuckles.

"Come on down to the spa when you are dressed. A day of leisure awaits." Alex hopped up and fired an imaginary pistol at me before leading Dmitri into the hallway and back down the stairs.

Did Sin give me friends for Christmas? The thought made me laugh, mostly because it was true. I rose and dressed simply, knowing full well I wouldn't be wearing clothes for long.

I skipped the empty breakfast room and hurried straight to the spa. The cloudy sky imposed on the glass panes above and cast a gray gloom on the usually sunny room.

A small table was laid out with croissant, fruit, and juice. Alex had already powered through some strawberries, and Juliet was mid-chew on a chocolate croissant when she saw me and squealed. After an intense hug, she allowed me to take a seat. It felt natural—all of us eating, drinking, and laughing.

"Did you win the beauty pageant thing we did you up for last time, or what?" Alex downed his coffee and poured more.

I shifted in my seat. "Umm, the results aren't in yet. I'll let you know, though."

"Well, if you didn't, then I'd like a word with the judges because you were amazing." His eyes lit. "Do you still have the dress?"

I dropped my eyes. I hadn't seen it since the ball. "No, I think the designer took it back for a show or something."

"Well, shit." He leaned back and murdered another strawberry.

"You win, *Krasivaya*. I know this." Dmitri had some new ink along his neck, something in Russian.

"What's that say?" I pointed to it.

"Oh," he laughed, the sound almost nervous. "Nothing."

Juliet raised an eyebrow, met my eye, and sipped her juice.

"Embarrassed?" I asked, teasing in my tone.

"No." He straightened in his chair, the joints creaking under his weight. "It is not meant for ladies such as you to hear."

"Oh my god, Dmitri! Are you blushing?" I asked.

Alex crowed with laughter and I couldn't help but join in. The big Russian rubbed a hand over his shaved head and grinned.

"Dmitri went and got something inappropes tatted on his neck and won't share." Alex giggled some more.

"It say." Dmitri shook his head. "It say my *chlen*

proud."

"Your what?" Juliet asked through her smile.

"My—" He gave an obvious look down to his crotch and then back up. "It is proud."

"What is your dick proud of, exactly?" Alex snickered.

Dmitri waved his meaty palm at Alex and let out a string of Russian.

Alex nodded. "Right, right. Very proud. I'm not denying it. So is it cut, or are you sporting foreskin?"

Juliet spit a mouthful of orange juice back into her glass, and I examined my feet.

"Let's get you buffed up, shall we?" Juliet rose and, thankfully, saved me from any further discussion about Dmitri's 'chlen'.

An hour later, I sat comfortably as Juliet buffed my legs, the sensation refreshing but also intense.

"Damn, Russian. If your hands feel this good, I can't imagine how your chlen must feel." Alex lay on the massage table, having talked Dmitri into warming up by massaging him first. Alex grinned at me and then grunted as Dmitri used his elbow on his lower back.

"Turn it on over," Juliet instructed.

I flipped on the table, staying under the towel as best I could, but I lost my grip and it fell to the floor. I winced, knowing what was coming. I'd already made an excuse about running in the wrong shoes about my feet. Now I had to explain the rest.

"What happened to your back?" Juliet ran her fingers over one of the scars. "Is this why Renee asked me for the scar serum?"

Dmitri loomed up next to me. "Who has done this, *Krasivaya*? The *suka* who came before?"

"Lucius? No. It doesn't hurt. Not anymore. Please don't worry about it. It doesn't bother me." I looked over my shoulder, my eyes pleading with Dmitri to leave it alone.

"It bother *me*." Dmitri smoothed his wide palm down my back and frowned.

"I don't want to talk about it." I rested my forehead on my hand.

"Come on, big guy. You heard her. Take it out on me," Alex said.

I breathed a sigh of relief as Dmitri's shadow receded, and Alex's deep grunt of pain filled the room.

"From the looks of them, the serum helped. But this should make them even less noticeable." Juliet patted my shoulder and started doing her thing. Coarse crystals rubbed against my skin, then finer and finer until it felt like she was floating thin sheets of silk across my body.

Once it was Dmitri's turn, I was in heaven. What little muscle soreness I had left was worked away by his strong hands. Alex snored on the table next to me, his hand on his stomach and his silver nipple rings rising and falling with each breath. I could relate. Dmitri worked magic.

When he was done, he draped my towel up over me and I remained in my haze of relaxation.

"Juliet. Your turn." Dmitri waved her over and smacked Alex on the arm. "Up!"

"Hey!" Alex sat up and rubbed his eyes.

Juliet shook her head and backed away. "I'm not doing that."

"You shy, baby girl?" Alex asked.

"No." Juliet dropped her gaze to the river-rock floor, her blonde bob hiding her face.

"It okay." Dmitri frowned. "I understand."

"I'm sorry. I'm just not…" She gestured toward my body.

"What? You're beautiful." I looked in her eyes. "Inside and out."

"Yes, beautiful," Dmitri said, and stared at Juliet as if this were an obvious fact.

"Me three." Alex stood and smacked me on the ass. "Get up, woman. Let's go in my room and play with hair stuff. Leave these two alone to negotiate."

"What?" Juliet's big blue eyes widened.

Dmitri smiled. "Yes. You go, Alex. I handle."

I tucked my towel around me and rose before pointing my finger at Dmitri. "Go easy on her, Russian."

"Of course." Dmitri smiled down at me as he motioned an unmoving Juliet to come to him.

I wanted to stay and watch, see if the large Russian could coax the skittish Juliet, but Alex pulled me into his booth and shut the door.

He clapped. "This is going to be good. You think they'll fuck?"

I cocked my head at him in the mirror. "Of course not. She'll probably run screaming before he even gets a finger on her." The words came out and whistled around my consciousness, a flash of barren tree limbs darting across my mind and the scent of earth and rotting leaves in my nose.

"Hey, you okay?" Alex patted my shoulder.

I forced a smile. "Fine."

"Let's give you a cut. Spruce up these ends. And, just for you, I'll tell you all about my newest boyfriend while I do it." He whipped out a black cape and tied it around me. "Have you ever seen a pierced dick?"

I spent the next forty-five minutes laughing and telling Alex just how bad he was after he regaled me with tales of his conquests, the most recent being a TV star on some show about zombies.

When he was done, I felt lighter, and my hair was cut, shampooed, and styled to fall in waves.

I ran my fingers through the strands. "Thanks, Alex. I'm a new girl."

He bent over, caught my eye in the mirror, and kissed my cheek. "No. You're the same one I fell in love with a couple months ago."

I smiled. This was by far the best Christmas present I'd ever received.

"Let's see if the coast is clear or full of Russian dick." Alex silently opened the door and crack, then swung it all the way. "What the—"

I peeked over his shoulder. Dmitri and Juliet had disappeared.

A smell wafted to my nose, something rich and delicious. My stomach growled.

"I think lunch is ready." Alex walked into the room and grabbed my clothes from the nearest rack before tossing them to me. "Get dressed. I'm starving. And please tell me I'm invited."

I dropped my towel and pulled on my underwear, jeans, and t-shirt. "Of course. But we need to find Juliet and Dmitri first."

Someone cleared their throat. I stared around. The sound came from a closet along the front of the room. The door opened and Dmitri stepped out, his eyes everywhere but on Alex and me.

"Where's Juliet?" Alex asked.

The door opened again and she hurried out, though Dmitri slapped her ass as she went by.

"I'm not discussing this." Her face was on fire.

I grinned, happy that the simple enjoyment of another person, no dark motives at play, was possible under this roof. "Fine. Come on. I bet you two worked up an appetite."

Juliet tucked her hair behind her ear before thinking better of it and plucking it back out. I led the procession, up the main hallway, past Sin's study, past the breakfast room, and to the large dining room where I'd signed the contract that fateful day. It seemed so long ago now. So much had changed.

Laura puttered around adjusting plates, but the table was perfect. A large roast sat in the middle, flanked by sides of green beans, mashed potatoes, corn, sweet potatoes, and any number of foods placed around like decorations.

"Wow," I said. "This is beautiful. I almost hate to eat it."

Laura smiled and motioned to the chairs. "Everyone sit. I already told the boys it's ready."

We took our seats, leaving the three spots around the end for Sin, Lucius, and Teddy. There were three more places set, and I wondered if Renee would join us. I missed my friend something terrible, the loss a nagging ache.

Deep male laughter bounced into the room for the foyer, Teddy and Lucius appearing in the doorway.

Lucius' eyes opened wide as he surveyed the room. He clearly had no idea there was company.

Dmitri growled.

"Keep it civil." I laid my napkin in my lap as Laura poured the wine.

Lucius leered at Dmitri before sitting in his usual chair. "Yeah, keep it civil, *comrade*."

"Very nice to see you again, Lucius is it? I'm Alex." Interest lit his face, the charm switch flipped.

I smothered my laugh as Lucius simply eyed the eager stylist.

Teddy bumped my elbow and grinned at me. "Have a good night?"

Lucius shifted in his seat and scowled at Teddy.

More steps in the hallway saved me from having to respond. Sin walked in, his black button down open at the throat with the sleeves rolled up. He wore a pair of perfectly fitting jeans with a familiar belt. Was the room suddenly warmer? My heart skipped a note as he strode to the head of the table.

"I'm not much for ceremony…" He paused when I raised my eyebrows at his words, but then continued, "But seeing as how we have this lovely meal—thank you Laura—and seeing as we have some of Stella's friends over, we may as well indulge in a little tradition." He sat and motioned for us to dig in.

Alex wasted no time grabbing some rolls and scooping mashed potatoes. Laura helped everyone fill their plate.

"Laura, please sit," Sin said. "Where's Farns?"

"Here, sir. Sorry for my tardiness. My knees, you know." Farns walked in slowly and took his seat. Laura fixed his plate and then sat next to him. Only one place remained empty.

"Renee?" I asked.

Sin cut his eyes to the ceiling and then back to me. "She may come in later."

I stared at the empty place setting for a moment before the clatter of silverware and the rhythm of small talk filled the room. I didn't know why Renee had stayed away, though it obviously had to do with Rebecca. I decided it was long past time for me to find out.

I spent the afternoon with Dmitri, Alex, and Juliet, just talking and laughing. It was as if we'd known each other for years, not just the small space of months. Dmitri and Alex competed on their storytelling abilities.

Dmitri kicked it off by explaining how he became the most skilled rabbit skinner in his town when he was five years old. Then he shared how he was a well known prize fighter in Russia, replete with lots of muscle flexing for emphasis.

Juliet and I, bundled up on the couch in the library, giggled as Dmitri puffed out his chest with pride, and told yet another tale about how he was the first boy to ever talk the town prostitute into giving him a free ride. When he was twelve.

"Was it the pride down below that got her?" Alex snorted.

"Yes." Dmitri grinned.

Juliet sank back into the cushion next to me and I wrapped my arm around her. "No shame in your game," I whispered in her ear.

She nodded and snuggled into me. Alex started into a story about the time he went skiing, ran into a tree, and wound up in an infirmary with a ski patrol dick in each hand. We laughed until the sun fell, though the clouds made it impossible to tell whether the gloom was true night.

On Juliet's turn, she shared her most embarrassing moment—the time she went to a red carpet event with her skirt tucked into her panties. When I was laughing so hard my ribs hurt, Sin walked in.

His stern face softened as he watched me. "I hate to do this, but our guests have to be on their way. The snow is supposed to start in an hour, and they need to be on a plane by then."

I knew they'd have to leave today—they had other family and friends to visit over the holidays—but I was beyond grateful that I got to see them, even if for such a short time. I forced myself not to cry as I hugged them goodbye and reluctantly let them go. Luke was already waiting outside with their things packed in the limo.

After saying our farewells on the front porch, Dimitri's face darkened as he approached Sin. Sin met his eyes, not even the slightest hint of fear in his demeanor. I supposed there wouldn't be, not after what he'd done in Cuba. Sin was capable of horrible acts if something important to him was threatened. The thought sent a shiver through me as sure as the chill wind that promised snow.

"If you hurt her, comrade, I come back here for you."

"You do that." Sin gave him a shit-eating grin.

Dmitri glowered, but backed away before squeezing me into a bear hug one last time and stomping down the stairs to the car. He ducked inside and closed the door. I fought back more tears as the car pulled away. Sin walked over and placed his arm around my shoulders as the first flakes of snow fell, the weather arriving earlier than expected.

"Thank you." I leaned into him.

"You're welcome." He kissed the top of my head and led me back inside.

CHAPTER TWENTY
STELLA

THE FUN DAYDREAM over, I stared up into Sinclair's eyes as he pushed my hair behind my ear. He leaned down to my lips and hovered just out of reach.

"Sin?"

He closed his eyes, as if just hearing me say his name was pleasurable.

"I want you to tell me about the last two trials."

His eyes opened and he straightened, the link between us broken with a string of simple words.

"We have time enough to worry about that, Stella." His voice was cold.

"Please, just tell me."

He rested his palm against my throat. "What did I tell you at the ball, Stella? Anticipation just makes it worse. You have three months before the trial. Don't spend them worrying."

"But I worry more when I don't know." I gripped his wrist and slid my hand down his forearm. "Please."

He opened his mouth to speak and then closed it. His grip tightened at my neck. "No. I'm not discussing this. Don't ask again."

Stung at his harsh tone, I backed away. He let his hand drop, but he followed my steps until I was backed against

445

the front door.

"Sin, pl—"

"I'm doing the best I can." He pushed me into the door, his gaze singeing me with its intensity. "I can't explain it to you, but I'm doing everything I can to keep you safe. But nothing has changed." His hand was back at my throat, the touch rough as he pressed me against the wood panel. "I still have to win. You aren't going to stop that. Understand?"

"No. I don't." I tried to shove him off but he didn't let me go, just came right back and pressed me harder, his chest crushing into mine, taking my breath away. I dug my nails into his hand.

Tears welled and ran down my cheeks. "Why is winning more important than me?"

"Because nothing is more important to me than winning the Acquisition, Stella. Nothing."

"Not me?"

"No." He said the word with a sharp edge that sliced me so fast I didn't feel it at first, but then the blood ran from my heart. "Do you think some fucking makes you more important to me than my name, than my own blood?"

I couldn't catch my breath. He scowled at me—the man who'd just given me the happiest Christmas I could remember, who'd given me more pleasure in one night than a lifetime of nights. Nothing but disgust was written on his face.

"Why can't you love me?" My voice was choked with tears, but I asked the only question I had left. The only one that needed to be answered.

"It's not that I *can't*, Stella. It's that I *don't*."

I pressed forward into his hand, forcing him to hold me tighter to keep me in place. I wanted to see his eyes. "You're lying."

"You don't know me, Stella. You've only ever seen what I wanted you to. What I needed to show you to keep you in line. Don't think for a fucking second I give two shits about what happens to you."

My tears turned to laughter, and I didn't care if it sounded insane. "You're *lying*, but not to me."

His body vibrated with rage, a frenzy of emotions churning from him. "Shut the fuck up."

I kept laughing. There was nothing else. He cared about me. I'd seen it. I knew it, and he couldn't take it away from me no matter what he said or did to me. He loved me.

"I don't love you, Stella." But he backed away, only his palm still making contact.

"You're a fucking liar. Don't touch me." I dug my nails in and wrenched his hand away.

I shot past him, darting up the stairs as I felt his eyes on my back. I ran to my room and sank onto my bed. I felt as if I were in shock. There were no more tears, only an empty expanse where my hurt should be. I felt nothing. Had he ripped it all out? Was I broken now? Is this what being broken meant? I lay that way for a long time, seeing nothing, hearing nothing.

Something, some sound—maybe the grandfather clock chiming—woke me from my reverie. I sat up, the night dark and a light layer of snow on the lawn. No moon, just black nothingness above. I let my eyes wander the window sash and then back to my own ceiling. *Upstairs. Answers.*

I opened my door slowly and peeked into the hall. It was clear, so I crept down the runner and hesitated as I eyed the rest of the way up to the third floor. My spine tingled, but I took the first step. Then another, then more until I was at the top.

The doors were closed up here, and the air was stale with disuse. The lights overhead were dim, but gave enough of a glow that I could creep along and listen at each door. Nothing. I kept moving until I heard a humming sound coming from the end of the hall. I moved closer, a cold sweat breaking out along my forehead.

I forced myself onward, looking for Renee, looking for some sort of answers.

The last door on the left hung open. I peeked inside. Renee sat in a rocking chair and hummed as she did needlework. The white-haired woman, Mrs. Vinemont, slept peacefully.

Renee must have sensed me, because the humming stopped and her eyes opened wide.

"Stella!" Her voice was a harsh whisper.

She dropped her needlework and hurried over to me. She wrapped her arms around me, but I didn't return the embrace, my arms numb.

"Why haven't you come to see me?" I asked.

"I couldn't bear to leave her. You shouldn't be here." She tried to guide me back into the hallway and pull the door closed behind her, but I pushed past her and into the room. Photos lined the walls. So many of Sin, Lucius, and Teddy—beautiful boys who grew into young men as the images continued from one corner to another. Another, larger photo was framed and hung above the fireplace. It was a young woman, her hair almost the same shade as mine, but her eyes the same light blue as Lucius'.

"Cara?" A scratchy, unfamiliar voice.

I turned to find Mrs. Vinemont staring right at me, her mouth gaping.

"Cara, is it you?"

Renee went to her side and gripped her hand. "No, your sister's gone. Remember, darling?"

"But she…" Mrs. Vinemont pointed a wizened hand at me.

"No, that's Stella." Renee's voice was gentle, as if speaking to a child. "Stella. Remember?"

"Stella." Rebecca's eyes cleared the slightest bit, then narrowed. "The peasant?"

"Rebecca, come on now."

"No, it's fine." I crossed my arms over my chest and stared down at Rebecca. "Her attitude helps."

"My *attitude*?" The older woman sat up in her bed, her familiar eyes perusing me from head to toe. "No wonder my son is having such trouble with you."

Her voice was brittle, like a dry, crumpled leaf being crushed under a boot.

"No trouble. I just want answers."

"Well, Stella, let me get up and pour you some tea and serve you some scones while I'm at it." She cackled.

Renee stroked her hand, but Rebecca ripped it away. "Get out of my room. Both of you are a curse. One after another. A curse!" She repeated "a curse" until the sound trailed off and she glared at me.

"I'll leave," I said. "I won't bother you again. But I have some questions first."

Renee put her hand up, as if warding off an attacking foe. "Please, Stella. Don't. Just go. I'm begging you. She can't handle any talk about it."

"About the Acquisition?"

Rebecca flinched at my words. "Let her ask her questions. We'll see if she likes my answers." She smiled, and I realized what a beautiful woman she must have been. But now, she was nothing more than a ruined, haunted wreck.

"What is the next trial?" I asked.

She hummed some bars of a song I didn't recognize and said, "Spring is the time for family."

"What does that mean?"

"I answered your question. Isn't my fault if you aren't smart enough to follow it. Next." She held her hand out, as if scooting me along, and I observed the same smattering of scars on the back of her hand that I'd seen on Sinclair's.

"What are those scars?" I pointed.

"These?" She held her hand out like she was showing me an engagement ring and batted her dark lashes. "These are from one wonderful night in Brazil. Shall I tell you about it?"

Renee blanched, the color draining from her face in an instant as she shook her head. "Please don't do this, Rebecca. Please."

"Have you ever been cut by a sugar cane leaf?" Rebecca's eyes drew me in, and I found myself walking closer until I stood at the foot of her bed.

"No."

"It's a very particular sting, you see?" She ran her fingernail across the lines, retracing whatever pain had put them there. "I took my eldest, Sinclair, to Brazil for a short vacation one time." She grinned. "He watched me kill a man. I had never killed anyone before. But I killed Mr. Rose. Shot him dead. Do you know why?" She didn't let me answer. "Because he was trying to tarnish my name, to take what was mine." Her voice hardened. "No one takes from us. Not again. Not ever. We are the ones who take things."

She leaned back, her face wistful, though she still watched me. "My son didn't understand. He kept crying." She threw her hands up. "The gunshots, the blood, the killing, the bodies—he couldn't handle any of it. He was weak. He was afraid. He clung to me like I was some sort of safety in the storm." She laughed, the sound harsh and jarring.

I put a hand to my throat, my hackles rising and my palms going cold. I could see the boy in the photos around the room, the one she spoke of. He'd been so happy, but something had changed, something was different in his older photos. Now I knew what.

She shook her head. "But I *was* the storm. So, after I'd gotten the Roses straightened out, I sat him down and took a sugar cane leaf. I retold the horrible things I'd done, the things he'd witnessed. Every time one of his tears fell, I cut him, and then I cut myself." She slid her nail sharply across her hand. "I cut and cut until I could make him relive it without a single tear, until he could recite it all himself without blinking an eye—how Mr. Rose had begged, how I'd shot him in the face, how the workers had run and screamed as my men hacked them to death. And then he was strong. Like he is now." She beamed, pride in her eyes.

My gorge rose, and I grabbed the footboard to steady

myself. A bead of cold sweat ran between my shoulder blades.

"Ask your next question." She folded her hands in her lap, clearly pleased with herself.

Renee cried softly into her palms.

I didn't know if I could stand another answer. Could I bear more truth from the malice-filled creature before me?

"What are the rules of the Acquisition?"

Another song erupted from her lips, but this one with words, *"Seven rules to see you through. Seven rules to live by. Seven rules to make it hurt. Seven rules to kill by."*

I shuddered and my knees buckled, but I didn't fall, despite the heavy weight of dread crushing down on me.

She grinned, her teeth like tombstones in moonlight. "Let's start with the first, and most important rule of the Acquisition. If you lose, you must kill the last-born child of your line. Weeds out the weak, you see."

The floor moved under my feet, and I gripped the footboard with both hands. "If he loses the Acquisition, Sin has to kill Teddy?" My voice was far away.

She nodded, her grin growing wider and filling her face like a garish caricature. "Teddy dies."

SOVEREIGN

CHAPTER ONE
STELLA

THE GROUND RUSHED UP to meet my face, but I turned my head just in time to avoid a busted nose. I wheezed as all the air was crushed from my lungs by the impact. Rolling to the side, I barely missed a large boot that stomped the grass where my torso had been.

I got to my feet and backed away toward the house, trying to catch my breath and ignoring the pain in my ribs. Sweat stung my eyes, and the warm sun peeked from a behind a cloud.

I focused on the massive man who rushed me, his arms spread wide and ready to capture me in what I already knew would be a painful bear hug. Ducking under his right arm, I turned, giving him a hard kick in the ass.

He grunted and took a lunging forward step to avoid falling.

"That's a point for me." I bounced on the balls of my feet.

"No *Krasivaya*. I no fall." Dmitri pointed to the grass and squared up with me again, the tapestry of tattoos on his bare torso rippling as he moved.

"You will." I grinned and ran at him, jumping at the last moment and landing a vicious elbow to his chest.

He grabbed for me and managed to get one of his bear paws around my ponytail. I landed on my feet and tried to back away, but he whipped my head around and placed his other hand at my throat. He squeezed, attempting to force my submission.

I brought my knee up and slammed my heel down onto his foot with all my strength. He yowled, but didn't let me go. The air in my lungs was trapped there, and Dimitri made sure I couldn't get any more oxygen. I struggled—kicking, punching, and clawing. I wouldn't submit. I'd fight until he choked me out rather than tap out.

Lucius clapped. "All right. She's had enough."

Dimitri released me and slapped me hard on the back as I bent over and took in huge gulps of air.

"Sorry, Krasivaya." Dimitri had made clear ever since we started training that he took no joy in hurting me. All the same, the past two months had left me bruised, strained, and exhausted. But I was better, faster. I could escape him, though I wasn't able to take him down. Not yet.

"It's your hair." Lucius ignored my sputtering and walked up behind me. "You may have actually had a chance this time if he wasn't able to grab hold of you so easily." He yanked my ponytail.

I whipped around and threw my leg out, swiping his feet out from under him so he landed on his ass.

"Ow, fuck." He looked up at me with his light blue eyes, irritation and amusement mixing in the quirk of his lips. "Uncalled for."

"Good." Dimitri patted me on the back one more time, his palm slapping on the exposed skin above my sports bra. "But he is correct. Your hair. It is weakness."

"I'll tie it up in a bun. Hell, I'll cut it." I didn't care. Winning was more important than my vanity.

"No way." Lucius got to his feet and brushed the grass off. "Cal loves redheads. It's an asset. Trust me. Besides, I wouldn't like it if you cut it."

"Thanks for your input." I arched an eyebrow at him.

The sun bore down on the back of my neck like a warm weight. Or maybe the vines tattooed there were growing, getting bigger and thornier every day I spent as an Acquisition. "Your approval of my looks is really key for figuring out how to win this fight."

He shook his head. "I think I liked you better when you were scared."

"I think I never liked you." I crossed my arms over my chest and stared him down.

He smirked. "A woman not liking me? Impossible." He stepped closer, almost within my reach. "Besides, I think it's pretty obvious you like me quite a bit."

Dmitri put his hands on his hips. "Leave her alone."

"Fuck off, Russian." Lucius flipped him off without even looking in his direction.

"This isn't helping." I brushed past Lucius and walked to the little water cooler set up under the oak tree. Pouring myself a cup, I sank down onto one of the collapsible chairs and replayed the fight over in my mind. Where had I gone wrong, other than my hairstyle?

"I could take you." Lucius pointed at Dmitri.

"You always say this. You always lose." Dmitri cracked his knuckles.

"Depends on your definition of losing."

"You flat on back like good little bitch."

They circled each other and then tangled, wrestling before separating and doing it again. Like animals butting heads, both too stubborn to back off and call a truce.

It was the same dance the three of us had been doing for the past two months. I trained. Dmitri taught. Lucius played. Sin... I didn't know what Sin did. After the night of his mother's revelations, he spent all his time in town, not even visiting on the one weekend when Teddy came home from school.

Though he maintained his distance, I knew he kept tabs

on me. I could feel it whenever Lucius took a phone call and glanced my way before leaving the room.

It was Sin. Skirting around my periphery, always watching. He'd chased me, caught me, and trapped me in his web. Once I was snared, he ran.

The last time I'd seen him was stuck on repeat in my mind. That night. I shook my head. The last night before he'd left the house for good. I rubbed my upper arms, a chill rushing through me despite the warm breeze.

He was gone, but I haunted his room, sitting on his bed and staring at my paintings. He'd seen every bit of me, all of my weaknesses, my dreams, and my thoughts. Each piece of whatever made up Stella Rousseau was spattered across his walls like blood at a crime scene. I'd seen him too. Knowing there was a splinter of a good man left beneath all his darkness had done me no favors. All was revealed, the masks gone. He still shut me out.

There were no secrets anymore, not from me. I roamed the house as if I belonged in it, as if it were mine. When Lucius was gone on business, which was often, I had the run of the entire estate. A prisoner with the keys to the castle.

The only place I didn't set foot was the third floor. I'd had enough of its occupant for a lifetime. Sin's mother's revelations were freeing, but they were also a cage, one Sin had been living in since being chosen for the Acquisition. Now I could see the bars clearly, examine each one for a weakness.

After the initial shock of what she'd told me, I'd become focused. Sin would win the Acquisition. Teddy would live. I would do everything in my power to protect him. Endure what I had to do and survive. My sacrifice for my father had been made through deceit. The one I'd make for Teddy was of my own choosing. I would fight for it. I would see him live a long, happy life. Then I would set my sights higher. Dismantling the Acquisition was no longer a wish; it was my true goal. The reason I still drew breath.

Dmitri flung his arm out in a vicious jab, catching Lucius in the mouth.

"Fuck." Lucius darted back and spit a wad of blood into the grass. "That's cunt shit."

"Come closer. We see who is cunt." Dmitri lumbered toward Lucius, the men unevenly matched in almost every way possible.

"Hang on." Lucius held up a hand. "It's hot out here."

Dmitri stopped and waited. "I tire of hitting this clown. You ready for another round, Krasivaya?"

"Almost." I sipped the cold water as Lucius unbuttoned his shirt and pulled it off one arm. He began to pull it from his other arm then rushed Dmitri when he was halfway through the motion.

Lucius' trick worked, and Dimitri groaned as the smaller man's fist collided with his ribs.

"*Blyad!* Little prick." Dmitri whirled and thundered after a retreating Lucius.

Lucius tried to spring back, but it was too late, Dmitri tackled him. They fell with a thud and Dmitri pinned him.

"Who is bitch now, eh?" Dmitri grinned and slapped Lucius playfully before squeezing his cheeks.

"Get the fuck off! You're crushing my nuts."

The Russian sat back and got up before offering Lucius his hand.

He took it and stood. "You need to lay off the fucking protein." Lucius craned his head and tried to wipe the stray grass off his naked back.

"Protein make man strong. You too skinny."

Lucius may not have had the larger build of Sin or the hulking Dmitri, but he wasn't a small man by any means.

"Skinny huh? I'll still kick your commie ass. Come on. Let's do this." He put his fists up, his abs and chest glistening with a light sheen of sweat.

"Again, then?" Dmitri shook his head but squared his shoulders.

"Okay, that's enough of a pissing contest." I stood and

stretched, my muscles aching. "I need to get back to training."

"She just doesn't want you to get hurt, comrade." Lucius dropped his fists and walked past me, plopping in the chair I'd just vacated.

I pulled the elastic from my hair and wrapped the strands around in a tight ball before re-tightening the band. Once satisfied it wouldn't serve as an easy grip, I walked back out into the sun to take position.

I bent my knees and pulled my hands up. I was too small to win a straight-up brawl, but Dmitri had taught me to grapple and strike just enough to get my enemy into a submission move. Get them to tap out. But first, I had to get close enough. So far, I'd only gotten close enough to Dmitri to get my ass kicked. Bruises colored my legs, and no amount of warm baths and massages could erase the tenderness in my muscles from day after day of training. It was worth it. I had something to fight for. Something I would fight until my last breath to keep safe, as well as something to destroy.

"Ready, Krasivaya?"

"Bring it."

CHAPTER TWO
STELLA

TEDDY DIES. THE WORDS lingered as I woke in a sweat. Like I did most mornings. Another dream—blood on my hands and screams in my ears. I rose from the bed, not content to stay where my fears manifested in my subconscious. Stripping, I walked to the bathroom and climbed into the shower.

The warm water rushed down my body, waking my senses and washing away the terror of the dream. It was always Teddy. His innocent brown eyes staring at me, lifeless. His blood coating my hands, seeping into my white dress from the last trial. I swore I could even taste it, coppery and hot.

I leaned my head against the cool shower tiles, willing the feelings away. Instead of fear, I put resolve in its place. I had a month.

One more month of training. One more month before the spring trial. What would it be? I wasn't sure. All I had to go on was Renee's memories about her year—a physical competition of strength and stamina. She never told me how it ended, only that I needed to be stronger and faster than she had been.

And so I trained. Weights, swimming, running, and sparring. I couldn't guess what Cal had cooked up for this year, but I knew it would be worse than what happened to Renee. Cal always made it worse. I could see why Rebecca had chosen him to reign. He was the perfect Sovereign, cruel and calculating. The system needed a firm hand to rule it, and Cal didn't hesitate to crush anyone who stood in his way.

I finished showering and dressed in what had become my uniform—a sports bra, t-shirt, and gym shorts. Snagging my tennis shoes, I pounded down the stairs to the breakfast room.

Laura served my usual fare of eggs, smoothie, and a flax seed waffle. Dmitri was already seated and powering through an immense pile of sausage. He'd stopped shaving his head since he'd moved in, and his dark hair was finally laying flat. It made him look younger and a little less intimidating. But it didn't matter. I already knew he was a big softy, with or without hair.

Lucius strolled down the hall, his voice carrying as he talked business. "No, I don't give two shits what the distributor charges, the price of sugar doesn't change based on some dipshit middleman. I'll handle it."

He walked into the sunny breakfast room dressed for travel in a navy suit, light blue shirt, and dark tie. His medium brown hair was cut neatly and smoothed back. Professional and suave, he fit perfectly as the business head of the family. Sin was wilder—something in his eyes, or maybe his bearing, gave him away as a threat.

Like water circling a drain, my thoughts always found their way back to Sin.

I shook my head slightly, as if that could erase memory of him, and took a drink of my banana, strawberry, and protein smoothie. "Where you headed?"

"New Orleans for the next few days." He sat across from me and flipped his tie over his shoulder as Laura served him. "Contracts and lawyers and shit. Nothing interesting."

I pointed at him with my fork. "Don't forget Saturday."

"I won't. I'll be back with bells on."

"Bells?" Dmitri stopped mid-chew and drew his thick brows together.

"Just an expression. He means he'll be sure to be here for Teddy's birthday." I reached behind me and felt along my left shoulder, the tenderness bothering me more than when I woke.

"Why don't you go easy today?" Lucius texted with one hand and ate with the other.

I stopped rubbing my shoulder. "Because I can't."

"You haven't had a break since…" He stopped texting and looked up. *Since Sin left.* "You need a break."

"No, I don't. I need to keep getting better. I'm still not strong enough. What if I have to climb, what if I have to swim for hours, what if—"

"Stella." Lucius glanced to Dmitri and went back to texting.

We'd told Dmitri I was training for a triathlon and wanted to throw in some self-defense just to help with coordination. He went along with it, though I often felt he suspected there was more to it, especially when he ran his hands over the scars along my back.

"Just think about it, okay? You can't keep going like this. You're a rubber band that's about to break."

"I'm not going to break. That's the last thing I'll do."

Lucius stopped texting again and caught my eye. "I know the heart inside you believes that, but you're just a person. You're a body, a mass of organs and muscles and whatever the fuck else Teddy studies in school. Your heart may stay strong, but the rest of you—" He let his gaze slide down my body then back to my eyes. "—doesn't have the luxury of whatever it is that drives you. Your body can be broken."

I downed my smoothie and stood, pushing my chair back with a harsh scrape. "I know my limits. Dmitri, you ready?"

He gestured to his half-full plate.

"Fine. I'll get a head start on stretching. Meet me on the

461

porch when you're done." Without giving Lucius another look, I strode through the hall and into the foyer. The chandelier caught the morning sun and sent fractals of light glinting in all directions.

Lucius followed, and it wasn't long before he grabbed my shoulder. I turned, staring up into his sky blue eyes that never seemed to give me any hint of truth.

"What?"

"Why are you doing this?"

"You know why." I swiped his arm off my shoulder.

"No. This isn't for Teddy." He gripped the collar of my t-shirt and pulled it to the side, getting a look at the bruises along my shoulder from sparring. "You don't have to run yourself into the ground."

"Stop." I shrugged him off.

"No." He stepped closer and glared down at me. "You're acting like an idiot."

"Trying to save your brother's life is me acting like an idiot?" I tilted my chin up, giving him nothing but disdain.

His jaw tightened, the sinews in his neck thrown in sharp relief. "That's not what you're doing."

I could have fought him. I didn't. Something about his words disturbed the numbness I'd drawn around myself like a cloak.

He grazed his fingertips up my arm and gripped my chin lightly between his thumb and forefinger. "I know you. I've seen you. I…" He paused and leaned closer. "You aren't mine. It was foolish to think you could ever belong to me. Even so, I don't want you hurt, self-inflicted or otherwise." His gaze bored into me, and he let his hand drop to my waist. "Lay off for a day. Please. That's all I'm asking."

He was pleading with me as if we were equals, as if he had some say in my life other than the simple illusion of ownership.

I fought the urge to slap him, claw him, make him hurt just so his cries could blot out the turmoil that ruled in my mind. "How many times do you think Gavin or Brianne begged 'please' while your friends violated them? Care to hazard a guess?"

He cocked his head. "Is that what this is? Don't blame yourself for all that, Stella. You didn't—"

"Shut up!" I exploded, his words like a match to a barrel of gasoline. "You don't know what we did, what happened. You weren't there. You didn't leave Brianne behind. You didn't send Gavin off alone. You didn't—" My voice cracked and I quieted.

His expression softened and he put his palm to my cheek. "No. I don't know. I wasn't there in the woods. But none of this is your fault."

"Whose is it, then?" I challenged. "Sin's? Your mother's? Whose—"

His phone rang in his pocket. Biting out a curse, he pulled it out and checked the number.

Glad for the reprieve, I sat on the bench by the front door and pulled my shoes on. "I'm training. You can either help or stay out of my way." I tied my laces, not even looking at Lucius as he answered.

"Yeah. Hang on." He turned and strode down the hall to Sin's study. I knew who was on the phone. It was as if I could sense his presence even across the miles separating the two of us.

Dmitri hadn't emerged from the breakfast room yet. I opened the front door and slammed it shut, though I still stood in the foyer. Then I crept down the hall toward the sound of Lucius' voice. The runner quieted my steps, and I eased to the closed study door.

"It's taken care of. I just have to go make a show of negotiating, sign the final contracts, and then I'll be done... No more than two days." His voice quieted, as if he were pacing away from me.

I pressed my ear to the door.

"Fine. Well, not fine. I mean she's training, but she's not being smart. It's like she, like she wants it to hurt. I don't know... Yes. Saturday." His voice grew nearer and I side

463

stepped, hugging the wall.

"Do you think that's wise? I fucking don't." Lucius voice turned darker. "I'm not telling her shit. You need to sack up. I'll put her on the phone right now… Coward. You know what this is going to do, right? You know what Stella will… Fine. I *know* she's yours. Jesus fucking Christ how many times… Yeah, go fuck yourself, too." Something crashed, and then the room fell silent.

I slipped back the way I'd come and quietly left the house.

I swam one more lap, pushing myself until the tips of my fingers and toes tingled. Pulling myself up on the edge of the pool, I took in breath after breath. Dmitri lazily swam in circles, floating on his back and keeping an eye on me.

"Running, you okay. Swimming, you good. Fighting, you worst." He splashed me before flipping under the water so I couldn't retaliate.

I glanced to the clock above the door leading back into the house. It was time to start setting up for Teddy's birthday party. He was a grown man, so it wasn't anything too over-the-top, but a small family to-do was well deserved.

Laura spearheaded the cake, and all I had to do was decorate a little and show up.

Dmitri surfaced and began his leisurely circle again.

I rose and wrapped a towel around me. "I'm going in. You coming?"

"Soon."

"Okay. We're done for the day, but I'll need you in the dining—"

"Yes, yes, Teddy's birthday, Krasivaya. I know. Every woman in house cannot stop talking about that *malchik*."

"He's a good malchik. He deserves a special day. When's your birthday?" I padded around the pool, leaving wet footprints on the grainy concrete.

"Real men no have birthdays."

"Here we go again." I laughed. "We'll continue this later. See you inside. And put on a happy face for the party."

"My face always happy." He frowned.

"Yes, I'm convinced." I pushed through the side door into the house and took the back stairs up to my room.

After a quick shower, I dressed in jeans and a black, flowy blouse. I dried my hair and applied minimal makeup before heading down to the dining room.

My decorations—a simple happy birthday sign and silly party hats—were laid out on a sideboard. I grabbed the sign and, after a trip to the library for tape, I climbed up on a chair and started to hang the sign over the wide windows.

"This seems familiar. Like the first time we met. Though that time you weren't wearing so many pesky clothes."

I glanced over my shoulder at Lucius. "I was standing on the table, not a chair."

He shrugged, his black polo and jeans giving him a casual but put-together air. "Still a nice view, all the same."

"Grab the other side and help." I secured the 'H' to the window casing.

Lucius leaned backed against the table and darted his tongue out to his bottom lip. "I prefer to watch."

"Suit yourself." I dropped to the ground and pushed my chair to the right before climbing back onto it.

"I still have your panties from that morning."

My hand faltered and I missed the 'Y' with the tape. I tried again and got it pinned.

"That's gross." I dropped to the floor and pushed the chair back to the table.

"They smell like you, you know?" He moved around so he stood at my back. "I only had a little taste that night at the cabin, but it was enough... And it wasn't."

I turned, the heat in his eyes impossible to miss as his

gaze flickered to my lips. "Lucius, we aren't doing this. I thought I'd already made that clear. I'm done playing this game with you."

"You say that now." He towered over me and ran a finger down my jawline.

Slight tingles rushed through me at his touch. "Stop." I slapped his hand away.

"We'll see. You might have a different answer for me later. I can't wait to hear it." He gave my lips one last look before he turned and walked toward the hall.

I gave Lucius credit for his single-mindedness, but not much more than that.

Laura pushed through the door from the kitchen and carried a two-layer cake to the table.

"That looks amazing." I walked over and helped her center it. It was done in a sky blue, with navy piping, and a white doctor's coat design on the very top.

"You think he'll like it?"

"He'll love it. I just don't know what we're going to do with all the leftovers."

She smoothed down her black maid's uniform. "Well, I was told to make enough for the family and two guests."

"Guests?" I asked.

"Yes. Those were the orders from Mr. Sinclair. I have to get the hors d'oeuvres set out." She retreated to the kitchen.

"No, go. That's fine." I walked to the powder room off the main hallway and ran my fingers through my hair, just to make sure I looked presentable.

After all, company was coming.

CHAPTER THREE
STELLA

THE STEADY RUMBLE OF a motorcycle told me that Teddy had arrived. I peeked out of the music room window and saw his sleek black form cruise down the oak-shrouded lane and into the garage.

"He's here," I called, loud enough for Laura and Farns to hear. Excitement welled up inside me. I hoped Teddy would enjoy his sweet surprise.

Glancing back up the drive, a black limo moved slowly toward the house and parked out in front. Luke, the Vinemont driver, got out and opened the back door. A heeled foot hit the ground, and then Luke helped a woman from the rear of the car as Sin exited the other side and came around.

Curiosity turned to something slimy in my gut the moment Sin's hand touched the small of her back. He led her forward, smiling and gesturing at the house as if he were some sort of salesman. The smile never reached his eyes. His dark gray suit created sharp, masculine lines against his broad shoulders and trim waist, and his dark hair shone in the sun.

The woman was tall and willowy, her long hair cascading down her back in ebony waves. Her sapphire wrap dress accentuated her long legs. She raised her perfectly arched eyebrows at the house, but had a smile for Sin. He led her up the stairs as another car pulled down the drive, the polished metal glinting in the noonday sun.

Farns walked past me as I stood motionless and unseen in the music room. He opened the door and greeted Sin and his guest with a "welcome." The woman didn't speak, only walked to the center of the foyer and turned her head back and forth, sizing up the elegance in every fine detail.

She swept her gaze into the music room and narrowed her eyes when they met mine. Something about her was familiar. Not her face, in particular, but her eyes. I'd seen them before, though I couldn't place where.

Sin walked up beside her and placed his hand at the small of her back again. He followed her gaze and froze, his eyes locking on mine for a split second before he turned away.

"I believe I saw Teddy riding ahead of us. The dining room is this way. If you'd care to freshen up before the lunch, there's a powder room down and to the left."

"Thank you, Sin." She gave him a kiss on the cheek, shot a scowl in my direction, and strode down the hall, her hips swaying with each step.

The door opened again, and Farns gave a stiffer "welcome" than usual. I'd been so preoccupied with Sin and the woman that I'd forgotten about the other car.

A man strode forward, his hand extended. Sin shook, and my breath caught. It was Cal Oakman. I remained still and forced the surge of hate and rage just seeing him brought to the surface back down inside. It wasn't time yet. Not until Teddy was safe.

"Sophia is freshening up. Shall we go in?" Sin kept his eyes on Cal.

"Sure." He followed Sin down the hall. "I don't believe I've been here in, what is it, ten years or so? Still looks the same."

"We try to keep it up as best we can."

"Well, not everywhere can be the Oakman Estate, especially given your family's late arrival to the game. Still, it could be worse. You seem to have…"

Their voices faded. I was trapped in ice. The joy at Teddy's birthday party had been quickly erased by unease. What was going on? Was this another test?

Lucius came down the stairs and turned toward the dining room.

"Lucius," I hissed.

He changed course and walked to me, his face inscrutable.

"What's happening?"

"A birthday party. You set it up, remember?" He took my elbow and pulled me along with him into the foyer.

"Why is Cal here?"

"The Sovereign can't attend birthday parties?"

I stopped at the foot of the stairs, forcing him to stop with me. "Stop playing games. Tell me."

He lowered his voice. "I just did. Cal wanted to attend Teddy's birthday party."

"The woman?"

He couldn't hide his smirk, not that he would ever try. "That's Sophia, Sin's date for the lunch."

My fingers grew cold, the tips of my ears hot as I digested the information. It was a punch in the gut. It shouldn't have been. I had no claim on Sin. The entire rulebook these people lived by had as its first and foremost tenet that certain people—like me—were nothing more than chattel. Was she the reason he stayed away?

Our last night together was seared in my memory, but perhaps I had mistaken Sin's words, his touch, for more than they really were. The thought rang hollow and false. I knew he meant all of it, that he'd given me everything he had. That knowledge was the only thing that had stopped me from seeking him out during his long absence. I trusted him. But he was here with another woman—one who gave me an unsettling sense of familiarity.

"Why didn't you tell me earlier?" I glared at him and let the hurt ferment into anger.

He shrugged and snaked his arm around my waist. "I figured it was best for you to see for yourself."

"This changes nothing between us." I stepped away from him and eyed the stairs. A retreat seemed like a good idea. Then again, Teddy was more important than any of it.

"We'll see. Come on. Cal will want to get a look at you." He took my hand and pulled me with him down the hallway. "And don't forget what I did to you in the woods."

I closed my eyes and tried to stop the murky thoughts—the ones that lived in my nightmares—from rising up and taking my sanity away. The woods, the cabin, the screams. Brianne's and Gavin's rapes, and my supposed violation by Lucius. He dropped my hand as we entered the room.

"Stella, so nice to see you again." Cal grinned and walked over, embracing me and running his hands down my back. My skin crawled, and I fought the nausea that rolled through me.

Sin was engaged in a conversation with Sophia and didn't even look in my direction.

"I'm still sad I missed out on you at the last trial. Maybe I'll have to arrange a little in-between treat." Cal whispered in my ear before releasing me.

The kitchen door opened and a grinning Teddy walked in, his cheeks rosy, and Laura in step right behind him. The smile died on his lips when he saw Cal.

"Happy birthday, young man." Cal skirted the table and shook Teddy's hand.

Forcing the smile to return to his face, Teddy said, "I didn't know you'd be coming, Sovereign. It's an honor."

"Whoa, look at the manners on this one." Cal laughed and slapped Laura on the ass as she passed with a serving dish.

Teddy balled his fists but did nothing.

"Sophia, how are you doing these days?" Lucius smiled easily and poured himself a drink at the sideboard.

"Same old, same old, really." Her voice was low and husky. I'd heard it before. A memory darted along the edges of my mind, but it was gone before I could grasp it.

"Jet-setting as much as you used to?"

"No." She tossed her hair over her shoulder. It looked effortless enough to be completely calculated. "Daddy didn't like me spending so much time away. So, I've been assigned to the New Orleans office. I still manage to get in a trip to Europe every couple of months, and of course, I spend a great deal of time in New York with Mother."

Lucius sipped his drink. "We're glad to have you here for Teddy's celebration."

"I wouldn't miss it." She scanned my decorations and the cake, her mouth turned down in distaste. "How quaint."

Laura bustled back in with the final dish and backed away from the table to wait.

"Shall we?" Sin motioned for everyone to sit.

Cal took the head of the table as if it were his house. Sophia stood at his side and waited for Farns to pull her chair out before sitting down. Then Sin sat to her right. I followed Lucius and sat between him and Teddy, still trying to get my bearings on what was happening.

"You seem to have recovered well, Stella." Cal lay his napkin in his lap as Laura began serving.

"Have I?"

Lucius gripped my knee.

"Yes, you don't look quite as fresh-faced as you were at the ball, of course, but you are holding up."

I darted my eyes to Sin. He ignored me and whispered something into Sophia's ear. They were close, their body language telling me that they knew each other far better than just as friends—the way their shoulders touched, how he nuzzled into her dark hair, and the way she smiled at his every word.

"She's been a bit more pliant since Christmas, I can tell you that." Lucius slung his arm around the back of my chair.

"What happened at Christmas?" Teddy asked, his voice quiet and his gaze fixed forward.

"You haven't told him about the fun?" Cal tsked and

471

took a drink of wine. "That doesn't seem very fair."

"I tire of Acquisition talk," Sophia said. "And frankly, I'm not certain why this one is allowed to eat with us." She waved her hand at me. "I mean, really, are we going to have the hunting dogs at the table with us next?"

I held my tongue. Not for my sake, but for Teddy's.

Sin laughed, his booming amusement like a knife twisting in my back. "We simply thought the Sovereign might enjoy a look at Stella."

"If you tell a redhead joke, so help me—" She leaned in and kissed Sin, their lips meeting and taking my breath away. It was obvious this wasn't the first time.

They were together. My mouth went dry as she gave him another peck and pulled away.

Cal sighed. "Fine, darling, if it's going to bother you that much, we'll send her out."

"Thank you, Daddy."

Daddy. It all clicked into place. Sophia was Cal's daughter.

"Stella will take lunch in her room. Thank you, Laura." Lucius kicked my foot.

I stood and squeezed Teddy's shoulder before walking from the room. He needed to stay silent, to sit through the meal and pretend to be one of them. Despite his goodness, he had to know that a certain level of acting was necessary just to survive in the world of Sovereigns and Acquisitions.

Just as I reached the door, Sophia called, "How's your arm?"

I turned to her, confusion and déjà vu mixing like a molotov cocktail in my memory. "What?"

Sin draped his arm across her shoulders and pulled her closer, dropping a kiss in her hair.

She laughed, as if I were behaving like a silly child. "Your arm. Don't you remember?"

"That was you." She'd been disguised by a mask at the Christmas trial, but I recognized her voice and eyes. When I'd tried to dress for the cold and give Brianne my sweater,

Sophia had hit me with a black baton. It took a month for the bruise to heal, for the bone to feel strong again.

"That was me. Too bad I didn't break it." She leaned back into Sin, her dark eyes sparkling with malice. "Now get out of here before looking at you puts me off my lunch."

CHAPTER FOUR
SINCLAIR

Three months earlier

"IF HE LOSES THE Acquisition, Sin has to kill Teddy?" Stella's weak voice floated down the hall.

My steady steps turned into a sprint until I was at my mother's open door.

"Teddy dies." Rebecca's voice, wizened and brittle like a fallen leaf, cut through the air.

Panic sliced my heart when I saw Stella standing at the mouth of hell, her skin pale, her eyes wide.

"Stella!" I rushed to her.

"I see no harm in telling the peasant girl the rules." Mother smiled, hate in every wrinkle, every line.

"Tell me. Tell me all of them." Stella stared up at me, her green eyes watering, though not a single tear fell. "I have to know." She gripped my arms, holding me tight and pinning me to the spot with the anguish in her voice.

"Tell her, son. Tell her." My mother's gleeful cackle was too much to bear.

I wrenched myself free of Stella's hold and went to the medicine cabinet. *Locked.* I gripped the handles and yanked, pulling until the wood splintered and the doors flew open. Grabbing a syringe, I turned and approached the demon on the bed.

"Please don't." Renee cried, but didn't rise to stop me.

"No." Mother tried to scoot away, fear darkening her wild eyes.

I grabbed her arm and pulled it straight. She slapped me and scratched my neck. I ignored it, just like I ignored every bit of pain she'd caused since that hellish night in Brazil. Even as she struggled and screamed, I hit her vein and depressed the plunger.

Her motions slowed, her words ceasing, and then she collapsed back into the bed, finally asleep. Finally silent.

Renee shoved me aside and sank down on the bed, stroking Mother's face and crying. "How could you?"

"It needed to be done." I tried to clear my head, to douse the fire of emotions that raged inside. I usually had an easy time of it. Not now. Not when my mother had seen fit to shove Stella into the same razorblade straightjacket I wore.

Renee smoothed Mother's hair, doting on her as if the woman were anything other than a venomous snake. "She was fine. She wasn't hurting anyone."

I threw the syringe in the garbage and looked at Stella, her eyes haunted.

"She's hurt plenty." I took Stella's hand and pulled her from the room. She didn't resist, shock settling on her like a lead weight.

I took her to my room and locked the door behind us. She sat on the bed and leaned over, her head cupped in her hands.

"Stella?" I knelt in front of her.

"Why Teddy? Why? He's the only good thing in this house, in this entire godforsaken family." She shook her head and still wouldn't look at me.

I pulled her hands from her face. They were soft, so easily broken. But nothing about her was in pieces, not shattered the way I was.

"The rules. It's what makes us compete. It turns us against ourselves until the strongest comes out on top."

That was the explanation, but not the reason. Was there any reason for this torment other than providing entertainment for the depraved lot of us?

"Why didn't you tell me?" A tear rolled down her cheek and hovered at her jaw line before dropping onto my scarred wrist.

"Power. If you'd known that from the start, you would have had the upper hand. Teddy is the heart of this family. You didn't know that when you arrived. You could have used that information against us."

"But after? When you knew how much I cared for him?"

"I didn't tell you for the same reason I didn't tell Lucius." I grazed my thumb along her cheek, wiping her tears—the ones I'd caused—away. "How do you feel now that you know? Stronger? Better?" I shook my head. "You are weaker. It's meant to be a spear in my side, as the Acquirer, to know what will happen if I lose. By the time you'd come to care for Teddy, I realized telling you would give you the same pain, the same weight, the same fucking dread that's crushing me."

She put her warm palm to my cheek. I pressed into it, needing so much more from her than I could even admit to myself.

"You've had to bear it alone."

The pity in her eyes, pity for me, almost broke what little of a heart I had left. "I've done what I had to do. I've been the man I had to be. I can't lose Teddy. But you... You were the best choice and also the worst for my Acquisition. If I'd only known..."

"What?" She edged off the bed and sank to the floor in front of me, her body pressing against me and her mouth tantalizingly close. "If you'd known what?"

I couldn't help myself. She was my weakness, my downfall. Everything about her was my undoing. I pulled her to me, her scent of vanilla and lavender filling my nose as her very essence filled my soul.

I stared into her green eyes. Her heart was laid bare,

though she'd never spoken the words to me. I'd acquired her, but she owned me. "If I'd known I'd fall in love with you." I kissed her, needing her past all reason.

She opened her mouth, and I slanted over her, punishing her sweet lips with my rough kiss. She was mine. I couldn't give her up. I needed her raw and wild, rough and passionate. Grabbing a fistful of hair, I pulled her head back and bit her neck like a savage leaving his mark.

She clutched at my shirt. I hated the feel of fabric between us. I needed her satin skin, her hot, wet cunt. I needed to bury myself in her and forget everything else except her taste, her breath, her life.

I pulled my shirt off and yanked her to her feet before shoving her down on the bed. "Strip. Now."

I unbuckled my belt and slid the leather between my fingers. It spoke to me, told me to punish her. But I couldn't wait, couldn't stop myself from having her. Not this time.

She bit her lip, her eyes half-lidded. I kicked my jeans and shorts away as she pulled her pants and her panties off.

"On your back, head on the pillow, and spread your legs wide." I gripped my shaft until it almost hurt, and stroked slowly as she lay back and spread. Her pink pussy glistened, wetness there for me.

She was perfect, her skin luminous and her breaths coming in shallow pants. I wanted to hurt her, but not just that. I knew she would take some of my pain and turn it into her own pleasure.

"Touch your pussy."

She kept her eyes on mine as she reached down and slid her fingertips across her slick clit. My cock leaked at the sight and I slowed my strokes, needing to be inside her.

"Tell me who you think about when you touch yourself."

She swirled her fingers around the tight little nub. I wanted to bite it.

"You," she breathed.

"Finger yourself. Two fingers."

She slid her fingers between her folds and sank them inside, her hips rising from the bed as she did it.

I dropped to my knees and moved between her thighs. Her soft moans echoed through my mind until I seethed with need. "What do I do to you?"

She bit her lip and pulsed her fingers in and out. Watching was torture, but I had to feel the sting before the pleasure. She would, too.

"You push me down and take me rough."

The words were like a lash at my back, driving me closer to her. "What else?"

"Y-you hurt me." The words were barely a whisper.

The animal that clawed at the inside of my chest howled at her admission. I gripped her wrist and pulled her fingers away. I licked them, savoring her taste.

"Grip the headboard." I devoured every inch of her skin with my gaze, searing her pale flesh into my memory.

Her hands wrapped around the antique wood, and I ran my palm from her chest to her pussy. I hovered my hand over her heat, never breaking eye contact. Then I drew back and slapped her wet folds.

She moaned and tried to close her legs. I wrenched them apart and slapped her again.

"Sin."

"Fuck, yes. Say it again." I licked her wetness off my palm and sank two fingers inside her.

"Sin!" She writhed, her back arching, her hips pushing down onto my fingers as I roughly pushed in and out. Her tits shook as I leaned over her, bracing myself with one arm while using the other to finger fuck her.

"This? Do I do this to you in your fantasies, Stella?"

"Sin, please. Don't stop."

The heel of my palm slapped into her clit again and again, and I leaned down and pinned one of her hard nipples between my teeth.

She moaned, low and long, and spread her legs even farther. I sped my pace and she froze, her hips seizing as her

479

pussy clamped down on my fingers. I withdrew and slammed my cock into her as she writhed beneath me, her orgasm squeezing me as I started a pounding rhythm.

Her throat; I had to take it. I wrapped my fingers around her neck, her life, and squeezed. I lowered myself to my elbow and gripped her hair so she had nowhere to go, nowhere to look but into my eyes as she rode the wave of her pleasure.

I shoved into her, jarring the bed with how much I needed to mark her as my own. She needed to feel me for days, to wear my bruises on her thighs. She didn't look away, didn't try to move her hands from the headboard. Even as I stole her breath and refused to give it back.

"Sin." A strangled whisper from her lips that turned me into a demon. Because I needed to hear it again. I needed my name always on her mind, on her tongue.

I released the pressure at her neck and she gasped, but I stole her breath again by kissing her hard and biting her bottom lip until I drew blood. She moaned and opened her mouth, the coppery taste mixing with her sweetness as I took everything from her.

Her blood was honey on my tongue, and her pussy heaven on my cock. I was never free, not until I was here with her. Just the two of us. Just her locked in a cage with the beast who lived inside me. She was unafraid. Even from the start, from the moment I'd seen her, she had been a piece of steel that I railed on, beat, and tried to break. She would never break. Instead, I'd shattered against her like glass against a stone.

Her tongue snaked inside my mouth, and I wrapped my arm under her back. I wanted to feel every bit of her skin I could, to meld her into me until we were one—my darkest elements wrapped in her light.

"Touch me." I growled against her lips and moved to her neck. She obeyed, her nails streaking down my back, the pain heightening the pulse in my cock.

I thrust into her and stayed there, pushing against her

deepest parts as I rocked my hips. She clawed my ass as I bit her shoulder, sinking my teeth in until I almost broke the skin. Pushing my hand between us, I stroked her clit with my thumb as I thrust deep.

"Come for me. I need to feel you." I dragged my teeth up her throat and rested my forehead against hers. "Give me all of you."

We panted, our breaths mingling as we surged into each other. Her body tightened and my cock thickened even more.

"I'm there. I-I'm coming."

"Say it, Stella." I shoved harder into her as her walls clamped down. "You know what I want."

"Sin. I'm yours." She repeated my name.

The sound was the richest aphrodisiac, one that sent my hips into a frenzy as I came, my release ripping through me as I shot deep inside her. I grunted as she moaned, her pussy still spasming as I emptied everything I had into her, coating her with me.

Her lips were swollen, the bottom one red and angry from my bite. I grazed my mouth across hers gently, the need to hurt her momentarily extinguished. I let go of her hair and put my palm to her cheek. She answered by wrapping her arms around my neck and pulling me into a possessive kiss. Her tongue sought and took, and I was more than willing to give. I'd already given her everything.

I pulled away so she could take a breath. So much emotion flitted across her eyes, but mostly the one that spoke to my soul. The small flame of something I'd tried to stamp out, to destroy. Somehow, it burned still. For me.

"I love you, Sin."

Her words were a balm and a barb. Just as she had always been both.

I slid out of her, hating the loss of her tight warmth. I dropped onto the bed next to her and pulled her to my chest. She lay her head over my heart. Could she feel my fear in its rapid beat?

I had to stop it all. To bottle my feelings back up and stow them away. Was it even possible anymore? "I have to do things, Stella. I have to hurt you. The spring trial."

"I know." She said it as if it were simple, as if me harming her were as normal as the sun shining or the breeze blowing. "And now I know why."

"I have to win."

"Yes." She nodded against me. "*We* have to win."

I clenched my eyes shut. "You don't understand."

"I do." She craned her head back to look me in the eye. "I will do anything to keep Teddy safe. Just tell me what to do. Tell me about the trial. Give me the rules. All of them."

"They won't help."

"Then what will it hurt? Tell me." She pushed away from me and sat back, pulling the sheet to her neck.

I wanted to yank her back down and cover her body with mine, but I stayed my hand.

Her jaw was set and she cocked her head slightly to the left. I knew the look—it meant she wasn't going to relent, no matter what I said or did. Her stubbornness was beyond even my comprehension.

I took a deep breath and let out a shuddering exhale. "The trial has to do with some sort of physical contest. I believe Cal's year was an obstacle course that turned into a grueling competition for the Acquisitions."

She nodded against me. "I can train for that. I'll start tomorrow. Do we know anything else?"

We. The word was so small, but nothing had ever held more meaning for me. "Red told me at Cal's party that the competition is to be held at Fort LaRoux."

"Hmm, that's familiar." She quirked her lips as she thought. "I think I know which one you mean. I thought it was abandoned to the state as some sort of historical site."

I laughed, the sound hollow. "The governor has no problem allowing use of government lands for this little game. He'll likely be standing at Cal's right hand."

"Does it mean anything? I mean, the location—what

does it tell us?"

"Yes, it means something. The terrain isn't made for any sort of obstacle course. It's more suited as an arena, the battlements serving as seating for the open center area."

"You think they'll have us fight each other?" She lay back down and snuggled in closer to my side.

"Maybe. Or it could be some series of tests or feats the audience could watch. I don't have enough information." And wasn't that always the fucking problem? Cal had obscured this year's trials more so than any in the past.

"And why would Red tell you any of this?"

"He thinks I'm the frontrunner." I shook my head. "He thinks if he helps me, I'll save his sister when I become Sovereign."

"Will you?" Her voice quieted even more.

"No. Not if it means I put my family in danger. The rules are quite clear on the penalty for losing, and I won't risk any challengers to my reign. I'll take her life to spare mine, Teddy's, or yours."

"How old is she?"

Eighteen years, six months, and seventeen days. I knew the length of her life as well as that of Eagleton's younger brother, Carl. Counting down the days to their deaths was the only way I knew to accept the inevitable—I would see them dead by their siblings' hands or my own. "It doesn't matter."

"Please, how old?" She rested her hand on my chest, her delicate fingers pulling the information from me bit by bit.

"Eighteen."

"Jesus." She buried her face in my neck, and I pulled her to me. "You can't kill her. She's so young—"

"I will. For Teddy. For you. I will. I'd kill her ten times over."

She pressed her fingers to my lips and looked at me with troubled eyes. "Don't say that. Please don't say that. You can't. We'll think of something, some way out."

Her fingers stilled my lips but not my thoughts. *There is*

no way out.

She lay back against me and dropped her hand to my chest. "Now the rules. I need them all."

She already knew the worst. The rest just completed the depraved puzzle. "First rule." I swallowed hard. "Is Teddy. Second rule, you know as well—the Acquisition can choose between first and second born. Third, an Acquirer may not harm an opposing Acquisition except during trials."

She nodded. "That's why Renee told me I would be safe the night we went to the party at Cal's."

"Yes. Fourth is that maiming an Acquisition or permanent loss of limb is not allowed."

"That's comforting."

"Fifth, we can't kill you."

"Even better."

"Sixth, the current Sovereign is the sole vote on who becomes the next Sovereign."

"Renee mentioned that. Cal wields all the power."

"And now that he's brought in your stepmother's family, he's solidified his stranglehold on the power structure. He'll only choose someone he trusts to keep him at the top."

"Makes sense." A shadow fell across her eyes. "He's our target, the one we're trying to convince."

"Yes, but a large part of that is putting on a show for the rest of them. We have to make it look good. Keep them entertained."

She sighed. "So what's the seventh?"

I glanced to the ceiling, as if I could see through it to my mother's suite. I hadn't known the seventh rule until after I'd been chosen. That particular cut of the knife was a master stroke by my mother. As chaotic as her mind was, there were still plenty of sharp edges.

"Sin?" Stella asked again.

"The seventh is that the previous Sovereign, not the current Sovereign, chooses the competitors."

She jolted, as if she'd touched a live wire. "You mean your *mother* chose you to compete?"

The weight of my mother's legacy crushed both of us, leaving nothing but destruction in its wake. "She did."

CHAPTER FIVE
STELLA

"WHO IS WOMAN?" DMITRI sank onto my bed, the antique wood groaning under his weight.

"Sophia."

"Why so rude? I go to party. She say I don't belong."

I reached over and patted him on the back. "Same here."

"*Pizda.*" He shook his head. "And why she with Sinclair?"

I tried to brush away my feelings, like crumbs off the bedspread. "I assume they are together. Like a couple." The crumbs were still there, grinding into my skin no matter which way I turned.

"Foolish man." He glanced at me, his scowl deep. "Now I all dressed up. No party. No nothing." He lay back on my bed and laced his fingers together over his chest. "We should train, eh?"

I lay next to him, and we both stared at the ceiling fan's lazy circle. "Yeah."

Neither of us moved. My body was tired, sore, and losing an afternoon of training was beginning to look like not such a bad thing. My thoughts strayed back to Sophia. She'd taken such pleasure in hurting me at the last trial, and now seemed to delight even more in rubbing it in my face. She and her father topped my list of people I would seek vengeance on once Teddy was safe.

After a few quiet minutes, Dmitri began to snore, softly at first, and then growing louder over the span of half an hour until I began to fantasize about smothering him with a pillow. A bump at the door had him awake and on his feet in a second.

"Who?"

"Just me." Teddy's voice. "Can you get the door? My hands are full."

Dmitri opened it for him, and Teddy entered carrying a large plate full of cake, another large plate full of sandwiches and some silverware, and a bottle of wine with red cups under his arm.

"This pleases me." Dmitri grinned and closed the door as Teddy laid the food out on the bed.

"This is a feast." I hugged Teddy as soon as his hands were empty and kissed him on the cheek. "Happy birthday."

"Thanks." He squeezed me tightly and then shook Dmitri's hand.

"Happy birthday." Dmitri pulled him in for a bear hug.

Teddy laughed and escaped. Then his face grew somber. "I'm sorry about downstairs."

"Don't worry about it. I know it's not you."

"No." He ran a hand through his unruly blond locks. "It's not, and I really didn't appreciate them showing up here like that. They're not the ones I want to spend time with."

"Have they gone?" I eyed the croissant sandwiches, and Dmitri's stomach rumbled.

"Yes. Well, Sin's still here. He's staying for the weekend." Teddy pulled the loosened cork from the wine bottle and poured us each a cup of red. "Dig in. I'm hungry, too. Cal and Sophia turn my stomach, so I didn't eat much."

We settled around the platters, Dmitri eating two sandwiches in one go.

"Anything important discussed while we were hiding up here?" I tried to make it sound as nonchalant as possible.

Teddy wasn't fooled. "No. I didn't get any information. You're the one who knows things. I'm in the dark." He put his sandwich down. "I wish you'd tell me."

I shot a look to Dmitri and back to Teddy. "You already know I'm training for the triathlon in the spring. I don't know what it will entail, exactly. So, we're on the same page."

"What else?"

"Like what?"

"How many more—" He glanced to Dmitri, who seemed to remain oblivious while munching away. "—*competitions* are there?"

"After this triathlon, only one more in late summer." I took a bite of sandwich despite the tightness in my throat. I wouldn't tell him everything, just enough to keep him even-keeled for the time being.

"That's it? Then you're done? Win or lose?"

I nodded and forced myself to chew. "Right. Win or lose, I'm done."

"That's more than anyone else tells me." He nodded and sat back. "Thank you."

"You're welcome."

I changed the subject to his time at college, and Teddy lapsed into how excited he was to start med school.

"When you doctor, you prescribe medications?" Dmitri asked and forked a chunk of cake into his mouth.

"Yes, that's part of it."

"Hard stuff?"

Teddy cocked his head. "Narcotics, you mean? Yes."

"I have friends. You make good money. All you have to do is—"

I stood and clapped my hands. "Well, I think I'm stuffed. Since they're gone, want to go downstairs? Maybe go outside and let me show you my skills?" I brought my fists up.

"You're kidding, right?" Teddy laughed.

"She no kidding." Dmitri puffed his chest out. "She taught by best fighter in all Russia."

"Well, hell." Teddy downed his wine. "On that note, let's do it."

Dmitri laughed as we walked into the hall and down to the front door.

"Your ass is going to be on the grass, pretty boy." I punched him in the shoulder.

"Ow." He grabbed his arm as we strolled out into the sunny yard, then dropped his hand and rolled his shoulders. "Just kidding. I didn't feel a thing." He grinned and pulled his hands up, palms open. "Come at me, bro."

I rounded up my hair into a ponytail and tied it with an elastic from my pocket. "I didn't realize you wanted an ass-whipping for your birthday."

He smiled bigger, getting into tough-guy character. "I hate to hit a girl, even one with a mouth like yours."

"Don't worry. You won't." I easily moved away from his first swiping grab.

"Can't catch me that way." I circled him, my knees bent and my hands up.

He darted toward me. I ducked and shot my foot out, tripping him. He hit the grass and rolled from his momentum.

"Damn." He laughed and got to his feet, slivers of grass hanging from his otherwise neat button-down shirt and jeans. "Slippery. You come get me instead."

"Okay." I advanced.

He backed away a step and barreled into me, tackling me to the ground. I landed on my back, him on top. He sat on my hips and put a hand on each side of my head, smiling and proud of himself. I held my arms out and he fell into them for a friendly embrace.

"A hug for the victor."

"Don't feel bad. I'm pretty strong." He returned my squeeze.

I slung my right arm over his shoulder, linked my hands, and shoved up from the ground with my left leg. He cried out in surprise as I flipped him and wrapped both hands around his throat.

"Yes! Krasivaya, yes!" Dmitri walked to us and towered overhead. "Now, Teddy. You must get free. Knock her off."

"Well." Teddy grabbed my wrists. "I wouldn't want to hurt her."

"Pussy." I grinned down at him.

He wrenched my hands from his throat and wrapped an arm around my neck, pulling me down into a submission move so my head was trapped between his torso, his arm, and the ground.

"Oh. No, Teddy." Dmitri laughed.

"What? I got her."

"Look down, comrade."

My hand was snugged in his crotch ready to squeeze as hard as I could to get out of the hold.

Teddy let me go. "Oh, fuck no."

"That's why you got a warning." I kissed the tip of his nose and got up, offering him my hand.

Teddy pulled himself to his feet. "You weren't kidding about the training."

"No. She fighter now."

"Let's test that theory, shall we?" Sin's voice whipped around my heart like a lasso, constricting and pulling at the same time. No longer dressed in a suit, he wore jeans and a dark t-shirt.

He studied me as if he were ticking off a list against his memory of how I looked the last time he'd seen me.

I balled my fists. He thought he could parade Sophia Oakman in front of me and treat me like the dirt under his shoe. And now he was taunting me?

"You game?" His eyes challenged me as much as his tone.

I was more than ready to hurt him any way I could. I met

his dark gaze.
"Let's do this."

CHAPTER SIX
STELLA

"YOU SURE YOU WANT to fight me?" I re-tightened my hair in the bun, taking my time as I tried to figure out how to best him.

"I want to take you down." He gave a predatory smile as his gaze raked my body again.

"You no hurt her." Dmitri stabbed a finger at Sin.

"But she likes it when I hurt her." Sin smiled.

Dmitri glowered and stepped toward him.

I put my palm to Dmitri's chest. "I can handle him. Go on inside. This won't take long."

Dmitri mumbled some curses in Russian. "Come, Teddy. Let's eat more cake."

"Go easy on him. He's not as tough as I am." Teddy swiped the rest of the grass off his shirt.

"Come. Come." Dmitri led him away as Sin circled me, sizing me up.

Teddy threw a worried glance over his shoulder as Dmitri herded him into the house.

"Why was Sophia here?" Of so many questions that bounced around my mind, the pettiest one came out first.

"Because she was my date for Teddy's party." He dashed

toward me.

I backed up, trying to time what his moves would be.

"Nice decorations, by the way." He smirked and circled me slowly, like a bird of prey.

I wouldn't wait for him to come to me. I rushed him and gripped his shoulders, throwing my weight forward and swinging my legs up. It would have been the perfect take down if he hadn't seen the move coming and twisted so I couldn't maneuver my legs around his neck.

He held me for a moment before taking me to the ground, his heavy wait crushing me as he knocked the wind from my lungs. The sun was high overhead, and I remembered this. I remembered the first day when I'd run for freedom but found only him.

Not this time. I wrapped him in my arms and did the same move on him as Teddy. Though Sin was bigger, he flipped just the same until I was straddling him, my hands at his throat. I pressed hard, far harder than I'd done with Teddy.

Sin didn't fight back, only slid his hands up my thighs.

"Where have you been?"

"Wooing Ms. Sophia Oakman." His voice was terse, the words barely passing my palms.

"Do you love her?"

His hands roved higher until they were at my waist. He pulled me down onto him, rubbing me back and forth against the hardening length in his pants. "No. Just courting an alliance, something like a business arrangement."

I eased my grip as he kept rocking my hips against him. "Are you dating her to help us win?"

"You're getting smarter the longer you stay with us, Stella. I applaud your love for learning, even at this late juncture."

I slapped him hard across the cheek and he growled before flipping me and pinning my hands next to my head.

"Asshole." Tears stung my eyes as he stared down at me, his brows drawn together. "You didn't have to stay away. You could have said something. You just left."

"No. I did what you needed me to do. You've been here, training every day and getting stronger and better. I would be a distraction. I already am, and I've only been back for a few hours. My time was better spent away, trying to catch Sophia's eye, and your time was better spent here with that fuckwad Dmitri." His jaw tightened. "Has he touched you?"

I laughed, the sound maniacal. "Yes. Every day. We spar and swim, and he gives me a massage."

"You know what I mean." He leaned closer, his sapphire eyes becoming my whole world. "I will kill him with my bare hands if he's tried anything."

I glared at him. "You show up here with that psychotic bitch on your arm, treat me like I'm beneath you, and then have the nerve to ask me if I'm fucking one of my only friends?"

"I have more nerve than that. I want to fuck you, and I have half a mind to strip you right now, flip you on your stomach, and punish you until you scream. So, answer my question. Has he touched you?"

"You wouldn't dare!" Heat rushed through me at his threat. Because I was fucked up. Because I wanted him to want me. Because he was all I could think about—his face, his body, his scent, his twisted mind.

"Wouldn't I?" He got to his knees and pulled me up before throwing me over his shoulder.

"What the fuck are you doing?" I beat at his back as he got to his feet and headed away from the house and toward the oaks that lined the driveway.

He ran his hand up my thigh and pressed hard against my pussy. "Hot and wet, just like I thought."

"Put me down."

"I will." He strode into the shade of the oaks and pushed me up against one of them. The oak's wide trunk hid us from the house.

I pressed my palm against his chest. "I'm not—"

He kissed me, pinning me between his chest and the tree. His hands roved me, and before long, he had one up my shirt, palming my breast through my bra. I dug my nails into his chest, but he only leaned in harder, as if he wanted my violence.

He ripped up my bra, exposing both breasts, and groaned into my mouth as he squeezed them. My knees went weak at his touch. Every thought of anger or hatred burned away as he consumed me as surely as fire does black powder. Breaking our kiss, he whipped me around to face the tree.

"Pull your pants down or I'll do it myself."

I glanced over my shoulder as he unfastened his belt. He ripped the elastic from my hair and tossed it aside.

"Do it, Stella." He growled and slapped my ass.

I fumbled with my button and unzipped my pants. He did the rest, ripping them down my legs to my knees.

He pressed his palm flat to my back, bending me over as I braced against the trunk. In one harsh movement, he entered me, his cock embedded deep as I moaned.

"Give it to me." He thrusted hard and slapped my ass, the sting mixing with the pleasure until I was panting, my pussy slick and wanting. "This is how you like it, isn't it?" He gripped my hair and pulled me to him, walking me forward until my breasts pressed against the bark as he fucked me in punishing strokes. His lips blazed a hot trail down my neck as he cupped my breast. "Tell me."

"Yes." I craned my head back and kissed him, his tongue darting in and setting the same pace as his cock.

"Touch yourself." He pushed me harder into the tree, the bark scraping against my nipples.

I ran my fingers down my stomach and rubbed them against my clit. He kissed my neck, sucking my skin between his teeth and biting down, his hand still tangled in my hair. I moved lower, brushing my fingertips along his cock as it surged inside me.

"Fuck." He groaned and squeezed my nipple, twisting it between his thumb and index finger and pressing me into the tree. "This is all I could think about. Every day. Every night. Every time I closed my eyes. You." As if the admission made him angry, he bit my shoulder.

My body was drawing into itself, the pressure sweet and tense between my thighs. I stroked my clit to his harsh pace. He maintained the bite on my shoulder, like an animal in heat, a wolf pouncing on its mate.

"Give me your fingers."

I pulled them away and lifted them over my shoulder. He sucked them into his mouth, his tongue licking them clean as he groaned and pounded me harder. My body was strung tight, his tongue on my fingers kicking my heat up a notch.

Once satisfied, he released them. "I want you to come on my cock."

I snaked my fingers back down and rubbed my swollen nub. He sank his teeth into my shoulder again and fucked me roughly as I cried out and scraped against the tree. My pussy constricted and my hips tensed.

The tiny explosions grew inside me until I couldn't stop the cresting wave.

"Sin!" My body shuddered as I came, and my mind went completely blank.

He growled into my skin and slammed inside me, staying deep as his cock kicked and shot in strong spurts. I let my hand fall and leaned my head against the tree. He grunted and thrust one more time before kissing the vicious bite mark that would surely bruise.

"I needed that. You. I needed you." He rested his forehead against my shoulder and steadied his breathing.

I turned to him. "I needed you, too."

He kissed me softly, his lips a gentle melody instead of the crashing crescendo of a few moments earlier.

"Stella?" Dmitri's voice drifted on the warm air.

"Shit." I pushed back against Sin.

He didn't move, just shoved his hips forward, his half-mast cock sending a tingle through me.

"Krasivaya? We train?" His voice sounded closer.

"Sin, he's going to see. Get off."

"I already got off once. I'd like to do it again." He smoothed a hand down my stomach and rubbed my too-sensitive clit.

"No." I jerked at his touch.

"I like it when you fight." His voice was a low rasp.

"You haven't seen me fight. Not yet." I tried to buck him, but it only pushed him in deeper.

He grunted and pulled my hair, still thrusting his cock slowly inside me. "You'll have to do better than that."

"Krasivaya?" Dmitri was close and getting closer.

Panic rose right along with my embarrassment at the thought of getting caught.

"Fight some more. Come on. You know I enjoy it." Sin's voice in my ear was hell, his mastery of my body, heaven.

"You asked for it." I reached over my head and grabbed a fistful of his hair, yanking viciously while I simultaneously threw my elbow back.

He grunted and backed off enough so I could spin to face him. The move dislodged his cock, but I scraped my side on the tree bark as I went.

His eyes were full of amusement, even as he tilted his head to the side because of my grip of his hair. He shoved me back into the tree. "What now?"

"Now she throat punch you." Dmitri walked around the trunk, and I scrambled to pull up my pants. My shirt had thankfully fallen to cover my breasts.

Sin, not caring about his state of undress, glared at Dmitri. "Get the fuck out of here. We're busy."

"She need practice." Dmitri looked everywhere but at me.

"No shit. You've been teaching her to pull hair? That's it?" Sin tucked his cock back in and zipped up. "That's not good enough."

"Not good enough for what?" Dmitri exploded forward until he and Sin were almost nose to nose. "What you do to her? What?"

"Fuck off, Russian. This won't end well for you." A wave of menace rolled off Sin like heat rising from pavement.

"Stop." I pushed at their shoulders. Neither man backed away.

"Stay out of this, Krasivaya. If he will not tell me truth, I beat it from him." Dmitri's scowl would have made even the fiercest fighter balk, but it seemed to only make Sin angrier, more ready to spill blood.

"Let's show him. Come on, Dmitri." I backed away from the shadow beneath the tree and out into the sunny grass. An ache shot between my legs thanks to Sin's attentions, but I had to separate the bristling men before they fought. "Let's spar."

"I rather *spar* with Sinclair."

Shit. "Please?" I tried my best wheedling tone. "Don't you want to help me get better?"

Soft-hearted Dmitri broke his death stare with Sin and glanced at me. "I do."

"Come on then." I brought my fists up. "I need help."

Dmitri snarled at Sin. "This not over."

Sin grinned. "Go on. Show me the tricks you learned in your Russian gutter. Let me see what I've been paying for."

"Sin!" I hissed.

"What?" He shrugged as Dmitri turned and entered the sunlight with me. Crossing his arms over his chest, Sin tilted his chin up. "Show me what you've got besides hair pulling."

"Position one, Krasivaya."

I bent slightly at the knees and kept my hands up, palms open. Dmitri ran at me. I shifted my weight to the side, let him barrel past, and aimed a kicked at the back of his knee. He stumbled and then straightened.

"Good. Position Two."

I straightened, hands still up, as Dmitri approached. He drew back his right fist and aimed it at my face. He jabbed and I dodged, slapping his fist away and shoving hard against his arm to throw him off balance. He took a step and caught himself.

"Attack." He bent at the knees and waved me to him.

I edged to his right and darted in, aiming the tips of my straight fingers at his throat. He swung when I got close. His fist grazed the top of my head as I ducked and stabbed upward with my hand, but he caught my wrist before I made contact.

"Good." He grunted his approval.

"Your greatest strength is surprise. Your greatest skill— speed. Do not forget, Krasivaya. You look weak. You small." He tapped the side of my head. "Use to your advantage."

Sin approached. "She's got a few moves. I can see that. But I think you could have done more to—"

I exploded off the ground and kicked my legs up. Sin wasn't quick enough this time, so I was able to straddle his neck and take him down. Landing on his back, he tried to shove me off. I tightened my legs around his neck as I sat on his chest, pinning him.

I pulled my fist back and smiled in triumph. "I could break your nose if I wanted to."

He glanced between my thighs, his eyes sparkling in the sun, before staring up at me. "I think I like this brand of training."

CHAPTER SEVEN
SINCLAIR

I RAN MY FINGERS through her hair, sifting the strands while my mind did the same with memories. She slumbered at my side, snuggled up to my darkness as if it gave off some sort of heat. The only warmth I had was a reflection of hers. Nothing more.

Sun streamed through her bedroom windows, lighting the bed and the quilts along the walls. Mother still asked every so often if I would make one to commemorate my Acquisition, as if it were a badge of honor. I enjoyed disappointing her each time she brought it up. If it were up to me, I'd destroy every one of them.

I studied the oldest one, the seams still tight. Its artistry reminded me of what we once were—sharecroppers and seamstresses. When my great-great-grandfather unwittingly saved the life of the reigning Sovereign, he'd damned us to this life. Seeing us now, raised so high amongst our wicked cohorts, would he regret his act of mercy?

I closed my eyes, blocking out my history, and relished every point of contact I had with Stella as her breath tickled my chest.

I'd been back for two weeks, ignoring my work and,

instead, focusing on her. She trained and fought, thriving despite the hellish environs of the Acquisition. I wondered at her strength, where it came from, why I didn't have it. But I also saw her self-destruction—how she pushed herself further to the brink every day. Her torment was mine. It pained me to see her so hell bent on punishing herself for wrongs she never committed. Still, trying to stop her was like trying to stop the Acquisition itself.

She shifted and her breathing quickened. Perhaps my shadowy thoughts had invaded whatever pleasant dream she'd been having.

"Who was Cora?" Her voice was still thick with sleep. "Renee told me she was your aunt, but nothing else."

"What makes you think of that?" I ran my fingers along her smooth side.

"I dreamed of that night. The one with your mother." Her eyelashes fluttered against my chest.

That hellish night. I sighed. I kept nothing from her anymore. She knew me, all of me, and yet she still lay here in my arms as if I weren't a twisted monster. I kissed the crown of her head. "My aunt, yes. She was the youngest in my mother's family. The one my mother fought to save."

"She was Rebecca's Teddy?"

"Yes."

She rolled back so her head was nestled on my shoulder, her green eyes piercing even as she emerged from the cobwebs of her dreams. "But Rebecca won. So, what happened to Cora?"

"Cora witnessed it all. She saw what Rebecca and Renee went through. She knew from the start that it was her life on the line. Years after it was all over, she hung herself in the woods."

Stella clenched her eyes shut. "God. I'm sorry, Sin."

"I don't remember her much." Her red hair and warm smile were almost lost to me, just like my mother—both women erased by the Acquisition. "My mother took it in, ingested the blame like a fine meal, and let it drag her down even further. *It was all for nothing.* My mother screamed those words at Cora's funeral." The memory of her, all in black, sinking to her knees and screeching at the clear blue sky, passed before my eyes before disappearing.

Stella scooted on top of me and cupped my cheek. "You were too young." The unshed tears in her eyes glistened, and I wanted to take them away.

"That's why Teddy can never know." I smoothed my palms down her back. "That's the past. We have plenty to think about without it."

Resting her chin on my chest, she said, "One more week. I just wish we knew what the trial will be."

"So do I." I'd tried to get information from Sophia, but she was almost as cold as her father. I still had my claws in her, I knew—she'd been texting me while she was in New York for the past few weeks. I hadn't failed with her, not yet.

Even if she agreed to an alliance with me, I still had the problem of her lover, Ellis, to deal with. If Cal found out she was seeing him instead of setting her cap at the next Sovereign, his displeasure would be lethal. So, if she wouldn't go along with my plans of her own accord, I could always dangle Ellis in front of her like a tasty lure. I would be the hook.

Still, she'd divulged nothing about her father's plans. The trial was almost here, and I hadn't been able to divine the actual mechanism Cal would use to wreak havoc on Stella. Rage exploded in my chest, and I beat against the cage I was born into like I'd done so many times before. In the end, I was still trapped, still lying here with the woman I'd kill to protect, but harm to save Teddy.

A light knock sounded at my door.

I pulled Stella next to me in the bed and covered her with the blanket. "Yes?"

"I'm sorry, sir. There's a man at the gate demanding to see you." Farns' voice wavered through the wood.

"Who?"

"Red Witherington."

"Fucking hell." I moved to the edge of the bed and stabbed my legs in my jeans. "Farns, let him in."

"Very good, sir."

Stella rose and pulled her tank top over her head.

"You're staying here."

"Like hell I am." She yanked on her panties and jeans.

I turned. "He hates you. If he has even a shred of information that can help us, then I need you out of sight. Understand?"

"What makes you think he came here to help?" She threw her hair over her shoulder and pulled her top down the rest of the way, covering the sight of her mouthwatering breasts.

I strode to her and grabbed her shoulders, holding her gaze. "I don't know why he's here. But if he sees you, it won't matter. It will all go to hell."

She opened her mouth to argue, then closed it.

"Do you trust me?" I asked the question I had no right to even think in her presence. I held my breath, wishing we were different people in a different life. Even as we were, could she give me the trust I didn't deserve but desperately wanted?

She rested her hand against my chest, over my heart. "Yes."

She must have had something in her palm, because warmth spread from it as surely as if she were the sun on a hot day. I kissed her harder than I'd intended. I must have put the weight of everything I felt, everything I was capable of feeling, into it. She wrapped her arms around my neck, pulling me closer, matching me with the same fiery intensity I'd seen in her the very first day we met.

She broke the kiss and stepped back. "Okay. I'll stay away, but I won't promise not to eavesdrop."

I took her hand and kissed her palm. "I would expect nothing less."

I turned and strode out and down the hallway to the

main stairs. I met Lucius on the landing. Dragging his carry-on behind him, his clothes were rumpled and he needed a shave.

I smirked. "You look like hell."

"Thanks. Just got back from Brazil. Rough fucking flight."

"Everything all right?"

He shrugged. "Nothing I can't handle."

"Good." I dropped down the next few steps.

"What are you up to?"

I glanced over my shoulder at his curious expression. "We have a guest."

"Who?"

"Red."

He let go of the handle on his carry-on. "Fuck yeah. I'm dying for a fight."

"We aren't fighting."

"Since when?" He raised an eyebrow and stripped off his jacket.

He had a point. We'd never gotten along with Red, even before the Acquisition.

"I need to see if he has any information about the trial. That comes first."

"So we're just going to take his shit?" Lucius shook his head.

"Of course not. Still, we will listen to what he has to say."

He followed me down the stairs. "I can live with that, but if he pulls anything, I'll knock his goddamn teeth out. Where's Stella?"

"I just left her in her room. She's getting dressed."

His jaw tensed, and I felt a decidedly non-brotherly satisfaction in him knowing I spent the night with her.

Farns waited at the door in the foyer and swung it open before Red had a chance to knock. He barreled inside, his hair mussed, and with dark circles under his eyes.

"What the fuck, Red?" Lucius stepped ahead of me, already itching for confrontation.

"You." He pointed at me. "I need to talk to you."

I smirked. "It may shock you to know this, but there are phones for that very purpose."

"Fucking prick." Red stepped forward, and Lucius matched his advance until both men stood nose to nose.

"Let him through, Lucius. He can say what he came to say before we come to blows."

I walked down the hall, feeling Red following at my heels as Lucius trapped him between us. "State your business, Red. I assume this isn't a friendly visit."

Turning into my study, I waved Red to a seat as Lucius closed the door behind us.

"Is that bitch here?" He looked around, as if Stella might be hiding in the drapes. My hands itched to crush his voice box, but I remained still and stared him down.

"Cut the shit. What do you want?" Lucius crossed his arms and leaned against the door.

"Evie." Red turned his bloodshot eyes to me.

"What about her?" I sat on the sofa across from him.

"Promise me you won't—you won't—"

"Kill her if I win?" I finished for him. "I can't promise that and you know it."

"But I'll promise I won't kill your brother if I win."

"That's not really an issue for me. You aren't going to win. I am."

He shook. I couldn't tell if it was from fear or rage. I hoped it was the former. "I know what you did at the last trial. I know it was you who caught her and brought her back."

An icy trickle of unease slid down my spine, but I affected an air of nonchalance. "What of it?"

"I'm sure Cal would like to know of the rules violation."

"I'm sure he would, too. Then what? I'd be disqualified?" I steepled my fingers and drew out the logical conclusion that he feared most. "You'd have to go up against Eagleton alone. Eagleton would win, obviously. You're already coming apart, and your Acquisition broke in the first trial. Eagleton won't cut a deal with you, but he will cut your sister's head off and hand it to you by the hair."

Red dry heaved and clapped a hand over his mouth.

"Vomit on this rug and you're buying a new one, asshole." Lucius curled his lip in distaste.

Red swallowed hard and tried to compose himself. "P-please. I have information."

"Why this sudden urge to work together?" Lucius asked. "You've always been a royal fucking prick, and now, out of the blue, you want to be a helpful fucking prick instead? What changed?"

"What you said. Brianne is broken. She's not strong enough. She's not like your bi—"

"Call her a bitch, cunt, or anything other than Stella or Ms. Rousseau, and I can promise you, you will not like the results." My words were calm and even, though my need to do violence increased with every syllable of weakness Red uttered.

"N-not like Stella. I can feel it. You are going to win. I know it. But if you do… I can't close my eyes without seeing Evie dead, and I-I'm the one who…" He ran a shaking hand over his face.

"What's the information?" Lucius walked over to stand behind Red. "What did you want to tell us?"

"Not until you promise. You have to promise me Evie's life. Please." He leaned forward, his hands clasped.

I glanced to Lucius. He shrugged. If Red told me and I won, my promise wouldn't matter. I could kill Evie and kick Red's family out of the aristocracy. Then again, I never broke my word.

"If I promise you that, and I win, they would rip me apart. The rules are clear. If I win, Evie has to die. No losing last born has ever lived past the coronation."

"Fuck the goddamn rules!" He screamed, his voice raw and explosive.

I studied him as he took a deep breath, torment in every movement from the shake of his hands to the sorrowful look in his eyes.

"Please, Sin. Please. I can't kill her. I can't let you kill her. I'd rather die. I thought I had a chance to win. I thought I could save her myself. I can't. I need you. Please." He slid to his knees. "I'll do anything you ask, give you whatever you want, just please—spare her."

"Fucking pathetic." Lucius slapped the back of the sofa.

Red didn't move from the floor, only stared up at me with watery eyes. I liked him broken and begging. Even so, I needed whatever scraps of information he'd brought me. If it would help Stella and Teddy, I had to have it. I would sort the consequences later.

I leaned forward. "The deal is this. You win, you spare Teddy. I win, I spare Evie. But the upfront price for this bargain is that you tell me everything you know about the remaining trials."

"I know what happened ten years ago. I can give you the details."

"That's it?" Lucius pushed off from the back of Red's chair and walked around to glare at him. "Some shitty intel from ten years ago?"

I held up my hand. "Let him talk." Any shred of information was helpful at this point.

"Okay, okay." Red pushed himself from the floor.

"No. Stay there and tell me." I pointed to the rug beneath him. This brief negotiation had done nothing to wipe away the insults and threats he'd made to Stella. He would pay for each of them in time.

Red slid back down to his knees and glared up at me. "That year, there was this hellacious obstacle course. Crawling through glass, swimming in a leech pit, climbing barbed wire."

"Jesus Christ." Lucius sat next to me.

"The winner was the only Acquisition who made it through."

"I suspected something like what you've described." I would deal with all of the horrors later, when Stella and I were alone. The thought of her suffering through any of it made acid boil in my stomach. "But why does this trial focus on family? I didn't hear any family angle whatsoever."

Red rubbed his eyes, grinding his palms into them as if trying to erase an image. "Because the last-borns were part of the trial. The two losing families had to send their youngest through the same obstacle course as punishment."

CHAPTER EIGHT
STELLA

"HOW WILL WE KEEP it from Teddy?" I punched Dmitri's palm and ducked as he swung.

"I've called him home from school. He'll stay here with Lucius." Sin walked around us in a wide circle as we sparred.

A courier had arrived earlier in the week carrying a missive with the familiar Oakman seal. The trial was set, and my time was up.

"He hasn't been summoned with us tomorrow?" I dodged Dmitri's hand and smacked him on the back of the head as I dashed past. "For the triathlon?" I added for Dmitri's sake.

"No." Sin stopped as my opponent and I circled each other.

"Isn't that odd?" I lunged at Dmitri. He caught me around the waist. I threw my hip out and tried to pull him over and flip him, but he kept his balance and shoved me to the wet ground. "Fuck!"

"Patience, Krasivaya. Must wait for right opportunity." Dmitri helped me to my feet. "Surprise, remember?"

"I know." I shook it off and backed away to start again. The clouds overhead threatened another downpour. I wanted to keep practicing. I had to get better.

"It's not odd per se. It means there's still a chance we

could spare him from it. We'll leave him here with Lucius who'll get word to me if and when Teddy is sent for. Then Lucius can explain to Teddy as best he can, so he's not walking into it blind."

"Won't that be too much for him?" I tried to grapple Dmitri into an arm bar, but he pushed me away and I sank to my knees. The grass gave way to mud the more we practiced, and large drops of rain began to fall.

"Let's go in. This was supposed to be a light day, anyway." Sin offered his hand. "It's getting dark."

I took it and pulled myself to my feet, my muscles protesting. "No, just a little longer."

"Stella." Sin smoothed some stray hairs from my face as the rain intensified, the oak leaves whispering above us. "You've done all you can. You're as prepared as you're going to get. You need to rest for tomorrow."

He was right. I knew it, but I couldn't stop. I darted past him and launched myself onto Dmitri's back. Taking him down was the one thing I'd never been able to do. And maybe if I could get him on the ground, I could make it through whatever the next Acquisition trial threw at me.

He whirled, and I dug my heels into his sides and constricted my arms around his neck. Reaching back, he gripped my upper arm and yanked. I held on, cutting off his airway even as he pulled at me. A primal grunt ripped through me as I fought to stay on his back.

"Stella! That's enough." Sin's sharp voice cut through the rain, but I held onto Dmitri, refusing to let him go, refusing to fail this time.

I closed my eyes. All I saw was Brianne's frightened face and Gavin's kind smile. I'd let them down, failed them when they needed me most. Squeezing tighter, I put all my strength into my arms. Not again. I wouldn't let Teddy down. I would do whatever I had to do to keep him safe. Something clicked under my forearm, my enemy's throat on the verge of giving way as I maintained my hold.

He pawed at my arms, his movements slowing. Strong

hands gripped my waist and pulled until I was forced to let go, my arms finally giving up. Sin and I fell back into the muddy grass. My heart hammered in my chest, fear and anger washing through me as Dmitri bent over and wheezed breath into his lungs.

Sin wrapped his arms around me, holding me steady as a deluge fell around us. "You could have killed him. Generally, I'd be all for it. Though I think you would have regretted it in this instance."

Shame rose, drowning out the faces and the pain. Dmitri wasn't my enemy. What was I doing? "I-I'm sorry, Dmitri." I tried to get up, but Sin held me fast.

"Is okay, Krasivaya. I fine." He stood tall and took an unsteady step before regaining his balance.

"Sin, please let me help him." At my request, he got to his feet and helped me up.

Dmitri took a few more steps, surer this time, and shook his head as if to clear it. "Is okay."

"Come on. Let's get out of the rain." Sin held my elbow with one hand, and I grabbed Dmitri's with the other.

"I'm sorry." I blinked against the rain, or maybe it was tears. I didn't know. Was I even capable of that act anymore? Crying?

"No, no. It was good move." He patted my hand as we walked to the front porch. "I be fine. I strongest man in Russia."

Sin snorted, and Dmitri glared at him over my head as we entered the house. After removing our shoes, Dmitri headed down the hall to his quarters while Sin and I climbed the stairs.

"Will he be okay?" I wiped the wetness from my cheeks.

"Sure. He's *strongest man in Russia*." Sin mimicked him perfectly, and I felt even worse.

"I didn't mean to hurt him, to do that. I was just trying to…" What was I trying to do? Win? Knock him down so I could stop feeling like something was broken inside of me?

"You can't keep blaming yourself for the Christmas

trial." Sin pushed through the door to my room and pulled his soaked shirt over his head.

"I-I don't." I stripped, tossing my clothes into the hamper in the bathroom before turning on the warm water in the shower.

He padded in behind me. The vines seemed more alive on his damp skin, the ink even more indelible.

"Come on." He pulled me under the water and into his arms.

Warmth enveloped me and I could breathe again, could think again.

"I know you feel guilty. I know." He smoothed his hands up and down my back as I lay my head against his shoulder. "But you did what you had to. Everything else that happened isn't on you. It's on us. The Acquisition."

"I can't stop thinking about it. About how they looked at me. Brianne and Gavin, the way they screamed." My lip trembled, and I hated my weakness, hated that I had the luxury of falling apart when Brianne and Gavin were the ones who'd suffered.

He wrapped his arms around me. "I know. Time is the only way to soften memories like that. Things you've seen that you can never un-see. They'll still be there, but they won't be able to hurt you anymore."

I pulled away and took his hand, pulling it to my lips. I kissed the criss-cross of scars on the back of his wrist before putting his palm to my cheek. "You're strong. Maybe I can be, too."

He leaned in and kissed me with a gentleness I didn't know he possessed. He rested his forehead against mine. "You are everything. If I could run with you, I would." He closed his eyes, as if thinking through the possibility again. When he opened them, they were stark. "We can't. They'll find us, hurt us, and kill Teddy for spite."

I pulled away and held his gaze. "I'm going to end it. All of it. *We* are. Together."

The water splashed down my back, warming me even as

514

goose bumps rose along my skin from the nearness of him, the heat that lit his gaze at my words.

"It won't be easy. You'll have to kill." He pulled me to him roughly, his hands going to my ass. "You would have their blood on your hands?"

I bit his chest and ran my nails down his back. "Yes."

He groaned, as if my assent pleased him more than he could stand. "This is a dark path. One I'm well acquainted with." He pushed me against the tiles and met my eyes. "Are you sure it's what you want?"

"I want to burn it all down." I pulled him down to me and kissed him with every bit of fierceness I had.

Lifting me, he pinned me against the wall and shoved inside me as I cried out from the pain and pleasure.

"We'll have to destroy every last one of them." He thrust hard, my back slapping against the frigid tiles. "I will never give you up. Nothing can keep me from you."

He plunged deeply again, and I clawed at his shoulders. His eyes were two dark gems, sparkling with intensity. "Because you're mine. You've always been mine, long before any of this." He bit my neck. "And I will always have what's mine."

CHAPTER NINE
STELLA

SIN SQUEEZED MY HAND as we pulled through the gate onto the Fort LaRoux property. Cars formed a line ahead of us as Luke rolled down his window to converse with the guard. All I could think about was the rapid beat of my heart. I kept taking deep breaths, but couldn't seem to stop everything from moving too fast.

"Calm, Stella. Calm." Sin ran the back of his hand down my cheek. "We can do this." The strain in his voice told me he felt the same rush of adrenaline and fear. He was just better at hiding it.

Teddy and Lucius remained at home, no last minute summons disturbing them. All the same, a sense of foreboding took hold in me. Rebecca's sing-song about spring being the time for family played in my mind, sending a shiver through me.

Sin kissed the back of my hand, his face drawn and starkly handsome. "The trial won't last more than a day. It can't. Cal hasn't set up any local accommodations."

"One day. I can do this. One day for Teddy." I took another deep breath and tried to school my features. Even if I was coming apart on the inside, I wouldn't let the circling vultures sense my weakness.

The narrow road to the fort curved through stands of

517

pulpwood on either side, the monotonous pines growing straight and tall for row after row. The rain hadn't let up; a light mist still floated on the air, coating everything with clammy wetness and hiding the early afternoon sun.

We cruised through the pines until the fort rose from the ground ahead of us. I'd studied it for hours, analyzing photos of the layout, trying to determine what Cal had cooked up for the trial. It was circular, built at a time when muskets and gunpowder were the only thing to stop invaders.

The rounded walls were made of large, square stones, but over time they'd become covered with green moss, the surface alive. The field around the structure was all high grass except for some older oaks, gray moss hanging wet and thick from the low branches.

An expansive red tent, bigger than most houses, was set up against the side of the fort. Luke pulled up, and a valet opened my door. Sin squeezed my fingers until they almost hurt before letting me go. I stepped out, my boots solid on the pavement.

I wore dark canvas pants and a long-sleeve sports v-neck, breathable and warm. Despite the pragmatism of my outfit, Renee had done my makeup and curled my hair into flowing ringlets for Cal's benefits. I had elastics in my pocket for when the competition began.

Sin strolled around the car, his mask firmly on as he gave me a derisive glare. "Let's go."

He took my upper arm and pulled me along with him into the tent. Chandeliers hung overhead, and a band played in one corner. Long tables overflowing with food ran down each side, and a bar was set up at the very back beside the fort entrance. The ragged wooden doors were wide open, people steadily making their way into the fort once they'd had their fill in the tent. Overhead lights glowed on the spiral stairs that disappeared upwards beyond my view.

The receiving line was long, Cal shaking hands with everyone who set foot inside. Dread and anger danced inside me as some of the decked out party-goers gawked at me and whispered amongst themselves. Sin shook a few hands and chitchatted as we moved steadily forward.

"I heard Lucius gave it to her good at Christmas." A wizened old man patted Sin on the elbow. "I bet you were sad you missed it."

Sin smiled. "Don't worry, Governor Treadway. I still manage to have plenty of fun with her. She's got a little fight left. Just enough to make it interesting."

Governer Treadway? I didn't recognize him by sight, but I knew him through my history lessons in school. He was one of the staunchest anti-integration governors in the South during the Civil Rights era and was still reviled for that legacy.

The old man eyed me up and down. "Interesting, huh? I can sure see that. I remember back in my day, they strung the bitches up and let us—"

"Barton." Sin clapped the next well-wisher on the back as the former governor gave me one last look before speaking to a man in line behind us.

"You're looking good this year," Barton said. "I may have a side bet on you. But don't tell Cal. He'll want a cut of the action." He winked at me.

I had the urge to knee him. Instead, I stared placidly ahead as we finally reached Cal.

"Welcome." Cal greeted Sin with a handshake. He pulled me into a hug. "And, my goodness, Stella. Glad to see you looking so fetching." Putting me at arm's length, he ran his gaze down my body before grabbing a tendril of my hair and smelling it. "For me?"

I fought my gag reflex but flinched when he rested his hand on my shoulder.

"She still seems to be in fighting form. Well done, Sin." Cal smiled, looking like a toothy shark.

"As whores go, she's not so bad." Sin took a glass from a passing attendant's tray and downed it.

Cal nodded. "Are you a whore, Stella?"

Sin tensed at my elbow and covered it with a laugh. "Answer him."

"No." My voice was barely a whisper, the sound stolen by the rage that constricted my lungs.

"No? Come now. What would it take for me to get one night with you?" Cal tipped my chin up, and I met his eyes. I hoped he could feel every ounce of revulsion that pulsed through me at his touch.

I didn't respond. He wasn't asking me anyway.

"That's something we could negotiate." Sin's fingers dug into my arm despite his words.

"You'd share?" Cal's eyes were still on mine, testing me.

"Hell, if it meant I was the next Sovereign, I wouldn't just share, I'd give her to you." His words rang false to my ears, but I couldn't tell if Cal heard the lie as easily as I did.

"Would you like that? Wouldn't it be nice to be mine? Fancy clothes, big house, warm bed." He grabbed my palm and placed it on his crotch. "This in your mouth, pussy, and ass every night." Cal raised his eyebrows, looking for a response I wouldn't give him. I focused on getting through the trial, not on the foul words falling from his wine-stained lips.

Sin's fingertips pressed deep enough into my arm to hit bone. "Cal—"

"Shh, I'm talking to Stella." He moved my palm up and down his hardening shaft as my stomach churned. "Tell me how tight your pussy is. If I stuck two fingers in there right now, would it hurt? Could I add one more and make it three without you crying? I bet your ass could use a proper fucking. I wouldn't be gentle. A filly like you needs a strong hand. I'd have to break you in. My come mixing with your blood, your tears, your screams—all of it sounds like heaven to me—"

"Daddy, the line." Sophia walked up, a flute of champagne in her hand and a forced smile on her elegant face.

Cal cleared his throat, snapping out of his fantasy of

horrors. "Right you are, darling. Can't keep our fabulous guests waiting." He let go of my hand.

Sin eased up on my elbow. "Looking forward to the game as always, Sovereign."

We walked past Cal as he continued greeting newcomers. Sophia joined us and took Sin's arm. She gave me a look so full of venom that the hackles on my neck rose.

"Sin, how are you?" She pulled him away, her short emerald dress and high black boots showing off her hourglass figure and long legs.

Sin glanced at me and continued along at her side. "Fine. Ready for the show. How was New York?"

I wanted to wash my hands, to erase every touch, every word from Cal. Still, I knew it would take more than soap to rid me of his vicious intentions.

Sophia led Sin into the crowd. Left alone for the moment, I kept my head down and walked out of the main aisle toward a bare area against the fort wall. Turning my back against the moss-covered stones gave me some sense of security. It was a ridiculous thought, as if having a centuries-old wall at my back could stop these people. I peered out at the crowd—the rich elite all in one place. I wished for a grenade.

A few moments passed, and I was glad for each second I was left unmolested. I feared my luck was at an end when a man stopped near me. I looked up at him, dreading a confrontation, but he took no notice of me. His eyes were trained on Sin and Sophia several feet away.

He was handsome, his hay-colored hair short and neat. Tall and wiry, he was older, perhaps forty. I wished him dead, just like everyone else here.

"Ellis, my man! How are you?" Another man of about the same age walked up and shook hands. Even with the distraction, it took Ellis more than a few beats to turn away from Sophia and Sin. They fell into conversation and melded into the mix of people in the center of the tent.

"Ma'am?" A server with black hair and dark brown eyes

walked up and offered me a flute of champagne.

I took it with a shaking hand. "Thank you."

He stopped and glanced back at me, his eyebrows raised in surprise. "You're welcome."

I supposed no one ever thanked the servants, never said a kind word. Vultures weren't known for their warmth. And here, where they could be themselves, their worst was on display.

He tilted his head to the side and glanced around before approaching me again. "Are you in some kind of trouble? Do I need to do something?"

"I'm fine." I whispered. "But you shouldn't talk to me. You'll get in trouble."

"It's just, I've heard things. This is my first time working one of these events. Money was too good to pass up. And you look...scared."

"Shh." I shook my head and grabbed another flute from his tray to make it seem like I was keeping him. "Stop talking. You're in danger."

He furrowed his brow. "If you're in trouble, I know people. Something doesn't feel right." He glanced around.

"Go. Now." I wouldn't meet his eye.

He shook his head and backed away. After giving me another long look, he continued his round of offering drinks.

The crowd swelled, overdressed people talking, eating, and drinking to the jazz from the band. I went almost unnoticed, pressed up against the cool stones, until I saw a flash of light red hair and heard Cal greeting, "Red, welcome, my friend."

Red surveyed the crowd, his gaze seizing on me for a second before roving elsewhere. Brianne walked behind him, her head down, her blonde hair hanging in curtains on either side of her face. She was a wreck, even more so than the last time I'd seen her. My stomach sank, and I leaned against the wall for support. The ages-old chill seeped into my bones, and I dreaded Brianne more than Red. Her judgment was far worse than any vitriol Red could spout at me.

Once their introductions were complete, Red dragged Brianne into the mix of people. He glanced at me again, but didn't seem inclined to engage for once. I sagged with relief and edged closer to the bar, toward Sin.

He was in a close conversation with Sophia. He smiled for her as she touched his arm and whispered something in his ear. Jealousy crept along the periphery of my thoughts, but I already had too many emotions competing for my attention. I hid the shake in my fingers by downing the champagne, setting the glass down, and stuffing my hands into my pockets.

The ghouls swirled around me, their vapid conversations focused on either themselves or the trial. I bowed my head to avoid their rude stares, though I could still hear their comments about my "chances," and how much fun the Christmas trial had been.

"Hey, Stella." Gavin approached, the only friendly face I'd seen.

He was like an oasis in a desert of sand and snakes. The warm smile on his gaunt face made tears sting my eyes. His smile faded as he neared.

"What is it?" He smoothed his hands down my upper arms.

"I'm sorry." I finally said the words I'd been wanting to say since that horrible day in December.

"For what?" The concern in his eyes made me want to vomit. I didn't deserve it.

I shook my head, willing the tears away. "For what happened to y-you."

He pulled me into a hug, his arms strong around my back. "That wasn't you, Stella." He kissed my hair and whispered into my ear, "It was them. Not you."

"I know, but it didn't happen to me. I didn't get…"

He hugged me harder. "How? Wait, it doesn't matter. I'm glad. Don't feel guilty about that. I've got your back, remember?"

"I've got yours, too. I'm so sorry—" My chest shook, and my unspent tears welled up inside me and threatened to overflow.

"Shh, it's over now. I don't talk about it or think about it. It's done." He rubbed my back, and I relaxed into him. Despite his words, I wasn't absolved. But it took some of the weight away to know he didn't blame me.

"I'm going to get them. I swear it. For you, Brianne, and me. They won't get away with it." My voice was a harsh whisper, and I meant every word.

"Let's just get through it. All I want is to get through it."

"We will. All three of us will make it." I nodded against his shoulder.

Letting go, he stepped away and furtively wiped at his eyes. "Have you seen Brianne?"

"Yeah. She came in, but then I lost her. Do you know anything about the trial?"

"Miss Rousseau?" Judge Montagnet moved through the nearest group of people, leaning on his cane as he walked.

Gavin scrubbed a hand down his face and blanched.

"Go. He just wants to torment me," I said quietly.

Gavin gave me a curt nod and walked away toward the band.

"Judge." I crossed my arms over my chest and stared into his faded eyes.

"How are you coming along? Recovered from Christmas?" He grinned, one of his bottom front teeth showing a filthy shade of green.

"Fine." There was no other answer—except the truth. And if I told him how I really was and what I really thought of him, I'd be putting Teddy in danger. So, "fine" it was.

He reached out and pinched my arm. "You seem thinner. Sin not been feeding you well?"

"He has." Though civil, I kept my words clipped. The sooner he was gone, the better.

"Good. Wouldn't want him starving you out. Not until

the trials are done anyway. How's your father?" He was nothing more than a self-satisfied cat playing with its food.

"Fine."

He cocked his head, perhaps unsatisfied with my short replies. But, it didn't matter. The sound system clicked on with a feedback hum. It was show time.

"All right, everyone." Cal's voice boomed over speakers nestled along the metal tent supports. "We have a wonderful show for you today. I can't wait to get started. Make your way up the stairs to the seating along the battlement. Don't worry, we've had special awnings installed as well as heaters, couches, beds—anything you'd want to get comfy on this rainy day."

People began streaming through the door and up the stairs as Cal continued. "I think you'll be pleased at the entertainment. We also have plenty of servants to accommodate your every desire. Even yours, Judge Montagnet."

The crowd laughed, and the judge swiped his hand through the air. "You joker," he called.

"Acquirers and Acquisitions, make your way to me. Announcements are over. Let's get the party started!"

CHAPTER TEN
STELLA

SIN FOUND ME AND took my hand, pulling me from the wall where I'd taken refuge. He squeezed my cold fingers as we made our way back to Cal.

His touch—the same one that once chilled me to the bone—now gave me a slight warmth. I would be the one suffering today. It would likely be my blood spilled, my body broken. The touch of his hand told me that he would be right there with me. Every stab of pain inflicted on me would be mirrored in his mind. I wished I could save him from it even more than myself.

We walked against the flow of people heading to the battlements until we reached Cal. Sin dropped my hand, and I was alone again. Brianne, Red, Gavin, and Bob were already assembled. Gavin gave me a slight nod, but Brianne kept her head lowered.

"We're all here. Excellent." Cal smiled, still in showman mode. "Acquisitions, head into the fort, turn left, and go down the stairs. An attendant is waiting for you. The three of you lucky Acquirers will stay with me. I have a real treat for you." He rubbed his hands together, the machinery in his conniving mind clicking and scraping. "Go on." He jerked his chin toward the door.

Sin gave me one last look, his eyes saying nothing, but I

527

still felt the warmth of his fingers on mine. I followed the crowd through the wooden doors into the fort. They turned right and climbed the curving stairs as Gavin, Brianne, and I turned left and descended. The air was dank, the rain running down the walls and feeding the moss. Naked light bulbs hung in a string along the curving ceiling, and my boots squeaked on the slippery stairs.

Foreboding rose inside me with each step, but I kept going. When we reached the landing, two attendants waited for us. I recognized one of them from the Christmas trial. Mr. Tablet, the one I'd embarrassed in front of Lucius. He didn't have a tablet for me to destroy this time, though he wore the same sense of smug satisfaction.

Gauging by the smirk on his almost-purple lips, he recognized me, too. "Right this way."

I reached for Gavin's hand. He took it as we marched around behind Mr. Tablet, the curving wall obscuring the way ahead of us.

"We'll get through it," Gavin whispered.

I glanced to Brianne. "Are you okay?"

She didn't respond, only darted her eyes up and then back down. She reminded me of a wild animal that had been caught in a trap. One that would gnaw its own leg off just to be free.

"I need to talk to Stella." Dylan's voice cut through the damp air. He leaned inside a dark alcove along the interior wall.

Mr. Tablet stopped our march. Gavin gripped my hand tighter.

"I don't believe we have time. The trial is about to—"

"I didn't ask." Dylan rose to his full height and stepped into the light. He was imposing, a brute with a malicious glint in his eye. "Take the rest of them. She'll be along shortly. Stella, come here." He gave a little smile after the command, as if the power he wielded was some sort of shiny new toy.

I didn't know what his game was, but I knew I didn't

want to be alone with him. I edged closer to Gavin.

"I'll come over there and get you. Is that what you want?" Dylan stepped toward us.

"Back the fuck off." Gavin moved in front of me.

"This is going to be fun." Dylan swung his arms over his head, stretching. "Let's go, big guy."

"Wait." I stepped around Gavin. He was strong, but Dylan was a wall of muscle and spite. Gavin wouldn't stand a chance. "I'll talk to him. Just go."

"No." Gavin gripped my elbow. "You don't have to."

"I'll be fine. I'll catch up." I disentangled my arm and walked to Dylan, despite the instinctive desire to run as far from him as I could.

Dylan nodded. "That's right. She'll be just fine with me. Go."

I glanced back to Gavin, his lips pinched and his brows drawn in concern. Then he glared at Dylan. "If you hurt her—"

"You'll what?" Dylan grabbed me around the waist and pulled me back into the shadowy alcove. "Fuck off."

Mr. Tablet pulled a black baton—the same one from the Christmas trial—from his belt. "Come on."

Gavin took another step toward Dylan and me. I shook my head. "I'm fine. Please go."

"I won't tell you again." Mr. Tablet held the baton at the ready.

"If he hurts you, yell. I'll come. I don't care about the consequences." Gavin said the last sentence to Mr. Tablet.

Satisfied he'd won, Mr. Tablet turned and led Brianne and Gavin away.

"Why is it so hard to get to you these days?" Dylan kept one arm around my waist and ran his fingers through my hair. "I couldn't get you at Christmas, though I was so close. And now I still have to fight just for some alone time with my sis."

I tried to push away from him, but he was too big. He may have even been more muscled than the last time I'd seen him. "I'm not your *sis*. Just let me go."

"Why would I do that? You're mine." I couldn't see his eyes in the dimness, and my skin crawled at what I knew I'd find there.

"I'm not."

"You are. I was cheated at the last trial. I still intend to have you, all of you." He gripped my hair and pulled my head back hard enough to hurt.

"Dylan!" I gasped as he bit the side of my neck. When he clamped down hard enough to break the skin, I tried to scream, but he clapped his hand over my mouth.

I struggled, trying to break free. He only bit harder. Tears rose in my eyes at the searing pain. Then he let up and pulled me to him again. My blood coated his lips, and he kissed me, smearing it onto my mouth.

He ran his hands to my ass and squeezed, pulling me forward and rubbing me against his erection. I turned my head and pushed away before he could sink his tongue between my lips.

"There now." He grinned, my blood between his teeth. "I can't wait for the Vinemont boys to see my mark on you. The next time Sin and Lucius are in your cunt, they'll think of me. And then, before long, the Acquisition will be over and you'll belong to me. My little whore to use and abuse. I've already ordered a cage for you. It's custom made. You'll sleep in it every night at the foot of my bed."

"I will never be yours." I couldn't comprehend half of what he'd said. "A cage?"

"I own you." He bent his head to my mouth and pulled my hair again. "Cal gave me a little welcome gift. You. I can't stop the Acquisition. It's too late for that. But once the new Sovereign is chosen, you're mine. You can run. You can try and hide. Don't doubt that I'll find you. Not even the new Sovereign can break this deal. It's done."

Loathing invaded every cell of my body, and my fight kicked in. I balled my hand into a fist and aimed a hard hit at his ear. He howled and shoved me back. I took off down the curving corridor, sprinting toward whatever trial awaited me. I didn't care. I had to get away from Dylan, from the twisted ghost of my former friend.

Voices rose ahead of me, and I ran headlong into Gavin's back. He turned and put his palms on my face, tilting my head as he stared at my neck.

His lips turned up in a snarl. "That motherfucker. Where is he?" He looked over my head, spoiling for Dylan to try and follow me.

"I left him. I d-don't think he followed." The tremor in my voice matched the chaos in my mind. I wiped my sleeve across my mouth.

"Hey, asshole, do you have a first-aid kit or something in this hell hole?" Gavin asked Mr. Tablet.

"Oh, I'm afraid not." Mr. Tablet smiled sweetly and strode to a wide wooden door.

"It's okay." Gavin turned back to me. "It's not that bad." He yanked his sleeve down to cover his hand and pressed it over the wound on my neck.

It stung, but I tried to calm my breathing, calm my mind. Dylan was just an appetizer for the main course of the trial. I couldn't fall apart before the real game even began.

The door had a sliver of space I could see through. It led outside, the low light of the cloudy day filtering through. The ground beyond was grassy, and there was some sort of narrow, circular platform in the very middle. I assumed Cal stood atop it, per his usual.

"Ladies and gentleman! Get your popcorn and take your seats because the entertainment is about to begin." Cal's voice boomed through the door, the speaker system at full volume. "As you all know, the classic theme to the spring trial is family. I've stuck to the theme, but I gave it my own little twist. Are the Acquisitions ready?"

Mr. Tablet swung the door open. "Yes sir!" He called.

"Perfect. Bring them out."

Brianne whined like a dog kicked by its owner.

I tried to grab her hand and squeeze it. She pulled away

CELIA AARON

as if I'd slapped her.

Gavin pressed into my wound one more time and dropped his arm. "I think the bleeding's stopped. Damn. I can tell it hurts."

"I'll live. Thank you."

"You're welcome. We'll get through it." His warm brown eyes still held the same optimism as they had before the Christmas trial. I didn't understand it, but I was comforted by it all the same.

"Go." Mr. Tablet motioned for us to walk through the door.

I took Gavin's hand and stepped into the arena.

CHAPTER ELEVEN
SINCLAIR

"RIGHT THIS WAY." CAL led us up the battlement and around to the side opposite where the spectators lounged.

I scanned the crowd, the ground below, and the central platform for Teddy, but he wasn't there. Relief couldn't take hold in my chest, though. Cal was far too gleeful. Whatever he'd cooked up must have been beyond heinous for him to prance along the stone steps as he did.

There was no point asking questions. He would reveal the game when he felt like it, and in a way that had the most impact. As Sovereigns went, I had no doubt he made an excellent one, despite my constant desire to snap his neck.

"Here we are." He stopped and turned, letting us go ahead of him.

I stepped around him and proceeded forward. I halted in surprise, but then shored up my mask. "Mr. Rousseau. Lovely to see you again."

Stella's father sat on a wooden bench, his hands and feet shackled. A chain ran from the binds to a metal ring affixed to the stone beneath him. Two others—a middle-aged woman and a dark-haired girl of no more than twelve—sat beside him. The girl sniffled quietly and the woman stared, a blank look on her face.

"Where is Stella?" Mr. Rousseau's voice was weak, his

skin sallow, and his eyes red and watery. He looked much the worse for wear since the night he had sold me his only child.

"She'll be out shortly. Don't you worry." Cal clapped him on the back, and the old man almost fell forward. I imagined kicking him when he was down, and it warmed me only a little. I was far more concerned with what Cal intended to do with Stella.

Bob walked past the prisoners to a stainless steel cart. Shiny instruments—scalpels, plyers, knives, metal knuckles—were laid out along the top. Rope and other, larger, weapons sat on a bench behind the tray.

"What are these for?" Bob, as usual, asked the dumbest question possible.

"Simple. Annie here is Gavin's little sister. Sin, you already know Stella's father, Mr. Rousseau. And, Red, this is Twila, Brianne's mother." He bent over and patted the woman on her cheek. "Sorry for the less-than-flashy introduction, but you understand, don't you?"

She stared silently, her mind far away from the fort and the cold stone beneath her feet. She and the girl must have been taken while they were sleeping. The girl wore a pair of too-small pajamas and the woman was dressed only in an oversized t-shirt.

Cal grinned and straightened. "I knew you would. We're going to have a round-robin of bouts amongst the Acquisitions. If your Acquisition fails the match, you will have to harm their family member. The more creative the harm the better. So, really, if you think about it." He tapped his finger on his chin. "Your Acquisition could lose, but you could still win if you really go to town. The rest of the rules don't even apply, since their relatives aren't truly Acquisitions. Maim them. Do whatever. Just do it with flair is all I ask."

"Ingenious." I could appreciate his brutality, though I still wanted to grab the closest knife, gut him, and make him chew his own intestines.

"Well, thank you. Means a lot coming from you." Cal grinned and headed back the way we came.

The child shivered and huddled closer to Brianne's mother. Bob ran his hand over the implements, eagerness in his eyes.

"Let me go. Please, I won't tell anyone. Just let me go." Stella's father clasped his hands together, the chains dragging and clinking across the stone.

"Just you? Not the child? Not the woman?" I asked.

He swallowed hard and darted his beady gaze from them to me. "All of us. That's what I meant."

"No it isn't. You chose this far more than they did. Deal with it." I inspected the courtyard two stories below. It was bare. Un-mowed grass covered the ground. The stark walls of the fort rose in a circular barrier, and a wooden platform made to look like a thin oak trunk with a small canopy presided in the center. Nothing to help Stella, but nothing to hurt her, either.

Her father stared up at me. "Stella wouldn't want you to—"

I backhanded him, the slap satisfying on so many levels. "You don't deserve to say her name. Speak again, and I'll use my fists."

The crowd across the way cheered lightly as the old man cowered against the girl, his cheek turning red. I resumed my stance behind him, straightened my shirt sleeve, and twisted my cuff link back to perfection. It was all about the show, after all.

"No head starts now, Counsellor Vinemont." Cal laughed atop the oak platform, his voice booming in all directions.

"Ladies and gentleman! Get your popcorn and take your seats because the entertainment is about to begin. As you all know, the classic theme to the spring trial is family. I've stuck to the theme, but I gave it my own little twist. Are the Acquisitions ready?"

A door beneath the spectators opened, and a round,

balding man yelled, "Yes sir!"

"Perfect. Bring them out," Cal replied.

Gavin and Stella walked out first, their hands clasped as they moved cautiously through the wet grass. Brianne followed behind, her head bowed.

The light rain fell at a steady pace, though we were covered by an awning similar to the one over the crowd. The Acquisitions kept up with the attendant until they stood at the base of the platform, about twenty yards away.

From my vantage point, I saw blood along Stella's neck, red tingeing the fabric of her shirt. I balled my fists. They'd already hurt her. *Fuck.*

"All looking fit and ready. Excellent. Before we get started, I'd like to thank Governor Elliot for allowing us the use of the fort."

The governor stood in the spectator section and waved. A woman knelt in front of him, her blonde head bobbing furiously on his cock. The crowd clapped, and the governor gave Cal a small salute before sitting down and focusing on the woman at his feet.

"Okay, folks, we are going to do a little Louisiana Gladiator. How's that sound?"

The crowd roared, the sound echoing around the fort and up into the cloudy sky.

"Family. Is there anything better?" Cal laughed, the sound hollow, like the man. "No. So, in keeping with our theme, here's the rules. Each Acquisition will fight the others one on one. Bare fists only—"

The crowd broke out in boos and jeers.

Cal held up his hand. "Wait, wait, let me finish. There are rules. We can't very well let them run around with machetes like the Vinemonts back in the day, now can we?"

Laughter erupted, and Cal had them in his palm once again. "So fist fights are the order of the day. *But,* if an Acquisition loses, then one of their beloved family members will be harmed by one of our competitors." Cal pointed toward us. "We have three new guests with us today. Twila,

Brianne's mother, Annie, Gavin's sister, and Leon, Stella's father."

"No!" Gavin turned, seeking and finding his cowering sister. He took two steps before the attendant brought a baton down on his shoulder, sending Gavin to his knees.

Stella gazed up at me, her heart-shaped face set in lines of determination. She dug in her pocket, pulled out a hair tie, and began finger combing her hair into a tight bun. Brianne peeked up and locked eyes with her mother. A litany of "no, no, no" came out of Brianne's mouth, growing stronger with each repetition.

Stella glanced at her father, but kept her face stoic. When she looked at the child, she winced. I shook my head at her. Pity had no place in the trials. Only strength.

"So, first up. Let's go ahead and see what Brianne and Gavin can do, shall we? I want to save the catfight for last." Cal saluted the crowd and motioned to the attendant who shoved Stella inside the hollow oak.

After a few long moments, she stepped onto the top platform. Cal pulled her to his side, their backs to me. I hoped for a second she would shove him off, but that was foolish. I needed Cal alive to win the Acquisition.

He glanced over his shoulder at me before running his hand to her ass and palming it. "Gorgeous redhead, I hope you like to watch as much as I do. Oh! Oh my goodness." He slapped his forehead and guffawed into the microphone. "Oh, dear me. I almost forgot to tell everyone the most important rule of the competition. Can you guess what it is, Stella?"

She squared her shoulders and said nothing.

"If an Acquisition loses both rounds, then their family member dies."

CHAPTER TWELVE
STELLA

THE SPECTATORS SCREAMED, BLOODLUST in their shrieks of approval at Cal's words. Death, misery, ruin—this was their currency. Hate burned in my heart, stripping away everything soft and gentle and turning me into nothing more than a brand of rage.

The child shivered, her eyes wide as she stared at her brother. Her lips moved, but I couldn't hear her words. Maybe they were silent. I knew what she said all the same. The same litany of fear I'd recited until the Acquisition transformed me from fearful to vengeful. Even so, I wanted to weep for her. I wouldn't.

"Mommy?" Brianne yelled up to the woman who sat catatonic.

The sound roused the woman and she leaned over and stared at Brianne. "Bri?"

"Mommy!"

Despite my efforts to avoid it, I glanced at my father. He was a shell of the man I'd seen only a few months before. His hair was faded to white, his cheeks sunken, and his eyes bugged in his too-thin face. Something moved in my heart—sadness or regret, I didn't know which. But I wished he weren't here, for his sake and mine.

"It's going to be okay, Annie. Don't be scared." Gavin called to his little sister, whose terrified eyes darted from him to Bob.

An attendant brought a chair to the top of the small platform, and Cal sat. He pulled me into his lap so I was angled sideways to him. Raising his hand, he pointed to the attendants stationed at the door where we'd entered the arena. They rushed out into the courtyard, batons at their sides.

"KO preferred. Incapacitation acceptable. If you don't fight, we'll hurt you *and* your family members. Red, give them a little taste so they know we aren't just teasing." Cal clicked the microphone off.

Red reared back and sank a fist in Brianne's mother's stomach. Brianne screamed. Bile rose in my throat as Cal dug in my hair and undid my bun, my hair falling messily down my back.

"Isn't that better?" He stroked my hair as Brianne's scream broke when one of the attendants cracked his baton across her back. She fell to her knees.

Cal clicked the microphone back on. "That's enough. I think they're ready."

The attendants hurried back inside the wooden door as Brianne struggled to her feet.

Gavin was still consoling his little sister when Brianne launched herself onto his back.

"That's more like it. Enjoy the show, folks." Cal dropped the microphone and ran his hand along my thigh before peering at my neck. "What's this here? Who bit you?"

I didn't answer, only watched as Gavin yanked Brianne from his back and tossed her to the ground. She scrambled up and rushed him again, her blonde hair flying out behind her. He had at least fifty pounds on her. There was no way she could win. But she fought, screaming and clawing at him as he tried to ward her off.

"Something about you. The more I see you, the more I

want you. I *covet* you. I'm not the only one, either. Why is that, do you think?" Cal's voice slithered into my ear.

I kept my mouth clenched shut as Brianne kicked at Gavin's shins. He yelled and shoved her back.

"I find myself wondering if your snatch is covered with the same color hair as this." He twisted a lock between his fingers. "You were bare last time I saw you."

I focused on Brianne and Gavin, analyzing their movements, looking for weaknesses. I could do it. I could fight and win. The only thing I couldn't do was look at Gavin's sister. Her frightened eyes were already etched in my mind, her youth ruined by this foul tournament.

"Hey." He yanked my hair and moved his hand under my shirt. "I need your full attention. Gavin and Brianne can work out their differences without you."

"You have it." I darted my eyes over to Sin. He cut an imposing figure, standing completely still, his eyes on me.

"I don't think I do." He worked his hand up my shirt to my sports bra and pinched my nipple through the fabric. "But I know how to get it."

I froze, humiliation washing over me at Cal's unwanted touch. Even as Brianne screamed below, I met his eyes, the dark pupils wide.

"Was that so hard?" He eased up on my nipple and palmed my breast. "I just wanted to talk to you a little. I feel like I haven't gotten to know you as well as Brianne."

The crowd roared as Gavin let out a shriek, but I kept my eyes on Cal.

"Very good. See? You can be taught." He pulled his hand out of my shirt and rested it on my thigh again.

I fought the urge to watch what was happening on the ground below. *Think*. I had to take this opportunity to learn what I could from Cal. "Dylan told me he owns me."

"Ah." His eyes went to the mark on my neck. "So I assume this is his handiwork?"

I nodded. "Sin owns me. Dylan owns me. You don't. There's no point coveting something you will never have."

"I wouldn't be so sure. I'm still Sovereign for some time yet. Besides, 'never' is such a broad term, don't you think?" He leaned over and licked along the bite mark. I bit my lip to keep from crying out at the sting.

Brianne's shriek got her mother to her feet as the crowd laughed and jeered. I glanced down. She was on her stomach, crawling toward Gavin. Bloodied and grim, he backed away from her.

Cal took my arm and wrapped it around his neck. "What if I said Sin would win if you'd be mine for the rest of the contract year? Voluntarily agree to do whatever I asked. I don't want to fight you. That's not my kink. I want total and utter obedience."

I stilled and stared into his face, trying to measure the weight of his words. Was he lying? "Why do I care if he wins or not? I wish him dead every morning when I wake up."

He smiled. "You aren't fooling me. I can see you're considering it. Good. Though it's not up to you, really. Sin would have to agree since, technically, he owns you now."

"How do I know you'll keep your word?"

His face hardened, and he slapped me. "Don't ever question my honor, you little cunt."

My ears rung but I tried not to react to the pain along my cheek.

Gavin yelled, the sound throaty and full of rage.

The crowd roared.

Cal's sneer turned into a smile. "I think that's my cue." He scooted me off his lap and stood.

Brianne lay motionless in the grass, her eyes closed. Gavin knelt beside her, tears streaming down his face as he stroked her hair. Her face was bloodied, his knuckles red.

"Looks like we need a medic. Get her revived for her bout with Stella. In the meantime, Red, you're up."

Two attendants rushed out and grabbed Brianne under her arms before dragging her back through the door we'd entered. Gavin sat heavily and stared up at me, his eyes open windows of pain and regret. I kept taking deep breaths, refusing to panic at the rising tide of horror around me.

Red walked to a steel table along the battlement, though I couldn't see what was on the top. I shivered as Cal came up behind me and lay his forearm across my chest above my breasts.

"You're really going to love this part." He held me in place so I was looking right at the chained victims.

Red picked up something that looked like a monkey wrench, the metal dull and heavy.

"Oh, good choice, my man. Let's see what he can do with it." Cal laughed, and the rest of the audience laughed with him.

My blood turned to ice as Red approached the bound woman. She tried to stand and back away, but she was chained to the floor. I glanced to Sin. He shook his head almost imperceptibly. Maybe he was telling me not to watch. It didn't matter. I had to see it, to witness every last disgusting act. It was the only way to keep my fire burning, the same fire that would destroy these animals.

Red pulled the wrench back and swung as Brianne's mother screamed. The sound was cut off as the wrench made contact with a wet thud. Her teeth flew out, like white pearls in the low light of the clouds. Blood poured down her face.

Gavin retched into the grass, and I bit my cheek hard enough to draw blood.

The crowd leapt to its feet and screamed with approval. Brianne's mother screeched and fell to her hands and knees. The child wailed, covered her face, and scooted closer to my father. He didn't comfort her, only stared at Brianne's mother as she moaned and touched her ruined nose and mouth.

"Well, well. Red's been working on his aim." Cal patted my ass. "Good show. Now let's move on to the next round. Gavin and Stella." He pushed me toward the stairs and lowered the mic. "Go on, and don't forget what we talked about. I only hope Gavin doesn't mess up your pretty face

543

too much. I'd like to do the honors on that."

I descended the narrow spiral stair and walked out onto the grass, the turf soft beneath my feet as the light mist continued to drizzle down around me.

Pulling another elastic from my pocket, I wrapped my hair into the same tight bun. Sparring with Dmitri was one thing. Fighting a stranger was something else. But having to fight Gavin when the consequences were torture and death?

Gavin still sat in the grass, head in his hands.

I glanced up to my father. He leaned forward, his eyes imploring me. Sin stood behind him, his arms crossed and his mask inscrutable. The child cried and clung to my father. I'd trained, struggled, and pushed myself so I could win any match. But the more I looked at the child, the more I questioned my desire to win.

I stopped in front of Gavin, my hands at my sides. "Gavin, you need to get up."

"Did you see what he did? Did you see what *I* did?" He turned his hands over and showed me his bloodied knuckles.

"You did what you had to do." Just like I was going to do what I had to do. "Get up or I'll kick you in the face."

"No." He shook his head.

"Bring out the batons, boys." Cal's voice drew the attendants, weapons at the ready.

I let out a breath, steadied myself, and aimed a kick at Gavin's ribs. He clutched the spot and fell to his side.

"Oh, we've got some fireworks."

The attendants retreated as Gavin struggled back to his knees, then his feet. He finally met my eyes. I wanted to hug him. Instead, I raised my hands, ready to fight.

"Are we really going to do this?" His question was more sorrow than anything else.

"We have to." I tilted my chin toward the captives. "For them."

He glanced to his sister and brought up his fists. "I'm sorry."

"Me too." I charged him and darted to the side at the last second, punching him in the side of the head. Pain shot through my fist and radiated up my arm, but I turned to face him again.

He shook his head as if he had water in his ear. "Fuck."

"Come on." I waved him to me.

He looked to his sister again before pounding across the grass. I dodged, letting his weight carry him forward, and jumped on his back. He flailed, grabbing at my arm as I brought my elbow down on his shoulder again and again.

He slapped my face and finally got hold of my arm, then threw me over his head. I hit the ground with a thunk. The wind rushed out of my body as the crowd tittered. I rolled before his foot came down where my stomach had been. Climbing to my feet, I backed away, breathing hard and looking for an opening.

Then I glanced up at my father. The girl sat next to him, frightened and alone. My father ignored her and watched as I fought to keep him from harm.

Gavin leapt toward me, but I backed away, curving around the platform as he followed. He sprinted at me, and I feinted right before kicking his shin as hard as I could. He fell to his knees, and his sister screamed. The sound was piercing, far too powerful for her small body. My father smiled down at me, triumph in the tilt of his head.

And then I knew what to do. My father had made his mistakes, committed his sins. Gavin's sister hadn't. I wouldn't let her suffer. I could lose this battle, but win the war by giving in to Cal's demand.

Gavin clambered to his feet and I kicked him in the stomach. He stumbled back as I launched myself onto him, wrapping my legs around him as he staggered back into the unforgiving wall. I took his head between my hands and knocked it against the stones.

"Fuck!" He grabbed my waist and tried to pull me off.

"You have to win this." I hissed in his ear.

He stopped struggling against me, so I punched the side

of his head. "Don't stop. Make it look good. But win. For your sister."

He punched me in the ribs. I gasped and fell back, landing on my feet. I brought my hands up.

The wails of Brianne's mother carried down to our ears as we circled each other again. The crowd went silent, and the rain began to intensify.

He lunged at me, but I sidestepped easily and swung around, landing the back side of my fist into his kidney. Stumbling forward, he doubled over. I kicked his legs out from under him and jumped on top. The crowd roared as I rained blows down on his face. He threw his arms up and tried to block me.

"Fight back." I said through clenched teeth.

He rolled to his right, throwing me onto my back and climbing on top of me. His palms slid against my wet skin as he wrapped his hands around my throat.

"Squeeze harder. Leave marks." I gasped, and he obeyed.

I clawed at his hands as the cold rain soaked into my clothes. When my vision began to dim, I pushed one arm between his and wrenched his elbow out to the side. It gave me the opening I needed to flip him and climb off. I backed away, my neck burning from his pressure.

"We still have a live one down there, my friends." Cal laughed.

I bent over and put my hands on my knees, taking deep breaths as Gavin scrambled to his feet and approached me. We were both wet and muddy as the rain began to pour. "Just give up now. You've put on a good enough show."

I shook my head. "More. We need more. We can't risk it." I exploded off my back foot and nailed him in the jaw with my right fist. Pain burst along my knuckles as he stumbled backwards.

Aiming a kick at his side, I struck him squarely with the tip of my boot. He howled and tightened up, pulling his arm in close to the injured spot. I darted away, adrenaline making my movements even faster.

Tracking my arc, he tackled me and we rolled until I was able to crawl away. He grabbed my ankle and hauled me back. I rolled onto my back and kicked at him, but he grabbed my knees and pinned me between his thighs. His fist came as a blur, and pain radiated from my eye and across my face.

I screamed and fought as he tried to get his hands around my throat again. Another burst of pain at my temple and my vision went dark for a moment before brightening almost unbearably.

"I'm sorry." He hit me again, this time lighting my ribs on fire. Another blow on my other side had me writhing and trying to dig my elbows into the soft ground and slide away from him. Rain pelted my face as he loomed over me, his fist drawn back. I covered my face, but he connected with the back of my forearm. Crying out, I scratched deep gouges in his neck. He slapped me, the sound like a shot, the pain bringing tears to my eyes.

I bucked hard and pushed with my right foot. He toppled sideways, and I scooted back from him. Turning to get on all fours, I tried to crawl away. His weight landed on my back, crushing me as his forearm went around my throat.

"Pass out." He hissed in my ear. "I can't hurt you anymore. I won't. Please don't make me."

I struggled, digging my nails into his arm and trying to roll him off me. He was too big. My breathing became labored simply from his weight on my back.

"That's enough. They'll buy it. Please. It's enough." He squeezed a little. "Just stop."

I slowed my movements and let my head loll to the ground.

"Thank you," he whispered as the crowd roared.

CHAPTER THIRTEEN
SINCLAIR

STELLA STOPPED MOVING, AND the crowd erupted in cheers. Her pain had me stretched tight, every fiber I possessed pulled to its breaking point.

"Well done, Gavin! You've made Bob proud. Head on back inside while they attend to Stella. She needs to get ready for the bitch fight."

The crowd chuckled.

"It will be a fun one. I saved the best for last." Cal turned toward me. "Sin, my fellow redhead lover, you're up."

Stella's father cowered as I strolled to the tray of implements. Some of them were far too coarse for my tastes, tools made for rough trades when I was more of an artist. I played my fingers along the handles and blades until I came to a particularly sharp set of pruning sheers. They would have been appropriate, given the vines that snaked their way around me, caging me even as I was out in the open air, but I needed to go bigger.

"Please…" Mr. Rousseau shook and stared at me, his eyes wide and his chains jingling with each shudder.

I ignored him and continued down the row of tools. A particularly sharp cleaver glinted in the low light, the blade covered with tiny droplets of mist. I gripped it and pulled it from the tray. Heavy in my hand, the blade would do well for what I had in mind. Red sat on the bench in front of me, Brianne's bloodied mother lying at his feet, her eyes open and glassy. The child cowered as I walked past, but Red sat still, eyes forward. Crimson marred his white button-down and a few splatters had crusted on his face.

I stopped in front of Stella's father. He grimaced and leaned away from me. His lip trembled and a line of spit oozed from one side of his mouth.

"Mr. Rousseau, hold out your hand."

"N-no." He shook his head. "Please don't."

"If you make me tell you again, I'll take two hands instead of one." I turned the blade this way and that, watching the light play along the razor sharp edge.

The girl whimpered and tried to scoot away. It was futile. Her chains kept her close.

I glanced at her. "Look at your feet and cover your ears."

Her chin trembled, but she did as instructed.

"Good girl. See? Mr. Rousseau? It's not hard to comply. Do you want me to tell you again, or would you like to lose just the one hand?"

A high-pitched strangled sound came from his throat, and he locked his terrified eyes on mine.

"Tense." Cal's hiss oozed through the speakers.

A tear rolled down his paper-thin cheek and he held out his shaking left hand. "Stella wouldn't want you to—"

I slapped him hard enough to split his lip. The crowd tittered at my back. "I told you never to say her name. And another thing—" I wrenched his hand to the side and pinned it to the bench next to him. "—Stella may as well have told me to do this."

I lowered my voice. "She lost on purpose. She wanted this for you. She knows you deserve it instead of the child. She knows doing this to you doesn't pain me at all. She's saved me. Again. Choosing you to suffer means that neither the child nor I have to suffer. Don't you see?" I pressed the cleaver to his wrist. He tried to hit me with his free hand, but I pushed back, my full weight crushing him as I lined up my stroke on his age-spotted skin.

"No, no, please. I'm sorry. I'm sorry. Please don't—"

I held the blade up high so everyone would see. The crowd gasped, anxious for the severing stroke.

"She's chosen me over you." I brought the cleaver down hard. His scream of pain pierced the air and rent the darkening sky. Cheers went up from the spectators.

The hand pulled away cleanly. I rose and grabbed it by the fingers, lifting it above my head as his agonized screams fed the bloodthirsty crowd. Then I tossed it down into the grass like a piece of garbage.

"Oh ho-ho, Sinclair came to play." Cal gave me an elaborate bow from his platform. "Well done."

Stella's father screamed again before huddling over his maimed limb and rocking back and forth. Satisfaction welled inside me, though I knew Stella wouldn't approve.

"Amazing. Ladies and gents, give Stella's father a hand!" Cal laughed, practically screaming at his own joke.

I leaned down so only her father could hear me. "That was a small price to pay for betraying her. I almost hope she loses again so I can finish the job."

.

CHAPTER FOURTEEN
STELLA

ROUGH HANDS DRAGGED ME back into the stone walls of the fort. I kept my eyes closed even as they dropped me on the hard floor. Footsteps clacked along the stones, and then I was doused with freezing water. I opened my eyes and sputtered, no acting necessary.

Sophia stood above me, hands on her hips. "Sit up."

I struggled to a sitting position, my body aching, my face especially.

She knelt and wrinkled her nose in distaste before waving the attendants away. "You will win this."

I stared at her, unsure of what sort of pep talk this was.

She grabbed my chin, her nails digging into me. "You will win this." Her voice was a threatening whisper, her eyes malevolent. "Sinclair will be the next Sovereign with me at his side. If you fail me, the consequences will be beyond your worst nightmares."

I laughed and spit in her face. "Get the fuck out of here."

"You little bitch!" She screamed as if I'd burned her, and wiped my bloody spit from her cheek. "Sinclair will hear about this."

I shrugged, the simple movement sending shooting pains down my spine. "Yeah, go ahead and tell him I think you're a cunt while you're at it."

She raised her hand to strike me, but paused as I stared her down. She was beautiful, her face a perfect oval, her eyes dark and sultry, her lips an indulgent red pout. My hands itched to destroy all of it.

She seemed to rethink the idea of hitting me, and dropped her hand. "I'll make sure you regret that."

"Put it on my fucking tab." I would fight to the death to keep Teddy safe, but this bitch would never be a part of that calculus. She was just a grasping climber, trying to hang on to the man she saw as the next Sovereign.

I looked past her and saw Brianne leaning against the wall by the door, her eyes closed. Sophia rose and stormed away, her heels echoing on the cold stone.

"Brianne?" I crawled over to her.

We would have to fight. One of us would lose. I clenched my eyes shut. The knowledge that more blood would be on my hands made the room spin. My actions to protect Gavin's sister had led to this, but was I strong enough to follow through and let my father meet his fate?

A scream sounded, followed by the roar from the crowd overhead, loud enough to make it through the heavy doors and thick walls.

She mumbled and didn't open her eyes.

"Brianne?" I got to my knees in front of her and stroked her hair from her face.

Mr. Tablet walked up behind me. "Let's go. It's time."

"She can't go again. Look at her."

A shooting pain in my ribs took my breath away. I fell to my hip. Mr. Tablet had kicked me.

He tried to grab my hair, but he was slow. I shot my legs out and sent him toppling over. Wrath coated every one of my senses as I climbed on top of him, pinning his arms to his sides with my knees. I nailed him with a right, breaking his nose as he screamed. I hit him again and again, my aching fists making fleshy sounds against his pudgy face.

Two other attendants grabbed my arms and ripped me off him, though I got in a good kick to his ribs before they threw me to the floor next to Brianne. My ass hit the ground hard, and a shooting pain tore up my back.

One of the attendants opened the door.

"Bring them out. We're ready for the bitches to go at it." Cal's irritated voice filled the air.

I got to my feet again as an attendant yanked Brianne up by her arm.

She flailed for a moment and opened her eyes. She looked everywhere, but seemed to see nothing. Despite her reticence, she fell into step with her attendant, and we walked out onto the muddy grass.

"Ah, here we are. Two beauties ready to fight it out. May the best bitch win." Scattered applause rang out as the attendants retreated through the doors and closed them.

"Brianne. We have to do this, okay?" I hadn't formed a plan for her. The knowledge of what would happen if I lost blinded me too much to think.

My father was doubled over, his face hidden. Sin stood behind him, his eyes on me. He lifted his chin toward Brianne, silently telling me to attack her.

"Bri, we have to. Come on."

"Do you need the attendants to beat you into it, ladies? Get to it." Cal's voice was a harsh bark, as if he were worried he was losing the crowd.

A high pitched whine came from above. Red grabbed Brianne's mother and shook her. "Fight, bitch, or I kill her right here, right now."

Brianne raised her face toward her mother, and her eyes widened. "Mommy."

Red threw her bloodied mother onto a bench, and Brianne lowered her gaze to mine. "I'll kill you." She took a step toward me, her knees wobbling and her eyes focused.

"I always love encouragement, Red. Works for me." Cal laughed. "I can't help but notice poor Brianne isn't doing so well. I don't think this is a fair fight. Do you?"

The crowd booed.

"I know. Let's make this more interesting. Give Brianne

a baton and one of those shocker things. You know what I mean."

The doors opened, Mr. Tablet hurried over to Brianne. He gave her his black baton and drew a hand-sized device from his belt. She took the weapons but kept her eyes on me. Her face was blank. I could feel her resolve. There was no other way this could end. Either her blood would die, or mine.

"I have to do it." She pressed the button and an electrical current shot through the tines on the end of the taser.

I backed up, trying to buy time. "Briann—"

"I have to." She rushed me and swung hard with the baton.

"And we're off to the races!" Cal cried.

I ducked and threw my shoulder into her stomach. She grunted and fell back, but held the taser out so I couldn't get close. Getting to her feet, she squared herself and followed me as I backed away. She was thin and weak. Even so, her love for her mother fueled her forward on unsteady legs.

Keeping my hands up, I waited for her swing. When it came, I darted close to her body and punched her in the back. She screamed and fell to her knees, but recovered before I could attack again.

"I won't let you kill my mother. I won't." She swung the baton in front of her, as if she were warming up.

The accusation was a deep wound, a slow bleed. "I'm not killing her. They are."

"No!" She screamed. "If you win, it's *you*. You did it." Her voice broke as she advanced.

I'd backed halfway around the courtyard when she sprinted at me. The baton was a dark blur as it struck the side of my neck, and I narrowly dodged her extended hand holding the stun gun. I tried to grab her as she shot past, but she was already out of range by the time I'd recovered from the hit.

She came again as a close bolt of lightning blinded me. I

tried to grab for the baton as she swung, but it connected with my fingers. I didn't know I'd screamed until I pulled my hand back, my index and middle fingers bent at unnatural angles, both numb and yet excruciating at the same time. Clutching my injured hand to my chest, I turned and ran, the soggy ground sucking at my boots. There was no escape, just the circle that endlessly led me back to suffering.

I spun, and Brianne collided with me, both of us falling in a tangle. Crawling away, I got to my feet. She was still on all fours, trying to get up, her breaths labored. I kicked her in the side, and she flipped onto her back. It was my chance to end it.

Dropping on top of her, I pressed my forearm against her windpipe and tried to hold her stun-gun-hand with the other. The baton cracked across the back of my head and the world went dark for a moment. Then a burning sensation rushed up my side and I fell over, my entire body sizzling like a steak in a pan.

Brianne let up with the stun gun and beat me with the baton, her blows raining down on my side and my head as I tried to cover myself. She shrieked with each swing, primal fury rolling off her as agony bloomed everywhere the baton struck. I curled into a ball, and the distinct cracking sound and burst of misery as she nailed my ribs made me scream.

I had to get up. If I didn't, my father would die at Sin's hand. I couldn't let it happen. I took a pained breath and shot my foot out, striking Brianne in the knee. It caved inward and she fell, still flailing with the baton. Darkness crept in at the edges of my vision, and everything was hazed in red. I crawled on top of her as she swung again with the baton. Something snapped in my upper arm on the impact. She'd dropped the stun gun when she fell.

Lightning blasted nearby, and the deep roll of thunder shook the earth beneath us. She swung again, slower this time, and I grabbed the baton and ripped it from her grip.

Tossing it away, I leaned over her and ignored her

clawing fingers. I gripped her throat with my good hand and pressed as she scratched at my face. She was too weak, the fight leaving her as surely as the oxygen left her bloodstream. I bore down on her throat with my weight as she stared up at me.

Her movements grew more and more sluggish until the crazed light finally left her eyes. They closed, and she was at peace, as if I'd soothed her to sleep with a caress instead of the bleakest violence.

The crowd erupted in cheers as I collapsed onto the wet ground beside Brianne. Rain poured down my face, but I would never be washed clean of what I'd done.

"It looks like Sin's feisty redhead has won this round. Team Vinemont sure knows how to pick 'em." I could hear the leer in Cal's voice, his words snaking down my body like the rivulets of rain.

"Red, get to it. Give us a grand sendoff for this riveting trial."

I turned to where my father sat in a huddle. The child rocked with her hand over her eyes. Red was bent over, and he bobbed up and down, working on something. He rose, yanked Brianne's mother to her feet, and pushed her over the side of the battlement. But she didn't hit the ground. The rope around her neck stopped her halfway down.

My mind seized.

She clawed at her neck and kicked. It was no use. Red had tied her tight. Her face was a ruined crimson mask, everything obliterated but her eyes. She stared down at her daughter as she gave a few more futile kicks.

The crowd sat in silence—her strangled noises the only sound other than the thud of her feet against the stone wall.

When she quieted, her dead eyes still stared at Brianne. Or was it me? I couldn't tell. I couldn't exist there anymore. The spectators roared with approval, and I screamed until my chest burned and the attendants dragged me away.

CHAPTER FIFTEEN
STELLA

"I TOLD YOU CHRISTMAS was the worst." Renee pressed cold compresses to my face. "It was. For me. But you, I think—no, I *hope*—this was the worst of it."

I could barely see her. One of my eyes was swollen shut, and the other gave me only a sliver of vision. Everything ached, especially my arm. I couldn't lift it. Reaching across my body with my left hand, I ran my fingers down the rough material of a cast.

Sin drugged me the second I got into the car after the trial. I should have been livid. Instead, I was thankful for the brief reprieve from reality. Had my dreams been happy? I didn't know. All I knew was that I was awake now, thrown back into the hell of Acquisitions and trials.

"Sin?" My voice was a rasp, sandpaper scraping rough wood.

"He's gone to town. Work."

I tried to shake my head clear, but shooting pains rushed up my neck at the movement. "How long?"

Renee moved the compress so it was against the eye that wouldn't open. "Two days. The doctor came and set your arm and your fingers."

Right. Brianne's eyes, the swing of the baton, and the sharp crack of bone that I could still hear. She was always there now—crying in the woods or screaming at me that it was my fault. Was it?

"Brianne has her mother's eyes." My words slurred and fuzzed, my tongue too thick and my lips too swollen.

"Shh, don't talk about that now. You're here safe. The worst is over."

I wanted to believe her. I didn't. Cal's proposition floated through my mind like a bloated body on a bayou.

A knock at the door sounded. I tried to look, but my neck muscles wouldn't cooperate. Instead, they ached and burned.

"It's me." Teddy's voice was like a burst of sunlight through the vapors of hell.

"No." I couldn't let him see me like this.

"Not now, Teddy." Renee rose to go to the door. "Stella isn't dressed."

"Get dressed. I want to see you. I came all the way home for the weekend just to check on you. The trial was a few days ago, wasn't it?" His voice fell.

"Don't come in." Renee grabbed the door handle right as it turned.

Teddy peeked through.

"No!" My vision blurred even more, my eyes swimming with tears. He couldn't see me broken and bruised.

He shoved the door open, knocking Renee back, and came rushing into my room. "Oh my god. What did they do to you?"

He dropped onto the bed next to me, his kind eyes surveying my face, neck, and arms. Tears flowed down my cheeks even as I tried to stop them, to stop the anguish from infecting him.

"Please go." I couldn't see any more, my eyes useless.

"God, Stella." His voice broke as he put a gentle hand to my cheek. "They did this. Why?"

"It doesn't matter why. It's done." Renee spoke from my side. "You need to go, Teddy. She needs to rest so she can recover."

"No shit!" The ire in his voice reminded me of Sin. He took my hand, his palm warm and soft. "You won't tell me, will you?"

I stayed mute, unwilling to give him any scrap of information he could use to blame himself.

"It doesn't matter. I'll get them for you. I don't know how, but they'll pay for this. Sin will pay for letting this happen to you."

"No." I squeezed his hand. "Not his fault."

"Bullshit. He dragged you here. I saw how he treated you. I know he's making you do these things. He didn't have to pick you." His grip on my good hand tightened until it ached. "He probably volunteered. He wants to be Sovereign so bad that he doesn't care who gets hurt."

"It's not true. Not his fault." I pushed to get the words out, the pain in my throat growing worse.

"Don't defend him. He doesn't regret a thing. I passed him on the way here. He was in the convertible with Sophia Oakman, both of them smiling. Makes me sick."

"Teddy, that's enough." Renee's voice rang out strong, but I heard the tremble. "She's had enough. Please, go."

He let my hand go and patted it. "I'll be back soon to check on you." He rose from the bed, his steps retreating to the door. "I'm sorry about this."

I couldn't respond. I couldn't say it was okay or explain it. The door clicked shut, and Renee took her seat on the bed beside me.

"Is it true? He's with Sophia?"

She sighed and smoothed the blanket over my legs. "Yes."

Her reticence told me she knew more. Renee always knew more.

I wouldn't stay in the dark on this, not when what little was left of me started to quake and shatter. "Tell me."

"I think you should rest—"

"Tell me!" I tasted copper, and my throat scorched.

"I-I overheard them talking. They're on their way to the airport." She brushed a hair out my face and put the compress on my cheek. "They'll be gone for two months. She's attending to some Oakman family business in Paris for two weeks, and they intend to spend the rest of the time in Cannes."

A laugh tried to loft from my lungs. It couldn't make it. Instead, it turned into a strangled sound that seemed more like a sob. He'd put me through a house of horrors, and then left for a vacation with the daughter of its architect.

"I'm sure he's only doing what's best."

"What's best? Right." I was glad I couldn't see her face, because I may have tried to claw her eyes.

"You have to understand. They have their own customs, their own ways. I have no doubt Sophia is making a power play. That's the way of it. Think of what it could mean for the family if they—"

"Get out." I couldn't hear it from her, too. Strategy, lies, and deceit were Sin's specialties, not Renee's.

"I'm not finished with your—"

"Go!"

"Please." She let her hand fall. "I didn't mean to hurt you. Only to explain. I just want to help."

There was no help for me, for anyone caught up in this damned competition. But there was information, and Renee had it. I would twist whatever screw I had to if it meant she'd open up to me.

"Tell me…" I swallowed, my throat clicking and burning with the effort. "…what the final trial is. Or get out."

She remained silent and still for what seemed like minutes. Finally, she spoke. "It's different every year. It's always different."

"Leave." My voice receded to a whisper.

She stood, but hesitated next to the bed. I could sense her wringing her hands. "There's a theme. It's always the same. Love."

"Love?" The word had no place amongst these people. It was meaningless.

"Yes."

"What happened your year?"

"My year." She cleared her throat. "My year, I was forced to choose between hurting two things I loved. That's all I'll say. I can't relive it, not even for you."

"Renee, please."

"No. It won't help you. It will only hurt me. I've already given you what you need to know. What do you love? It's what they will take from you." Her skirt whispered as she walked around my bed and to the door. It shut softly behind her.

They'd already taken so much. What was left? What did I love?

CHAPTER SIXTEEN
STELLA

MY RECOVERY HAPPENED SLOWLY. First, my bruises healed, and then my fingers. My cracked rib and my arm would take more time, though I was no longer stuck in a cast. The aches faded the further I got from the trial, but not the nightmares.

Teddy visited every weekend, bringing me treats from Baton Rouge. He didn't mention Sin again, but his ire bubbled under the surface. I couldn't explain it to him, no matter how much I wanted to. The truth would destroy him the same way it had the rest of his family.

Dmitri was gone, having caught a flight out on the same day as the trial, but I fell into our old routine. A relaxed version of it—light exercise and easy swims to help my body heal.

I often walked around the property, the sun growing hotter with each passing day as spring turned to summer. Every time I passed the levy or the house hidden in the woods, I felt a pull on my heart. But Sin was gone.

He hadn't called, and he hadn't even spoken to Teddy. He was on the beach with Sophia. Did she warm his bed at night? It would be foolish of me to think otherwise. The pain the realization caused just layered on the rest, like sand falling in an hourglass. I was buried beneath it, time weighing down on me as each second ticked closer to the final trial.

After one of my walks, I climbed the stairs to find Lucius waiting for me on the front porch, a glass of Scotch in hand.

"What?" I wiped the sweat off my brow with the back of my forearm.

"I have some news." He stared ahead at the row of oaks. "Sit down."

A stab of worry cut through me. "Teddy?"

"No, he's fine." He patted the seat next to him on the swing.

After considering for a few seconds, I sat, my feet dangling above the floor as he rocked us gently.

"Sin called." He took a long draw from his glass.

I tried not to spend my days wondering what Sin was doing or imaging him with Sophia. I still wanted to believe that his courting of her was done out of the desire to win. It hurt, even if it was a charade. Every day that passed without a call or even a letter made my hopeful fire burn lower.

"What is it?" I kept my tone even.

"He and Sophia are coming back in three days."

I pressed the tip of my toe to the floor, stopping the sway. "Cutting their trip short?"

"Yes."

"Why?"

"I'm not sure. He said they'll be returning and to have the house ready for guests." He didn't look at me, his gaze still on the oaks.

Foreboding swirled in my stomach. "So?"

"So, he'll be bringing her back here with him. He wants to have a get-together with the Oakmans and a few other families. Something to impress everyone."

"What aren't you telling me?"

The distant rumble of thunder foretold a storm brewing.

Afternoons in the early summer always progressed too quickly, the volatile air mimicking the tumult inside me. Clear and sunny turned into dark and stormy in a matter of moments. Lucius swirled his drink around in his glass instead of answering me.

"Lucius?"

"Nothing. That's it." He downed the rest of his drink, his brown hair lifting in the warm breeze. "I just wanted you to know she'll be here with Sin. Together. And he wants a welcome party and for you to look like a million bucks." The corner of his mouth lifted in a small smile. "Shouldn't be hard."

He turned to look at me, finally giving me a glimpse of his sky blue eyes. "How are you?"

I studied him, his square jaw and full lips. "Why?"

He set his glass on the small side table and slung his arm across the back of the swing. "Can't I ask how you're doing without some ulterior motive?"

"No." I moved to get up.

"Wait. I'm not going to do anything. I just want to talk."

I arched an eyebrow at him. "Talk?"

"Yeah."

"You sure?"

"Of course." He smiled.

Though I knew he wasn't capable of such an innocent motive, I didn't care. Some sort of contact that didn't involve Renee's subterfuge or Teddy's pity was more than welcome. I eased back down and let him push us back and forth. The cicadas sang in the trees along the edge of the grass that was freshly mowed in a diamond pattern. Despite his desire to talk, we sat silently for a while, the rhythmic creak of the swing the only sound between us.

Relaxing back into the cushion, I pulled my feet up under me and let him do the work. The movement was soothing, and despite our past, his presence was, too. I lay my head back on his arm and closed my eyes. We rocked as the sun fell behind the treetops and the rumbles of thunder grew louder. Rain scented the wind as flashes of distant lightning lit the sky.

"I feel like we should be drinking mint juleps or something."

I snorted. "What even is that?"

The swing stopped as the wind picked up, whistling along the high eaves. "Are you kidding?"

"About what?"

"Are you sitting here telling me you've never had a mint julep?" His eyes rounded, as if it was the most preposterous thing he'd ever heard.

"No. I'm not from here." I shrugged. "I don't drink mint juleps and play the banjo on the front porch."

He rose and stretched, his muscled body fitting perfectly in his button-down and dress slacks. "Get up. Time to drink."

"We haven't even eaten dinner yet."

"So what?" He held his hand out for me.

Would drinking be so terrible? Maybe it would take my mind off the news of Sin and Sophia. I took his hand and rose. The rain began to fall as I followed him into the house.

"The key to a mint julep, as you may have guessed, is good mint."

"So what's a julep?"

"You'll see."

We walked down the hallway and entered the kitchen. Pots and pans hung above a wide, wooden island, and a gas range, two large refrigerators, and a freezer lined the walls. It was tidy, Laura always keeping it in top shape, and some sort of beef stew simmered on the stove top.

"Mint, mint, mint." Lucius mumbled and opened the nearest stainless steel fridge. "Must be in here somewhere." He dug through one drawer and then another.

"Can I help?" Laura walked through the door from the dining room.

"Thank god." Lucius tossed some celery back into a drawer and turned to her. "Mint?"

"Oh." Laura smiled, her rosy cheeks giving her a youthful glow I feared I would never have again. "Here." She walked to the farmhouse sink and reached up to the window sill lined with small pots. "How much do you need?"

"This is going to be an all-nighter." He began to roll up his sleeves, his movements methodical and sharp. "So, give me all you got."

"No all-nighter." I crossed my arms over my chest. "One drink."

"Right." He smirked. "Just one."

Laura tore off the tops of the mint, the earthy smell permeating the air. He took the bunch from her and rummaged around in a drawer. "Glasses and ice." He pulled out a small mortar and pestle as Laura fetched me two highball glasses with ice. "Go ahead and take an ice bucket to the library for me, would you?"

"Yes sir." Laura turned to a cabinet and plucked out a silver pail.

"Stella, come with me." He pushed through to the dining room and opened the sideboard. "Where's the good bourbon?" After leaning over and inspecting each bottle, he shook his head and grinned. "I know where it is. I'll meet you in the library. Put on some music."

Usually, I would have snapped back at orders from him, but the fact that he seemed intent on actually making something for me had me complying and strolling, glasses in hand, to the library. Laura had already placed the ice on the table beside the sofa, and I set the glasses next to it.

The library had a small music console, the speakers hidden in the bookshelves. I flipped through several internet stations before settling on something I figured Lucius would like. Classic rock.

He walked in with a large bottle under one arm, and the mortar, pestle, and mint in his hands. I sank onto the sofa and watched him with interest.

"I didn't know you were a Boston fan." He smirked and

got to work on the mint. "Some people think that crushing the mint ruins the drink. They're idiots." He dropped pieces of mint into the small bowl, his long fingers tearing the leaves. Then he grabbed the pestle and began to twist it. "You want the mint to infuse the bourbon, not just serve as a garnish." The mint crunched under his attack until it was wilted and the library smelled like an herb garden.

Lightning struck close by, the windows rattling from the ensuing boom. He gave the pestle a few more turns before he scooped the crushed mint into the glasses. Then he poured the bourbon over the tops and swirled them.

"Garnish is for pussies. Let's drink." He handed me a glass and held his out.

I clinked with him and took a sip. The mint was strong, the bourbon stronger. "Whew." I took another drink and let the heat race into my stomach and expand from there.

He plopped down next to me. "This is the good shit. No joke." He took a large swig and settled into the couch, his warmth radiating along my side as the wind howled outside. "Sin's going to kill me when he gets home and goes looking for his hidden bourbon stash."

"It's good. Minty. Definitely strong." I took another sip. "And I think you enjoy pissing him off."

"Indeed I do. I had to do a little lock picking to get ahold of this bourbon, so enjoy it." His tone turned dark even as he smiled at the taste of his drink. "I intend to make sure the bottle is done for by the time Sin gets back."

Just hearing his name set off a reaction inside me— longing and something akin to being stung. But then my thoughts turned to Sophia. He was with her, maybe fucking her right this moment. I took another pull on the mint julep, the taste less bitter this time than the first.

Lucius got up and went to the fireplace. The muscles in his back pressed against the soft material of his shirt as he leaned over and reached for some wood. Before long he had a fire going and had finished his drink.

He claimed my glass and fixed two more mint juleps.

After killing the lights, he sat even closer to me as the fire blazed orange, keeping the clammy air at bay. My head swam, but I enjoyed the lessening ache in my heart. Dulling my senses seemed to be the only way to look at Sin's conquest of Sophia objectively. It was a ruse. It had to be. He loved me. I'd seen it in his eyes, felt it in his touch.

Before long, Lucius made me another drink and put his arm around me. We didn't speak, just watched the fire and listened to another storm roll past with a rock tune thumping in the background. I was as content as I could be under the circumstances.

Uncertainty still ruled my future, but I had a trump card—Cal's proposal.

"You know." I snuggled into his side, enjoying his familiar sandalwood scent. "Cal made me an offer."

He tensed. "What sort of offer?"

I giggled, the sound foreign to my ears, especially because what I was about to say didn't strike me as humorous in the least. I blinked my eyes to clear my swimming head, but it didn't work, only made it worse.

"Stella." He gripped my injured upper arm and I yelped.

He eased up. "Fuck, sorry. I forgot. What did Cal say?"

"He said all I have to do is give myself to him for the rest of the contract year and Sin will win."

He finished his drink and slammed the glass onto the side table. "Drink up."

My glass was half full, and my eyelids were heavy. "I don't think I should."

"Drink it, Stella." His voice was an insistent whir when I wanted silence.

"Fine." I drained my glass, the taste barely registering. He took it, set it next to his, and turned to face me.

"Tell me *exactly* what Cal said. Don't leave anything out." His light eyes were close, his brow wrinkled as he focused on me.

"I did. He said he wanted complete obedience. Said Sin would have to agree to give me to him and then Sin would win." I tried to make my mouth stop moving, to stop giving away my secrets, but the gates were open and I was gone. Why did telling someone make it easier?

"Complete obedience?"

"He wants to hurt me." I shuddered, my body quaking as if another peal of thunder had sounded overhead. "And it'll save Teddy."

His jaw tightened, and he put his hand to my cheek. "It won't come to that."

I leaned into it, suddenly desperate for a touch that was gentle instead of cruel. "I was going to tell Sin, but he ran away from me. Went to *her*." I loathed the sorrow in my heart that leeched into my voice.

He put his palm on my other cheek and kissed me. I tried to lean away. He held me steady. His lips were soft, his kiss gentle. It felt like a caress, not him trying to take something from me. He licked my lips, asking instead of forcing. I opened my mouth as he deepened the kiss, his tongue sinking into my mouth as he wrapped one arm around me and pressed me close.

I ran my hands along his shoulders and then trailed my fingers through his hair. He groaned into my mouth when I tugged lightly. His tongue flicked against mine as he lifted me so that I straddled him. Emotions flashed through me— desire, guilt, and anger chief among them. I didn't love Lucius. My heart belonged to his brother, and there was nothing either of us could do to change it.

I pulled back, breaking the kiss and breathing deeply as he moved to my neck. "I can't."

He gripped my ass and ground me against his cock, the movement sending tingles and heat through me. "You can." He ran his teeth along my throat. Gripping the hem of my shirt, he tugged it until I lifted my arms. He pulled it over my head and tossed it to the floor.

"No." I protested as he wrapped his arms around me and turned, laying me on my back.

"Yes. Stop fighting it." Settling between my thighs, he

shoved my bra over my breasts and sucked a nipple into his mouth. I moaned and arched off the couch, clawing at his scalp as he bit and licked.

He worked his way back to my mouth, his kiss no longer gentle as he ground his hips into me. My skin crackled like the heat from the fire, and I gave in, letting his hands rove me as his mouth slanted over mine.

As if he sensed my defeat, he gripped my wrists and pinned them over my head. His kiss intoxicated me more than the mint juleps, and I craved the contact, the closeness, the heat he offered. But I didn't crave it from him. Could I take it anyway? The same way Sin was taking it from Sophia?

His tongue swirled in my mouth as he kissed me with more passion than I'd ever seen from him. His movements became rougher, rawer. I knew he could give me pleasure, make me forget, if only for a few fleeting moments. It was right in front of me, mine if I would have it. But even as he set me alight, my mind whispered another name and my heart spoke of someone else.

"I don't love you." The words flew out as he kissed to my ear.

"You don't have to." He nipped at my earlobe and palmed my breast. I made an *mmm* sound as he ghosted over the healed bite on my neck. Reaching between me and the couch, he crushed me to him, as if he wanted every bit of closeness he could get. Even as Lucius promised me a respite from reality, Sin was there in my memory, his eyes open, and his soul bare. I had to stop.

I embraced Lucius and buried my face in the crook of his neck. "Please don't. I can't say no. I need you, but please don't make me do this."

He stilled and nuzzled into my hair. My chest constricted, because I needed him more than I desired him. More than that, I was asking for something he'd never offered. Comfort.

He thrust his hips against me, and I bit my lip to stifle my moan at the naked want the friction created.

"You don't want this?" He nipped at my throat. "You sure? I can feel how hot you are."

"I want…" I swallowed hard. "I want you, but not like this."

He stilled. "You've got to be fucking kidding me. Again, Stella?" He groaned. "You're going to cock block me again?"

I nodded and clung to him even harder. "I'm sorry. I just can't."

"Fucking hell." He pried my arms off him and sat back, eyeing me with open irritation.

I yanked my shirt down as he let out a large exhale. I expected him to storm out or start destroying things. Instead, he stared, his face unreadable in the flickering firelight.

After several uncomfortable seconds, he shook his head. "Goddammit." He pressed the heels of his palms to his temples. "I can't believe I'm doing this. Go upstairs. Get in bed. I'll be there in a little while. I have some fucking blue ball business to take care of first. I'll be there when I'm done."

He stood, his erection noticeable in his pants, before helping me to my feet. I walked past, relieved that my freedom was so easily won.

"Wait." His strained voice stopped me. "One more kiss. That's the price."

I could say no and sleep alone like I'd done so many times already. The nightmares were always there, as if they fed on my loneliness. Paying for a night of solace with a single kiss wasn't too much to ask, especially not after what almost happened on the sofa. Mind made up, I turned and walked back to him.

He put his palms on my cheeks and stroked my hair behind my ears. "Why do I feel like this is the last time? The last chance I'll get to keep you for myself?"

I gazed up at his thoughtful expression, but I had no answer. He brought his lips to mine and kissed me with a surprising reverence. His touch stayed gentle, and his eyes remained closed. It lasted only a moment. When he pulled away, I could sense he wanted so much more. I couldn't give it to him. My heart was long since gone, grudgingly given to another. I wanted to take it back. Especially when the thought of him with Sophia hurt like someone was searing my insides over a spit. Still, it was too late.

"Go." He dropped his hands and kicked his chin up.

I turned, and he smacked my ass. I yelped at the sting.

He held his hands up, his signature smirk back in place. "Sorry. I deserved at least a little something for my troubles."

I made my way up the stairs, though they seemed far more uneven than usual. Once in my room, I stripped off everything but my panties and donned a tank top and shorts. I crawled into bed and waited.

Then I realized I'd invited a viper into my bed during a haze of drunken lust and sorrow. I rolled over and sank to the floor. Pulling out the bottom drawer, I felt around for my knife, wanting the cold comfort it provided by just being there. Sin had returned it to me after the Christmas trial, his blood dried on the blade.

It was tucked against the bottom of the drawer. Next to the familiar metal, I felt something else. A piece of paper. I gripped it between my thumb and forefinger and pulled it loose. Clicking on the lamp, I winced away from the glare and stared at the paper until Sin's dark, slanting handwriting materialized.

Trust me. Everything I do is for you and Teddy.

I stared at the letters, trying to ascribe every meaning possible to them in the hopes I'd land on the right one. Was this about Sophia? About how he was with her to solidify his future as Sovereign? I shook my head. If he'd only spoken to me instead of running off with her, I could have told him about Cal's proposition, about how I already had the key to winning.

The words blurred again as my eyes began to close of their own accord. Alcohol and fatigue warred inside me, but I would sleep no matter which was victorious. I stuffed the piece of paper into my nightstand and crawled back into bed, the knife forgotten. Trusting Sin was all I could do. I had no choice. I'd already decided to trust him the moment I left my father's house. This was just more of the same self-inflicted torment.

The minutes ticked by, and I dozed off. I woke as the bed shifted. Cool air wafted over me as Lucius climbed into bed beside me. He pulled the blanket back up and ran his forearm under my neck, pulling me to him.

"You're not wearing a shirt." I rested my head on his shoulder and threw my arm across his stomach anyway. I was too tired to care about what he'd done to alleviate his blue balls, or worry about the fact he was shirtless. Maybe just having a warm body next to me could keep the nightmares at bay.

"You are an astute observer. I sleep naked."

I tried to pull back.

"Calm down. I kept my boxers on for you."

"Oh." I settled against him again and inched my fingers down to check. They met fabric at his waist.

He ran his hand through my hair. "I think you were hoping I was lying."

I snorted. "No. I just assumed the worst."

"Maybe you shouldn't do that about me anymore. I'm in your bed after all. Dick dry as a bone. All because you asked and looked up at me with those goddamn green eyes. I feel like I'm pussy whipped, but I don't even get the pussy."

I was already drifting back to sleep as he complained. "I'm sorry."

"Don't be. I'm betting you'll let me fuck you in the morning."

I passed out mid-laugh.

CHAPTER SEVENTEEN
SINCLAIR

I SPED DOWN THE narrow lane, pleased to have control once again. The time spent with Sophia had been full of appointments, duties, and requirements that chafed even the deep-seated decorum I'd been taught.

More than the freedom, I wanted Stella. Not on the phone. Not across a table from me. Not in a fucking first class seat next to me. I wanted her beneath me, crying my name in pleasure and pain. My moods grew darker each day I was away until Sophia declared me "insufferable" and demanded I return home and wait for her arrival.

I was more than happy to oblige, leaving for the airport that night and returning even earlier than expected. My tires hummed on the pavement as a warm summer sun began to heat the muggy air. Impatience stalked back and forth through my mind, and I sped even faster, desperate to hold what was mine.

The gate swung open too slowly for my tastes, but before long I was cruising under the familiar Vinemont oaks. I parked in front and took the steps at a run. The house was quiet, everyone just waking up for the day. I couldn't stop the smile that quirked my lips as I approached Stella's door. I slowed my steps, creeping along the runner, not making a sound.

577

Turning her door handle, I pushed the door open and peered through.

My stomach sank, and every bit of anticipation running through my blood turned to ice. She lay on her side, face angelic in sleep, as Lucius slept beside her, his arm slung across her waist, his face buried in her hair.

They were beautiful together in the morning light. A stunning pair who encompassed so much—pure and corrupt, light and dark. My hand tightened on the doorknob until my bones pressed into the glass. Something this lovely needed to be destroyed. I followed the line of Stella's body, the curve of her breast through her top, the blanket pulled just to her hip. Lucius's tan arm stood in contrast to her fair skin. My fingertips remembered her smoothness. I'd traced her face every night in my dreams.

My palm grew warm, blood coating the door handle as I took in every breath, every curve, and every hair on her head.

I had two options. I could kill them both as they slept and bring the entire Vinemont line to ruin. Or I could walk away. I stood for long minutes, just listening to them breathing deep and even, no doubt exhausted from a long night of fucking.

Lucius had finally won out, taking her from me while I was busy solidifying our family's safety. She'd chosen him over me yet again, and I was the fool who hadn't seen it coming. I studied the back of my hand, the scars there visible, but not as deep as the ones that remained hidden inside me.

Of course she'd turned her back on me. I was a demon. She'd said it in her sleep on dark nights when she would cry out and awake in tears. I'd cradled her in my arms, fighting off the nightmare version of myself. But as I watched her and Lucius, I realized there was only one me. I was the nightmare version, the one who terrified her, haunted her— who took everything from her and left her broken.

My head pounded, and each beat of my heart was an

individual torment. A maelstrom of dark thoughts rained down and swirled in my mind, each one worse than the last. Pity was that I couldn't make good on any of them. Even as she lay in another man's arms, I still wanted her.

Long minutes slipped by as I weighed my need for retribution against the lives of my two brothers and Stella. Could I destroy it all, killing what little was left of me in the process?

Murder whispered to me. After a few more moments, I shoved the dark thoughts down. Molten lead poured over my heart, charring it and sealing it in an impenetrable tomb. When it cooled, I would finally be the man I needed to be to win the Acquisition.

I closed the door.

CHAPTER EIGHTEEN
STELLA

"SO, ABOUT THAT MORNING fuck we discussed." Lucius ran his fingers down to the small of my back and tucked them into the waistband of my shorts.

I groaned and rolled away from him. It was too early, though bright rays of sun streamed through the window. My head pounded along with my pulse, a hangover already setting in.

"Nuh uh." I buried my face in my pillow and stretched my legs all the way down to my toes before relaxing again.

"Come on." He propped on his elbow next to me and squeezed my ass. "It'll be fun. I don't even care if you just lay there. Go back to sleep. I'll handle the rest."

I snorted and reached back to slap his hand away. "Asshole."

"I've never met a girl who jumps right to anal, but sure." He smoothed his hand down farther.

"That's my cue." I slid out of bed and stretched, my arm aching where the break had been. My stomach churned—the bourbon had transformed to acid. He lay back in a huff, his erection noticeably tenting the sheet. Climbing back into bed and sleeping in was preferable, but there was no way I was going anywhere near him.

He sat and pulled his knees up. "How did you sleep?"

"Good, actually. Better than when I'm alone."

"You cried a little." He glanced away. "I woke up and you were talking about leaves and then rope. I said something to you, and you quieted down."

I should have been embarrassed about it, but I wasn't. He knew what I'd gone through at the last two trials. Besides, there was no way I could control what I did in my sleep.

"What did you say to me that helped?" I asked and walked to the bathroom.

"I don't know. I was half asleep. I guess my voice or something made you feel better."

"Maybe. Hey, I'm going to shower." I turned and pinned him with a glare as he smirked. "*Without* you. Your sleeping buddy services, while very much appreciated, are no longer needed."

"Don't get used to it. The next time I'm in this bed, I'll be between those legs." He licked his lips. "Also, I'm about to be out of the country for a week or two."

I peered at myself in the mirror, the circles under my eyes still apparent though not as dark. "You'll miss Sin coming home."

"Yeah, I'm real bummed about that. I'll cry into my mojitos over it." His voice receded, and I heard my door click shut.

"Thank you."

He didn't hear me, but I meant it all the same. Somehow, I'd spent the night with Lucius Vinemont and made it through unscathed.

I laughed at the thought as I stripped and stepped into the shower. Halfway through soaping up I heard a knock at the bathroom door.

"It's me," Renee called.

"Hey. What's up?" I rinsed off and stepped out, taking the towel she proffered.

"Nothing. Just wanted to come by and see you." She smiled. Her warmth had dimmed as of late, but it was still welcome.

I glanced to the ceiling. "How is she?"

She lowered her head. "Worse, I think. Lucid less and less."

"Did you know she chose Sin to compete this year?" I toweled off and snagged some lotion from the counter.

"What?" She canted her head at me. "No, she didn't."

"Yes." I walked into my bedroom. "She did."

Renee followed and sat on my bed, her mouth drawn into a frown. "That can't be true."

"Sin said so. The previous Sovereign chooses who will compete."

She shook her head slowly as I dressed. "Cal Oakman visited last summer. It was odd. He only came to see Rebecca. The boys weren't even home." She lifted her wide eyes to me. "She did this? How could she do this to her own blood?"

I'd never seen a good side to Sin's mother. When Renee described Rebecca talking and laughing about the boys when they were little, I couldn't picture it. The cruel old crone on the third floor was the boogie man to me, but Renee still believed there was some good left inside her.

"This is what she does. What she's become." I sat next to her and took her hand. "Rebecca set this in motion. I don't know if it was to keep the Vinemonts in power or what, but she chose him. I'm sorry she kept it from you."

She stayed silent, though her thoughts were loud enough I could almost hear them.

I squeezed her hand. "Let's go down to breakfast. Maybe Lucius can shed more light?"

"No. I'm going upstairs. I need to hear it from her." She set her lips in a thin line.

I knew the look. There was no arguing with it. We stood and walked into the hall. She took the steps to the third floor as I descended to the first. The scent of bacon drew me toward the kitchen, but I stopped as I passed the dining room. Sin sat at the head of the table, his eyes already focused on me as I rounded the corner.

I couldn't stop the happiness that swelled in my heart, but he regarded me with a cold stare. My joy at seeing him faded like leaves in the winter. Had he fallen for Sophia after all?

"When did you get here?" I strode toward him, wanting to touch him. Instead, I stopped and sat at my usual place. I couldn't gauge him. The look on his face was stony, but the fire in his eyes was hot enough to burn.

"This morning."

"Why didn't you tell me?" I lay my napkin across my lap and met his glare.

"Why would I have to tell you anything?"

"What?" I stopped what I was doing as anger overtook my earlier happiness. "You watch me get beaten to within an inch of my life, watch me choose between killing my father or Brianne's mother, and then you leave for a European vacation with that Oakman bitch? And now you're back and don't feel the need to even mention it to me?" My voice rose to almost a yell.

He stood and towered over me, hell in his eyes. "Don't you *ever* refer to Sophia in that manner. You aren't fit to speak her name, much less stand in her presence. In fact, get the fuck out of here. You can eat with the dogs where you belong." He swiped my table setting onto the floor. My plate shattered at our feet.

I rose and stood toe to toe with him, craning my head back so I could look him in the eye. "You asked for my trust. I gave it. I believed this entire time that you were cozying up to Sophia to save Teddy. To save *me*."

He gripped my throat, his palm clammy. "I *said* do not speak her name."

I couldn't see him anymore, not the real him. The devil who'd come to my house and offered me the contract was back, his mask firmly in place.

"What is wrong with you?"

He leaned down until we were nose to nose. "What is

wrong is that I ever thought you were anything more than the whore daughter of a petty criminal." The hand at my throat tightened. "Now get out of my sight."

He shoved me back, and I stumbled into the sideboard. Lucius walked into the dining room and looked from me to Sin.

He bristled. "What did you do?"

Sin calmly returned to his seat at the head of the table. "Get your whore out of here before I do something she'll regret."

"What?" Lucius took my elbow and steadied me. "What the fuck are you talking about?"

"You heard me." Sin leaned back and gave me a withering glance. "I'd do it quickly, if I were you. Otherwise, there will be a bloody mess to clean, and that just wouldn't do."

"Wait just a fucking minute. You need to explain—"

"No." I pulled away from Lucius's grip. The room spun, but not from my hangover. "I'll go. I don't want to be in here anymore. I don't want to be here at all." I turned and ran as my heart hammered, my ears burning.

Bounding up the stairs, I almost bowled Teddy over. I'd forgotten school was out for a few weeks before summer term.

He put a hand on my shoulder. "You okay?"

I couldn't look at him, couldn't bear his kindness right after Sin had treated me so horribly. I refused to cry, especially in front of Teddy. Explaining it wasn't an option.

"I'm fine. Hungover is all." I side-stepped him and continued climbing the stairs. "I'll catch you later today. Promise."

"Okay." His voice remained uncertain, but once I reached the second floor landing, I heard his steps retreating downward.

I turned toward my room and hesitated. Raised voices from the third floor caught my ear. Throwing another glance toward the sanctuary of my room, I took a hesitant step up the stairs.

"Why?" Renee's yell had my feet moving faster.

Was she asking about why Rebecca had chosen Sin to compete? I wanted to hear that answer. I hurried up the stairs and down the hall, the yelling covering any noise I made.

"Because he's strong." Rebecca's screech raised the hairs on the back of my neck.

"You've doomed him. You've killed Teddy."

"No, no, no. Don't cry. Come here. Let me hold you." Rebecca's voice switched to something soothing. The sweet timbre drew me closer and I peeked between the hinges as Renee sat on the bed. Rebecca pulled her into a hug and rocked her back and forth.

"Why?" Renee's question was thick with anguish.

"I had to. It's the only way." Rebecca smoothed Renee's hair. "Do you know I've always thought your hair is the most beautiful I've ever seen? The softest I've ever touched?" Tenderness suffused every word.

I blinked hard, trying to reconcile the calm, attentive woman before me with the raving lunatic of a few months ago.

"You've told me, yes."

"I'll tell you again and again, because it's true. You're the best thing in my life. You and my boys." Rebecca continued rocking Renee, the two women locked in a loving embrace.

"But Sin, he could break. The same thing that happened to us could happen to him."

"No." Rebecca shook her head. "He's strong. He can end it."

"End it?" Renee pushed back and stared into Rebecca's face. "What do you mean?"

"I mean he's strong enough and smart enough to win. And once he does, he will bring it crashing down."

"How?"

"He already has what he needs to do it. Stella. He loves her." Rebecca cupped Renee's cheek. "My love for you broke me. His love for her will save him. I know it. He's stronger. You'll see."

Renee shook her head. "But what do you mean by—"

Rebecca's kind face twisted in disgust, and she slapped Renee hard across the face. "Goddamn bitch. Who let you in here? Why are you in my room?"

"Rebecca, please."

She slapped Renee again, and I was about to walk in and restrain her, but Renee rose.

Rebecca wielded her harsh words like a bludgeon. "You're a curse. I wish I'd never laid eyes on you. I wish I'd left you where I found you so you could die in the gutter where you belong. You shouldn't be here."

Renee calmly walked to the repaired cupboard, unlocked it, and pulled out a syringe.

Spit flew from Rebecca's lips. "Answer me! Where are my boys? Where's Cora? What have you done to Cora? It's all your fault. All of it. You did this."

Renee returned to the bed, and before long, the screaming stopped as Rebecca drifted off to sleep.

Renee pulled the blanket to Rebecca's chin and smoothed the hair from her face. She kissed her on the forehead and curled up in the bed next to her, holding her hand. "I hope you're right about Sin and Stella, my love. For all our sakes, I hope you're right."

CHAPTER NINETEEN
STELLA

SIN LEFT THAT MORNING. I pressed my fingertips to the window pane as his sports car retreated down the long drive.

"He thinks we fucked." Lucius walked up behind me. "Wouldn't listen to a word I said, but that's nothing unusual."

"He didn't even ask. Just assumed." I bounced my forehead on the glass. "And he's been fucking Sophia this whole time so he has no right—" I bit my cheek to stop the waterfall of bitter words.

Lucius squeezed my shoulders and turned me around to face him. "I know, but I also know that when he gets like this, there's no talking to him, no explaining, no nothing."

"I've gathered." I let him pull me into a hug. "Why are you being so nice to me?"

He smoothed his palms up and down my back. "I figure if he already thinks we fucked then we may as well do it, right?"

"Lucius—"

"Or look at it as getting back at him." He gripped my ass and pulled me up his body until I was eye level with him. "Don't you want to?"

Yes. I wanted to punish Sin for assuming the worst, for

being with Sophia while expecting me to stay behind, pining for his return. *Trust me.* His note asked for something he wouldn't give me—trust.

I wanted to hurt him. But I wasn't like him. I couldn't turn off one emotion and turn on another like water from a spigot. He could exchange one mask for another as easily as changing clothes. I'd never had the luxury of a disguise. I was always out in the open, my heart on my sleeve. The foolish thing was, I didn't want to change. I wanted to remain the same. At the end of the year, when I walked away from this cabal of vultures, I still wanted to be me.

I answered Lucius's questioning look with a shake of my head. "Put me down."

"Fuck, Stella." He set me on my feet and scowled.

"I thought you were leaving on business."

He sighed. "I am."

I lay my hand over his heart and got to my tiptoes to kiss his rough cheek. "Thank you for last night."

He peered down at me. "Nothing to thank me for."

"It's okay to be a decent person every so often, you know?"

"Keep talking like that and I'll throw you on the bed and show you just how decent I'm not." His eyes flickered to my lips in his usual, wolfish way.

"Stella?" Teddy pushed through my half-open door. "Oh, hey. Sorry. I didn't know you two were—"

Lucius gave me one more long look before turning and walking away. He clapped Teddy on the back as he walked past. "No, it's cool. I've got a plane to catch."

"Where you headed?"

"Cuba for a little while."

"Is everything okay there?" Teddy sat on my bed.

"Nothing me and a .45 can't fix." Lucius strolled out the door and down the hall.

"Is he kidding?" Teddy raised his eyebrows.

Definitely not. "Yeah. I think so. He's just in a mood."

Teddy lay back and ground the heels of his palms into

his eyes. "Seems like everyone is. Sin bit my head off about talking to Laura before tearing out of here. What's going on?"

I plopped next to him. "Sin thinks I slept with Lucius."

He stopped rubbing his eyes. "Oh, well then that makes more sense. Wait, did you?"

"Yes. I slept with Lucius as in he literally slept in my bed with me last night because I needed someone. No, we did not have sex."

"Thank god. I was beginning to question your judgment."

"Shut up." I swatted his leg.

"What about Lucius? What's his problem?"

"Naturally, he's mad that he got to spend the night but didn't get any."

He laughed. "He's such an ass sometimes."

"He isn't as bad as he seems." I lay back so we were shoulder to shoulder.

"Huh. I thought I was the only one who knew that."

"Nope. I know it now, too."

"Neither of them are bad. Not really. Sin can be sort of…"

"Psychotic?"

"Yeah, something like that. But it's because he's had a lot of pressure, I think. Dad died when we were little, and then Sin became the man of the house. And then there was the Brazil thing that we don't talk about." He drummed his fingers on his chest. "And Mom. And now the Acquisition. He's just really strong, and it makes him sort of, I don't know, focused and driven to the point of seeming cold and, like you said, psychotic."

"Not to bring up old wounds, but you seem to have changed your mind since our last conversation about him."

He shrugged. "I'm doing what he didn't do for you. I'm giving him the benefit of the doubt. There *has* to be a reason, some really good reason, for the things he's done to you. Right?"

"There is." That was the closest I'd ever come to telling him the stakes. I couldn't say more.

"I *knew* it. If you think it's worth it, then it has to be."

I took his hand and squeezed it. "It is."

"And the thing with Lucius... We'll get it straightened out."

"Sin didn't even ask me. He just assumed the worst and stormed off."

"Give him a minute to cool off. He'll come back. And then you can explain it to him and see if he'll, I don't know, grovel or something to get back in your good graces."

I laughed. "I don't think Sin has ever groveled in his life."

"He'd do it for you. I know he would. He loves you. He may be too caught up in this Acquisition bullshit to see it clearly, but I know he does."

"You try to see the best in everyone. Sometimes it isn't there. You know?" I sighed and shifted, my arm beginning to ache.

"It is."

I had my doubts. But then I remembered the conversation I'd overheard between Rebecca and Renee. Maybe Teddy was right. Rebecca wanted Sin to bring the Acquisition down. There was light left in her despite the dark roads she'd travelled. I wanted to tell Sin what I'd heard, to let him know what his mother intended. Would it change anything?

"Maybe you're right about seeing the best in people. Though, I must say, I've seen some pretty horrible human beings over the last few months."

"I know. But maybe some of them could change?"

"What about Cal Oakman?"

He stopped drumming his fingers. "Okay, yes. I'll give you that one. He is, without a doubt, an evil person. When Sin wins Sovereign, maybe he can clean house or something?"

My thoughts turned murkier as my mind clicked and

whirred about how to end the Acquisition. I hadn't seized on any solution yet, though I'd contemplated contacting authorities in Washington. Sin's warnings that some of the most powerful people in the South, and the country as a whole, attended the trials tempered the idea. Maybe the only way to dismantle it was from the inside.

Farns cleared his throat in the doorway.

"What's up?" Teddy asked.

"I've just received a phone call from Mr. Sinclair. He gave me instructions on how he would like the house prepared for the luncheon on Saturday. And…" He scrubbed a hand down his face in a move that was utterly un-Farnsian. He was always so put-together and stoic. "Mr. Sinclair also gave me specific instructions on how you are to be prepared, Stella."

"What luncheon?" Teddy sat up. "What do you mean 'prepared'?"

Dread settled in the pit of my stomach.

Farns continued, "Mr. Oakman wishes to celebrate his daughter's return from Europe. The families and a few close friends will be here for the party Saturday afternoon."

"Party?" Renee's voice sounded from the hallway. She scooted past Farns and came to stand beside me.

"Yes." Farns nodded. "But there's more." His eyes watered. "He asked me to-to tell you…" He sagged against the door frame and Renee rushed over and took his elbow.

"Are you all right?"

"Fine." He straightened. "I'm fine. Mr. Sinclair instructed that you are no longer to have this room. Instead, you will stay in the barn, beginning today. He also said that you are to wear servant's attire for the party and that you will wait on Ms. Oakman exclusively."

Not only would Sin not speak to me, he also set out to humiliate me in front of the very people who saw me as nothing more than a plaything. I was stunned into silence, disbelieving what I was hearing.

"No. She stays here." Teddy put his arm around my

shoulders.

"Teddy, it's best you don't get involved. Mr. Sinclair's word goes." Renee knit her brows together, as if she disagreed with her own statement.

"I don't give a shit. He can't just order her around like this. She's a person."

"He can." I found my voice, a thin, fragile thing. To disobey would make Sin look weak, lessen his stature in the running for Sovereign. I was caught between wanting to fight him and wanting to keep Teddy safe. I would always choose the latter. "I'll go."

"No." Teddy tightened his hold. "This is yours."

"It never was." I disentangled myself from him. "I don't belong here."

Farns clutched his hands in front of him. "We are going to have several people in and out doing cleaning and such for the next three days. So the barn will be quieter." Then he bowed his head. "I truly am sorry. I tried to talk him out of it, but that has never worked."

"It's all right. I appreciate it." I scanned the room, trying to decide what to take with me.

"You know what?" Teddy walked to the door. "If you're sleeping in the barn, so am I. I hope you're cool with a roommate. I'm going to pack."

"Teddy, you'll just piss him off—"

"I don't care! He's being a dick. I won't let you stay out there alone. No one is going to change my mind. So don't bother trying to talk me out of it. I can make my own decisions." He stormed down the hallway as Renee and Farns watched me grab a few items from my drawers.

"At least come down and eat before you go." Farns squared his shoulders. "I know you missed breakfast. I had Laura keep a plate on the stove for you."

I threw some painting supplies into the same piece of luggage I'd brought when I first came to the house. "I'll take it with me. Thanks."

"Very good." He left.

Renee wrung her hands. "This isn't what I was hoping for. I hoped he would—"

"Fall in love with me?" I zipped up my bag and pulled out the handle.

She nodded.

"I think he did in his own way. But he's made up his mind. I can't change it. He won't even speak to me. And now…" I looked around at the room I'd come to call home that he'd so easily taken from me. "I don't know if I want him to. Maybe it's better this way." I lowered my voice. "I'll do what I have to do to keep Teddy safe. And when it's done, it's done. I'll leave here. There's nothing to keep me."

I only hoped Dylan wouldn't come after me, but even if he did, I'd handle it. Fearing him wasn't high on my list of concerns, not when Teddy's life still hung in the balance. And, no matter what, I could still give myself to Cal. Sin wouldn't object. Not anymore.

I would suffer, Teddy would live, and then I would escape and never look back.

CHAPTER TWENTY
STELLA

TEDDY'S BLONDE HEAD APPEARED at the top of the
ladder. "Hey, the guests are arriving."

"Great." I smoothed down the plain maid outfit Sin
had sent out to the barn for me. It was an ill-fitting white
button down shirt and a black skirt.

"You don't have to do this."

"You keep telling me that. If you're awake, you're
saying that. If you're asleep, you're snoring the words out
and waking me up." I glanced to our cots. The barn loft had
turned out to be not so bad. My easel and paints were set
up next to the wide barn window. I left it slung open to let
in sunlight and fresh air. Teddy would play on his laptop
while I sketched his profile. His face was plastered all along
the wall around the window.

As far as punishments went, this was one I could bear.
The lack of air conditioning could be a problem, but it
wasn't full on summer yet and the barn stayed relatively
cool. Teddy treated it like a tree house more than anything
else, as if we'd run away from home and were hiding out
until the grown-ups found us.

The afternoon storms made the straw smell sweet, and
the chickens pecking around below kept things interesting.
The roosters crowing at daybreak, though, I could have

done without.

"I don't snore," Teddy said.

"Ask Laura. I'm sure she can independently verify."

He grinned. "She may have mentioned it in passing. I'm sure she thinks it's cute."

"She's mentioned it. She says the only way to stop it is to poke you in the ribs until you sputter and wake up a little." I smirked at him. "Not that I've done that at least once every night or anything."

"Jerks." His smiled faded. "Come on. Let's get it over with. I hope it only lasts for an hour or so, but who knows?"

"Remember what we talked about." I clambered down the ladder, my heels hooking on each rung. "It's not going to be fun for me, but you have to play along like it's cool with you. No matter what they do to me, just act natural."

He took my hand and helped me off the last step. "I'll do my best."

"Do better than even that. Put on a show. That's all I'm doing." My show would consist of feigning obedience and pretending my insides hadn't been shattered by Sin. I'd broken so many times in the past few months—I feared my pieces had become too small to put back together.

We piled onto his ATV and sped up the winding drive to the house. Cars were lined up out front near the oaks, their polished metal glinting.

I took a deep breath as we entered the back door. He squeezed my hand and walked down the hall toward the dining room while I went into the kitchen. Several hired workers bustled about, their attire the same as mine. Laura directed all of them, the kitchen running smoothly under her guidance.

"Stella!" She stopped mid-order and gave me a hug.

"What can I do to help?"

"Nothing. But Mr. Sinclair has already asked for you. Best if you go on in." She shook her head at a man who was ladling soup. "Hey, not yet. That won't be ready to go out until after the salad course. It'll be cold by then. Put it back."

I threw my shoulders back and pushed through the doors leading to the dining room. The guests chattered amongst themselves as I entered. Every seat at the table was filled. Four servers, two on each side, stood against the walls, staring straight ahead.

"Stella!" Cal sat at the head of the table, a wide grin firmly in place. Sophia sat at his right already glaring at me.

Sin sat directly across from her, his eyes boring into me, disgust writ large in the tilt of his head and the slight wrinkle of his nose. My fingers went cold, and I could hear my blood pumping over the sounds of talk and clinking glasses.

"About time." Sophia tossed her raven hair over her shoulder and held out her empty drink. A diamond the size of a marble graced her ring finger, and she tapped the band on the glass.

It wasn't an ordinary ring.

My body chilled. I closed my eyes, letting the pain rip through me as my heart struggled to beat. This was an engagement party, not a welcome home lunch.

Sin's betrayal was complete. Sophia wasn't simply a ruse to solidify his position. He'd chosen her to be his wife.

"Stella, Sophia needs a refill." Sin's voice struck me like a shard of ice. "Get to it."

I glanced from her to Sin before taking the glass to the sideboard and refilling it. My hand shook as I poured her tea. I needed to hold it together. I would mourn later, once I was hidden from Sin's cruel stare.

Taking a deep breath, I set the pitcher back down. I spied Teddy sitting halfway down the table, watching me as an attractive young woman spoke in his ear.

After placing the glass on the table next to Sophia, I backed away.

"You seem to have trained her well." Cal smiled.

"She doesn't listen worth a damn, and takes direction even worse, but when put in a situation befitting her station, she reverts to true form." Sin sipped his coffee. I had the

599

brief mental image of taking his cup and dousing him with the steaming liquid.

The kitchen door swung open, and servers poured out with salad plates, waking me from my fantasy. Once the servers placed the dishes, they disappeared back into the kitchen.

"Stella, where is Sophia's salad?" Sin's voice was hollow, cold.

"I-I—" I rushed into the kitchen. "Laura? Sophia's salad?"

"There." She pointed to a plate on the island.

I snagged it and hurried back into the dining room, placing it in front of her. Before I could back away, she grabbed my hair and yanked, the burn at my scalp forcing a yelp from my lungs.

"Make me wait again and I'll have you whipped." She pulled me closer so only I could hear. "I'm nowhere close to repaying you for what you did at the trial." She let me go, and I backed away until I bumped into the wall.

Sin made no move, though his eyes narrowed as he stared at Sophia.

They began to eat, the conversation picking back up. I glanced down the table and gave Teddy a reassuring nod. His face was pinched, but he picked at his salad and tried to continue the conversation with the pretty girls at each elbow. Looking farther, I recognized some faces from the trials, and one in particular caught my eye—the blond man from the tent outside the fort. His gaze was glued to Sophia again. Who was he? I continued along the row. My eyes stopped when they met Dylan's. He sat next to Red, both of them staring me down. Loathing slithered through my stomach, and I forced myself to look away.

Cal stood, and the table went silent. "I'm afraid I've invited you here under false pretenses." He gave a grin.

Some of the guests shifted uncomfortably in their seats.

"Don't worry, the actual reason is to celebrate the

engagement of two people who are very dear to my heart. I confess I was a bit surprised at how quickly love bloomed between these two, but if you've seen them together, you just know it's right. No point in stalling. I couldn't be more pleased to announce that Sophia and Sinclair will be wed next spring."

A smattering of polite applause sounded and then died out.

He raised his glass along with everyone else at the table. "To my beloved Sophia and my soon to be son-in-law Sinclair."

"Sophia and Sinclair." They echoed in unison before drinking to the couple of the hour.

I hid my hurt as best I could, standing still and keeping my eyes up like the men along the sides of the room. I wouldn't let them see me suffer.

After the salad course, the servers brought out a shrimp appetizer. I retrieved Sophia's from the kitchen and set it before her.

"There's something on this plate." She pointed to a stray grain of rice along the lip of the plate.

"It's rice."

"I didn't ask what it was. Take it back." She picked it up and shoved it against my stomach, some of the broth staining my oversized shirt.

I bit my cheek and took the dish back to the kitchen. Laura whipped up another one and made sure to wipe the rim of the plate before sending it out. "Chin up. You're doing fine."

"Thanks." I took it and set it in front of Sophia again. She found no fault with the food, but turned her sights on me. "You look disgusting. Go change. Now." She waved me away with a flick of her wrist.

Pushing back through to the kitchen, I found a rack with white shirts for the staff. I chose one in my size and darted into the powder room off the main hall. As I stripped off the stained shirt, the door opened.

"I'm in here." I tried to push against it, but the intruder shoved harder. I shrank back when Dylan appeared and closed the door behind him, clicking the lock like I should have done.

I held my hands out in front of me as my bare back hit the wall. "Don't."

He slapped my hands away, a cruel smirk on his face, and grabbed me by the throat. "You do well as a servant."

"Stop. I have to go." My voice came out as a hushed croak. Fear controlled my thoughts, and all I wanted was to run.

He worked his fingers between my bra and my skin and yanked, the material stinging across my back as it pulled away. Palming a breast, he squeezed my throat and lifted until my feet dangled from the floor.

"Stop," I squeaked and tried to scratch him, but I couldn't get a grip on him.

"Fuck, I've been waiting for this. And here you are, right place, right time." He hiked my skirt up and slipped his fingers in my panties. I jerked as he pushed lower, seeking my entrance. "Not even wet for me? That's okay. Your blood will work just as well."

He dropped me and I gasped for breath. He bent me over, my hands on the toilet as he pushed my skirt up.

"No!" When I tried to stand up, he punched me in the back. I cried out and fell forward, hitting my head on the back of the toilet. He took the opportunity to rip my panties off. I tried to turn and fight, but I wasn't used to close quarters, and he was too big.

"Shut up." He clapped a hand over my mouth. "Get loud again and I'll knock you out. Either way, this pussy is mine. Maybe your ass, too, you filthy slut."

His belt buckle rattled and my gorge rose.

"Stella?" Teddy knocked.

"She's not in here." Dylan pressed his hand harder to my mouth. I flailed my hands out and knocked the soap dispenser from the sink. Anything to make noise.

"Stella, are you in there?" Teddy knocked harder.

Dylan inched his hand up so his palm covered my nose and mouth. I tried to pull in air, but his large hand blocked any breathing.

"Go the fuck away, man. I'm trying to take a shit." Dylan pulled his dick out and rubbed the wet tip down my ass.

I bucked forward, shaking the toilet, but not breaking his grip.

"Teddy, what are you doing? Get back in the dining room." Sin's voice wafted through the door as Dylan tried to push his cock down to my entrance again.

My vision faded and I could feel myself going limp.

"No. I think some guy has Stella in there."

"What?" The question was sharp, but not as loud as the splintering sound of wood as the door burst inward.

Dylan was ripped away from me and I fell against the sink, trying to get air into my burning lungs.

"Stella!" Teddy yanked my skirt down and turned me to his chest, wrapping his arms around me. "Jesus, what did he do to you?"

Thuds and yells erupted from the hallway, and the wall shook, plaster dusting from the ceiling. My throat ached, and I buried my face in Teddy's shoulder.

"It's okay. Shh." He shook his blazer off his shoulders and wrapped it around me, drawing it tight at my front before pulling me to his chest again.

"Don't you fucking touch her!" Sin's rage-filled roar shot to every corner of the house as the servers rushed past in the hallway.

"Boys, boys! This is why we can't have nice things." Cal's laugh rang out and was followed by cackles from the dining room.

After the servers were gone, Teddy peeked out the door toward the foyer. He scooped me into his arms and ran for the back stairway. I held onto his neck as he took the steps two at a time.

"What happened?" Renee hovered at the top step.

"Some guy attacked her in the bathroom." Teddy rushed down the hall and carried me to my room, sitting me on the bed as I clutched his jacket to me.

I couldn't stop shaking. He sat next to me and pulled me close again, rubbing my back and shushing me as I trembled. Renee knelt in front of me, and tilted my chin up. She gasped when she saw my neck.

"He could have killed her." Her voice was unforgiving. "Who was it?"

"I don't know, but he was big."

"Dylan." My voice croaked through my teeth.

"Your stepbrother?"

I nodded. Renee and Teddy exchanged a look as raucous cries erupted from downstairs.

"We have a victor!" Cal's showman voice lofted to our ears. "Congratulations, Sinclair. Well done. Somebody get Dylan cleaned up. He gave a good showing. Now, let's finish our lunch."

CHAPTER TWENTY-ONE
SINCLAIR

I TOOK ANOTHER SWIG of brandy as Farns did his best to patch up my busted knuckles. I barely felt it.

The party was at an end, and the last guest had left hours ago. I glanced at the stairs. Teddy still hadn't come out of Stella's room.

"I heard what that nasty fellow tried to do. I am proud of you, Mr. Sinclair."

I shook my head. "I'm the last person in this house for you to be proud of. I can promise you that."

"Don't be so hard on yourself. You didn't choose this." He glanced up at me, his blue eyes faded while the man inside was still sharp. "You are doing well."

Steps on the stairs had my heart speeding up. But it was only Renee. Stella remained above, hidden from me.

"Did you kill him?" The steel in Renee's voice sent a chill through me.

My memory flickered alive like a beast needing to be fed. When my mother and I returned from Brazil, Renee met us at the airport. She rushed up and kissed me on the forehead before taking Rebecca in her arms.

"*Did you kill them all?*" She'd whispered. I'd barely heard her, but the timbre was the same as what she'd just asked me.

605

"No." I finished my glass and slammed it on the table. "I damn well would have if Red hadn't pulled me off."

Renee gripped my chin and pulled my face up to her scrutiny. All pretense of being anything other than my second mother fell away as she perused my black eye and bloody nose. "You'll heal."

"How is she?" I knew I shouldn't care, that I should keep up the charade that I was only angry with Dylan for trying to take what was mine or for tampering with my Acquisition. Instead, the thought of him harming her churned my stomach and fueled my fury. I wanted his blood, all of it, on my hands.

"She's been better. Her throat is swollen and bruised. Teddy is comforting her."

A stab of jealousy punctured the careful cocoon that wrapped my heart. "The same way Lucius comforted her?"

"Yes, as a matter of fact." She frowned and dropped her hand.

I stood so fast that Farns would have fallen if I hadn't caught him. Murder roiled in my breast, emotions spilling into my heart through the cracks of jealousy etched into my armor.

"Calm down. You've misjudged her *and* your brother, for that matter."

"What, by seeing them in bed together?" I forced myself to stay put even as I imagined Teddy on top of her.

"That's all you saw. Maybe if you'd asked her instead of going off half-cocked, or maybe if you'd listened to your brother—"

"Lucius was telling the truth?" The ice water running through my veins grew colder. "They never—"

"No. And now you've punished her, nearly got her violated, and driven her away. And all the while you were courting that fork-tongued Oakman girl. How do you think she felt? You need to fix this." She pinned me with a fierce gaze. "For all of us, but for yourself most of all."

She took Farns' elbow and helped him through the

dining room and out the door. He walked with slow steps, his age creeping up on him like a masked assassin.

I lolled my head back and stared at the coffered ceiling. Had I misjudged her? I tried to put myself in her shoes—not something I'd ever even thought of before, much less attempted. Maybe Renee was right. But surely, Stella knew I only dated Sophia for show, a business arrangement, nothing more.

Sophia treaded a fine line as it was. Her lover Ellis stayed with us the entire time we travelled Europe, the two of them dining together and spending the night in a tangled heap as I smoked, drank, and thought of nothing except Stella.

During the day, Sophia and I made a handsome pair, and the deal had been struck. I would marry Sophia, set her up with a trust fund flush with Sovereign cash, and we would go our separate ways for the majority of the time, or at least until we were needed for events. She could live happily ever after with that ponce Ellis, and I would keep Stella.

I'd left Stella a note telling her to trust me. I didn't dare call or write any other way. Ears were everywhere, and I had to keep Sophia—and by extension, Cal—happy by acting the perfect son-in-law. I knew my trust was broken the second I'd seen Stella in bed with Lucius. But maybe she'd trusted me after all.

I was no longer content to wait for answers. I stalked into the hall and up the stairs. Her door was closed, but I heard voices. I huddled close and listened.

"Just tell me what it is. Why do you stay? We could run away. I can take Laura. What keeps you here?"

I couldn't hear her response. My fists tightened at the thought of her voice being taken by Dylan's rough hands.

"Fine." He sighed. "I just wish you would share it with me. I could help, you know?"

Another pause.

"Yes, I'll stay the night. Let me go to my room and get

out of these stuffy clothes. Renee already laid some PJs out next to you. Do you need help changing?"

After a moment, Teddy laughed. "Busted. Okay, I'll be right back."

I stepped aside as the door opened. Teddy closed it softly and gave me an unforgiving glare. "What do you want?"

"I want to see her."

"No." He crossed his arms over his chest and blocked the door.

"What are you doing?"

"I'll stand out here for as long as it takes. You aren't seeing her. You don't get to see her after what you did." His temper reminded me of my own.

"If I have to go through you, I will."

"Fuck off, Sin. You leave her here beaten and broken. You take off to Europe with Sophia fucking Oakman while Stella has to heal from whatever torture you put her through. Then, you never give her a chance to explain what happened with Lucius." His brows lowered, actual rage coloring his face. "And then you force her to sleep in the barn and wait on that cunt Sophia hand and foot." His voice turned into a hiss. "She was almost raped because of *you*."

He'd only told a fraction of my actual sins against Stella. I was heartened that he didn't know the rest.

"All that may be true. Even so, I *will* get through that door." I'd never hit Teddy, and I didn't want to start, but the roaring need inside me to be with Stella drowned everything else out.

Teddy huffed his breath out through his nose. "Are you going to hurt her?"

Not today. "No."

"Are you going to apologize?"

I tasted the word, bitter and rotten. Still, if it would get me past Teddy without violence, I'd do it. "Yes."

"For everything?" He leaned closer.

"Yes."

"I have your word?"

I nodded. "Yes."

"Then you can go in. Just know that if I hear from Stella that you even *said* something to upset her, I am going to do my best to kick your ass. I know I won't win, but I will give it all I've got. Understand?"

How did this fucked up family ever turn out a beautiful soul like Teddy?

"I understand."

"Good. Give her a minute to change clothes." He shuffled away from the door and gave me one more pointed scowl before heading to our wing of the house.

I waited for a few moments, the anticipation pacing in my chest like a lion on a leash. The bed creaked, and then silence. I waited a while longer to be sure before wrapping my palm around the door handle.

I turned it and eased inside. She lay curled up in a ball, her back to me. Her soft breaths were deep and slow.

Her resting form was beyond tempting, and I'd thought of nothing except her for so long—either with longing or hatred—that all I could do was stare. She was all mine now. No one else's prying eyes watched her. I grew hard in my pants, but chided myself for already treading too harshly on Teddy's rules.

Quietly, I removed my shirt and pants. Sliding into her bed felt like coming home, and for the first time in months, the hellfire that leapt in my heart quieted to embers. I moved my arm under her head and pressed into her back. I wanted to groan from the feel of her. My skin was numb until it touched hers, and then it was alive with every sensation.

She mumbled something and snuggled back into me, her hair tickling my nose as I pulled her close. I didn't care that she thought I was Teddy. All I wanted was her in my arms. Everything quieted inside me, the sections of my mind that were always calculating or planning finally clicking off.

Her breathing changed, and she stirred. "Teddy. You're um, you're sort of poking me." Her voice was a scratchy whisper, and I wished all over again that I'd killed Dylan.

She turned to face me and shrank back with a gasp. "What are you doing here?" She pushed at my chest, but I trapped her in my arms. I was never letting her go again.

"Stop, please. You'll only hurt yourself more."

She didn't stop, only struggled harder, like a wildcat in my arms.

I nuzzled into her hair. "Stella, please. I'm sorry. I'm so sorry."

"Sorry?" She froze. "That doesn't even begin…" She swallowed hard. "To cover what you've done."

"I know. But I will make it up to you somehow. All of it."

"You can't make it up to me." Her voice broke, the pain in her piercing me more deeply than I thought possible.

"I can." I stroked her cheek. "I will. You'll see."

She pulled away from my touch. "By marrying Sophia?"

"I'll never marry her."

"But you've been with her this whole time." Her eyes shimmered in the low light.

"I've never touched her. I swear. She's with someone else. I've only been with her to please Cal. They think I'll marry her, of course, after I become Sovereign. I won't." Spending time with Sophia had been my personal ninth level of hell. Vapid, selfish, and cruel—we were a perfect match. I already wanted her dead for harming Stella, and having to spend time with her only made me come up with various gruesome ways for her to meet her end.

"I didn't sleep with Lucius." She shook her head. "I mean, I slept with him, but we never—"

"I know." I kissed her forehead. "I'm sorry."

"I believe you." She relaxed into my arms more, though she still held back. "So what will happen when you don't marry Sophia?"

"I don't care. Cal will try to retaliate. I'm not sure what

he'll do. It won't be pretty. Nothing approaching all-out war between our families, but things will be strained."

"He's promised me to Dylan."

I froze. "What?"

"Cal is going to give me to Dylan once the Acquisition is over." She shuddered.

"You're not his to give." I clutched her tighter and wished, once again, that I'd killed Dylan downstairs.

"They've made some sort of deal. I don't know the details."

"You don't have to. It isn't going to happen. I don't care if it results in all out war with Cal after I become Sovereign."

"Could you boot Cal's family? Stop the infighting that way?"

"Yes, but playing that card early could lead to trouble later. I'd prefer to keep that in my back pocket. The very threat of it will help keep him in line." Or so I hoped. Cal had consolidated power during his reign. He would be a particularly vicious adversary.

"There will be fighting. You and Lucius will be in danger, like in Cuba?"

I brushed my hand down her hair. "Yes."

"Then no."

"What?"

"I don't agree to this plan at all." She chewed her bottom lip.

I arched an eyebrow. "Are you saying you *want* me to marry Sophia?"

"Of course not. But you simply winning isn't going to be enough. Not for me, anyway."

I took her hand and pulled it to my heart. Her palm was warm and small, but she held me in it. "Anything you want me to do, I'll do it." I inhaled a deep, shuddering breath. "I'm yours. I've been a fool and treated you worse than you deserved—"

"Sin—"

"Let me finish. Even if what I'd thought was true—that you'd slept with Lucius—I should never have punished you like that. I'm sorry. And when Dylan..." My jaw tightened, and I struggled to continue. "When Dylan tried to hurt you, I realized I didn't care anymore if you had or hadn't slept with Lucius. You are mine to protect, to cherish, and to love." The last word was one I said with the same care I would use in handling a live grenade.

I cleared my throat as her expression softened, and she stroked my cheek. That feeling welled up inside me, the one I only had when I thought of her. It was my drug, far more intoxicating than anything else I'd found. "After I had a moment to calm down, I decided that I would only have killed Lucius. Not you."

She tilted her head. "I think that's one of the nicest things you've ever said to me."

I covered her hand with mine. "I don't know what else to say or do to prove it, but I love you. All of you. I will gladly kill for you, buy you whatever your heart desires, and show you the world. Anything. If I have it or I can get it, it's yours." My heart constricted. Is this what love felt like? Like you were on fire, and instead of turning to ash, your mate only made you burn brighter?

"I love you, too." She kissed me, soft and chaste. "But I need something from you before I can forgive you."

"Anything. It's yours. Just name it."

Her eyes narrowed. "Promise me that we will burn it all down. Every last piece of the Acquisition. Or we will die trying."

I couldn't look away from her, my vengeful queen. "How did I never know when I first set eyes on you that you were the strongest person in the room?" I kissed her, not chaste, not gentle. She moaned in my mouth and tangled her fingers in my hair. I needed her taste on my tongue, every inch of her body beneath my fingertips, but she pulled away.

"Promise me." She dotted kisses on my cheek and bit

my ear. "Promise, because you never break your word."

I slid my hand down her body and into her panties. She was wet, and I needed to be inside her.

She grabbed my wrist. "Promise me first."

I got to my knees and yanked her panties off before shucking my shorts away. Lining up at her entrance, I stared down at her, the warmth in her flowing to me and making me more than I ever thought possible.

"I promise." With one hard thrust, I seated myself deep inside her. Leaning down and claiming her mouth was the sweetest reward I'd ever tasted.

I pushed harder, needing to give her every bit of raw aggression I'd felt for anyone who thought to hurt her or take her from me. She clawed my back and I kissed to her collarbone, careful on her neck. It was too dark to see, but I knew she was bruised there. I would have Dylan's head for it.

"Sin." She clung to me as I slowed my pace and wrapped my arms around her.

"Do you trust me?" I teased at her lips.

"Yes."

I rested my forehead against hers and kept my thrusts smooth and even. I wanted it to last, to stay inside her for as long as I could.

She was my home, where I belonged. And I would never doubt her again.

CHAPTER TWENTY-TWO
STELLA

THE SUMMER ARRIVED WITH full force, the hottest on record. I spent the days with Sin, except on the odd times when he was called to make an appearance with Sophia. He always came back irritable, but after some particularly enjoyable attention from me, he was back to his usual dark and brooding self.

Sin showed me more of the estate and even took me to see his office in town. He barked at his staff to get to work as they gawked at the "mystery woman" on his arm. He hid me away in his private office. I ran my fingers over his many diplomas and reveled in his plush domain.

"Not bad for government work."

He sat in his desk chair and pulled me into his lap. "Have you ever played a game called naughty secretary?"

"No." I laughed. "Have you?"

"Of course not." He ran his hands to my hips. "Though I'm quite disappointed to hear you're unfamiliar."

I rubbed my ass back and forth over his growing erection. "I've never heard of it, but that doesn't mean I wouldn't be good at it."

"I like it when you're up to a challenge."

"Always." I stroked his dark hair, the strands soft on my fingertips.

He pulled me in for a kiss, his hands roving my body as he bit my bottom lip. The singular sensation of tingles and warmth, one that only he could draw from me, ricocheted around my stomach.

"Mr. Vinemont." A woman chirped through his phone.

He growled into my mouth before reaching over and pressing a button. "What, Kim?"

"You have a visitor."

"I don't have any appointments today." His tone turned cold, displeasure coating each syllable. "I checked."

"He's a walk-in. He believes you'd want to speak with him."

"Who the fuck is it?" He clicked off the speaker and kissed me again, his impatience growing by the second.

"Leon Rousseau. He specifically asked to speak to the young lady you're with."

My heart fell at my father's name. I hadn't seen him since the trial, though Sin told me what he'd done to him. It had been gruesome, but I understood why it had to be.

Sin leaned back and looked up at me, his lips pressing into a thin line. "Fuck. He must have seen us arrive. I'll send him away."

"No. He can see me if he wants to. Both of us, I mean." I took his hand and laced our fingers together. "He can see both of us."

"Are you sure?"

"Yes. I think I'll be fine. And maybe it will be a good thing, to finally see him face to face on equal footing. No more pretending." The certainty in my tone wasn't matched inside my heart. My love for my father had grown stale and brittle, but something remained. Would it always be there?

"Send him in." Sin shoved the phone away.

I tried to stand.

He held me in place. "He can see you here with me, where you belong."

"Claiming your turf?" I leaned my shoulder into his

chest.

"If you'd rather I piss on you to mark you as mine, I will." He dug his fingers into my sides and I squirmed, trying not to laugh. "Is that a yes?"

"No." I grabbed his hands as the door opened.

My short-lived amusement died away as my father hobbled in, his back hunched and his face sorrowful. So many emotions rushed through me that I thought I might burst at the onslaught. Of all of them, pity won out.

He sank down into a chair across the desk as the secretary closed the door.

His bloodshot eyes found mine, and he held out his left arm, the end covered in graying gauze.

"Look at me. Ruined."

Sin spoke through gritted teeth. "You got what—"

"Let me, okay?" I squeezed his forearm and he quieted, though he wrapped his hands around my waist. Meeting my father's eyes again, I said, "Go on."

"I need you, Stella. I need someone to take care of me. The money…" He shook his head, unshed tears wobbling in his eyes. "It's all gone. No one cares about me. Dylan hasn't spoken to me in months. I need you to come home. Please."

"To the home you burned to the ground?"

His eyebrows rose, but he shook his head. "Who told you that? Him?" He shot a glance to Sin. "It was lightning. The damned insurance people wouldn't pay up." His tone turned bitter and his top lip curled into a sneer. "Only gave me half what it was worth."

I saw right through him as if he were a pane of glass on a sunny day. "Can you still not tell me the truth, even now?"

"What lies has he told you? He poisoned you against me. You're sitting in his goddamn lap like a pet!" As his voice rose, Sin tensed beneath me. I smoothed my hand up and down his arm, trying to tamp down the beast I could feel raging beneath his surface.

"Sin told me the truth. He showed me your signature. Stop lying to me." The brittle love I had for him was breaking into pieces, disintegrating into the wind of his lies.

"That stuff can be forged. You know that. Why do you believe him? He's the one who framed me, hounded me, convicted me based on lies. Don't you remember?"

"I remember believing in you so much that I sacrificed myself to save you. I remember accepting my fate if it meant you would be safe." I rose and stared him down. "And then I was told the truth. You brought all of this on us. Your lies, your schemes." I flattened my palms on the desk. "How long until the million ran out?"

"What? No. There was no million." He glared at Sin. "What have you told her?"

"Look at me. He told me the truth. How. Long?"

He sputtered and shook his head. "N-no. It wasn't like that. I was—"

I slapped my hand on the desk. "How long!"

He covered his face with his hand. "Just a few months. I-I thought I could get you back somehow. Keep the money and get you back, but he took you and told you lies about me."

"Do you even hear yourself?" Realization hit me, and I straightened. "You believe your own lies, don't you? You actually think you were innocent, that you could somehow sell me and keep me at the same time."

"I just need you. My hand. He took it, and it's all his fault. He caused every last bit of it." He vacillated between crying and yelling, and pointed a shaking finger at Sin. "He wanted you all along, from the first moment he saw you."

"That's the only true thing you've said." Sin stood behind me and put his hands on my shoulders. "I think it's time for you to leave, Mr. Rousseau."

"She's mine." My father snarled, more animal than man. "You can't keep her from me. Her mother tried to take her from me once. That didn't work out very well for her."

"Take me from you? She never tried…" My knees

went weak and I leaned against the desk for support. "Did you—was it you? What did you do to her?" My mother's face flitted across my vision. "What did you do?"

He changed yet again, the vehemence gone and weakness in its place. "Please, Stella. I need you. Please."

My head spun, the room flickering light to dark. "You said it was suicide. It was ruled a suicide."

He nodded. "Yes, suicide. Come with me."

"Liar!" I screamed and tried to get around the desk. I wanted to rip him open until the truth finally spilled out. Sin wrapped his arms around me and held me in place.

"I suggest you leave now, Mr. Rousseau. I'd love to watch her destroy you, but it may cause her pain, and I can't have that."

"I need you. Please, come with me. Please." His teary plea made bile rise in my throat, and all I could see was my mother, her warm smile and sad eyes.

"I'm warning you, Mr. Rousseau." Sin spoke quietly, hatred infusing every word.

"You killed her. You killed her, didn't you." It wasn't a question, but the answer was in his bowed head. The lies were finally at an end.

"I thought we'd get more money to live. Stage it like a break-in. It didn't work. Insurance wouldn't pay because it was deemed a suicide, and I had debts. I'm sorry. I would never hurt you. Please—"

"I warned you." Sin released me.

I tore around the desk and shoved my father to the ground. Dropping to my knees, I hit him as tears blurred my vision and rage lit me up like a house on fire.

"How could you? I loved you!" I hit him as he covered his face, cowering beneath my onslaught. My movements slowed as sobs rose in my chest. I kept swinging even as my arms tired and my knuckles burned. And then, after I'd worn myself out, I was done. Finished with him.

Sin lifted me to my feet and picked me up, cradling me in his arms as I cried into his chest.

"Get out." He turned to the door and yelled. "Kim!"

She hurried through as if she'd been waiting just outside. "Have Burt or Clancy escort Mr. Rousseau to his car. Call the sheriff and make sure he is escorted to the parish line."

"Yes, okay." She bustled out of the room.

"The next moment I set eyes on you will be your last." Sin backed away, holding me close.

"M-Mom." I sobbed.

"Shh, it's all going to be all right."

A man walked in and helped my father to his feet. His cheeks glowed red from my fists and one eye was already starting to swell shut. The man asked no questions and hustled my father out the door and closed it behind them.

I clung to Sin, the world ripping to shreds around me as he stood firm.

"I'm sorry." He kissed my hair. "I'm so sorry. If you want me to have him killed—"

"No. There's been enough blood. Too much." I calmed my breathing, taking gulps of air to stop the tremors.

"I'll do anything to make you happy. Anything." He was a wild, tormented creature, but everything about him soothed me, lulled me.

"I know."

Another knock and then Kim's voice. "He's out of the office, sir, and the sheriff is on his way to escort him away."

"Good."

The door closed and another round of sobs shook me. "He took her from me. She loved me, Sin. I remember her. Her smile, her hair, the way she would sing while I played with my finger paints." Her yellow dress with the blue checks, the time I got into her makeup and painted my lips and cheeks with her red lipstick, choosing my dress for my first school dance, playing in her garden—so many memories welled up inside me. How many more had my father stolen from me? "She'd still be alive. She'd be with me. H-he took her."

Sin rocked me back and forth, trying to ease the ache that could never fully be erased. "Shh, I've got you."

I cried for the parents I'd lost as he held me close, his strong arms cradling me until my tears finally subsided. He kissed my hair.

I leaned back to look up at him. "Thank you."

"I'm sorry." His face softened, and his tenderness made my tears threaten again.

I cleared my throat to try and stave off another crying fit. "Is all this going to be a p-problem with your staff or anything?"

He laughed, a deep rumble in his chest. "After what they've heard about Judge Montagnet, my eccentricities seem rather run-of-the-mill, I'm afraid."

"I hate that man."

"We'll get him." He dropped a reassuring kiss on my lips. "We'll get them all."

One stormy afternoon, Sin, Lucius, and I climbed the stairs to the third floor. Renee had interrupted our strategy session with Lucius to let us know that Rebecca was back—the real Rebecca.

I followed Renee, both Sin and Lucius on my heels. We moved quickly. Catching Rebecca lucid was like trying to see a shooting star. Spotted rarely, and only briefly before burning out.

Though I'd witnessed her change for Renee briefly, I couldn't imagine her as anything other than spiteful toward me. My trepidation grew as we approached. But when I walked in with Sin and Lucius, she smiled without a hint of malice.

"Boys." Rebecca motioned them over, her joy like a mirror to her past when she was young and full of life.

I hid my surprise and stepped aside so Sin and Lucius could go to her bedside.

"Mom?" Sin hurried to her, Lucius on his heels.

"Sit. Let's talk before I go back under. Hurry. We don't have much time." Rebecca patted the bed.

They sat as I hovered at the door.

"Stella? Come here. Let me look at you." I walked over, Renee at my elbow.

"See? It's her. It's my Rebecca." Renee dabbed at her eyes.

"Rebecca." I nodded in greeting, still unsure if I was going to get a kind word or a kick in the teeth.

"You are beautiful. Almost the spitting image of my sister, Cora. And I hear you have her spirit, as well." The woman in front of me wasn't the same one who'd run into the dead of night screaming, or who had told me with glee about the trials. She was warm, friendly—a total stranger.

"Thank you." I didn't know what else to say.

"Renee, leave us for this part. I know how it upsets you." She reached out and squeezed Renee's hand before letting it go.

"I'll be just down the hall." Tears rolled down Renee's cheeks, joy mixing with sorrow.

Once Renee was gone, Rebecca turned back to me. "The final trial is more of a mental test than anything else. Stella—"

"Is it true?" Sin asked. "That you want me to end the Acquisition?"

She took his hand. "Yes. I've never wanted anything more in my life. If I had any strength left, I'd do it myself. We don't belong. The Vinemonts were never meant to be a part of this." She shook her head, her white hair flowing around her shoulders. "We were poor sharecroppers. Your great-great-great grandfather unknowingly saved the life of the Sovereign, who repaid him by adding us to this disgraceful club. Don't you see? It's not in our blood. We don't belong here."

"But you always said we were better, that we were above everyone else—"

"Forget what I said." Her tone turned desperate, and her bottom lip shook. "Forget everything I ever told you. Forget everything I've done to you." She ran her fingers over the scars she'd cut into the back of his hand. "But remember what I tell you now. The final trial will force Stella to sacrifice something she loves." She turned to me again. "Child, what do you love? Tell us."

"I-I love Teddy and Sin and Lucius. I love Renee, Farns, and Laura."

"Is there anyone else they could try and take from you?"

"Dmitri." Lucius glanced at me. "And the rest of them. The flaming hair guy and the blonde."

"Yes, them too."

Lightning crackled through the sky, and the boom of thunder shook the house.

Rebecca leaned back, her eyes beginning to dim. "So many to choose from. So many. I'm afraid I'll be no help. But Cal is the worst of them all. He will make it hurt. He will try to turn you into something you're not." She held her hand out to me.

I took it, the skin thin, and the bones frail.

"Don't let it happen to him. Please. Don't let him turn into this." She looked down at her withered body beneath the covers. "I couldn't bear it if I'd doomed him to live this way. He's a good boy. They're all good boys. Please help them."

"I'll try. I promise. I don't want anyone else to suffer ever again in the Acquisition. We have plans. We—"

She snatched her hand away. "What are you doing in here?"

Sin's face fell, and Lucius stood.

"You two just let anyone in my room?" Her voice cut through the air, shrill and poisonous. "Servants and riffraff from the street?"

623

"Mother, please."

"Get out!" She turned her face away, staring out the window as the rain hammered against the glass.

Sin sighed and rose. We trudged back down the stairs, silence enveloping us like a too-warm blanket.

"After that exciting interlude, I'm calling it a night." Lucius gave us a two-finger salute and strode toward his side of the house.

I stroked Sin's cheek, but his gaze was far away, likely in the past. "Hey. It's going to be okay."

He blinked and kissed my palm. "I know. As long as I have you, it will be." Striding off toward his room, he pulled me behind him.

When we got there, he shut the door and locked it. Pushing me down onto the bed, he went for my neck, his teeth sliding over my pulse.

I stared up at the canvas I'd done of the first trial, the dark vines swallowing me whole. "You never told me what you did with the North Star. My painting."

"I know what the North Star is, and I sold it. Why do you insist on wearing so many clothes?" He yanked my top over my head.

I laughed as he kissed my chest. "I'm wearing a t-shirt and jeans."

"That's the problem. Nothing is preferable."

"You want me to walk around the house naked for Teddy and Lucius to see?"

He bit my breast, and I yelped. "No. But in my room, or your room, or any room with just the two of us, is nude really too much to ask?" His tongue grazed my nipple.

"Stop trying to distract me. What about the North Star? Why did you sell it?"

He sucked my nipple into his mouth and swirled his tongue around the hard tip. I raked my fingers across his scalp as he kneaded my other breast.

He switched to the other nipple, licking and sucking until I was panting.

Kissing to my lips, he continued, "I sold it to a very high end collector. It's on prominent display in his Manhattan home. I hated to part with it, but I had to sell it to launch your career. Last I checked..." He nipped at my lower lip. "You were still the talk of the art scene, your mystery only enhancing your reputation."

"You did that for me?" I stroked my fingers through his hair, wondering at the softness that lived at the very heart of him.

He kissed me, hard and possessive, before gazing down at me with an intensity that belonged only to him. "I would do anything for you."

I laced my fingers behind his neck. "Do you think we can do it?" Doubt flittered around my mind, worry as well. "All of it, like we planned?"

"Of course. Lucius has already moved our money." He got to his knees and yanked my pants down before tossing them to the floor. He stripped his shirt and pants off, his muscles rippling. "We've stockpiled everything we need for the coronation ceremony. Teddy will be safely stashed at our compound in Brazil. All we have to do—"

"Is win the final trial." I finished for him, the words far easier than the deed.

"And we will." He sank back on top of me, his weight keeping me grounded.

"What if we don't? What if—"

"Shh." He stroked my hair. "Everything will fall into place. If anyone so much as talks to Dmitri, or Teddy, or Alex, or anyone you love, we'll know."

"Knowing won't stop me from having to hurt them." The whispered truth roared in my ears.

"I could win it. I could give myself to Cal—"

"No." He gritted his teeth. "We'll win without it. I won't give you away. Not to anyone, but especially not to him. There's no point discussing it."

"I'd do it. To save Teddy, I would."

"I know you would. I can't let you. I couldn't stand it.

He would do horrible things, and I would know. Every night, I would know you were being tormented because I wasn't strong enough to save you."

"Even so, I'd do it."

He peered down at me, disbelief in his eyes. "How did I ever manage to catch you?"

"If I remember correctly, you didn't play fair."

He smirked.

"Just tell me we'll be okay, that Teddy will be okay." I pulled him closer and rubbed my cheek against his stubble.

"We'll get through it. Together. The same way we've done each trial." He kissed to my mouth.

"I'm scared."

"I know." He kissed my forehead. "But they're the ones who should be afraid."

CHAPTER TWENTY-THREE
STELLA

"STELLA!" SIN'S VOICE HISSED in my ear, and I shot up from his bed. "They've sent a car. The trial's today. Fucking Cal surprised us." He dropped a kiss on my lips. "This changes nothing."

"They're coming." Lucius stood in the doorway, peering down the hall.

"Hurry to your room. Get ready. I'll meet you downstairs." He kissed me again quickly and pulled his sheet free, wrapping it around me.

I rose, clutched the sheet closed at my chest, and hurried away with Lucius.

"What's going on?"

"Just more fucking dickishness by Cal." Lucius' back was tight, his pace hellish as we turned the corners toward my room.

"Get in your bed, quick. Cal wants to surprise you himself. I held him off with coffee. Go." Lucius pushed my bedroom door open. I slipped through and jumped into my bed as he closed the door. The sheet slipped off and I kicked it down beneath my blankets.

My heart raced, and I glanced to the dresser. I hated the thought of Cal catching me naked. The hall was quiet, so I slipped out of bed and pulled my drawer open. Then I heard footsteps.

Fuck. I crept back to my bed empty-handed and slid under the sheets. Feigning sleep with my eyes barely open, I turned my head toward the door and lay on my back.

I breathed long and steadily, completely at odds with the frantic beat of my heart. When the door handle turned, I clutched my pillow. It opened farther and Cal peeked in, a large grin spreading across his face as he "caught" me sleeping.

Lucius peered at me over Cal's shoulder, his face pinched. Cal opened the door the rest of the way and eased toward my bed. Chill bumps broke out across my skin, and I wanted to curl up into a defensive ball. Instead, I closed my eyes so he wouldn't realize I was awake.

The bed shifted, and his hand brushed the hair from my face.

"Stella." His voice was soft, with a hint of merriment.

I opened my eyes and tried to shrink away from him, but he closed his fist in my hair.

"That's no way to greet the day." He tsked and let his gaze slither down my neck to my bare shoulders. "Sleeping nude?"

I pulled the blanket to my chin. "Why are you here?"

"Today's your big day. The final trial. Excited?" He rested his hand at my throat.

I didn't answer, silently willing him away.

It didn't work. He leaned closer. "I thought you'd at least try and convince Sin to let me have you." He wrapped his fingers around the blanket and pulled it down.

I resisted, trying to keep myself covered. When he pulled my hair so hard I thought it might rip out, I let go. He shoved the blanket away and surveyed my body. I crossed my arms over my breasts. He pulled them away and pinned my hands to my sides. I was helpless, the same way I'd been so many times at the hands of these people. I wouldn't let my fear win. Hatred burned brighter.

"It doesn't matter now. It's too late. The last trial is

here." His malicious eyes took in all of me. "Still, I have a few tricks up my sleeve." He let one hand go, and I moved to cover myself.

He slapped me, my cheek stinging as the crack shocked the still air. "Don't fucking move."

I lowered my hand back to my side, humiliation burning and rising to the surface, painting my skin red.

"Better." He trailed his hands around my breasts and down to my waist and then lower. He smirked and ran his fingers across my pussy as I clenched my legs shut. "Red like I thought." He met my eyes again. "As I was saying, I have a trick or two left. Your stepbrother has been kind enough to let me have you for a week before he takes delivery."

I fought the instinct to hit him as he took my nipple in his mouth. He groaned and bit down on it as I tried to keep breathing.

"Lucius?" Sophia's voice carried down the hallway.

Cal popped his head up and winked at me. "I'll taste the rest soon enough."

He stood, and I wrenched the blankets back in place.

Sophia and Lucius air kissed in the hallway as Cal strode out. "Get ready, we're leaving in ten minutes," he called over his shoulder.

I rolled into the fetal position, holding onto myself because there was nothing else. I wanted to scrub every square inch where Cal had touched me with steel wool. Instead, I gathered my wits and got out of bed. Considering the hot weather, I would have dressed light in a tank top and shorts. Given the twists of the trials, I dressed in layers— tank top, light jacket, jeans, and boots.

Once I'd tucked my knife into my boot, I whipped my hair up into a ponytail. My stark refection in the mirror barely resembled me. What little curves I possessed had turned to muscle, my eyes had grown colder, and my cheeks were almost gaunt. But it was the woman inside who'd changed most of all, to the point where I felt I was looking at a stranger. Would I ever get myself back?

"Stella." Sin stood in the hall, his medium gray suit hitting in all the right places. He didn't even throw me a glance. "Let's go."

I followed him down the stairs and into the breakfast room. Cal held sway over the table, ordering Laura around and discussing the sugar business with Teddy. Sophia met Sin's eyes as we entered and gave him a chilly smile.

I sat, trying to keep calm despite my growing sense of dread. Laura poured me an orange juice and set down a plate of my favorite breakfast—bacon, two eggs over-easy, and fresh fruit. My hand shook so badly I almost knocked my glass over.

Cal smiled. "Calm down, Stella. My goodness. Would you like to sit on my lap? See if that makes you feel any better?"

"Oh Daddy, you're the worst sometimes." Sophia tittered what I assumed was a laugh.

"I was just trying to be nice. Comfort her a bit." He watched me over his coffee cup as I sipped my orange juice.

"What's the plan?" Lucius leaned back in his chair, giving off an air of relaxation.

"We'll be taking the lovely Ms. Rousseau and Sin to an undisclosed location for a little fun. They may be back by nightfall. They may not." Cal shrugged. "So, what wedding plans have we settled on?"

My stomach turned. I forced myself to eat. I couldn't be certain what was in store, but keeping my energy up was key.

Sophia sighed as if shouldering a heavy burden. "We'll have the wedding at our chateau of course. I haven't decided on much else."

"You'll need to get to work as soon as the Acquisition is over. I want some grandsons sooner rather than later."

"Daddy, there will be plenty of time for that." She turned to me. "I hear you'll belong to your stepbrother after the coronation." She simpered. "I hope he treats you as you deserve."

"I hope you choke on your coffee."

"Stella!" Sin slammed his hand on the table. "Apologize."

"And there it is. The fire that's never been snuffed out. Will today be the day?" Cal laughed before turning icy again. "Apologize to my daughter."

I clutched my napkin in my fist and stared at her, hoping she'd fall over dead as I'd said.

Lucius squeezed my knee, and I knew I had to do it.

"I apologize."

"More punishment is needed, to be honest, but we simply don't have the time. I think it's best we be on our way. The guests will be waiting for us." Cal rose, as did the rest at the table.

Lucius waited for me to walk past and fell into step behind me. "You can do this," he whispered as we entered the foyer. I glanced over my shoulder. His light eyes weren't fearful, but they weren't colored with his usual mischief, either.

I gave him a small nod as Sin strode past, Sophia on his arm, and walked onto the front porch.

"Go on, now." Cal shooed me out to the waiting limos. "Stella, honey, ride with me."

"Actually, I apologize, Cal." Sin helped Sophia into the car, her lemon yellow sheath dress perfectly accentuated with narrow floral pumps. "But I did have some business I'd like to discuss. The Cuba conflict brought up some information you'd likely find of interest."

Cal wrinkled his nose and stared at me, as if trying to decide if hurting me was more important than Cuban business deals.

"Fine, fine. Business before pleasure. Besides, I'm sure Sophia would enjoy Stella's company just as much as me." He laughed and slid into the back seat.

Sin shot me a look, his face hard but his eyes warm. *Together.* We would get through this together.

631

I walked around and sank into the backseat next to Sophia. She was speaking fluent French into her phone and paused, craning her head to watch as Sin got into her father's car.

"*Merde!*" She swiped her phone off as the car started moving. "Why?"

"I guess Sin got tired of your sparkling personality." I grinned as she balled up her fists. "Daddy's not here to make me behave, so do me a favor and shut the fuck up for the ride. Sound good? Good." I leaned back and turned my head, watching the oaks recede and the woods encroach.

She fumed beside me and finally found her voice. "I will tell them both that you spoke to me like this. You *will* be punished."

"Then I'll tell your father you've been fucking Ellis. So go ahead, be a bitch. See where that gets you." I raised my voice as she sputtered. "Hey, can we get some music back here? I don't think I can even stand listening to her breathe."

The chauffeur raised his eyebrows at Sophia and she stammered out "f-fine."

The music rose, classical and airy, as we hit the main highway. Sophia didn't speak for the rest of the trip. It was only a small victory, but it was mine.

CHAPTER TWENTY-FOUR
STELLA

THE JOURNEY ENDED AT a sprawling Tudor mansion surrounded by a lush lawn dotted with shade trees. No gate stopped entry from the main road, but a guard stood at the ready to check our credentials. Several cars hemmed us in as we approached the mansion.

We pulled through the roundabout and stopped in front of the massive dark wood doors as people climbed the shallow front steps. I opened my door, happy to be away from Sophia's presence. Sin and Cal walked up behind us, Cal greeting everyone in his usual jovial manner. He stationed himself outside the doors and waved us through.

"Whose house is this?" The interior was dark. Heavy curtains and old, faded paintings gave it an 18th century feel.

"Judge Montagnet's." Sin took my arm as Ellis walked up to Sophia. The two of them slipped into a side room.

Sin led me toward a bar set up in a stuffy sitting area. The room wasn't large enough to hold the number of people, and we had to wade past several well-wishers and gawkers before making it to the bar.

"How was your car ride?" Sin pointed to a bottle and held two fingers up. It should have come off as rude, but seemed more authoritative than anything else.

"Blissfully quiet."

He snorted. "What did you do?"

"Nothing." I snagged a strawberry from the nearest serving platter and bit into it, the cold, sweet juice running down my throat.

The barman poured two reds and handed them over.

"What's this?" I sniffed, the odor strong and almost bitter.

"Port." He tipped his glass, and I took a sip, the flavor overpowering.

"That's kind of intense." I shook my head and set my glass down.

He smiled and drained his.

Was it always like this? Us talking like two normal people in a normal house surrounded by normal guests? We couldn't be further from reality.

Sin set his glass on the bar and leaned close. "Have you found him?"

"No." I scanned the crowd, looking for a particular server.

"Let's mingle. Maybe you'll see him."

I pulled the card with Sin's cell number and instructions from my pocket and lodged it in my palm. Following him through the throng of people, I kept an eye out for the server who'd spoken to me at Fort LaRoux. My hope faded each time a server passed and it wasn't him.

Sin stopped and talked with different groups of people, laughing and joking about the trials. It gave me the opportunity to continue my search. I tried not to meet anyone's eyes, but the occasional guest leered at me or tried to touch me. Sin moved us along to prevent any scenes and to keep the too-eager at bay.

We'd made the circuit through the room with no luck.

"He's not here."

"He has to be. Let's keep looking." Sin pulled me along behind him through the crush of bodies.

My name whipped through the surrounding crowd as the guests voiced their ugly thoughts. I ignored them and focused on finding the one friendly face.

We wound around through another sitting area, a library, and past the door to the kitchen.

"Stop. Let me look in there."

Sin glanced around at the almost-empty back hall. "Make it quick."

I pushed through the door and darted to the side as a server with a tray full of crawfish barreled past. The kitchen was all sound and smells—too many people cooking, chopping, and layering food onto trays. Everything was stainless steel, and the room was almost unbearably hot. I peered at the workers, hoping to see him.

There. He was busy adding garnish to a platter full of bacon-wrapped scallops. I bypassed someone flaming up a pan on a wide range and several servers carrying trays. A man in a high chef's hat stood toward the rear of the kitchen barking orders. Something told me I didn't want to be noticed by him.

I stood at the server's elbow. "Hi."

His brown eyes met mine and his fingers stilled. "I remember you. You okay?"

"Yes. I think the guests said they wanted more of the bruschetta." I pressed the card into his hand and turned.

"O-okay. I'll get right on that." I didn't look back as I slipped out the door.

"Success," I whispered as Sin took my hand and led me back to the foyer. He glanced to the sweeping stairs to the second floor, wider at the bottom than the top, as people climbed.

I took the lead and joined the steady stream, approaching my destiny step-by-step and surrounded on all sides.

The second floor gave way to a series of rooms down the hall on the left and a walkway overlooking the foyer to the right. I followed the crowd to the right until the tight corridor opened into a ballroom almost as big as the one at the Oakman Estate. Wide, sunny windows looked out on the swath of green lawn, and chandeliers glowed warmly overhead.

Plush couches and chairs were situated around a raised platform only a few feet off the ground. A single metal chair sat atop it, open shackles attached the arms and legs. My knees tried to give way and my heart faltered, but Sin pushed me farther along until we stood in front of one of the windows. Other guests walked past and chose their seats.

"Keep it together." He lifted my shirt and pressed his palm to my lower back.

The contact helped, and just knowing we were a team made it more bearable somehow. I lowered my head to focus on breathing, and also to keep the chair from my view. Would I go first? Would my skin feel the initial bite of the metal as the crowd roared and salivated for my blood?

He rubbed my back slowly enough that no one would notice. He even shook hands with a few people, all the while soothing me. I focused on thoughts of Teddy. The pain would keep him alive. His fate was in my hands, and I couldn't break now.

"Ms. Rousseau?" Judge Montagnet's bony fingers wrapped around my elbow. "Welcome to my home. I hope you enjoy your stay." He smiled, his face striated with each year of his horrible existence. "Sin. Doing well, I heard. Just one more task. Cal told me his plans for the day. Exciting." He scratched his ear. "It should make for one hell of a show. Best of luck. I've got my money on you, young lady."

I forced my mouth to stay shut, but every vile curse I'd ever learned swirled on the tip of my tongue. Control was imperative if I were to succeed, and I couldn't let this ghoul shake mine.

Sin gripped his shoulder. "Thanks, Judge. I'm glad for your support."

He smiled, and then moved into the rows to sit next to a young man in servant's attire. He couldn't have been more than twenty. The judge's hand darted between his legs, and the man stared at the ceiling, as if he switched himself off. I turned away and caught Gavin staring at me from across the room.

His lips creased, a fraction of a smile for me. I did the same, letting him know I was here and that we would get through this. Guilt pounded in my veins as I scanned the crowd for Brianne. I spotted her sitting in Red's lap as he chatted with some people. Her face was blank. No words passed her lips, and her skin hung from her bones.

"Don't look at her. It wasn't your fault." Sin kept easing his hand back and forth.

"She blames me."

"She's foolish. She should blame everyone in this room except you and Gavin."

"Even you?"

He nodded. "Even me."

I wanted to pull him close and tell him he wasn't bad, that he didn't suffer from the same evil that infected these people. He wouldn't believe me. The scars on the back of his hand and the ones in his heart were too old, too thick for me to break through completely. But I would keep working until he saw his own light, his own goodness.

A too-loud laugh crackled through the room, and Cal bounded up to the platform.

"Ladies and gents—this thing on?" He tapped the microphone until feedback kicked in. "Ladies—ah that's better—and gents, welcome to the final Acquisition trial!"

Whoops and yells went up from the crowd as Cal smiled and turned in an appraising circle.

"We've had some *stiff* competition this year—looking at you, Judge." He pointed to Montagnet, and the room erupted in laughter as my blood turned to acid.

"I don't think I've ever seen a stronger slate of competitors. The highlights—Stella's whipping, Gavin's time in the woods, and Brianne's mother. Could we have wished for a better year?"

"No!" The crowd roared.

"That's right. *So* right. On to the delights of the day.

637

The theme for this trial, as we all know, is love. This is my favorite one, because I love all of you." He kissed his palm and spun around to blow it to the entire audience as they laughed. "I do. Same faces I grew up with, here supporting me as my reign slowly comes to a glorious end. I appreciate you all and look forward to many, many more fabulous years."

More applause and yells erupted before Cal put his hand out to quiet them down.

"But you know, love is a two-sided coin." He pulled a quarter from his pocket and flipped it into the air, catching it with ease. "And on the other side—" He held the coin up. "—is hate. Now, without further ado, let's get started! Sin, Red, Bob—come on up with your Acquisitions."

Sin dropped his hand and straightened my shirt. I lurched forward, the floor seeming to give way under my feet. Dizziness swirled through me as he took my elbow and led me through the seating area and to the platform. To the chair.

"That's it. Come on, come on." Cal waved us up to stand beside him.

I edged closer to Sin who stood rigid and still. Brianne was already crying, her sunken eyes clenched shut and her nose running. Gavin stared at me, his eyes warm but tired. His clothes fit loosely now, the Acquisition taking a toll on him just like Brianne and me.

"You three—Sin, Red, Bob—have pleased me beyond my wildest dreams. You made excellent choices of whom to acquire. You've put them through their paces. I couldn't be prouder. Show them some *love*." Cal held his hand out as if he were displaying a prize on a game show as the audience responded with thunderous clapping and crowing.

"Perfect. Now, perhaps I'm getting a bit old fashioned, but I believe that if you truly love something, you will suffer for it. You will do what you must to keep it safe. Nurture it. Never harm it—well, unless she asks for it. Am I right?" Chuckles rose from the crowd as he went on. "So I've created a special task for this final trial. It's going to be a surprise for our competitors."

He snapped his fingers. Three attendants rushed to the stage. "Go with them. All three of you have separate rooms. Wait there until I send for you. And no peeking. I don't want anything ruining the surprise."

Sin and I dropped off the platform and followed an attendant out of the ballroom. The doors to the ballroom closed once Brianne, Gavin, Red, and Bob stood in the hallway with us. The attendants herded us back across the walkway over the foyer and down to the end of the far hall. We were divided among three rooms, and an attendant took position outside our door as it swung shut.

"That chair." I rushed into Sin's arms. "Oh, god." My voice caught, and I fought away tears. Not here. I wouldn't cry here. Not until the pain was too great and I couldn't take it anymore.

"Stella." He put his palm to my face, and I realized it was trembling. "The chair. They'll make me hurt you."

"I know." I looked into his wild eyes as he scanned the room, like an animal seeking escape through the bars of a cage. But we were in a bedroom, high on the second floor. "Hey." I got on my tiptoes. "We can do this."

"I don't think I can bear it." He scooped me into his arms and sat on the bed.

"We can."

He rocked me and rested his lips in my hair. It was as if I could feel him coming apart beneath me, the layers of armor he usually wore stripping away until a broken boy stood there, begging me to save him.

"You don't understand. I can't hurt you again."

"Shh." I scooted so I sat upright in his lap and pressed my lips to his. "When this is over, I will still love you. Nothing will ever keep me from loving you."

"Don't say that." He glanced to the window again. "You don't know what's going to happen."

"I know they won't make you kill me or maim me. It's

639

against the rules to do it to an Acquisition, right? And anything else, I'll heal from it. Sin, please just look at me."

He brought his tortured gaze back to mine.

"I'll be alive on the other side. I'll be with you. Do it for Teddy."

He didn't respond, only pulled me to him. We sat in silence for over an hour. I thought I heard footsteps and the doors close from the adjoining rooms, but I couldn't be certain.

Random bits of noise filtered down from the ballroom, but not enough for us to have an inkling of what was going on. After another two hours had passed, our door opened. Sin set me on my feet as the attendant motioned for us to follow him back to the ballroom.

We entered, and the coppery scent of blood surrounded us.

"Our final competitor at last. Come on up."

My feet didn't want to move, but Sin pushed me forward roughly. He was back in character, which was a good sign, though I feared how he'd react when he had to hurt me.

"Oh, Stella." Cal pulled me into his side. "Have I mentioned that I have a thing for redheads?"

The crowd laughed as I stared at the blood on the platform, red streaks on the chair, and what looked like a tooth on the smooth ballroom floor. My stomach heaved, and I vomited. Cal backed up as it splashed onto the floor, and the ladies in the front row all broke out their fans.

"Clean this up." Cal motioned over some attendants who used dirty, bloody towels to mop up my mess. He slapped my ass. "Feeling better? Where was I? Right. The final show. Bring the goodies over."

An attendant wheeled a small cart to the edge of the platform. It was littered with various tools—some bloody, some untouched, and none of them pleasant. Sin's eyes were wide, terror written there like I'd never seen before.

Cal continued talking, the speakers booming his voice

across the crowd. "You can do this," I whispered to Sin.

He met my eyes and calmed as I held his gaze, his face returning to its cold mask. To show him I could take it, I stepped to the chair and sat down, resting my wrists in the shackles.

Cal turned around. "Oh, no, no darling Stella. The chair is for Sin."

CHAPTER TWENTY-FIVE
STELLA

I SHOOK MY HEAD, my ears ringing as if a bomb had gone off.

"Look, she doesn't believe me." Cal laughed and took my hand, ripping me up from the chair. "See? Not you, gorgeous." He turned to Sin. "You."

The room fell silent as Sin looked down his nose at Cal. Then he smirked and whipped off his jacket.

The crowd cheered as Sin sat down with dramatic flair and placed his wrists and ankles in the restraints.

"Could you at least tell her to go easy on my face? A, it's a handsome face, and B, I want to look good enough to marry your daughter."

Cal roared with laughter as an attendant snapped Sin's shackles closed. "You are one cheeky asshole, you know that?"

I rested my hand on the back of his chair. Maybe it would stop the room from spinning. Sin tilted his head back and met my eyes. A quick nod, and then he was facing forward again, smiling.

"You amaze me, Counsellor. You really do. Do you have any idea how Bob quaked and cried? How much Red begged Brianne to go easy on him? Did she go easy on him, y'all?"

The crowd laughed, and several cries of "no" rang out.

"Indeed, she did not. It seems Red underestimated her. But here's the rules. Stella can visit any harm upon you she sees fit, with any of these tools I have at her disposal. Like I said, love and hate, same coin. You understand, right Sin?"

"I understand that you better have lunch ready when I get out of these restraints. I'm going to work up a real appetite." Sin's voice, confidence dripping from the words, boomed over the crowd without the benefit of a microphone.

"Damn. That's my man. I'd like to shake your hand right now." He glanced to the shackles at Sin's wrists. "Too bad on that one, my friend." Cal smiled. "Rules are simple, Stella. You can't kill him. He can't lose parts."

"The same rules." I gripped the back of the chair harder.

"Exactly, the same rules. It's up to you. Have your revenge. All I ask is that you make it good enough for our entertainment. Brianne and Gavin sure did." With that, he hopped off the platform and took a seat between two redheads, throwing an arm around each of them.

The room quieted until I could hear my breath, the steady pump of blood in my ears. I walked around to Sin's front.

"Do your fucking worst, cunt." He flashed his eyes at me. No fear. Instead, relief sat in the crease of his mouth, the turn of his chin.

"Damn. I love this guy." Cal stage-whispered.

So do I. I stepped down to the cart of tools. I clasped my hands in front of me, my fingers shaking and frozen.

"Pssst."

I turned toward the sound. Dylan sat two rows back, leering at me. I ignored him and went back to perusing the weapons. A scalpel was coated with blood, and a larger pocket knife was, too. The claw hammer had bloody fingerprints along the handle, and a vicious-looking set of needles sat neatly to the side.

"Come on, Stella." Cal's tone lost some of its showman quality, impatience seeping through. "I'm beginning to feel a bit peckish. It's after lunch. Get to work."

I glanced up to Sin. His face was calm, his body relaxed. This felt right to him. He was used to someone he loved bringing him pain. Not just the back of his hand, but the wounds that went so much deeper. He was calm in the face of what he knew, that love was pain. Would I be that to him? Someone he trusted who ultimately made him suffer because of the Acquisition?

I backed away from the cart. "No. I won't."

"Stella." Sin leaned forward. "Do it."

"No."

Cal stood. "Why on earth not?"

"I can't." I lowered my head.

"Stella!" Sin barked. "Do it now!"

I stared at the bloody floor.

"Oh, dear me. This is a problem. Stella, doll, look at me." Cal put his finger under my chin and brought my face up to his. "If you don't do this, you'll take his place. Is that what you want?"

I shook, my teeth chattering as my body trembled.

"Stella. Stop this prideful refusal or I swear that I will beat you again as soon as we leave here!"

"Sin, she just doesn't have the stomach for it. Totally understandable." He turned back to me. "Now, it's up to you. Either you take your revenge on Sin—the one who stole you, who whipped you, who let his brother rape you—or you let me take my aggressions out on you."

Sin growled and his shackles rattled. "Stella. Do as I say." It was a harsh command, but I felt the fear in it.

I wouldn't hurt him. Showing him that love didn't always end that way—with pain and torment—was more important to me than an hour of suffering. I took a deep breath, and exhaled only one word.

"No."

"You heard the lady. Unlock Sin and put her in his

place." Cal began to roll up the sleeves of his dress shirt.

"Goddammit, Stella. Do it!"

"Too late now. I appreciate your efforts to make a good showing, Sin. I sure do. But I suspect Stella and I will make the best showing of all." He plucked at my jacket. "Go ahead and take your top off. I want more canvas to work with."

"No!" Sin pushed the attendant away and dropped down to the floor. "Stella, don't."

"I have to." I couldn't meet his eyes.

"No, I can take it."

"I know you can." I looked up at him, his brow furrowed. "But you shouldn't have to," I whispered.

"Enough chit chat. Let's get going." Cal ripped me away and pushed me up onto the stand.

Sin grabbed Cal's arm and whipped him around. He pulled his fist back.

"Sin!" I cried.

He turned to me, his fist still cocked, and I shook my head. *Teddy*, I mouthed.

"What do you think you're doing?" Cal recovered from his defensive posture and shoved Sin away.

"Sorry Sovereign. I guess I just hoped I'd get to do it myself is all." Sin opened his fist and dropped his arms to his side.

Cal considered him for a moment, the room tense. Then he rolled his shoulders and smiled. "All worked up, eh? Good man." He motioned to the redheads on the couch. "Sit with the girls and enjoy yourself, but not too much. He's taken, ladies. Stella, why's your shirt still on?"

He climbed to the platform and yanked my jacket off my shoulders. Gripping my tank top at my chest, he ripped it apart in one harsh movement and threw the tatters to the ground. I couldn't stop the squeak of fear that caught in my throat. He didn't stop, only slid my bra straps off my shoulders. "Unhook it." His voice was thick with lust.

I reached behind my back, but my fingers were too

numb to do anything.

"Allow me." He hugged me to him and undid the clasp. My bra dropped to the floor and I crossed my arms over my breasts. "Have a seat."

I backed up and sank down into the chair, the sticky blood of its last occupant coating the bottom of my arms. Cal knelt down and locked me in. I trembled and closed my eyes.

"Girls, I said go easy. He's engaged."

"Sorry." One of them giggled as a sharp sting erupted across my cheek.

Cal's hand turned into a blur as he slapped me again and again until I tried to loll my head forward to stop his attacks.

"Hold her head."

An attendant climbed up behind me and grabbed a fistful of my hair, pulling my head back so I had no choice but to see Cal.

"That was just foreplay." He balled his hand into a fist, his eyes sharp and focused. "Let's go all the way."

CHAPTER TWENTY-SIX
SINCLAIR

HER STRENGTH FAILED, HER will dissipated, and no more screams passed her lips. Even when Cal took a scalpel and sliced across her left breast, she remained silent, her eyes open, though no spark lit them.

The whores on either side of me had finally given up trying to entertain me. All I could see was Stella, suffering in front of me while I sat in comfort. I only remained still because of her. She'd committed fully, sacrificing herself for Teddy. I had to see it through. For her.

The devils surrounding me would pay, but I couldn't take comfort in the promise of violence.

I had never prayed in my life. Perhaps when I'd been younger, before Brazil. But at no time in recent memory. I prayed as Cal hit her, lashed her body with his belt, split her lip and broke her nose. I prayed he would stop. I prayed she would recover. And I prayed for their deaths. The litany was on a loop in my mind, and it was the only thing that kept me sane.

Cal continued his expansive carving, ending the cut on her stomach at the edge of her jeans. He stood back and admired his handiwork as her blood oozed from the sweeping curved lines. Wiping the sweat from his brow with a bloodied sleeve, he stepped down from the platform. The attendant let Stella's chin drop to her chest.

"I think my masterpiece is done. What do you all say?" He scrubbed the blood from his hands with a towel as the crowd cheered, though their zest had died down over the hour of torture.

"Thank you. I take pride in my work. We have a delightful lunch prepared downstairs. Please make your way down, and I'll be there shortly after I get cleaned up. Don't worry, I still have enough left in me to carve the roast." He grinned and bowed as the applause swelled once again, and the guests began to leave.

Stella didn't move even as the attendant unbuckled her manacles. She sat as if she were still tied down.

"Sin, let's chat."

I finally stood, but forced my feet to take me to Cal instead of Stella. Everything inside me screamed and demanded vengeance.

Instead of snapping Cal's neck, I smiled. "Good work. You certainly have a knack."

"I knew you'd appreciate my art." He finished wiping the blood from his mouth, the bite marks along Stella's right breast and upper arms still red and angry.

Once the final guest left, Cal clapped me on the back. "What's it feel like to be the next Sovereign?"

"So, you've chosen?" I scrubbed a hand down my face, my relief for Teddy doing nothing to ease the burden weighing down on my mind, my heart.

"No, she chose." He pointed at Stella who sat like a pool of water, flat and motionless.

I peered into his taciturn eyes. "I'm not sure I follow."

He sank onto the nearest chair and let out an exhausted sigh. He stalled, wanting to provide more theatrics. I was desperate to grab Stella and run with her, get her help and save her. But, as she'd done from the moment I met her, she'd saved me, instead.

"The theme of the final trial is love for a reason. Every trial has its purpose. As Sovereign, you will tell your

650

competitors that the purpose in the end is to break their Acquisition, to be the worst son of a bitch south of the Mason-Dixon."

"Yes?" I wanted to know. I wanted Stella more. The quicker Cal explained, the quicker I could get her out of here.

"That's not the trick of it, in the end. Think about it. Your mother, for example. She had a special relationship with her Acquisition. Still does, am I correct?"

"Yes." My gaze flickered to Stella, who remained impassive.

"You won't remember my Acquisition. She certainly had a special place in her heart for me. Redhead. Anyway—"

"Yes?" My impatience overflowed.

"She chose you. You who whipped her, allowed her to be raped, made her fight to the death, forced her through so many horrors. But still, she chose you. She chose to take your beating. Usually, the winner of this trial is the one whose Acquisition does the least damage to the Acquirer. No one knows that except the Sovereign of course, and it's a closely guarded secret."

I pinched the bridge of my nose. "What are you saying?"

"I'm saying the fact that you were able to mistreat Stella beyond all bounds of cruel and unusual, but that she is *still* loyal and protective, makes you the winner. She went one step further and actually took your punishment." He raised his eyebrows in chagrin. "That is unprecedented in trial history. You made her fall in love with you, even though you tortured her and even though she knew you could never love a peasant like her. You have twisted and broken not only her body, but her mind, her spirit. That's the sort of strength we need as Sovereign. Congratulations."

No wonder Mother had won. Renee was devoted to her. How had I never seen it as the key?

He rose and popped his neck. "The coronation will be

651

in a month at my estate. I'll take delivery of Stella then, as well."

"Delivery?"

"Oh, yes, forgot to mention. I'm taking Stella for a week or two before giving her to Dylan. I enjoyed our time today, but I want more of a private session. You don't mind, do you?"

My hands demanded I choke the life out of him. "No, of course not. I will turn her over then."

"Good man. I'm very pleased about your elevation, and I'll let Sophia know. Just keep it under wraps until coronation day. You know I love surprises." He grinned and turned to leave. "You coming to lunch? We don't want to start off on the wrong foot."

"I'll be down in a moment. Just want to get her handled so she doesn't bleed all over my suit."

"You are such a dandy." Cal laughed and walked out. As soon as he was gone, I jumped up to Stella and wrapped her in my suit coat.

When I picked her up, her head lolled back, her eyes still a glassy green. My chest burned as if my heart was being dipped in a vat of acid.

"Stella?"

She didn't respond.

"Stella, please."

Still no words as a tear rolled down her cheek. No, not hers. Another one landed at the corner of her lips, mixing with the blood there before moving down to her jaw. I blinked hard. My tears. The idea was so foreign to me. I hadn't shed a tear since Brazil, and now the floodgates were opened. Tears flowed down my face as I clutched her to me, her bloodied and broken body drawing breath but otherwise devoid of life.

I rushed through the ballroom and kicked the doors open, knocking an attendant on his ass as I rushed past. It seemed like days had passed since we'd been in the bedroom at the end of the hall, waiting to meet our fate. I pushed through the door and lay her on the bed.

"Is she okay?" Gavin walked in behind me.

"Get the fuck out." I picked the bloody strands of hair away from her busted nose and tried to gauge what sort of medical attention she needed. Not that I could give her any. I had to show my face downstairs. *Fuck!*

"There's a medic next door, fixing Bob up. I can get her in here."

"Get her. Now. Bob can wait." I turned back to her. "Stella, can you say something?"

She hadn't blinked. He'd hit her in the head so many times. I wanted to scream and rage and burn the entire fucking house to the ground. But I had no right. I'd just sat there, the whores pawing at my dick as Stella took hit after hit. For me. "Oh god, Stella, please."

"Move away from her." A woman's harsh voice cut through my misery. She wore bloody scrubs and had a flowery carrying case in one hand. "I said move."

"Can you help her?"

"Up. Go."

I stood, but wouldn't leave.

She pushed past me and inspected Stella's face, then opened my jacket and looked at the bloody wounds along her torso. "Jesus. At least she's not the worst I've seen today."

She set her bag on the bed and dug out a syringe. "Night night." She hit a vein, no problem, and let the meds fly.

Stella's eyes finally closed, and I was back in my mother's room as she screamed and railed until I drugged her to sleep. "Not her, please not Stella."

"I'll need to set her nose, clean her wounds, and bandage her up. Some of these cuts could use stitches, but stitches aren't my specialty." She dug several implements from her bag, including alcohol, gauze, tape, and what looked like a tongue depressor. "I tend to leave ugly scars. So if in doubt, I'll leave them out."

"Will she be okay?" Gavin stood at my elbow. I'd forgotten he was there.

"Mister." She shook her head, her black braids swaying. "I've seen some fucked up shit today that I hope I never see again for as long as I live. No amount of money is worth this. Don't ask me stupid questions like that."

She got to work as I stood glued to the spot.

"Why is she hurt?" Gavin shoved me back. "Why? I beat Bob unconscious. Brianne had to be pulled off Red. But you stand here without a scratch."

"Get off me." I couldn't see Stella.

"No. Tell me why!" He shoved harder until my back hit the fireplace.

I swung hard and fast, my fist crunching into his cheek. He fell away, and I rushed forward to Stella again as the medic dabbed her wounds with alcohol.

"Stella, please." I rested my hand on her shin.

"Motherfucker." Gavin got to his feet and brought his fists up.

The medic turned a harsh eye on both of us. "If you two are going to fight, get the fuck out. The last thing this poor girl needs is more violence."

I didn't give Gavin so much as a glance. "Don't try to keep me from her. I'll kill you." It wasn't a threat, only a simple fact. If he tried to come between Stella and me again, I'd pound his face into a bloody pulp.

"Mr. Vinemont?" Someone spoke from the hall.

"What?" I couldn't take my eyes off Stella as the medic wrapped a blood pressure cuff around her arm.

"Mr. Oakman is asking for you."

I ground my teeth so hard I thought they might crack.

"I'll stay here with her." Gavin walked around the bed and sat next to her, taking one of her bloodied hands in his.

I wanted to kill him, to show Stella I could protect her. But that's what he was doing. Protecting her. I'd failed. I'd watched it all. I'd done nothing.

"Go." He didn't look at me when he spoke. He blamed me.

He was right to. I was at fault for all of it.

I stared, wanting to will some sort of comfort into her as the medic listened for her heartbeat. I rubbed my eyes.

"Mr. Vinemont?"

"I fucking heard you." I whirled and walked to the door, but turned back before going through. "Don't let anyone touch her or hurt her while I'm away."

Gavin caught my gaze, hatred written in the narrowing of his eyes. "She'll be safe as long as you're gone."

I turned and left. The worst part was that he was right.

CHAPTER TWENTY-SEVEN
STELLA

THE HOT BREEZE ROCKED the swing as I watched Lucius and Teddy toss a football back and forth in the yard. I stretched my arms above my head, ignoring the burn of pain that still sizzled from my healing wounds. Sin came out the front door, two glasses in his hands. He passed one to me, and I sipped as he settled next to me.

He pulled me gently into his side. "It's not too hot out here, is it?"

"No. I'm glad to be out of the house." I rested my head against his shoulder.

"Go long!" Lucius pointed to the tree line.

"I am long," Teddy called back.

"Longer than that, asshole. I can throw farther than a peewee league quarterback."

I laughed. Sin laced his fingers through mine as Lucius threw to a distant Teddy. He caught it, but had to dash up a few yards first.

"Fingers slipped." Lucius threw his hands up and turned around to look at us. "Fingers slipped. That's what that was."

"Sure." Sin nodded.

"You want to try it?"

"No." He hadn't left my side since we returned from

657

the trial. I didn't remember much. From what I could tell, my faulty memory was a blessing. My nose was still swollen, and Sin had taken me to a plastic surgeon in New Orleans to repair the cuts. The scars would be barely noticeable, but I would always know they were there.

Sin watched over me day and night during the weeks since the trial, letting his prosecutor position go untended. Sometimes, it was as if he were afraid I'd disappear if he weren't looking right at me.

"Go on and throw the ball around. Show Lucius up." I pulled my hand away. He took it back.

"No."

"Don't want to embarrass him?"

He kissed my forehead. "Exactly."

The days were already growing shorter, the trees casting long shadows over the lawn. Sin rocked us slowly as the sun made its retreat down the sky. After a while, Lucius and Teddy, winded and sweaty, bounded onto the porch and collapsed into the rocking chairs. We chatted as the fireflies began to glow, an intermittent symphony of tiny lights.

"I think I'm going to go see what's cooking for supper." Teddy stood and made a show of rubbing his stomach.

"Try not to fuck her against the stove. It's dangerous." Lucius grinned.

Teddy's cheeks reddened, and he hurried into the house.

"That wasn't very nice." I shook my head at Lucius.

"He'll live."

"Yes, he will." Sin kissed my hair.

Lucius glanced to the door and then back at us. "He's gone now. Let's talk. I have all the goods collected and ready to be rolled into the estate as soon as the gates open."

"Stella, is your guy on the inside ready?"

"Quinlan, yes. I spoke to him earlier. He took the money and hired his own trustworthy people for the job.

They know the score and will get out of dodge when it all goes down. Some of the attendants won't know, but he's promised to keep them out of harm's way when all hell breaks loose."

"How do you know we can trust him?" Lucius asked.

"We don't. But he's an ex-Marine, and his uncle runs a security firm. They're working together on this, and we're paying them both a small fortune. They won't get the money until the job's done."

Lucius seemed appeased and moved on. "The supplies?"

"Already loaded up in the caterer's vans, ready to go."

I'd been over the plan so many times in the past three weeks that it was in my mind like a well-worn path through grass. There was no missing it.

"I still think you should stay here." Sin sighed.

"No." I was going. I didn't care how many times Sin tried to talk me out of it. Besides, it would look fishy if he showed up without Cal's prize.

"Lucius, tell her she should stay."

"You'll get no help from me. She's right. She deserves to be there."

"She deserves more than that. Much more." Sin pulled me into his lap.

Lucius scowled. "If you're doing this, I'm out."

"We'll talk business later." Sin waved him away.

Lucius grumbled and slammed the front door on his way in.

"Are you tired?"

"No." I leaned against him and watched the fireflies spark. "I feel good."

"What hurts?" He ran a hand up and down my thigh, goose bumps rising under the thin material of my pajama pants.

"Nothing."

"Are you sure?"

"Yes. Stop worrying."

He kept rocking us at a leisurely pace. "I'll never stop worrying about you."

"I know, but I'm fine now. I'm healing. I want to get back to painting and walking and riding with you and Teddy. And mainly, I want you to stop feeling guilty." I kissed his neck.

"I don't think I'm capable of that."

"You didn't think you were capable of love, either."

He canted his head to the side, the stubble along his cheeks looking even darker in the low light. "Touché."

"You don't have to be careful with me, you know? I won't break."

"I can't hurt you." He peered down at me, worry wrinkling the skin near his eyes.

I nibbled at his neck. "Take me upstairs."

"No, you're still healing. I can't."

I twined my arms around his neck and pulled myself up to his mouth. I licked along his bottom lip and bit down on it.

"Stella." His voice lowered to a growl. "Don't."

"Make me stop." I kissed him and ran my fingers through his hair, pulling close to the scalp where I knew it would hurt.

He slid his hand up my thigh and gripped my ass, then lifted me so I straddled him. He kissed me hungrily, like he'd been starved for me. I caressed his tongue with mine and moved my hips back and forth over his growing erection.

He dug his fingers into my waist and moved me faster on top of him.

"No." He pulled away. "We can't. You're hurt."

"I'm not." I kissed down his neck.

He gripped the collar of my shirt and pulled it aside, the ugly red scar from Cal's cut curving around my collar bone. "You are."

"It's almost healed. Give this to me. Please?" I dropped my eyes. "Unless you don't find me attractive any longer, now that—"

"Don't be an idiot." He crushed my mouth with his, one of his hands tangling in my hair. Lifting me with ease, he walked to the door, his lips still pressed to mine, his tongue ruling my mouth.

I wrapped my legs around him as he pushed through the door and into the house. Making quick work of the stairs, he carried me to my bedroom and lay me down.

He pulled his shirt over his head. I stared at the broad expanse of his chest, the masculine V of his torso. I took the hem of my shirt and started to pull it, but he stayed my hands with his.

"I want to do it." He pushed my shirt up slowly, dropping soft kisses along my skin with each inch he exposed.

By the time he reached my breasts, I was clutching his hair and arching my back. He kissed around the bottoms of each, keeping his slow pace. He paid extra attention to my scars, his breath tickling me as his mouth sealed his love to my skin.

He kissed my nipples, still taking his time as my shirt moved higher and higher until he pulled it over my head and tossed it to the floor. His eyes were reverent as he kissed my lips with the same soft pressure he'd used on the rest of me. My thighs were on fire, and I wanted him, all of him.

He ended the kiss too soon and dropped to his knees, pulling my pants and panties off. Starting at my toes, he kissed up each leg. The gentle caresses multiplied and reverberated through my body until all I could think of was him.

Spreading my legs, he lay his palms flat against my inner thighs. His warm breath grazed my pussy, and he kissed my bare skin, up and down until no spot was left untouched. I jolted when he slipped his tongue inside me.

He hesitated. "Is it all right?"

"Better than all right. Please don't stop."

He gave me the devious smile—the one I once loathed and now loved—before diving back down. His stubble scraped against my thighs as he licked me from entrance to clit. I moaned at the overwhelming rush of sensation. He did it again and put his hands under my ass, lifting me to his face as he devoured me.

I clutched the blanket as he licked and sucked, his tongue darting inside me and then swirling around my clit. He groaned into me as I spread my legs wider, my body opening for him. He wrapped his lips around my tight nub and sucked.

I raised up on my elbows and met his eyes as he shook his head back and forth, his lips rubbing against me and his scruff prickling my most sensitive skin.

"Sin." I gasped and let my head fall back as he attacked my clit with his tongue again.

When he sank a finger inside me, I dropped back down on the bed. When he added another, I worked them like they were his cock. My hips moved to his rhythm, a slave to his fingers, his wicked mouth. I tensed as he gave me no quarter, every move designed to send me rushing over the edge and into the deep abyss of pleasure below.

My hips jerked, and I came, the release exploding through me as I rubbed myself against his mouth. His name rolled through me on a moan as my pussy convulsed again and again, the orgasm thumping through me as he continued fucking me with his fingers.

When I relaxed back onto the bed, he crawled on top of me and ran his fingers around my lips. I sucked them, licking myself off him before he kissed me and shared the taste. He rested his weight on his elbows, careful not to crush me. I didn't want careful or tentative. I wanted Sin.

"Fuck me." I yanked on his hair for good measure as he kissed to my neck.

"Stella, I'm warning you."

I pulled harder until he met my eyes. "Don't warn me. Fuck me."

He tangled a hand in my hair and pulled until I had to arch my back. "Is this what you want?"

"Yes."

He ran his lips down my throat and bit. "This?"

"Yes."

He thrust his hips against me. "This?"

"Yes, please."

He stood and removed his belt, tossing it on the bed next to me. Then he freed his cock and crawled back on top of me. When his tip hit my clit, I moaned and tried to kiss him. He pulled away and grabbed his belt.

"Hands together, over your head."

I arched an eyebrow. "No."

"Stella." His voice was gravel as he rested his weight on me and wrenched my hands above my head. He looped the belt around my wrist and pulled tight, then kept the slack in his hand. He kissed me hard, the way I remembered— the way I wanted.

I spread my legs as wide as possible, and he slid his tip down to my entrance.

He blinked and hesitated. "Am I hurting you?"

"Not enough," I breathed.

"Fuck, you were made for me." He thrust inside me halfway, pulled out, and then slid all the way in as I moaned.

He reached under me and lifted, moving me to one of the bed posters, his cock still inside me. He wrapped the free end of the belt around the wood and tied it in a loose knot. Then he yanked my hips down, the knot tightening and holding me in place as his cock surged even deeper inside me.

"I didn't want to hurt you." He settled on top of me and pumped slow and deep.

"I trust you."

He kissed me, just a taste. "I never want to lose that trust."

"You won't."

"I don't want you to go to the coronation. If I lost you, I don't know what I'd do."

"You aren't going to lose me." I captured his lips,

kissing away his fear as he thrusted harder.

His tongue warred with mine, and he picked up his pace, making my pussy grow tighter with each impact. I raised my hips so every surge of friction caught my clit. He slid an arm under me and wrapped his fingers around my shoulder, taking complete control as he fucked me hard, finally taking what was his.

I moaned as he kissed to my neck and palmed my breast. He squeezed and then pinched my nipple as I pulled at my restraints. It was useless. I wanted to be caught.

"You're everything to me." He buried his face in my neck and nipped at my earlobe. "I can't be without you ever again. Promise me."

My heart—the one that had been betrayed, broken, and abused—suddenly beat with renewed purpose. I lived for him, for a life together outside the world of the Acquisition.

"I promise."

"Thank you." He dropped kisses along my jaw. His eyes glittered in the dim light as he took my mouth and ran his hand to where we were joined.

His thumb found my clit, and I lit up, every cell in my body focused on his movements. He swallowed my moan and stroked me insistently, demanding I come with each swipe of his thumb. My body tensed, the wave cresting. He must have felt it—he sped faster, his cock filling me again and again until my body gave in, my legs shaking and my hips locking as I came.

He groaned into my mouth and pressed deep inside, his cock kicking as I milked him, my orgasm rolling like waves crashing on the shore.

"Sin." I panted. My thoughts flew away, and he was the only one left.

He thrust once more and rested his head on the bed next to mine.

"I love you." His words were barely a whisper, but they spoke to me in a way nothing else ever could.

CHAPTER TWENTY-EIGHT
STELLA

FARNS SHUFFLED INTO THE breakfast room, his pace growing slower each day. Even as his age turned to infirmity, he refused to retire and simply live at the house. Though I wasn't sure if the earth might spin off its axis if Farns wasn't up at daybreak, dressed in crisp attire, and setting the house to rights from front to back.

"A messenger brought this." He handed a piece of parchment to Sin. The oak seal was unmistakable. Cal.

He broke the wax and unfolded the missive, his brows drawing down with each line he read.

"What?" Lucius glanced to the hall. "Say it before Teddy gets in here."

"All the last-borns have to attend the coronation. Even Teddy." Sin tossed the paper down on the table and leaned back in his chair, the heels of his palms against his eyes.

"Oh, god, we can't keep it from him." My appetite vanished, and I flinched when I heard Teddy's steps on the stairs.

"No, we can't. And I thought Cal would let him stay away. Fuck. We'll have to make adjustments."

Lucius pushed his chair back and rose. "I'll get in touch with Quinlan, let him know we'll have one more on the list."

"Do it." Sin nodded and gripped the arms of his chair.

Lucius disappeared toward the study as Teddy walked in. He wore a Led Zeppelin t-shirt and jeans riddled with holes. He yawned and stretched his arms over his head as he approached.

He was the heart of the family, a pure soul. Would the knowledge of the trials hurt him? I knew it would. I only hoped it wouldn't destroy him.

Sin grimaced, dread shrouding his features.

"Sin." I took his hand. "Let me. Go with Lucius and get the plan straightened out. I'll do this part."

"What part? What plan?" Teddy sat beside me.

Sin squeezed my fingers. "Are you sure?"

"Yes. I think it'll be better. Go on."

He rose and kissed me on the forehead before walking out, his steps stiff, worry sitting heavy on his shoulders.

"What is it now? Something bad?" The sleepiness had fled from Teddy's eyes, and only fearfulness remained.

How could I explain? I had to keep him grounded, give him just enough knowledge to know the score, but not too many details.

I began where it all started, where it would make the most sense. "There are seven rules to the Acquisition."

He paled. "It must be really bad if you're going to tell me."

"I have to." I took his hand and pressed it between my palms. "I don't want to, but Cal has demanded your presence at the coronation. So you're going to find out some things. I'd rather tell you now. Just the two of us. And I-I'm afraid. So I'll need you to help me. I don't want it to change you or hurt you."

"Tell me. I can take it." He scooted his chair back and pulled mine around so we faced each other. "No matter what, I'll deal."

"The first rule, and the only one you truly need to know." I cleared my throat and gripped his hand tight. "Is that if an Acquirer loses, he has to kill the last-born of his line."

Teddy knit his brows together for a split-second before his eyes widened and his jaw went slack. "Me?"

I nodded. "If Sin were to lose, he would have to sacrifice you as punishment." The words were so harsh, so steeped in evil, but they had to be said.

He shook his head, disbelief and shock in the slow back and forth movement. "Oh, god. No wonder. No fucking wonder. And all this time, I've been blaming him."

"And you?" His eyes watered. "How long have you known? What did they do to you? What have you gone through for me?"

I leaned forward and pulled him to me, wrapping him in a hug as the pain washed over him like a pelting spring rain. "I would do it again if it meant keeping you safe."

A sob rocketed up from his lungs, and he clung to me. "I'm so sorry. God, Stella, I'm so sorry. I don't even know what to…"

"No. It's not your fault. You have to know that. You didn't set any of this up. It isn't your fault. I swear. I love you, and I never wanted you to know."

He shook, sob after sob breaking him down until tears wet my cheeks, too.

"It's okay. Shh." I stroked his hair and whispered what few words of comfort I could.

We sat for a long time as anguish poured from him. I recognized it all, the feelings he cycled through like gears in a car—anger, sorrow, fear, rage. I knew them by heart. I held him as Sin and Lucius milled outside the doorway, their faces set in grim lines of worry.

When Teddy's tears subsided, he let me go and cradled my face with his hands. "Thank you." His voice shook, but his resolve was certain. "Thank you, Stella. I can never repay you. Never."

"You already have." I smiled and wiped his tears away. "That was the bad news. I've got some good news, too."

I motioned for Sin and Lucius to come in.

"Good news?" Teddy rose and embraced Lucius and

then Sin. The three of them stood together, brothers with a bond that could never break.

"Yeah, little brother. This is my favorite part." Lucius cracked his knuckles.

"We're going to kill them all." Sin spoke of mass murder with a gleam in his eye that would have chilled even the stoutest heart.

All I felt was pride. "We are."

"Good." Teddy nodded and stood straighter, the Vinemont steel strengthening his spine just as it did for Sin and Lucius. "I want them to suffer. For Stella. What can I do?"

Sin smirked and clapped him on the back. "I knew it was in there somewhere."

I stared up at them. I was caught in the web, surrounded by three deadly spiders, and there was nowhere else I'd rather be.

"I think that about does it." Tony clicked the tattoo gun off and sat back. "I can easily say this is the best work I've ever done. Here." He handed me a mirror.

Sun filtered through the glass panels in the spa room and lit the ink along my skin. I followed the swirls of vines curving gracefully from my collarbone, across my breast, down to my stomach, and ending with a flourish over my heart. "He's going to love it. Just don't tell him you saw my nipples or things might get ugly."

"Oh, I'm well aware. I could tell that night at the party with the masks."

I peered up at him. "You could?"

He dabbed some ointment along the fresh ink. "Are you kidding? He couldn't take his eyes off you. I thought he might take me out just for touching you. If that wasn't love, then…" He shrugged. "I don't know, maybe it was some sort of unhealthy obsession?"

I smiled. "A little bit of both."

"Sounds about right. He's a strange guy." He met my eyes and hastily continued, "I mean, I dig him. No offense meant."

"None taken. He's definitely strange." I sat up and pulled my t-shirt back on.

He leaned back and twisted one of the piercings in his eyebrow. "You sure you're okay? I know you said you got into a car accident, but the scars I covered—perfectly, I might add—look sort of, I don't know, intentional?"

"Don't worry. No one's hurting me. I promise." I smiled to reassure him. "It was a car accident."

He twisted the loop a few more times before dropping his hand. "Yeah, you seem like the sort of woman who gives as good as she gets." He packed up his tattoo gun. "Anyone else and I'd keep pressing, but I get the feeling you might put a hurting on me if I pry."

"Your instincts are spot on." I kissed him on the cheek. "Send Sin the bill. He'll pay up."

"He always does."

"And I'm glad you'll be far away from here when he sees our little secrets." I'd added in a couple of piercings especially for Sin, ones that he might strangle poor Tony over.

"Me, too." He shuddered, the tattoos along his arms dancing as he cleaned up his work space in the spa room.

I stood and stretched, ignoring the stings along my skin.

"Make sure you follow up with my aftercare instructions," Tony said as I retreated back into the main hallway.

"I'm all over it. Don't worry. And if I'm not, Sin will be."

The boys were in town finalizing preparations. I'd bowed out at the last minute, claiming I needed some "me" time. Sin didn't want to go without me. After a lot of convincing, I eventually shooed him out the door along with Lucius and Teddy. I hated for him to worry, but I was safe at home and wanted the new ink to be a surprise.

Laura bustled around the kitchen as I entered. She'd made a platter for sandwiches, so I fixed a ham and cheese and grabbed some chips from the pantry.

"How's Teddy been the past few days?" I tried to keep my tone nonchalant.

"A little distracted. Otherwise, fine." She hit some buttons on the dishwasher and turned to give me a smile. "You're looking happy today."

"I am. I got Sin a surprise."

"Oh, do tell." She walked over and leaned on the island.

I grinned and put my sandwich down. "Brace yourself."

She smiled and clasped her hands together. "Consider me braced."

I lifted my shirt, and her eyes went wide.

"Did those hurt?"

"Hell, yes, they did." I smoothed my shirt back down and ate some more of my sandwich as Laura stole a few of my chips.

"Do you think Teddy would like it if I did that?"

I laughed. "I'm beginning to think I'm a bad influence on you, and I like it."

A loud thunk sounded in the hallway.

"What was that?" Laura cocked her head to the side.

"I don't know. Stay here." I grabbed a knife from the butcher block and walked into the dining room. I crept to the hall door, holding the knife at the ready. Peeking out, I saw Farns lying in the foyer.

"Oh shit, Laura!" I dropped the knife and ran to Farns. He lay on his side, blood running from a wound on his forehead.

He tried to sit up, but I pushed him down. "Don't

move. Let us look at you."

"No." He pointed up the stairs, and his eyes swam. "Rebecca. Help her."

"Help her?"

Laura knelt and pressed a dishtowel to his forehead.

"Take care of him. I'm going to see about Rebecca." I darted up the stairs and dashed down the third floor hall.

Renee's sobs sounded clearly from Rebecca's room. I rushed through the door and stopped. The matriarch of the family lay still in her bed, her face turned toward the sun and her eyes closed. Renee sat next to her, gripping Rebecca's hand between hers.

"Renee." I walked over and rested my palm on her back. "I'm so sorry."

"Sh-she spoke to me this morning. It was her. The real her. She told me she loved me and the boys and to watch over you. And then she said she wanted a-a nap." Renee pulled Rebecca's hand to her lips and kissed it. "I thought she was sleeping. I didn't even notice." She stroked Rebecca's hair. "Please don't. Please come back." Her tear-filled pleas tore at my heart, but all I could do was be there for her as she cried.

I pulled a chair up next to the bed and sat as Renee smoothed Rebecca's hair and talked to her. Some of the most beautiful things I'd ever heard passed Renee's lips. The love between them was stronger than even I realized, and the well of grief inside Renee seemed to have no bottom.

After a while, Laura crept through the door. When she realized Rebecca was gone, she put a hand to her mouth. I stood and went to her.

"Farns?" I whispered.

"He's fine. Just came down the stairs too fast and slipped." She didn't look away from Rebecca. "I-is she?"

I nodded. "Go take care of Farns. I'll wait here with Renee."

She wiped at her eyes. "All right."

Hours passed before I heard the familiar roar of a

motorcycle. Teddy had returned, Sin and Lucius likely with him.

"Renee, honey. I'm going to go tell them. I'll bring them up in a few minutes, okay?"

She didn't respond.

I left the room and headed for the foyer. Teddy was the first one through the door. The smile on his face faded as soon as he saw me.

"What? What is it?"

There was no other way to say it. "Your mom. I'm sorry, Teddy. But she's passed."

He looked up the stairs. "When?"

"This morning." I hugged him. "I'm sorry."

Sin walked in, Lucius right behind him. I went to Sin, his strong arms encircling me.

"Mom's dead." Teddy ran a hand through his hair and began to climb the stairs.

"What?" Lucius turned to me.

"She passed in her sleep this morning. Peacefully. Renee is up there with her."

Sin held me close, his heart beating wildly as if he'd been shot full of adrenaline. Lucius followed Teddy to the third floor.

"In her sleep?"

I swallowed hard. "Yes. She was kind to Renee this morning and then took a nap. She didn't wake up."

"Renee? How is she handling it?" He absentmindedly rubbed his hands up and down my back.

"Not great. I haven't been able to pull her away. Are you okay?"

"I can't tell. My mother's dead, but…"

"It's all right to have mixed emotions."

"My problem is having emotions at all. You've changed me somehow. Before… Before, I don't think I would have felt this sort of, I don't know what it is. I can't put it in words." He sighed in frustration. "There's an ache where there used to be nothing."

I pulled away and met his eyes. "It's sorrow."

He stroked the back of his hand down my cheek. "I think so. And I always knew she would die. I assumed it would be in some horrible fashion." He shook his head. "But in her sleep?"

"It's a good thing."

"Yes. I suppose we should go up."

"I'll be with you the whole time. I'm here for you." I got on my tiptoes and kissed him. "Anything you need."

He squared his shoulders, took my hand, and led me upstairs.

CHAPTER TWENTY-NINE
STELLA

MY DRESS ARRIVED ON the morning of the coronation. Its emerald silk gleamed in the rays of sun filtering through my window. I walked around it, making sure it was perfect for the night. I would know for certain once Sin saw me in it.

After his mother's funeral, he'd gone to New Orleans for two days to clean up financial and legal matters concerning her estate. He was set to arrive at lunchtime.

I smiled just thinking about what he'd say about the dress. I drew it myself and sent the specifications to his seamstress. She'd whipped it up in record time. The bodice was a black corset with a neckline that skirted the tops of my breasts in a straight line. My vines would be on full display, and the back was low enough to show my scars. The skirt flowed out in deep green silk, with a slit up one thigh for easy access to my knife.

"Stella?" Sin's voice had my heart racing. He was home early.

I took off toward the stairs and flew down them. He caught me as I jumped into his arms from two steps up.

He laughed, the sound warming me more than a summer sun. "I missed you, too." He kissed along my cheek to my lips and ran a hand to my hair. His tongue swept into my mouth, and he backed me into the wall next to the music room. He moved a hand to my breast and I squeaked when he ran his thumb over my nipple.

He broke our kiss and looked down. "What's this?"

"I…" Color rose in my cheeks, which was odd given that he'd seen and tasted every inch of my body. "I got my nipples pierced."

"You what?" He set me down and yanked my shirt up.

"Sin!" I tried to pull it back down and glanced around for Farns or Laura. We were, thankfully, alone.

"Jesus." He bent his head to my left breast and licked along the metal barbell.

My pussy clenched at the mix of pleasure and pain. "Ow. They're still healing."

"That's a *you* problem, not a *me* problem." He licked again and pulled my shirt to my collarbones. "Ink, too? This is beautiful. Here." He pulled my shirt up to my neck and caged my throat with his palm.

"Tony's work?" He inspected the vines and licked my other nipple as I made an *mmm* sound.

"Yes."

"He touched you?"

"He wore gloves."

His palm tightened. "He touched you?"

"He had to. But he knows I'm yours. He was a consummate professional the entire time."

"Mmhmm." He traced the vines with his index finger. "I love it, though I may still kill him for it."

"Sin, don't be mad—"

He rubbed the flat of his tongue along my left nipple, and I pressed my lips together to keep from moaning. Footsteps in the hall had him whirling, covering me with his broad body. I hastily lowered my shirt. Farns rounded the corner, a bandage still affixed to his forehead.

"How are you feeling?" Sin asked.

"Much better, thank you."

"Maybe we should have that talk again. The one about

you taking it easy while bossing a younger man around."

"No sir. Not a chance. Not while there's still breath left in this beat up old body."

"It wouldn't be so bad." Once my shirt was straight, I walked over and squeezed Farns' bony elbow. "It's not like you'd be going anywhere."

"All the same, I prefer to continue my duties for as long as I'm allowed."

"Suit yourself. Come on, Stella, I have some estate particulars to go over with Lucius and Teddy."

I followed him down the hall. Laura had prepared an early lunch. We told her we'd be leaving in the afternoon and attending an all-night party. Teddy and Lucius sat at the table, Teddy chatting with Laura as Lucius spoke Spanish on his phone.

When we walked in, Teddy said, "We're going to need some family time, babe. I'll catch up with you before we leave this afternoon."

Laura's cheeks turned pink, but she nodded and went to the kitchen. Sin closed the door behind us, and Lucius ended his phone call.

"What's the word?" Lucius popped a cheese straw into his mouth.

"Mother's estate is taken care of. I checked her holdings in the city—all the safe deposit boxes are secure. She left it all to me, but I saw fit to divide the estate equally three ways. However, the business won't be quite so easy to divvy up, so all three of us will remain on the board. Also, I kept the house for myself, because I can."

"That all sounds fine by me." Lucius nodded.

"Does that mean I'm rich now?" Teddy asked.

Sin smirked. "Oh, forgot to mention, your third is held in trust. Lucius and I are the trustees."

"Aw, shit." Teddy took an angry bite of his baguette to the point it was almost comical.

"Good one, Sin." Lucius laughed.

"Now, let's get down to more pressing business." He

sat at the head of the table. "I've checked with Quinlan, and everything is on schedule. He's adjusted arrangements to add Teddy; otherwise, the plan is the same."

A knock sounded at the door.

"Yes?" Sin barked.

Renee poked her head in. Though her eyes were ringed with dark circles, her hair was fixed and her clothes clean and neat. I dropped by to see her more frequently over the few days after Rebecca passed. She made a habit of sitting by Rebecca's grave under an oak near the levee, often taking a blanket and lying in the shade for hours.

Sin, Lucius, and Teddy were grim for the brief funeral, but Rebecca's death seemed to bring as much relief as grief for them. Renee, however, was inconsolable. The love she'd shared with Rebecca—even when it was twisted and ugly—was one that even death couldn't snuff out.

"What can we do for you, Renee?"

"I'd like to help, if I can."

Sin nodded. "Come in."

She closed the door behind her and came to sit next to me. I held her hand under the table as Sin continued.

"Once Quinlan gets everything in place, I'll give my coronation address. Lucius, Teddy, and Stella will stick close to me. I don't want to lose sight of any of you. Not for a second. When things start to happen, it will go quickly. There's no room for error. Teddy, you'll handle helping the last-borns and Acquisitions out. Lucius will remain hidden and aid Quinlan. Stella will warn Brianne and Gavin. And that's all we can control."

"What can I do?" Renee asked.

Sin tapped his fingers on the table. "Until you, we didn't have anyone here at the house who could keep an eye out. If things turn out badly, we'll regroup here in a hurry and then scatter. All of us are packed and ready to go should the need arise. Just be ready. If we don't show back up by daybreak, you will need to take Farns and Laura and get as far away as you can. I've already set up my bank to wire money into your account should that happen. I was going to leave instructions, but now you know."

"I'll kill anyone who tries to set foot here." Renee squeezed my hand.

"It won't come to that."

"Are you going to kill them all?" Her voice rose.

"We're going to make a run at it."

"Good. I hope they rot in hell." The acid in Renee's voice reinforced my own conviction that we'd made the right choice. Not that it mattered. Right or wrong, we were committed.

"We could still fail." Sin ran a hand through his dark hair. "Even though we've planned it all right down to the last detail. If anyone gets wind of it, we're dead. Everyone at this table knows the stakes. One misstep, and it's all over before it even began."

"I'm all in." I held his gaze.

"I wish you weren't."

"I'm going." I didn't want to have this argument again, but I would. Nothing could keep me from bringing the Acquisition down, and I wanted to be there when it crumbled.

He sighed. "I know."

"To the death. Theirs or ours." Lucius stood. "That's the way it's got to be. I think everyone is on the same page."

Sin rose. "Let's go get ready. Make it look good. We don't want to tip anyone until the right moment."

"I got this. And I'll even tie your bow tie for you." Lucius smirked at Teddy.

"I can tie my own tie."

"And end up looking like a circus clown? Dead giveaway."

"Dick." Teddy stood.

I laughed and got to my feet.

"Oh, and one other trifling detail I shouldn't overlook." Sin walked to me and dropped to one knee. He pulled a ring from his pocket. It had the biggest emerald I'd ever seen, surrounded by diamonds.

My heart seemed to stop and I couldn't catch my breath. I stared down at him, my mind spinning as I tried to understand what was happening. The sharp lines of his face softened and his eyes glimmered as he offered the ring. I covered my mouth with one hand, disbelief rolling through me like a turbulent wave.

"Will you marry me?"

I grabbed the back of the nearest chair. "Are you serious?"

"I don't get on my knees for anyone—except you." He lifted the ring higher, and the gems caught a ray of sun and scattered a prism of light against the dining room wall.

"Smooth," Teddy whispered.

I stared into his eyes, his soul laid bare. He was the one I needed, the man who loved me more than his own life. It was all written there in the deep blue, the open heart, and the proffered ring.

I held out my shaking left hand. He kissed it and slipped the ring on my finger. My heart upped its pace to a hectic beat as he rose and pulled me to him. He hesitated before giving me the kiss I would kill for.

"I think you forgot something," he whispered against my lips.

I smiled and wrapped my arms around his neck. "Yes."

CHAPTER THIRTY
SINCLAIR

I PULLED THROUGH THE gate and sped past the line of cars.

"Is that wise?" Stella smoothed her dress down. She didn't need to. Everything about it, about her, was perfect.

"I'm the new Sovereign. If anyone has a problem with it, they can take it up with me."

"Good point." She held her left hand out and admired the ring.

The Vinemonts owned several priceless gems, but this one spoke to me the moment I saw it in the safe deposit box in New Orleans. It had been in my family since the 1920s, and had never looked more stunning. She was born to wear it. My chest swelled with pride that she liked what I'd picked for her. Then again, I always did have impeccable taste.

I pulled up to the valet in front of whoever had been patiently waiting and got out. An attendant helped Stella from the car.

"This is the one." I handed the attendant my keys.

The attendant stopped and nodded, recognition firing in his eyes. He whistled two notes—the signal—to let me know he understood. Quinlan's men were in place.

I helped Stella to the curb, and we climbed the stairs. We were two different people since the first time we'd done this a year ago. A cool wind whipped around us, and Stella's skirt flowed to the side as I wrapped my arm around her bare shoulders. She trembled.

"Are you all right?"

"I'm perfect. I can't wait, to be honest."

I smiled at her bloodlust, and we continued to the top of the stairs. Dropping my hand to her waist, we entered the chateau.

Cal stood in the foyer greeting guests with his usual aplomb. "Hello gorgeous," he said and shook my hand. "Stella, you look nice, too." He laughed and took her waist.

My hands fisted, the need to destroy him rising like a ship on an ocean wave.

"I can't wait until I get you home, beautiful." He kissed her neck, and then held her at arm's length. "And what's this? New ink?"

"I had her branded a bit more. Just so everyone knows I had her first." I kept my tone cold, though my hatred seethed, red and smoldering.

"I'll take your sloppy seconds any day. Go on in. Your seats are on the stage. Where's Teddy?"

"He's arriving separately, but he'll be here."

"Perfect!" Cal slapped me on the back and waved us toward the ballroom.

Stella walked ahead of me, her red locks cascading down her back in a soft wave. I took her elbow and guided her through the groups of people, each of them whispering about us, each of them dying to know who the Sovereign would be.

We entered the ballroom—this time devoid of the enormous oak in the center. A stage stood along one wall. Red, his younger sister Evie, and Brianne sat in a huddle, as did Bob, his brother Carl, and Gavin. Three seats to the left of the podium remained empty.

Servers whisked by with drinks and hors d'oeuvres. Every so often, one of them would whistle from high to low, assuring me that the preparations were in order.

"Have I mentioned how beautiful you look?" I whispered in Stella's ear.

"You may have mentioned it about a dozen times. But it can't hurt to hear it again." She smiled. That simple turn of her lips, nothing more than a reaction to stimulus—I lived for it. Her happiness was as necessary as the air in my lungs.

We made our way through the chattering throng toward the stage.

"Sin?" Sophia's voice clawed at my eardrum.

I spun, keeping Stella shielded at my back. "Sophia."

I turned my head and whispered, "Wait for me by the stage."

"Okay." Stella backed away.

"Sin, where have you been? We were supposed to brunch on Sunday with Mother." Her displeasure was eclipsed by mine. I hated the sight of her.

Even so, I masked my disgust. "My apologies, but my mother passed. I should have sent word."

"She's dead? Yes, you should have sent word," she hissed. "Now it will look like I didn't care."

"When I'm Sovereign, will that matter?"

She opened her crimson lips, closed them, and then re-affixed a smile to them. "You're right." She kissed me on the cheek, and I wondered if her lips were still warm from being wrapped around Ellis' cock. Not that I cared. Her lips would be forever stilled within the next few hours.

"Sin." Teddy walked up and took Sophia's hand, kissing the back of it.

"I'm glad to see at least one of the Vinemont men has manners." She smiled, her dark eyes taking Teddy in from head to toe.

"When I see a beautiful woman, my first thought is to kiss her." He shrugged, his boyish charm now an act, but just as convincing as the real thing.

"Oh, you flatter me. Keep it up." She shifted her gaze to some point behind Teddy.

I followed her line of vision to Ellis.

"Excuse me for a moment." She walked around Teddy and beelined for her lover.

Teddy shifted closer and eyed the crowd. "Where's Stella?"

"In front of the stage." I turned and scanned for her. My heart chilled when I realized she was gone.

Guests milled around, and I pushed through them until I stood at the stairs. She wasn't there.

"Fuck!" I couldn't breathe, couldn't think.

"We'll find her. Calm down," Teddy leaned this way and that, trying to see through the mass of people.

"Welcome!" Cal's voice carried over all others as he made his way to the stage.

"We don't have time." I wanted to scream for her, to knock down anything that blocked the path to her, but I couldn't.

Cal waved us on. "Come on fellas, get up there. Where's Stella?"

"Powder room." Teddy lied almost as easily as I did.

"We'll have to start without her. Shame." Cal pushed us up the stairs ahead of him.

At the top, I turned and scrutinized all the faces. I finally found hers, a look of horror on it as Dylan dragged her into a side room, his hand clapped over her mouth.

CHAPTER THIRTY-ONE
STELLA

I SCREAMED AS DYLAN threw me to the floor in a small sitting room off the ballroom. His weight crushed down on top of me, and he pinned my hands to the floor.

"No one here to save you now." He smiled as I tried to free my hands.

I should have been afraid. I wasn't. Anger boiled over, scorching my insides with naked hatred.

"Get the fuck off me."

"Shut up." He let one hand go and slapped me. "I wanted to get my taste before Cal. I'll have you after, too. But something about being inside you first just does it for me." He pushed his hips into me for emphasis.

"You're fucking pathetic!"

He backhanded me this time, his knuckles busting my lip.

I spat my blood in his face.

He wiped it away with the back of his sleeve as I inched my hand down to my thigh where my blade waited. Cal's amplified voice came through the door clearly as he went over the trials of the year and built up to announcing the victor.

"I'm going to rip you apart for that." He yanked my dress up and fumbled at his zipper.

"I'll kill you." I palmed my knife.

He stopped and wrapped his large hand around my throat. "I could snap your fucking neck right now. I should. You deserve it."

Thunderous applause erupted from the ballroom and I swung, stabbing him in the side over and over before he even realized I'd done it.

"What are you—?"

I bridged up, shoving him off me. He clutched his side and brought a bloody hand to his face.

"You cut me." He shook his head in disbelief as I got to my feet.

"That's not all." I aimed a kick at his face and delighted in the sickening crunch his nose made during the impact.

He fell back sputtering. The applause died down, and his cries grew louder. I had to shut him up so he could bleed to death quietly. I kicked him in the side of the head with all my strength. He went limp.

I wiped my blade on the window curtain and stuffed it back down in the garter on my thigh. My hands were steady, my heart in a calm rhythm. I dabbed my busted lip on the inside of my skirt and traced the outline of my lips with my finger to wipe away any smeared lipstick.

Opening the door, I saw Sinclair at the podium. He spoke of history and the importance of tradition, but his eyes were fixed on me—his future. I gave him a nod to let him know I was okay and pushed my way through the throng before climbing onto the stage and taking my seat next to Teddy.

I glanced at Gavin and Brianne. They both watched Sin. I hadn't had a chance to warn them. Dylan had grabbed me soon after Sin began speaking with Sophia.

Red cradled Evie in his arms as she sobbed, and Bob's brother cried quietly to himself. Teddy rested his arm along the back of my chair as the faceless mob in the darkened ballroom stared up at us.

"You okay?" He whispered.

"I could take them all on, bare handed. I'm that okay right now." Getting the best of Dylan shot me into the stratosphere, especially when his was only the first blood that would be spilled tonight. I'd killed a man, and instead of regret, all I felt was triumph.

"And now, I'd like to thank my Acquisition, Stella Rousseau. Without her, this win wouldn't be possible. I'd also like to thank Red and Bob, and let them know their sacrifices are appreciated. Bring the knives." He waved toward an attendant who climbed the stairs and gave long, curving knives to Red and Bob. Red's hand shook as he took the blade, and Bob grabbed his with a chilling nonchalance.

The crowd began to chant. It started as a whisper in the corner of the room and grew until the entire room filled with the word "blood" on a never-ending loop. Sin whistled two notes, the sound carrying across the speakers and over the sounds of the continuing chant. Red held his sister, the knife shaking in his hand as he gave me a vindictive glare. I shook my head. *Wait*, I mouthed to him. His eyes narrowed.

Doors along the back and sides of the ballroom opened, and attendants wheeled in several carts covered with black cloths. They spaced them out amongst the guests and then retreated back through the doors. I couldn't see it, but I knew lengths of chain were being affixed to all the exits. There was no escape for any of the people below. A small, hidden door behind the stage remained unbarred. That was it.

Sin held up a hand and the chant died down. "Patience. I have one more official act before the blood will be spilled."

Cal stood at the foot of the stairs, his brow wrinkled in confusion at the change of plan.

"As you all know, being Sovereign comes with amazing benefits. I take a cut from each of you every year. My wealth grows and grows, and I have the power to end whichever one of you I see fit. Sovereign is a time-honored role, one that is coveted beyond all others. Wouldn't you agree?"

CELIA AARON

Some of the guests applauded, though I could sense unease begin to build. I wanted to smile, but kept my face impassive.

"The reason we have a Sovereign is, of course, to prevent infighting and to consolidate power in one principal place. But have you ever wondered what would happen if there were no Sovereign?"

Whispers rippled through the crowd.

"That would lead to a power vacuum. That would mean the strongest of you would be the next Sovereign. There are plenty of people in here who could claim the throne—Cal, for instance; he's strong. Sophia, his daughter, very smart and wily. Look at your neighbor. Would they take it from you? Your chance to be Sovereign? Would you let them? Or would you claim it for yourself and have everything you've ever dreamed of?"

Sin let the crowd ruminate for a moment. One of the guests pulled the sheet from atop a cart and a collective gasp sounded from everyone close enough to see what was there.

"As some of you have discovered, there are weapons scattered throughout the room. Knives, hatchets, hammers, bats, daggers, axes—you name it, it's there."

All around the room voices rose, and even in the glare of the spotlight, I could see people snatching weapons from the carts.

"Now, look around you. Who will reign? You best decide quickly, because my first act as Sovereign is to banish the Vinemont household from the nobility forever."

Cal sputtered and shook his head as Sin continued.

"This is *your* chance. You want to reign? Take it. You want the spoils? Take it. You want to decide who lives and dies? Take it. Because if you don't, someone else will. Pick up the knife and strike down anyone who tries to take what's yours. There is no Sovereign anymore, except whoever is strong enough to claim it."

The stage lights went out and the room became steeped in gloom. Screams erupted from all sides.

Cal groaned and fell forward, a dagger glinting in his back. Teddy jumped to the floor and yanked a cart full of guns from beneath the stage and sent it skittering into the crowd.

I darted to Gavin. "There's a door behind the stage. Go. Take Bob's brother."

Bob tried to get up, too, but Gavin punched him in the side of the head. He fell to the floor and began to cry, the sound drowned out by the screams.

"You're staying." Gavin kicked him in the stomach and led Carl down the back of the stage.

"Brianne, go." I pointed to where Gavin had disappeared. She rose and followed, though she seemed to have no idea what was going on.

"Evie, you too."

She clung to her brother. I pulled my knife out and shook my head at Red. I couldn't let him go.

He glowered and tried to dislodge Evie. "Go sweetheart. I'll be all right."

She wouldn't budge. "No."

Gunfire erupted, and Sin grabbed me. "We have to leave, now."

I pointed my knife at Red. "Take her and go."

He picked her up and fled down the back stairs as more gunfire ripped through the air.

"Stella, now!"

I surveyed the room, a mass of bodies caving in on itself. Some ran for the doors and screamed to be let out. It made them easy targets, and they fell in heaps as their former friends and allies fought to claim the throne. Every time someone fell, or a cry of agony pierced the air, I felt a sliver of comfort. I wanted to stay, to watch all of them suffer.

Judge Montagnet tried to scramble up the stage steps, his eyes wide and a bloody slash on his cheek. I tightened my grip on my blade, but a young man behind him swung swift and sure with a double-sided axe, almost severing the judge's head completely. The man yanked the axe free and climbed to the platform. Sin pulled out a revolver and fired two rounds. The man fell backward as others began to rush the the stage.

"Let's go." Sin threw me over his shoulder and dashed down the back stairs.

I got one more glimpse of the gratifying chaos before he carried me through the hidden door. Quinlan swung it shut behind us, and he and another larger man chained and barred it. The noxious scent of gasoline filled the air, and rows of gasoline cans lined the carpeted hall, a stark contrast to the hand-drawn walls and ornate chandeliers.

Sin put me on my feet. All eyes turned toward the door as pounding sounds and screams poured through it. The cries were silenced one by one.

I covered my nose, a futile attempt to avoid the gasoline fumes, and looked down the hall. Red lay on the floor in a puddle of crimson. Lucius stood over him, a bloody knife in his hand.

I nodded. "Good."

Evie cried on Gavin's shoulder as the screams rose and fell within the ballroom. Brianne clung to Carl, her stare far away. Gunfire continued sporadically, the stately chateau devolving into a slaughterhouse floor. My heart sang with each life that was snuffed out, their blood slowly dousing the rage burning inside me.

"It worked." Teddy ran a shaking hand through his hair. "I can't believe it worked."

Sin whipped me around to him and pulled me into a kiss. I closed my eyes and reveled in our victory, in the turmoil and death beyond the door, and most of all in the man I loved.

"We need to get out of here." Lucius knelt and wiped his blade on Red's pant leg.

"Quinlan, are we good here?" Sin asked.

"It's ready to burn."

Sin pulled a roll of hundreds from his inner suit pocket.

"Make sure no one gets out alive."

Quinlan took the money. "Not a problem. Everyone's cleared out, and I've got men with eyes on this place."

"Thank you." I met Quinlan's eyes.

"After that last thing, in the fort." He shook his head. "This was my pleasure."

"Come on." Lucius pulled Teddy down the hall. "We have to go."

Sin scooped me up and ran with me, my heels clattering to the floor. Gavin, Evie, Carl, and Brianne followed. Quinlan and the large man brought up the rear.

We burst out into the cool night, but Sin stopped and set me on the ground.

"Stella gets to do the honors. Give them to her."

The larger man pulled a book of matches from his pocket and handed it over. I turned the matchbook over in my hands, amazed at how light total destruction could be.

I opened the pack and pulled out a single match, the tip green. With a single flick of my wrist, the head flamed, a bright orange burst in the evening gloom. Time stopped, and only I and the flame existed, both burning, both bent on annihilation. I threw it, the flame flickering in the light wind. It bounced off the door, landed on the carpet, and then multiplied into a snakelike inferno. Orange flames raced down the hall in a whoosh, the carpet catching and the walls bubbling.

Quinlan slammed the door, and Sin scooped me up again and ran to the cars waiting for us.

"You." He pointed to Gavin and then a car. "That one. Key's in the ignition. Money's in a bag in the trunk. Get far away from here. Take them with you."

Sin tucked me into the passenger side of his sports car.

"Wait." I got to my feet and dashed to Gavin, wrapping my arms around his neck.

He held me close. "I got your back."

"I got yours."

"You did it. I can't believe you did it. You burned them

the fuck down."

"Be safe."

"You too."

"Stella!" Sin banged on the hood of his car.

I gave Gavin one more hard squeeze and ran back to Sin. He dropped into the driver's side, waited for Teddy and Lucius to pull away, and then tore down the drive.

The gate was wide open, and we followed Lucius's taillights down the main road, away from the chateau, and back toward home. *Home.*

I looked at Sin, his jaw set tight and his eyes flicking to the rearview.

"It's over."

A loud boom rumbled through the air. I craned my head back. Smoke rose over the trees, blotting out the stars and hazing across the moon. An orange glow marked the Oakman estate, fire wiping the slate clean.

Sin shifted into another gear, speeding faster, and took my hand, bringing it to his lips.

"I would gladly kill a thousand more for you."

"Let's hope we don't have to. Do you think anyone will come for us?" We'd discussed it before, but tonight we had just tried to get through the coronation alive. This was a whole new reality.

"I don't think anyone's left to retaliate. If they do, we'll be ready." His tone was full of malicious promise. He kissed my hand again, his gentle lips at odds with his dark words.

"The police?"

"Anyone who's left will kill any investigation into the Acquisition. The governor won't want anyone digging too deeply into this *tragedy*. Besides, every sheriff from the surrounding parishes was in the crowd."

I relaxed back into my seat, staring ahead as we raced off into the night. Into our future, while the world of the Acquisition turned to ash behind us.

CHAPTER THIRTY-TWO
STELLA

"NO, TO THE LEFT." I put my hands on my hips. "No, Teddy, your other left. And they're really going to let you operate on people?"

He laughed and adjusted the star atop the Christmas tree more to my liking. "How about that?"

"It looks straight to me."

"The top is cocked to the left." Sin wrapped his arms around me from behind.

"No it isn't." I ran my hands over his arms.

"Yes, it is. Angle it to the right more, Ted."

Teddy looked at me for permission.

"Fine, to the right. See how that looks."

He tweaked it and stood back on the ladder. "I've only changed it five times so far."

"See, now it's perfect. Like you." Sin kissed my neck, and I sighed.

Teddy climbed down and pulled the ladder away. Sin reached over and hit the lights. The tree glowed white, the lights glittering amid the silver and gold ornaments.

"Beautiful. Also like you." He nibbled at my ear, sending goose bumps running down my arms.

Teddy sank into an arm chair and threaded his fingers behind his head. "This is pretty much my best work yet."

Laura walked into the library and clapped. "Oh my god, it's perfect!"

I smiled. "It was all Teddy."

"Liar," Sin whispered in my ear.

I melted into him, leaning back as he held me. He was everything; I couldn't even fall asleep without him now. He kept the nightmares at bay—the faces, screams, and flames. He'd given up his position in town and focused on the sugar business. Where he went, I followed, though I drew the line at returning to Cuba.

After the coronation night, the news ran several stories about the "tragedy in the bayou," the fast-moving fire that had trapped many fine and upstanding members of Southern society. At first, it seemed like coverage would never end, but after a couple days, the world just seemed to move on.

The house was on high alert the first month, hiring Quinlan's men to keep watch at the front and back gates. But after a while, it appeared the entire power structure had collapsed, leaving no one to retaliate.

Fall turned to winter, and as Christmas approached, I wanted to change our history, mold the season into a happy time.

Laura walked to Teddy, who pulled her into his lap.

She protested. "Stop. Not in front of them."

Teddy scoffed. "Stella and Sin don't care. They're practically doing it standing up over there."

She laughed as he ran his hands around her waist and pulled her down to his mouth.

"Jesus, that tree is overdone." Lucius walked in and plopped down on the sofa, drink in hand as always. "Did you raid the north pole or something?"

I arched an eyebrow. "Shut up. It's gorgeous."

"If you say so." Lucius saluted me with his drink and downed half of it in one go. "Farns would have a heart attack if he saw it, for the record." Lucius kicked his feet up on the coffee table.

"Well, then it's a good thing we sent him on a vacation to a sunnier clime." I refused to let Lucius bring down my Christmas spirit.

Teddy came up for air. "Lucius, don't be such a dick. It's Christmas."

I walked to Lucius and pulled his glass away. "I think what we need is food instead of alcohol. Maybe it will improve your mood."

He glanced to Sin and then stared at my chest. "I'd love to tell you what would improve my mood, but Sin probably wouldn't like it."

"Don't talk to her like—"

"Sin, it's fine. He needs to eat. The liquid diet makes him grouchy. I'll go get some snacks from the kitchen."

"There's a roast on the stove." Laura started to get up.

"No. Stay. I'll make a plate and bring it. Lucius and Sin, play nice while I'm gone. Laura and Teddy—" I smiled. "—carry on."

I hummed "Last Christmas" as I entered the kitchen. Renee stood in the pantry, her back to me.

"Oh, hey, I was wondering where you were. We just decorated the tree. I'm going to take some—"

She made a strangled noise and fell forward.

"Renee!" I rushed to her and turned her over. A knife protruded from her chest. I drew air into my lungs to scream, but Dylan lunged from the darkness of the pantry and clapped a hand over my mouth.

He shoved me until my back was against the island, his knees straddling me.

"Miss me?" He licked my cheek and pressed something metal against my chin.

"If you make a sound, I'll pull the trigger and splatter your brains on the ceiling. Nod if you understand me."

I nodded, too afraid to blink. His hand crushed my lips, but the gun barrel was still foremost in my thoughts.

"You're coming with me. I own you. See, I'm the Sovereign now. You're going to serve me until your cunt is worn out and your will is broken. Then I'm going to spill your blood for all to see. Like christening a boat. I'm going to rebuild it all." A crazed light burned in his eyes. "And your boys in the library? They'll be punished, too. But you're the prize, the one I want. They'll try to come after you. I'll kill them and make you watch." Spit flew from his lips, and he almost vibrated with excitement.

"Come quietly, or I'll kill them all now. So what's it going to be? Will you behave and come with me?"

I nodded.

"Do you promise, Stella?"

I nodded again.

"I'm going to take my hand off your mouth. Make a sound and I'll kill you. No hesitation." His soulless eyes made me believe every word.

He pulled his hand away slowly. I took a shuddering breath, but didn't make any noise.

"Good girl. Now get up." He pulled me to my feet and leaned close to speak in my ear. "I'm going to fuck you as soon as I get where no one will hear you scream. Keep that in your mind. Hold onto it for me." He pulled me away from the island. "Out the back door."

Pushing me ahead of him, he shoved the barrel between my shoulder blades. Blood pooled around Renee as her unseeing eyes stared straight ahead. I walked past her, biting back my grief, and turned toward the rear of the house.

The door from the hall opened and Teddy walked in. "Stella, Laura sent me—"

The gunshot deafened me. Teddy fell to his knees, crimson spreading along his stomach as he stared up at me.

"Teddy!" I whirled and knocked the gun from Dylan's hand, and then darted to the knives lined up along the wall over the stove. I pulled two down as yells erupted in the hallway. Dylan ran. I followed.

His feet thundered down the back steps and out onto the lawn. I couldn't let him get away. He was fast, but I was faster. His bulk slowed him down as I sprinted after him, his blond hair glowing in the bright moonlight. Everything inside me was numb—everything except the need for vengeance.

I gained on him, my feet sure on the grass as he ran past the garage toward a car parked under the oaks. I pushed harder until everything burned. When I finally caught up with him, I cut a slashing arc across his back.

He screamed but kept running. I shoved my hand out, embedding a knife in his thick torso. He slowed and stumbled. I slashed him again and dropped to his knees, only a few yards shy of his car.

I circled to his front and kicked him so he landed on his back, the knife penetrating deeper. Bloody bubbles rose from his lips as I settled on top of him.

Someone yelled my name. I stabbed downward. Dylan screamed weakly. I withdrew the knife and did it again. I stabbed and stabbed until Sin grabbed my wrist and pulled me to my feet.

"Stop. It's over. Stop."

"Renee? Teddy?" A car reversed out of the garage and squealed tires, passing us and almost knocking us over with the draft.

"Renee is gone. Teddy—" His voice broke.

I dropped the knife and wrapped my arms around him.

"Lucius took him."

"I left Dylan alive. This is my fault." I shuddered, everything shaken all the way down to my soul.

"No." He stroked my hair as Laura ran out the front door and collapsed on the stairs, head in her hands. "You didn't do this."

"Renee." A flash of her kind smile on the first day we met struck me like a slap in the face. "Are you sure? Maybe she—maybe…"

"No. Shh. She's gone. I'm sorry."

I stared down at Dylan, blood covering his throat and face. Pulling back, I looked down at my red hands, the blood

697

seeping into my shirt and jeans. I shook even harder.

"You're in shock. Come inside."

"We need to go to the hospital. We have to help Teddy."

Sin locked his arm around my waist and guided me to the porch. "We will, but we can't take you like this."

"We have to—"

"Lucius has him. We'll leave as soon as you're okay." His voice remained calm as he hurried me up the front steps.

"Laura, I'm going to get Stella cleaned up. Pull my sedan around. We'll all go to the hospital as soon as we're done."

Sin picked me up and carried me to my bathroom. He turned on the shower and stripped me. All I could do was stand, my teeth chattering. He stripped his clothes and got in with me.

The red bloom on Teddy's shirt spread larger and larger in my mind. His wide eyes full of pain and surprise. "Do you think Teddy—?"

"I don't know." He hastily lathered a washcloth.

The blood sluiced down into the drain, a crimson river that would never run clear again.

I covered my face with a shaking hand. "It should have been me."

"Don't say that." Sin pulled my hand away. "Never say that. We'd all be dead without you. Either from the hell of the Acquisition or Dylan's bullets."

"But Teddy—"

"No!" He slammed his fist into the tiles hard enough to break one. "Never wish yourself away from me."

He crushed me to him, our battered souls clinging to one another as they had done from the start. "Never."

EPILOGUE
STELLA

"TEDDY, COME IN. IT'S time for lunch." I called loud enough for the dark-haired toddler on the lawn to look up at me.

"Mommy!" He grinned and did his best to navigate the grass toward me. Lucius ran up behind him and scooped him into his arms, tickling him as they barreled through the sunny morning.

I rubbed my stomach, the twins growing inside me apparently engaged in a fistfight. I turned as Lucius stomped up the stairs behind me.

Teddy giggled like a maniac. "Again, Unky Lusus!"

"Lunch first."

"Mommy's a buzzkill, little man." Lucius set him on his feet in the foyer. He toddled off toward the kitchen. I may have been his mother, but he knew Laura had all the snacks.

"When are you going to pop?"

"Two weeks. You know that."

"You keep telling me that, and I keep disbelieving that you can *still* be pregnant. Huge, is all I'm saying."

"Beautiful, he means." Sin came down the stairs and gave me a kiss. He peeked down the hallway and saw Teddy.

Giving me a grin, he turned and crept along behind his

son, then grabbed him up and blew raspberries all along his stomach as he giggled.

"Are you sure they're both girls?" Lucius matched my lumbering pace toward the breakfast room.

"That's the word at the doctor's office." I trailed my fingers beneath my mother's portrait that hung in the hall. I'd painted it from memory, and her smile greeted all guests to the house.

"Do you think maybe you could name one Lucia or something?"

"Not a chance." I eased into the breakfast room. Lucius pulled out a chair for me, and I sat, my feet thanking me for the brief respite.

"Here." He scooted out the chair next to me, and lifted my feet up.

I leaned back and closed my eyes. "Thank you."

"Welcome."

Sin came through from the kitchen and started rubbing my shoulders.

"He's not eating sweets, is he?"

"Not really. Laura knows he's supposed to eat lunch first. She only gave him a handful of jellybeans." He kissed my forehead and kept rubbing.

"That's sweets." I threw my hands up. "Whatever. No one listens to the preggo lady around here."

"Yes we do." He dug his thumbs in, unwrapping my tight muscles like a Christmas present.

"I'm just irritable."

"We know." He laughed and kissed me again.

"Twins are your fault."

"You may have mentioned that a couple hundred times. Though, I don't think it's true."

Sin moved around and sat opposite me, putting my feet in his lap. He knocked my house shoes off and rubbed my swollen feet. "Spread your legs a little more."

I tilted my head at him. "What?"

"You heard me."

"I did but—"

"Do it." He used that tone—the one that sent a thrill through me every time.

I slowly opened my legs.

"Pull up your skirt more."

"Sin." I shook my head.

"Stella. Do it now." He dug his thumb into the bottom of my foot.

I grabbed the material and pulled until my skirt hit midthigh.

"Much better." He continued rubbing, his gaze vacillating from my eyes to between my legs.

My body warmed as he watched me. "You're a bad man."

"So I've been told." He switched feet. "As soon as Teddy's down for a nap, I'll be going down on you."

My temperature kicked up a notch. "Bad, bad man."

He shrugged. "What? I can't give my pregnant wife the special attention she deserves?"

One of the babies kicked what must have been a vital organ. I groaned and rubbed my belly with a vengeance. "Twins are all your fault."

"Actually they're not." Teddy walked into the dining room, his green scrubs making him look older.

I closed my legs and wrinkled my nose. "What do you know? You're not even a real doctor yet."

I huffed as he leaned down and pecked me on the cheek.

"Okay, you're right. It *is* all Sin's fault."

"Much better. I thought you were in rounds or something all day?"

"Nope. Got done this morning. Wanted to come by and see little T. And check on you, of course."

"I'm fine. I mean, I would like to have my body back to myself, but other than that, I'm good."

"I could do like a check or something. See how your cervix is dilating—"

"Don't even think about it." Sin squeezed my foot tighter.

"Teddy was kidding. Right?"

"Yeah, kidding. Little T in the kitchen?"

"He takes after his namesake. He's in there charming Laura right out from under you." I smiled up at him.

"That's my man." He pushed through the door to the kitchen.

Sin rubbed my feet for a little while longer. "Have you thought any more about names?"

"Yes." I set my feet down and leaned forward, resting my head on his chest.

"I know we discussed lots of different ones, but I've been thinking... What about Rebecca and Renee?"

He stayed silent and pulled me closer.

"If you don't want to, that's okay. Those names obviously carry some baggage. But I thought it would be—"

"I love it." He tilted my chin up and pressed his lips to mine.

Little Teddy toddled in, both uncles hot on his heels.

"Mommy, jay bees!" He held out a hand with two jellybeans stuck to it.

"I see that." I shook my head.

He ran to Sin, who picked him up and sat him in his lap. Sin whispered in his ear. Teddy's eyes lit up, and Sin pointed at me. "Tell her."

"I love you, Mommy." His smile, so much like his father's, was infectious.

"I love you, too."

Sin cupped his hands around Teddy's ear and whispered again.

"Daddy love you, Mommy."

"I love Daddy, too."

Laura bustled in from the kitchen with lunch, and before long we were all laughing at big Teddy's and little Teddy's antics.

I lay my head on Sin's shoulder, and he pulled me close. The long shadow of the Acquisition no longer darkened our doorstep, and the nightmares were nothing more than ghosts.

ROMANCE
BY CELIA AARON

Kicked

Trent Carrington.

Trent Mr. Perfect-Has-Everyone-Fooled Carrington.

He's the star quarterback, university scholar, and happens to be the sexiest man I've ever seen. He shines at any angle, and especially under the Saturday night stadium lights where I watch him from the sidelines. But I know the real him, the one who broke my heart and pretended I didn't exist for the past two years.

I'm the third-string kicker, the only woman on the team and nothing better than a mascot. Until I'm not. Until I get my chance to earn a full scholarship and join the team as first-string. The only way I'll make the cut is to accept help from the one man I swore never to trust again. The problem is, with each stolen glance and lingering touch, I begin to realize that trusting Trent isn't the problem. It's that I can't trust myself when I'm around him.

Tempting Eden

A modern re-telling of Jane Eyre that will leave you breathless...

Jack England

Eden Rochester is a force. A whirlwind of intensity and thinly-veiled passion. Over the past few years, I've worked hard to avoid my passions, to lock them up so they can't harm me—or anyone else—again. But Eden Rochester ignites every emotion I have. Every glance from her sharp eyes and each teasing word from her indulgent lips adds more fuel to the fire. Resisting her? Impossible. From the moment I held her in my arms, I had to have her. But tempting her into opening up could cost me my job and much, much more.

Eden Rochester
When Jack England crosses my path and knocks me off my high horse, something begins to shift. Imperceptible at first, the change grows each time he looks into my eyes or brushes against my skin. He's my assistant, but everything about him calls to me, tempts me. And once I give in, he shows me who he really is—dominant, passionate, and with a dark past. After long days of work and several hot nights, I realize the two of us are bound together. But my secrets won't stay buried, and they cut like a knife.

***

EROTICA TITLES

Forced by the Kingpin
Forced Series, Book 1

I've been on the trail of the local mob kingpin for months. I know his haunts, habits, and vices. The only thing I didn't know was how obsessed he was with me. Now, caught in his trap, I'm about to find out how far he and his local cop-on-the-take will go to keep me silent.

Forced by the Professor
Forced Series, Book 2

I've been in Professor Stevens' class for a semester. He's brilliant, severe, and hot as hell. I haven't been particularly attentive, prepared, or timely, but he hasn't said anything to me about it. I figure he must not mind and intends to let me slide. At least I thought that was the case until he told me to stay after class today. Maybe he'll let me off with a warning?

Forced by the Hitmen
Forced Series, Book 3

I stayed out of my father's business. His dirty money never mattered to me, so long as my trust fund was full of it. But now I've been kidnapped by his enemies and stuffed in a bag. The rough men who took me have promised to hurt me if I make a sound or try to run. I know, deep down, they are going to hurt me no matter what I do. Now I'm cuffed to their bed. Will I ever see the light of day again?

Forced by the Stepbrother
Forced Series, Book 4

Dancing for strange men was the biggest turn on I'd ever known. Until I met him. He was able to control me, make me hot, make me need him, with nothing more than a look. But he was a fantasy. Just another client who worked me up and paid my bills. Until he found me, the real me. Now, he's backed me into a corner. His threats and promises, darkly whispered in tones of sex and violence, have bound me surer than the cruelest ropes. At first I was unsure, but now I know – him being my stepbrother is the least of my worries.

Forced by the Quarterback
Forced Series, Book 5

For three years, I'd lusted after Jericho, my brother's best friend and quarterback of our college football team. He's never paid me any attention, considering me nothing more than a little sister he never had. Now, I'm starting freshman year and I'm sharing a suite with my brother. Jericho is over all the time, but he'll never see me as anything other than the shy girl he met three years ago. But that's not who I am. Not really. To get over Jericho – and to finally get off – I've arranged a meeting with HardcoreDom. If I can't have Jericho, I'll give myself to a man who will master me, force me, and dominate me the way I desperately need.

***

A Stepbrother for Christmas
The Hard and Dirty Holidays

Annalise dreads seeing her stepbrother at her family's Christmas get-together. Niles had always been so nasty, tormenting her in high school after their parents had gotten married. British and snobby, Niles did everything he could to hurt Annalise when they were younger. Now, Annalise hasn't seen Niles in three years; he's been away at school in England and Annalise has started her pre-med program in Dallas. When they reconnect, dark memories threaten, sparks fly, and they give true meaning to the "hard and dirty holidays."

Bad Boy Valentine
The Hard and Dirty Holidays

Jess has always been shy. Keeping her head down and staying out of sight have served her well, especially when a sexy photographer moves in across the hall from her. Michael has a budding career, a dark past, and enough ink and piercings to make Jess' mouth water. She is well equipped to watched him through her peephole and stalk him on social media. But what happens when the bad boy next door comes knocking?

Bad Boy Valentine Wedding
The Hard and Dirty Holidays

Jess and Michael have been engaged for three years, waiting patiently for Jess to finish law school before taking the next step in their relationship. As the wedding date approaches, their dedication to each other only grows, but outside forces seek to tear them apart. The bad boy will have to fight to keep his bride and Jess will have to trust him with her whole heart to make their happy ending a reality.

F*ck of the Irish
The Hard and Dirty Holidays

Eamon is my crush, the one guy I can't stop thinking about. His Irish accent, toned body, and sparkling eyes captivated me the second I saw him. But since he slept with my roommate, who claims she still loves him, he's been off limits. Despite my prohibition on dating him, he has other other ideas. Resisting him is the key to keeping my roommate happy, but giving in may bring me more pleasure than I ever imagined.

***

Zeus
Taken by Olympus, Book 1

One minute I'm looking after an injured gelding, the next I'm tied to a luxurious bed. I never believed in fairy tales, never gave a second thought to myths. Now that I've been kidnapped by a man with golden eyes and a body that makes my mouth water, I'm not sure what I believe anymore. . . But I know what I want.

ROMANTIC COMEDY
BY CELIA AARON
& SLOANE HOWELL

Cleat Chaser

Kyrie Kent hates baseball. She hates players even more. When her best friend drags her to a Ravens game, she spends the innings reading a book... Until she gets a glimpse of the closer—a pitcher who draws her like a magnet. Fighting her attraction to Easton Holliday is easy. All she has to do is keep her distance, avoid the ballpark, and keep her head down. At least, all that would have worked, but Easton doesn't intend to let Kyrie walk so easily. When another player vies for Kyrie's attention, Easton will swing for the fences. But will Kyrie strike him out or let him steal home?

Cleat Catcher

What happens when an unrepentant Cleat Chaser meets the player of her dreams?

Nikki Graves has a history of going through the baseball roster with an eye for talent--the kind of talent that keeps things spicy between the sheets. But, once she meets Braden Bradford, catcher for the Ravens, her talent scout days are done. He's the one.

Braden has never met a woman like Nikki, and he can't get enough of her smart mouth and big heart. But life isn't always as direct and certain as the connection between Braden and Nikki. When family objections and career trajectories begin to crowd the plate, will Braden be able to keep his catch of a lifetime?

About the Author

Celia Aaron is the self-publishing pseudonym of a published romance and erotica author. She loves to write stories with hot heroes and heroines that are twisty and often dark. Visit me at aaronerotica.com. Thanks for reading.